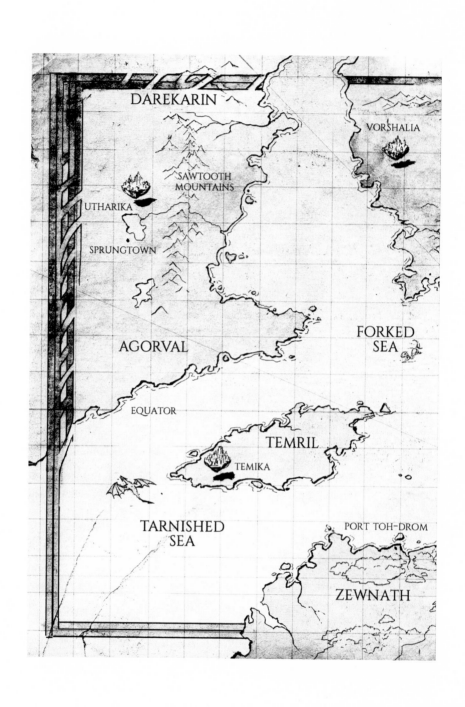

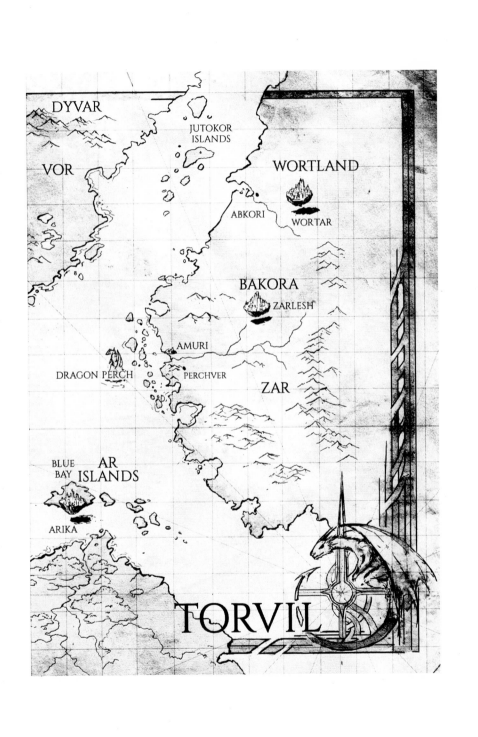

1

As the mageship *Dauntless* flew southward high above the Forked Sea, Jakstor Freedar stood inside the ancient dragon portal lying flat on its deck. He leaned his hip against it, using the surface like a desk as he painstakingly drew a waterfall flowing down a mossy cliff into a pool surrounded by a lush green jungle.

Actually, it was a *gray* jungle, since all he had for the task was a pencil. The deep-blue pool, verdant foliage, and fresh spray glistening on the rocky perch beside the water were much more vibrant in his mind than on the page.

"There's no way a stranger is going to recognize this place based on my memory of it from a dream," Jak muttered.

Jak glanced up, as he reminded himself to do every couple of minutes, to make sure a mage with inimical intent wasn't sneaking up on him. Captain Toggs, the surly captain of the ship Jak had bluffed his way into commandeering, was glaring at him from across the deck.

Toggs didn't seem to have sneaking in mind. He was, however, drumming his fingers on the sleeve of his green uniform and possibly contemplating launching a fireball at him.

"But you'll protect me from that, right?" Jak patted one of the four blue-black dragons that were linked together to make the circular frame of the portal.

It pulsed blue, the magical flash noticeable even under the sweltering equatorial sun. Jak *sensed* it as well as seeing it with his eyes. That was still a novel feeling for him.

It had only been two days since he and his mother had fled the sky city of Utharika, and not much longer since he'd learned he had an aptitude for magic, something he'd been blissfully unaware of as a university student in his extremely mundane and unmagical home of Sprungtown. He hadn't yet grown accustomed to being surrounded by magical people and magical objects—or being able to sense them.

The portal warmed under his hand and slid a vision into his mind. It wasn't anything to do with Toggs or the rest of the mage crew of the *Dauntless*, so maybe the ancient artifact wasn't concerned about them. The vision featured the actual waterfall and pool that Jak had been trying to draw. It was vibrant, crisp, colorful, and included monkeys hooting, parrots squawking, and a snake slithering along a branch.

"That helps," he murmured. "Thank you."

Jak hurried to draw the extra details before the vision faded. The indigenous fauna might help a native of the continent of Zewnath recognize the place.

While he worked, the mercenary unit that was politely *not* helping the mage crew subdue Jak and his mother came on deck and started doing calisthenics, not minding the sun or the increasing humidity. Meanwhile, Jak tried not to dribble sweat onto his paper.

"This is looking... almost decent," he decided as he sketched the finishing touches.

Maps were his passion and his specialty, but he could manage a landscape or a portrait when he had a model in front of him. Or a model magically inserted into his mind by an intelligent artifact.

"I don't suppose you could put a *map* into my mind?" Jak whispered after the vision faded. "Then we wouldn't have to find a guide or speak to anyone. We could fly straight to where you need to be placed in order to operate."

A sensation came from the artifact. It might have been confusion. It returned the vision of the pool to his mind.

Jak smiled. It was better than nothing. That an artifact could understand and communicate with him at all was amazing. Or *creepier than the slavemasters in Hell licking human blood off their whips,* as Captain Toggs had put it.

The salty sea breeze shifted, carrying faint murmurs to his ears. Toggs had called over two of his crewmen, younger mages with goatees that they stroked as they eyed Jak.

"...get back control... Has to be before... get to Zewnath," the words floated to him.

Pretending he was engrossed in his drawing, Jak didn't look at them, but he strained his ears, willing more of their words to carry to him.

From what he'd heard earlier, the *Dauntless* would reach the port city of Toh-drom on Zewnath's northern shoreline that evening. If the mages meant to wrest control from him—or *do* something to him—before then, he needed to know about it. So far, the artifact had pulsed a few times and helped make the crew believe Jak could use it as a weapon if the mages attacked him, but it hadn't hurled lightning bolts the way it had in the battle in King Uthari's courtyard. Because of that, the crew had been growing more brazen.

Or maybe they were more desperate. Jak didn't doubt that Toggs had received orders from his commander to return to Zarlesh with the portal. That was the whole reason the *Dauntless* had been sent to invade Utharika. If not for Jak and his mother—

and the will of the portal itself—Toggs would have succeeded with his mission by now.

"...shoot him... before the artifact... It won't defend him if he's dead."

"I'm tempted." That was Toggs. He didn't bother to lower his voice to a whisper. "It would be nice if those mercenaries would *assist* us with this difficulty. After all, they took King Zaruk's payment and signed a contract to help retrieve the portal."

Captain Ferroki, the commander of Thorn Company, was in the middle of performing push-ups with her unit, but she looked over at him. "Actually, we haven't been paid yet."

"That ought to incentivize you to help us solve this *problem*." Toggs pointed at Jak.

Ferroki, a dark-skinned woman of about fifty, was hard to read, and Jak had no idea what she was thinking when she gazed over at him.

During the voyage, he'd tried a few times to make eye contact and say witty and amusing things to Rookie Tezi, the youngest and prettiest of the mercenaries. Too bad she usually made an excuse and scurried away when he spoke to her. She was in the back row of the formation now, her blonde braid dipping to the deck with each push-up, and she didn't look over at him. He chose to believe that was because one of the grumpy sergeants was stalking around the formation, razzing anyone who paused, rather than an utter lack of interest in his fate.

"I may need your help in a moment." Jak again rested a hand on the smooth blue-black dragon steel, its surface warm and tingly under his palm. The confused feeling that emanated from the portal wasn't comforting.

A hatch opened, and Jak's mother walked out from belowdecks, the breeze tugging at her thick brown braid and loose trousers, tunic, and vest. She clinked as she moved. Jak wondered how many vials weighed down her pockets today, and if they held acids, liquid smoke, or some other concoction that could act as a weapon, or if she'd been scraping interesting plant or fungi specimens off the ship's hull.

She looked at the mercenaries and the mages as she walked toward Jak, and the concerned expression in her blue-gray eyes wasn't that reassuring.

"Problem?" Jak asked as she stopped in front of the portal. He remained on the inside, as he had for most of the trip, choosing to sleep and even eat in the spot, since he felt safer and more protected there. He had a hunch that one of the mages would risk attacking him if he went belowdecks—or anywhere out of sight of the artifact. "*New* problem?" he clarified, since they both knew their existing problems well.

"An extension of the same one. I thought I should tell you..." Mother glanced around again. Several people were watching them, and she lowered her voice. "I've had some dreams the last two nights."

"Dreams about how we'll succeed in getting the portal to this spot?" Jak tapped the pool in his drawing. "And how we'll slide the key into the keyhole?" He tapped the dragon-headed medallion affixed to the band in the hat he always wore, the hat that had once been his father's. "And how the portal will activate, so we can jump through it together and find some *amazing* dragons who have missed humans terribly these past ten thousand years? Dragons who are eager to return to Torvil to help us defeat all the wizard kings so we can bring peace and prosperity to all the terrene humans who are tired of living as serfs and slaves?"

"I'm afraid not." Mother smiled, but it was fleeting, and the concern remained in her eyes. "I dreamed—I'm not positive they *were* only dreams—that Malek was in my cabin."

"Oh."

Jak remembered the last time they'd seen King Uthari's loyal zidarr, a warrior and wizard of unparalleled skill and power and someone Jak dearly hoped wouldn't be sent after them. Malek had been recovering from a magical lightning bolt to the chest, and he'd held up a pistol as the *Dauntless* flew away from Uthari's castle. Malek *could* have fired at Jak or Mother, but he hadn't. Because Uthari wanted them alive, not dead. He wanted them to figure out how to open the portal, not for the good of mankind but for his own gain.

"Uh, what was Malek doing?" Jak asked. "And what do you mean you're not sure if they were dreams?"

Her next smile was bleak. "I don't know the full extent of zidarr abilities. I think it's possible he may have used magic to reach out to me in my sleep. He was asking me where we're going."

"Fortunately, you don't know." Jak turned over his drawing to hide it from her.

She snorted.

"Did he ask anything else? Did he say he's coming after us?" Jak also didn't know the full extent of a zidarr's abilities, but he'd seen Malek fight, and he'd experienced Malek reading his mind, so he had no trouble believing the man could reach out to them in their sleep, even from hundreds of miles away. Or maybe it was thousands of miles by now.

"Not exactly, but he said he would make sure we weren't harmed if I told him where we were going, so that implies he would be there." Mother wiped away the sheen of sweat on her forehead. "I hope he doesn't bring that awful General Tonovan with him if he comes."

"Me too. Mention that to him in your dreams, will you? Dear Lord Malek, you're invited to stalk us at a distance, but leave your general behind, please."

"I wasn't planning to invite *him* either."

"I know. Malek could drag us and the portal back to his king easily; I doubt I could talk the portal into attacking him." Jak doubted he could talk the portal into attacking *anyone* unless it was to defend itself or to defend him. For whatever reason, the artifact was interested in keeping him alive, probably because it knew he wanted to take it to its home and set it up. But Malek didn't want to kill Jak or his mother; he wanted to *use* them. The portal wouldn't object to that.

The mercenary Colonel Sorath walked past the plotting mages —or tried. Toggs reached out and gripped his arm, the normal arm, not the one that ended in a pickaxe head.

Toggs whispered harshly, the words too low for Jak to hear, but when Toggs pointed at him, there was little doubt about the topic of the conversation.

"I think the crew is a more immediate problem than Malek," Jak whispered.

"I think so too. You've been wise to sleep up here." Mother touched the portal. "I've wondered if I should too."

"Have any of the crew threatened you?" Jak hadn't been without dreams himself. The night before, he'd woken with a start, believing Toggs had grabbed Mother and pressed a dagger to her throat.

"No, but they haven't been that hospitable. It was the mercenaries who gave up one of their allotted cabins so I could have a bunk. Captain Ferroki has been sharing her food with me."

"Something Toggs looks irked about."

Toggs released Sorath with a shove, not that it budged the big fighter. Though in his fifties, with gray mingling with black in his wiry hair, the scarred Colonel Sorath was fit and muscular. Given the sword across his back, the pistol at his hip, and the sharp point of that pickaxe, even a mage would be foolish to pick a fight with him. He always had a pocket full of tiny spheres that exploded on impact with the ground—or a person—and he was an expert at wielding them to distract mages trying to use their power against him.

"I believe that man is irked about everything," Mother said.

"He probably has an inadequate drawing tool."

"Are you making penis euphemisms again?"

"Of course not. I'll be nineteen later this week. I'm told it's an age of maturity."

"I've spent most of my career on a university campus. I know exactly how mature nineteen-year-olds are." Mother glanced at the still-exercising mercenaries. "Have you made any inroads with them?"

He and Mother had agreed to try to befriend the fighters, figuring they were more likely to switch sides than the military mages loyal to their rulers.

"I've succeeded several times in causing Rookie Tezi to look awkwardly away from me and make excuses to hastily depart my presence," Jak said.

"That's not something a mother likes to hear."

"I'm just trying to start a conversation with her."

"Well, stop it. If she's interested in talking to you, she'll come to you. But chances are all of those women have had rough lives. Taking up arms and risking your life on a daily basis isn't a career you sign up for if everything has always been wonderful at home. Besides, *he's* the one you should befriend." Mother nodded toward Sorath as he left the mages and headed in their direction.

It wasn't clear if he wanted to talk to them or was simply walking the deck for exercise. Hours a day of walking, jogging, calisthenics, and sparring seemed a requirement for the mercenaries.

Jak eyed the scar on Sorath's face that ran from his eyebrow halfway down his cheek. Numerous bumps on his nose suggested it had been broken many times.

"Tezi seems a lot more approachable," Jak admitted. "I haven't noticed her driving pickaxes into people's skulls or otherwise garishly slaying them while being spattered in her enemy's blood."

Jak *was* intrigued that Sorath carried a pen in his bushy hair.

He'd heard a rumor that the man was writing a book. That seemed at odds with the garish pickaxe slaying.

"The lowest-ranking mercenary isn't the one we need to establish a rapport with," Mother said.

"I know." Jak had seen her speaking with Captain Ferroki several times and might have asked her how their *rapport* was coming along, but Sorath stopped in front of them.

"Your artifact keeps glowing," he remarked.

"It's giving me tips on my drawing." Jak started to point to it, then realized that if he and his mother escaped with the portal, the mercenaries might be paid to hunt them down. Giving them tips on their destination wasn't wise. He flipped the paper over again before Sorath got a good look. "But my work isn't ready for a gallery showing."

Sorath arched his eyebrows. "I've heard of artifacts made from lesser dragon steel being able to share visions with their owners. It's not surprising that full dragon steel could have even more magical properties." He scratched his jaw with the tip of his pick. "I admit I was startled when it hurled lightning at our enemies. And was it also responsible for destroying the tool that kept the castle shield in place and allowed us to escape?"

Given how chaotic the battle in the courtyard had been, Jak wouldn't have expected Sorath, who'd been busy fighting guards, to notice all that. Maybe he'd pieced it together based on the timing.

Jak had little familiarity with the various mercenary units in the world, since Uth and Sprungtown had been protected under King Uthari's rule for all of his life, but he'd heard the Thorn Company women talking about how Sorath was, or had once been, a brilliant commander who'd won numerous battles against impossible odds. Even if he looked like a bruiser, Jak couldn't let himself think of Sorath as a dumb thug.

"I didn't see that particular blow," Jak said, though the portal had shared a vision with him, "but I believe so."

"Interesting. I've read about the dragon portal, and I don't think any kind of sentience or ability to do more than open passageways to the dragon home world was ever mentioned."

"You've read about it?" Mother asked. "Do you have an interest in archeology?"

"It's been a hobby for me over the years. I'm certain I haven't anywhere near your knowledge." Sorath nodded politely, not only to Mother but to Jak as well.

If Sorath weren't a potential enemy, who might have come over here at Toggs's request to gather information, Jak would have been flattered. Neither Uthari nor anyone else had seemed to believe that *he* had any knowledge worth anything. As far as they all believed, he was tagging along to hold his mother's pencils. That Sorath, through very few interactions, had come to believe Jak knew something was more concerning than flattering.

"It was built and abandoned before humans had a written language," Mother said, though she glanced at the phrase in Ancient Zeruvian engraved at the bottom of the portal. *Gateway to the stars.* "Our knowledge of its abilities is limited. We also don't know why it was buried on that volcanic island, far from where it originally stood."

"I wondered how it came to be there if it was built, or at least operated, on Zewnath." Sorath's brows rose again. "Was it? Or am I making too many assumptions based on the direction you're sending us?"

"We believe it can operate there, yes," Mother said tersely, glancing at Jak.

Maybe she also wondered if Sorath had been sent over to pump them for information.

"And it won't operate anywhere else?" he asked.

"We don't know that for certain yet," Mother said, "but there have been clues to suggest it needs to be in the Southern Hemisphere."

"Oh? We're almost there now. Maybe we could try it from the ship." Sorath eyed Jak's hat. No, he was eyeing the *medallion* in the headband.

"Maybe." Mother shrugged.

"Please forgive my interest." Sorath inclined his head again. "As I said, archaeology is a hobby, and this is quite a find. That hobby is why Captain Ferroki originally came to ask me about that medallion."

It hadn't occurred to Jak to wonder how Sorath had gotten involved with Thorn Company—Zaruk's alliance had hired numerous mercenary companies to attack King Uthari's city—but maybe it should have.

"What was your assessment of it?" Mother asked.

"Just that it's dragon steel and possibly the key to the portal." Sorath extended a hand toward it. "Do you think that's the only one or that there were once many in existence? If a key is required for use, there might be numerous keys out there. Unless that one goes into the hole and remains there all the time. Then there might be only one per portal. That seems unlikely though, doesn't it? What would the point be of even having a key?"

"We don't know," Mother said. "That's interesting to consider though."

Jak hoped Sorath was wrong. *He* wanted to be the one to go through the portal to another world. If there were dozens of keys out there, that meant dozens of opportunities for others to beat him through and contact the dragons first. Hopefully, if many keys had once existed, they'd all been lost, or at least were not anywhere that the kings—or Malek—could easily find them.

"I said to figure out how to get *rid* of them," Captain Toggs called to Sorath's back, "not chat with them about archaeology."

Exasperation flashed in Sorath's dark eyes, but it was gone by the time he looked over his shoulder at Toggs. "I'm being friendly and lulling them into believing I'm not a threat."

Jak exchanged a long look with his mother. Just because Sorath was being open and sarcastic didn't mean the statement was untrue.

"Oh, carry on then," Toggs said. "Do you want me to have a crewman fetch you some tea for your lulling? A tropical juice beverage?"

"We'll take papaya juice," Sorath called before turning back to Jak and Mother. "You may have guessed that he's plotting to get rid of you and change course."

"We didn't have to guess," Jak said. "I heard him talking to his men. He's not being subtle."

"Those who can hurl fireballs to incinerate their enemies rarely bother with subtle," Sorath said.

"Malek does," Jak said.

Mother gave him a sharp look. A warning not to speak of her dreams?

Sorath's expression grew bleak. "He isn't always, but he can be subtle, yes. I would prefer not to see him again, or any other zidarr, but I'm sure I won't be that lucky."

"I guess that means you'll be offended if he shows up," Jak said, "and I point him in your direction instead of mine."

He'd meant it as a joke, but Sorath's face only grew darker. "Very offended, yes." Sorath headed toward the hatch leading belowdecks. "Watch your back, killer," he said over his shoulder.

"Was that a warning or a threat?" Jak asked.

"I don't know," Mother said, "but you could work more on your rapport-building skills."

"Maybe when I'm nineteen and more mature, they'll come more readily."

"Let's hope." Mother looked toward the southern horizon, probably hoping to spot Zewnath's northern coastline. Unfortunately, the *Dauntless* was still hours away. "They probably don't know that *we* don't know where on the continent we need to go. They may feel the need to act before we reach Port Toh-drom."

"Meaning we should both stay here hunkered in the middle of the portal?"

"It might not be a bad idea. I wish we had money so we could hire another ship once we get there. As long as we're surrounded by men loyal to King Zaruk's alliance, we'll be at risk."

"I know." Jak leaned a hand on the portal.

Surprisingly, it shared a new vision with him, one of three blue-hulled mageships flying above the sea. Zaruk's people. Judging by the position of the sun, and assuming the vision indicated something in real time, the three ships were flying south— the same direction as the *Dauntless*. Mage soldiers in uniforms prowled the decks, and the ships' artillery weapons were manned.

Jak spun to peer behind them, afraid the vessels might even now be in sight. They weren't, but that didn't mean they wouldn't be soon.

"Do you think..." Jak shifted his weight. "Do you think Zaruk's people can track the portal?"

From his own meager ability to sense magic, Jak knew it had a powerful signature. What he didn't know was how far away one could sense it from. It couldn't be *that* far, or mages living in Perchver would have detected it buried under the rock on one of their nearby Dragon Perch islands. Unless the rock had insulated it. Or it had been dormant then and not given off much of a signature.

"Possibly," Mother said.

"Because the portal is showing me three ships that might be pursuing us."

"Ah." She didn't sound surprised. "I think that was inevitable. Toggs surely has a dome-jir and can communicate with his people. He's likely been updating Queen Vorsha on exactly where we are, and she's aligned with King Zaruk. It was only a matter of time before they sent more ships after us. I'd hoped we would reach land first and figure out a way to slip off into the jungle with the artifact."

Slip off? With a twenty-foot-wide metal portal?

"What happens if we *don't* reach land first?"

"Our day gets a lot worse."

2

ZIDARR MALEK SIFTED THROUGH THE RUBBINGS, ATLASES, AND archaeology books on his desk in his cabin on the *Star Flyer*. For the last few days, he'd been using his magic to help with repairs of Utharika's city walls and the mageships in King Uthari's fleet, so he hadn't had much time to research the portal or the hunch that had come to him as soon as Professor Jadora Freedar and her son had escaped with it.

He believed they weren't letting the mercenaries and crew of the *Dauntless* take it back to King Zaruk. Why would they want to go from being prisoners in Utharika to prisoners of another king in another sky city? He didn't know how they had convinced that ship's crew to take them somewhere else, but he was certain they had.

Admittedly, he had no proof. Uthari's intelligence agents in other cities and in other rulers' fleets hadn't reported seeing it. Malek was basing his belief on what he'd come to know about Jak and Jadora and on what he'd dreamed about her the last couple of nights.

In the dreams, she'd been in a cabin on a mageship—the *Dauntless*, presumably—on a long journey, a longer journey than they would have needed to reach Zaruk's kingdom. He'd asked her where they were going, and she'd refused to respond, but then he'd touched her mind. In her thoughts, he'd seen a lush jungle and a waterfall, and he'd sensed she was heading south. To the continent of Zewnath or somewhere nearby.

There had been a time when Malek wouldn't have relied on his dreams for anything, since they'd been meaningless drivel spawned by his subconscious, but a few years into his career as a zidarr, he'd won first his main-gauche and later his longsword in battles against mighty warriors. The weapons were made from lesser dragon steel and had, as he'd learned, a few properties beyond being useful as unbreakable blades.

He sometimes received warnings from them, flashes of insight that alerted him when an enemy was targeting his back. His dreams had also changed after he'd had them for a while, shifting from meaningless imagery quickly forgotten upon waking to highlights of possible futures as well as glimpses of what his enemies were plotting. Sometimes, he could even go to sleep thinking about what he wished to learn, and the weapons would accommodate. It didn't always work, but when it did, he almost always found out later that what they'd shown him had been the truth.

Dreaming of a woman was a first, especially since he didn't consider Jadora an enemy, but he did feel a link with her, so maybe it wasn't surprising. And since he'd failed to keep her from getting away with the artifact, and felt the need to find it for his king, his subconscious mind was no doubt dwelling on that.

Still, without actual evidence, Malek couldn't order his ship off to the Southern Hemisphere, especially not when Uthari had commanded him to stay here. He had to finish helping with repairs and ward off enemies if anyone returned to lay siege again to the city. Not that such seemed likely to happen. It had been quiet since the *Dauntless* escaped with the portal.

Malek lifted one of the rubbings he'd taken of the collections of symbols on the inside of the portal. It was the only one that reminded him of a written language he'd seen in an archaeology book.

The leaf and branch accents were distinctive and favored by the druids that lived in several regions of Zewnath. The journal he'd copied said in several places that the portal was believed to be older than any of the written languages of Torvil, and yet... there were at least two examples to the contrary. It would be interesting if the languages had been *based* on the symbols on the portal and not added to it later, but he wasn't enough of a student of the topic to guess if that was plausible.

He caught himself wishing he could discuss it with Jadora, then snorted at himself. He was a warrior and a wizard, having spent thirty years of his life training in those areas to best serve his king. It had only been at Uthari's behest that he'd started studying archaeology. This wasn't his passion, nor would Jadora enjoy discussing it with him. Or discussing *anything* with him. Despite Uthari's suggestion, Malek hadn't managed to gain her trust while she'd been imprisoned here. Even though it had been an impossible task—how did a captor gain the trust of a captive?—he couldn't help but feel he'd failed his king in that regard as well as in keeping the portal.

A knock sounded at his door, and he sensed Captain Rivlen in the corridor, no doubt here to make her daily report.

Three days before, she'd been Lieutenant Rivlen, second-in-command of the *Night Falcon*, where she'd apparently performed spectacularly during the siege, helping take down numerous enemy ships. Meanwhile, the *Star Flyer* had lost Captain Korthan during the battle with Stone Heart's ship and needed a new commander. General Tonovan had ordered Rivlen's transfer to the *Star Flyer* and promoted her to captain. The choice surprised Malek, since he'd assumed the *Star Flyer*'s more experienced Lieutenant Yardrakan would be granted the position.

Malek was suspicious of Tonovan's motives, assuming he had chosen Rivlen either because she was loyal to him and would spy on Malek or because she was an attractive woman he hoped to have sex with when he was aboard, but he hadn't cared enough to object. Tonovan's machinations kept Malek on his toes. Besides, Rivlen had an exemplary record and was a powerful mage in addition to being a capable officer and warrior. At twenty-five, she was now the youngest mageship commander in Uthari's fleet, but as far as Malek knew, her promotions hadn't been without merit.

"Come, Captain," he said.

Rivlen opened the door, stepped inside, and saluted. "I have your report, my lord."

"Go ahead."

"Repairs have been completed on the *Star Flyer*," she stated in a professional, matter-of-fact tone that matched her tight brown bun, pressed uniform, and polished boots, "as well as the *Comet Chaser,* the *King's Courage,* and the *Dragon Dart.* The city wall, watchtowers, and infrastructure are also as new again. The city's defensive shield is being reinforced and extended out over the docks. We've also, as you requested, reinforced the *Star Flyer*'s engine, power infrastructure, and hull with layered magic superior to what existed before." She inclined her head toward him. "The crew are appreciative that you helped with that work and are somewhat bemused that you picked up a hammer and mage wrench."

Rivlen looked him up and down. Nothing prolonged or rude, but he had the sense that she was assessing him. They hadn't worked together before, though most people in Uthari's employ were familiar with Malek.

"The *crew* are?" he asked.

He'd helped with repairs to the *Star Flyer* before. It was the ship he flew on most often, so he had reason to want it to be as well-maintained and impervious to attacks as possible, but he would have helped anyway. If he wasn't training to maintain his fitness as a mage and warrior, he had to do *something*. Under the Zidarr Code, idleness was frowned upon.

"*I* am appreciative. I *was*." Rivlen looked flustered as she shook her head, but she quickly regained her professional reserve. "Lord Yidar is the zidarr who usually traveled on the *Night Falcon*."

"Did he not lend his assistance when repairs were needed?"

"He was too busy training. Usually with his shirt off out on the deck in front of the female officers." Rivlen kept her tone passive, as if she were simply delivering facts without condemnation, but it was hard to miss her distaste.

Even though Yidar had proven himself too ambitious to be trusted of late, and was even now getting a second chance to prove himself to Uthari by finding the archaeologists and the portal, Malek would not speak ill of his fellow zidarr.

"He is young," was all he said.

"Of course."

Rivlen probably knew better than to be too disparaging of a zidarr, for she went back to her report, letting him know the *Star Flyer* had been resupplied and was ready for a trip, should that be required. She sounded hopeful, like someone who longed for battle and action rather than lurking around the city on the off chance that enemies returned.

Malek understood the feeling perfectly well.

As he listened, he picked up more of the rubbings, now eyeing the ones that contained groupings of dots. He hadn't thought much of them when he'd made the rubbings, using a charcoal pencil to gather them in case a time came when he didn't have access to the portal. Little had he known that it would be so soon.

Only when Jak had opted to do his own rubbings with a blue crayon had Malek gotten the clue that these dots might represent constellations. But he recognized only one of them, the Dragon's Tail, a grouping of stars visible only from the Southern Hemisphere.

The urge to order the *Star Flyer* to carry him to Zewnath was difficult to resist, especially since he doubted Yidar had gone in that direction. Malek understood why Uthari had ordered him to stay here, but he longed to find the portal and Jadora and Jak before his colleague.

Should Yidar find them first, he might not let Jak live. He'd wanted to kill Jak as soon as he'd realized Jak was a wild one—an untrained boy with magical power who'd been raised by terrene humans.

Jak didn't mean anything to Malek, though Malek also felt no ill will toward him, but Jak and Jadora were both knowledgeable about the portal and could be useful in achieving Uthari's goals. It would be a shame to kill him. Malek also didn't want to see Jadora hurt by losing her son. If one of Uthari's people was responsible for that, it would be even more challenging to get her to work for them.

"Finally," Rivlen finished, "I have informed General Tonovan that I will not have sex with him."

Malek, realizing his mind had drifted from her report, focused on her again. Puzzled by the statement, he said, "Tonovan is currently riding along with Yidar on the *King's Courage*. I suspect that will not be an issue."

Rivlen's brown eyes narrowed. "He let me know when I assumed command of the *Star Flyer* that he travels on this vessel frequently and expects to have his *needs* attended whenever he's here. He went on to remark on my tits and ass and how much *other* female officers have enjoyed his cock lately." She said this in the same matter-of-fact tone with which she'd delivered the rest of the report, though indignation had found its way into her eyes. "I told him I would launch a fireball at his cock and char his balls to ash if he touched me again."

Again? Malek raised his eyebrows, but when Rivlen continued, she didn't go into details on any past encounters she might have had with the general.

"In response," she said, "he told *me* that I would fail utterly at said ball-charring and that such an attempt would result in disciplinary action, that I would be drummed out of the fleet, if not outright slain for attacking a superior officer." She paused and looked Malek in the eye—previously, she'd been delivering the report to his collar bones. "You are wondering why I am telling you this, my lord, when you are outside of the fleet and not in my chain of command."

It had crossed his mind. She didn't seem to be the type who would ask him for protection.

"I wanted someone with King Uthari's ear to know that if I end up killing General Tonovan, it will only be to keep him from pawing over me like a rutting baboon, and that it would not be right for my superiors to punish me for defending myself, even from a superior officer."

"Do you think you can kill him?" Malek asked curiously.

"I am aware that he is very powerful with the designation of not only mage but *wizard*, and that I am young and only a mage, but I am not weak. Also, he is a pompous, arrogant blowhard with more weaknesses than a sandbag wall facing a flood."

"I assumed Tonovan was the one responsible for your promotion." Malek, recalling his earlier thoughts that Rivlen might be a spy for Tonovan, wondered if her indignation might be a ruse. Had Tonovan put her up to this? "Is that not true?"

"He signed my orders," Rivlen said shortly. "I do not know if they were his idea or came from someone else."

"Only King Uthari outranks him."

"I do not know if the king is aware of me or not, but Tonovan does not like me because I speak my mind about what an ass he is. It is possible he gave me this command because I am young, and he believes I will fail and embarrass my family." Rivlen lifted her chin. "I will *not*."

"Good."

Rivlen saluted him again. "My report is complete. I look forward to serving on your ship, my lord, and I trust I will have the opportunity to prove to you that I am a worthy commander for the *Star Flyer*."

She walked out, closing the door and leaving him more aware than ever how little familiarity he had with the ways of women. Mind reading did not work on fellow mages, who were adept at walling off their thoughts, so he was left with only physical and verbal cues. He still didn't know if Rivlen was genuinely upset with Tonovan or if they were working together to deceive him.

It was no wonder he had been clueless when it came to figuring out how to earn Jadora's trust.

Malek, King Uthari spoke into his mind. *Are you busy?*

Malek sensed that Uthari was in his suite in the castle. The *Star Flyer* was close enough that telepathic communication was a simple matter, though it was likely Uthari could have reached him from hundreds of miles away.

I have been receiving Captain Rivlen's report, but she just finished, so I am not busy.

Ah, good. I was the one to recommend her for command of your ship, though I left it to Tonovan's discretion. I have not spoken with her personally, but she has an exemplary record.

Does it involve frying the balls of her superior officers?

I don't believe so. Did she threaten your nether regions? That seems unlikely.

No. Tonovan's if he molests her.

He prefers prey that he can cow easily.

I am aware. Malek attempted to keep judgment from accompanying the thoughts, not because he believed he was wrong to condemn Tonovan for his tastes, but because it wasn't his place to complain to Uthari about his officers. Besides, Tonovan was not the only high-ranking mage officer who traveled with a harem of terrene humans. Uthari allowed his officers pleasurable indulgences if they distinguished themselves in battle.

I would appreciate it if you kept an eye out for Rivlen, Uthari surprised him by saying. Malek wouldn't have guessed he cared. *At least in regard to Tonovan and his sexual appetites. She is young, but she has great potential as an officer, both because she is competent as a leader and because of her growing power. Perhaps she even has the potential to take Tonovan's place one day.*

Malek would not miss Tonovan if he retired—or was killed in his sleep by a slave. *It is unlikely they will encounter each other soon,* was all he said.

They might. Yidar and Tonovan reached Zarlesh and discovered that the portal is not there. The city was also not well-defended. They believe that King Zaruk and his allies have sent many of their mageships in search of our wayward archaeologists and the portal.

I suspected they would not find it in Zarlesh.

Do you know where they're taking it?

Malek eyed the rubbing. *I believe Zewnath, but I don't know where on the continent.*

Why there? Because no king claims that land?

Because there are symbols on the portal suggesting it originated there or perhaps must be used there.

Interesting. I will tell Yidar and Tonovan to head in that direction. How long have you known about this?

Malek couldn't tell if there was judgment in Uthari's words. *Not long, and I am not positive, but I have clues that lead me to believe they went south.* He didn't bring up the dreams, though Uthari also had artifacts made from lesser dragon steel, so he might understand.

Even so, it seemed like a silly thing to admit. The rubbings were more concrete evidence. *Do you wish me to go after the portal as well? And the archaeologists?*

He'd wanted to from the beginning, and an unexpected eagerness filled him at the thought. Because he worried that Yidar would kill Jak and Jadora, he told himself. There was no other reason he should want to be the one to recapture them, other than because it was his duty to do as Uthari wished.

Yes. With repairs nearly finished, I no longer need you here. Help Tonovan reacquire the portal, find out if it must be used on Zewnath and where, and get the archaeologists. Keep the professor, in particular, alive. Remember, I need her because of her knowledge of the Jitaruvak plant, not only archaeology. She must be kept alive at all costs.

I will find her and the portal. Will you recall Yidar?

No. As I said, there were fewer ships than expected around Zarlesh. I believe that Zaruk, his allies, and perhaps by now all the other kings and queens are aware that the portal is out there somewhere for the taking. More than that, Zaruk and Vorsha should know exactly where it is, since the archaeologists left on one of Vorsha's ships. Entire fleets might even now be descending on Zewnath. It is likely you will need Yidar and Tonovan, and the ships I sent with them, to help against so many. I want you to make sure that we are the ones to get the prize.

Malek grimaced, not certain that Yidar would work *with* him rather than against him. As much of an ass as Tonovan was, Malek didn't think he would betray Uthari, but Yidar had already proven once that he would.

You mage-marked Yidar before he left. Can you punish him from afar if he betrays us again?

I can. And you can trust I will be paying close attention to his actions. This is important, Malek. I am tempted to leave Utharika to go myself, but I would be foolish to believe that none of my enemies will take this opportunity to attack when I am distracted and many of our forces are away from the city. I am depending on you, my old friend.

I understand. I will not fail you, Sire.

On the deck of the *Dauntless*, Tezi Tigan parried a sword thrust with a sideways jump and a twist of her wrist. She came down in a crouch, ready for the next attack, but her opponent halted, lowered her blade, and propped a fist on her hip.

"What was that?" Sergeant Tinder demanded over the sword clashes from the other mercenaries paired up around them for weapons practice.

"What?"

"That bunny hop. And that little flick." Tinder emulated the wrist twist with far more flamboyance than Tezi had used.

"Uhm, flair?"

"Well, knock it off. You perform the moves like we show you, as fast, accurate, and as efficiently as possible. If you deflect the parry correctly, you won't need to jump back and give ground. And adding *flair* will get you killed. I could have swept your leg when you jumped, and you'd be on the deck on your back right now."

"Yes, Sergeant. Sorry, Sergeant."

Since the infiltration of King Uthari's castle, Tezi had felt slightly better about her abilities as a mercenary, but leave it to the tall, burly Sergeant Tinder to knock her back down to inept beginner status. Tezi had helped Colonel Sorath in the tunnels, and even kept Tinder and the others from being hurt by a grenade hurtling toward them, but maybe she would never be anything but a rookie in the eyes of the others. At least Sorath had acknowledged her help. He called her *killer* instead of rookie. Granted, he called everyone killer, but it was still more flattering than anything Sergeant Tinder called her.

"Let's do it again. *Seriously.*" Tinder lifted her sword.

Before they came together for another round, an angry male voice distracted them.

"I want to talk to you mercenaries." It was the perennially cranky Captain Toggs. He'd singled out Captain Ferroki and was gesturing for Colonel Sorath, who'd been sparring with Lieutenant Sasko, to join them.

Tezi thought Tinder would want to continue their practice and leave the meeting to the officers, but Tinder paused to watch, her fist finding her hip again. "This won't be anything good."

"I'm tired of you supposed *fighters* lounging around on my ship all day, doing nothing while that kid sits over there hugging the priceless artifact that Queen Vorsha and King Zaruk ordered us to bring back to *them*." Toggs pointed toward the great portal taking up substantial room on the deck of the mageship.

Jak and Jadora were both standing inside it, comparing notes and looking at maps. Tezi hadn't seen Jak climb out of the center since he'd threatened to have it attack the crew if they didn't fly the ship to Zewnath. A wise choice, because everyone aboard wanted to throw him over the railing and finish the job they'd been hired to do.

Sorath was the only mercenary that Tezi had seen speak to Jak. Jak had attempted to draw *her* into conversations a few times, but she'd hurried away. She didn't think he was a villain, not exactly, but she worried she would get into trouble if people witnessed her speaking to him. The mercenaries were already receiving ferocious frowns from the mage crew members.

"We're practicing, not lounging," Captain Ferroki said, calm in the face of Toggs's bluster. "Like the panther in the Kraetorian Forest, we're poised to attack when our prey presents itself."

"Uh huh. Your prey is right *there*." Toggs pointed to Jak again.

He didn't bother keeping his voice down, and Jak and Jadora looked warily toward him.

Tezi had no idea if Jak could truly command the artifact to spit lightning at anyone who crossed him. She'd seen the amazing destruction it had done back at the castle, but that might have been a simple defense mechanism magically imbued into the portal.

"I've had word—numerous times a day—from Zaruk and Vorsha," Toggs went on. "They want the artifact back, and they want it *now*. They've sent more ships after us, and if we can't resolve this problem on our own, they have orders to attack us and resolve it *for* us. Which will mean the *Dauntless* and everyone aboard, including lounging mercenaries, will end up dead at the bottom of the sea."

Most of the sparring matches had stopped, and the Thorn Company women exchanged low mutters and uneasy glances.

"You people should have attacked those two and gotten rid of them *days* ago," Toggs continued, "not sat here and eaten our food and done *nothing*."

"We signed on to help invade Utharika and retrieve the artifact from his castle," Ferroki said. "We've held up our end of the deal, and we haven't yet been paid. It is your people who are in breach of our contract."

"I'm sure King Zaruk will pay you as soon as you help us *get the artifact back to his city*." By now, everyone on the deck was looking at Toggs. Sweat dampened his brow, and he kept pushing a hand through his gray hair in agitation. That threat from his superiors must have come in recently.

"What do you want us to do?" Ferroki looked at Sorath, who'd stepped up to her side.

Toggs lowered his voice. "Kill those two or at least dump them overboard."

"And if the boy commands lightning to shoot out of the artifact?" Sorath asked.

Tezi had seen some of those lightning strikes land. Zidarr Malek had survived being struck, but several guards in that courtyard had been killed, their heads blasted clean off or torsos horribly charred by great power.

"Maybe you'll lose some people," Toggs said, flicking a hand toward Tezi, "but that's how it is. You're mercenaries, and this is war. Just get rid of those two before that portal can kill everyone. I'm sure once the kid is gone, it won't attack us."

"How can you be sure of that?" Ferroki's voice was impressively calm, considering he was asking her to sacrifice her troops.

Since Toggs had pointed to *Tezi*, she felt anything but calm.

"I'm not sure he has the power to do *anything*," Toggs growled.

"Here's an idea," Sorath said. "Why don't you send some of *your* people at him to find out?"

"We're not sacrificing *mages* when there are expendable terrene humans here." Toggs pointed again, not just to Tezi this time, but to all of Thorn Company.

"Expendable," Sorath said. "Right."

Tezi tightened her fist around her sword hilt, though she wouldn't dare attack Toggs. She'd killed mages before—and not only as a hired mercenary in combat, when the Rules of War allowed it—and thanks to that, she had to spend the rest of her life watching over her shoulder, hoping they didn't find out.

"Can't your mages raise barriers to protect themselves?" Ferroki asked.

"I don't know. That *thing*—" Toggs's hand flick went toward the portal this time, "—nailed King Uthari. And it wasn't so instantaneous that he couldn't have seen it coming. I'm positive he and some of the others in that battle had their defenses up, and it *still* zapped them." He brought his pointing finger back to them, to Ferroki's chest. "You pick some people to send in as fodder, and then you shoot those two while the artifact is busy zapping others. Shoot them, and throw them over the side. If you don't, we'll *all* have to face a bunch of mageships, not to mention the zidarr that my commander said Zaruk is sending along. We'll *all* end up dead, mages and mercenaries alike. You've got ten minutes to figure something out."

"What's the hurry, killer?" Sorath drawled, as calm as Ferroki.

"They're less than an hour from catching up to us is *the hurry*." Toggs waved toward the horizon behind the ship. "I can sense them coming. The zidarr is using his magic to propel them along at a faster speed than should be possible. We're not going to make it to land, and there wouldn't be any escape from them there anyway. Ten minutes, Thorn Company." Toggs stalked off, rejoining a group of his crew.

"I hate those bastards," Tinder growled. "They all think they're some evolved form of humans and so much better than the rest of us. Let him sacrifice *his* people."

Tezi shook her head bleakly, certain that wouldn't happen. Even if Sorath and Ferroki had been willing to look the other way when Jak and Jadora had first convinced Toggs to change course, they wouldn't dare continue to do so now.

"Do you think the captain will send me in?" Tezi whispered to Tinder. "As a sacrifice? Because I'm new and... expendable?"

"If she sends you in, it won't be because you're new. It'll be because of your ill-advised flair."

Tezi turned her bleak expression on Tinder.

"I'm kidding." Tinder thumped her on the shoulder hard enough to make Tezi take a step to brace herself. "Even if she does order us to attack and puts you at the front of the charge, you'll be fine."

"What? Why?"

"The kid over there drools every time you walk by."

It took Tezi a moment to realize what she meant. "I doubt the *artifact* is attracted to me."

"Yeah, but if he's controlling it, he's not going to let it zap you. If the other ships attack, you can hop in the middle with him, stroke his hair a little, and bask in his ardor while he protects you."

Tezi knew it was a joke, but she couldn't keep from frowning. "I don't need a boy to protect me. I'm here with you, learning to protect myself."

"Sorry, Rookie. None of us can teach you how to protect yourself from magical lightning bolts hurled by a pissed-off ancient portal. We should *all* get in the middle with him and hope for the best. Maybe it'll go after the mages instead." Tinder tapped her chin. "Do you think we could all fit?"

"I doubt he would let us all in, even if we could."

"Sure he would. You just do your part." Tinder stroked her own hair to demonstrate.

"Funny, Sergeant."

"Keeping the rookies entertained is my job." Tinder pointed at Tezi's sword. "Do some shadow sparring. I'm getting my grenades. Just in case." She eyed Sorath and Ferroki, who had their heads together as they debated their options.

Tezi worried that they didn't *have* any options. Fighting mages wasn't impossible—she'd learned that when she'd gone into battle with Sorath—but it wasn't wise. And they would never survive against far superior numbers. Even one-on-one was iffy. They had *so* many advantages.

The first time Tezi had killed a mage, it had only been possible because he'd been drunkenly asleep on top of her after raping her. She'd tried to fight him off when he'd first collected her, after he and his buddy had killed her parents, but she hadn't been strong enough. Even drunk, he'd been too much for her to handle, too impossible to stop. She hated those people and hated that she had to live in fear of them.

She happened to be looking toward the artifact when Jak glanced over, meeting her eyes. Usually, he smiled at her, but he only grimaced and looked past her to the officers—Sasko had joined Sorath and Ferroki. Since Toggs hadn't bothered whispering, Jak had probably heard the captain's ultimatum.

"We're going to have to subdue them somehow," Sorath told Ferroki with a sigh. "I was willing to look the other way in the hope... you know what those two want to do, right?"

"I know," Ferroki said, "but their plan is naive at best."

Tezi listened to them but also mulled over Tinder's comments. If Tinder was right, would Jak let her get close, and could she... use that somehow?

Tinder had grenades. Did she have anything sneakier? Smoke bombs or some chemical concoction that could knock people out?

Maybe if Tezi could do that, and take Jak by surprise before he could order the artifact to attack, the company could capture those two and lock them up below. If Jak was unconscious, he couldn't make the artifact zap people, right?

That would be better than Jak and Jadora being killed, and Zaruk could still get the artifact, the company could be paid, and maybe Tinder and the others would think of Tezi as a worthy addition, not an expendable rookie.

The idea of tricking Jak didn't appeal to Tezi, but she nodded to herself as she solidified the plan. This was better than death. By the time Tinder returned with her grenades, Tezi was ready to share her idea.

She walked over to the officers and lifted a finger, hoping they would hear her out before shooing her away. "Captain? Colonel?"

They looked at her. She licked her lips—strange how dry they'd just gotten—and explained her idea.

"Now you're thinking," Tinder told her, grinning.

Sorath and Ferroki exchanged long looks. They didn't appear as delighted by the plan, and nerves tangled in Tezi's belly. Maybe it wasn't as clever as she'd thought.

"I think," Sorath said slowly, "we should have tried this last night if we were going to do it. They know everyone is angling for them now." He tilted his head toward Jak and Jadora without looking in their direction.

"I agree that it's unlikely you'll be able to trick them now," Ferroki said.

"Not *them*," Tinder said, taking position as Tezi's advocate. "Only the kid. Even if he sees it coming, he's not going to order the artifact to attack her. His penis won't let him."

Ferroki rolled her eyes. Tezi blushed.

"His mother is standing right next to him," Ferroki said. "Even if he's too full of lust to think straight, she won't have that problem."

"It could still work." Sorath stroked his chin thoughtfully. "Rookie Tezi would only have to get close to them, not physically knock them out or convince them to leave the portal. I agree that he's not likely to attack her, and I like the idea of locking them up instead of killing them. It's not our job to kill civilians."

"It's not our job to kill anyone," Ferroki said with a sigh. "Not now. As I pointed out to Toggs, we *did* our job."

"I don't disagree," Sorath said, "but if he's not lying to us about ships coming, we don't have a choice. We have to wrest those two away from the artifact."

Ferroki didn't look happy, but she raised her eyebrows toward Tinder. "Do you have anything that could knock them unconscious?"

"Actually, *I* have something." Dr. Fret was the one to raise a finger. She'd been listening from the outskirts of the group. "Sedatives in my medical kit."

"Can you teach the rookie how to deploy them without knocking *herself* out?" Tinder asked.

"Certainly. If the captain agrees."

"Go ahead," Ferroki said. "It beats the other options we were discussing."

Like shooting Jak and Jadora? Tezi nodded. She hoped to avoid that.

They would be furious when they woke up to find their precious artifact gone, but so be it. They'd been foolish to believe they could keep it away from mages. Mages always won. That was just the way the world was.

3

A SEAGULL SQUAWKED SOMEWHERE BELOW THE MAGESHIP. THE sound of the bird might have filled Jadora with hope, since it meant they were close to land, but she'd heard the ultimatum Captain Toggs had given the mercenaries, and she'd seen them over there plotting. She doubted she and Jak would make it to Port Toh-drom with the portal. Even if they did, they didn't have a way to get it off the ship or know where to take it.

"We're so close," she whispered, slipping her late husband's journal and the maps they'd been perusing into her pockets, "and yet so far."

Jak, who'd already put away his drawing and pencils, crouched low and rested his hand on the portal. His head was below the surface, meaning the crew and mercenaries couldn't see him. He might be communicating with it. Trying to convince it to attack? His lips were pulled back, his face a rictus of concentration.

"What are you doing?" Jadora watched the mercenaries as she asked. The young blonde woman—Rookie Tezi—was being singled out for something.

"Trying to either convince the artifact that it needs to fly itself to land or channel my nascent magical powers to levitate it overboard myself."

Jadora raised dubious eyebrows. "Maybe you should start by trying to levitate something smaller. Like a pencil."

"I don't need my *pencil* to escape our enemies."

"Starting with a five-hundred-pound artifact is ambitious."

Dragon steel weighed a lot less than regular steel, but it still wasn't *light*.

"I know, but wouldn't it be great if it worked?" Jak asked, eyes squinted shut. "I could be like Malek and lift it wherever I wanted. Maybe while we ride it. All the way to safety."

Jadora, doubting he would be able to lift it an inch, didn't point out that all the other mages on the ship could probably levitate it too. At best, they would end up in a tug-of-war. Assuming they didn't take advantage of Jak's distraction and shoot him.

Tezi smoothed her hair, lifted her chin, and strolled toward the artifact.

Before this, Jadora hadn't seen her sway her hips, thrust her breasts out, or do anything remotely flirty, so the fact that she did so now sounded alarms in her mind. Jadora knew exactly what the mercenaries were going to try. They'd gone back to sparring with their swords, but several had pistols on their hips, and they were all watching Tezi while pretending not to watch her.

Jadora started to reach for Jak, to warn him that she was coming, but maybe it was better if he didn't see her at all.

"We're not interested," Jadora told Tezi and made a shooing motion, trying to send her back to her people. Toggs and his wizards were watching her even more closely than the mercenaries. "Thanks."

Tezi stopped, her determined expression faltering, but she took a breath and kept approaching the artifact. She glanced warily at it and stopped short of touching it.

"I came to talk to Jak." Tezi clasped her hands behind her back. Was she holding something?

"He's busy."

"I wanted to know if he'd like to join me for a drink."

"He wouldn't."

Jak bolted upright. "What?"

"It's hot out here on the deck," Tezi said. "I thought we could go below and have a drink."

Jadora put a hand on his head and tried to push him back down. "You're busy. Nascent magic, remember?"

Tezi smiled warmly at him.

"Uh." Jak looked longingly at that smile, his eyebrows rising hopefully, but they soon drew down. He glanced at the mercenaries and mages. Disappointment made his shoulders slump as he—thankfully—caught on to the ruse. "I think that might be the last drink I ever had."

Tezi shook her head. "Nobody wants you dead. *I* don't want you dead."

"That's good to know, especially given how many times you've brushed off my awkward but earnest attempts to engage you in conversation."

Her cheeks grew pink, and she bit her lip. Jak watched that lip with the rapt attention of a hawk. Or, more accurately, a horny teenage boy.

Jadora frowned, concerned that Tezi seemed to be fiddling with something behind her back. Jadora slipped a vial of acid out of her pocket, though she was reluctant to throw it at one of the mercenaries. Captain Ferroki had risked much to keep Jak's medallion safe. She could have sold it, or she could have thrown it in the sea, but she'd kept it until she could return it to them. Jadora didn't want to be enemies with Ferroki or any of her people; she wanted Thorn Company for allies.

"Don't side with the mages," Jadora whispered to Tezi. "You're terrene, like us. You can't want them to have the portal, to have *more* power."

"That's right," Jak added. "You know what we want to do, don't you? To use the portal to find allies—to find *dragons*—and bring them back to help us end the wizards' rule. To stop them from bullying us and enslaving us and forcing us to abide by the laws of a government *they* created. Don't help them against your own kind." Jak pressed a hand against his chest.

He *was* earnest. It warmed Jadora's heart that he cared so much, though she couldn't tell if his words moved Tezi at all. So far, of all the mercenaries who'd heard what they wanted to do, only Sorath had been visibly wistful, as if, under different circumstances, he would have sided with them against the mages.

"You can't succeed against them," Tezi whispered. "They're too powerful. If you don't give up that artifact, they'll kill us *all*." Another emotion replaced the determination in her eyes. Anguish?

"We *can* win against them," Jak said. "There are more humans like us than there are like them. All we need is some powerful allies, allies strong enough to win against wizards, even against zidarr. And I *know* they're out there."

Jadora didn't know that—none of them truly could—but she didn't naysay Jak. They both hoped their dreams would be proven correct. It had been her late husband's dream too, one he'd died for.

"I can't let your plans cause deaths to the company." Tezi started to pull the item out from behind her back, but she glanced past Jadora and let out a startled gasp. "Ships."

Jadora resisted looking, suspecting it was a ruse to distract them, but Jak peered back and swore.

"Zaruk's people," he said. "Toggs was telling the truth."

Tezi lifted a hand to throw whatever she held. Jadora lifted her vial, but Jak reacted first. He vaulted over the portal and tackled Tezi. She managed to throw what looked like a glass bottle with a gray liquid inside, but it went over Jak's head. It went over Jadora's head too and smashed down inside of the portal.

Suspecting it a sedative, or something more deadly, Jadora held her breath and also sprang over the portal. She came down beside Jak and Tezi as they wrestled on the deck. Footsteps thundered toward them—dozens of the mercenaries charging.

"Jak, the portal," Jadora blurted and grabbed his arm to press his hand to its side as Tezi tried to force him to roll away from it.

"Let her go," Captain Ferroki barked.

A dozen firearms came up as the mercenaries aimed at Jak.

"She attacked *us!*" Jadora lifted her vial again, but it was pointless against so many.

Farther back, the mages raised their hands as they also prepared to attack.

The mercenaries held their fire—Jak and Tezi were entangled on the deck, and they didn't want to hurt one of their own. But the mages didn't care about Tezi. Toggs glanced at the oncoming ships —three blue-hulled vessels flew toward them from the horizon— and his fingers blazed with orange flame as he formed a fireball to hurl at Jak and Tezi.

Jadora threw her vial at Toggs, but she was too far away, and it fell short.

She grabbed Jak again, hoping to pull him out of the way before the fireball struck. But it was too fast. The flaming ball blasted at them like a charge from a magelock rifle.

No helpful streaks of lightning flew out of the artifact, and Jadora knew she and Jak would be incinerated. Frustration and fear filled her as she threw herself on Jak, trying to protect her son, hoping vainly that this wouldn't be a fatal blow.

But the fireball never reached them. The spinning flames

halted a few feet away from Jak and Tezi and spread, as if they had splashed against a glass wall, and dissipated.

Tezi and Jak, who'd stopped wrestling to fling up their arms defensively, gaped. So did Jadora.

Toggs swore and launched another fireball.

"*Kill* them," he roared in frustration.

Several other mages launched attacks that ranged from fireballs to lightning bolts to raw gusts of power that knocked over the nearby mercenaries. Nothing reached Jak, Tezi, or Jadora. Nothing even stirred their hair.

She reached back, resting a hand on the artifact, certain it was responsible. *Thank you,* she thought emphatically, though she doubted it could hear or understand her.

A little buzz—of warning?—ran up her arm.

She yanked her hand back in surprise. It hadn't objected to her touch before, but it had given her visions of warning with people dying in them, much different visions than it had given to Jak.

I mean you no harm, she thought, though this wasn't the time to figure out her relationship with an ancient artifact. *I'm Jak's mother. We're trying to take you back to your pool where you can be activated.*

Toggs was still launching magic at them, fury contorting his face. His crewmen lowered their arms and stopped, and the mercenaries had never fired, but Toggs yelled at them all.

"If we don't gain control of that thing, the zidarr and all the mages on those ships are going to *kill* us." Toggs stabbed a finger toward the horizon; the blue-hulled mageships were gaining quickly.

Jak and Tezi released each other and knelt back, peering warily at the mages and mercenaries.

Though Jadora no longer touched the portal, it put a vision in her mind, the same pool that Jak had seen several times now. She recognized it immediately from his drawing. A question seemed to accompany the vision, as if the portal wanted to verify that Jadora did indeed want to help it return to its home.

Yes, she thought. *I want to help you get there.*

Another sensation came from the portal, and the faintest foreign touch stirred in her mind. That made her uneasy, more uneasy than the frustrated fireballs that Toggs was still throwing toward them. It felt like the portal was reading her mind, or maybe even something beyond that. When Malek read her thoughts, she never felt it.

Something that might have been acceptance or agreement came from the portal. This was the first time she'd received what she could only think of as *feelings* from it.

Jak gasped and grabbed the side of his head. He bent over so sharply, almost smashing his face into the deck, that she thought an attack had slipped through and he'd been *shot.*

"Walk away from the artifact, boy," one of the mage crewmen said.

Jak gasped in pain again and rolled toward the portal, his back clunking against it. He reached out, patting it with his hand.

"Help," he wheezed.

Even though she knew he wanted the artifact's help, Jadora dropped to his side. "What is it? A mental attack?"

The barrier was still up, but they'd found another way to hurt him. Jadora glared at the mages, resenting that she could do nothing to protect her son from them.

Jak groaned, rolling on his side, and didn't answer her.

"What are you doing to him?" Tezi called, rising to her feet and facing the mages. "This wasn't our plan."

"Stay out of it, Tezi," Lieutenant Sasko said.

The crewman who was attacking Jak gasped and jerked back so hard he almost fell over. Toggs grabbed him, but a second later, Toggs dropped to his knees and grabbed his own head.

Jak looked over, the pain no longer contorting his face.

"Are you all right?" Jadora gripped his arm.

"Yeah, it stopped." Jak glanced at the portal. "I think it's stopping them. It's attacking them back."

The artifact didn't keep up the attack for long, but it left an impression. When Toggs and the crewman lifted their heads, fear lurked behind their scowls.

"Those ships are getting closer," one of the mercenaries said. "Do we have another plan?"

"All of our plans plummeted off a cliff as soon as we got the artifact on board," Captain Ferroki said, "and it took over."

"Is it *it*? Or the boy?"

"I wish I *could* do something," Jak grumbled, pushing himself to his knees.

Tezi gave him a pitying look. "I'm sorry I tried to trick you. I'm just trying to help the company. To protect them. They're all I have."

"No problem," Jak said, though he was wobbly as he got to his feet, his hand resting on the portal for support. "Can we still have drinks later?"

Tezi's expression shifted from pitying to bewildered. "I punched you, and you're getting a black eye."

"I don't hold grudges."

Jadora gripped his shoulder. "Now that the portal is active again, is there anything it would be willing to do to get us to its home? And stop these mages and *those* ships—" she pointed to the blue-hulled vessels, "—from capturing us? Capturing *it*?"

"I've been trying to talk it into that all day," Jak said, "but it doesn't know how to get to the pool."

"What, did they blindfold it when they removed it?"

"Maybe it's forgotten the way. Ten thousand years is a long time. As to the rest..." Jak shrugged. "It's still not willing to do anything but defend itself against attackers. And, for whatever reason, defend me."

Jadora held up a finger and tilted her head toward Tezi to remind Jak that they'd been bluffing about what the portal would do since they left Utharika. The mercenaries didn't know the truth. Or they *hadn't*.

"Maybe because you've got the key," she said quietly.

The mages were all on their feet and muttering again. Tezi poked the invisible barrier that protected them, testing its boundaries.

"I didn't have it with me in the courtyard," Jak said.

"True."

"My charm must be what's winning it over."

"Funny."

Jadora looked to the south, hoping to spot land on the horizon —and hoping that getting to Zewnath would somehow make a difference.

Her breath caught. Not only had a green shoreline come into view, but a city rose on hills to either side of a river spilling into the sea. Port Toh-drom. Far inland rose high green mountains shrouded in fog, the kind of mountains where waterfalls might tumble into pools.

Before Jadora could say anything, the *Dauntless* started turning away from land and toward the other ships. To surrender?

"Uh oh," Jak said.

"You're going to have to bluff again," Jadora whispered. "Look, we're so close. Try to get Toggs to land, lift the portal off the deck, and let us go with it. We'll find another way to transport it once they're gone."

"That's not going to work. Even if we convinced this crew to do that, what about all those new crews?"

"If you can't bluff them, there aren't many other options. I don't suppose you can convince the portal to knock all the mages off the ship so we can take over the *Dauntless* and fly to the pool without impediment."

"If I could do *that*, I would have on the first day and saved us being glared at throughout the journey."

"Just try the bluff. You're the only one who has a chance."

Jadora couldn't stomach the idea of getting so close and then being dragged back to one of the sky cities and imprisoned once more. Last time, she'd lost Darv, her friend and colleague of decades. What—or who—would she lose this time?

The ship had turned halfway around. Soon, they would be flying farther from Zewnath.

"I'll try." Jak climbed onto the side of the portal and puffed out his chest. "You've tasted a hint of the pain that the artifact can deliver, Captain Toggs," he tried to boom with a voice that lacked the depth for booming. "You will *not* turn this ship around, or it will attack you again."

"We're not doing it, kid." Toggs lifted his hands.

Colonel Sorath frowned and jogged to the hatchway of the navigation cabin. "Nobber, are you turning the ship?"

"I'm not doing it, sir," came the squeaky voice of the mage helmsman who wasn't much older than Jak. "And I can't stop it."

"*Who's* doing it?" Toggs demanded.

Jadora looked toward the oncoming ships. People were visible on the deck now, blue-uniformed mages and one man in black with a cloak that flapped in the wind.

"What new zidarr tormentor is this?" she whispered, certain he was the one controlling their ship, forcing it to turn.

"Nobody I want to meet," Jak said glumly.

A cannon boomed on the closest enemy ship. Several fireballs flew from mage hands. Jadora sank low beside Jak and behind the portal as the projectiles flew close.

The mercenaries and mages ran to the railing to defend the

ship, but the bleak expression on Toggs's face said it all. There was no hope against so many enemies.

"They'll crash us." Jadora groped for something they could do to stop this. "They'll crash their own people to get the artifact."

"I know." Jak's eyes were locked on the new zidarr. "And I don't think bluffing is going to work with them."

4

A FIREBALL SLAMMED INTO A BARRIER THE MAGES HAD ERECTED around the *Dauntless*, and the mercenaries were lined up at the railing, weapons aimed at the three enemy ships closing on them. No, not *enemy* ships, Jak amended silently. At least not to Toggs and the *Dauntless*. Zaruk's ships *should* have been allies to Captain Toggs's ship, sailing under Queen Vorsha's flag.

Several of the mage crewmen paused to look back at Captain Toggs. He hadn't said anything, at least not out loud, but Jak guessed he was communicating telepathically with his people. Colonel Sorath and Captain Ferroki also looked back, frowning at Toggs, and then sharing frowns with each other. They must have been included.

Only Jak and his mother were excluded. And maybe Tezi. She still stood next to the portal with them, trapped within the barrier it had erected.

Slowly, the mercenaries lowered their weapons and backed away from the railing. The crewmen did the same.

Jak didn't know what was happening until a fireball made it through the ship's defenses, the magical flames slamming into the hull of the *Dauntless*. The deck shuddered as the mageship rocked. The mercenaries spread their arms for balance as they exchanged worried expressions. With the *Dauntless's* barrier down, they could have fired back, but none of them did.

"They're surrendering," Mother said quietly. Grimly.

She wrapped a supportive arm around Jak's shoulders.

Tezi distanced herself from them. She prowled around the portal, poking its barrier with her rifle and trying to find a hole so she could escape. Nobody wanted to be standing next to Jak and his mother when those ships closed on them.

"They didn't say that," Jak said, though he feared his mother was right. "Not to us, anyway."

"No, because they're afraid you'll talk the artifact into attacking them if they openly defy your wishes."

Even if the artifact would have obeyed such a request, Jak couldn't have punished the crew for not wanting to be obliterated. But how were he and his mother supposed to get out of this situation?

If the *Dauntless* crashed, they might all die. If Zaruk's people overtook it and captured it without crashing it... Jak didn't know if the artifact would be able to protect them indefinitely against so many mages. Especially with a new zidarr here. It had effectively zapped Malek when he'd been caught off-guard, but Jak wouldn't bet against Malek—or a zidarr with power similar to his—being able to protect himself if he were prepared. A zidarr might also be able to tear away the barrier protecting them.

Cannons enhanced with magic boomed, and more fireballs streaked toward the *Dauntless*.

Jak braced himself, expecting the attacks to crash through the deck around the artifact—or target it directly. But the attackers focused on the same spot, and each blast crashed into the hull well below him. Wood splintered and flew, and the ship shuddered again.

From Jak's spot, he couldn't see over the railing to the sea below. He didn't know how high up they were... or how far they would fall. All he knew was that someone had taken over the tiller, and the *Dauntless* was heading away from land and closer to its attackers.

"Surrender, boy," Captain Toggs called, meeting Jak's eyes, "or you doom us all to death. They've told me they'll completely destroy us if we don't hand over the artifact."

Instead, Jak rested a hand on the portal and willed it to grasp the situation and the fresh danger it was now in. He urged it to extend its barrier around the entire ship if it could.

To warn it of what could happen if it didn't, Jak envisioned the ship crashing and the artifact sinking to the bottom of the sea. The water below them was deep, and if it sank here, it might never be recovered. It might never make it back to its rightful spot by the waterfall in the jungle.

A feeling of distress emanated from the artifact.

"What's he doing?" one of the mercenaries asked.

"Is he going to make it attack us?" one of the mages asked.

Someone on the deck launched another magical attack at Jak. Thankfully, the portal's barrier was still up.

The ship rocked, its frame creaking ominously. The smell of burning wood tainted the air, and smoke wafted up from the damaged hull. Another volley of magic and cannonballs sailed toward them.

The *Dauntless* turned again. Startled oaths came from dozens of mouths as the bow pointed toward land once more. Though it was damaged, and though fire kept raining down on it, the ship picked up speed, going faster than it had at any point in their journey.

The artifact was responsible. It didn't want to sink into the sea and be lost forever. It wanted to make it to land.

Unfortunately, the *Dauntless* started losing altitude.

"The engine is almost dead," a crewman said. "They've hit it directly several times. We're going to crash if we don't land first on our own."

"We don't have control of the ship!" someone else yelled.

"It's that damn boy again. Someone get him away from the artifact."

"We *can't!*"

The frustration in their voices was palpable. If Jak hadn't been certain they would shoot him the second he stepped away from the artifact and its protection, he might have felt bad for them. They were only obeying orders from their king.

But they were mages—the *enemy*—and they thought nothing of killing people like him. He wouldn't sympathize with them. He would do what he had to in order to escape.

"We're dropping fast," his mother said over the booms of cannons and the roar of the sea—that roar grew louder as they descended. "I don't see how we can get away with the artifact."

Tezi glanced over at her.

Jak shook his head, wanting to disagree, but he also couldn't think of a way out of this. "We can't let them take it back to their city. That's thousands of miles in the wrong direction."

"If they do, they won't be able to operate it. It'll be useless to them. A huge paperweight to sit in their king's courtyard."

Jak didn't know why his mother was repeating what they both knew, but it prompted Tezi to look over again, her brow furrowed. Did Mother hope she would pass that message along to her superiors? Who would then tell the mages and the zidarr? To what end? To keep the mageships here in Zewnath, toting the artifact around to figure out where it could be set up?

He thought of Colonel Sorath, the hobbyist archaeologist, who'd glimpsed Jak's map. Would *he* be able to figure it out? And did Mother want him to? If they could get away themselves, and maintain possession of the key, maybe they could make plans to reunite with the artifact later. So long as it stayed here in Zewnath, they might have another opportunity to get it.

As if his mother were reading his thoughts, she nodded at him.

"I guess as long as they can't use it, losing it isn't the worst thing in the world for our people," Jak said, speaking loudly enough for Tezi to hear him over the noise.

Wood snapped somewhere under them, and the deck lurched. They'd descended far enough that Jak could see the tops of trees beyond the railing, and they were close enough for him to make out leaves and vines. Maybe if they crashed this close to land, he and his mother *could* escape.

Can you help us get away? Jak silently asked the artifact, his hand still on it. *The ship is going to crash, but we've got the key, and we'll figure out a way to get back to you and get you to the right spot. We'll—*

"Brace yourselves," Sorath yelled to the mercenaries.

Jak opened his eyes in time to see the ship plow straight toward the tops of trees lining a beach. Tall trees with stout trunks. The *Dauntless* smashed into them hard enough to knock over everyone on the deck. Jak hit the artifact, then pitched down next to Tezi. She smacked down hard, chest first, and her magelock rifle went clattering across the deck.

Jak's hat almost flew off, but he mashed it down on his head. He dared not lose the medallion, or they would have lost everything.

The ship, no longer able to continue forward, plummeted to the beach. When it struck down, with a cacophonous smashing and cracking of wood, Jak flew upward. Even the heavy *artifact* flew upward.

Tezi rolled sideways away from it, and Jak realized as he thumped down again, pain battering his body, that its protective barrier was gone. As soon as one of the mages realized that, he and Mother would be targets.

Jak scrambled toward her, fear overriding his pain, and he lurched to his feet. Aware of the mages and the mercenaries recovering, he grabbed her and pointed at the railing. They only had seconds to get over the side and escape before someone realized their intent.

Thankfully, Mother hadn't been seriously hurt, and she knew exactly what he wanted. Using the artifact for cover, she ducked low and ran around it and toward the railing. Tezi must have taken a harder hit when they landed, for she was groaning and grabbing the side of her head. Jak resisted his urge to help her, instead grabbing her fallen rifle and following his mother.

She vaulted over the railing with impressive alacrity for someone more than twice his age. Jak scrambled over after her, a blast of acrid smoke hitting his face.

They were above the portion of the hull that had been targeted, and fire burned around the holes that had been blistered into it. He didn't sense any magic coming from what had been the engine.

The drop was farther than Jak expected, the smoke making it hard to see the ground. He landed awkwardly, one foot coming down on a piece of driftwood.

Agony struck his ankle like a hammer, and he pitched into the sand. He couldn't keep from gasping and grabbing his ankle, terrified their escape would end before it began. His mother couldn't *carry* him.

"They're getting away!" someone yelled.

Mother swore, grabbed Jak's arm, and dragged him to his feet. He gritted his teeth and hobbled with her toward trees and dense foliage that lined the beach. He willed the pain in his ankle to go away and for his leg to support him.

"Get them!" someone yelled.

"*Shoot* them!" That was Toggs.

As Jak and Mother rushed around burning wreckage dotting

the beach and toward the trees, Jak glanced left and right, hoping to spot the city they'd seen earlier. But they must have crashed miles from it. Damn it. It would have been easier to hide out in a city than a jungle. Some of those mercenaries would be trackers; he had no doubt.

His shoulder blades itched, some instinct warning him of danger. When Jak glanced back, the smoke didn't quite hide the railing and the deck of the ship. Several of the mercenaries were lined up, aiming their firearms at his back.

"Almost there," Mother said, tugging him along. "Hurry!"

He ran faster, trying to ignore the pain in his ankle, but he feared he was too slow. They wouldn't make it.

One of the mages attacked first—Toggs. With fury contorting his face, he launched a gout of fire at them.

Jak saw his death as the writhing orange flames streamed toward them. But the attack halted twenty feet away. A barrier. Someone had erected another barrier. He could sense it. The artifact. It had to be. Nobody else on that ship would protect them.

His heart ached as they ran farther from the portal, ducking between trees and scrambling over coconuts and palm fronds littering the ground. He couldn't help but feel that they were abandoning a friend. They *were* abandoning it, and yet it was still protecting them.

Thank you, he thought to it as Toggs roared with frustration. *We'll come back for you*, he promised. *We'll find a way.*

Tears leaked from Tezi's eyes, and she kept coughing as she patted about on her hands and knees on the tilted deck of the *Dauntless*. Countless holes had been smashed into the planks, and mages worked to put out fires in the hull. She was looking for the valuable magelock rifle that Captain Ferroki had lent her before the invasion. Even though it might be understandable that she'd let go of it when they crashed not once but twice, first into the trees and then onto the beach, shame burned her cheeks with each passing minute that she didn't find it.

"The kid got it," came Sorath's voice from behind her. "I saw him limp into the jungle with it."

The feeling of shame intensified. Not only had she been too busy clutching at her battered ribs and skull to notice Jak and Jadora escaping, but she'd let him steal her weapon. "I'm sorry, sir."

"Come on." Sorath gestured for her to follow him. "Your unit is forming up. The mages will have directions for us, I'm sure." He eyed the artifact darkly, then turned toward the rest of the mercenaries.

Sergeant Tinder was ordering them into formation while the mages used their power to funnel nearby seawater to the ship, splashing it down on fires. That made more smoke, and Tezi wasn't the only one coughing.

The sun had set during the battle, and dusk encroached on the beach. Inland, the dense jungle looked to exist in perpetual twilight. Unfamiliar animals hooted while birds cawed from the treetops. This was a foreign place to Tezi.

As she walked toward the formation, movement in the sky startled her. Even though she'd known the other mageships were still here, it was disconcerting to see them close overhead, hanging in the air above the beach.

"Take your time, Rookie," Sergeant Tinder yelled from the front of the formation.

Lieutenant Sasko and Captain Ferroki talked quietly off to the side. Everyone's uniforms were covered with soot and ash, and some were ripped open. More than a few people were scraped and bleeding, and Tezi decided she'd gotten off better than most in that crash.

She jogged into place at the end of the squad at the front of the formation. She wished she could have slunk into the back, since she felt conspicuous with her rifle missing, but the others had left that spot open for her.

"At least they've got their artifact now," Sasko said.

"Do they?" Ferroki dabbed at a gash on her jaw that was dribbling blood down the side of her neck. "Are we sure it'll let them touch it?"

"I say we volunteer the mages to do any touching."

Captain Toggs strode over to them, and Thorn Company fell silent. "I want you people to go after those two and find them. You haven't done anything for days. You can damn well hunt down a pair of ungainly scholars."

"Will you wait for us to return?" Sorath asked, joining Sasko and Ferroki.

"Of course. We've got to repair this ship so we can sail home. We—"

A grating sound came from the side, and Tezi wasn't the only one to jump. It was the artifact. It wobbled, then rose up into the air.

None of the mages on board appeared to be responsible. On the closest ship, a zidarr in black clothing with a matching cloak stood at the railing, a short sword and a mace hanging from his weapons belt. His hand was outstretched as he focused on the artifact, levitating it into the air. It rose slowly toward the deck of his ship.

"Good," Toggs muttered. "Let someone else be responsible for that thing."

The zidarr was too far up to have heard Toggs, but the man's gaze settled on him. He had a chiseled jaw and cheekbones, along with icy green eyes that stood out against his olive skin and short black hair.

Tezi had never met him before, but she tried to still her mind of thoughts, lest he be skimming them. As she'd learned from experience, any zidarr—any *mage*—who learned about her past would punish her for it.

By the luck of Thanok, she hoped the man took the artifact and never came down to the *Dauntless*. Stone Heart, the other zidarr who'd learned her secret, was dead now, and she couldn't feel anything but relief about that.

"Will they take it back to King Zaruk?" someone asked.

"Yes," Toggs said. "That's where it should have gone to start with. This detour was a waste of time, and *look* at my ship." He thrust his arm out to encompass the smoke and the damage. "They're not even planning to stick around to help with repairs. They blame *me* for this. And they expect *me* to retrieve those two archaeologists." He scowled at the mercenaries, as if he were looking for someone to take his anger out on.

When his baleful expression landed on Tezi, she braced herself, again wishing she weren't in the front row.

"I thought you were going to knock them out, girl. What happened to that *genius* plan?" Toggs shared his glower with Sorath and Ferroki. "You gun huggers are the most worthless bunch of supposed fighters I could have gotten stuck with. If I didn't know better, I'd think you *wanted* those two to get away. Were you sticking with your own worthless kind on purpose? That'll only get you killed."

Since it had been her idea, Tezi felt responsible. Sorath and Ferroki didn't appear that concerned about being yelled at, but that didn't make Tezi feel any better.

Before she could think wiser of it, she lifted a hand. "Captain? Uhm, I heard them talking."

"About what idiots we are?" Toggs asked.

"No, sir. They said they didn't care if you took the portal back to King Zaruk, because it won't work in his city. They said it'll be a giant paperweight."

"That's not my problem," Toggs snapped.

"It could be mine," a new speaker said from behind the formation.

The zidarr had jumped down without anyone noticing.

Several of the mercenaries glanced back, but Tinder barked, "Eyes front."

Tezi obeyed and abruptly wished she hadn't spoken. If she'd known the zidarr was back there, the very person she'd been praying wouldn't notice her, she would have kept her mouth shut until later.

The zidarr strolled around the formation, his hands clasped behind his back, and came to a stop beside Tezi. She froze like a statue, though panic made her want to bolt.

"Lord Night Wrath." Toggs bowed to the newcomer. "We are pleased to hand the artifact over to someone with your power so that you can more successfully take it home to the alliance."

"Ready to make it someone else's problem, are you?" The zidarr—Night Wrath—only looked at him for a moment before regarding Tezi.

As ordered, she kept her eyes forward, but she had no trouble seeing him staring at the side of her head from only a few feet away. A bead of sweat trickled down her spine, and she couldn't blame the tropical heat.

"What do you mean the artifact won't work anywhere else?" Night Wrath asked her.

Tezi licked her lips and attempted to keep her mind clear of any thoughts except the conversation between Jak and Jadora. "They said it could only be activated somewhere here on Zewnath."

"*Where* here on Zewnath?"

"I don't know, my lord. I don't think they know either."

Long seconds trickled past as he kept staring at her.

Tezi couldn't feel him trying to read her mind, but she knew he was. Likely, all he wanted was to see her memory of the conversation between Jak and Jadora and assess it for himself. All she had to do was keep her mind focused on that and not let herself think of other things like the hotel where she'd shot a mage or the night she'd fled her village after stabbing her rapist to death. But the thoughts refused to be locked away. It was as if he was sifting through the sand of her mind, stirring up all her most condemning memories to examine.

Night Wrath's eyes narrowed. Tezi barely breathed.

"We'll capture them again and find out what they know," Sorath said, stepping toward Night Wrath.

Without looking at him, Night Wrath lifted his palm. Sorath halted as if he'd smacked into an invisible wall.

"You have killed mages," Night Wrath said softly, his eyes focused on Tezi.

"We've *all* killed mages," Ferroki said. "It's what we're hired to do by other mages."

"This one has killed them outside of a contract," Night Wrath said, not looking at her. He was still sifting through Tezi's thoughts. "She killed a mage to avoid the *honor* of being chosen to serve a king."

Sorath's jaw clenched, and he seemed to be straining against the barrier. His hand dipped into his pocket. For one of his explosives?

Tezi swallowed and shook her head. As much as she wished Sorath would stop this zidarr from rifling through her mind, if he attacked, he would be killed. There were far too many mages here for even a full mercenary unit to fight. And as good as Sorath was, he couldn't beat a zidarr. He'd lost his battle with Stone Heart.

"Stone Heart," Night Wrath whispered, sifting through her mind further. He found the day she'd gone with the others to see the magistrate in Perchver, the telepathic conversation she'd had with Stone Heart. "He learned of your crime, and he let you live?

Just because you hadn't killed a mage in *his* realm? Well, he paid for not enforcing the rules, didn't he?"

"Do not harm her, my lord," Ferroki said. "She is under my command. If there is to be a punishment, I'll take it."

Tezi shook her head again. She didn't want to be punished, but she also didn't want the captain or anyone else hurt on her behalf.

"Not punishment but *death*." Night Wrath lifted a hand, and power wrapped around Tezi and forced her to her knees. "That is what we do if you kill a mage, if you *dare* believe you are the equal of a mage, if you think your meager life is worth more than one of ours."

Pain blasted Tezi as every nerve in her body lit on fire. She couldn't keep from crying out.

Several of the mercenaries turned toward her and tried to grab her, to pull her away from his fury, but Night Wrath used his magic to shove them back without releasing his grip on Tezi. An invisible hand wrapped around her throat and tightened.

Tears pricked her eyes, tears that had nothing to do with the smoke. Captain Toggs and most of the mage crew watched impassively. Only Nobber, the young helmsman, shook his head sadly and looked at Sorath, as if the colonel might be able to do something. But this wasn't a battle; he couldn't cleverly arrange troops on the battlefield to defeat this foe.

"It'll be easier to catch the archaeologists if you let her live," Sorath said. "We can use her as bait."

"We have the artifact," Night Wrath said. "We don't *need* them."

With waves of agony coursing through her body, Tezi barely heard them.

"Don't you know about the key?" Sorath asked. "The boy has it."

"What key?" Night Wrath snapped, looking at him.

His grip on Tezi didn't loosen, but the pain grew less intense.

"Haven't you been chatting with Malek?" Sorath asked.

"I don't *chat* with other kings' zidarr."

As Night Wrath focused on Sorath, Sasko and Ferroki edged closer to Tezi. She had no idea what they wanted to do, but she shook her head again, as much as she could while bound by the zidarr's power. The last thing she wanted was for the whole company to be punished—or worse—for trying to help her.

"Maybe you should," Sorath said. "Then you would know what Uthari knows, that you people need the archaeologists. They've been studying the portal for years and know how to operate it, and they probably know where to put it so it *can* be operated. You definitely need the key."

"Are you *lying* to me, Colonel?"

"No. You can check the truth in my mind. You need them, and you can use the rookie to catch them. The boy has a crush on her. We can use her as bait and lure them into a trap."

That was as unappealing as it had been the first time she'd tried to ensnare Jak, but a hint of hope rose in Tezi's chest. If it meant living another day, she would let Sorath dangle her at the end of a fishing line.

"You need *bait* to catch a boy with no power?" Night Wrath asked. "If that's true, you're not half the man your reputation suggests, Colonel."

"If my reputation has anything to do with tracking people through dense unfamiliar jungles, I'm going to have a word with the bards who've been singing about me."

"She *could* be useful," Ferroki said. "Would your rulers truly want you to throw away a useful tool?"

"A tool that has *killed* our people?" Night Wrath clenched his fist, and the invisible hand tightened around Tezi's throat again.

Sorath shrugged. "Use her first, and kill her later, if you must. I'll point out that our escaped prisoners are getting farther and farther away every minute we waste. If they're eaten by predators in the jungle, we'll lose the only people who know how to work the portal."

A salty breeze stirred the smoke as Night Wrath stared at Sorath. Silence had fallen over the ship, neither the crew nor mercenaries whispering a word, only the sound of waves breaking and birds squawking audible. Even the mages watching from the ships above were deathly quiet.

Tezi closed her eyes, trying not to think about anything that would upset the zidarr further, trying not to think about how much she hated these people and this world.

Night Wrath released her so abruptly that she fell, barely catching herself before smashing her nose against the deck.

"Use her then, mercenary," he told Sorath. "Take her and fetch the archaeologists, and bring them to me to question. Do not waste time. Zaruk and Vorsha are not the only ones who've sent mageships and zidarr after this artifact."

"As you wish, my lord."

"Captain Toggs," Night Wrath said. "You'll repair your ship while we wait."

"Yes, my lord," Toggs said.

Night Wrath strode across the deck, sprang onto the railing, and paused to look back at Sorath. "I will go into Port Toh-drom and perform a search of my own. If I find the archaeologists before your people do, we'll consider you superfluous and leave you here without pay." He pointed at Tezi. "Except for that one. She *will* see the executioner's axe as soon as this is resolved."

He jumped down to the beach and started walking east.

"I love dealing with mages," Sorath growled.

Two mercenaries helped Tezi up.

"You've killed mages, Rookie?" Sergeant Words asked. "Before you joined us and started training? You've got a lot more gumption than I would have guessed."

"Yes," Tezi said bleakly. For months, she'd been hoping to prove herself and win the regard of the mercenaries, but she hadn't wanted her past to get out. With another zidarr in on her secret and promising to kill her, the probability of her surviving to see her next birthday had plummeted. "Thanks for trying to help," she told Sorath and Ferroki.

"*Trying*? I'm positive we *did* help." Sorath nudged Ferroki with his elbow. "We helped, right?"

"Temporarily," Ferroki said. "And you were on the verge of getting yourself killed too. I saw you reaching for your explosives."

"I reach for those all the time. They comfort me in difficult situations."

"Huh," Tinder said. "I never would have thought me and the great Colonel Sorath were so similar."

"Quit blathering," Captain Toggs said. "If a zidarr tells you to hurry, you hurry. Leave some of your people here to help if enemy ships show up while the rest of you get out there and catch those two." He pointed toward the jungle, then at Sorath's chest. "Especially *you*, Colonel."

Toggs left them, stomping around the deck, issuing orders to his crew regarding repairs. Tinder dismissed the formation, ordering people to grab their weapons and whatever gear they had, since they might have to spend the night in the jungle.

Ferroki murmured something to Sasko, then went belowdecks, but only for a minute. She came back carrying her rifle—the twin of the fancy one she'd given to Tezi—and a little suede pouch.

"Uhm, Captain?" Tezi asked. "I lost my rifle. I'm sorry. Jak took it."

"I saw. I want you to get it back, but you can take mine for now." Ferroki handed the rifle to her and also put the pouch in her hand.

It had the heft of coins, and Tezi frowned in confusion. "Captain?"

"Help Sorath find Jak and Jadora, and do whatever he asks as far as being *bait*—" Ferroki's mouth twisted with distaste, "—and then disappear."

"Disappear?" Tezi mouthed.

"Those coins should be enough for food for a couple of months and maybe passage to another continent. I won't tell you where to go, because that zidarr will question me when he realizes you're not coming back. But it's been good knowing you, and I hope we've given you a few skills to help in life."

Tezi stared at her, slowly grasping what the captain was saying.

"You're kicking me out," she whispered.

"For your own good. If we meet again at some future date, once that artifact is out of all our lives, and zidarr aren't breathing down our necks, we'll gladly take you back, but I don't want to stand helplessly by and watch any of those bastards kill you. You don't deserve that."

"Captain, I—" Tezi's throat closed up, and she couldn't get more words out. She was touched that the captain cared but distressed that she was being asked to leave. She'd only just begun to prove herself worthy of a position in the company. She didn't want to quit *now*. "I—"

Ferroki raised her eyebrows.

Tezi stepped forward and hugged her.

"Shit, is that allowed?" Tinder asked. "LT, what's the mercenary handbook say about hugging?"

"On the eve of a hurricane, even the wolves huddle together in their dens for warmth and comfort," Ferroki said.

"*That's* what the handbook says?" Tinder asked.

"The *Parable of the Woodland Creatures*," Ferroki said dryly. "There is an unfortunate lack of proverbs, maxims, and apothegms in military handbooks."

"Yeah," Sasko said. "I remember reading ours and thinking exactly that. Not enough apothegms."

Tezi stepped back, glad the captain hadn't minded the hug, even if the others were being silly. "Thank you, ma'am."

Sorath returned with his weapons and gear. "You ready, killer?"

"To be bait? I guess, sir."

"Better to be bait than to be dead."

"Yes, sir."

As she followed Sorath off the ship, Tezi looked over her shoulder toward the rest of the company. Several groups of mercenaries were forming search parties, but she couldn't help but fear she wouldn't see any of them again.

5

JADORA KNELT IN THE DARK, HER KNEE RESTING IN SQUISHY decomposing foliage, and gently probed Jak's ankle. It was swollen, and he hissed when she flexed it for him, but she didn't feel evidence of fractured bones.

He'd been walking, but he grunted in pain every time he came down on it wrong. And with twilight deepening into full night and nothing but uneven jungle floor around them, it was hard *not* to come down on it wrong. Jadora had twisted her knee as they'd been running from the ship, and she feared it would also be swollen soon.

"I've had an epiphany," she admitted, glancing back the way they'd come.

They'd moved deep enough into the jungle that the lamps from the ships were no longer visible through the trees, but not five minutes ago, she'd heard branches snapping and an ominous rattling of foliage. It was *possible* it had been an animal chasing after its prey, but she suspected search parties were hunting for them.

"That twisted ankles should be avoided at all costs?" Jak asked.

"I think that's your epiphany, not mine."

"I'm sharing it so you'll know about it too."

"That's considerate. Thank you."

The thunderous calls of howler monkeys proclaiming their territory echoed from the treetops, hopefully not acting as a beacon to the mages or mercenaries or whoever that zidarr had sent after them.

Jadora pulled down Jak's trouser leg, reluctantly admitting there was nothing she could do for him out here. All she had were the sample vials and handful of belongings she'd had in her pockets when they fled the ship. It was more than *most* people kept in their pockets, but she had nothing that could fill the role of Dr. Fret's medical kit.

Once they found their way to the city, maybe they could find a healer who would take pity on them. Unfortunately, neither of them had money. They didn't even have food or water. Any sane person would have called their escape ill-advised, and she didn't know if she would disagree. At the least, Jadora knew an apothecary in Port Toh-drom—if she still lived and worked there.

It had been years since Jadora had visited Zewnath on her way to study herbalism at one of the druid temples near the coast. If that temple had been closer, she would have tried to reach it instead of the city, but it was dozens of miles away, and she didn't know if one could walk there. Last time, a guide had taken her team by boat, traveling upriver and turning into a maze of swampy channels.

A great cat roared in the distance, and the monkeys fell silent. A tiger? Jaguar? Numidoran? All three large feline predators were native to the continent.

What if, after all this, she and Jak died to some predator's fangs?

She thought of her father back in Sprungtown, wishing she had a way to let him know what was going on. Even though they had more differences than commonalities and rarely spoke anymore, he would worry when he found out her home had been empty for months, and nobody knew what had happened to her. If she and Jak died down here, would word ever find its way back to him?

"What's your epiphany?" Jak grabbed a tree trunk and used it to push himself to his knees.

Jadora pushed her dark thoughts to the back of her mind and helped him the rest of the way up. She put his arm around her shoulders and wrapped her arm around his waist. "Do you know which way the city is?"

It had been obvious from an elevated position out at sea, but she wasn't sure if the *Dauntless* had crashed east or west of Port Toh-drom, nor was she positive she could find her way back to the beach in the dark. They'd run blindly into the jungle, worried more about escaping than mapping their route.

"That way." Jak pointed, seemingly at random.

"You're sure?"

"Yes. I saw the city right before we crashed. And you know I have a good sense of direction."

"I do, but I'm hoping you're wrong, because I think the roar came from that way."

He sighed. "It did."

They hobbled in that direction, moving far more slowly than Jadora wished, the damp foliage drenching their feet through their shoes. She hoped the search parties would also struggle to maneuver through the jungle in the dark. And that any mages who joined the search couldn't use Jak's medallion to find them. It didn't give off anywhere near as much of a magical aura as the portal, but mages could sense even small trinkets if they were close enough.

"My epiphany is one I should have had weeks ago," she said quietly as they walked. "I *had* been thinking—maybe because it was what your father always talked about—that if we could find the portal, travel through it, and find powerful allies, it would be enough. We could bring them back and gather the armies we would need to battle the mages and wrest control of our fates away from them."

Admittedly, Jadora had never thought of herself in that *we*, assuming that if she could find the portal, someone else would handle the raising of armies and the fighting. That she was wrapped up in this at all was ludicrous. But a lack of foresight about how things would turn out had gotten her entrenched in the mess.

"That's how I saw it too," Jak said.

"I think that we need the army first, and we were—*I was*—foolish to believe we could activate and use the portal without a lot of help."

"You didn't know we'd have to carry it halfway around the world to a remote location."

"True, but it still seems like hubris for me to have believed we could do this with only a small team of archaeologists. It isn't as if I didn't know that the mages were interested in your father's research."

"If we'd been able to activate it right there in the Dragon Perch Islands, we wouldn't have needed anyone else. We could have gone through ourselves. We could have already been *heroes*."

The longing in Jak's voice made her realize that he'd been dreaming of far more than riding a dragon.

"I don't care about being a hero," Jadora said. "What I want is a world where nobody is enslaved by anyone else, nobody is considered a lesser human being, and we all have the freedom to pursue our dreams and enjoy the fruits of our own labor."

"Making all that happen sounds harder than just becoming a hero."

"Likely true."

After a pause, Jak added, "Is it all right if *I* want to be a hero?"

"I thought your dream was to explore long-forgotten ruins and map interesting new places."

"Yeah, but *heroically.*"

"Ah."

They paused to rest, breathing in humid air laden with pungent floral and fruit scents. Between brushing against foliage heavy with water droplets and Jadora's own sweat, her clothing was wet enough to cling to her. She'd forgotten from her earlier expedition to Zewnath how hot and thick the air was and how frequently it rained. At least they wouldn't have to worry about drinking water.

"I don't know how we would have raised an army beforehand," Jak said, whispering in case anyone was nearby. "And it may be hard to do now. You wanted us to try to win over the mercs, but that didn't work that well."

"I'm not positive we didn't make any headway there." Jadora ducked under a branch, bumping the large green fronds with her head, and water dribbled down the back of her neck. "I could tell they didn't want to work for the mages or get rid of us. They were stuck in a difficult position because of their prior obligation. Maybe if we'd had more time with them, we could have swayed them to our side. We would likely only need to get Sorath, since the others were following him. Or Captain Ferroki, since it was her company."

"I think I got Tezi to agree to have a drink with me."

"Was that before or after she punched you in the eye?"

"Both. I'm appealing in both states."

"I'm going to choose to believe you're making jokes to keep my spirits up and aren't truly so motivated by your hormones that you think she'd be better to get on our side than one of the leaders."

"I didn't say she'd be better to get on our side, just that she'd be more enjoyable to have a drink with. It doesn't matter anyway. We can't let any of them catch up with us or—" Jak hissed and lurched as he came down badly on his swollen ankle again.

Jadora tightened her grip on his waist, wishing she could help more.

"I wouldn't refuse help from trained mercenaries," Jak said, "but what we *really* need are mages on our side. An entire company of mercenaries can't stand up to a single zidarr."

"They were successful in fighting mages in the castle. With the right gear and weapons, there's hope."

"Not much. I think all the mages we faced in Uthari's castle were the weaker ones who didn't get sent out to attack the invaders."

"You can't be grudging about small victories."

"All it would have taken was one zidarr to blow away all of Thorn Company. You *saw* Malek single-handedly defeat a ship full of mages. He was fighting four at a time at one point, and he beat them all."

"There aren't that many zidarr. If we can avoid them—" Jadora stopped as Jak halted abruptly. "Are you all right?" She glanced toward his ankle.

"He's the one we need," Jak said.

"What?"

"Not what. *Who.* Malek."

"Uh."

"If we could get the mercenaries, I won't deny that it would be useful, though I don't know how we would lure people who fight for money over to our side when we don't *have* money. But imagine if we could get *Malek* on our side. He could probably twitch a finger and make the mercenaries follow us. Or he could gather a new army, maybe here in Zewnath."

A weird little zing went through Jadora as she imagined Malek working *with* them instead of against them, but that would never happen. He wasn't one of them, and he never would be.

"Jak... Malek isn't going to leave Uthari and join a quest to help us defeat *his* people."

"I suppose not, but that's not the first thing we need, is it? We need to get the artifact back, then figure out where to take it and how to go through it. But there's no way we're going to defeat four ships full of mages to get it."

"If Tezi shares what we were talking about in front of her, those mages should figure out that the artifact needs to stay in Zewnath. They may even find the pool and take it there themselves. At which point, if we later show up with the key, we can go through."

"How are they going to find the pool when I've got the only picture of it?"

"The artifact could share visions with them. It's not your loyal pet dog that's only going to do tricks for you."

"Thanks, Mother. But let's say that your idea works. We find Zaruk's people at the right spot in the jungle, and they've got the portal set up. They'll be watching for us. They'll be able to sense the medallion. We'll never get through. Not without help."

"Malek isn't going to help us. He isn't even here."

"What if he could be?" Jak grunted and reached up, clasping a hand to his hat to keep from losing it to a branch. "I've communicated messages to him before. Remember when we were in the courtyard, and another zidarr had a dagger to your throat?"

Jadora shuddered. "I'll never forget that moment."

"I planted the idea in Malek's head for him to convince the zidarr to threaten the artifact. And it wasn't the only time he said he heard me, er, *thinking* at him."

"I remember," she said. "The mages call it telepathy, right? But you did it from ten feet away. I highly doubt that if you *think* at him from across the world, he's going to hear you. I know you've got some fledgling magical power, but you're not trained to do anything, and I don't think even trained mages can speak to each other at great distances. That's why they've got those communication devices—dome-jir—on their ships."

"It wouldn't hurt to try. If you agree that I should reach out to him. Wouldn't it be better to work with him than these other people we don't know? Captain Toggs wanted to *kill* us. His commander and the new zidarr might not realize that we have value."

Jadora thought of the times they'd interacted with Malek. If they *had* to pick a zidarr, he had been the most reasonable to work with thus far. But that didn't mean he wasn't utterly loyal to his master. The only reason he'd been protecting them was because King Uthari wanted them alive.

"Not just for what we know about the portal though," she mused.

"Hm?"

"Uthari wants us—or at least me—because of my herbalism and chemistry background. He wants me to find Jitaruvak and synthesize a drug for him, a hypothetical longevity potion."

"Right," Jak said, more excitement in his voice. "Uthari doesn't care about the dragons or getting powerful allies, at least if he was telling us the truth. He's an old man who wants a way to live longer. What if we told Malek that we would help him activate the portal, go through and find that plant, and give it to him freely? Do as King Uthari wanted."

"He can read our minds. We would genuinely have to be willing to do that."

"Couldn't we be? Would creating a longevity potion be so bad? And in the process, we would learn about the portal, figure out everything we need to know about traveling through it, and we could look for the dragons. Like you said, we might not be able to do this without help, and who better to help than the most powerful zidarr out there?"

There was reverence in his voice as he spoke about Malek, and that worried Jadora. This wasn't the first time Jak had brought up Malek's role in the battle they'd witnessed that night on the *Star Flyer*.

The idea of her son idolizing a zidarr would have been concerning under any circumstances, but it worried her more given his newly discovered proclivity for magic. The thought of Jak starting to identify with mages and wizards—and zidarr—and possibly losing his interest in identifying with normal humans distressed her. He was her only son. She couldn't lose him to them.

Hopefully, he would remember that the majority of them would want him dead for developing that latent power. As a wild one, he would be a threat to them, or so they claimed. They *killed* wild ones. For whatever reason, Malek hadn't threatened to do that, but another of Uthari's zidarr had. Yidar. Further, she had little doubt that if Uthari ordered Malek to kill Jak, he would.

"How do we escape Malek after he helps us?" Jadora swatted away a large insect buzzing by her ear. "And let's be clear. If he worked with us, it would be because he believed we were helping *him* and doing what he wishes. He may very well have orders from Uthari to kill us after we do everything they need. Neither he nor any other mage is going to stand by and let us talk dragons into attacking their cities and overthrowing their governments."

Jak didn't answer right away, and more crunches sounded in the jungle somewhere behind them. A monkey hooted, then fell silent.

"We'll have to part ways with him before then," Jak said. "Maybe we can slip away from Malek and hide out on another world with the key until they forget about us."

"What other world? If we traveled with Malek, he would be with us on the dragon home world."

"I don't think that's the only place the portal goes."

Jadora paused and looked at him. "No? All of your father's work and all of the stories he collected speak only of the portal opening a magical passageway between Torvil and the dragon home world of Ezarith."

"There are thirty-two star constellations and thirty-two symbols linked to them that we believe represent languages, right? And we only recognized one set."

"Just because we didn't recognize the other languages doesn't mean they're from other *worlds*. They could have existed here at one time, then faded away and been forgotten. There have been many civilizations in our history that rose and fell." Even as she spoke, Jadora admitted she'd had a similar thought back at Uthari's castle. It was surprising that she, with all her familiarity with dead languages, hadn't recognized more than one.

"And did the *constellations* also fade away? Ten thousand years is a long time, but it's not like the stars would have changed that much. I flipped through the atlas of star charts in the library. The only match was the Dragon's Tail constellation. Those other ones have got to be some other world's stars. Or other *worlds'* stars."

"If that's true, that's remarkable, amazing, and another reason to explore all the portal can offer, but unfortunately, it doesn't help us with our current situation."

"Any luck?" came a call from behind them.

Jadora froze.

"Not yet," someone replied. "Ssh!"

They had been female voices. Two of the mercenaries.

Jadora poked Jak to get him walking again. The mercenaries hadn't been *right* behind them, but they also weren't that far away. Maybe a quarter of a mile back.

"Malek could help us with our current predicament," Jak whispered. "Do you want me to try contacting him?"

"I don't think that will work," she whispered back.

"But do you want me to *try*? On the off chance it works, are we willing to help him get that plant?"

Jadora released a slow breath. If a sample of Jitaruvak was

truly all that Uthari wanted, she wouldn't object to handing that over to the old wizard. Maybe she could hand some over to Sprungtown University too. Such a plant could help all people, mages *and* terrene humans.

But she feared Uthari wanted more than that and hadn't told her. Why would he detail all of his ambitions to a captive?

Still, would it hurt to let Jak try to reach out to Malek? She couldn't imagine that it would work, and even if it somehow did, would it make their situation any worse? Not likely. And Malek *could* protect them from the mages hunting them.

"Go ahead," she whispered. "But make it quick. We need to reach the city, evade the mercenaries, talk someone into bandaging your ankle, and find a map or guide to the pool."

Not at all a daunting list.

Jak paused with his hand on a tree. Jadora looked back, thought she saw a light, and grimaced. She feared that even in the city, a city where they would stand out as pale-skinned foreigners from the north, it would be hard to shake their pursuers. She didn't know whether to hope Jak succeeded at contacting Malek or not.

As the sun sank below the horizon, Malek wielded wooden practice swords on the deck of the *Star Flyer*, battling any crew members willing to spar with him. Nobody would fight him one-on-one, but that was fine. He liked the challenge of multiple opponents, and it simulated conditions he faced in real battle. Few besides other zidarr sprang to engage him without numerous allies at their sides.

Now, as the light faded, some of the heat bleeding out of the day, he fought four opponents, the rat-a-tat-tats from their lightweight wooden weapons echoing from the walls of the aftercastle and forecastle. The crewmen did their best to coordinate their strikes so Malek couldn't defend against them all at once, and he did his best to zip around, keeping them in each other's way so he faced no more than two at a time.

Whenever one of their wooden swords slipped in close, he had to resist his instincts to use magic to hurl his opponents back. They'd all agreed ahead of time that their sparring match would rely on physicality only.

He didn't mind. It was a good workout this way, and he could practice his magic without opponents.

One of his foes, a maintenance officer who'd grown up in a family of swordsmen, glanced to the side. Surprisingly, he tripped over his own feet, even though Malek had been focused on another man and hadn't struck him. When the officer stumbled, Malek thought about teaching him a lesson with a quick thwack—a reminder that distraction could get him killed—but he stepped back and waited for him to recover instead.

However, one of his allies grinned and took advantage, slipping in to smack the officer on the ribs with his practice sword.

"Ouch." The officer stumbled back, gripped his side, and glared at Malek, not realizing *he* hadn't done it. "My lord, that's not fair."

Malek eyed the mischievous crewman, causing him to shrink back and lose his grin.

"He didn't do it," the crewman admitted. "I did. But it's fair to take advantage of someone's distraction. And remind you that there's never a good reason to turn your back on a zidarr."

"There is when you're looking at a *girl*." The officer glanced back again.

"A girl? I trust you're not referring to your new commanding officer." Malek hadn't looked, but he was aware of who was around them.

Captain Rivlen had passed through numerous times during

their sparring match. She was overseeing, and occasionally help-ing, a team of crewmen painting trim that had been replaced during the repairs. Despite the heat, she was in her full uniform, so Malek didn't know why the officer was ogling her.

"Er, right, my lord. She's a woman, not a girl."

"Definitely a woman." One of the men dragged his arm across his face, then puffed out his chest, and looked at the captain.

She was ignoring all of them and, as far as Malek had noticed, had been doing so every time she passed through. She disap-peared belowdecks, carrying paint cans and brushes.

Malek lifted a hand to signal a halt to their exercise session. They'd been at it for an hour and could use a rest, especially if people were tripping over their own feet. And he was breathing as hard as any of them, with sweat streaming down his bare chest. Even though he kept himself in good shape, the heat and humidity of this latitude sapped a man of his energy more quickly than the brisk northern air.

"She's an improvement over our old commander," the officer whispered.

"Definitely," a crewman said.

"I considered Captain Korthan a competent officer." Malek didn't appreciate the disparaging of a dead man, even if he recog-nized that the men's comments were born not out of disrespect but of a vain hope that Rivlen would have a sexual encounter with them.

"Oh, yes, sir," the officer hurried to correct. "He was a good captain. Just not an *attractive* captain."

"I wish Rivlen would come out here and spar with us," another man said. "With her shirt off."

That earned snickers.

"I suggest you not make that suggestion to Captain Rivlen, since she is your commanding officer, and the Code requires respect of one's colleagues and superiors." Granted, that was the

Zidarr Code, and these men were military officers, but they had their own set of regulations that contained a similar policy. Malek opened his mouth to say more but paused. A faint tickle at the back of his mind made him think someone was trying to communicate with him telepathically.

Uthari? He had the power to speak with Malek from across the world.

But no words formed in Malek's mind, and he wondered if he'd imagined it. Or maybe it was someone like Yidar, who had reason to reach out to him but didn't have quite the range of a wizard. There had been something familiar about the touch.

"Yes, my lord," the officer said.

"We're sorry, my lord."

Barely hearing them, Malek lifted a hand. "That's enough for today. Dull the blade without leaving time for sharpening," he quoted a zidarr text, "and the morn's battle will go poorly."

The men rushed away, relieved to depart.

Malek dropped the practice swords in a rack, grabbed his shirt, and put on his weapons belt with his real sword and main-gauche. He rested a hand on the hilt of the larger weapon, sensing the power of the lesser dragon steel, and calmed his mind, trying to open himself for communication.

If Yidar was trying to contact him with important information, Malek had to do his best to amplify his awareness and ability to receive it. He could also reach out to Yidar himself, but as he felt that faint, distant touch again, he decided it wasn't Yidar.

Who was trying to reach him? A zidarr loyal to one of the other kings? He had no doubt that other ships and other zidarr would be sent after the artifact—by now, word about it had likely gotten out to everyone on Torvil—but it surprised him that one of them would contact them.

This touch could also be a sign of someone attempting to spy magically on him, to ascertain his position and see if the *Star Flyer* would be a threat soon. If so, he should send back a mental attack to punish the spy for his presumption.

A paintbrush clattered to the deck, and two men started shouting at each other. Malek headed to his cabin, both for quiet and so he could meditate. That was the surest way to open his mind and sense who was reaching out to him.

Captain Rivlen had finished her errand and was heading to her cabin, and they reached the corridor at the same time. She stepped aside, hands clasped behind her back in a professional parade rest, and made room for him to pass. He nodded to her and thought nothing of their chance encounter, but she surprised him by speaking as he reached his cabin.

"You were skilled and fit during your practice, my lord. It is clear you keep yourself in shape."

He paused with his hand on his door and looked back at her. "I do. It is my duty."

Belatedly, he wondered if he should thank her for what might have been meant as a compliment rather than a statement of fact.

"Of course." Rivlen glanced at him—at his chest—but only for a second before looking toward the wall. "I look forward to serving with you." She saluted, then hurried off, not toward her cabin, the direction she'd originally been going, but back the way she'd come.

Odd. Maybe she'd forgotten something.

Malek stepped into his cabin, dried himself with his towel, and put his shirt back on. He removed his weapons belt again but took the sword with him and knelt in the corner of his cabin where he meditated. The lesser dragon steel had been known to enhance his meditation as well as his dreams, and it might help him figure out who was trying to reach out to him—or spy on him.

He closed his eyes, relaxed his body, and slowed his breathing as he emptied his mind, opening himself to the world and to the magic that permeated all. Thoughts could flow across nature's waves of magic, from one person to another, if only they had enough power to transmit them. The medium was conducive to it, for those who sensed it and could manipulate it.

The presence brushed him again, a little clearer now that there were no distractions.

Lord Malek? Distinct words formed with the presence, though they were very weak, very distant.

Yes, he answered, though he hadn't yet identified the speaker. It was someone familiar but not any of his regular contacts.

Can you hear me, Lord Malek?

Malek's eyes flew open in surprise and recognition. *Jakstor Freedar.*

Jadora's son. Even though Jak had demonstrated that he could transmit telepathically back in Uthari's castle, Malek wouldn't have guessed the untrained boy could reach out across such a great distance. Though maybe it was possible the *Star Flyer* had caught up to the enemy ships and was closer than he'd assumed. But he swept out with his mind, magically searching the skies within a hundred miles of the *Star Flyer*, and he didn't sense any other mageships or any sign of magic at all. He certainly didn't sense the portal within that range. Its great power could call to him from a long distance.

Uh, yes. You can call me Jak. Uhm, my lord. The voice was as tentative and uncertain as the words. Was Jak afraid of how Malek would respond to this contact?

Malek's first thought was that he had underestimated the boy and his potential—anyone with the ability to speak to him across such a distance had *much* potential. He'd known when he told Uthari the boy wouldn't be a threat that it was possible it hadn't been an entire truth, but he hadn't realized how much of an untruth it had been.

His second thought was to realize that one of the very people he sought was reaching out to him. Why?

Jak might have gotten in trouble and thought Malek could help. Maybe he'd been imprisoned by Yidar or one of Zaruk's zidarr, and he now realized he'd made a mistake in running, that he couldn't escape all the mages in the world, and Malek was better to work with than most. Or, as Jak would more likely think of it, Malek was the lesser of two evils.

Are you in trouble, Jak? he replied.

Technically, we escaped from the trouble, but it's looking for us and wants us back.

Zaruk's people?

Yeah. The Dauntless *crashed, but there are three other mageships, and there's another zidarr. They have the portal.*

Malek tensed at this reminder that he'd failed to keep others from stealing the artifact, but he forced his muscles to relax with more slow breaths. For him, nothing had changed. When this day had started, his duty had been to get the artifact back. That was still his duty. That Jak was contacting him was a good thing. It sounded like he was still close to the artifact. Perhaps Malek could find it, them, *and* acquire the medallion.

He resisted the urge to ask the boy where he was. That might make him wary.

Do you want my help? he asked simply.

Are you on the way?

To Zewnath? Yes.

A long pause followed. *Is that general coming?*

Tonovan? Malek considered if it would be a betrayal to warn Jak of the other ships, ships that were closer to Zewnath than his own *Star Flyer.* Perhaps not. If he could win the boy's trust by sharing nonessential intelligence with him, Jak might guide Malek to him. To him and Jadora and the medallion. The artifact itself would be simple to find. Perhaps not simple to steal back from other zidarr, but as long as they did not have the key themselves, there wasn't a rush. *He is heading your way on another ship.*

Ugh, that's not going to make my mother happy.

I imagine not. It occurred to Malek that Uthari might have asked him to gain the trust of the wrong person. It might be easier to win over Jak than his mother. *If you tell me where you are, I won't allow him to hurt her. Or you. You know King Uthari wishes me to protect you and your mother.*

I didn't think he cared about me.

True. Though Malek had figured out through watching them work in the courtyard that Jak knew as much about the portal as Jadora. They were both valuable for their knowledge.

Uthari has no ill will toward you, Malek said, *and I do not wish your mother to lose someone else she cares about. She should not have lost the professor. It's not my intent to torment you two. I seek only to follow the orders of the king I'm sworn to serve. And all Uthari wants is to gain control of the portal so he can use it to obtain that plant.*

Malek didn't truly know if that was *all* Uthari wanted the portal for. He wagered his king also wanted to control it so none of his enemies could use it against him, but he hadn't voiced that to Malek.

That's what we were talking about, Jak said. *And how maybe there's nothing wrong with that.*

Malek stifled indignation that the boy would presume to *judge* Uthari. He had to be careful here. Jak hadn't yet given him their location. Like a man holding out seeds to lure in a wild bird, Malek embraced calm and patience.

There is nothing wrong with it, he agreed. *The Jitaruvak could be a boon to all of humanity.*

Does King Uthari know about me?

The change of topic threw Malek off, and it took him a moment to realize what Jak was asking. *That you have the potential to be a mage? Yes, he noticed before I did.*

Will he kill me? Or order you to kill me?

The boy's frankness was interesting. He hadn't spoken so

openly with Malek before. Maybe he felt bolstered by the distance between them. Or maybe he wanted to make sure Malek wouldn't kill him after he finished Uthari's task and they no longer needed archaeologists. Since integrity was one of the core tenets of the Zidarr Code, and Malek did not care to lie, he debated how he could answer truthfully without scaring the boy away. He told himself that even if Jak didn't tell him where they were hiding, he knew enough now that he could find them.

It is the way of our kind to kill wild ones. Those who have grown up with terrene humans are steeped in their beliefs and might use their power against us. But Uthari did not order me to kill you now or at any point. If you do not prove yourself a threat, I believe he will continue to look the other way, especially if you assist us in this matter.

I've seen you people throw lightning bolts around. There's no way I'd ever be a threat to you. Jak seemed relieved... as if he genuinely believed that.

Malek wasn't so sure. The fact that Jak, completely untrained, was able to reach out this far to communicate with him suggested not modest potential but great potential.

Malek was surprised Jadora didn't have any ability to sense magic. Usually, it took two gifted parents to produce a strongly gifted child. But unless someone mentored Jak, he wouldn't likely develop more than a few intuitions about magic and the ability to sense others' thoughts.

You will need to be careful around other mages and especially zidarr and wizards, Malek warned. *Since you are past the age when wild ones can be reliably brought into our world and trained, many would kill you simply for your potential.*

Like your buddy Yidar. I hope he's not coming.

Malek almost didn't comment on that. For him to tell Jak that Yidar was coming for him at Uthari's behest could be considered treasonous, but he'd already admitted Tonovan was on the way. If Jak was worried about Yidar, that might prompt Jak to give Malek his location and wait for him. Uthari would not care which of his people obtained the artifact and the archaeologists, only that they were obtained.

He is with Tonovan, Malek said.

Shit.

As I said, I will protect you if you tell me where you are and wait for me. Is that not the reason you contacted me?

There was a long pause. Again, Malek forced himself to be patient, to quietly hold his hand out with the birdseed on it, not to try harder to coerce Jak.

Yes, Jak finally said, a whisper in Malek's mind. *We're in the jungle outside Port Toh-drom, but the mercenaries and maybe the mages from the* Dauntless *are trying to find us. Mother knows an apothecary in the city. Niva Treetangler. We're going to see her and hope she can fix my ankle, help us get supplies, and figure out my vision.*

Malek burned the apothecary's name into his mind. He hadn't spent much time in Zewnath, but he'd traveled there on errands for Uthari before and could navigate Port Toh-drom.

Vision? he asked.

The artifact showed me where it wants to go.

Where it must be set up for operation? Malek asked.

Jak hesitated again.

I saw the constellations, Malek said. *I know one of them is in our Southern Hemisphere, and that we'd need the help of an astronomer to guess what worlds the other ones apply to.*

You figured that out too, huh?

Yes.

You'll come for us? And do like you said, protect us from those who want to kill us?

Kill you or capture you?

We may have frustrated Captain Toggs with our bluff. He was definitely trying to kill us in the end.

Malek almost growled, annoyed that some idiot would try to

kill people with valuable information in their minds. He lamented that Uthari hadn't let him leave immediately on this quest.

Since he was behind Yidar and Tonovan, they would have a full night and day to locate Jak and Jadora before Malek arrived. He didn't know whether to hope Yidar and Tonovan found Jak and Jadora before their enemies or not, since they wouldn't necessarily be safe with Malek's colleagues. Yidar had threatened to kill the boy, and Tonovan might enact some of his sexual fantasies on Jadora.

Malek clenched his jaw, wanting neither event to come to pass. *Find your apothecary, and if you can, learn specifically where to take the portal. Wait for me. I have funds to buy supplies. We will regain the artifact and set it up together.*

Good. Jak hesitated again. *Thanks.*

As his presence faded from Malek's mind, Malek opened his eyes and focused on the wall opposite his meditation corner. He considered contacting Yidar or Tonovan and threatening them if they harmed Jak or Jadora, but neither liked him, and Tonovan especially might go out of his way to torment them if he believed it would annoy Malek.

Better to say nothing and trust that Jak and Jadora could manage to hide for a day. They were clever.

He smiled slightly, thinking of all the concoctions Jadora had made to throw at enemies, even when she'd had nothing more than lavatory and kitchen supplies. He remembered the insanely strong glue she'd made to climb the walls out of her cell. If she had the opportunity to visit an apothecary shop, it would be the equivalent of a soldier resupplying in an armory.

6

Lieutenant Sasko found Captain Ferroki leaning against the railing of the *Dauntless* and looking down the dark beach in the direction Tezi and Colonel Sorath had gone. While search parties of mercenaries and mages had entered the jungle to look for Jak and Jadora, those two had headed straight toward Port Toh-drom. It was probably the right move. Even with magic, it would be hard to find someone in the jungle, but Sasko doubted Jak and Jadora had any supplies with them, so they would be forced to visit the city before heading anywhere else.

"You think it's safe to get some sleep, Captain?" Sasko looked up, toward the three mageships hovering a couple hundred feet above the beach over them.

Everyone here was supposedly on the same side, but the new ships had wrecked the *Dauntless*, and Zidarr Night Wrath had threatened Tezi. Sasko worried he would change his mind about letting Sorath use her as bait and would kill her if he found her. Couldn't a zidarr easily capture a couple of archaeologists on his own anyway?

"I don't know." Ferroki's elbows were on the railing, one hand clasping something. "I heard Toggs talking about more mage-ships being on their way here. Enemy ships, not more from Zaruk's alliance. He sounded like it was a certainty, not a possibility."

Sasko groaned. "Does that mean we'll be expected to fight them?"

"Likely."

"Are you sure we should? We did our job. It's not our fault Toggs couldn't convince two puny nonmagical humans to let him take the artifact back to his masters. We haven't been paid for risking our asses to get it in the first place, and unless you're keeping secrets from me, nobody's offered to pay us for continuing to help him."

"Toggs has been feeding us."

"Oh, yes. His canned sardines and tins of pulverized salty meat are what men dream about in bed with their hands around their cocks. Don't think I didn't notice that his mage crew gets a lot better food."

"You're grumpy tonight, Sasko. We're on a beautiful beach in an exotic tropical location with nature giving us a symphony." Ferroki waved toward the jungle and the surprising number of vociferous animals making sounds, even though the sun had gone down hours ago.

"I'm pretty sure those are just gorillas mating."

"Night monkeys."

"What?"

"I believe that's the species responsible for those trills and grunts. During the flight down, Professor Freedar told me about the native flora and fauna we could expect to encounter here. I've never been."

"And she has?" It hadn't occurred to Sasko that the archaeologists might have the advantage of being familiar with the area.

Ferroki opened her palm to eye the dark item in her hand.

Some charm? Not that medallion again, Sasko trusted. She'd seen it in the kid's hat right before they'd crashed.

"Yes," Ferroki said. "Apparently, there are a lot of useful medicinal plants to research down here."

"What does an archaeologist need with plants?"

"That wasn't her original field of study or an interest at all for her until a few years ago. She gave up her career to finish her husband's work after he was killed by King Uthari's loyal minions."

Sasko slanted her a long look. "Should you be spending time getting to know people we might have to... capture?"

She *hoped* they didn't get orders again to kill them, but she couldn't be sure. When Toggs had been ranting and raving as the other ships approached, he'd shouted for everyone to kill Jak and Jadora and take back control of the artifact.

"I've been thinking about that." Ferroki was looking down at the charm again. "About what they're trying to do and the fact that, as you pointed out, we've completed what we promised to do, haven't been paid, and are not at this point obligated to do anything Toggs or that zidarr asks." She glanced upward at Night Wrath's mageship.

"Are you regretting sending the search parties out? And Tezi?"

"I sent her off so she would be safe. Hopefully. As to the rest, I gave them orders to capture, not kill Jak and Jadora, but yes, I do regret it. I'm considering what the ramifications might be if we simply say we're leaving, get off the ship, and go to town. We could find work here."

"In an isolated city in the middle of a jungle? What *kind* of work?"

Sasko didn't object to a change, but she was aware of how little money was left in the coffers—it didn't help that the captain had given Tezi a big pouch of coins—and she hadn't heard of any wars being fought here in Zewnath. As far as she knew, there wasn't much in the way of ore, gems, or coal deposits in the mountains, and the jungle grew back as quickly as it was cleared, making farming and raising livestock difficult. In short, few powers were fighting for resources down here. Hundreds if not thousands of miles separated most of the city-states, and they tended to leave each other alone.

"There aren't any kings vying for power down here," Sasko added, "nor any ambitious mages of note who might hire us."

"That wouldn't be so bad. Working for mages is deadly. As Corporal Jinx could attest." Ferroki held up the charm.

Sasko realized then what it was. The charm necklace that the tough corporal had worn, her one feminine item. It was, if Sasko recalled correctly, something a relative had given her for luck. Unfortunately, it hadn't helped Jinx during the battle outside of Utharika. The company had been lucky to only lose one soldier, but losing anyone was always tough.

They'd had a funeral on the flight down, the captain saying a few words over Jinx's ashes. The mages had insisted on incineration for disposing of the body, even though that wasn't how the company usually did funerals. In the southern deserts, bodies were buried under rock cairns while everyone sang and prayed to Thanok or Shylezar, depending on the deceased's beliefs. But there were no cairns to be made at sea.

"You've pointed out yourself that there aren't many other options," Sasko said, "not for mercenaries who want to eat."

"The locals do have some problems with pirates. They might be interested in hiring us."

"*Roamer* pirates. You think Sorath is going to sign on to fight his own people?"

"Just because he has roamer ancestry doesn't mean he's loyal to them or even that he grew up with them. I don't know if he did or not, but he doesn't have an accent and seems more like one of us." Ferroki waved vaguely in the direction of the continent of

Bakora and the southern deserts. "Either way, he's not a part of Thorn Company, so we can't base our future contracts on his desires. Like us, he's also done what he was asked, so he might leave at any time." A hint of sadness lurked in Ferroki's voice, but Sasko didn't know if it was for Jinx or the idea that Sorath would leave. "I do hope he stays out of Zaruk's kingdom. Stone Heart offered him a pardon, but with Stone Heart dead, Zaruk might not honor that bargain."

"He should be wary of Zaruk, yes, but we shouldn't need to be. Listen, Captain. Not only have we succeeded at everything we've been asked to do, but the artifact is back in Zaruk's people's hands now." Sasko waved up to the mageship where the portal now rested on the deck. "There's no reason that Zaruk's people should betray *us*. They shouldn't know you helped Sorath in that hotel. Even if Stone Heart did, he's gone now. And we signed a contract. All we should have to do is kiss up a little to stay in these mages' good graces, help them round up the archaeologists, and go back with them to collect our pay. Very *good* pay, as I'm sure you recall. Captain, we could be set for the rest of the year once we collect that. We could take a month or two and relax back at our head-quarters."

"You make a good point. They *should* pay us. That said, I know it's silly, but I can't help but wonder *what if* when it comes to that portal. What if we could somehow help Jak and Jadora travel to another world, gather dragon allies, and bring them back to change things here?"

"You don't *really* believe that's possible, do you? Nobody has seen a dragon for ten thousand years. They're probably all dead."

"Or the portal between our worlds has simply been closed."

"Captain." Sasko gripped her shoulder. "We're not dreamers. We're realists. Let's go get the money we're owed. Don't let Jinx's death be for nothing."

"I suppose you're right. We need to at least attempt to collect our payment. And I need to send the death benefit back to Jinx's family. She has a mother and younger sister back home. I'm sure they need the money."

Sasko opened her mouth to reply, but a groan came from behind them.

It was the young helmsman, Nobber. He wasn't looking at them but off to the side, out to sea. "They're coming."

Sasko didn't see anything, but it was dark out there. The stars were out, but no moon had come up.

"Who's coming?" Ferroki asked him.

"More mageships. They're heading straight toward us. The captain was right."

"No chance they're more of your allies?" Sasko asked.

"No. I think the ones that are getting close belong to King Uthari's people. And the captain said even more ships may be on the way from other kingdoms who heard about that artifact and want it. Either way, we're going to have to fight again soon. We better finish repairs." After another groan, Nobber headed to the navigation cabin.

"At least what they want isn't located on our ship now," Ferroki said.

"I hope Toggs is bright enough to stay down here on the beach looking crashed and defenseless," Sasko said.

As if he'd heard his name, Captain Toggs strode out of the darkness toward them. He stopped in front of Ferroki.

"We've got enemies on the horizon. You're in charge with the colonel gone, right?"

"It's my company, yes." Ferroki didn't sound irked—she rarely did—but she was probably affronted that Toggs didn't know that she was *always* in charge of Thorn Company.

"All right. I've gotten orders from Zidarr Night Wrath." Toggs touched his temple to indicate telepathic communication. "He wants your remaining forces, anyone who isn't involved in the search, to head up to his ship to help defend the portal from the newcomers."

"What about this ship?" Sasko asked.

"We likely won't be targeted since we're already crashed, but my crew will defend us if we are. They want the extra hands up there."

"How are we supposed to get up there?"

"They'll take care of that." Toggs started to turn away.

Ferroki lifted a hand. "Captain? We haven't been paid for the *last* mission we went on for the leaders of your alliance. If you wish to engage our services again, we need to agree on payment and create a new contract."

"You can take that up with Night Wrath. He's in charge now."

Before Ferroki could answer, an invisible power gripped Sasko. She swore as it lifted her from her feet. Ferroki rose right beside her. Just as the artifact had been levitated from the deck to the mageship above them, magical power carried them upward.

Sasko groaned. "I'm sorry, Captain."

"For what?"

"I think maybe you were right and that I should have encouraged you to grab everyone and take off for the city while we could. We're going to be stuck fighting now." A battle that Sasko didn't know if they could win. She shuddered at the idea of facing Malek. They'd avoided facing him during the invasion, but they'd seen him defeat the powerful Stone Heart. *Twice.* The second time, Malek had cleaved Stone Heart's head off. Sasko didn't want to face him or any other zidarr in battle.

"It's what we do." Ferroki sounded defeated rather than determined.

More of their people were levitated from the deck of the *Dauntless.* Sasko highly doubted Thorn Company would be given the option to negotiate a new contract.

Jak's ankle throbbed like a red-hot poker in a smithy's furnace. He sank to one knee, leaning against a moss-draped tree for support, and waited for his mother to return.

They'd reached the edge of the city, a few limestone buildings visible through the foliage ahead, their sides as leaf-covered and vine-draped as the trees. Mother had gone ahead to check for guard towers or patrols that they might have to slip past. Throughout the night, they'd managed to avoid the mercenary search parties, but that didn't mean Captain Toggs or someone else hadn't warned the city watch—or whatever equivalent Port Toh-drom had—to keep an eye out for them.

His mother returned, carefully picking her way over roots and through the dense undergrowth to him. This close to the city, there were trails through the jungle, the vegetation recently burned back to keep them clear, but they'd been afraid to use them. With dawn approaching, others might be traveling the paths.

"Are you all right?" she asked for the dozenth time that night as she touched his shoulder and crouched beside him.

Even though Jak appreciated her concern, he was tempted to answer with a frustrated *no*. The ankle wasn't the worst injury he could have received, and he was thankful that nobody had succeeded in incinerating him with a fireball, but it made walking difficult at a time when all they needed to do was walk. Or run at a dead sprint.

"Yes," he made himself say.

"I didn't see patrols or any other sign that the local law enforcers are worried about invasion, at least not from the direction of the jungle. I climbed up in a tree with a view of the river and their docks, and the city is very quiet."

"You climbed a tree?"

"I'm forty-two not eighty-two," she said. "I'm capable of pulling myself up a tree."

"Did you do it because you wanted a good view or because there were some medicinal flowers that you wanted to pick sprouting from its branches?"

"They're medicinal *berries*."

"I knew it."

"Here." Mother opened his palm and pressed some mushy fruit into it. "Hirithisa berries. They're tart but dull pain. I had some myself. My knee aches, and I've developed a headache for some odd reason."

"I can't imagine why. Thank you."

Trusting her ability to identify berries—and everything else in the world that grew out of the ground—Jak didn't hesitate to eat them. Tart was an understatement. His face puckered up so hard his eyes threatened to pop out.

"I also gathered some dycha grass seed that I chanced across. It's a powerful dewormer that costs a fortune back in Sprungtown. It's somewhat common here, so far less valuable, but I plan to offer it in trade for supplies and medical attention for your ankle."

"Are worms a big problem down here?"

"All manner of parasites thrive in the jungle and are easy to pick up."

"Maybe I shouldn't have been licking rainwater off the leaves."

"Better rainwater than puddle water stagnating on the ground with mosquito larvae floating in it."

"Ew. You've put me off *all* water."

"There are armored ships moored at their docks," Mother said, "and I saw cannons and other artillery weapons on elevated platforms pointed out toward sea. More than I remember from my last trip here ten years ago. They were having problems with pirates then. That may have intensified."

"*Pirates* aren't what I'm worried about." Jak peered back toward the jungle and also glanced at the sliver of starry sky he could make out over the city. It hadn't been visible all night, thanks to the dense canopy above them, and he didn't know how many mageships were out there, but he doubted any of them had left.

"I know. If you're ready, we'll head for Niva Treetangler's apothecary shop."

"I am." Jak used the trunk to push himself to his feet. "And I hope your acquaintance is still here after ten years. Especially since that's where I told Malek to meet us."

In the dark, he couldn't see if his mother grimaced, but she hadn't been happy when Jak had admitted to having a lengthy conversation with Malek and telling him their destination. At first, she'd been shocked that Jak had been able to communicate with him, especially when he'd told her how far away Malek had seemed. Then she'd been worried.

She hadn't accused him of giving away too much, but he'd gotten the sense that she was afraid he had. He hadn't pointed out that *she'd* been chatting Malek up in dreams and letting him read her mind. Jak didn't know if that was true or even possible, or only a reflection of her worry.

"I hope she's here," Mother said, "because she's the only person I know in this city who might help us. Assuming we're not going to resort to thievery, we need someone to trade supplies to us at an extreme discount. The grass seed is valuable, but since it would be easy for her to collect herself, I fully admit it would be a pity trade."

"Malek will help us when he comes."

"I'd prefer not to *need* his help."

"I don't think we have that option. Unless your friend is a powerful mage, she's not going to be able to protect us from everyone searching for us."

"I know." Mother took his arm and draped it around her shoulders again. "But I'm still hoping we can find out where that pool is and get there ourselves."

"I told him we'd wait for him. He asked for us to."

"Oh, I have no doubt."

"Mother." Jak wished he didn't need her support, but he was forced to lean on her as they maneuvered over roots and uneven ground. He used the magelock rifle he'd taken from the *Dauntless* to support himself on the other side, though he felt bad that he had turned Tezi's fine weapon into a crutch. "You said I could reach out to him. You *agreed* that we need help to evade all those mages and gain access to the portal again."

"I know, but I didn't actually think you'd be able to speak telepathically to him across the entire Forked Sea."

"It was only *half* of the Forked Sea."

"So, a thousand miles instead of two thousand?"

"Probably." Jak shrugged.

"I'm concerned for you," she said quietly, glancing toward his hat, where the medallion remained nestled. "I don't think that's a normal ability for even a trained mage."

Jak shrugged again, though her observation made him uneasy. Was he... some kind of freak?

In truth, he hadn't expected to be able to reach Malek either. He'd figured it was a long shot.

"I think it only worked because I was trying to contact someone extremely powerful and able to sense... a lot." Jak admitted he had little idea how telepathy and mind reading worked, but that seemed plausible. "Not because I'm so powerful."

"I hope so. It terrified me when Yidar detected you sending your thoughts to Malek and instantly learned that you have power —and instantly wanted to kill you."

"That terrified me too." Jak said it lightly, but he meant it. During their conversation, Malek had hesitated when Jak had asked if Uthari would kill him, or order Malek to kill him, because he was a wild one.

The answer hadn't been that reassuring. *If you do not prove yourself a threat, I believe he will continue to look the other way.* Malek *believed*. A hedging word. That meant he wasn't positive.

And what happened if Uthari decided Jak *was* a threat? Jak couldn't imagine ever developing the kind of power that Uthari or Malek had, but what if they considered even small displays of magic a threat?

"Not so much that you've been assiduously reading *The Mind Way*, I noticed," Mother said.

"That's because *you* were reading it. I figured you needed to learn to protect your thoughts even more than I did."

"Why? My thoughts aren't as irreverent as yours."

"I don't believe that's true. And you're a woman. If you piss them off, they could hurt you more."

Mother sighed. "They can hurt you every bit as much as they can hurt me. And I don't want to see that."

"Me either. That's why we're going to wait for Malek and hide behind him all the way to our reunion with the portal."

She managed an amused snort. "I just worry that we're making a deal with one of the slavemasters in Hell. Just because he's not as openly vile as some of the other mages doesn't mean we can trust him longer than he has a use for us."

"I know, but I think we can trust him as long as he *does* have a use for us. And since Uthari wants you to make that longevity potion, he should need us longer than the kings who just want to figure out a way to open the portal."

Jak decided not to point out that Uthari and Malek didn't need *him* for that. There was no need to worry Mother more than she already was.

The jungle gave way to a cleared area, though bamboo recently hacked down to nubs promised that it wasn't easy to keep that area cleared, and they walked on to a concrete paver road winding between the first buildings. The stone walls and terra-cotta tile roofs reminded Jak of Perchver, but the lush vines growing up the sides of many of them were nothing like he'd seen on the stark desert dwellings. Here and there, stinky lanterns burned on street posts. Whatever was in the reservoirs wasn't kerosene. Maybe whale blubber?

Even though it was early, the predawn light barely creeping into the streets, Jak was surprised at how empty the city was. Maybe all of the people were staying inside because they were worried by the mageships that had shown up on their beach. It felt like Jak and his mother had walked twenty miles last night, but that was because the undergrowth and uneven terrain had been so difficult to navigate, and they'd been forced to take a roundabout path. He was positive the ships were only two or three miles up the coast. They would be in view from the hilltops within the city.

If anyone bothered looking for them. Not only were all the doors shut, but the shutters were pulled on the windows of every building they passed. It was as if the citizens were expecting a storm.

Only once did someone open a shutter long enough to peek out at Jak and Mother. The person in the shadows didn't look for long before pulling it back closed.

"You'd think *we* were the evil mages here to wreck their lives," Jak murmured.

"I'm sure they're hoping the evil mages leave them alone entirely," his mother said. "On this continent, most of those who develop magical power are taken off to the druid sanctuaries deep in the jungle. They're not known to interfere much with the terrene denizens."

"I'm envious."

"Me too."

They took lefts and rights, alternating between walking down wide boulevards with merchant stands not yet open for the day's business and narrow alleys between buildings. Here and there, the pavers turned into stairs, and Jak couldn't imagine a wheeled conveyance doing well on most of the routes through the city. Maybe Port Toh-drom was compact enough that everyone traveled on foot.

Though Jak carefully noted everything they passed, imprinting landmarks in his mind so they could find their way again later, he was glad his mother seemed to remember where she was going. When they reached an inauspicious three-story building on a hill at the end of a street, she pointed to three signs on the wall at the bottom. They were in a language Jak couldn't read, but the one at the top displayed a mortar and pestle, indicating the apothecary shop was on the top floor.

His ankle hurt less after chewing the berries, but the climb up the narrow steps on the outside of the building wasn't easy. He paused to rest on the landing at the top.

Vines wound all along the railing, and no fewer than twenty pots of various sizes hung from it and from the walls to either side of the door. Floral scents from pink, purple, and yellow blooming flowers perfumed the air.

The landing looked out over the city, the river, the sea, and a wide boulevard running along the base of the hill perpendicular to their street. Since there were still so few people out, he immediately spotted a couple walking down there.

He slumped against the railing. It was a *familiar* couple. Even in the dim light, that blonde hair was hard to miss. And Colonel Sorath's bush of dark wiry hair was equally identifiable.

There weren't any mages with them, but Jak didn't call out. Judging by the way they peered into alleys and doorways, they were looking for more than an eating house serving breakfast.

He eased back into the shadows near the wall, his ankle twinging as he put weight on it. He jerked at the reminder of pain and bumped Mother's shoulder. She was looking out toward the city too, and hadn't yet knocked on the door.

"We'd be foolish to try to contact them, right?" Jak whispered, admitting that he was only tempted because one of the mercenaries was Tezi. But he'd stolen her rifle. She wouldn't be pleased to see him. Jak wouldn't be surprised if Sorath had picked her deliberately to try to trick him again. There could be mages about, ready to pounce if Jak approached the pair.

"Yes, but I'm more worried about those ships right now." Mother pointed toward the horizon over the sea.

Jak expected to see Zaruk's three blue-hulled vessels, the crews perhaps coming to the city to look for him *personally,* but two black-hulled mageships were flying toward land. Uthari's people. For a moment, he thought Malek's *Star Flyer* might be one of the vessels, but Malek was still farther away.

Jak's gut twisted. This had to be General Tonovan, Yidar, and whatever other loathsome mages they had along.

"My eyes aren't playing tricks on me, right?" Mother asked. "Those are black ships, not blue ships?"

"I'm afraid your eyes are still as good as your tree-climbing skills."

"That's a relief. I think. I hope General Tonovan isn't on one of those ships."

Jak slumped against the wall. "He is. Yidar too. Malek told me."

She frowned at him. "He gave you intelligence on what the rest of his fleet is up to?"

"Well, I asked."

"I wouldn't have expected him to tell you anything. You are— we are—the enemy."

"No, we're his once and future captives. Also, I'm not positive Yidar and Tonovan aren't also his enemies."

"Malek and Yidar sparred together all day outside of the library when we were inside trying to work," she pointed out.

"They're at least rivals. Didn't you get that impression from them?"

"Yes. But you're…" Her frown returned. "I hope he wasn't setting a trap. Trying to lure you into complacency."

"I'm not an idiot, Mother."

She lifted a hand. "I know you're not. You're smart, but you're also young, and I've been afraid…" She eyed him with uncharacteristic wariness. "You get a little dreamy-eyed when you talk about how good a fighter Malek is."

"You saw him. He *is*. But it's not like I'm some enraptured *girl* fawning over him. I know he's our enemy and would do anything his king says. I get it."

"Good. I'm glad."

"I was holding back the information *he* wanted so he would tell me more. I wanted some assurances before giving him our location, even though I had a feeling he could find us whether I told him where we were or not. But I intentionally asked him a bunch of stuff before letting him get what he wanted. Aren't you glad we know Tonovan and Yidar are on those ships? So we can better avoid them?"

"Let's hope we can." Mother knocked on the door.

"I do believe, even if he's our enemy, that Malek is honest. Don't you think?"

"I don't know, Jak. He doesn't seem shifty, but he's smart. We can't underestimate him."

"Oh, I know. He also figured out the constellations and what they imply."

She squinted at him. "The ones from the artifact?"

"Yes. He either memorized everything, or he made his own rubbings when we weren't around. Either way, he's had time to think about what they mean. And because only one is recognizably based on *our* stars, he also believes there might be thirty-two different worlds."

"Damn," she whispered, staring at the door. "I don't think your idea to want to work with him is bad, but I don't know how we're going to out-clever him and get away in the end."

"We just need to stay alive and go through the portal. Once we see what we're dealing with and if there *are* dragons, we'll figure something out."

"I hope you're right." Mother knocked again. "I don't hear anyone moving around inside."

A shutter opened in a building on a nearby hilltop, and a woman peered out at them. As with the last person, she pulled her head back in quickly. The shutter banged back shut.

Jak looked toward the boulevard, but Tezi and Sorath had disappeared. He didn't think they could have spotted him and Mother in the shadows, but not knowing where they'd gone made him uneasy. As if he needed more to be uneasy about. Even in the couple of minutes they'd been on the landing, the black ships had grown larger. They were flying this way fast.

"If I had someone else I could visit, I would, but..." Mother tried the door. It wasn't locked, but it appeared to be barred from the inside. "That's a big gap between the wall and the door. Can you fit your caliper through? Do you still have it?"

"Of *course* I have it." Jak fished in one of his pockets. "What kind of cartographer goes to a continent he's never visited without mapmaking tools?"

"The kind who's been searched and imprisoned as many times as there are weeks in this month?"

"Yeah, but Malek keeps giving me my stuff back. He's a really weird captor."

"And here I thought you liked him because of his fighting skills."

"I don't *like* him." Jak slid his caliper into the gap between the door and the wall. It barely fit, but it did reach the bar on the other side. "He's just less odious to work with than the other zidarr, and he's not actively trying to kill me."

"That is a point in his favor." Mother plucked a couple of purple flowers from a bush with plenty to spare and slid them into her pocket.

"Are you out of vials?"

"Yes."

"Are those also painkillers?"

"Daraviva pollen reduces fatigue and stress levels."

"Is it for us or for our enemies?" Jak eased the wooden bar upward and tried to figure out how he could unseat it without dumping it on the floor and making noise.

"Us. Unless you think lowering General Tonovan's stress levels would make him less of an ass."

"I doubt it."

"I'd rather drench him in erithra tea."

"What does that do?"

"Lowers one's libido."

"I'm not going to ask why you know about his libido." Jak said it lightly, because he didn't want to gawk in horror at his mother, but he hadn't forgotten the leer Tonovan had given her in Uthari's castle. If Jak ever got the chance, he would stab his caliper in the general's nuts, consequences be damned.

"It's all right," Mother said quietly. "He didn't have time to do anything to me on the *Star Flyer*, but I feel horrible for the *children* he has on that ship to service him."

"Gross." Jak scowled. Maybe stabbing the general in the *heart* would be a better goal. "This is going to make noise." Jak had been shifting the bar around, but he didn't have the reach to lower it silently. "Is that all right?"

"It'll have to be. We knocked, so it's not as if whoever's inside doesn't know we're here."

Jak nudged the bar off, pulled his caliper back, and hefted his borrowed rifle.

Mother held up her hand. "This was an acquaintance. No firearms."

"What if *she* has one?"

Mother shook her head and eased the door open, the fallen bar scraping on the tile floor.

"Hello?" she called softly. "Niva? It's Professor Freedar from Sprungtown University. Are you home? My son and I could use some help."

Jak wanted to push past her and go inside first with his rifle at the ready, but she quickly stepped across the threshold, and his ankle kept him from pushing anything.

"Niva? Do you still live here?"

A woman inside barked a warning in a language Jak didn't understand. His mother had been speaking in Dhoran, the trade language spoken most widely in the world, but if the person who lived here didn't understand it, then that opening might not have been reassuring.

But Mother switched languages to respond. Her pronunciation was halting and rough, but it sounded like she knew and understood enough to speak with the locals.

The woman inside replied, her voice panicked. A clack sounded, and Mother halted, raising her hands.

"Does she have a *pistol*?" Jak tried to peer around his mother. "That sounded like a flintlock."

"It is. And it's a musket, not a pistol."

"That's not *better*." He stared over his mother's shoulder at a woman barefoot in a dress, gray hair tugged back in a hasty bun.

As promised, she was pointing a musket at them. Jak tried to surge in front, wanting to disarm the woman and make sure she couldn't shoot, but his mother shifted to the side, blocking him. He came down wrong on his ankle again, and pain jolted up his leg.

"I agree." Mother smiled and launched into a lengthy explanation while she kept her hands up and nodded around the room toward shelves, cases, and open cupboards overflowing with powders, dried herbs, strings of tubers, and who knew what else. The floral-scented landing had held only the faintest of aromas compared to this pungent mix of odors.

The woman answered, jerking the muzzle toward a shuttered window. Jak didn't know if she was saying the shop was closed or if she planned to shoot them and throw their bodies over the railing outside.

Mother asked a few questions, though judging by the furrow to her brow, she wasn't completely following the rapid-fire words. She reached slowly into her pocket, drew something out, and showed some of the seeds she'd collected.

Finally, the woman lowered her musket, resting the butt on the floor. She pointed for Mother to put the seeds on a counter, then at Jak and finally to a stool.

"This isn't Niva," Mother said. "My old acquaintance left Port Toh-drom a few years ago and moved to a small village to live with her adult children. This is Merija, the new owner. She says to sit down, and she'll look at your ankle, but that we have to leave soon. Nobody is allowed to be out in town until the curse goes away."

Mother waved Jak inside and closed the door, but not before glancing again toward the horizon and the black ships flying ever closer.

"The curse?" Jak hobbled to the stool as his mother deposited her seeds on the indicated spot on the counter. Payment for wound treatment.

"The *Telvik-arukvar*. The ring of the evil dragons, the destroyers of the old cities."

"Uh. *Evil* dragons?"

"That's what she said. And what she calls the portal. It seems the locals remember it, and they don't like it."

That worried Jak, and he scowled at the floor as Merija pulled up another stool and waved for him to lift his foot into her lap.

All along, they'd been wondering why ancient humans had removed the portal from its jungle home and buried it on a distant island. The visions of playful dragons that he'd seen didn't suggest any evilness, and he didn't want to believe they had been enemies, but if these people had old stories of dragons destroying cities, that was an ominous sign. How could both versions of dragon lore be true?

Mother spoke again in the local language as the woman examined Jak's ankle.

Merija shook her head vehemently.

Jak winced through more probing, but tried to be patient for the exam and the continuing conversation that he couldn't understand.

"She says the seeds will pay for your treatment but not anything else," Mother said quietly. "Unless you can think of something to trade, we're not going to be able to buy food or medical supplies for a trip." She gazed longingly at the jars and bags around the shop. "I also asked if she would look at your drawing and see if she recognized the place, but she refuses. She says it's forbidden to go into the jungle while the *Telvik-arukvar* is here. Also that the evil mages from the north are going to battle. The people of Port Toh-drom are praying to Thanok and their jungle gods for protection. They're terrified that the arrival of so many threats signifies the end."

"I guess Shylezar isn't a popular god here if they believe dragons are evil."

"No, no!" Merija jerked her head up to look at him. She used two fingers to make a gesture like horns and X-ed them over her chest, then switched back to her native tongue.

"It's also forbidden to speak of the dragon god," Mother said. "I remember from my last visit that he isn't worshipped here, but I didn't realize they felt that vehemently toward him. I guess dragons didn't come up much in my chats about flowers back then." Mother pointed to little dried cones in a jar on the shelf and asked Merija something.

Merija answered calmly, less disturbed when speaking about her ingredients. More questions followed, and Jak guessed Mother was trying to establish a rapport with the woman. Maybe one that would lead to them getting free supplies.

Merija placed a poultice on Jak's leg and wrapped it with a bandage. As she was tying the knot, a pounding came at the door.

Jak lunged for his rifle and sprang up as Merija grabbed her old flintlock. She yelled a question at the door. Probably *who is it.*

Mother took powder from one of the jars and lifted her arm to throw it.

The door opened to reveal another gray-haired woman standing on the threshold. The closest thing to a weapon she had was a broom, and she wasn't pointing it at them, but at the sky. She shouted a long stream of words to Merija and shook the broom, as if trying to scare away invisible enemies. Jak only recognized one word in the mix. Zidarr.

Jak leaned to the side enough to see out the doorway, and he groaned. One of the two black ships had disappeared, but one was hanging in the sky right over the city, close enough for its red-uniformed crew to be visible on the deck.

Amid cursing, Merija ran forward, grabbed the woman, and pulled her inside. She shut the door, barred it, said something to Mother, and ran into a hallway, gesturing for her friend to follow her. They opened a door, disappeared into a back room, and a thunk sounded as another bar slammed into place.

Merija shouted something that might have been for Jak and Mother.

"She said we could take a few medicinal supplies but told us to see ourselves out and suggested we find our own place to hide. The zidarr are coming."

"For us?"

"*They* don't know that, or they probably would have shot us, but..." Mother's gaze lifted to his hat and the medallion. "I'm positive that's the case. Hold on."

She ran around the room poking into cabinets and peering into boxes.

Jak took off his hat and looked at the medallion, afraid that Yidar, Tonovan, or whoever else was on that ship would be able to track him by it. There had to be plenty of magical things in the city, so that might make it tricky to single it out, but he couldn't be sure of that. Dragon steel might feel differently to them than more mundane materials that crafters imbued with magic.

"Here." Mother had found a square of fabric that looked like canvas. "Wrap this around it." She also grabbed powders, herbs, vials, and a couple of small tins and jars from around the room. "This is more than she implied I could take. I'm going to have to find a way to pay her back someday. I hope we live long enough to do so."

"Me too. What is this?" The material didn't feel magical to his untrained senses, but that didn't mean much.

"Dark-eye fabric. It's supposed to insulate magical items to hide them from mages. We'll cross our fingers that it works—and that they can't track us through other means."

Jak wanted to point out that it might keep *Malek* from finding them too, but they had better get away from the apothecary first. Even without magic to guide them, their enemies might guess that Mother would come to such a place.

"Where are we going to go?" Jak's ankle didn't feel much better, and he winced at the idea of sprinting through the jungle.

"I don't know." Mother sounded as weary as Jak felt, and it didn't look like they would get to rest anytime soon.

7

LIEUTENANT SASKO FOLLOWED CAPTAIN FERROKI AND A GUIDE toward the captain's cabin on their new ship, the *Tempest*. Once again, they were stuck with the artifact. It was lying on the deck in much the same spot it had been on the *Dauntless*. This was Night Wrath's ship, and Sasko didn't look forward to seeing him again, not after his threat to kill Tezi had made Ferroki send her away to keep her safe.

Originally, Sasko had been skeptical that Tezi would ever be tough enough and strong enough to make it as a soldier, but from what she'd heard from Tinder and Sorath, she'd done well on the incursion into Uthari's castle. And the other mercenaries had started speaking more with her and including her in their activities. Just as Tezi had started to prove she had what it took... they'd had to let her go.

And what a place to let her go. Even with coin, Sasko wouldn't enjoy being abandoned and left to fend for herself on a foreign continent where she didn't speak the language. She silently wished Tezi luck and hoped to see her again.

The crewman who'd been leading Sasko and Ferroki waved for them to enter the captain's cabin.

"Ask for payment," Sasko whispered.

"And a new contract," Ferroki murmured back. "I intend to."

They found the captain inside, his clean, high-collared blue uniform suggesting he hadn't seen any fighting yet, nothing that would cause a wrinkle or dirt stain. The black-wearing Night Wrath stood at his side, his arms folded over his chest. He must not have found Jak and Jadora when he'd gone into Port Toh-drom to look.

Another man in a rumpled blue uniform with grease spattering his torso stood—no, *slouched*—on the other side of the desk, swinging a wrench and an unfamiliar glowing tool, as if he were already bored with the meeting. A mage mechanic? He was a touch scrawny, though he had a handsome face, with the same olive skin and green eyes as Night Wrath.

"Captain Ferroki. I am Captain Myroth. A *real* captain of an elite flying mageship with a crew of more than a hundred." The snobby captain was a gray-haired man with a trimmed beard and mustache, and he exuded power in the way the zidarr and wizards did, something tangible—and tangibly dangerous—even to Sasko.

Ferroki's eyebrows twitched, but she didn't otherwise comment on the distinction between their ranks. As a mature commander, she probably wasn't fantasizing about throwing him out the port-hole behind his desk.

"My understanding is that you are second-in-command of the mercenaries," Myroth continued, "that were sent to help our alliance invade Utharika and retrieve the artifact. Where is Colonel Sorath?"

"The artifact you've brought up to your ship and that is now resting on your deck, yes." Ferroki extended her hand in that direction. It was doubtful the man needed a reminder that they had it. Maybe she wanted to point out that Thorn Company had been instrumental in acquiring it, despite this diversion to the Southern Hemisphere. "I am the leader of Thorn Company. Colonel Sorath was given command of that specific mission, which we have accomplished and have not been paid for. I must request that we receive payment and negotiate a new contract before we engage in any more fighting."

"Mercenaries do like money, don't they?" The captain tilted his nose upward, nostrils flaring.

There was a pencil on his desk. Sasko fantasized about shoving it into one of those nostrils.

"It is how we feed our people and buy weapons and supplies," Ferroki said.

"You like money too, Captain," the mechanic drawled. "I've seen your house. Other than the servants you've got slave-banded and slavishly obeying you like a god, you've got a staff to pay."

The captain's big nostrils flared again as he sniffed disdainfully and noisily. Maybe he would inhale the pencil without any effort required from Sasko.

"You will be silent, *Lieutenant* Vinjo," Myroth said. "Or I will punish you personally. Just because your brother is here does not mean he will interfere with punishment."

"No, I wouldn't think so. He enjoys seeing me punished. He hasn't forgiven me for being Mother's favorite." Vinjo saluted Night Wrath with his wrench, then winked at Sasko, as if including her in the secret.

"I *do* enjoy seeing you punished," Night Wrath told him without any humor twinkling in his dead zidarr eyes. "Because you're obnoxious, irreverent, and don't apply yourself."

"And I'm Mother's favorite."

"*Father's* good opinion means far more."

"I disagree. Mother is the one who bakes cherry turnovers when we come up. When *some* of us come up. Having a zidarr for a son makes her uncomfortable, and she hides in her suite when you're there." Vinjo nodded at Sasko, bewildering her until he also checked out her chest. At least that explained the winks, though Sasko would have preferred to be left out of... whatever this was.

"Gentlemen," Myroth rumbled. "If you don't mind, I'm trying to question the mercenaries."

"We don't mind." Vinjo smiled. "Carry on, Captain. I believe they're enjoying your pomposity."

Myroth slanted him a dark look as Night Wrath also glared at the lieutenant—his brother.

Vinjo winced in pain—as someone magically delivered punishment?—then hefted his glowing tool, as if it might give him strength. "Why don't I get back to work? Save your punishment if you want that artifact tie-down system installed." Vinjo's previously affable expression turned hard as he glared at the captain. "And if you don't want anything inimical to happen to your recently finely tuned *tyronda* engine."

"If anything happens to it," Night Wrath said, "we'll know where to look."

"But would you know *what* you're looking at? I know you struggle to grasp the function of objects with more parts than your sword." Vinjo saluted them, then trotted out, sneaking a peek at Sasko's backside on the way, and closed the door before the mages could do more than exchange exasperated looks.

"He must be trying for your family," Captain Myroth said.

Sasko hoped she didn't encounter the mechanic lieutenant again. Given that mages all seemed to believe that any women they encountered should be theirs if they wished it, she would prefer not to star in any of their fantasies.

"Very much so," Night Wrath said. "Mother only bakes for him so she has something to shove in his mouth to shut him up."

"I'll instruct the cook to try something similar."

Myroth and Night Wrath focused on Ferroki again.

"Where is Sorath?" Night Wrath asked. "Still searching for the missing archaeologists?"

"As far as I know, yes," Ferroki said. "Many of our people went after them, per your orders, my lord."

"My understanding is that they are integral to the operation of the portal and should be recovered." Captain Myroth glanced at Night Wrath.

"Yes." Night Wrath pointed at Ferroki. "I'll leave your people searching for them. It would be better to acquire them than to let our enemies have them. But we will need to recover Sorath and his supposedly brilliant tactical mind. How many of your troops are left here to assist with defense? Enemy ships are on the way."

"We've about forty people here."

"Forty? That's it?"

"Twenty more are on the search."

"Such meager forces." Myroth picked up the pencil and scratched his jaw through his beard.

Sasko refrained from smirking, but she was amused that the pencil was so close to one of those big nostrils.

Night Wrath frowned at her. Cursed mind readers.

She clasped her hands contritely behind her back.

"Our company is modest but effective," Ferroki said. "Should you *pay* us for our last mission, we can talk about ways we can assist you with your defenses and sign a contract for this next endeavor."

Sasko nodded, relieved Ferroki was negotiating. The night before, Sasko had been concerned she would take Thorn Company and walk away from the mageships, leaving them stuck here without pay and desperately looking for work.

"Maybe we can get some roamers," Night Wrath told Myroth, "to round out their numbers. I've sensed some of their fishing vessels in the nearby waters. I'm sure some of those are *pirate* vessels and have combatants trained sufficiently enough to throw at our enemies as distractions to their mages."

Ferroki's face grew bleak, as she doubtless envisioned being stuck in command of a bunch of wild roamers with no allegiance to anyone. Would they even accept her as a leader?

"Pawn it off on Sorath," Sasko whispered.

"If you'll pay us and negotiate a new contract," Ferroki told Myroth, "we'll discuss how we could integrate more troops into your defenses if necessary."

"Yes, yes, we have coin for you." Myroth waved at Night Wrath.

Sasko watched curiously as he withdrew a heavy sack from inside his cloak. She had been skeptical they had money or would pay Thorn Company if they did.

Night Wrath tossed the sack to Ferroki, and it clinked with satisfying heft as she caught it.

"The agreed upon amount from King Zaruk and his allies," he said.

"Thank you, my lord."

Myroth opened a desk drawer and removed a piece of paper and a couple of pens. "And here is the contract we propose for your continued services. King Zaruk wants to keep Sorath—and your company—with our fleet until this matter with the artifact is settled. If we find some more men to bolster your ranks, you will have to split the pay with them."

Ferroki skimmed the contract. "We agree to continue working for you, but we insist that the contract is *only* for Thorn Company and Colonel Sorath. You'll need to negotiate with the leaders of the roamers and give them their own contract."

"They don't *read,* Captain Ferroki. It's difficult to make contracts with such people."

"I'm certain that verbal agreements work for them. Nonetheless, I will only sign a contract related to my company specifically."

"You're already aboard our ship, Captain," Night Wrath said coolly. "It wouldn't be wise for you to refuse our employment. Should you ask to get off, it's a long drop to the beach."

Ferroki gazed at Myroth without replying to the zidarr's threat. "We have experience with the artifact and Uthari's troops. You would be wise to keep us here and treat us well."

"Oh, I'm sure." Myroth's voice leaked sarcasm, but he did cross out the lines about adding troops, initialed the alteration, and pushed the contract back to Ferroki.

She read it through more carefully a second time, to the impatience of the mages, and finally signed it. Sasko tried not to feel bleak about the commitment. They'd been paid, and she had argued for this. She couldn't regret not walking away now.

Besides, they couldn't do that. They were mercenaries. This was what they did. Had Sasko wanted less dangerous work, she could have been a barmaid.

Once they'd been dismissed and were out in the corridor, Sasko muttered, "I guess that's what we wanted."

"Some of us more than others, but the rabbit wishing that winter won't come starves at the changing of the seasons."

"Now that we're in the tropics, you should use other animals in your platitudes."

"Such as night monkeys?"

"What are their opinions on winter?"

"I think they just have a rainy season and a slightly less rainy season here." Ferroki led the way back up to the main deck. "I hope Colonel Sorath returns soon."

"Because you miss his company or because you want *him* to deal with any roamers those two scrape up?"

"Yes to both."

~

Tezi had never been to Port Toh-drom or Zewnath or even the Southern Hemisphere, and she tried to make herself look around with interest at the city as she and Colonel Sorath walked along its roads, but all she could think about was that she was soon to be stranded here with no place to go. Captain Ferroki had given her money—her full pay and some extra—but she would rather have remained a part of the company.

"You don't have to stay with me, killer." Sorath glanced at her, though he went right back to scanning their surroundings as he drummed his fingers on the black-powder pistol hanging on his belt.

He also bore a sword and more of his pop-bangs, as he called them, in his pockets. She didn't know how many he had left, since he'd used many in Utharika and had brought them all the way from Perchver.

"Don't you need my help, sir? To be bait? The captain said I was supposed to do this last mission with you before disappearing."

"That's because the mage crew was in earshot. She just wants you to be safe. Somewhere that zidarr won't stumble across you."

"I wouldn't mind being useful one more time before... before they go, and I don't see them again."

"Well, if you spot Jak, you can try some flirty moves on him."

"Flirty moves?" Tezi touched her hip, wondering if she was supposed to walk with more of a sway. Her Thorn Company uniform didn't show off her curves, and given all the scratches and cuts she'd received in the past few weeks, she was surprised any man would think she was cute.

"Sure. I'd do them, but I don't think I'm Jak's type. Why is there nobody out in this town?" Sorath pointed his pickaxe hand toward the empty streets and the plethora of fishing boats at the docks. "Because of us? The mageships?" He squinted out to sea. "Or because of *them*?"

Tezi had noticed two black mageships—Uthari's colors—on the horizon earlier, and they grew closer with every passing minute. "Probably a combination of all of that, sir. When I was a regular person, I would have hidden inside my house if even *one* mageship showed up." And she had. Not that it had helped.

A pang of loneliness went through her as she thought about being alone again. Just as she'd started to feel she might have a home among Thorn Company...

"Mercenaries aren't regular people?"

Tezi looked at his oft-broken nose and scarred cheek. "No, sir."

"I suppose not. Still, you'd think there would be some kids out on the beach with spyglasses, wanting to see what's going on." They were walking along a wide boulevard lined with shuttered shops, but Sorath peered back at that beach, as if such youths might have scurried out. "Being visited by a bunch of mageships from the north has to be interesting. Worthy of gossip, at the least."

"Yes, sir. Do you truly think Jak and Jadora came this way? All the search parties headed off into the jungle."

"Even if they have another destination in mind, they wouldn't have gone deep into the jungle without supplies."

"They've got my rifle," Tezi said glumly. "They could have hunted."

"For how long before it ran out of charges?"

"Uh, not long, I guess."

"They'll come to town. They're probably already here somewhere."

"Are you sure we need to find them, sir? I... Captain Toggs tried to get us to kill them."

"That's because he's an idiot. I doubt Night Wrath has that in mind. But they've got that medallion—the *key* to making the portal work."

"Maybe we could get that and let them go," Tezi suggested,

then regretted it. Sorath might consider it dishonorable or unprofessional to do anything less than his best.

"That's crossed my mind," was what he said. "Especially since we're not being paid for this, but if I don't get them, I'm worried that zidarr and all of his people will take it out on Thorn Company."

"I understand, sir. I don't want that."

Sorath had been peering down every alley they passed, but he tapped her arm, then turned a corner. He led her around another corner, jogged down an ancient cobblestone street, then turned again. At first, Tezi thought he'd spotted Jak and was chasing after him, but after the next corner, he stopped and put his back to the wall. He pulled her against it beside him and lifted his pickaxe as he waited.

Several long seconds passed, but Tezi didn't budge, trusting Sorath had legitimately seen something. Even so, she was startled when he lunged around the corner. A startled squawk sounded.

"Stop, or we'll— Colonel?"

"What are you two doing?" Sorath demanded.

Tezi peeked around the corner.

Sorath had a familiar man shoved up against the wall, a fist knotted in his green uniform tunic, and his pickaxe lifted warningly toward the second man. They were mages from the *Dauntless*. One had gone into the tunnels and infiltrated Utharika with them.

"Captain Toggs said to follow you, Colonel. In case you found the archaeologists but didn't do the right thing."

Sorath squinted but let him go. The other crewman, one Tezi didn't know well, was eyeing him contemplatively, perhaps remembering that he was a mage and shouldn't have to answer to a mercenary without magic. Of course, if Sorath used his distracting explosives, he was good at taking down mages, at least the less powerful ones.

"What's the *right thing*?" Sorath asked.

"Bringing them back to the ship. Zidarr Night Wrath called the captain an idiot for losing them. We're also supposed to hurry up and get back to the ship because Uthari's people are on the way. There's going to be another fight over the artifact."

"I have no doubt. If our trap works—" Sorath waved at Tezi, even though he'd already told her she could leave, "—we'll get both of them and bring them back. You don't need to follow us."

"Uhm." They looked at each other. "Captain Toggs didn't give us a choice, Colonel."

"Do you want *me* to not give you a choice?"

Tezi didn't know what that meant, or if Sorath even knew, but he gave the men dark, threatening looks.

"No, sir," the one who'd fought alongside them before said.

The other mage looked like he might protest, but his buddy gripped his arm and jerked his head back toward the way they'd come. "We'll look for them on the other side of the river."

"Good plan," Sorath said.

They trotted off.

"It's useful to learn how to menace mages," Sorath told Tezi and pointed toward an alley that would take them back to the main boulevard.

"I can't even menace shopkeepers who cheat me out of the proper change," Tezi admitted.

"Why not?"

"I don't know. Either my face isn't scary, or they aren't looking at my face."

Unfortunately, Tezi didn't know how to make her *breasts* menacing.

He grunted. "Probably the latter."

As they stepped back onto the boulevard, Sorath glanced toward the beach again. The glance became a long look followed by a curse.

Tezi peered around him and did a little cursing of her own. One of the mageships had veered off, no doubt going to challenge the *Dauntless* and Zaruk's ships, but one had come to the city and hovered a hundred feet above the river and the docks.

Even as they watched, a few red-uniformed men and someone dressed all in black leaped onto the railing with large oval disks in their hands. They sprang off into the air, and Tezi gaped as they plummeted downward. She knew the zidarr had unbelievable otherworldly abilities, but only the black-clad man looked to be one of them. As far as she could tell, the others were normal mage crewmen.

As they fell, they maneuvered onto the oval disks, and their descent slowed. More than that, the disks started sailing sideways and flew off with the men riding them, arms spread for balance.

"I've seen those before," Tezi whispered, "back at the Dragon Perch Islands when the *Star Flyer* arrived." She started to feel vulnerable, for they were out in the open boulevard, and Uthari's people were heading in their direction.

"They're called skyboards." Sorath pointed toward an awning in front of an eating house with tables out front, and they stepped into the shade under it.

As the uniformed mages rode the disks—skyboards—over buildings and streets, they scanned the city below, searching for someone.

Strangely, the zidarr wasn't peering around. He gazed toward a hill on one end of the city, as if he knew exactly where he was going.

"I hope they didn't see us," Tezi whispered as the men passed over the boulevard without glancing toward their awning.

"They were sent for other prey," Sorath said.

"Jak and Jadora?"

"That's my guess. Come on." Sorath trotted across the boulevard to a street heading toward the hills.

"Where are we going?" Tezi was too much the proper soldier to think of disobeying a senior officer, but she remembered Tinder's advice from the time she'd helped Sorath battle eight mages: *Never run into battle with someone crazier than you are.*

"Where *they're* going."

8

JADORA LEANED AGAINST THE SIDE OF A WATER TANK ON THE FLAT roof of a large building with public baths inside, her cheek to the cool stone. Jak had picked this spot because it was on a hill with a view of the water, the apothecary building, and the black mage-ship floating over the docks. Maybe it wasn't wise to be out in the open, but they wanted to know if anyone was coming.

The weary part of Jadora that hadn't slept the previous night wanted to give up and let them find her. These were Malek's people, so it seemed bizarre that they were hiding from them while waiting for him. If Tonovan captured her and Jak, Malek ought to be able to get them away from him. Of course, there was a question about what Tonovan would do to them in the meantime. And then there was Yidar, who might kill Jak on sight for being a *wild one.*

No, they couldn't let themselves be captured. They had to avoid that, hope Malek could find them, and hope he had been speaking honestly to Jak and not setting a trap. Since Malek, Tonovan, and Yidar all loyally served Uthari, Jadora had no problem imagining them strolling up side by side by side to apprehend her and Jak.

"They're coming," Jak whispered.

He was kneeling in front of her, trying to rest his ankle while keeping an eye on the ship. Feeling guilty that she'd had her eyes closed while wallowing in grim thoughts, Jadora leaned around the water tank to look.

Two red-uniformed mages and a zidarr—that looked like Yidar—were riding skyboards. The men were soaring over the buildings toward their part of the city.

"I can't tell if they're coming straight toward us or going to the apothecary shop." Jak pressed himself against the water tank, hiding in its shadow. "They may be able to find us because they're familiar with us, but I'm hoping the gong tower will keep them from sensing the medallion, in case the fabric isn't enough."

"Gong tower?" Jadora glanced behind them at the only structure rising higher on the hill than their building.

It was an eight-story brick tower with leafy vines growing like a carpet all the way to the top, to an open area under a pointed copper roof where a bell would have hung if it had been a tower back home. Here, a large golden gong hung on chains.

Jak nodded. "The gong is magical. I was able to sense it from several blocks away. Its aura should drown out lesser ones." He lifted the rifle he'd taken from the ship. Was it magical too? "The gong is much more noticeable than the medallion. It doesn't have as strong an aura as the portal, but few things do."

And here she'd thought he chose the spot only for the view. "It's a Gong of Thanok. They were built over the centuries in towns and cities Thanok's priests were attempting to convert to their religion. Originally, anyone who converted was allowed to climb up the tower and ring it to receive a blessing. These days, a priest has to ring it on your behalf, and they're usually only used at ceremonies."

"Shylezar's followers have never bribed people with blessings to convert to their religion." Jak sniffed, a reminder that he preferred Torvil's only religion with dragons, perhaps because of his boyhood desire to ride one.

Jadora had never tried to convince him to follow another path —much to her father's consternation. Her father, a devout priest of Thanok, had expected her to raise her son to follow the One True Religion, even though she herself was agnostic. Father had given up on her soul some time ago, as he informed her at every family gathering, but he'd been jaded anew when he learned that Jak prayed to a flying scaled god with fangs.

"We should have looked for a druidic tower," she murmured, thoughts of religion making her wonder if they could find clues about where the portal needed to be placed for operation. Given the fear the locals had of it, finding a guide to that pool would be more difficult than she'd realized.

"Do druids have towers?"

"No. It was a joke. They have temples and meeting stones, usually in the swamp or jungle, but some cities have them. Port Toh-drom might. It's quite populous by Zewnath standards. The classic configuration for their meeting stones is four rectangular granite or limestone slabs tipped inward to lean on each other at the top. From a distance, they look like narrow pyramids." Jadora had visited one during her previous trip to Zewnath. Unfortunately, they were easier to find than actual druids, whose settlements might or might not be anywhere near the stones. "Given that the language next to the Dragon's Tail constellation on the portal belonged to the ancient druids, modern druids may be our best bet."

They fell silent as Yidar and his two mage soldiers rode their skyboards closer. Jadora rose to her feet, about to tap Jak on the shoulder and suggest they climb down the back of the building to find a less open place to hide.

But Yidar led his people to a rooftop farther down the hill. Jadora closed her eyes. The apothecary shop.

"I hope those women got out of there," Jak whispered. "I doubt a locked door is going to keep a zidarr from getting to them."

"I know. Can the zidarr sense places we've been? How did they know to go straight there?" She wondered at what point Jak had become her resource about the magical world. Since he'd admitted he could sense magic, she supposed.

"I don't know. You'd think if they could sense that, they could sense us up here, and would have come straight here."

"They may be checking all of the apothecaries in the city, guessing I'll have contacts here or will show up at one." Jadora knew there were four or five apothecary shops in town and found it suspicious that chance had taken the mages first to the one she'd visited. As soon as they questioned the women—an easy task with their mind-reading abilities—they would have proof that Jadora and Jak had been there.

Jak gazed out at the city. "I wish I had a map. I'm looking for druid stones."

Jadora almost pointed out that they would be of little use and that they needed to find *actual* druids, but she didn't know that. The stones she'd visited before had been covered in runes, ancient messages that might contain something useful to their quest. Besides, it wasn't as if they had anything else to try.

"How's your ankle?" she whispered as Yidar and his assistants hopped from the roof down to the balcony she and Jak had been on a half hour earlier. "Can you climb again if we need to?" She tilted her thumb toward the back side of the building.

"Not much better, but I'll have to."

Jadora stood, figuring they should move while Uthari's people were inside, but a voice spoke into her mind.

Well, good morning, Professor Freedar. It was General Tonovan.

She slumped against the water tank.

What ever are you doing down here in Zewnath? My king is quite put out that you left the luxurious suite that he gave to you and the boy.

She didn't answer. Maybe it was delusional to think that it mattered, but it might be harder for him to pinpoint her if she didn't reply.

She squinted toward the black mageship floating over the docks, expecting to spot him standing at the railing and gazing up at her and Jak. But if he was aboard, he wasn't visible. Other red-uniformed mages stood on the deck, but their focus was to the west rather than the city. Toward the rest of the mageships and the artifact.

Yes, we are dealing with that first. Reacquiring the artifact is my priority. I will drop it at Uthari's feet and remind him that it was taken out from under Malek's nose. Tonovan chuckled, the sound ringing in her mind as if he were physically beside her, laughing in her ear. *I've sent my young zidarr traveling companion to see if he can locate you. If he can't, that will be an embarrassment for him, one I'll be sure to point out to my king. I do love seeing those pompous zidarr fail. If I must, I'll get the artifact myself and then come for you. This time on our ride back, I'll ensure we have plenty of time alone together without interruptions, during which I can show you how to be properly respectful to a powerful wizard.*

Tonovan chuckled again, then forced sexual imagery into her mind of what might have happened last time if not for Malek walking into the cabin.

Jadora clenched her eyes shut and attempted to wall off her mind and drive him out, but the handful of exercises she'd tried from the monk book that Malek had given her weren't enough. Closing her eyes only made it worse, because all she could see was him and his lurid fantasies of what he wanted her to do for him.

"Mother?" Jak had risen, like he was ready to leave, but he paused to prod her shoulder. "We need to go. They came back out."

Jadora nodded jerkily, focusing on him and the rooftop around them. "Lead the way."

"Is someone attacking your mind?"

"Something like that." She scowled. "Tonovan."

"That bastard." Jak clenched his rifle tighter. "Where is he?"

"Hopefully busy with the artifact."

Though not nearly busy enough if he had the time to torment her telepathically from a distance.

"Follow me. I have an idea." Jak took her arm, as if he were afraid she wouldn't be able to come if he didn't guide her.

He might have been right. She couldn't get Tonovan out of her mind. Even with her eyes open, she saw double, an overlay of him in his pornographically decorated cabin with all of his enslaved sex servants—and her.

As she stumbled after Jak, not toward the ladder they'd climbed to reach the rooftop but toward the back of the building, she broke her resolve not to respond to Tonovan. She needed to say something that would distract him from his torment.

Zaruk's people have a lot of powerful mages and a lot of mageships, she told him. *You better call your zidarr to help you, or they'll destroy you, and King Uthari will never get the artifact back.*

Their mages are weak. We'll have no trouble with them. I could single-handedly destroy all of their ships. You'll be permitted to witness my prowess.

Why haven't you started the fight if you're so wonderful? In truth, Jadora had no way to know if the battle had begun, but she believed they would hear cannons firing and explosives detonating, even from miles down the beach, if the mageships were battling. The crews might sling fireballs and lightning bolts, but they also used black-powder weapons. *Are you waiting for Malek to arrive to do the real work? That seems to be how it goes.*

Screw that sanctimonious ass. A burst of hatred and rage flooded Jadora's mind.

Due to its intensity, it was painful, almost an attack in its own right, but the sexual imagery disappeared, so she preferred it. She put an image of Malek in her mind, her memory of him battling numerous mages the night the *Star Flyer* had been attacked and taking over an enemy ship by himself. With luck, it would repulse Tonovan.

Jak reached the edge of the rooftop and pointed across a three-foot gap between the bathing house and the vine-covered wall of the tower. "Can you jump across this, Mother?"

She stared at him. "Jumping across is less the problem than whether those vines will support our weight. What was wrong with the ladder?" She pointed toward the other side of the building.

"I want to go up, not down."

"Uh." She gaped up to the top of the tower. It was more than twice as high as the bathing house.

"From up there, we'll have an even better view of the city, and if there are druid monuments, we'll be able to see them." Jak pointed at the wall. "Those vines are thick and anchored to the mortar and wrapped around the railing up there. I know it won't be easy, but we didn't pass any map vendors on the way in. The sooner we figure out where we need to go, the sooner we can get away from those hunting us." Jak glanced in the direction of the apothecary shop, though it was no longer in view. For the moment, the mages weren't either. "Besides, the gong's magic might help hide us. We'll maneuver around to the back so we won't be visible to those mages if they ride into view again."

"We could end up trapped up there. I don't think—"

Is he the one you want to writhe in sexual ardor with? Tonovan had recovered from his repulsion, though the rage was still there, simmering now. *I believe you'll find the prudish zidarr a disappointment. From what I've gathered, he's not very interesting or creative.*

Jadora kept the memory of Malek in her thoughts, using it like a shield in the hope that it annoyed Tonovan enough that he would stay out of her mind.

Do you think he would defend you from threats? Tonovan asked, amusement accompanying his words now. *He is Uthari's man, more loyal than a hound. He follows all orders from his master without question. He killed your husband, you know.*

Jadora froze.

Was that true? Or was Tonovan lying to annoy her? Or to *distract* her until his allies found her? He might even now be directing Yidar to her location.

Tonovan forced more imagery into her mind. This time, it was more horrifying than before, because it seemed to be a real memory of an actual event.

Loran's face filled her mind, identical to how he'd appeared five years earlier. He was in his office, working late at the university, researching by lamplight. The details of the office were so accurate, exactly as Jadora remembered it, that she knew without a doubt that Tonovan had been there.

Of course he had. He'd collected Loran's severed head and brought it to her at home. She grimaced, remembering that night as if it had just happened.

Loran was at his desk, scribbling notes, when a man in a brown jacket with a glowing sword stepped out of the shadows. Malek.

He demanded Loran's journal, but the journal was nowhere in sight, and Loran refused to say where he'd put it. Malek thrust a hand out, trying to read Loran's mind, but some magical trinket kept him from succeeding. He snarled, then sneered and sprang onto the desk and swung his sword. The magical blade cleaved through Loran's neck, blood flying everywhere.

Jadora lurched forward, gripping her knees. Tears streaked down her cheeks as she tried to shake the vision—the mental attack.

Not only did he slay your husband, Tonovan said smugly, *but he'll slay your boy too. We only need* you *to assist with the artifact. You are all Uthari cares about, and he will have you. As will I.*

Distant booms rang out, the cannons and explosives she'd expected earlier. Tonovan's presence in her mind faded. Thank the gods. All of them.

Fearing it was only a temporary reprieve and that the zidarr was on the way, Jadora wiped the tears from her eyes and straightened. The vision lingered even without Tonovan actively manipulating her mind, and she couldn't shake the notion that it might be true. Early on, Jak had voiced concern that Malek might have been the one to kill Loran. If he had... they had agreed to meet up with her husband's murderer.

Jak slung his rifle across his back on its strap, then startled her by springing across the gap to catch two of the vines. She barely kept from lunging to grab him, especially when the foliage rattled, and a snap sounded, roots ripping away from their tenuous grips.

Swearing, Jak rearranged himself by grabbing a different vine. The foliage stilled, and nothing else snapped.

"Easy," he whispered back. "Follow me."

"That didn't look *easy.*"

"Anyone who can climb trees can climb vines."

"Trees don't fall apart when you ascend them."

He smiled back, a confident and encouraging smile.

Jadora growled.

Before heading upward, Jak eased sideways toward the corner of the tower, his boots braced against the wall, all of his weight hanging from the vines. Belatedly, Jadora thought about saying they could have climbed down to the street, walked to the tower, and gone up to the top via a door and what were likely stairs inside.

But when she glanced back, she saw one of the red-uniformed

mages riding over the city on his disk. The others had to be out there too—looking for them.

After Tonovan's cruel taunts, the last thing she wanted was to be captured by his people. Now, she also had no wish to end up with Malek. If they could find a druid and get directions, maybe they could slip off into the jungle and avoid all the mages. With luck, the battle over the artifact would take a long time and be devastating. Someone would eventually emerge victorious, but maybe she and Jak could be gone by then.

Making sure the water tank blocked her from the mage's view, Jadora sprang across the gap and grabbed one of the vines. It shifted under her grip, and she lurched downward. She thrust one hand to the side and gripped another one, trying to distribute her weight evenly. Roots on the first vine ripped free, and pieces of mortar crumbled and hit the street below, but the second one was solidly anchored. She shifted her weight to it and then to another.

Jak had already disappeared around the corner, and no cries of alarm suggested he was having trouble. If he could do this, she could do it.

With her neck craned to keep an eye on the mage, she crept closer to the corner. He flew out from behind the water tank, but he wasn't looking in her direction.

She hurried around the corner in time to see Jak skitter around the next corner. Far below, she spotted a wooden door, and her fantasy about going inside and using the stairs returned, but it might be locked more securely than the door at the apothecary shop.

"I'm going up," Jak whispered, his back to the jungle now. The mages wouldn't see him unless they circled the tower. "There are even more vines on this side."

Jadora made herself follow, her arms already growing weary from supporting all of her weight. When she reached the corner and spotted Jak again, he was already ten feet up and climbing for the top, moving fast for someone with a sprained ankle.

"I've never had to work so hard for a view of a city," she muttered, maneuvering after him.

Since they were on the back side of the tower, their enemies couldn't see them, but they also couldn't see their enemies. Worried about what the mages were doing, Jadora climbed more quickly. Leaves and pieces of mortar broke away and rained down on her as Jak neared the top.

He pulled himself over the railing. Somewhat reassured when he didn't gasp or cry out, Jadora hurried after him.

By the time she reached the top, the golden gong gleaming in the morning sun slanting into the tower, her forearms were shaking. Jak grabbed her and helped her over. As soon as her feet touched the solid wood floor, she slumped against the railing with relief.

The Gong of Thanok, a concave, ten-foot-wide plate hanging on two golden chains, continued to hide them from view. Jak patted her arm, then turned to step around the gong so he could see the city, but he halted. Alarm flashed in his eyes.

Before Jadora could ask what was wrong, a black-clad figure stepped out from behind the gong, the skyboard he'd been riding tucked under one arm. Yidar.

A dagger and a short sword hung in scabbards from his belt, but he hadn't bothered reaching for them. He had no need.

With a nod, Yidar wrapped power around them that forced them to their knees with crushing force. "Did you think you could hide from a zidarr? We can hunt down anyone."

He eyed them with haughty disdain, the same expression he'd worn back in the foyer of Uthari's library. Yidar wasn't that much older than Jak, perhaps twenty-five, but his fitted black clothing made his imposing musculature prominent, and he radiated the same kind of power as Malek.

The sea breeze stirred the muggy air, rifling through his short brown hair as he considered them. No, he was considering *Jak*.

Tonovan's words that Uthari didn't need Jak, only Jadora, sprang unbidden to her mind. She wanted to step in front of her son, to block the zidarr's view and distract him, but they were both on their knees, and she couldn't move more than her head.

"Where is the medallion? The *key*." Yidar pointed to the empty spot on Jak's hat. "I know you recovered it from the mercenaries."

"I lost it in the jungle," Jak said. "Darn."

Anger flashed in Yidar's eyes, and he lifted a hand.

"Don't they need you for the battle?" Jadora blurted.

The booms were continuing, and from the top of the tower, she could see over some of the trees to the west. Two of the mageships were visible, one blue-hulled and one black. Fireballs hurtled from the deck of one to the other and also downward. She couldn't see the *Dauntless* and had no idea if it was still wrecked on the beach, nor did she care, other than to hope the mercenaries would survive—and that Yidar would be summoned to help.

"Not yet," Yidar said, not focusing on her. He had gray eyes like storm clouds, and they remained locked on Jak, even though he wasn't looking back.

He was peering out across the city. Looking for the druid stones? This wasn't the right time, Jak...

"Have you been trying to develop your powers, boy?" Yidar asked.

"Nope," Jak said. "I'm not interested in magic at all. Your ship is leaving. Don't you need to be on it?"

The black mageship above the docks *was* moving, heading to help with the battle, but Yidar didn't glance back at it. With his skyboard, he could zip up the beach in minutes if needed.

"Malek said you have little potential," Yidar said skeptically, "but I sensed you sending your thoughts to him, trying to make him suspicious of me."

Less than a foot from Jadora's knee, an open trapdoor led to stairs that wound down eight stories to the door she'd seen from the outside. If they could distract Yidar somehow, maybe they could escape that way. Assuming Jak was paying attention. His gaze had latched on to something in the distance. She saw it too. A set of druid stones rising up from a merchant square deep within the city.

Jadora jerked her gaze from the monument, willing Jak to ignore it. Yidar *had* to be monitoring their thoughts.

She tried to inch her hand toward one of the pockets she'd stuffed with useful powders and herbs from the apothecary. But Yidar's power held her arms fast.

"He's wrong," Yidar whispered. "I can tell you have potential. Malek must have known. Why did he lie? Why was he protecting you?" He glanced at Jadora.

She masked her face and emptied her mind. "Jak isn't a threat. As powerful as Malek is, he's not worried about my son, and neither is your king."

"It doesn't matter if he's a threat now or not. He has the potential to become one. Those who aren't brought into the fold young enough must be killed. That is the way."

Yidar drew his dagger, a blade made of lesser dragon steel. It flared to life, glowing white in the shadow of the roof, as he eyed Jak's neck.

"No!" Jadora attempted to lunge to her feet, but Yidar's magical grip continued to hold her powerless.

Somehow, Jak broke free of it. He surged at Yidar, trying to bowl him over, to knock him over the railing.

Even though surprise flashed across Yidar's face, he darted aside quickly enough to evade the attack. Jak was the one to end up hitting the railing. Yidar lifted his blade to drive it toward the back of Jak's neck.

The power gripping Jadora lessened as Yidar focused on Jak,

and she managed to rise. She lunged for his arm, hoping to deflect the blow. Again, he was too fast, and she only connected with air, but she'd disrupted what would have been a killing blow.

Yidar launched power at her, and it struck like a battering ram. She flew backward, slamming into the gong. It rang with a shudder, and she tumbled downward.

Jadora cried out in terror as she fell through the open trapdoor. She flailed, trying to catch the railing of the stairs that wound around the inside of the tower walls. Her knuckles cracked against wood, but she missed her grab. As she tumbled past the next level of stairs, she lunged again and hooked her arm around a wooden railing.

It shuddered and creaked as all of her weight hung from it, but it held. Panting, she swung her leg up, trying to scramble onto the stairs.

"Now you *die,* boy," came Yidar's words from above.

"No!" she shouted again, hoping vainly to distract him as she clawed her way under the railing.

Something hit the gong, and an explosive went off. The boom hammered her eardrums. The wooden staircase trembled under her, and a great snap came from above. A shadow fell across her, and instinct warned her to sling herself toward the wall.

The huge gong plummeted through the trapdoor and crashed downward. The wind from its passing tugged at her hair and clothes. It struck railings and stairs and broke wood as it clattered all the way to the stone floor, where it hit with a clang almost as loud as the explosion had been.

"Run down!" someone called, the voice muted. Whoever it was —Malek?—was down below and outside the tower.

Another explosion thundered at the top. As Jadora jumped to her feet, broken boards clattered down. One clipped her shoulder hard enough that she almost dropped to her knees again.

"Hurry!" the man shouted.

The voice was familiar, but it didn't belong to Malek. He wouldn't be throwing explosives.

Colonel Sorath?

Jadora wanted to obey, but she had to get Jak. Thick smoke hazed the air above the trapdoor, and she couldn't see him through it. What if the explosions had knocked him and Yidar over the railing? Jak couldn't survive a fall like that.

Even as she started upward on the trembling stairs, the smoke stirred. Someone charged through the trapdoor. Jak.

"Go, go," he whispered, spotting her.

She needed no further urging. She raced down ahead of him, the multiple levels of stairs taking a ridiculously long time to navigate. The door was still shut at the bottom. If it was locked, she hoped they could open it from within.

Another boom came from outside the tower, the noise deafening as it echoed from the brick walls inside. Jadora glanced up, but if Yidar was still up there, he wasn't charging down after them.

When they reached the bottom, the door was locked. There was a keyhole but no latch, bar, or anything they could unfasten from their side. The hinges were on the inside, but Jadora didn't have a screwdriver.

Jak rammed the door with his shoulder. The heavy wood shuddered, but it didn't give, and his face contorted with pain.

"Hold on." Jadora tried tugging on the pin tips of the hinges but wasn't surprised when they didn't budge. "Do you have a pen?"

"Always." Jak fished one out and handed it to her.

"And your caliper again."

"Uh." He hesitated to give her the tool. "Are you going to break my gear?"

"Hopefully not." She took it, placed the pen like a narrow chisel to the bottom of one of the hinge pins, and was about to whack at it with the caliper.

"You *dare* attack a zidarr?" Yidar yelled, not from the top of the tower but from the other side of the door.

Jadora froze, afraid to make any noise. He couldn't be more than five feet away.

"You will die for your presumptuousness, mercenary!" A wrenching sound came from outside.

"We're paid to be presumptuous," Sorath yelled. He was farther away from the tower now, maybe taking cover at the corner of the bathing house or one of the other nearby buildings.

Weapons fired, and another explosion shook the ground.

Jadora used the noise to cover the sound of her clunks as she hammered the pin loose. She tugged it out, tossed it to the ground, and hurried to strike the pin from the second hinge before the clamor outside stopped.

She needn't have worried. A black-powder weapon cracked, alongside the *thwumps* of a magelock. Something ripped free of the ground, followed by a great shattering noise. Jadora imagined Yidar out there using his magic to hurl entire buildings at Sorath and however many mercenaries had come with him. Hopefully more than Tezi.

Jak shifted impatiently from foot to foot as the sounds of battle continued. Someone cried out. A woman.

"That's Tezi," Jak whispered, distress in his voice.

Jadora thrust his tools back at him. "Help me unseat the door."

They eased it off the hinges and peeked out. Yidar stood ten feet away, his arms raised as he cast magical attacks at a nearby stable, one of its walls torn down and half of its roof tumbling inward. Someone fired at him from within the building, but the blue charges struck an invisible barrier and never hit him.

Jadora and Jak slipped outside. Now was their chance to get away.

But Yidar started to turn. Damn it.

A small sphere sped out from behind the stable. It landed in front of Yidar and exploded, drawing his attention.

Jak and Jadora sprinted around the corner of the tower. In case Sorath could see her, Jadora waved her gratitude.

Running when he and the other mercenaries might need help didn't feel right, but Yidar meant to kill Jak. They had no choice.

Jak glanced back several times, probably worried for Tezi, in particular, but he must have had similar thoughts, for he didn't suggest they slow down.

As they sped into the city, Jak leading them in the direction of the druid monument, running awkwardly to favor his ankle, Jadora hoped they could avoid being found again. Unfortunately, that seemed a vain hope.

Sorath fingered the last of his pop-bangs. Since leaving Perchver, his supply had been dwindling rapidly, and he'd used four of his last five trying to help Jak and Jadora get away. At his side, Tezi kept firing at the zidarr, though it did little good. The magical blasts from her rifle bounced off the man's equally magical defensive barrier.

"Nothing hits him," she whispered.

"I know." Sorath gripped her shoulder and jerked his head toward the back of the stable. "We have to run."

A moment ago, Sorath had seen Jak and Jadora slip away, somehow unlocking the locked door that had kept him from charging into the tower earlier. There was no reason for Tezi and him to stick around.

A gust of power like a hurricane gale slammed into the stable where they crouched. Already, a wall and part of the roof had caved in, but this new attack tore support posts from their foundations and knocked over two more walls. Roof tiles and boards struck down all around, pummeling them as surely as weapons.

Sorath tried to protect Tezi, his arm over her head, as they darted toward the back, but debris crashing down impeded them. A beam snapped and slammed to the ground inches from his side, hurling dust into the air. A smaller board cracked Sorath on the head, and he stumbled, tripped over broken tiles, and went down. Pieces of the roof landed on top of him. All he could do was protect his head and hope that so much didn't fall that it crushed him.

He hated mages, and he hated zidarr even more. As always, he resented how indestructible they were. He'd managed to surprise the zidarr with one of his explosives, blowing up the railing and knocking him off the top of the tower. As the man tumbled down, Sorath had been certain he would strike the pavement headfirst and die, but the zidarr had twisted in the air and used his magic to soften his landing, coming down like a cat jumping from a bookcase.

"This wasn't your fight, mercenaries," the zidarr called as the rubble settled, half the roof feeling like it had fallen on top of Sorath.

The weight pressed down on him like an anvil. Sorath hoped the smaller and more fragile Tezi hadn't been crushed. Nothing was stirring now in the flattened stable.

"It was pointless for you to get involved," the zidarr added. "All you've done is put a trip wire in my path. I'll still find those two. And you will *die* for your interference."

Sorath had been hoping the zidarr already thought they were dead. As he tried to squirm out from all the boards, tiles, and broken beams on top of him, a magical vise wrapped around his neck.

"Lord Yidar!" someone called from an elevated position. One of his allies riding a skyboard?

The pressure around Sorath's neck disappeared.

"What?"

"General Tonovan needs us at the battle. The defenders are putting up more of a fight than he expected."

Sorath managed to squirm out from under some of the rubble. Dragging himself along on his belly by his elbows, he found spots with less debris than others and wormed his way through the flattened stable. He glanced toward where he'd last seen Tezi, but there was no sign of her.

"My lord?"

"Yes, yes, I'm coming."

Sorath paused, deciding it might be better to wait for the zidarr to leave. If Sorath didn't make a move or noise, maybe his enemy would believe him dead or unconscious. He emptied his mind and closed his eyes.

Raw power blasted into the remains of the stable. A final support post snapped, and the last beam crashed down. Something landed on Sorath's back, and a sharp corner bashed his temple. Pain lanced through his skull, and black dots swam through his vision.

Ten feet from him, rubble shifted loudly, debris being knocked to the side. A feminine yelp of surprise sounded. Tezi. Still alive but in trouble.

Though Sorath tried to lift his head to see her, whatever had fallen last on him kept him from rising up far enough. Warm blood ran down the side of his face.

"And so is our new prisoner," the zidarr said with a chuckle.

"That one is more to the general's tastes than an ugly old soldier," the other mage said.

Fear for Tezi gripped Sorath, and he pushed at the ground, trying to shove the beam off his back with pure muscle and frustration. But too much weight pinned him down. He couldn't move it.

"Yes," the zidarr said, "his tastes are what we should be prioritizing right now."

"I just... know what he likes, my lord."

"Let's hope she has some use beyond as a toy for him."

With blood dripping from his jaw, Sorath tried to squirm forward. He couldn't rise up, but maybe he could slither out like a snake.

Another beam blocked his way. He gripped it, snarling, and shoved it aside. Sunlight filtered in through the rubble above him. He clawed his way upward over heaps of wood and tiles and finally rose above the rubble. He jerked around to point his pistol toward the tower and the spot where the zidarr had been.

But he was too late. The zidarr and the other mage were on skyboards, flying up and over the buildings and toward the coast. Tezi was on the disk with the zidarr, his arm wrapped around her waist, her blonde braid sailing out behind her head.

Sorath aimed at them, but they disappeared over a rooftop before he could get a shot off.

He slumped back on the rubble, frustrated and furious and wishing Captain Ferroki had never walked into his shop back in Perchver. The blackness that had been threatening swept over him like a blanket, and he lost consciousness.

9

As Jak and his mother navigated through the city, his ankle throbbed, the poultice and bandage wrapping it doing little to help. Since he couldn't stay off it while it healed, he couldn't expect it to get better, but the constant pain mingling with weariness from being up all night made it hard to stay alert to his surroundings.

His mother looked just as tired, sweat gleaming on her forehead and dampening her hair as they made their way toward the druid monument. They had slowed from a sprint to a walk, gradually coming to believe the mercenaries had effectively deterred Yidar—or that he'd been called away to help with the battle.

Now that they were out of the hills and in the core of the city, they could no longer see over the trees to the mageships, but cannon blasts continued. Now and then, when the wind shifted, they could hear orders being shouted amid cries of pain.

"Think there's any chance Yidar was killed back at the tower?" Jak kept checking the sky, but from the streets, with buildings rising up all around, not much of it was visible. Yidar and his mages could have been flying all over Port Toh-drom on their skyboards, and he might not have seen them.

"By a few mercenaries? Doubtful." Mother's hand twitched toward Jak as he stumbled.

She kept trying to help him, to offer him support, but he'd let her do that all night. He could tell she was exhausted, and he didn't want to be a burden on her or slow them down. That battle couldn't go on forever, so they had to take advantage of this reprieve, learn what they could, and get out of the city. They could hide in the jungle until Malek arrived.

"I am very thankful that those mercenaries intervened though," Mother added. "I thought Yidar was going to kill you."

"Me too."

"I am worried that Yidar might have killed *them* for helping."

"I think the one yelling at us to get out of the tower was Sorath." Jak was positive he'd also heard Tezi. He hoped they hadn't been alone. What could two mercenaries do against a zidarr?

"It was," Mother said with certainty. "I wish we could have talked with him."

"Still thinking it would be good to get him on our side?"

"Yes."

Jak almost mentioned that they would have Malek, and he would be plenty, but he was distracted when the street they had been following curved and opened up into a square. A fountain burbled in front of massive rectangular slabs of stone, all leaning together at the top, as Mother had described and as he'd seen from the tower.

"There it is," he blurted.

Already, Jak could make out symbols carved into the slabs, words written in the ancient language of the druids. That monument might have been here longer than the city, maybe even since the days when the portal had been in use.

Excitement thrummed through Jak as he recognized the writing as being similar to what he and Mother had looked up in the book back in Uthari's library. It had the same leaf and branch accents as one of the symbols on the portal.

"We're going to find an answer here," Jak said. "I'm sure of it."

Mother's expression was dubious, or maybe concerned, and she didn't say anything.

"Are you all right?" He squinted at her, surprised she wasn't delighted by this discovery. "You said Tonovan was pestering you before. Did he do something... I need to kill him for?"

Alarm replaced the concern, and she whispered a harsh, "*No.*"

"That's a yes, isn't it?"

"You're not killing anybody or trying. We couldn't even handle Yidar."

"He's a zidarr. That means he's more powerful than a mage soldier, even a general."

"I don't think that's necessarily true. Anyway, we couldn't fight either of them." She took a deep breath and forced a smile. "You're right that there may be answers here. Now I wish I'd taken that book from Uthari's library. We have no way to translate this."

"Don't you speak and read the druid language?"

"One of the modern languages, yes."

"*One* of? There's more than one?"

"Yes," Mother said, "and this is an ancient language. I don't think anyone speaks it anymore, though some of their scholars can likely read it. If we could find some local druids, we could ask for help."

They gazed around the square, at vendor stalls still closed even though the sun had been up for hours. One with a bright blue dragon painted on a sign caught their notice, but it was as closed as the others. All around the square, benches sat empty, the nearby fountain burbling softly.

"This is a market area," Mother said. "I doubt we'll find druids here."

Despite the words, she walked up to the stones. She rested a hand on one as she looked up and down, perusing the symbols carved into the ancient slabs.

Jak realized she hadn't answered his question about what Tonovan had done to her back by the water tank. On the one hand, he didn't want to hear details if he'd thrust sexual imagery into his mother's head, but he also didn't want her to suffer that torment alone. He wanted to *do* something.

Back atop that tower, he'd managed to summon some power from deep within him, and he'd briefly broken Yidar's grip on him. It had only been for a second, and the zidarr had been too fast for him to take advantage, but didn't that imply he might be able to learn to eventually? That he had the potential to fight them?

Never in his life had Jak dreamed of becoming a mage and a part of their tyrannical world, but the way he and his mother had been trapped and imprisoned these past weeks made him long to be able to defend himself from them. To defend *his mother*.

"Maybe there *is* a sanctuary nearby," his mother mused as she moved around the monument, pausing here and there to examine one symbol or another. "I associate druids with living in nature and being expert herbalists as well as users of magic, but it's possible one or more could live in the city to tend this place." Her voice turned wistful. "Maybe they would take us in and hide us. Their leaders have power that's supposed to rival that of great mages, maybe even wizards. It's why Zewnath was never conquered by any of the kings or queens, and pockets of druids remain free and unmolested even in the various kingdoms around the world."

"At the least, they ought to know where the portal used to be set up."

"If they'll tell us. Some of these symbols are familiar. I remember them from that book, but I don't see any that match the writing on the portal." Mother slid a hand over a grouping of runes. "This is close but not quite a match. If there's a sanctuary nearby..." She paused to ponder something.

"We don't need a sanctuary right now, Mother." Jak, realizing he sensed faint magic emanating from the monument, stepped closer to search for the source. "We just need to avoid capture until Malek gets here. Then he can get the portal, and we've got the medallion and—"

"I don't think we should go through with that plan."

"What? Why? Three hours ago, you were all right with it."

"No, I wasn't. Three hours ago, I was horrified that you managed to contact him."

Jak waved a hand in dismissal. "But you *agreed* that working with him was our best option. Or at least *an* option superior to being captured by any of these people who want us dead."

When Mother looked at him, her eyes were haunted.

He'd intended to argue further, but he hesitated. "Did Tonovan say something about Malek? Give you some new information on him?"

"Have I mentioned that it's a blessing and a curse to have a teenage boy who's oddly perceptive for his age and gender?"

"No, but whatever Tonovan said, you *can't* believe him."

"I know. And I don't... necessarily, but the details suggested..." She lowered her face and rubbed her forehead. No, she rubbed her *eyes*. Because she was crying?

"Mother." Jak rested a hand on her shoulder. "I'm *sure* Tonovan was lying. About whatever it was. He hates Malek. You could tell just by standing in the same room with them."

"I know." She wiped her eyes and tilted her face back to look at symbols higher up on the slab. She was avoiding his gaze.

He wanted to comfort her, but there was so little comfort to be had in this situation.

"If we can't find an alternative, we'll work with him. But we have to be very careful and escape as soon as it makes sense." Mother pointed upward at a dragon carved in the slab. Two crudely drawn men were facing the winged creature with spears. "I *really* wish I'd taken that book from Uthari's library. The few words I recognize make me believe this monument was built to tell a story from the past. A *warning* from the past."

"Hold on. There's something magical here." Jak let his senses guide him around the corner to another slab, to more symbols and... a *map*.

He rested his hand on it, devouring it with his eyes. It represented the continent of Zewnath, showing the rivers and swamps and jungles and mountain ranges all across the land, though it didn't mark any cities. Maybe it had been carved in the stone before cities had existed. Or maybe the druids hadn't *cared* about including population centers. They'd marked things more important to them.

At least twenty little formations on the map seemed to represent monuments similar to this one, most located deep inland. The magic that Jak sensed emanated specifically from them. In other spots on the map, there were distinctive leaves and flowers. Guessing they might indicate the location of medicinally significant plants, he waved for his mother to join him. Two stars marked opposite ends of the continent, though he couldn't guess what they might signal. Ancient observatories?

With so many things on the map, Jak almost missed a little ring far inland from the northern coast. It was his mother who reached past him to touch it with her finger.

Jak sucked in a breath. "Is that the portal?"

He also touched it, and a tingle of magic ran up his arm. It was nothing like the magic of the artifact, so that was disappointing, but maybe this was what druid magic felt like.

"The map doesn't show a pool or waterfall or anything from the vision, but the ring is at the base of this mountain range." Jak traced the crude carvings with his finger. "Those things *could* be there."

"If there were a dragon next to it, I'd be certain that was the spot," Mother breathed, excitement distracting her from her earlier concern and distress.

"There are dragons elsewhere on the monument."

"With people jabbing spears at them. It's similar to the warnings the portal gave me. I wish we could spend the whole day with the monument, that we dared." Mother looked upward.

There were no mages on skyboards in view, but Jak was also aware of how out in the open they were. If Yidar or one of the others sailed past, Jak and Mother would be easy to spot in the middle of the square.

"There's no legend." Jak dug out his folding ruler to measure the total distance across the continent and then the distance from their position to the ring at the base of the mountains.

Port Toh-drom wasn't marked, but the river it was situated on was. That was enough. Since he'd studied a modern map of Zewnath before arriving, and knew how many miles the continent spanned, he could run a mental conversion to figure out how far it was to the ring—to the place the portal had once been placed.

Maybe. This map wasn't very accurate, with the shoreline all around the continent far smoother than he knew it to be. That lack of precision concerned him, because it could indicate all the sites marked inland might be off by hundreds of miles. Or more. Whoever had carved this had done it before modern tools had been invented to allow cartographers greater accuracy.

"Judging by known distances, it should be about nine hundred miles to that location from here." Jak touched his finger to the ring.

"A long walk."

"But not that long of a flight on a mageship."

Mother grimaced. "Let's make sure we get on the right one."

"Malek's *Star Flyer*, yes."

She slid her hand over nearby carvings. "I wish I had paper and charcoal and time to take rubbings of all this."

"I have charcoal if you have paper." Jak didn't know if he had time.

Her gaze shifted upward toward another dragon. That one was on its back with more humans with spears above it, stabbing downward. "And I'd *really* like to talk to a druid or read an accurate history of this continent that could explain these dragons."

"Maybe humans decided it was a challenge to hunt them." Jak said a silent prayer of apology to Shylezar. The dragon god would have been horrified by these depictions, he was sure.

"From everything we know about their power, that seems suicidal. Carving victories in stone would be a lot easier than actually being victorious in battle against dragons."

"Are there any blank pages in Father's journal? I could copy this map quickly." Jak glanced skyward again, but he caught movement from the side, not from above.

Several dark-skinned people in loose tunics and dresses were creeping toward them with rusty swords and crude clubs fashioned from chair legs.

"Uh." Jak pointed toward them to warn his mother even as he took a long look at the map and tried to burn it into his memory. Something told him these people weren't going to give him a chance to copy it.

Mother turned, raised her hands, and called to them in their language.

A graying man in the lead pointed his sword at them, barked something angry, then pointed it at the monument, and finally waved it in the direction of the mageship battle.

Mother tried asking a couple of questions. But the people only shook their heads in anger. More than anger, Jak decided. *Fear.* They were as scared as the apothecary had been.

"They're telling us to get out of the city." Mother held up her hands and nodded to the people, gesturing that they would leave. "They know we came with the mageships—and the portal."

"They know about it too?"

"Their magic users felt it before we reached shore, and they warned the entire populace." Mother backed slowly away from the monument and the mob, nodding for Jak to do the same.

He cast a last longing look at the map. With his rifle, he might have scared the mob off, but they looked like simple people with little to their names, and he would feel like a bully doing so. Besides, the rifle didn't have indefinite charges, and they hadn't yet passed any recharge points in the city. It was possible these people didn't use magical firearms, and the rifle was only of use as long as it had charges.

"They believe the portal is cursed," Mother added as they continued backing away, toward a different street than the one they'd come in on. "They think having it nearby will bring ruin to their whole city."

"Uh, why?"

"They're not articulating that part well. I also don't understand their language perfectly, so I'm missing a lot of words."

The group had stopped advancing, and they spread out around the monument, as if to guard it from intruders.

Jak and Mother kept backing away until they reached the edge of the square. They passed close to the vendor stall he'd noticed earlier with the dragon painting on the sign out front. Before, he'd only been able to see the front of the stall. Now, as they passed it to enter another street, the back came into view. And he almost shrieked.

"Mother!" He pointed at a dead man pinned to its back door, by what looked like a wrought iron fence pole jammed through his throat.

His mother swore and gripped Jak's arm.

His first thought was that it was someone else who'd come on the mageships, and this was an example of the citizens punishing an outsider for the *curse*, but the man looked like a local, not a mage or mercenary. He wore the same type of tunic as the other people.

One of those people shouted angrily and pointed a sword at Jak, then waved it at the stall.

"Come on." Mother patted Jak and pulled him farther up the street.

"What did they say? Why did they kill that man?"

"He sold dragon statues and toys to children."

"And that's a *crime*?"

"They blamed him, and those like him, for the return of the curse." Mother's eyes were haunted again as she led him swiftly away from the square. "Those people were terrified. I don't think they know exactly what the portal is, and they may only know to fear dragon steel, but they believe its return means that dragons will come to their world again."

"Why are they so sure that's a bad thing?"

"I don't know."

Yidar caught up to the *King's Courage* as it sailed toward the battle booming farther up the beach between their *Dread Arrow* and three of Zaruk's mageships. A fourth craft, the green-hulled *Dauntless*, already lay wrecked in the sand below.

Even though Yidar's skyboard was fast and capable of flying him many miles, irritation flashed through him that his ship's captain hadn't waited for him before leaving Port Toh-drom. Having a prisoner aboard the skyboard slowed it down.

The mage crew of the *King's Courage* also hadn't waited for him before raising a defensive barrier around the ship. Perhaps it made sense since they were approaching enemy vessels, but Yidar felt affronted nonetheless. It was as if they did not *want* a superior zidarr warrior-mage battling at their sides.

With a surge of his power, Yidar tore a gap in that barrier so he could fly through.

One of the mages on deck cringed and sank to one knee, clutching his head. No doubt, he had been the one responsible for forming that portion of the barrier, and the tearing had caused a backlash of pain in his mind. That would teach him the folly of not watching for a zidarr's return and pulling down his barrier on his own.

Yidar's prisoner twisted and squatted low, trying to slip away from him. To do what? Jump into the ocean? They were hundreds of feet in the air. The fall would kill her. Foolish woman.

He glared over his shoulder at her, tightened his magical grip, and glided over the *Courage's* railing and onto the deck. On a whim, Yidar had captured the girl instead of killing her. He hoped he would not regret it. When he'd realized the archaeologists had gotten away—blast the mercenary commander and his suicidal willingness to hurl explosives at a zidarr—Yidar had almost killed them in a fit of fury, but he'd caught himself and checked their thoughts first. The girl had been thinking of the younger archaeologist—Jak—and how she hadn't been as useful as everyone thought for luring him into a trap. Through her eyes, Yidar had seen a flash of the boy drooling insipidly over her and immediately thought that he could do what the mercenaries had failed to do—use her to lure the archaeologists to him. Especially Jak.

Yidar curled a lip at the memory of the boy using raw untrained power to disrupt his hold. That Malek had known Jak had such potential and hadn't slain him immediately was infuriating. Yidar would report that information to Uthari as soon as he had a chance.

The lip curl turned into a smirk as he imagined getting the sanctimonious Malek in trouble.

As Yidar landed on the deck, General Tonovan walked out of the navigation cabin, his fur-lined cloak flapping around the legs of his red uniform.

Yidar started to grimace, as Tonovan had been on the other ship earlier, and Yidar had assumed he would lead the *Dread Arrow* into battle, but this was fine. They could fly into battle together, the better to cow their enemies.

"That's not an archaeologist." Tonovan folded his arms over his chest, seemingly oblivious or indifferent to the fact that the battle for the artifact was already engaged, and the *Courage* was about to join in. "Nor do I sense the dragon-steel key on her or on you."

"The archaeologists got away." Yidar hated to admit that, but what could Tonovan expect when he'd called him back so soon? "The boy has feelings for this mercenary though. I thought we could use her for bait to lure him out if necessary."

"Feelings?" Tonovan eyed the girl. "Feelings of lust, no doubt. I remember you from the beach, girl."

She bared her teeth at him, and he laughed.

"They've either hidden the medallion or used dark-eye fabric to shroud it," Yidar added. "I didn't sense it anywhere in the city and had to use my hunting skills to locate them."

"I'm surprised you caught sight of them at all. Or did you?"

"I caught both of them on a tower," Yidar growled. "I was on the verge of bringing them to the ship when a squad of mercenaries attacked, hurling explosives at me."

"There were two of us, not a squad," the girl said.

"Do not speak when you are not invited to do so." Angered that a terrene human dared open her mouth and interrupt a zidarr, Yidar flicked power at her, making her gasp in pain. She should not interrupt *any* mage.

"Two mercenaries derailed a mighty zidarr from his mission?" Tonovan laughed again. "It's shocking that Uthari didn't slay you instead of giving you a chance to prove yourself."

Yidar wished he could flick an attack at the pompous general and also inflict pain, but Tonovan radiated power almost to the extent that Malek did. He might be a mere soldier and not a zidarr, but he hadn't risen to be supreme leader over Uthari's military forces for no reason.

Ignoring the jab, Yidar said, "The boy also used power on me. Did you know he is a wild one?"

Tonovan blinked. "The professor's son? Jak Freedar?"

"Yes."

Yidar thought about explaining that it had only been a little burst of power, enough to distract him and break his hold on the boy, not a serious attack that either of them had to worry about, but maybe it would be better if Tonovan believed the boy was stronger than he was. When Yidar spoke to Uthari, he would give the full truth.

He did not yet know if he wished to beg and plead and obey every whim to attempt to win his way back into the king's good graces, but if Uthari had spoken the truth and would consider helping Yidar carve out a kingdom for himself, it might be worth being the obedient zidarr the king wanted.

"Isn't that interesting?" Tonovan glanced to the side as a fireball splashed against the invisible barrier surrounding the

Courage. He raised his voice to call to his troops. "Keep the barrier steady, and use mental attacks against the mages defending the ship with the artifact on it. We'll focus our efforts on one ship at a time, starting with that one. We have reinforcements coming, but I want the artifact *before* they arrive. Show Zaruk's feeble mages what we can do!"

A roar of agreement went up from their mage crew.

"What reinforcements?" Yidar asked.

"Malek and the *Star Flyer.*" Tonovan's lip curled, much as Yidar's had a few minutes ago. "I'd prefer *not* to need his help."

"As would I. Malek knew Jak was a wild one, and he let him live."

"Oh?" Tonovan raised his eyebrows.

"I felt it when I encountered them together in the castle the day before the invasion. I *told* him we had to kill the boy. Jak's far too old to let live. The mother threw a vial of acid at me." Yidar snarled and touched his cheek, though the wound had since healed. "Malek *defended* them. They dared attack a zidarr, and he defended them."

"Does Uthari know about the boy?" Tonovan ignored the rest.

"I don't know, but I intend to tell him."

"Good. Do it after the battle. Our enemies have brought at least one zidarr along—Zaruk's Night Wrath. You and I should be more than equal to him, and even though we have fewer ships and troops, our mages are more powerful than theirs. As they'll soon find out. Now, more than ever, I want to defeat Zaruk's fleet before Malek gets here. We'll figure out a way to use the girl to collect the archaeologists later. The portal is our primary concern. And grinding our enemies under the soles of our boots. Put the girl in a cell, and come back up to fight."

Annoyed at being given orders, Yidar thrust the girl toward one of the other mages. "Search her, remove her weapons, and imprison her."

"Yes, my lord."

Yidar strode up to the forecastle, drawing upon his power until it crackled in the air around him. He would defeat the other ships single-handedly if he could. Malek wasn't the only zidarr around with vast power, and Yidar would prove it.

10

MALEK STOOD IN THE FORECASTLE OF THE *STAR FLYER*, HIS HANDS clasped behind his back. As the sun set over the sea to the west, he watched the horizon to the south. Neither Zewnath nor any enemy or ally ships had come into view yet, but he sensed them ahead, multiple vessels engaged in battle. The *Star Flyer* would arrive soon.

Earlier, he'd exercised, meditated, and studied his notes on the artifact, and he was ready to join and do his part, but he found himself uncharacteristically antsy as his ship drew near. Though he maintained an outward calm, an unfamiliar feeling of anxiety simmered within him. He hadn't received another message from Jak, nothing since their conversation early that morning. Soon after that, he'd heard from Uthari that Tonovan and Yidar had reached Port Toh-drom. They'd had all day to battle Zaruk's people, claim the artifact for themselves, and find Jak and Jadora.

Had they?

Malek, knowing full well that zidarr could track down anyone, especially someone carrying magical items, worried he was too late. If Yidar had found them, he would have killed Jak promptly.

If Tonovan had found them, he might have killed Jak and dragged Jadora off to his cabin to torment. Usually, Tonovan favored those young, pretty, and too afraid of wizards to do anything but hurry to please him, but he also enjoyed being cruel to his prisoners for sport.

When he was on the *Star Flyer*, Malek could put a stop to it, but Tonovan frequently rode on other mageships. Malek hoped Tonovan didn't try to teach his perversions to Yidar. Malek already questioned whether Uthari would be able to trust the young zidarr again, and he wouldn't be surprised if those two came up with some seditious notions if they developed a friendship.

You will arrive soon, Malek? Uthari spoke into his mind, his telepathic voice distant but clear.

Yes, Your Majesty.

Good. Tonovan and Yidar need assistance. They are battling Zaruk's ships for the artifact, but they are outnumbered.

I will help them.

First, I want you to slip in with the Star Flyer *and get the artifact while the others are quibbling over it. Once you have secured it, Zaruk's men will be demoralized. They also won't be able to figure out how to use it as a weapon against our troops.*

It will be difficult to slip in, *Your Majesty. Already, I sense their ships, and it is likely some of their mages can sense the* Star Flyer.

I once taught you to camouflage your approach, and you had a knack for it. Amusement laced Uthari's telepathic words as he added, *I believe you envisioned weaving dark-eye fabric around yourself.*

Yes, but to camouflage an entire ship will be difficult. And the tactic is... not something I've practiced often. Malek couldn't keep the distaste out of his words. Even though zidarr were taught stealth and to track down prey without being noticed, he'd always preferred to openly challenge foes in combat, rather than springing from the dark in a sneak attack. To defeat a foe in honorable combat was superior to doing it with trickery.

Even with the addition of the Star Flyer, *our ships will be outnumbered. Put your pride aside and use stealth. You are one of the few people I've encountered who is talented enough to hide yourself—and your ship —from other mages. Take advantage of that.*

Malek sighed. *I will attempt it, Your Majesty.*

I have another reason for making this request. I would prefer that you be the one to acquire the artifact and secure it on your ship. As you know, I am keeping an eye on Yidar. I wish to give him his chance to redeem himself, but why tempt him with so great a prize?

I understand.

Once you have the artifact, fly away. I will instruct Tonovan to cover your departure. He will battle any who attempt to chase you down. He will protect you.

I'm sure that assignment will delight him. Malek imagined Tonovan sending him obscene gestures even as he fired upon enemy ships.

It will not, but he is loyal. He will do as I say, and I will reward him. Have you learned where to take the portal yet to operate it?

The answer is not in my notes, but I told Jak to figure that out while he waits for me.

There was a long pause as Uthari digested that. Did he not believe Jak and Jadora would be able to learn that information? Or did he not like that Malek was relying on them? That had always been their plan, hadn't it? To capture the archaeologists for their knowledge.

They would have sought out the information regardless of my instruction, Malek added. *If Tonovan and Yidar haven't captured them, they've had all day to do research.*

Malek waited, hoping Uthari would give him the answer he wanted, that Tonovan and Yidar had been too busy battling Zaruk's mages to search for Jak and Jadora.

Yidar almost captured them this morning, Uthari replied. *Apparently, some mercenaries intervened, but before that happened, the boy broke a pressure wrap Yidar had placed around him and his mother.*

An uneasy sensation squirmed through Malek's gut. *Broke it?*

With a burst of his own power. As you can imagine, Yidar was surprised. Uthari paused. *I am also surprised. You said the boy did not have that much talent and would not be a threat.*

I did not think he would be. Malek grimaced at the half-truth. *I sensed that he had potential, yes, but I would not have guessed he could do anything to a zidarr, or even a trained mage with modest talent.* That was closer to the full truth. He wouldn't have believed Jak could be a threat to anyone, not without training.

Are you being dishonest with me, Malek? That is unexpected from you and a little disappointing.

Malek closed his eyes. If Uthari punished him for this, he would deserve it. *I... underreported his potential. I did not wish you to kill him or instruct me to kill him. I apologize for not being more forthright. I am genuinely surprised he troubled Yidar in any way.*

You have feelings for him?

No, but, as we agreed, I did not want Professor Freedar to lose someone else she cared about. You've asked me to try to win her trust and get her to work with us. That would not have been possible if we took her son from her.

We did agree on that. Do you have feelings for her?

No. I hope I have not given you reason to doubt me, Your Majesty. My loyalty is to you.

I believe you, Malek. I am merely concerned about leaving alive an enemy who could become a potential threat one day.

I find it unlikely he will be. That day would be years if not decades off, if it ever came at all. It is likely Yidar was simply distracted by something and is not admitting it.

That is possible. He mentioned the mercenaries. Still, once this mission is complete, and the professor has synthesized the herb and made a medicine that my scientists can replicate, it may be necessary for you to kill the boy. You know what the terrene humans wish to do: to overthrow us. We cannot allow them to have powerful mages on their side.

Malek grimaced in distaste at the idea of convincing Jak and Jadora to work for him, knowing full well that he might end up being Jak's executioner. That doubly disturbed him because he had promised to protect Jak. He imagined the boy standing behind him, believing himself safe from their enemies, only for Malek to turn and drive a dagger into his chest. Jadora would scream and hate him, perhaps attack him, and would he then have to kill her as well?

He'd read so many of her papers, coming to know and admire her through her work. She was intelligent and did insightful research. She should be permitted to continue that. Malek neither wanted to kill her nor her son.

What if Jak could be made loyal to us? Malek asked.

Us?

To you ultimately, of course. But he reached out to me and asked for help. It occurred to me that he might be easier to win over to our side than his mother. He has power. He will be curious about it. These past weeks will have made him frustrated at how easily normal humans are pushed around by mages. He will want to learn how to use his power. I could bring him back to you, and you could teach him, as you did me. If he became loyal, his mother might lose the will to fight us. Perhaps she would willingly take the position you offered her, working in one of your universities. She could continue to publish and perhaps find other useful herbs on other worlds that could benefit you. Why kill potentially valuable resources?

Malek made himself stop, realizing he'd been thinking the words at Uthari at lightning speed. Trying to convince him.

Would Uthari question him and why these two mattered to him? Malek did not want that.

Of course, if you require that I kill them, I will, he added into the silence.

Perhaps that will not be necessary. I admit that my first thought is to push back because Jak is much older than you were when you came to me.

Not that much older. I was also beyond the age that wild ones are tamed, as you'll recall. You took me in anyway.

Because of your great potential, yes. And because you were earnest and honest. I should not have been surprised when Yidar betrayed me. He was never like you. A wave of fatherly warmth accompanied the words.

Malek bowed his head, sending back an emotional acknowledgement of gratitude to have been chosen long ago, along with his desire to remain loyal.

You have intrigued me, Uthari said. *As you said, the boy contacted you. Just as his mother stepped toward you for protection from Tonovan. It is possible you could win both of their loyalties.*

You know I do not seek to accumulate loyal followers of my own and that such is against the Zidarr Code. I would only seek to transfer that loyalty to you.

I trust that is true.

That was a relief. The last thing Malek wanted was for Uthari to believe he had some ambition, like Yidar, to gather followers and create his own kingdom.

Yes, Uthari added. *They need not be killed if they could be made loyal to us. Do what you can to charm them. I agree with your assessment that an impressionable young boy who's lost his father may be easier to win over than his mother. Perhaps I should have thought of that before. Collect them, the artifact, and complete the mission. Then bring them back to Utharika.*

I will do my best, Your Majesty.

"Land ahead," one of the crew called.

"A *battle* ahead," another called, eagerness in his voice.

Malek, distracted by his conversation with Uthari, hadn't noticed the green smudge of Zewnath's northern shoreline growing visible on the horizon. He couldn't yet see the mageships battling over one of the beaches, but he sensed them, sensed the magic filling the air ahead, and he also sensed the artifact.

Remembering Uthari's orders, Malek lifted his arms, letting his eyelids droop to slits as he envisioned dark-eye fabric weaving itself around the *Star Flyer*. He funneled his power into the vision to make it a reality while hoping he hadn't waited too long. With luck, the other mages were busy with the battle and hadn't been watching for the approach of other ships.

But even if they knew it was out here, they should have just lost track of the *Star Flyer*. At least for now. Already, he could sense the power required to maintain the facade draining him of energy. He would not be able to keep it up indefinitely.

A woman cleared her throat as she climbed the ladder to join Malek in the forecastle. Captain Rivlen.

"My lord?" She saluted, her uniform crisp, despite the humid air. Her boots gleamed from polish, and not a single stray hair had fallen from her precise bun. "I sense that you did something to the ship, but I'm not familiar with the magic."

"I have camouflaged it so that even mages should not sense our approach. Uthari commands us to sneak in and acquire the artifact while the others battle each other, oblivious to our presence."

"Impressive," Rivlen said, clasping her hands behind her back. "Were it not forbidden for zidarr to instruct other mages, I would implore you to teach me."

She gazed intently at him, as if hoping he would make an exception.

No, he would not break the Code and risk punishment. If she distinguished herself such that Uthari offered her a reward, she could ask *him* for the lesson.

When Malek did not respond to her statement, Rivlen asked, "Does this mean we will avoid battle while our comrades risk their lives?"

He considered whether her tone held censure. "Tonight, it may, if all goes according to plan. I am certain other battles will find us before we accomplish our mission."

"Is it wrong to be disappointed not to have an opportunity to pit oneself against the mages and perhaps zidarr from Zaruk's alliance?"

"It is not wrong. Battle is, after all, the primary way to prove oneself and earn prestige among one's colleagues and superiors."

"Yes. I long for this."

"And to fight zidarr apparently." He quirked an eyebrow toward her.

"*Zaruk's* zidarr. I am certain they are inferior to you."

"Stone Heart was a worthy opponent."

"That you slew," Rivlen said. "Were I to slay an enemy zidarr, perhaps I would be promoted again soon."

"You are ambitious."

"I am."

"I am certain that King Uthari will reward those who accomplish the mission he has sought to achieve for more than five years."

"Excellent. I am prepared to do as ordered to acquire this artifact." Rivlen saluted him and started for the stairs but paused to look back, her eyes narrowed. "It would also not disappoint me to accomplish what General Tonovan cannot."

"I will take note of that."

"Excellent."

An odd woman, Malek decided, but he preferred her over Tonovan as the commander of the *Star Flyer* and the troops aboard it. It would not disappoint Malek if Tonovan fell in battle, but he would not wish for that. He would hope for the best for all of his allies while he did what Uthari wished: retrieve the artifact, find Jak and Jadora, and win their loyalty so he would not have to kill them later.

He nodded to himself. He would accomplish these tasks.

"I wish a shop was open so we could buy paper, pens, and a good map."

Jadora glanced at Jak, noting that his limp was more pronounced as they clambered back uphill toward the gong tower. Feeling guilty that the mercenaries had risked themselves, and they hadn't stuck around to see what happened to them, Jadora wanted to check the area to see if any had survived and needed help.

"And food?" she asked.

"That too."

After studying the druid monument, Jadora and Jak had been forced to spend most of the day avoiding mobs of people driving strangers out of their city. When they hadn't been doing that, they'd tried vainly to find food, but with everything closed, that would have been difficult even if they had money. Their stomachs were growling, and her eyes were gritty with fatigue.

At least they hadn't seen Yidar again. He and the black mage-ship that had hovered over the docks that morning hadn't returned. She suspected he'd been called away to join the battle. General Tonovan hadn't telepathically sent any more distasteful messages or images, so she hoped he was busy too.

"We don't have any mo—" A yawn broke into her sentence, and she couldn't hold it back. "Money for maps," she finished, fighting back another yawn.

Spending the previous night fleeing from mercenaries in the jungle meant they hadn't slept since the night before last. Adrenaline had kept her awake earlier, but that had faded, and she longed for a safe, cozy bed in which to nap. She might have settled for a spot on a shady patio and a cool beverage. Even though the sun was creeping toward the horizon, it was still hot, and the humidity didn't keep her from feeling thirsty. They stopped to drink at every city fountain they passed, but the tepid water wasn't that appealing.

"We didn't have any money at the apothecary shop either," Jak said. "That didn't keep you from helping yourself to the wares."

"I'll pay the proprietor back when..." Jadora almost said *when all this is over*, but when would that be? How did this end for her and Jak in a way that they would once again have money and wouldn't be hounded by mages? "Someday, somehow," she finished with a mutter.

Jak smiled sadly at her and didn't argue further. "This is the street that leads to the tower. Are you sure we want to go back up there? I told Malek we'd meet him at the apothecary shop."

"I'm sure he can find us anywhere. Yidar did." Jadora checked the sky again, though the booms of the distant battle continued.

One would think all those mages would run out of ammunition and eventually grow too tired to cast magic.

"I'm asking because the mercenaries aren't necessarily on our side," Jak said. "Colonel Sorath was probably sent to retrieve us and take us back to Captain Toggs's ship. Or one of the other ships Zaruk's people sent."

"True, but for whatever reason, he helped us. And risked his life to do so." Jadora yawned again.

Jak stepped on an uneven stone, lurched, and hissed in pain.

Jadora reached out to steady him. "Do you need to rest? I have the ingredients to make another poultice and some anti-inflammatory medicine."

"More nasty berries?"

"I haven't seen another yindaki tree in town, but as you

pointed out, I collected supplies from the apothecary shop. We haven't seen any angry mobs for a while. Why don't you let me take a look at your ankle again?"

"The apothecary lady already looked, and her treatment hasn't done much."

"That's because we've been running around the city, leaping onto towers, and climbing up vines. That's not what healers mean when they say to rest and elevate your injury."

"It was elevated when we were up there." Jak waved to the tower, the gong no longer glinting from the top.

How long, Jadora wondered, before the priests who maintained that tower wandered up and found their gong mysteriously lying on the floor at the bottom?

"Dangling from vines eight stories in the air isn't what elevated refers to," Jadora said.

"Are you sure? It seems extremely elevated to me."

She squeezed his shoulder, glad he could still joke. She was too exhausted to manage a witty retort.

Jak veered down an alley. "Let's come to it indirectly. I don't think any mages are in the area, but I'm not positive."

"Agreed." She let him lead the way down the alley and up another street toward the hilltop, while fantasizing again about a meal and a place to sleep. If they went into the jungle tonight, could they find a safe spot? A spot where the winners of that battle couldn't easily find them? The idea of staying in the city worried her, especially after seeing the vendor at the dragon cart brutally murdered. She shuddered at the memory.

"Oh, Shylezar," Jak said, halting.

They'd reached an intersection, and the tower and bathing house were in view. So was what *had been* a stable. It was completely demolished, the supports, walls, and roof all collapsed.

Jak hobbled closer. He stopped next to rusty brown smears of blood on the street near the wreckage. It looked like someone had pulled himself—or herself—out from under the rubble.

Guilt washed over Jadora. Sorath had helped them escape, but at what cost to himself and whatever troops had been with him?

She frowned toward the river, the docks in view again from the top of the hill, and checked for the black mageship. She sucked in a breath. It wasn't there, but another one was. A blue-hulled vessel. That had to be one of the ones that had flown in to help Captain Toggs regain control of the artifact. What was it doing *here*?

The mageship was damaged, its sides charred, with holes blown in the hull, but it was still floating in the air. Had it fled the battle? Or was this the last ship flying? The lone survivor?

"Jak." Jadora tugged his sleeve. "Can you tell if that ship has the artifact?"

"Uhm." He'd been eyeing the blood and the destroyed stable, but he turned. "I don't sense it, no. When I concentrate, I *can* sense the magic of its engine and other magic-powered things aboard. I think... I'm starting to be able to do that from farther away. That makes me feel oblivious for not sensing Yidar on the tower this morning."

"Maybe the zidarr have ways to hide themselves."

"I guess."

"I didn't expect to see you two again," a rough male voice said from the shade of an alcove in the back of the bathing house.

Jadora and Jak jumped.

"Colonel Sorath?" Jadora recognized the voice, though there was an unusual hitch to it. A hitch of pain.

"That's right." He was sitting in the alcove, one leg stretched out, his back to the door inside. He'd been pointing a pistol at them, but he lowered it.

"When we saw that Yidar left, we came back to check on you and thank you for your help." Jadora noticed more dried blood between the stable and the alcove and realized it had to be his. She winced, regretting that they hadn't returned sooner. "I'm sorry we took so long."

"We had to check a druid monument in the city," Jak said, "and find a map."

Jadora made a cutting motion with her hand, feeling they shouldn't blurt what they'd found to one of the mercenaries, even one who'd helped them.

Jak bit his lip, seeming to realize his mistake.

If Sorath noticed the exchange, he didn't show it. His eyes were glazed as he stared out into the street.

Jadora started toward Sorath, hoping she could help him. Jak remained in the street, though he put his back to a wall and stood in the shade so he wouldn't be that noticeable as he kept an eye on Zaruk's ship. Good. Jadora doubted any of the mages were interested in this city for any reason other than finding the medallion —and them.

"I lost Tezi," Sorath mumbled.

Jadora halted mid-step. "She's dead?"

"Just as bad," Sorath said bitterly. "The zidarr got her. Took her to his ship."

She glanced back to check on Jak's reaction, but he hadn't heard. Maybe that was for the best. He would only worry. *She* was worried, afraid that Yidar taking Tezi to his ship would end with Tezi in Tonovan's clutches. Not that Yidar couldn't also be a bastard who would torment a woman.

"The roof fell on me." Sorath touched his temple. "Knocked me out, buried me. I couldn't get out in time to stop him. Not that such was in my power. I'm lucky he was called away to the battle. He was about to kill me with his magic."

Jadora hurried into the alcove and knelt beside him. Judging by the dried blood on his shirt, trousers, and the side of his face, the gouge at his temple was only one of many wounds.

"I'm sorry," she whispered. "Hold on. I'm not well outfitted right now, but I have some bandages and medicine to help you."

"Not well outfitted?" Sorath leaned his head back against the door and closed his eyes. He looked like he might pass out again. His lips were dry and cracked, and she wished she had a canteen of water to share with him. "You jumped from our crashed ship and fled into the jungle without outfitting yourself for adventure? Odd."

"We were somewhat pressed for time." Jadora pulled out a roll of bandage and poultice-making ingredients, then fished into the pocket that held ditherika root. She handed him a nub to chew. "This tastes awful, and the side effects can be thinner blood and thirst, but it should help with the pain from your injuries."

He gnawed on it without doubting she was giving him something useful. She appreciated that faith, especially since they weren't on the same side. But he *had* saved them that morning.

"I've been trying to muster the energy to walk back up the beach to check on the battle and let Captain Ferroki know about Tezi." Sorath winced. It was probably for his lost soldier rather than the bitter taste of the root.

"I don't know if it would be possible to reach them right now. I assume they've been pressed into battling Uthari's mageships."

"If that's true, I hope Ferroki got a new contract ironed out first." He shook his head slowly. "For their sakes, I hope they decided to get off the *Dauntless* and leave those people to battle each other."

"Do you think that's likely?" Jadora opened Sorath's shirt and found numerous scrapes, bruises, and punctures in addition to whatever internal injuries he'd taken. Unlike them, he had brought a canteen with him. She picked it up, intending to wash his wounds, but it was empty. "We gathered from the mercenaries out searching for us last night that they're still obeying Toggs and doing what he wishes."

Jadora caught Jak's gaze and hefted the canteen. She hated sending him on errands when he was limping, but she needed to tend Sorath as quickly as she could. She had no idea how long they had before people from that ship came looking for them.

"Toggs isn't in charge anymore," Sorath said. "One of Zaruk's zidarr showed up with the newcomers. He would have the power to ink out a deal with Thorn Company. Night Wrath is his name. He's the second-highest ranking of Zaruk's zidarr, and most powerful, after Stone Heart. I guess he's now *the* highest ranking and most powerful. He should be able to communicate directly with his master."

Jadora remembered Malek fighting Stone Heart in the court-yard of the castle while battle raged all around them, the two men slashing with swords and blasting their power at each other. In the end, Malek had lopped off his enemy's head and come out on top.

A part of her wished that she and Jak could trust Malek, at least within the parameters of them having a common goal for now, because Jak was right. He would be a powerful ally. A larger part of her was terrified that he knew where they were and was coming for them. If he'd killed Loran, she could never trust him, not for a second. She shouldn't even speak with him again.

Jak took the canteen and went to hunt for water. The city had numerous fountains, so it shouldn't take him long.

"Be careful," she mouthed to him.

He glanced toward the mageship but only nodded and limped off. The sun had disappeared, twilight descending upon the streets. Would it be easier to escape notice during the night? Probably not, but she hoped so.

"Zaruk or his allies could have sent even more zidarr than Night Wrath," Sorath said, his eyes still closed. His face was flushed, either fevered or sunburned, and his voice was a rambling mumble. At least the root would help with a fever. "That man we were fighting this morning is one of Uthari's young ones. Yidar. I hope those people all kill each other, and Ferroki and her company can get away without any more losses. One of her corporals was killed during one of the fights outside of Uthari's castle. She's lucky she didn't lose more. Working for kings and battling mages is always deadly."

"Then why do it?"

"They're the only ones who can afford to pay well," Sorath said. "And by well, I mean enough for a mercenary commander to keep her people outfitted and fed. Few of us ever get rich doing this. After a career of decades, I earned enough to buy a little shop with an apartment in Perchver, but most mercenaries don't live long enough for that. And my home was destroyed before I left, so now, I have nothing."

Jadora leaned out of the alcove to check on the mageship and look for Jak's return. "Since Jak and I also have nothing now, I can commiserate."

"Has your home also been destroyed?" Sorath asked.

"It's probably still intact, but we can't return to it. I worry that my friends will be in danger simply because they know me. And my father is back in Sprungtown. We don't interact often, so I hope the mages don't think to find him and use him against me. We have some philosophical differences, but I still care for him, and they've proven they'll kill people I care for." She lowered her voice. "They killed my husband five years ago for his research. No, because he wouldn't *share* his research."

Tonovan's imagery of Malek slicing off Loran's head reared in her mind again, and she froze, realizing it was the exact motion he'd used to behead Stone Heart.

She swallowed. That didn't mean it was what had happened. It was eerily similar, but Tonovan couldn't be trusted. It wouldn't bother him in the least to lie to her. But... he also might have told her the truth because he'd known it would hurt her.

"I'm sorry for your loss," Sorath said. "And that we've helped make your life more difficult."

"If you could stop hunting us, I'd forgive you for that."

He snorted softly. "Don't we get credit for helping you this morning?"

"Yes. I'll pretend you weren't nearby because you were looking to drag us back to Toggs."

"It was Night Wrath who ordered us after you."

"So much better."

Jak returned with a canteen full of water. "We might not want to linger, Mother. I had a feeling..." He twitched a shoulder. "I felt like someone was watching me."

"Someone magical? Or the people who warned us to get out of their city?"

"My feeling wasn't that precise. It was just an instinct."

Since he was developing new powers, she wouldn't dare dismiss his instincts. After thanking him for the canteen, she washed Sorath's wounds in the fading light. There were street-lamps at all the intersections, but they burned oil and had to be lit by hand. Given how few people had been out during the day, she doubted any maintenance workers would be by to tend to them.

"It's gotten quiet," Jak noted.

Crickets, cicadas, and other insects Jadora couldn't name buzzed and chirped loudly from the jungle, but she knew what he meant. The booms of the battle that had gone on all day had faded.

"Does that mean someone won?" Now that her patient's wounds were clean, she hurried to make poultices and bandage him.

"It would have to be Zaruk's people if so." Jak pointed toward the mageship. "If they'd been losing, that one wouldn't be loitering here."

"They're probably doing more than loitering," she said.

Another reason for her to finish with Sorath, so she and Jak could find a hiding spot for the night.

"It's also possible they've called a ceasefire for the night," Sorath said. "As powerful as mages are, they're still human. They get tired from having to maintain barriers and throw magical attacks all day. They might leave a few on duty to keep their defenses up while the others eat and rest so they can start in on each other in the morning."

"Uh." Jak pointed toward the river. "The mageship is coming this way."

Jadora swore.

Sorath patted her hand, then gripped his pistol and pushed himself to his feet. He groaned, winced, and used the alcove for support, but he stayed upright. "You two better get out of here. If they find me, I'll tell them I haven't seen you since this morning."

"Thanks, but I haven't noticed that lying to mages works well." Jadora packed her bandages and herbs back into her bulging pockets. "Also, you're wearing my handiwork. They might notice."

"Unless you stamped it with a logo, I can say some other healer in the city treated me."

"From what we've seen, those healers would be more likely to shoot strangers than help them right now." Jadora also stood up. "But I refrained from putting a maker's mark on my bandages."

"Good. If they try to read my mind to get the truth, I'll outsmart them by passing out." Sorath blinked slowly, as if such were a possibility right now. It probably was. He'd lost a lot of blood.

Jadora patted him on the chest and stepped out into the street to join Jak. Twilight was deepening, but that didn't keep her from being able to see the mageship flying slowly up from the river. He was right. It was heading in their direction.

"Let's go." She gripped Jak's arm and waved toward the jungle.

They had evaded people by spending the previous night out

there. Maybe they could do it again. She didn't point out that they'd only been evading terrene mercenaries the night before and that now mages were searching for them.

Before they'd taken more than a few steps, a man in black stepped out of the shadows by the destroyed stable. He held a lesser-dragon-steel sword, and as he lifted it, it flared with a white glow that brightened the side of his hard face. Jadora didn't have to recognize him to know he was a zidarr. He radiated the same power as Yidar had, maybe more. This man was older, more experienced, and would be harder to distract.

Jak glanced to their left, but two mages in blue uniforms stepped out from behind the tower, blocking escape in that direction. Two more mages appeared to their right, in the street that led down the hill. Several of their uniforms were charred and torn, and a couple had bruised faces, but Jadora feared this was the victorious party.

Behind them, the blue-hulled mageship flew closer.

"Professor Freedar," the zidarr said, "I am Night Wrath, and we've come to reunite you with the artifact. Colonel Sorath, I am pleased you've cooperated by locating these two and keeping them here for us." His tone was dry, and Jadora doubted he believed that had been Sorath's intent.

"You bet. You know I love serving your people." Sorath gripped his pistol as he stood in the alcove, still using the wall for support, but he didn't raise the weapon. What would be the point?

"Yes, I feel your love and adoration for us oozing from you like sweat." Night Wrath focused on Jadora. "Despite the feeble attempts of Uthari's people to defeat us, they've been unable to take the portal. They've backed off, and soon, they'll flee back to their homeland. We *are* the superior warriors, and we'll be taking our prize home tonight. And you with it."

Home. They hadn't figured out it had to be set up here in Zewnath to be used?

She didn't know whether to be relieved or depressed. After all this, to end up in another king's castle, far from where the portal had any use...

"Ah, interesting." Night Wrath was squinting at her.

Reading her thoughts, she realized.

"I'd wondered why you people fled here with it. I will have to consult with King Zaruk to see what he wants. Come." Night Wrath pointed toward the ship—it hung over them now like an ominous storm cloud, its belly almost scraping the tops of the nearest buildings. "I'll do my consulting while you two are tucked safely away in a cell."

"Uthari gave us a suite," Jak said.

"Clearly, *King* Uthari—you'll mind your tongue when speaking of our kind—was too lenient, since you escaped." Night Wrath narrowed his eyes. "You'll be shackled in my ship, and I intend to wrench every piece of information from your mind that I can."

Distant booms started up again. Maybe Uthari's ships hadn't backed off and fled after all. Sorath might have been right, that they'd only been resting.

Night Wrath frowned in the direction of the noise.

"No new ships have arrived," he murmured. "Why are they attacking again? Surely, they can't believe the outcome will be any different."

Take cover in the alcove with the mercenary, a voice spoke calmly into her mind, a voice she recognized even though he'd rarely spoken telepathically to her. Malek.

"Jak," Jadora whispered.

"I heard," he whispered, already backing slowly toward Sorath.

"Stay right there!" Night Wrath's gaze locked back on them. He lifted a hand and hurled a wave of power at them.

It struck Jadora like a tsunami, knocking her into the air, her feet leaving the ground. She flew back, slamming into the wall, pain blasting her.

But as she crumpled to the ground, a flare of orange light brightened the area. A fireball hurtled out of the darkness toward two of the mages.

Night Wrath spun to face a threat from behind. Malek ran toward him, wearing the same simple brown and tan clothing that she'd seen him in before, and his face was eerily calm as he sprang at Night Wrath, his main-gauche and longsword glowing.

Two mages in Uthari's red uniforms charged in, seemingly out of nowhere, to battle the blue-uniformed mages.

As the battle blew up all around them, Sorath grabbed Jadora under her armpits, helping her to her feet. He pulled her back into the alcove, then returned for Jak.

He'd also been slammed against the wall, and now, he stared, mouth dangling open as Malek and Night Wrath clashed, blades whirring too fast to follow, the white glows leaving streaks in the darkening night air.

Sorath pulled Jak into the alcove with them. It was a tight fit, especially when he mashed Jak and Jadora together behind him, but lightning bolts and fireballs were streaking everywhere now. As Malek battled Night Wrath, his mages fought Night Wrath's mages. There were more people in blue uniforms than red, but Malek evened the odds by casting lightning bolts and raw blasts of power at their enemies at the same time as he clashed swords with the other zidarr.

Shouts came from the mageship above. Before, its crew had been focused on the renewed sounds of battle farther up the coast, but they'd realized what was going on below them.

"That's Malek down there!" one cried.

"Get him!"

Jak swore. "Why'd he attack right under their noses?"

Sorath glanced back at him but only for a second. He raised his pistol toward Malek and Night Wrath. "I don't know, but I *hate* that bastard. He and his precious King Uthari were among those who betrayed me and slew my entire company."

As injured as Sorath was, he didn't have any trouble holding his arm straight and aiming at Malek.

"They're shielded," Jak blurted. "You won't be able to hit them with a mundane firearm."

"I'll get my chance," Sorath growled, keeping his arm up, tracking Malek.

For now, Night Wrath was in his way, his back to them as they fought.

The mages up above leaned over the railing and started sending attacks down. They had to worry about hitting their own people, so they didn't open up with all they had, but Jadora winced when something akin to a bomb landed beside Night Wrath and Malek.

It blasted a crater in the street, and the shockwave hurled the two zidarr into the air. Night Wrath flew into the destroyed stable. Malek flew upward and backward, twisting in the air.

"That's it," Sorath barked and squeezed the trigger.

Before his shot went off, Jak knocked his arm aside. The black-powder weapon cracked, echoing against the limestone buildings all around, but his round flew high.

Malek came down on his feet like a cat. He glanced toward the alcove as Sorath shouted, "What're you doing?" at Jak. "His defenses were down."

Jadora braced herself, expecting Malek to throw an attack at Sorath—one that would crush her and Jak as well—but after the glance, he sprang into the rubble of the stable. Night Wrath hadn't landed on his feet, but he recovered quickly and leaped up at Malek's approach. Once again, they clashed, swords screeching and clanging, drowning out the cicadas.

In the ship above, the mages prepared to throw more attacks.

Sorath was still glaring at Jak, looking like he meant to shove him out of the alcove, but a fireball streaked past parallel to their building and not two feet away from them. Sorath snarled and focused on the battle again.

Orange fire lit the night, driving the shadows out of the streets. At first, Jadora assumed it was another fireball, but it was so much brighter that it had to be more.

Sorath gaped and swore. He wasn't watching the zidarr fight now but the sky above.

Another mageship had appeared, its black hull coming out of nowhere. A woman in a red uniform stood on the forecastle at the railing, her hands outstretched as she hurled walls of flame at the blue mageship. The fire roared through the sky, striking the other vessel, almost swallowing it before its mages fought back. They must not have expected an attack, and they'd been so focused on Malek and Night Wrath that they hadn't had their barrier up.

"That's the *Murder Flyer*." Sorath swore. "It came out of *nowhere*."

The *Star Flyer*, Jadora thought but didn't correct. She remembered Ferroki saying that her people had their own name for Malek's fearsome ship.

"Who is that woman?" Jak asked.

The female officer sent another wall of flames toward the blue-hulled craft. This time, its mages were prepared, and they deflected the great fiery blast, but shouts of alarm came from their deck. Fires burned in a dozen spots from the first attack, and the *Star Flyer* was barreling down on their ship, its shark figurehead glowing at the point of its bow.

Zaruk's crew launched fireballs at the woman and the *Star Flyer*. Instead of raising a barrier, the red-uniformed mages on its deck used fireballs of their own to knock the magical projectiles aside. Once deflected, they streaked off over the city and the jungle.

The female mage shifted her hands, pointing at the figurehead. Was she funneling magic into it? The shark glowed even brighter.

"They're going to ram us!" someone cried.

"Put all power into the barrier!"

In the stable below, Malek hurled an energy blast at Night Wrath, knocking him into the air and sending him rolling all the way to the base of the tower. Instead of sprinting after him while he was discombobulated, Malek pointed his sword at Zaruk's ship. A beam of white light poured out of it, slicing into the air around the mageship.

"He's tearing a hole in their barrier," Jak said, his senses giving him more of a clue about the battle than Jadora had.

The *Star Flyer* sailed through the hole and rammed the enemy ship, smashing into its hull as the woman on the forecastle and her fellow mages cast attacks at individual officers on the deck.

Night Wrath jumped to his feet, roared, and ran back at Malek. But Malek, having shredded the defenses on the enemy mageship, turned calmly back to meet his charge.

Something about that calmness niggled at Jadora, as if there were significance in it that she couldn't quite grasp.

The two zidarr's glowing swords burned the night air as the men thrust, slashed, and parried. The blows were so swift that the clash of metal sounded like one continuous ring that bounced from the walls of the surrounding buildings, hammering the eardrums of the onlookers.

Above, the *Star Flyer* shoved the enemy vessel ahead of it, driving it over the bathing house and into the side of the tower. Panting, Night Wrath leaped back from Malek so he could check on his ship.

Malek took advantage of the pause, launching an attack at one of the blue-uniformed mages battling his own men on the ground. What had been an even fight between them quickly turned as the blast of incendiary power swallowed the enemy mage. It engulfed him like a sun, scorching the flesh from his bones, and a scream of sheer agony drowned out every other noise in the battle. The scent of charred meat assaulted Jadora's nostrils, turning her stomach.

Sorath growled and pointed his pistol at Malek again. "*Don't* touch my arm, Jak," he snarled without taking his gaze from the battling zidarr.

"His defenses are up," Jak said softly. "You can't hit him."

Sorath clenched his jaw and didn't respond, didn't take his eyes from his target.

Night Wrath scowled fiercely at Malek and raised his weapons to jump back at him, but more screams of agony came from the mageship being mashed against the tower. Its defenses must have been down, for the *Star Flyer's* mages were hurling attack after attack. Small fires turned into larger ones, and soon, an inferno burned on the blue-hulled ship.

Swearing, Night Wrath whirled and ran away. Not to help his ship but to sprint into an alley between buildings. Only one of his ally mages on the ground was still fighting, but when he saw his zidarr leader fleeing, he cursed and did the same.

Malek let Night Wrath go, but his red-uniformed mages weren't as lenient with their opponent. They ganged up to throw gouts of flames after the fleeing man, ripping through his defenses and lighting him on fire. Another screech of utter pain wrenched the night.

Jadora trembled as she witnessed the mage's agony. She'd always worked to help people, to make substances that could cure and *heal* them. Watching people being burned alive was horrifying.

Malek strode toward their alcove, unconcerned by Sorath aiming his pistol at his chest. He met Sorath's gaze, appearing indifferent to the fury blazing in the mercenary commander's eyes.

Over their heads, the *Star Flyer* drew back from its entanglement with the other ship. Once it was no longer being pressed against the tower, the blue-hulled vessel plummeted to the ground, the fire engulfing it so intense and hot that Jadora could feel it from the alcove.

"Step aside, Colonel." Malek continued gazing calmly at him. "You will not shoot me."

Sorath fired, the weapon cracking loudly in the alcove and making Jak and Jadora jump.

The bullet bounced off Malek's magical barrier.

"You will not *effectively* shoot me," Malek said.

Sorath growled like a bear.

"Step aside," Malek repeated. "Go join the rest of your people, and tell them to ally themselves no longer with Zaruk's troops. The artifact will be ours before the night is over, and there is no point in battling with them anymore, unless you wish to lose all of your forces."

Sorath didn't budge until Jak squeezed out past him.

"What are you doing?" Sorath blurted, reaching for him, but Jak jogged to Malek's side.

Confusion wrinkled Sorath's brow. When he glanced back at Jadora with bewilderment, she realized he thought he was defending them, that he believed it was his duty.

Afraid Sorath would do something to prompt Malek to attack —or even kill—him, Jadora squeezed his shoulder and also stepped past.

"Thank you for the help this morning," she said. "We have to go with him."

"You *have* to go?" Sorath demanded. "He'll torture you for everything you know, use you until he has no more need, and then kill you."

"We don't have any choice," Jadora said quietly, trying not to think about Loran's death, about how Malek may have done it.

Jak already stood at his side, as if he didn't even mind that they had no choice. For some reason, that chilled her.

"These bastards already got Tezi," Sorath whispered harshly to Jadora. "I can't let another zidarr take more of our people."

Jadora didn't want to argue with him, so she didn't point out that she and Jak weren't *his* people.

"We'll try to find her and help her," she said instead, though she didn't know if that would be possible. The *Star Flyer* wasn't likely the ship that Yidar had taken Tezi to, and if Tonovan had her, he wouldn't cheerfully hand her over to Malek.

Sorath took a step from the alcove after Jadora, like he wanted to protest further, but he looked toward the flaming wreck. Some of the men—the bodies—had been thrown clear and burned independently, charred husks no longer human as they smoldered in the street. The *Star Flyer* floated above, hovering over Malek.

Malek met Jadora's eyes, nodded once at her, as if they had some agreement, then used his magic to levitate her in the air. Jak floated up beside her, toward the deck of the *Star Flyer*. They'd tried so hard to escape that ship before, and now, they were voluntarily going up to it.

She glanced down, catching Sorath's gaze, reading the anguish and fear for them in his eyes, and she couldn't help but worry that they'd made the wrong choice.

11

JAK'S ANKLE STILL THROBBED, BUT HE DIDN'T CARE. HE AND HIS mother had escaped capture unscathed. Or at least no more scathed than they'd been before.

Now, he stood on the deck of the *Star Flyer* with her, leaning against the railing as it sailed out of the city and into the jungle, then turned west. Heading off to help in the other battle?

A shiver of magic rippled around the ship, something Malek was doing. It felt like his power.

Jak marveled that he could not only sense it but tell that it was different from other mages' power. Like a person's distinctive scent. Lately, he'd started sensing much more when it came to magic. Or maybe it was that it had never been a part of his life before, aside from the trinkets, tools, and magebands that proliferated in Sprungtown.

"Are you all right?" his mother asked quietly from his side.

She was staring at Malek and had been since he crouched and sprang more than thirty feet into the air to land on the deck with them. As the sea breeze riffled through their hair, he spoke to a few uniformed officers, including the woman who'd been throwing those walls of fire.

Jak had never seen that before and couldn't help but be impressed, especially since she didn't look to be that much older than he. Mid-twenties? She had several rank bands wrapped around her sleeves, enough to indicate she was the captain of the ship. As they spoke, she nodded politely and deferred to Malek, but all the other mages deferred to both of them. Jak hoped she was loyal to Malek. It worried him that Yidar and Tonovan acted like they would be as happy to kill Malek as work with him.

"Jak?" Mother prodded him and looked toward his injured ankle.

"Yes, sorry. I'm just—aren't they incredible?"

He shook his head, thinking of Malek battling Night Wrath as well as this new captain leading the attack on Zaruk's ship. A weird sense of longing filled him. Even though he didn't want to be a part of their world and resented that mages oppressed terrene humans, he couldn't help but wish he could develop the power to take care of himself like that. Take care of himself *and* his mother. He didn't want to incinerate anyone—that had been *horrifying*—but it would be amazing to have the ability to keep mages from pushing them around. Especially after the events of these recent weeks, Jak was tired of being helpless.

"Yes, but be careful." Mother spoke quietly, for the captain and Malek were looking at them now. "I understand that you made a deal, and hopefully, Malek will protect us, but we still can't trust them."

"I know. I don't. We'll use them the same way they want to use us." Jak smiled and patted her arm.

Malek walked over with the captain at his side. Despite the battle, her red uniform was pressed and impeccable, and she clasped her hands behind her back in a stiff parade rest as she faced them. She regarded Mother without notable change in her aloof expression, but her glance at Jak was more dismissive.

"Jak, Jadora," Malek said, "this is the new captain of the *Star Flyer*, Xeva Rivlen. Captain, this is Jak Freedar, cartography student, and Professor Jadora Freedar, herbalist, chemist, and archaeologist. She's published numerous respected papers in her fields, and she was the one responsible for finding the artifact after it had been buried." Malek glanced down at Mother's form, and that startled Jak. Before, Tonovan had been the one to leer at her, not Malek. Not that Malek was leering, nor was he looking at her curvy parts. He pointed instead toward her bulging pockets. "Those are usually full of vials, and she can make glues, acids, and other compounds she finds helpful in escaping and deterring enemies, using, as far as I can tell, dirt and lint."

Malek's eyes crinkled with amusement. Jak almost pointed out that Mother had gotten a much lengthier introduction than he had, but he felt self-conscious next to the impeccable officer. After his sword fight, Malek was a little more rumpled, with his short black hair tousled and blood spattering his trousers, but he was equally impressive. Jak felt scruffy next to them.

"Then she should be searched thoroughly and such items removed before she's locked up." Rivlen eyed Jak. "They both should."

"No." Malek lifted his hand. "I made a deal with Jak. They've voluntarily surrendered themselves to assist us with getting the portal operational. They are our guests."

Rivlen's mouth puckered, as if she were sucking something sour. "Of course, my lord, but might I suggest that even *guests* should have their pockets searched?" She looked from Mother's pockets to Jak's. His were full but lacked books, bandages, and poultice-making-ingredients, so weren't as noticeably stuffed. "Especially when they each look like they're carrying an armory's worth of grenades in them."

Mother lifted an empty hand, then slowly lowered it into her pocket and withdrew a rolled-up bandage. "I can see where this would be mistaken for a grenade, but I assure you I possess nothing so inimical."

"So, no acids?" Malek asked.

Mother hesitated. "*Mild* acids."

"Those aren't inimical?"

"Certainly not. Acids are simply molecules or ions capable of donating a proton or forming a covalent bond with an electron pair."

Malek's eyes gleamed. With... appreciation?

"They *sound* inimical," Rivlen muttered, glowering at Mother *and* Malek.

"It looks like your new captain isn't a fan of science," Jak said.

She glared at him. "I'm a fan of incinerating irritating enemies."

"But not treasured guests, I hope," he said.

"I'm positive Lord Malek did not say you were *treasured.*" Rivlen pointed to a hatch, the movement stiff. "If there's nothing else, my lord, I will show them to their cells."

"A cabin," Malek said. "Guests get their own cabin."

"Forgive me, my lord. Military vessels I've been on in the past rarely *entertained.*" Rivlen bowed formally toward him.

"I'll send them along with you in a moment, Captain. I want to question them."

Mother returned her bandage roll to her pocket, concern flashing in her eyes.

"Yes, my lord, but we need to attack soon if we're going to surprise the enemy." Rivlen glanced toward the jungle below them and the dark sea to the right. Orange lights flashed beyond the trees to the west, signaling that the battle for the artifact was still underway. "I grant that your camouflaging spell proved extremely effective—" she bowed less stiffly toward him, "—but it's a foregone conclusion that Night Wrath has warned the others that we've arrived."

"I am certain of that, but the longer they wait, poised for us to strike, the more tense and weary they'll be when we do. According to Tonovan, they've already been fighting all day. He and Yidar have kept them busy to wear them down for us."

Mother grimaced at the general's name. So much for their hope that Tonovan and Yidar had died in the fighting.

"I'm sure they told you that, my lord, but I wouldn't be surprised if General Tonovan was trying to defeat them without our help, so he could collect the artifact himself, claim all the honor, and besmirch our reputations by implying ineffectiveness."

"So long as we acquire it, it matters not who carries it aboard his ship. We are all loyal to the same king." Malek did not address the possibility of reputation-besmirching.

"I shall assume that as your new captain, it is not my place to point out that you are quick to trust people to be as honorable as you are, my lord." Rivlen glanced darkly at Mother.

"That is correct, but I will take note of your censure, regardless."

Rivlen bowed again and headed for the hatch.

"You are injured?" Malek pointed to Jak's leg.

Jak was leaning against the railing, but he hadn't realized he'd been so blatantly favoring the sprained ankle. He straightened and put as much weight on it as he could without wincing. For some reason, he was reluctant to show any weakness to Malek, maybe because terrene humans like himself were *already* so weak compared to zidarr.

"It's not a big deal," Jak said. "I twisted it a little."

"Sit." Malek pointed at the deck.

The command didn't include magical compulsion, but Jak felt compelled to obey, regardless. Besides, he was exhausted after not sleeping the night before. It felt good to sit down.

"Do you have any injuries, Professor?" Malek surprised Jak by kneeling beside him and placing a hand on his ankle.

"Just a few scrapes." Mother looked at her hands. "Some prickly slivers from thorny vines under my skin from when *someone* convinced me to climb up a tower... from the outside."

"Only because a *zidarr* was chasing us," Jak said before remembering he was in the presence of another zidarr who worked for the same king as Yidar.

Malek didn't acknowledge his comment, instead gazing up at Mother's hands. Trying to decide if she was injured enough to need help?

"It's nothing serious." She lowered her hands, started to put them in her pockets, realized they were too full for that, and instead clasped them at her waist.

"Very well." Malek focused on Jak, and a warm tingle flowed from his hand into Jak's ankle.

Immediately, the pain lessened. Jak slumped back against the railing, some of the tension ebbing from his body. Until Malek glanced at his hat.

"What happened to the medallion?" Malek's voice remained as calm as usual. If he was worried they'd lost it, it didn't come through. "I do not sense it on you."

"We have it," Mother hurried to say. "Wrapped in dark-eye fabric."

"Show me."

Maybe he wasn't as quick to trust people as the captain thought.

"Please," Mother muttered, digging it out of her pocket.

Malek's eyebrows twitched slightly.

Jak winced. They had enough enemies out here, and Malek had saved their lives. *Again.* They ought to act respectfully toward him and not make any demands. Given how other zidarr had treated them so far, Jak was delighted Malek didn't call them scum, force them to their knees, and make them grovel before his greatness.

"Doesn't your Zidarr Code say anything about social niceties?" Mother, oblivious to Jak's thoughts, unwrapped the medallion and showed it to him, the gold plating hiding the blue-black dragon steel underneath, the edges distinctly ridged to match a small indentation in the portal. "Or does it only apply to interactions between zidarr and powerful wizard rulers?"

The warmth faded from Jak's ankle, and Malek rose, taking the medallion from the thick fabric to examine it. Worried he wouldn't return it, Jak barely resisted the urge to lunge up and grab it. It wasn't as if he could wrest it away from Malek. Whether he called them guests or not, they were now trapped on this ship until they did what Malek and his king wanted.

"Our Code requires that we be honest and loyal, not socially nice." Malek turned the medallion over, not seeming to have trouble examining it in the dim light. Most likely, he used his magical senses rather than his eyes. "We need only respect our equals and superiors, not say please to them."

"Well, we wouldn't mind if you said please and thank you to *us*," Mother said. "It's in our code, and we consider it respectful."

"The code of... archaeologists?"

"Yes."

"I see." Malek looked at Jak. "Did you learn where the portal must be taken in order to operate?"

He wasn't asking Mother. It was as if he already knew Jak had been the one to find and memorize the map.

"We got a clue to what may be the location from a druid monument in the city." Jak pointed inland, though the mountain range was too far away to see. "It was a crude map, so I'm estimating, but about nine hundred miles that way."

"I'll have someone bring you paper. I need a map that I can hand my helmsman."

"I can draw a map. A *good* map." Jak smiled, already imagining ways he could improve upon what had been crudely carved into that stone, but he glanced at Mother, worried she wouldn't appreciate him cheerfully volunteering.

But she only nodded. It wasn't as if Malek couldn't pluck the image from the druid monument out of Jak's mind.

Malek handed the medallion back to Mother. "If we're successful in acquiring the portal, it won't likely matter, but keep it wrapped in that fabric so others can't sense it." He arched his eyebrows. "Please."

Jak couldn't tell if he was being sarcastic or not, since his tone didn't fluctuate much. Mother's lips pursed, and he didn't think she could tell either.

"I will," she said.

"My lord," Jak whispered up to her.

Malek's eyebrows arched again. Mother frowned down at Jak.

"They like that," he whispered. "It's respectful to *them*."

Judging by her scowl, she didn't appreciate his suggestion to employ zidarr-approved social niceties. Jak grabbed the railing to pull himself to his feet, expecting pain even though his ankle was no longer throbbing, but the injury didn't bother him at all. He stared down at his foot and rotated it carefully. It didn't so much as twinge. He leaned his weight on it. Nothing happened. He resisted the temptation to jump up and down on that foot while spinning in a circle—barely.

Even though some mages specialized in using their power as healers, he hadn't expected a zidarr to be one. A *good* one.

Jak also resisted the urge to hug Malek, but he did beam at him. "*Thank you*, my lord."

Malek inclined his head. Not quite a bow or a *you're welcome*, but Jak wasn't the stickler for courtesy that Mother was. A healing was courtesy enough. He wished he'd paid more attention to what Malek had been doing. If he could learn to heal himself and others, that would be an amazing way to put the power he hadn't asked for to work.

Mother gripped his arm. "He healed it?"

"Completely," Jak said.

Mother looked at Malek, who was studying Jak thoughtfully. Reading his mind? Maybe Jak shouldn't have been thinking about learning to use his power.

"Thank you for healing my son," Mother said formally to Malek. After a pause, she added, "My lord."

Malek inclined his head toward her, then surprised Jak by saying, "You are welcome."

Even Mother's eyebrows flew up.

"He's a better captor than Toggs," Jak whispered to her.

"You haven't threatened to flatten his crew and take over his ship with your artifact," she muttered back.

"He did have his artifact knock me across the courtyard while trying to blow a hole in my chest." Malek's tone was mild, but he rested a hand over his heart, as if the memory pained him.

Reminded that Malek had a reason to hold a grudge if he wished, Jak said, "It's not *my* artifact. Just the artifact I was standing next to."

"That you commanded to attack me and Uthari and help you escape," Malek said dryly.

"I *requested* that it do those things. And only because your king was about to kill me. He looked right at me and was about to fry me with that evil—*inimical*—red lightning." Jak touched his own chest, the memory still enough to shake him. He'd been close to dying that night.

"Lightning isn't inimical. It's simply an electrostatic discharge instantaneously releasing as much as one gigajoule of energy." Malek was replying to Jak, but he looked over at Mother.

She snorted softly.

"I guess your chest will forgive me then," Jak said.

"I believe all is fair in battle when you're fighting for your life or your freedom."

Mother's eyebrows went up again. The words surprised Jak too, since Malek hadn't previously been willing to acknowledge that mages were oppressing the terrene humans of the world or that terrene humans should *need* freedom.

Malek squinted at Jak. "Others may *not* forgive you for using your power against them. Yidar said you were able to break his hold when you faced him today."

"Uh." Jak licked his lips, his mouth abruptly dry. "I'm not sure what I did. Colonel Sorath threw some explosives at him, and things got a little confusing. I was only trying to keep him from killing me."

Malek's eyes narrowed further. "Did he say he would?"

"Yeah. Because I'm a wild one. I'm really not that wild, my lord. Other than occasionally staying up too late working on papers and turning books in a few days late at the library, I've never been a rebel, at least before all this started."

"He also told King Uthari of the incident."

"He's a big tattletale then, isn't he?"

His mother slanted Jak a warning look. Maybe he should have added a respectful *my lord* there.

"Jak." Malek looked around the deck—making sure nobody was listening?—before continuing. "I told Uthari it was unlikely you would ever have the power to be a threat. If he comes to believe otherwise, he may kill you. Or *order* you killed." Malek's expression didn't change that much, but his lips thinned in a hint of a grimace.

Did that mean Uthari would make *him* do it? That thought filled Jak with bleakness. He didn't want anyone gunning for him, but he especially didn't want Malek to kill him. Why it mattered who did it, he didn't know, but it did.

"I know you have only grudgingly agreed to work with me,"

Malek continued, meeting both of their eyes, "but I suggest you resist any urge to use magic against me, my crew, Tonovan, Yidar, or any other mage or zidarr working under Uthari. Cooperate, and I will protect you from our enemies, but I cannot protect you from my own king if he decides you're a threat."

"What am I supposed to do if one of your people attacks me?" Jak asked. "I can't just... let them kill me."

"I will prevent that from happening. Nobody on this ship will attack you."

Jak was more worried about Yidar and Tonovan and whoever was on *their* ships. Inspiration struck, and he blurted a request before he could think better of it. "Will you teach me how to defend myself? With my magic?"

Malek stared at him as if he'd requested him to pluck stars from the heavens and hand them over.

"Just to defend. And, uh, that healing thing would be super nice." Jak waved toward his ankle.

"It is forbidden," Malek said.

"Because I'm a terrene human and wasn't born in some hoity-toity sky city?"

Mother elbowed him.

"My lord," Jak added.

Mother gave him an exasperated look. Maybe that wasn't what she'd wanted. Still, if there was even a faint chance that Malek would teach him a thing or two, wasn't it worth asking?

"It is forbidden because I am zidarr," Malek said, ignoring his irreverence. "Our time and our full loyalty must be to our masters, those who taught us. We may not take apprentices of our own or instruct others, lest our loyalties be divided. It is for the same reason that we are forbidden to marry."

Mother stared at him and opened her mouth but must have thought better of speaking.

"I don't want to marry you," Jak said. "Just learn how to keep mages from putting a death grip on my throat with their magic."

"If you prove yourself useful to Uthari, he may teach you."

Jak barely refrained from saying he would rather be taught by a man-eating lion actively gnawing on his foot, but maybe Malek heard the thought in his mind, for his eyes narrowed again.

"Uthari took *me* in and taught me when I should have been too old as well," Malek said.

Before Jak could come up with another argument—he wanted *Malek* to teach him, not that old prune in his castle—Mother elbowed him again.

"There's no need for anyone to teach Jak. Thank you. But there is something else I need to ask you if you're done questioning us." She'd slid the medallion back into her pocket.

Malek started to respond but paused and looked in the direction of the battle. The fighting had escalated with more fire and lightning flashing, and the booms of artillery weapons ringing out again.

"General Tonovan requires assistance. We'll have to go in now and get the artifact." Malek waved toward a mage standing near the hatchway. "Forlith will show you to a guest cabin."

Mother frowned, looking like she wanted to blurt her request anyway, but Malek was already walking away.

The mage he'd called over eyed them with confusion. "Did he say *cabin*?"

"*Guest* cabin." Jak smiled. "It should be the best you've got. With plush blankets and towels and bars of soap and perfume for the ladies." He nodded toward his mother.

"You *are* grimy," the mage muttered, more to Jak than Mother. "Follow me."

After tramping through the jungle, climbing vines up towers, and fleeing irate natives with clubs, Jak couldn't argue with the assessment. His eyes were gritty and tired, and he was relieved they would get beds that night. Assuming the ship survived the battle. It didn't escape his notice that, as the mage led them belowdecks, the *Star Flyer* was sailing straight toward it.

As the mageships battled each other over the beach west of Port Toh-drom, Sasko crouched by the railing of the *Tempest* beside Ferroki, Tinder, and several other women from the company.

There had been no reprieve for the mercenaries. Few of them had slept since arriving in Zewnath; even during lulls in the battle, they were expected to remain at the ready and fire whenever the mages lowered their defensive barrier for an attack round. There had been talk of sending Thorn Company and some of the mage crew over to one of Uthari's vessels for a forced boarding, but so far, none of the ships had been able to draw close enough to one another for that. Mostly, they'd been launching magical and mundane attacks at each other's barriers all day.

"They're concentrating their firepower on us now." Ferroki waved her rifle at the numerous magical blasts slamming into the barrier protecting the *Tempest*, then looked at the mages standing rigid nearby, their eyes tense as they focused all of their energy on keeping it in place. "Before, they were spreading it across all of Zaruk's ships, even though they had to know the portal is on this one."

Sasko glanced at the artifact lying flat on the deck, the same as it had for their trip on the *Dauntless*. She was sick of seeing the thing and sick of fighting over it. At least the mages hadn't scrounged up any roamer pirates to add to Thorn Company yet, and that mechanic lieutenant—Vinjo—had strapped the artifact down, so it might be harder for an enemy to levitate off the ship.

"It's a little surprising they didn't focus on us earlier," Sasko said.

"I had the thought that they weren't trying as hard as I would expect," Ferroki said. "At first, I thought it might be because they knew they were outnumbered, but now, I wonder if they might have been waiting for backup. I heard one of the mages say something about sensing another ship heading this way."

"Wonderful. If we get out of this—"

A loud snap behind them interrupted her, and Sasko spun around. At first, she didn't know what had caused it, but then more snaps sounded. The straps the mechanic had bolted to the deck to hold the artifact in place were breaking.

"Uh." Sasko fingered her rifle, but she didn't see anyone to target. A mage had to be breaking them from one of the other ships, but which mage? And which ship?

As soon as the last strap snapped—that hadn't taken long—the artifact scraped across the deck away from them. It was as if the ship had tilted, and gravity was making it slide away, but that hadn't happened.

It took a few seconds for the mages to notice, but then one barked, "Stop that!"

The artifact lifted a few feet into the air and headed toward the railing on the inland side of the *Tempest*. Strange. There weren't any mageships in the jungle behind theirs. All of their enemies—Uthari's two black-hulled vessels—were out to sea. The only other ship in that direction was Toggs's *Dauntless*, but it was still crashed on the beach and hadn't been contributing to the battle. Even if it had been, the crew would have been aiding Zaruk's ships, not trying to take the artifact back.

Several mages who had been instrumental in keeping the defenses up spun around and focused on restraining the portal. It was floating over the railing now, but their magic wrapped around it, and it halted.

"Our barrier is down!" someone warned. "Mercs, fire!"

Sasko cursed and made herself turn her back on the artifact.

Uthari's ships were flying closer, emboldened by whoever was causing the distraction.

She aimed at red-uniformed officers on the deck of the closest vessel—there was their general with the flamboyant cloak who liked shouting taunts at them. Though it was likely pointless, as every other shot she'd fired that day had been, Sasko targeted him and squeezed the trigger.

Next to her, Tinder bellowed a battle cry and threw one of her grenades. Both of their attacks struck the invisible barrier around the enemy ship and bounced off.

A few feet away from the mercenaries, one of the crew screamed in pain and dropped to the deck, both hands clutched to her head.

"Get our barrier back up!" another mage ordered.

"Something's stopping us from forming it. There's another ship!"

Sasko swung around, certain the new threat was coming from behind.

A black-hulled ship that hadn't been there ten seconds ago— she was *positive* it hadn't—loomed fifty feet from the far railing. Several mages stood on its forecastle, their arms outstretched as the artifact lifted toward them. All were uniformed save one in a brown jacket. Malek. His hands rested on the hilts of weapons, though his eyes were intent as he focused on the artifact.

"It's the *Star Flyer*!" someone cried.

"Fire!"

Ferroki shot toward the enemies they'd been facing all day. Sasko, certain they would be in trouble if Malek succeeded in getting the artifact, fired at him.

The blue blast from her magelock bounced off the *Star Flyer's* barrier. Sasko growled but realized they would have to lower it to take the artifact on board. That might be her chance. She readied her rifle to fire again.

"Where'd that other ship come from?" someone demanded.

"It wasn't there a second ago!"

"I didn't even sense it."

"Well, it's there now. Don't let those bastards take our—" Lightning streaked across from one of Uthari's other ships and struck the speaker in the chest.

The mages with Malek in the forecastle launched fireballs toward those trying to keep them from getting the artifact.

All the deadly magic flying about made Sasko want to spring for cover, but it also meant the barrier protecting the *Star Flyer* from enemies was down. She focused on Malek again, aiming for his chest. Since his eyes were locked on the artifact as he continued to maneuver it through the air toward his ship, she might have a clear shot.

But when she fired, her charge exploded in the air halfway to him.

Malek glanced her way, only for a second, and a blast of power slammed into Sasko. Pain hammered her chest and threw her against the railing so hard that wood cracked. Ferroki lunged and grabbed her, then pulled her down to the deck.

"Hate them," Sasko rasped around the agony in her chest.

"Stay down until Fret can tend you." Ferroki patted her shoulder and started to rise, but a mage in a rumpled uniform ran into view. Vinjo, the mechanic.

"They broke my straps? Those bastards!" Vinjo glanced at the mercenaries as he started past, a toolbox in hand, but he spotted Sasko flattened to the deck and paused. "Here. Try this. Mobile defense shield." He opened his toolbox, took what looked like a folded tarp from the top, and tossed it in front of Ferroki. Without explaining what it did, he ran off to help the mages trying to tug the artifact back to the *Tempest*.

Sasko feared that was a lost cause.

Ferroki nudged the folded tarp, and it sprang open, like a coiled spring let loose. It formed a waist-high wall of fabric.

"Duck," came a familiar yell. Sergeant Tinder.

A fireball sailed toward them from the *Star Flyer*. With no other cover around, Ferroki squatted behind the fabric wall and adjusted it to cover Sasko as well.

If Sasko's chest hadn't been aching, she would have laughed at the ridiculous sight. What would a piece of fabric on a frame do against *flames*?

The fireball skimmed past above their heads, clipping the top of the frame. Sasko couldn't tell if the contraption was magic, but she assumed so.

After the fireball skipped off the top, it was deflected into the air. It sailed toward one of Uthari's other ships. Sasko doubted it did any damage, but she fantasized about it slamming into their general's chest.

"Not bad." Ferroki poked her head over the fabric wall. "But too late to help. They've got the artifact and are securing it on their deck. It looks like their barrier is back up too. And they're flying away, toward the jungle and inland, not toward the sea. That might mean we'll be sent after them."

Sasko grunted, her chest aching as if a dragon had smashed her with its tail. The last person she wanted to be sent after was Malek.

Ferroki turned the lightweight portable barrier to face in the other direction. Their barrier was back up, but Uthari's other two ships hadn't stopped firing at them.

Ferroki waved someone over. Dr. Fret appeared and dropped down beside Sasko.

"What hit you?" Fret rested a hand on her chest.

"Malek flicked a finger at me." Sasko eyed her chest. She wasn't bleeding, just battered. "Have you got a potion for that?"

"Maybe a swig of alcohol after the fighting is over."

"I doubt that will help."

Ferroki sank down beside them, swapping her rifle for her pistol. "I need to recharge soon. It looks like the ships that have been attacking us all day intend to keep doing so while the *Star Flyer* disappears with the artifact."

"What are the odds," Sasko muttered, "that Zaruk's ships will flee, slink home in defeat, and we'll be done with this battle?"

Bellows came from across the deck, Captain Myroth ordering the mages and mercenaries to crush their enemies, so they could get the artifact back.

"Not good." Ferroki sighed and pointed her pistol at some target.

Though Dr. Fret hadn't finished examining her, Sasko made herself push up to her knees and grab her magelock so she could do the same.

Captain Myroth jogged over to them, looking harried. "Recharge your weapons, and prepare for another round. One of our other ships is going after the *Star Flyer*. We're to keep the rest of Uthari's fleet busy so they can't help Malek. We *have* to get that artifact back."

Sasko groaned and sank back to the deck, worried they weren't done dealing with Malek after all.

12

Jak flopped back on the bed and wriggled around on the covers. It had been *days* since he'd slept on a mattress, and he immensely looked forward to it. Even before their night in the jungle, he'd been stuck sleeping on the deck in the middle of the portal, afraid Captain Toggs would shoot him if he didn't stay cuddled up to it.

"Perhaps you should wash before getting your grimy, sweat-stained clothes and stinky body all over the blankets." Mother went straight to a pitcher and basin and rubbed water over her face with relish.

"That little basin lacks the power to effectively lay siege to my stink. Besides, I'm sure mages can snap their fingers and poof everything clean again."

"I doubt it. They probably have terrene human minions locked in a laundry room in the bottom of the ship, scrubbing away *their* stink."

The thought that his moment of pleasure might cause work for someone else made Jak stop rolling. He sat up but only to lean against the wall. He couldn't bring himself to get off the bed. If not for the sounds of battle emanating through the hull and the flashes outside the porthole in their cabin, he might have already skinned out of his clothes and pulled the covers over his head. He knew they weren't safe, but under Malek's protection, they were safer than they had been for days.

As soon as Mother washed, she went not to the other bunk in the cabin but to the porthole to peer out. So far, not a single jolt had jarred the *Star Flyer*. They had to be under attack, since they'd been flying straight into battle the last Jak had seen, but the crew must have been fresh and able to keep their defenses up without trouble.

He closed his eyes, willing his mind to sense the magic around them, trying to tell how the battle was going. To his surprise, he detected a familiar powerful artifact lying on the deck not a hundred feet from him.

"They got the portal," he blurted.

"Already? There's still fighting going on out there, but I think I see the jungle under us again. Maybe they got it, and we're flying away while Uthari's other ships keep Zaruk's busy."

"I bet that was exactly their plan."

"I wish I'd asked Malek sooner," Mother said.

"Asked him what?" Jak remembered that she'd been about to request something when Malek had received word about the battle and strode off.

"I don't know if he can do anything, but they're his own people, so I thought..." She squinted at something outside.

"Thought what?"

Mother sighed and looked at him. "You probably didn't hear, but Yidar got Tezi."

Jak sat up straight. "*What*?"

"Sorath told me. He was upset that he was injured and hadn't yet been able to get back to Thorn Company to let them know."

"Wait. By *got* her, do you mean *killed* her? Or captured her?"

They couldn't have killed her. He hadn't even gotten to have that drink with her yet.

"Captured her. Before we left, I told Sorath I would try to get her back." Mother tugged on her braid. "I don't know why I said that, because I can't imagine how I'm going to manage it, but I had to say something. He looked so betrayed that we were willingly going with Malek. But if we hadn't, he would have gotten himself killed defending us for no reason."

Jak barely heard her. He couldn't keep from imagining that odious Tonovan putting his hands all over Tezi. Slavemasters in Hell, what if Yidar was into that too? Why else would he have grabbed her? Tezi was the lowest-ranking mercenary. She couldn't *know* anything or have any tactical value to them. Jak highly doubted Yidar had believed they could trade her for the artifact. And now they didn't need to do even that. *Malek* had the artifact.

"Why?" Jak whispered, his throat tight. "Why would he have taken her?"

"No good reason," Mother said grimly, maybe thinking the same thoughts as Jak.

"I *hate* them," Jak snarled as their door opened.

He sprang up, though he no longer had a weapon. The mage who'd put them in the cabin hadn't searched their pockets, despite the captain's insistence that guest pockets *should* be searched, but he had taken Jak's rifle. No, that had been *Tezi's* rifle that he'd stolen when they fled the *Dauntless*.

If she'd had it with her rather than some inferior substitute, would it have made a difference for her and Sorath in that battle with Yidar? Guilt swamped Jak, and he slumped back onto the bed, hardly caring if his impassioned words got him in trouble.

Captain Rivlen walked into the cabin with a clipboard holding a small stack of paper. She eyed them briefly but said nothing about what she must have overheard, only waving for a young officer to step inside with her, the man carrying a stained canvas sack. It looked like a trash bag.

"We're going to search their pockets and inventory everything. Anything *inimical*—" Rivlen squinted at Mother, clearly referencing her conversation with Malek, "—goes in that bag and gets incinerated."

Mother faced her with her hands clasped behind her back but didn't raise any objections at the idea of the valuable herbs, powders, and who knew what else she'd collected from the apothecary shop being destroyed. Jak hoped Rivlen didn't plan to incinerate anything in *his* pockets.

"Remove everything," Rivlen told her, "or Garun will, and he gets handsy with the ladies."

The young officer's eyebrows flew up. "That's not true, ma'am."

"There have now been three instances of you brushing against me as you've managed to need to go through narrow hatchways or down ship's ladders at the same time as me."

He shook his head vehemently. "Those were accidents. And only with you, not with all *ladies*." He glanced at Mother, his cheeks turning pink.

"Do you have such accidents with Malek?" Rivlen asked.

"No. I don't want to brush his anything."

Rivlen lifted her eyes toward the ceiling, then pointed to Mother's pockets and snapped her fingers. "Empty them."

Jak thought his mother might object—to the finger snapping if not the activity—but she must have decided to swallow her indignation and accept her fate on this trip. She dug into the pockets in her trousers, her shirt, and her vest and carefully laid Father's journal, *The Mind Way,* vials, jars, small pouches, packets, bags, and twists of dried herbs onto the desk. Careful not to pile things on top of each other, she filled the entire surface and set a few things on the chair.

"I can't believe that's all coming out of your pockets." Rivlen stared as her young crewman eyed his sack and seemed to wonder if there would be room in it. "Don't you people believe in backpacks or purses?"

"We had trunks, packs, and numerous other storage receptacles at our dig site," Mother said coolly. "When Malek and his minions came to capture us, they didn't allow us to pack and take our belongings with us."

"*Lord* Malek." Rivlen stepped forward with her clipboard. "Tell me what each thing is. Don't bother lying. I'll be able to tell."

"Hercampuri, lemon beebrush, zeath grass, erfarsik, tefti, sulfur, healwort gel, blackened bitter root, saltpeter, vine of the dead, cat's claw, tawari tree bark, dried jana berry, Zewnathian scorpion venom, darthan centipede venom, forked asp venom, dehydrated yova mushroom powder..."

Rivlen wrote quickly to list everything. Jak kept his mind empty as Mother shared everything without any explanation as to what each item did. He didn't know what most of her inventory was for, but a few he recognized as combinable into something *inimical*. If the captain—or her not-handsy crewman—didn't have a chemistry background, they might not know.

"Are any of those poisons?" Rivlen asked.

"I'm a healer, not a poison maker."

"What about the venoms? And the mushrooms?"

"I'm thinking of mixing them to make an intriguing after-dinner beverage."

Rivlen lowered the clipboard and glared at her.

Mother sighed. "The venoms *are* poisonous—technically, they're *venomous*—but they have medicinal uses. The centipede venom can be used as an anesthetic to dull pain and as an anticonvulsant to treat epilepsy, including epileptic fits induced by bites from the indigenous wraith tarantula. The scorpion venom can be refined into a compound that is a strong anti-inflammatory. And the asp venom, I simply picked up because those snakes proliferate the jungles here and bites are common. If I can obtain needles from your ship's doctor, I can start injecting whoever is interested with small doses that will allow the body to build up an immunity."

"That sounds useful." Rivlen glanced toward the porthole at the dark jungle passing below them, hoots, hisses, and howls audible through the hull.

"Of course."

Rivlen squinted at her. "Are you sure that's *all* they do?"

"The venoms? I admit a side effect of the compound made from the centipede venom can be priapism. Given the apparently handsy nature of your crew, you may not wish to employ that on them."

Jak doubted the crewman knew what the word meant, but his cheeks reddened again.

"Spell that." Rivlen probably didn't know what it meant either. Maybe it was for the best that Mother's references went over their captors' heads.

Mother did so.

When Rivlen finished writing, she eyed the desk, the trash bag, and the desk again. "I'll show Malek the list and ask his opinion."

Jak couldn't keep from snorting. It might have been an ineffectively repressed snicker.

Rivlen squinted at him.

"Make sure to ask his opinion on the venom's side effects," Jak said.

This time, Mother lifted *her* eyes toward the ceiling. What? If they distracted the mages with dumb stuff, that might keep them from noticing the more genuine threats.

"If I have to question you people later, I'll bring a dictionary." Rivlen pointed at Jak's pockets. "Empty them."

"Yes, ma'am."

Jak used his bunk to spread out his pens, charcoal sticks, pencils, compass, caliper, collapsible ruler, and a folded stack of drawings he'd worked on during the voyage to Zewnath. Sadly, he'd lost the sketch pads from the dig site. The map of the Dragon Perch island he'd been working on had likely been scorched to ashes by molten lava flowing over it.

None of the drawings were of anything embarrassing—he'd resisted the urge to draw Tezi, since she'd been ignoring him at the time, and it might have seemed too familiar—but he winced when Rivlen picked them up to look at them. He wagered she would have something snarky and dismissive to say about his talent.

She unfolded the pictures and looked through them. Jak had done one of interesting architecture in Utharika, one of a dragon, one of Captain Ferroki and Colonel Sorath standing shoulder to shoulder by the railing on the *Dauntless*, and one of Sergeant Tinder and Dr. Fret sitting on the deck, knitting and making grenades. It had been such a surprising juxtaposition of hobbies that he'd had to sketch it.

"These are good, but no maps?" Rivlen asked.

Good? Had a mage *praised* him? It had been quickly and matter-of-factly, but it was better than snark.

"Lord Malek said you would make one that shows where we need to take the artifact," she added.

"Yes, but he asked for that less than ten minutes ago." Jak smiled.

Rivlen didn't. "It was twenty minutes ago. Get to work."

She handed him a couple of thin sheets of writing paper from the bottom of the stack on her clipboard, then hesitated and offered him her pen.

"I see he's willing to supply the best materials."

"It doesn't have to be a masterpiece," she said.

"May I quote that back to him when he's punishing me for ineptitude?"

"It's more likely the *helmsman* will punish you."

"Comforting. Will you tell Lord Malek that we need a favor? A friend of ours is Yidar's prisoner. Maybe General Tonovan's prisoner by now. I know you people are all on the same team, so I thought maybe Malek could politely request that Tonovan send our friend over here."

"While throwing fireballs at him," Mother murmured.

Rivlen frowned at her, looking like she might say something about this inappropriate irreverence toward a superior mage, but Jak remembered her distaste for male handsiness and hurried to speak again, in the hope that she might care.

"She's one of the mercenaries, a young woman named Tezi. Pretty girl from the northlands. We don't want him to harass her."

"One of the mercenaries who helped you escape from King Uthari's castle and forced us to partake in this needless journey?" Rivlen asked.

Ah, all filled in, was she?

"Technically," Jak said, "the mercenaries had no interest in helping us escape. We invited ourselves along on their artifact-acquisition mission."

"The end result was the same. I'll tell Lord Malek about the prisoner, but if you consider one of the mercenaries that King Zaruk hired a friend, we may need to reconsider your status as guests." Rivlen looked at the desk full of herbalism and chemistry ingredients, then her crewman with the trash bag. Jak worried she had changed her mind and would insist it all be thrown out. But she shook her head and walked toward the door. "You can put that away for now. I'll see if anything on the list disturbs Lord Malek."

Rivlen and the crewman walked out, shutting the door with a thump.

"I doubt much disturbs Malek," Jak said, already thinking of contacting him directly to request assistance with Tezi. If he'd spoken telepathically to him from across the Forked Sea, he ought to be able to do it from two decks down in his ship. "Though he may want to avoid the venom with the weird side effects. I know *I* would."

"If it's at all heartening, the main effect is worse."

"Death?" Jak assumed that in large enough doses all of the venoms could kill a person.

"Yes."

Mother carefully sorted her collection, organizing the items as much as one could for storage in pockets. Chemical elements in one pocket, venoms in another, jars of corrosive acids in another... She truly did need a backpack. Or perhaps a large trunk and a few porters.

"Do you think the captain will relay our message about Tezi?" Mother asked. "I'm afraid for her."

"I don't know, but *I'll* talk to Malek." Jak touched his temple. "We're flying away from the battle. He can't be that busy."

Light flashed outside the porthole. The orange of a fireball? Jak could sense a magical barrier still protecting the *Star Flyer*. Maybe he'd assumed too early that they were safe. One of the enemy vessels could have slipped away from Uthari's other ships and be chasing them.

"I don't know if he'll help or not," Mother said. "He's been protecting us because his king wishes it, but I doubt he otherwise cares one way or another about terrene humans." She sounded a little sad.

Jak doubted zidarr in general worried about terrene humans, but maybe he could make a deal. Something along the lines of... *So, Lord Malek, I can draw a horrible map, as befitting the supplies your captain gave me, or I can try to make one your helmsman will actually be able to read...*

Since Jak was once again on the same ship as the artifact, he could also attempt to bluff Malek, the same way he had Captain Toggs, but Malek had a much better idea of what the portal could and couldn't do. He also had shown on numerous occasions that he could read Jak's thoughts like the large-print edition of a very remedial book.

"I'll see what I can do." He didn't expect her to believe he could do much.

But Mother considered him for a moment, then nodded. "Thank you. And here."

She withdrew something from a seventh small pocket that she hadn't delved into during the inventory. The medallion wrapped in dark-eye fabric. She offered it to him.

"I'll keep it if you want, but Malek said not to unwrap it." Jak waved at his hat, wishing he could slip it back into what had been its rightful place for so long.

"It belongs with you."

"You're not afraid it'll turn you into a mage if you carry it around for five years the way I did, are you?"

"No, though it *is* chilling to imagine it oozing magic and altering the biological material within your cells to irrevocably change you."

"It wasn't that bad. I barely felt it."

She snorted softly and sat at the desk. She hadn't put away the saltpeter and sulfur. "I need one of your charcoal sticks, please."

"Planning to make something to throw at enemies?"

"If necessary."

Tezi prowled around her cell, a strange oubliette with no windows or doors, save for an opening high above with a grate locked across it.

Her body ached from having half of a stable fall on it, and she should have rested, but the sounds of battle reached her through the walls. She couldn't help but feel she needed to escape before it ended. For now, Yidar and the mage crew were busy and hadn't bothered her, but once they were done fighting, they would have more time to contemplate their prisoner.

Guards had searched her before dropping her into the cell, taking her weapons as well as her money. She'd fought hard over losing that, biting and punching and kicking in frustration. It hadn't even been a full day since the captain had given her that coin, far more than she deserved and probably more than Ferroki should have parted with, and she'd already lost it. The only thing her flailing outburst had proven was that she could effectively bite the hand of a suitably distracted mage. It had been worth it, even though he'd punched her after that, hard enough that she'd bitten her tongue and left the taste of blood in her mouth.

It had faded, but her frustration hadn't. Tezi growled and thumped her palm against a wall as hard and unyielding as steel. Since it was made with magic, it might be even *harder* than steel. She had no idea why Yidar had taken her prisoner instead of killing her, but nothing good would come from it.

After a time, the sounds of battle faded. Faint voices drifted down from above, and boots came into view, two red-uniformed men standing on her grate. They stepped off it, and she thought they might leave her in favor of tormenting some other prisoner, but a clank sounded, and the grate scraped aside.

Magical power gripped her and levitated her into the air. She felt like a doll being manipulated by some divine master.

No, she told herself. The mages weren't that. *The Teachings* told that men were men, whether powerful or vulnerable, and nobody except the gods could touch the stars or should be worshipped. She couldn't let herself think of them as divine or superhuman, or she would be too afraid to act. She'd killed their kind before. Not only did they bleed, but they could die.

As the magic settled her onto the deck in the corridor, the two mages looked her up and down, letting their eyes brazenly consider her curves.

"That uniform is about as sexy as a canvas tote, but she'll do."

"Absolutely, she will." One leaned in and squeezed her butt.

Tezi whirled and threw a punch before she could worry about consequences. Unfortunately, it struck an invisible barrier inches from the man's broad smiling face.

"And she's spunky too. The general will like that. Or is she for Yidar?"

"I don't know. They're both up in the forecastle. Maybe they're going to enjoy her together."

"I can't imagine a zidarr going for that. They're all stiff and rigid."

"You're thinking of Malek, but he doesn't represent all zidarr. Besides, you wouldn't go for that either."

"Not with Tonovan, no. Disgusting."

Tezi sighed as one grabbed her arm and steered her down the corridor. It would be nice if the male representatives of the species, especially the arrogant *mage* species, would treat her like a person instead of a sex toy. Failing that, if they could leave her alone altogether, that would also be acceptable.

They led her through a hold glowing with magical objects that powered the ship, connected by strange pulsing tendrils that flowed through decks and walls like some bizarre growth. Finding the place eerie, she was relieved when they took her above decks. The moon glowed silver through the clouds, and she was surprised that the sea was no longer in sight. The mageship was flying inland over a dark, dense jungle that stretched in all directions.

Even though she wasn't any safer outside, Tezi couldn't help but look wistfully toward the trees, the thick canopy like a carpet. How high were those treetops from the ground? If she could escape and jump off the ship, was there any chance she would survive the fall?

"No," the mage gripping her elbow said. "It's hundreds of feet down. Even if you survived, something would eat you. The jungle hunts are a popular sport among mages in the southern kingdoms, those who want the trophies of something deadly and fearsome to hang on their walls back home. But it's dangerous even for our people. There are lots of critters down there that you can't take down with magelocks and that can kill you with a single venomous bite."

Tezi would prefer to take her chances with the *critters* instead of the mages, but since her guard was reading her mind, she tried to empty it, so she wouldn't give him any more fodder.

He pushed her up steps to the forecastle where Yidar stood with his hands clasped behind his back, looking toward the route ahead. General Tonovan was with him and had brought a bottle of wine and two gilded goblets.

"Have a drink, Yidar." Tonovan ignored Tezi and her two guards. He poured wine for himself and the zidarr, then offered him a goblet. "We succeeded."

Yidar scowled at the goblet. "We fought all day so *he* could slink in and get the artifact."

"As Uthari wished. I told you that was the plan."

"You don't even *like* Malek."

"Of course not."

"How could you want him to get the credit?"

"We'll all be rewarded. He's got the archaeologists too."

"And we've got *nothing*."

"You did bring me a pretty girl to play with." Tonovan smirked, met Tezi's gaze, and held it while he drank from his goblet. "And there are more mageships out there. It's always possible someone will get lucky and knock the *Star Flyer* into a volcano."

Did this discussion and flight away from the coast mean that

Zaruk's mageships had all been defeated? What about Ferroki, Fret, Tinder, and the rest of the company? Tezi's shoulders slumped at the thought that they might all be dead.

"I don't think there are volcanos here," Yidar said.

"A shame. But I suppose I shouldn't fantasize about his death anyway. After all, we've got orders to catch the ship chasing the *Star Flyer*. Maybe he'll be in trouble when we arrive. Then we can bravely save Malek and his crew from being pounded in the ass like slaves in the salt mines."

"Your mind is preoccupied with sex for someone so old," Yidar said.

"I'm not that old. My keen wit, ability to suck up to the right people, and well-honed power have propelled me up through the ranks at an admirable rate."

"Your hair is gray."

"Because my job is stressful." Tonovan flicked his fingers toward the guards. "But I know how to unwind. Will you join me, Yidar? I'll bring up some other women so we don't end up prick-fencing."

Yidar only glanced at Tezi before turning an incredulous look on Tonovan. "That's not why I brought her back with me. The boy cares for her. I thought we could use her to lure him to us."

"Had it proven necessary, we could have, but Malek has the boy now. There is no need." Tonovan tried again to hand Yidar a goblet of wine. This time, he accepted it.

Tezi listened bleakly to them, not sure whether to pity Jak for being Malek's prisoner—had his mother been captured too?—or to wish she were with them. She had no idea if Malek was more perverse than Tonovan or vice versa, but it would have been nice to not be alone in this misery.

She tried to bolster herself. She'd been forced by a man before, and she'd survived that. Thus, she could survive this.

Though a part of her that longed to avoid prolonged pain and wanted things to end quickly couldn't help but gaze toward the railing. Was it horrible that the mage's promise that she would fall far and die immediately was enticing tonight? The warm earthy air, scented with exotic blossoms and fruits, almost called to her. What did she have left to live for?

"Does it truly not bother you to play Antar the Helpful to his Bravork the Destroyer?" Yidar sipped from the goblet and grimaced. "This is a bad idea. We may have to fight again soon. We're trying to catch Zaruk's runaway ship, aren't we?"

"Yes, but if a sip of alcohol dulls your abilities, I'll be terribly disappointed in your vaunted zidarrness."

One of Tezi's guards had a dagger on his belt. She didn't look longingly at it or let herself think about it or what she wanted to do with it. She merely made note of it as she gazed past the railing.

"Maybe we should let it catch the *Star Flyer*," Yidar said, "and see how well he does without our help."

"You're so one-note, my young bitter friend. Come, enjoy some sex and wine. Didn't you say you were tired of your rigid Zidarr Code? Let me help loosen you up. You do know what to *do* with women, don't you? I know you boys can't marry or fall earnestly and poignantly in love, lest the king doubt your loyalty, but I truly hope you're not forced into celibacy."

"We're not."

"Good." Tonovan smiled at Tezi, his lips red from the wine. "One of you two remove her uniform, will you? That brown is dreadful and does nothing for her skin coloring."

"Uh, up here, sir?" One of the guards looked around at the open deck, numerous mages on duty below the forecastle.

"Indeed," Tonovan said. "Nature is so stimulating."

A monkey hooted.

Tezi couldn't resist the urge to look toward the dark depths of the jungle again, the canopy barely ten feet below the mageship as it adjusted altitude or steered around taller trees thrusting up above their peers. Maybe the helmsman was staying low to try to sneak up on their foes.

She didn't care why, only that there was a possibility she might grab a branch and survive a fall. Admittedly, a *poor* possibility. Those branches at the top wouldn't be strong, and it was more likely she would plummet straight to the ground.

But even if she did, would it matter? Her family was gone, save for a brother who'd been enslaved by mages years ago and may or may not be alive, and she'd been forced to leave the company. There was no one left who would miss her if she died.

Tezi didn't *want* to die, but she'd been tormented before by someone like Tonovan, and she didn't want to live through that again. Especially when there was no promise of reprieve. Uthari's minions had collected the artifact, the archaeologists, and would succeed in their mission and drag her back to their city as a prisoner. Or maybe Tonovan would simply kill her once he tired of her.

"Such *grisly* thoughts, pretty one," Tonovan crooned.

He'd prowled closer, like a panther stalking his prey. Prey incapable of moving, thanks to the mages using their magic to hold her in place.

She sneered at him, though he would probably be aroused by defiance. The perverts always were.

"Isn't that the truth?" He stroked the side of her face, his eyes mocking. "Meek women have their purpose in the bedroom, but they're not stimulating."

Tezi jerked her head back, as much as she could with the magical bonds around her, but it wasn't enough to get his hand off her. He smirked, then looked at the zidarr, who was more interested in watching the route ahead than in this display.

"Come, Yidar," Tonovan said. "Enjoy your prize with me. You brought her in, after all."

Prize, right. As if she'd been won in a great battle, not dragged half-unconscious out of a pile of rubble like a drowned rat caught in a dam.

"We'll catch up to the other ship soon and have to fight. Besides—" Yidar frowned over his shoulder at Tonovan— "your *prize* isn't interested in being enjoyed."

"So? I thought you wanted to give up your oppressive zidarr ways and conquer a kingdom of your own so you could enjoy women and riches mounded all about you."

Yidar's expression darkened. "Is that what Uthari told you?"

"Is it not the truth?"

"It *is* what I want, but I want willing women who long for me because of my power and prowess, not to rape some girl barely old enough to hold your dick."

Yidar looked at Tezi, and for a second, she thought he might do something to stop this, but he sneered as dismissively at her as Tonovan.

"Careful, Yidar," Tonovan said coolly. "You're in danger of sounding as sanctimonious as Malek."

"I'm *nothing* like that bootlicker." Yidar set the barely touched goblet of wine on the deck and stalked off the forecastle.

"Shaping young minds is so tedious," Tonovan said, talking more to himself than the guards or Tezi. "I don't know why I bother. But I'm just as happy *not* sharing my bedroom with obnoxious upstarts." His gaze returned to Tezi, and he lifted his hand again, sliding his fingers into her hair. "Now, where were we?"

She tried to bite him. Again, the magic kept her from getting close. He threw back his head and laughed.

"Uh, General?" came an uncertain voice from the ladder. Not Yidar again but a young, uniformed mage. "We've got Zaruk's ship in our sights. Their barrier is up, and I think we'll need you to help pull it down so our attacks can get through."

Tonovan huffed in annoyance. "With our zidarr pouting in his cabin, I suppose that's true. Very well." He released Tezi and told the guards, "This won't take long. Keep her here, and get her ready for me. Clothes off."

"Yes, sir."

Unfortunately, Tonovan didn't leave the forecastle. He only turned his back to them and strode to the bow, prepared to sling his magic from there.

The guards could have used magic to strip Tezi of her uniform, but they did the work with their hands, groping her along the way. She kept her mind blank as she eyed the dagger again. Maybe if she used her body to distract them, instead of standing there like a rigid stick, she could keep them preoccupied. Then she might slip that weapon free of the guard's belt as the ship engaged in battle.

Lifting her gaze to the stars, she mumbled a silent, *Thanok, give me strength*, and did her best to keep her plans out of her mind as she took action.

13

In the aftercastle of his ship, Malek lowered his hands and stepped back from the railing.

He'd been ready for battle, to attack the vessel that had given chase, soaring inland fast enough to catch up with the *Star Flyer*. But his allies had been flying right behind it, and before the ship could attack, Tonovan and Yidar had launched a barrage of magic, decimating the crew and lighting the craft on fire.

Now, flames roared and smoke wafted from the ship as it listed toward the trees. Distant scraping noises pierced the night as branches clawed at its damaged hull. Monkeys, insects, and various other nocturnal creatures fell silent at the ruckus. They hadn't minded the fireballs hurtling through the night sky, but scraping noises were alarming.

Malek kept the *Star Flyer*'s defenses up in case the crashing ship managed a final attack in his direction, but he doubted it would. His allies had been effective.

He appreciated that Tonovan and Yidar were here, doing the job that Uthari had asked of them, but he couldn't help but feel a twinge of disappointment that he hadn't seen more fighting this night. Skulking in to make off with the artifact while the enemy was distracted had been effective, but he would have preferred to win the prize in a straightforward and honorable battle.

Malek eyed the portal on the deck behind him, knowing he should simply be pleased that they'd acquired it. Also that it hadn't done anything to stop him from doing so. Since it was a dangerous and unknown entity—Malek rubbed his chest at the memory of the lightning bolt it had struck him with—he hadn't been certain that would be the case.

Did the portal know Jak was aboard the *Star Flyer*? Did it care? Malek didn't know, but he was relieved it hadn't zapped him again. At least not yet.

Captain Rivlen climbed the steps to join him, a clipboard in hand. She glanced toward their smoldering enemy as she saluted him. "I made a list of what our prisoners—your guests—had in their pockets."

Malek created a mage light so he could read it. "That's a long list."

"They have a lot of pockets."

He remembered that from his previous investigation of their belongings. Professor Freedar must have found the opportunity to resupply. He knew she hadn't found that much around Uthari's castle.

"I wasn't sure what a lot of the items were," Rivlen admitted. "Since you didn't want me to throw away everything they had, I thought you would want to take a look."

"Did you know what *any* of them were?" As Malek scanned the list, he recognized a few common elements but not many of the herbs. Even though he'd read a number of the papers Jadora had published before switching fields, he had, per Uthari's request, educated himself much more thoroughly on archaeology. Uthari had only wanted him to learn enough about herbalism and phar-macology to be able to recognize the plant he sought and grasp the value of others Malek might find when traveling through the portal to another world.

"Few. Mostly just the kid's stuff. I gave him paper so he can draw the map."

"Good. Three different kinds of venom, huh?"

"She said doses of the asp one can be given in small amounts to help a person build up an immunity. The asps are supposed to be common down here and have a penchant for biting people."

"I'm not that familiar with Zewnath, but that doesn't seem unlikely. I'll trust that I can heal myself with magic if a snake bites me."

"I'm not that strong in the healing arts," Rivlen said. "I've focused on battle magic."

"Once you've been scorched ten or twenty times by battle magic, you may find yourself with an interest in healing." Malek tilted the list toward her. "Sulfur and saltpeter can be combined with—" Malek ran his finger down the list to what had to be Jak's collection of drawing implements and found the third ingredient, "—charcoal to make black powder."

Rivlen swore and took back the clipboard. "I was too focused on the venoms. I'll go take those items immediately."

Before she could leave, Malek lifted a hand to stop her. "Let them have them. They're unlikely to be a danger to us." He pointed at Rivlen and himself. "And if someone gets past our defenses, we don't want our archaeologists to be easy targets. The goal is to keep them alive and also from being kidnapped by someone else."

"That won't happen, my lord."

"No? It happened in Uthari's castle. Admittedly, they were actively trying to escape at the time. Had they stayed in their suite, we wouldn't have lost them to a pack of mercenaries."

"What happens if they try to escape again? I know they came voluntarily, but they also don't adore us. What if what they think is a better offer comes along? They could want to team up with the mercenaries again. The kid has drawn pictures of them. He must not loathe them."

"I believe they'll stick with me." An uncertain presence tickled Malek's mind. Jak was reaching out to communicate with him again. His ability to do so reminded Malek of his earlier thoughts about Jak and the artifact. "One moment."

Hello, Lord Malek, Jak spoke telepathically to him. *Sorry to bother you. I'm not sure how to let someone know I wish to talk without rudely inserting my words into their mind. Is there a mental equivalent of a door chime?*

A mage or wizard can block you if they don't wish to speak. Has your mother absconded with one of your charcoal sticks yet?

Jak hesitated.

Malek thought it was a good idea to let his guests know that he knew what they were up to. He was willing to let them make black powder and whatever else, but they might be less inclined to try something on his crew if they believed Malek had his eye on them.

There wasn't any absconding, Jak said. *She asked first if she could borrow it.*

Borrow? Will she return it after she's ground it down into her explosive concoction?

I didn't ask. I'm busy drawing a map. Per your request. And if it's permitted, I'd like to make a request of you.

Go ahead.

Yidar kidnapped a girl my age. She was trying to help us get away from him earlier today and after dropping a stable on her, he took her off on his flying disk.

Is this girl one of the mercenaries? One who was helping Colonel Sorath against us?

Malek had almost killed Sorath when he'd seen the man, especially since Sorath had taken a shot at him, clearly longing to kill *Malek.* The only reason he hadn't was because Sorath had been protecting Jak and Jadora. Because his employers wanted them for their own use, no doubt, but if he'd helped keep Yidar—and through him Tonovan—from getting Jak and Jadora, that had made Malek's job easier. Also, he'd sensed that Jak and Jadora felt something akin to friendship toward Sorath, which had left Malek reluctant to kill him while they watched. However, if they met again in battle, he wouldn't hesitate to slay the nettlesome mercenary.

She is a member of Thorn Company, Jak admitted. *But she agreed to have a drink with me. Or she was on the verge of it when the* Dauntless *crashed.*

Thus I should bring her to this ship so you can more easily date her.

No, that's not what I mean. Jak's embarrassment came through the telepathic link. *She's pretty, and I'm afraid... Mother and I are afraid for her. There was no reason for Yidar to take her. If anything, he should have taken Sorath. Tezi is the newest and lowest-ranking member of Thorn Company. It's not like she's been privy to secret information or would know anything useful. There's only one reason why they would have taken her.*

Yidar's main reason might have been because *Jak* had feelings for the girl, and he'd thought he could use her as bait—Malek suspected the mercenaries had sent her along with Sorath for the same reason—but he was too familiar with Tonovan's tastes to dismiss the possibility that a pretty girl would end up in his cabin.

If you're open to negotiations, Jak continued, *I could make a vastly superior map instead of a mediocre one, and I'll communicate with the artifact on your behalf and do everything within my power to help you get it set up and working. If you'll rescue her.*

You were planning to make me a mediocre map?

The one carved into the druid monument is mediocre. It occurred to me to simply copy it.

I'm disappointed that you would give me substandard work. Malek debated the ramifications of flying over to Tonovan's ship to retrieve the prisoner.

Jak's next words seemed genuinely abashed. *I wouldn't have. Sorry. I just don't want anything to happen to her.*

Malek sighed.

"My lord?" Rivlen asked.

"My guests object to Yidar having taken a prisoner."

"The girl? They asked me to ask you to arrange a prisoner transfer to our ship."

"Were you going to tell me?"

"Yes." Rivlen shrugged. "Realizing they were making black powder down there drove the thought from my mind."

"Do you think it's a good idea?"

"To steal the bed toy of the general who's helping keep Zaruk's people off our butts and may end up buying the time we'll need to figure out how to get the portal working? No, I don't."

"Do you want me to do it anyway?" Malek remembered Rivlen introducing herself to him—and detailing her feelings on Tonovan.

"Yes. Or you could send me, and *I* could get her."

"I doubt Tonovan would relinquish a prisoner to you."

"Not without a fight, no."

"You are a talented mage but young. You might not survive a fight with him."

"Or he might underestimate me, and I might defeat him and throw his battered body over the railing where he'll land in a tree containing a nest of those asps. They'll promptly inject him with gallons of deadly venom."

"Gallons?"

"I'm envisioning a *lot* of asps."

"Your prior history with Tonovan must be more involved than I realized." Malek didn't ask, in part because he wasn't one to pry into people's pasts, especially new officers he barely knew, and in part because he had to work with Tonovan. He tried not to judge his non-zidarr colleagues by the Zidarr Code, but the further they strayed from it, the more challenging it was.

"It was more involved than anyone would wish," was all Rivlen said, her voice tight.

She turned a dark gaze toward the equally dark jungle. She might take this matter into her own hands if Malek opted to do nothing. It would be a shame to lose someone who seemed to be a quality officer and boon to Uthari's military. Further, if he didn't act, Jak and Jadora might rethink their willingness to work with him. Even if Tonovan was the deviant, if Malek stood by and did nothing when he had the power to act, what did that make him?

He'd already made up his mind to go get the girl when a distant scream floated across the night, a woman's scream. It came from the direction of Tonovan's ship.

Rivlen clenched her fist. "My lord—"

"I'll go get her." Malek didn't know if that was the mercenary, since Tonovan took many women to his quarters—it was also possible that he, Yidar, or another officer had captured a female mage from Zaruk's ship and was interrogating her for mission-critical information—but he didn't want to risk Rivlen getting herself killed or doing something that would end her career. "Stay here, get the map from Jak, and keep the ship on course to our destination."

"Yes, my lord."

"Also, keep a defense crew awake and a barrier up around the clock. In addition to needing to worry about other ships after the artifact, there are numerous flying predators on this continent."

"Yes, something that looked like a winged shark tried to take a bite out of the bottom of the hull earlier. Be glad we're not on foot here."

Malek nodded and jogged to his cabin to retrieve his skyboard. *I'm going to get her, Jak.*

Thank you, my lord. A flood of relief accompanied the words. Maybe Jak had heard the scream.

Malek, who mostly spoke telepathically to Uthari and other zidarr—trained mages who guarded their emotions as well as their thoughts—wasn't used to such raw feeling. He had the urge to rush and succeed at the task, so that Jak wouldn't be hurt by the loss of a friend. Then he questioned if Jak was intentionally—or, more likely, unintentionally—using that emotion to manipulate him. Malek didn't think he was susceptible to that, but those with less seasoned minds might be. Maybe Yidar was right that Malek had vastly underreported what Jak was capable of and how much of a threat he might one day be.

A problem to mull over later. Malek returned with his skyboard and leaped over the railing.

Jak sat in the cabin's lone chair, trying to focus on finishing drawing the map, but his mind refused to stop conjuring images of Tezi being tortured by General Tonovan. Malek had said he would go get her, and he might already have departed from the ship, but Jak had heard a woman's scream and worried it was too late. Even if Malek reached Tonovan's ship in time, would he be able to pry Tezi away?

Several times when he'd been aboard the *Star Flyer* last, Jak had seen Tonovan and Malek look like they were on the verge of coming to blows—Malek had even challenged the general to a duel. What if Yidar proved a friend of Tonovan's and was willing to gang up on Malek with him? If they seriously hurt Malek, they might end up in charge of the entire mission and with control over the *Star Flyer* and the artifact. And Jak and his mother.

Uneasy, he frowned over at her. After they'd shared a meal a crewman had brought, she'd started making something similar to

Sorath's pop-bangs, though without the assistance of a blacksmith to create a protective shell, they looked more like wads of chewed gum.

"I should be grateful that they left my ingredients and reactants," she said when she noticed Jak's glance, "and not frustrated that I don't have access to a lab."

Jak tried to put his worries aside and smile. "With as often as we're prisoners here, maybe you should request that Malek install one on his ship for you. Though we're technically guests this time."

"I think in this context a guest is simply a prisoner who surrendered voluntarily."

"I didn't surrender. I reached out and negotiated with him for our protection and safe passage."

"Next time, negotiate with him for a lab too."

"To get that, I might need more to trade than our delightful company."

"Hm." Mother looked toward the porthole.

She'd opened it, and the clicking and chirping of cicadas drifted into their cabin. It had been several minutes since the scream, but Jak didn't know if that meant Tezi was safe. He wished there were a way he could help Malek to make sure he succeeded. Chances were he didn't *need* help, but Jak couldn't get the thought of Yidar and Tonovan working together against him out of his mind. He wished he could hurl powerful lightning across the treetops to slam into them.

Wait, was it possible that he *could*? He was back on the same ship as the portal now.

It hadn't been willing to attack anyone except when it or Jak had been in danger, but maybe he could convince it that Tezi was an ally worth protecting. But even if he could, what was its range? Far enough to shoot lightning back to another ship trailing at a distance?

Jak pictured the portal up on the deck and reached out to it with his mind. In the past, he'd found it easiest to communicate with it when he touched it, but the artifact *had* shared visions with him in dreams from afar. The same night it had done that, he had asked it questions telepathically, and it had answered with pulses of light.

Hello, portal, he attempted to speak with it. *Are you awake?*

He rolled his eyes at himself. It was an artifact, not a person, and as far as he knew, it didn't understand his language. If it understood any language at all, it would be that of the dragons who'd built it.

Still, he received a response. Not words, but a pulse of awareness, followed by a hopeful sharing of the pool and the waterfall with itself set up beside them.

Yes. We're on our way there now. Jak thought of the map and the ship flying in that direction. *But I was wondering if you could help me with something. There's a ship behind us.* He formed a vision in his mind to accompany the words. *One of our allies is a prisoner on it and is in danger.*

Jak doubted the artifact had interacted with Tezi and would consider her an ally, but with images, he tried to convey that *he* thought she was an ally, and since he was an ally of the artifact's, he would appreciate it if it would help free her.

The door opened with a bang, and Jak almost fell out of his chair.

"What are you doing?" Captain Rivlen demanded, a dagger in her hand.

"Nothing." Mother surged to her feet, lifting her open hands and using her body to block the explosives she'd been constructing on her bed.

Rivlen didn't so much as glance at her. Her icy glare locked on to Jak.

Dread swam into his gut as he realized she might have sensed his telepathic communication.

"Nothing? I mean, I'm finishing your map." Jak plucked it off the desk, shifted in his seat, and waved it in the air so she would see it.

"I *sensed* you drawing upon magical power and trying to convince the artifact to attack our people." Rivlen stalked into the cabin, her knuckles tight around the haft of that dagger. It wasn't made from lesser dragon steel, like Malek's weapons, but Jak had no doubt it could cut his throat. "You're not even supposed to *have* magical power. What under the slavemasters' whips is going on?"

Damn it, he hadn't realized that other nearby mages could detect his attempt to communicate with the artifact. The last thing he needed was for more people—people who could *kill* him—to realize he had power. Malek might not care, but he was the only one. Yidar had tried to kill him not once but twice for being a wild one. And Malek had specifically warned Jak to be careful so others wouldn't find out.

"You're a wild one?" Rivlen demanded, glancing at Mother, as if this were her fault.

No, Father was the one who'd given Jak the medallion that he'd worn in his hat for years, the ancient dragon-steel artifact somehow imbuing him with the ability to use magic.

"I think you're mistaken." Jak smiled, attempting to appear affable and powerless, and stood slowly. He held the map out in front of him as if it could shield him. "We're just normal people. But the artifact has communicated with *me* in the past. It was doing so just now. Of course, it's very magical and powerful. Maybe that's what you sensed?"

"I'm not an idiot. I know what I sensed." Rivlen halted two steps from him, eyeing him up and down as if he were some viper who might strike. One she wanted to kill before he could. "Does Lord Malek know? It's clear you're untrained. You can't even pinpoint your telepathic thoughts to who or *what* you want to communicate with."

"Exactly. I'm a complete neophyte. Not a threat, not worth bothering with at all. Do you want your map? I was about to put a legend on it, but it's otherwise done. You might want to have your helmsman alter your course a bit. I think we need to go slightly more to the southwest than our current heading." It was hard to keep smiling as Rivlen kept staring icily at him.

Was she even blinking? This close, he could sense her power coiled in her like a loaded spring. She might not radiate as much pure power as Malek, but she wouldn't need that dagger to kill him.

Maybe Mother realized that too, for she moved to stand next to Jak, to support him. Too bad it would be impossible for either of them to do anything if Rivlen attacked. He remembered the wall of fire she'd cast at the other mageship, turning it into a floating torch.

"Does Lord Malek know?" she repeated, squinting at him.

A faint buzz reverberated in his mind as she scoured his thoughts.

"Yes," Jak said.

He sensed her surprise more with his mind than by reading her face.

"And he doesn't care?" Her surprise turned to incredulity. "And he didn't *kill* you?"

"He knew I'm not a threat."

"Not a threat? That's not what *I* sensed."

"I was just trying to chat with the artifact."

"You were trying to coerce it to attack us."

"Not *you*." Jak shook his head in exasperation. How could she have sensed so much of his message and not gotten all of it? "I wanted it to help Malek against Tonovan. I don't want that bastard to hurt Tezi. Or to hurt Malek. I know they hate each other."

Rivlen squinted at him, the buzz reverberating in his mind again. He didn't try to hide his thoughts, instead letting her see his memory of Malek challenging Tonovan to a duel. But after a moment, he wondered if it was smart to share any of that. He had just met this woman and had no idea if she was loyal to Malek. What if she didn't like him either and would rather see Yidar and Tonovan come out ahead?

"Why would you care about Lord Malek?" Rivlen asked quietly, her eyes still narrowed. She glanced at Mother. "You said yourself that he kidnapped you, that you're not working of your own free will for King Uthari."

"Well, he's..." Jak also looked at Mother, wondering how to explain his feelings for Malek. It was... complicated. "He's been protecting us, and we'd rather he not be killed and that he stay in charge. He's the lesser of two evils."

"He is not *evil* at all," Rivlen snapped. "He is a great zidarr, if not the greatest, and he is honorable and follows their Code like no other."

Even though she looked as pissed as she had been since entering the cabin, Jak released a relieved breath. This was confirmation that Rivlen respected and supported Malek. That should mean that he and Mother would be safe as long as they were under Malek's protection. Beyond that, Jak found it heartening that Malek had at least one supporter aside from his distant king thousands of miles away.

"That's why we would prefer he not lose in a fight against Tonovan and Yidar," Jak said reasonably.

"We've agreed to help Lord Malek set up the portal," Mother added. "We're not your enemies."

"Why did he let you live?" Rivlen's gaze remained locked on Jak. She wasn't willing to let that go. "The Zidarr Code requires that wild ones be killed, *especially* before they can become a threat, and you clearly have the potential to do so, if someone instructs you."

Clearly? Jak wished he knew why they all believed that. He couldn't do *anything* useful. If he could, he wouldn't have to beg an artifact for assistance.

"Does King Uthari know about your power?" Rivlen asked.

"Yes. I know they've discussed me. And I'm not sure why they're letting me live, other than that they need my mother's help. Tonovan already killed her good friend. They probably know there's no way she would keep helping if they killed me too."

Mother nodded firmly and rested her hand on Jak's shoulder. She eyed the dagger, though Rivlen had lowered it to her side.

Jak expected Rivlen to point out that she or Malek or any other mage on the ship could *force* Mother to help, no matter who she lost.

"Tonovan is an ass," was what Rivlen said. "Lord Malek went to get your friend back."

"I'm glad," Jak said.

"He doesn't need *your* assistance for that. Do not attempt to communicate with the portal again, not when your ignorance of telepathy makes you fling your messages all over the ship."

"All right. What's the secret to making them pinpoint?"

Rivlen opened her mouth, but she caught herself before replying, and scowled at him. "I will not teach a wild one. That is even more forbidden than letting one live. Why Lord Malek is risking himself for you, I can't imagine."

"Because I'm charming, a hard worker, and I have a sunny disposition." Jak beamed a smile at her, though he had a higher probability of melting a glacier with his warmth than this frosty woman.

"You're trouble."

"Yes, that too."

"Maybe Uthari wants to use you somehow." Rivlen sheathed her dagger and took the paper from him.

"Yes, to draw maps. I'm sure he could use a court cartographer."

Rivlen gave him another scathing look and stalked out the door.

"I didn't get a chance to add the legend," Jak called after her.

Without replying, she slammed the door shut.

"I think she's warming up to me." He looked at Mother. "What do you think?"

"That you have a better shot with Tezi." She looked out the porthole.

After enduring who knew what torment at the hands of these people, Tezi wouldn't want anything to do with Jak either. He would have to wait for some future day when his world returned to normal to ask a girl to have drinks with him. He looked sadly out the porthole. Would that ever happen?

14

THE *TEMPEST* THUNKED DOWN ON THE BEACH WITH A JOLT, NOT crashing, the captain assured the crew, but giving in to the need for a forced landing. *Very* forced, if the smoke wafting from the damaged engine was any indicator. Fortunately, some magic braced the hull so it didn't tip over.

Thorn Company and the mage crew had done their best to keep the enemy busy, but in the end, they'd all been too exhausted, and the *Tempest* had taken too much damage. Uthari's ships had escaped inland, the prized portal in their clutches.

Sasko's chest ached, but she was faring better than other mercenaries and several mages who had been injured in the battle, and she resented being left in an out-of-the-way corner of the deck with them. Ferroki had promised her duty was *keeping an eye on them* while Dr. Fret tended wounds, but Sasko knew she'd been relegated to the sick list.

Elsewhere, bangs and thumps sounded as the crew did repairs, pulling in mercenaries to help whenever "sense-dead humans would do." As far as Sasko could tell, that was when holding tools and fetching water were required.

"As long as we're on land," Sergeant Words said from beside Sasko, "is there any chance they'll let us amble over to the city for a drink from the pub, a gastronomically superior meal from an eating house, and a massage from a nubile young man with rippling muscles?"

"Can men be nubile?" Sasko usually trusted Words to be an expert in vocabulary usage, but she hadn't heard that adjective used to describe muscled men.

"The kind I like can be." Words winked.

"A mage tried to blow your leg off." Dr. Fret was bandaging that leg, the pungent vapors of one of her healing creams forming a cloud in the air around their impromptu sickbay. "You're not ambling anywhere for a while."

"He *tried*, but he was unsuccessful. I am certain that under the balm of your superior treatment, I'll soon be fully ambulatory. In the meantime, Lieutenant Sasko can carry me to the port for the enjoyments. She's barely injured. That mage didn't even blow her shirt off."

"That mage was Lord Malek, and I'm lucky I didn't fly over the railing to my death." Sasko touched her tender chest.

"Do you want me to rub cream on it?" Fret poked through a bag that held as many balls of yarn and knitting needles as medical appurtenances and hefted a fresh tub of the gunk that had been leaving a pall in the air.

"No." Sasko lowered her hand. "Tinder might get jealous and threaten to blow me up."

"Because your bare chest will so entice me?"

"Obviously. I wouldn't want to be responsible for breaking you two up."

"Your thoughtfulness knows no bounds."

"It's why I'm second-in-command."

Lieutenant Vinjo ambled past, the grease that had been on his uniform before having extended to smear his face and hands. He was still carrying his toolbox and had a harried expression on his face—Sasko had seen Night Wrath bellowing at him earlier as he ran about, directing and participating in repairs. That didn't keep him from pausing when he drew even with their group.

"Greetings, alluring female mercenaries. How did my portable thaumaturge-defier bulwark work?"

"Your what?" Sasko asked.

Vinjo pointed to the still-erect magical fabric wall. Earlier, Ferroki had tried to refold it, but she hadn't been able to figure out how. They would need it again for the next battle anyway. From what Sasko had heard, as soon as they repaired the *Tempest*, they were going after Uthari's ships to try to get the artifact back. Night Wrath had been livid when he'd found out Malek had gotten the best of them.

"The shield?" Sasko said when nobody else answered, aside from rolling their eyes at each other after the *alluring* comment. "A fireball bounced off it instead of incinerating it."

"That is the desired effect." Vinjo winked at her. "It keeps those crouching behind it from being incinerated as well. I invent things to help terrene humans who can't protect themselves with their own magic."

"You do?" Fret asked curiously. "That's unusual."

"What you mean to ask is *why*. And what's in it for him?" Sasko didn't want to encourage the mechanic to stick around. He was one of the mage crew, and if he deigned to talk to them, it was because he wanted something. And when he winked at her, she knew exactly what he wanted.

"Money, of course." Vinjo bowed. "Please tell your captain that I can mass produce the bulwarks and will give her the heavily-taxed-and-impoverished-terrene-human discount. I understand what it is to be poor, you see. Since I dreadfully failed to be accepted into the zidarr training program, made worse by having an older brother who was welcomed in and promised great honor for the family, my father disowned me. I've no access whatsoever to the family fortune. I'm on my own, and it's not easy to make enough to live the life to which one of my stature is accustomed."

Sasko eyed his rumpled uniform and grease stains. "Your military pay doesn't get you a nice pigsty in Zarlesh?"

"Indeed not. Have you *seen* the rents in our fine city? Dreadfully high. And since I have a vast tool collection and numerous projects in the works, I require a chicken coop *and* a pigsty."

Captain Myroth yelled at Vinjo from across the deck. Vinjo turned to yell that he couldn't get started on the engine until it cooled off.

Dr. Fret nudged Sasko. "I think he's flirting with you."

"I know. I'm trying to put a stop to it."

"Why? I've heard mage lovers can be appealing." Fret lowered her voice to a whisper. "They can use their magic to make areas deep in your lady garden tingle."

"Doesn't Sergeant Tinder do that for you with her explosives?"

"I don't allow her to apply those to my lady garden. Are you sure you don't want me to rub cream on your chest? To ensure painful and ugly bruises don't form?"

"That sounds like a stupendous idea." Vinjo had turned back in time to hear the part about bruises. Hopefully, nothing else. "Do you need assistance? I have excellent hands. I can heal the housing of a *tyronda* engine in under three minutes. There may even be tingling." Damn, he'd heard about more than the bruises.

"For the engine or for you?" Sasko asked.

"Well, *I* certainly enjoy it."

Fret, Words, and the six other people in their sickbay area, including two mages Sasko didn't know, were watching this exchange with fascination. She made a shooing motion at Vinjo. While this attention might be better than what she usually received from mages—orders to drop to her knees and acknowledge their superiority—she wasn't interested in him.

"You can go now," she said. "I hear your captain begging you to make his engines tingle."

"I have no doubt of that. But you *will* tell your Captain Ferroki about the deal I'm offering, won't you? Six bulwarks for... two hundred gold oronis. Is that less than my brother paid your company? I don't want to bankrupt you, but my devices are magnificent and well worth the money. I'll be happy to throw in sex as a bonus, and I won't even draw back in alarm at bruises or scars. One expects warrior women to be so adorned."

"No. Nobody wants anything from you. Shoo."

"We actually *should* tell the captain that we could get more of the shield things, shouldn't we?" Fret asked.

"Yes," Vinjo said as Sasko shook her head. "And they're called portable thaumaturge-defier bulwarks."

Words raised the finger. "I could be interested in sex with a mage engineer. Are you good at massages? And nubile under your uniform?"

"I am indeed nubile in a manly and masculine way. My offer of sex is only for Lieutenant Sasko though. She delighted me during the meeting with Captain Myroth."

"I didn't even talk to you."

"That's typical with women, but I meant the part where you envisioned pencils lodging themselves in Captain Myroth's nose. Since I have often entertained similar fantasies, I was smitten that we had this common interest."

Ferroki walked up, thankfully providing a distraction, so Sasko didn't feel compelled to respond to Vinjo.

"Captain," Sasko blurted with more enthusiasm than necessary. "Do you have orders? Do you need me for anything?" Sasko winced as she pushed herself to her feet, her chest aching at the movement. Maybe she would take some of Fret's cream after all.

"Just to keep an eye on things," Ferroki said, her face grim. "I've been ordered to step off the *Tempest* for a talk with Captain

Myroth and Night Wrath. They spotted roamer ships nearby, probably thinking to come in and loot the *Dauntless* before it could be repaired and lift into the sky again, and they want to recruit the pirates. Hundreds of them. They want me to help and expect me to take command of them unless we can find Sorath. I also need to round up our search parties. Night Wrath isn't worried about retrieving the archaeologists now, not until they get the artifact itself back."

"Uh," Sasko said. "That's a lot of roamers. Do you think you'll succeed in getting them to take orders from you?"

"No. They might follow Sorath, if we can find him, but I think he might have left the roamers a long time ago, and they're not known to like those who abandon their ways."

"So, this mission is about to get even more fraught," Words said.

"Captain Ferroki." Vinjo hadn't obeyed Sasko's wishes and *shooed*. "Would you like to purchase six portable thaumaturge-defier bulwarks including one that was slightly used in our last battle?" He pointed to the fabric shield they'd employed. "As you can see, it's still in good shape."

"How much?" Ferroki asked without missing a beat.

Sasko shook her head, not trusting the mechanic as far as she could kick his toolbox. If he tried to betray them, she vowed to take that wrench and shove it into one of his favorite orifices.

"A steal at two hundred oronis." Vinjo touched his chest. "And I've agreed to throw in sex with your lieutenant."

"Fifty, and no sex unless she wishes it."

"*Fifty?* Captain, the raw materials cost more than that, and of *course* I would not give myself in a manly manner to Lieutenant Sasko unless she wishes it. I'm not one of *those* types of mages. But I have much to offer, and my services are desired by many, so when I offer myself along with my glorious tools, I assure you it increases the value of my proposal immensely."

Ferroki looked over at the device. Other than the magic that held it together, it didn't look like more than a tarp.

"Didn't you take the materials from the ship's stores without asking permission from your captain?" Ferroki asked.

Vinjo blinked. "That's amazing, Captain. I didn't think terrene humans could read minds. How fascinating. For the record, I did ask. While he was in his cups and not paying attention."

"The ideal time," Ferroki murmured.

"Naturally. Eighty oronis, optional sex, and your doctor will throw in cream that I can rub on injured comrades." He bowed to Sasko.

"What's the fascination with my lieutenant?" Ferroki asked.

"She has terribly irreverent thoughts. Just a moment ago, I caught her imagining doing vile things with my wrench and my orifices."

Sasko closed her eyes and let her head thunk back against the railing.

"And you like that?" Ferroki sounded more bemused than appalled.

Later, Sasko would have words with her.

"Naturally," Vinjo said. "I'm *also* irreverent. You probably didn't notice since my work is sublime and distracts a person from what's coming out of my mouth."

"I noticed," Ferroki said.

"Oh? You're a perceptive mercenary then. I agree to fifty oronis for my fine devices."

"And no cream and no sex."

"You said *optional* sex." Vinjo beamed a smile at Sasko. "Not no sex."

"Fine," Ferroki said. "Optional sex. *Her* option."

"Yes, of course. And done." Vinjo clasped her hand, bowed, and started to say more, but Captain Myroth bellowed at him to finish the repairs. "I'll deliver them later," he promised and took off.

"I need to go too." Ferroki visibly braced herself as she gazed over the railing to where the masts of sailing ships were now visible anchored off the shoreline.

"I'd wish you luck, Captain," Sasko said, "but I think you just set me up on a date with an idiot."

"An optional date." Ferroki's smile was fleeting before she headed off.

"Roamer pirates." Words shook her head. "Not only are they unlikely to be nubile, but they could be as eager to kill us as Uthari's mages."

"Pirates," someone else said. "They'll kill us in our sleep instead of casting magic at us to our faces. I don't like anything that's going on here today."

"I'm moderately entertained by the lieutenant's allure winning her a mage engineer," Words said, "but I otherwise agree."

"I think he's just a mechanic," Sasko muttered.

"What's the difference between a mechanic and an engineer?" someone asked.

Words opened her mouth, probably to deliver a dictionary definition.

Sasko replied first, "The amount of grease on his face."

"Ah."

Malek wrapped his camouflaging magic around himself as he flew over the jungle, his skyboard supporting his weight. The lights of the *King's Courage* were visible ahead, but he wanted to check the enemy ship before confronting Tonovan and possibly becoming embroiled in a battle with his allies.

The battered vessel dangled sideways where it was caught

among several trees, the survivors scrambling as they tried to levitate each other down and figure out how to get out of their predicament. Their ship would take time to repair and shouldn't be a threat.

Malek adjusted course and let himself focus on the *Courage*. As he flew closer, he spotted Tonovan right away. He was up on the forecastle, lamps burning along the railing, illuminating him with his trousers sagging as he pinned down a naked young woman. A bottle of wine and goblets rested nearby, as if this were a *picnic*.

Fury at this flagrant dereliction of military professionalism flared in Malek almost as greatly as anger at the treatment of the prisoner. If the mages from the enemy ship *had* been less preoccupied, they were still close enough that they could have attacked. Anyone could have blasted a fireball at Tonovan, who was too distracted by his lust to have his defenses up.

Two soldiers knelt to either side of him, helping to keep the girl pinned and looking like they expected a turn afterward. The rest of the visible crewmen were doing their best to ignore the situation, though none stepped forward to try to stop it. None dared to interrupt the highest-ranking officer in the fleet, a man who should have been a role model to them, not an example of what they could get away with if they grew powerful enough.

As Malek flew closer, urging his skyboard to top speed, he was tempted to hurl a fireball and incinerate Tonovan and his helpers, but Uthari would be furious. During a time of peace, Malek might have gotten away with killing Tonovan, but the kingdom couldn't afford to lose high-ranking officers now. Worse, Malek needed Tonovan's help to fulfill his mission, to keep away further enemy ships that would try to catch the *Star Flyer* and take back the artifact. As much as it grated, Malek would have to be tactful about how he handled this.

But first, he would stop the poor girl's torment. He lifted a hand, intending to knock all three men away from her, but the

Courage lurched as it bumped a tree that grew higher than the surrounding canopy. Maybe the helmsman was getting drunk as well.

The jolt to the ship caused Tonovan to pause and lift his head. It was enough for Malek to see the woman underneath him and confirm that it was the blonde mercenary Jak and Jadora wanted rescued. He didn't know if he'd arrived soon enough to keep Tonovan from raping her, but he was surprised to notice a glint of metal in her hand. Had she gotten a *knife* somehow? From one of the guards? Too engrossed in their fantasies, neither had looked up at the jolt. They were staring at the woman's breasts, not the blade she hid with her hand.

As the ship sailed toward more tall trees, inspiration struck Malek.

The helmsman saw the threat this time and tried to navigate around them, but Malek reached out with his magic toward the jungle. He was no druid who knew how to use his power to make plants grow, but they were tall trees with enough flexibility to survive windstorms. He coaxed them to lean to the side, putting them into the ship's path again. The helmsman had been eating and drinking alcohol and not giving his full attention to his task, so it didn't take much for Malek to nudge his mind from wakefulness into sleep. His hand slumped away from the wheel.

When the mageship struck the trees, more than a jolt ran through it. Its defenders, believing their enemies vanquished, hadn't been keeping a barrier up, so the trunks and branches battered the hull. They wouldn't do serious damage to the sturdy material, but the collision knocked people off their feet and caused a tremendous scraping and wrenching sound that was likely heard back at the *Star Flyer*.

Even Tonovan pitched forward, falling across his prisoner. She must have been caught by surprise from the noise and jolt as well, but she reacted more quickly than the men around her. As

Tonovan planted his hands and pushed himself up, she struck with the speed of a viper. She stabbed the knife into his eye.

Tonovan jerked back, reacting quickly enough to keep it from plunging into his brain, but blood spattered onto her, so Malek knew he'd been wounded. Tonovan roared in pain and lashed out with his magic, an angry burst rather than a precise one. The guards, as well as the woman, flew into the air, tumbling all the way to the railing. One of the guards struck so hard that he crashed through it. He flailed and caught a post before falling off the ship.

Malek navigated the skyboard around the forecastle to come in from behind Tonovan, so his rival wouldn't find it suspicious that he'd arrived from another direction than the *Star Flyer*. No need for the general to believe that anything except his own people's ineptitude had put him in this predicament.

It only took Malek a few seconds to fly around to that side of the ship and jump off his skyboard behind Tonovan, and he'd assumed he would have time to protect the woman from retaliation, but she wasn't on the forecastle anymore. She must have jumped down to the main deck and run belowdecks to hide.

Tonovan was still there, clutching his eye and roaring at the night in pain and fury. His wine bottle and goblets had fallen, the dark red liquid almost matching the nearby blood droplets. The other soldier helped his colleague back onto the deck, and they collapsed against each other, panting and looking warily at Tonovan.

"General," Malek said, walking toward him with his skyboard under his arm.

Tonovan whirled toward him, blood dripping between his fingers.

"*Malek*," he snarled, far more furious than pleased at seeing him.

"You're injured." Malek looked from him to the jungle, in the direction of the enemy ship, though it was miles back by now. He thought about asking if one of Zaruk's mages had struck him, but he had no thespian training, and even if Tonovan deserved this fate, Malek was reluctant to outright lie about the role he'd played. He already doubted himself for using trickery instead of approaching Tonovan in a straightforward manner. It had been cowardly, a way to avoid a confrontation.

"No shit, I'm injured." Tonovan screamed with rage and pulled his hand down to look at the blood and gore.

Huh. The girl had taken out his eye. Good aim.

Malek might be able to heal the organ, but he wasn't sure. That was more complicated than healing flesh and muscle.

"Where did that bitch go?" Tonovan demanded, peering around the forecastle with his remaining eye. His gaze landed on the soldiers. "Go get her, you idiots. She *dared* attack a wizard. She'll pay dearly for that *gall*."

Surprisingly, the soldiers didn't spring immediately to obey. They looked at each other and glanced toward the broken railing.

Tonovan, already focused on Malek again, didn't seem to notice. An uneasy feeling formed in the pit of Malek's stomach. Maybe she *hadn't* fled belowdecks to hide.

"What are you *doing* here?" Tonovan demanded.

This was Malek's chance to confess, but Tonovan was so enraged that he would likely spring upon Malek if he learned the truth. Malek was prepared to defend himself, or duel the general to the death if needed, but if they ended up killing each other, what of the mission? Only Yidar would remain to carry out Uthari's orders, and he knew little of the artifact and nothing of the plant. And what of Jak and Jadora? Malek could not protect them if he was dead.

"I am here to check in on you, to see if you need anything, and to thank you for keeping Zaruk's troops occupied while we slipped in and got the artifact." The subterfuge would have to continue, at

least for now. Later, Malek could confess, and they could duel if
Tonovan wished it.

"See if we *need* anything? I need my damned eye fixed up. And
I need someone to bring that conniving prisoner to me."

"Calm down, General." Malek stepped in front of him. "I can
heal you, inasmuch as is possible."

"Inasmuch as is possible. What does *that* mean?"

Malek, realizing that Tonovan might not yet know that she'd
stabbed clean through the eye, created the illusion of a mirror in
the air in front of him. It was enough to reflect his bloody face
back at him so he could see the truth. Tonovan gaped in shock,
then roared into the night again.

"Can you fix it?" A note of desperation replaced the fury, and
Tonovan started shaking, the truth sinking in. He was familiar
with battlefield injuries and knew what magic could and could
not fix.

"It is unlikely I can repair your eye, but I can heal the wound
and take away the pain."

Tonovan's lips rippled with displeasure.

"You have a doctor aboard, do you not? Perhaps you wish to
see him instead."

"No, just do it. Your magic is more powerful than his. I know
that. As soon as it's done, I'll find my prisoner and punish her."
Tonovan glanced at his men, saw they hadn't produced her yet,
and roared, "Why haven't you found her and brought her to my
feet yet?"

"Uhm, sir? She jumped over the railing."

Malek kept from cursing aloud. He had been afraid of that.

Tonovan swore and stomped around the deck like a toddler
having a tantrum.

Malek halted him and gripped both sides of his head, so he
could study and heal the injury, even if Tonovan deserved to be in
pain for a while. Taking his eye had been a fitting punishment, but

Malek wished the woman hadn't jumped to her death afterward. Again, he regretted not handling this in a straightforward manner.

"There may be more enemy ships coming," Malek said as he healed the damaged eye. "Will you be able to continue to work?"

"Of course I can continue. I don't need my eyes to obliterate my enemies with magic." Tonovan's body shook with anger as much as acceptance. He clearly longed for *someone* to obliterate. "Do you think the girl could have survived jumping?" He sounded like he still wanted to punish her. "She's just a terrene. I can't sense her and tell whether she's alive or not."

"It's three hundred feet to the ground," Malek said. "She won't have survived."

"She better have died painfully."

"You're a bastard, Tonovan."

"Shut your noble hole, and heal my face."

"I'm working on it." Malek kept his features impassive, not allowing himself to show any sign that he believed Tonovan had gotten what he'd deserved. If he appeared smug, Tonovan would grow suspicious.

Malek worked as quickly as he could, wanting to fly down and check on the prisoner. He doubted he'd lied to Tonovan about her surviving, but there was a chance she'd caught in a branch and hadn't fallen all the way to the ground. Jak and Jadora would be disappointed if she was dead, and that bothered him. It bothered him that he'd failed to anticipate her reaction and stop it.

"I'm done." Malek lowered his hand.

"Good." Tonovan stomped off the forecastle and headed to his cabin. Maybe to check the damage in a real mirror. So long as he was back on deck by the time more ships caught up with them.

The two soldiers who'd been a part of all this stood in rigid attention poses, watching Malek warily. Not certain if they were dismissed?

"Unfortunately, not all officers behave professionally and

demonstrate proper moral conduct," he told them. They didn't have a Zidarr Code, but Uthari's militia had *some* standards of appropriate behavior. "You should avoid such men inasmuch as is possible and always seek to act honorably yourselves. Your actions and choices reflect on you, your families, and your unit."

"Yes, my lord."

Malek didn't know if the words meant anything to them, but he had no interest in spending more time lecturing them. He hopped on his skyboard and flew away from the *Courage*, wrapping himself in camouflage so they wouldn't know he was speeding back to the spot where the prisoner had gone over the side.

Since he hadn't seen her jump, he had to guess at the location based on how much time had passed and how fast the ship was flying. The darkness and dense foliage didn't help. A crashing ship would have broken numerous branches and left evidence of its passage, but a single person might have slipped through, barely stirring a leaf.

As he reached out with his senses, trying to pick out a human from among the myriad reptiles, mammals, and birds down there, he noticed a magical signature. That was surprising, since they'd traveled nearly a hundred miles from the coast and Port Toh-drom by now and seen little evidence of inland settlements.

The signature emanated druid magic, something he'd encountered only occasionally in the past. Druids were few and far between in Uthari's kingdom and most of the civilized world. The ones he had met before had made it clear they held no love for zidarr or their wizard rulers, so he'd never had a reason to seek them out.

The druid magic had nothing to do with the prisoner, so Malek made himself ignore it as he flew below the canopy and sought sign of her. He made a sphere of light to float among the branches, hoping his eyes might spot what he couldn't find with magic.

A bat squeaked and flapped away.

Something glinted, reflecting the yellow of his light. Metal in the wilds?

Malek flew closer. He spotted a broken branch and looked for torn clothing that might prove she'd been the one to break it before remembering she had been naked. As if being stranded in the jungle wasn't bad enough.

The glint came again. There. It was the knife she'd used to stab Tonovan, the edge sunken an inch into a branch. She must have hit her arm as she fell and lost her grip on the weapon. It also could have flown out of her hand as soon as she jumped from the ship, but either way, Malek was in her vicinity.

He peered toward the ground, expecting to see her broken body sprawled below, but the numerous layers of leaves made it impossible to see that far. He navigated them like a maze, making his way lower. There were more broken branches along the way, but when he reached the undergrowth below, her body wasn't anywhere in sight.

He poked around, thinking the foliage thick enough to hide it, until he spotted a trail. It wound through the undergrowth, the earth damp enough to show fresh footprints. Fresh *human* footprints.

Malek turned slowly around, his gaze drawn in the direction where he sensed the druid magic. He rode that way, guessing he would find one of the ubiquitous stone monuments that proliferated Zewnath. The trail also headed in that direction.

Four massive stone slabs leaned against each other, their surfaces engraved with hundreds, or maybe thousands, of runes. Interestingly, the surfaces were free of dirt, and no vines or other foliage snaked up the monument. Given how fast everything grew here, that meant someone tended the area regularly.

The monument rested in a cleared circle of river rocks, the trail ending at it. Four benches faced the slabs from what might have been the cardinal points. He half-expected to find the woman lying on one of them, but they were empty, and he neither saw nor sensed anyone around.

As Malek stood on his skyboard a few feet above the ground, he gripped his chin. As far as he could tell, there wasn't a door or tunnel entrance or anywhere a person could have *gone*. If someone with magical ability were nearby in the jungle, Malek should have been able to sense them, but whoever had made those footprints —and collected the prisoner?—had disappeared.

"Hello?" he called in Dhoran.

He didn't know any of the languages of Zewnath, so he wouldn't be able to communicate even if someone *did* step out of the trees to speak with him. But nobody answered.

Malek flew around the area, looking for evidence of a domicile or sanctuary, but the trails that led away from the monument soon ended, one at a pool surrounded by croaking frogs and the other at a salt lick. There wasn't magic anywhere else except at the monument.

He flew back up to the canopy, so he could return to the *Star Flyer*. Though he believed the prisoner was dead, that she couldn't have survived that fall, he would ask if Jak and Jadora wanted to come back here to see if they could, with their archaeological knowledge, figure out if there was an entrance to a secret sanctuary.

15

Night had grown deep by the time Sorath walked the three miles up the beach, hoping to rejoin the mercenaries, though he worried he was too late for that. Before leaving the city, he'd hunted around and found the druid monument Jak had mentioned. He'd scoured it until he found a map, one that showed a tiny ring that might represent the former resting place of the ancient portal—and the place where it needed to be erected once again in order to work. He'd tucked the information away, not sure if he wanted to volunteer it to Zaruk's people or not.

When Sorath had left the mageships, the *Dauntless* had been the vessel crashed on the beach, the crew working at repairing it. Now, it floated in the air off the coast, and one of the blue-hulled ships rested in the sand, repairs underway. Another of Zaruk's ships floated alongside the *Dauntless*. It looked like a new arrival.

In addition to the mageships, three sailing vessels were anchored beyond the waves, and at least a hundred brown-skinned warriors milled on the beach, wearing a mixture of leather and mesh clothing and carrying weapons ranging from spiked clubs to cudgels to black-powder pistols.

Before seeing them, Sorath's main concern had been how he would tell Ferroki that he'd lost Tezi. Now, he had another concern.

Most roamers were independent spirits who sailed the seas and minded their own business, refusing to be integrated into any wizard's kingdom, but enough were notorious pirates that it led outsiders to suspect *all* roamers of being cutthroats and thieves. Sorath knew better... but he also knew how to spot the type, and these were the type.

What were they doing *here*?

Sorath spotted Ferroki on the beach with the black-clad Night Wrath and a gray-haired man in a blue uniform with captain's rank markings. The trio stood shoulder to shoulder facing the large group of roamers.

Sorath rested his hand on his pistol as he approached and held his pickaxe arm away from his body so it would be visible.

It had been years since he'd interacted with any roamers, but he had little doubt they would recognize him as sharing their blood. Most of them shared his tall, muscular build, as well as his brown skin and black hair, but that was where the similarities ended. Since his mother had left their kind when he'd been little, all he knew of their culture and language he'd learned from her. Every time he'd crossed paths with roamers in the past, they'd accused him of being a traitor for not living among his own kind. They never cared that he'd had little choice in the matter, but he didn't resent his mother for that. She'd wanted him to grow up on land, going to a kingdom school and learning about more than fishing and sailing and the sea.

Ferroki spotted Sorath and waved. She didn't appear to be in danger, but her wave seemed one of relief as well as welcome.

Several of the roamers eyed Sorath as he skirted them to join Ferroki.

"Nice of you to return, Colonel," Night Wrath said. "Did you have a nice leisurely nap in the city?"

"Under a collapsed stable, yes." Sorath flexed his shoulders, frowning at the aches that came from all over his body. The root the professor had given him to gnaw had dulled the pain, and she'd bandaged the worst of his injuries, but it would be days before he could easily go into battle again.

Days he might not have. Judging by the number of crewmen working on the ship, the captain wanted it in the air again soon.

"Captain Ferroki," Sorath said before the zidarr could speak again, "I'm afraid I have bad news."

"You didn't find the archaeologists?" Ferroki asked. "Our search parties are back and reported the same thing. It's surprising those two were able to evade everyone, but we have a new mission."

"Getting this ship back into the sky and getting the artifact back. We have allies on the way, and we're hiring more fighters." Night Wrath pointed at the roamers.

Sorath had been afraid it would be something like that. Who would those roamers take orders from?

"I did find Jak and Jadora, but Uthari's younger zidarr showed up at the same time. Tezi and I tried to keep him from getting them, and we succeeded, but then Malek arrived and took them up to his ship." Sorath took a deep breath. "And the younger zidarr got Tezi."

"Got?" Ferroki mouthed. "Killed?"

"Took prisoner. I... don't know if she's alive or dead now. It was hours ago."

Ferroki's shoulders sagged.

"She's theirs now then, body and mind. You won't get her back." Night Wrath didn't sound like he cared, though he narrowed his eyes and added, "Did she have any mission-critical information?"

"*We* don't even have any mission-critical information." Sorath touched his chest, though that probably wasn't true. He knew more about the artifact than the other mercenaries and probably most of Zaruk's people. And now that he'd seen that map, he might know *more* than they did.

Ferroki shook her head. "She's our rookie. Our youngest and—"

"A killer of mages," Night Wrath said coldly. "Yidar will see that in her thoughts and kill her after he questions her. It's what she deserves."

Ferroki clenched her jaw to keep from protesting that, but her eyes burned with fire. Sorath understood perfectly, but he held a hand up to keep her from getting herself into trouble. When their eyes met, he tried to convey that he would help her get Tezi away from them if he could.

But how? He eyed the damaged ship. "How far ahead are Uthari's ships? Do you know where they're going?"

"Not exactly," Night Wrath said, "but I can find them."

"Do you have a better plan for defeating their ships this time? It appears the last battle didn't go well."

Night Wrath and the ship's captain glared at him.

"The plan has to be more than to fly up and attack them openly," Sorath said, accustomed to mages glaring at him. "Catapulting hordes of roamers at their ships won't be enough."

"We also plan to catapult mercenaries," Night Wrath said.

"That plan is as solid as dragon steel. It's sure to work." Especially since they'd already tried an open attack and were now repairing their ship on the beach. Sorath shook his head.

"You have something else in mind?"

Sorath eyed a crewman using magic to repair a hole in the hull of the ship. "Are zidarr too honorable for sabotage?"

"What *kind* of sabotage?"

"I've noticed your people—and presumably theirs—don't keep

magical barriers up around the clock."

"Not if there isn't danger within range, no," Night Wrath said. "It's energy-intensive."

"Maybe you can send a saboteur ahead on one of your ships that doesn't need repairs, someone who can sneak aboard *their* ships. We might have an easier time attacking them successfully if they're crashed in the jungle when we catch up to them." Sorath didn't *know* that was true, especially against Malek, but they would have the advantage if they could maneuver and their enemy couldn't. "Someone good might be able to sabotage all three of their ships, the *Star Flyer*, the *Dread Arrow*, and *King's Courage*."

Sorath smiled at Night Wrath, hoping the zidarr caught that he meant him. He couldn't imagine sending someone less capable to what might be his death. But a zidarr ought to be able to fight his way off a ship if he were caught. Unless he came face-to-face with Malek or Yidar. And if that happened... Night Wrath could get what he deserved for creating the situation that had forced Ferroki to send Tezi away.

Night Wrath glared at him, probably reading his every thought. Sorath didn't care. He wouldn't cry if the mages and zidarr ended up killing each other, though he hoped Ferroki and Thorn Company could avoid going down with them.

"I am a wizard and a warrior," Night Wrath said, "not a saboteur with expertise on how to damage engines."

"You could take your brother with you," the ship's captain said.

"I could send him in my place," Night Wrath said.

"Is he a zidarr with more mechanical aptitude than you?" Sorath asked.

"He is *not* a zidarr. He is a bumbling engineer who invents stupid things and is the disgrace of the family."

"That doesn't sound like someone who should go alone," Sorath said. "You better go together."

"You are not in *charge* here, Colonel," Night Wrath said.

"King Zaruk did want him along to advise," the ship's captain said.

"*Stone Heart* wanted him along to lead the mercenaries," Night Wrath said, "not advise *zidarr*. And now Stone Heart is dead."

"At the hand of the man whose ship I'm inviting you to sabotage," Sorath said. "You should enjoy the chance to avenge your colleague's death. Perhaps you can battle Malek while your engineer breaks their engine."

"That's not an abysmal idea," the ship's captain said. "It would be a simple matter to overpower them and retrieve the artifact if their ships were crashed *and* Malek was dead."

"Yes," Night Wrath said, "I'll challenge him to a duel while my brother rubs his hands on their engine. That will be good for my health."

"You don't think you're a match for him, my lord?"

"I could defeat Yidar in a fair fight."

"The artifact is on Malek's ship," the captain said. "I'm sure King Zaruk would be extremely pleased if you destroyed him and his flagship."

"Of that I have no doubt." Night Wrath shook his head and waved inland. "We don't even know where they're going. They flew into the jungle, not back toward Utharika." Apparently, Night Wrath wasn't positive he could find them after all.

"I know where they're going," Sorath said. "Jak was kind enough to mention a druid monument with a map on it, and I looked at it on my way out of the city. They're taking the portal to where it can be set up and used."

"Can you provide that location to our helmsmen?" the captain asked.

"Of course."

"I'll talk to my brother," Night Wrath said.

"Excellent, my lord. We'll find you two a fast ship to ride on for this mission. Our next battle is sure to go better than the last." The captain jogged off with a spring in his step.

Night Wrath glared at Sorath. "I am aware of your manipulation."

"The mercenary handbook advises us to sow confusion among the enemy through deception and sabotage," Sorath said.

"Deception? Do you want me to lie to Malek while I'm there?"

"I highly recommend it. Perhaps you could start your battle by telling him that his boots are untied."

Night Wrath scoffed and strode off, leaving Ferroki and Sorath on the moonlit beach. The horde of roamers muttering nearby kept any thoughts of romance from his mind, and probably hers too.

"I've met that engineer," Ferroki said quietly. "Unless he's a lot smarter than he acts, I'm concerned about sending him up against Malek and his people."

"My understanding of mageship engines is that they're technologically as well as magically advanced. If this engineer keeps his ship's equipment in good working order, he's probably not dumb. Besides, the plan is for him to sneak in, ideally while everyone is sleeping, not outsmart anyone."

"Let's hope it works. If not, he'll be captured and questioned."

"I don't think anything these people have done, or that they have planned, would impress Malek's people if it were revealed to them."

"Not even the roamer catapulting?"

"Doubtful."

Once Jadora slipped the explosives she'd made into a jacket pocket, she removed her shoes and lay on her bunk. After not sleeping the night before, she needed rest, but she didn't know if she would be able to fall asleep until Malek returned, hopefully with Tezi.

Jak must have had similar thoughts, for he was pacing the cabin. Had Jadora had more energy, she might have done the same. She was worried about him. Too many mages had figured out that he had power. Too many mages who would be happy to see him dead, if not kill him themselves.

"You're agitated," she said. "Do you want me to read to you?"

"Would it be from *The Mind Way*?"

"Are you guessing that because of our limited options for reading material or because you also feel that you need to learn to ratchet down your burgeoning skills to keep potential enemies from realizing you have them?"

"Subtle, Mother."

"I'm worried for you."

"I know." Jak pushed his hands through his hair. "Is there a chapter on that? Hiding burgeoning skills?"

"Chapter Seventeen, 'The Turtle Shell.'"

"Turtles come up a lot in that book."

"The monks admire them."

Someone knocked on the door.

Jadora tensed and rolled to the side to sit up, but she'd already put away everything she'd made. Her pockets bulged uncomfortably, making her long for the days when she'd had a nightgown and more than one set of clothing.

"It's Malek," Jak whispered, spinning toward the door with hope in his eyes.

Her first thought was that he knew it wasn't Captain Rivlen because *she* didn't knock, but she realized Jak could likely sense the auras of the mages—and zidarr.

"Come in," Jadora called, since Malek seemed to be waiting for an invitation. Such a polite captor.

Malek stepped into the cabin carrying two sturdy waxed

canvas backpacks.

Jak peered around him, looking for Tezi.

But Malek's face was grim as he held up a hand. Jak's shoulders slumped, and Jadora's heart ached for him, already certain they'd lost her. She wondered if Sorath and the rest of Thorn Company had made it, or if all the mercenaries had fallen battling Malek, Tonovan, and Yidar.

"I am not certain if she is alive or dead," Malek said. "When I landed on the ship to stop an incident, she sprang over the railing and fell into the jungle. I did not see her jump, or I might have reacted quickly enough to keep her from crashing down. I apologize for being distracted." He bowed not to Jak but to Jadora, as if she would be more aggrieved by this news.

She *was* aggrieved, but since Jak was the one with feelings for Tezi, it would hit him harder.

"But you're not sure she died?" Jak asked. "Did you check for, uhm, her body?"

"I did. Someone, possibly a druid, found her first and took her..." Malek turned a palm toward the ceiling. "Somewhere. I came back to see if you wish to assist me in looking for her. As I said, I do not know if she lived or died, since I could not find her body. Near where she fell, there is a druid monument covered in runes. I couldn't find anyone but spotted fresh footprints, so there may be a secret entrance. Perhaps with your archaeological knowledge, you may locate it more easily than I."

"Oh, absolutely. Mother will be able to decipher it." Jak waved at her. "I'm sure of it!"

Since Jadora only knew one of the modern druid tongues, and the monuments were carved in runes from their ancient language, she was less certain of it. She hadn't had much luck interpreting the runes on the monument in the square. It would be much easier if she had the book she'd used in Uthari's library to translate the symbol on the portal.

"Ah," Malek said, watching her. "I brought that book along."

"You did?" She stared at him. "I hid it so you wouldn't find it."

"I know." He smiled faintly. "I found the symbol in it and also translated it, though the artifact hasn't been giving *me* visions—" he glanced at Jak, "—so I'm not sure it would have helped me locate its home."

That glance seemed to imply there was something special—or peculiar?—about Jak. Jadora wished she hadn't noticed it. Rivlen's belief that he could be powerful was disturbing, not only because so many mages were sworn to get rid of threats but because having access to such power seemed to turn mages into arrogant bastards who thought nothing of stomping all over terrene humans.

Malek's faint smile turned rueful or maybe sad, and Jadora realized she was doing a poor job of hiding her thoughts from him. She and Jak *both* needed to read the turtle chapter.

"The jaguar one is also helpful," Malek said.

"Does it keep people from interrogating you in your dreams?" It wasn't the only question Jadora had for him, nor the most important, but she had been wondering about it.

Malek's eyebrows rose in surprise, though he soon recovered, and his face grew thoughtful. Not bewildered, as if he didn't know what she was talking about.

So, he *had* done it. Questioned her in her sleep somehow. Her subconscious mind hadn't made that up from nothing.

Knowing that made her uneasy, and she wondered if Tonovan might have been telling the truth about the rest.

"I am uncertain if exercises undertaken while awake could strengthen one's mental defenses while asleep," Malek said. "Guarding one's thoughts does become habitual for mages, and some keep their defenses up even during sleep. Others do not. Studies suggest it isn't based on innate power but is a combination of other biological factors."

Jadora didn't care about any of that, only that he'd essentially been interrogating her in her sleep. It had been a far less painful interrogation than anything physical—it hadn't been painful at all—but it had still been an intrusion. It was bad enough he read her mind while they were standing next to each other in the same room. If he could do it from thousands of miles away...

"Why do you need me here at all if you can just pluck the information you need out of my mind whenever you want?" she asked.

"Uhm." Jak looked back and forth between them. "What are we talking about?"

"The dreams I told you about where *he* came to me in my cabin while I was sleeping and demanded to know where we were taking the artifact. It was creepy. And an intrusion." She glared at Malek.

His eyebrows flew up again at the word *creepy*. She couldn't help it. The dreams had unsettled her.

"I apologize," Malek said. "I didn't realize you were experiencing the same dreams. I'm surprised that you were."

"Why? You meant to question me without me knowing it?"

"I had no control over them. They were dreams for me as well."

She shook her head, not believing him. Even if *mages* could somehow be linked and share dreams, there was no evidence to suggest normal human beings could experience that.

"Perhaps we can discuss it later," Malek said.

"In our dreams?" Jadora couldn't keep the words from coming out sarcastically. She was stung and worried anew about Malek and whether this alliance, or whatever it was, had been a good idea.

Jak frowned at her, as if to admonish her. *Her*. As if she were at fault here.

"I would say no," Malek said, a hint of sadness in his eyes that she found puzzling, "but I sleep with my weapons near my bed, so it's a possibility."

"Weapons?" she mouthed, confused.

Malek didn't explain further. He'd been holding the backpacks throughout the conversation, and now he handed one to Jak. He stepped closer to Jadora and offered her the other. She didn't take it, not because she wanted to be difficult, not when Tezi was still in danger, but because she was still trying to figure him out.

The sadness seemed to deepen, and he laid the backpack on her bed and stepped back. "They have food and water and basic medical supplies, as well as room for your belongings, should you wish to give your pockets a break."

"Do we get to keep them?" Jak asked.

"Yes."

"Thank you," he said.

Jadora nodded, accepting that they would be useful, even if Malek flummoxed her. He read her mind, infiltrated her dreams to question her, and might have killed her husband. Was that the reason he treated them better than other mages did? Because he regretted killing Loran? Or out of guilt?

"We need to leave now." Malek pointed toward the corridor without commenting on her thoughts, though it was hard to believe he didn't read them. "The skyboards are fast, but their range is limited. Like your magelock weapons, they need to be charged between uses. More enemy ships are chasing after us with orders to acquire the artifact, so I can't order Captain Rivlen to stop or slow the *Star Flyer*. We need to take the skyboards, search quickly, and return before the ship is out of range."

Jadora fought back a yawn and the urge to look longingly at the bed. It was worth giving up sleep again if there was a chance of finding Tezi. If she met Sorath and Thorn Company again, she would love to give them their rookie back.

"I'm ready." Jadora peeked into the bag to see how much room it had for her supplies and was surprised at how spacious it was. And was that a clean change of clothing? It was a military uniform without rank—far from her preferred style—but it looked like a woman's uniform, so it might fit. And there were even pockets. The outside of the backpack was full of extra pockets too. So many that it reminded her of Sergeant Tinder's bandolier for grenades.

Jadora avoided looking at Malek as she struggled to keep gratitude from seeping into her thoughts. He was not an ally, she told herself, and not any better than the rest of them. If he'd killed her husband, he might be the worst of all of them.

"Uhm." Jak's voice had an odd note, and he looked at Malek with atypical wariness. "Why is Mother's bag magical? Is it... so you can track her?"

Jadora looked sharply at Malek.

"No." Malek lifted a shoulder. "It *would* be easier for me to track, because it's magical, but I wove craft power into the fabric to make it stronger than typical and also give it more space than it should have based on its physical dimensions."

Jadora looked inside the pack again. She'd *thought* it had appeared extra spacious.

"Oh." The wary suspicion faded from Jak's eyes, though he looked a little disappointed in his own pack now. "Not to sound unappreciative, because I'm not, but how come *I* don't get a magic bag?"

"I didn't have time to make two, and your mother needs room for all of the explosives she's been down here making."

When Malek looked over at her, an eyebrow raised, Jadora felt heat rise to her cheeks, but he didn't say more, simply gesturing for her to follow him into the corridor.

Not wanting to delay finding Tezi, Jadora hurried out after him.

"If I make some explosives," Jak said, trailing them into the corridor, "can I get a magical backpack later?"

"No." Malek led the way to his cabin. "It's an effort to make them, especially for someone with as meager of crafting skills as I have, and your pencils don't take up that much room."

If not for everything else hanging in the air between them, Jadora might have been touched that he'd made the effort for her, especially since they were short on time. Actually, if they were short on time, it was shocking that he'd done it. Unless... had he started it for her earlier? Again, the urge to feel gratitude crept over her, but she reminded herself that guilt might be his motivation for doing nice things for her. What other reason could there be?

Malek looked back at her, as if in response to her thought, but once again, he didn't comment. Was silence acceptance? She hated to think she'd guessed the truth, but it all made too much sense.

They reached his cabin, and he stepped inside long enough to grab the ancient-languages book.

"I could get bigger pencils," Jak said, still dwelling on the difference in their backpacks.

"Drop it." Jadora was in no mood for humor.

"Sorry," Jak whispered as they followed Malek through the spacious hold and up the steps without rails. "I have bag envy."

They stepped through the hatchway and found Captain Rivlen waiting. She eyed Jak, having heard the comment, but only snapped a salute to Malek.

"Continue on course," he told her. "We should be back soon, but if we don't make it, locate the pool on the map, lower the artifact down, and set it up."

"Will it be... self-activating?" Rivlen asked.

"Doubtful," Malek said as Jadora shook her head.

"Then, with all due respect, my lord, you should leave one of them here. Whichever one knows most about how to get it working. While I doubt a druid will be able to best you in a battle, if you fall behind and the skyboard runs out of its charge... it's a long walk on foot."

Jadora wasn't surprised that Malek had briefed his captain on everything, but the words about a druid and a battle concerned her. Was that likely? That whoever had taken Tezi wouldn't want to give her up? What if this druid ended up being as much of a pervert as Tonovan and fancied the idea of an exotic foreign slave for his bed?

Or what if the druid refused to help a zidarr on principle? Jadora knew that it wasn't only terrene humans who feared and hated the zidarr.

"You make a valid point," Malek said, "but Professor Freedar is more likely to be able to decode the druid monument, and I doubt Jak will let me go off alone with his mother."

"He won't *let* you, my lord?" Rivlen gaped at him.

"He wouldn't approve of it," Malek corrected himself.

"So what? He's a prisoner."

"He's a guest," Malek said.

Rivlen looked like she was about to roll her eyes, but she restrained herself and stared at Malek's chin instead of challengingly into his eyes as she said, "I respectfully object to this line of reasoning, my lord. If both of them are gone and *you're* gone, there's nobody left onboard who knows anything about that." She pointed at the artifact gleaming on the deck under the moonlight.

"I want to go along to help Tezi," Jak said.

Jadora also wanted him to go along. She didn't want to be alone with Malek, especially after their chat in the cabin and all the uncertainty around him. She also hated the idea of being separated from her son.

"Besides," Rivlen added, "a skyboard will only carry two."

"I'd thought to see if Jak could command one," Malek said.

"They only work for mages."

"Anyone with power and the ability to use magical tools," Malek said quietly.

Rivlen's lips thinned. "I guess he was telling the truth that you know he has power."

"I know," Malek said.

"And King Uthari?"

"He also knows."

"I see." Rivlen looked like she wanted to say more on the topic —complain more on the topic—but she took a deep breath and said, "The sooner you leave, my lord, the more likely you'll return before we fly out of range."

"I know." Malek turned to look not at Jak but at Jadora. He raised his eyebrows. "Will you go without him?"

"Do I have a choice?"

Jadora couldn't argue against Rivlen's reasoning, but she worried trouble would find Jak if he didn't have anyone to watch out for him. What if Rivlen arranged for some accident to befall the vile *wild one*? Jadora couldn't keep from thinking about Darv's death. That had happened during a handful of minutes when Malek had been belowdecks.

"He'll still be under my protection," Malek said. "Captain Rivlen is *not* General Tonovan."

Rivlen's eyebrows snapped down at the mere suggestion.

"She will obey my wishes and protect Jak," Malek continued. "As she pointed out, if anything happens to us, she'll need him so our people can succeed at this mission."

Rivlen nodded once. "Yes, my lord."

That only partially assuaged Jadora's concerns, and it did nothing to address the fact that she truly didn't want to be alone with Malek. Oh, she didn't believe he would do anything untoward. She was just afraid... Hell, she didn't know what she was afraid of. The discomfort and distress of being with the man who might have killed her husband, she supposed.

But she made herself nod in agreement. She didn't want to be the reason they didn't find Tezi or make it back in time to rejoin the ship.

"Obey Captain Rivlen while I'm gone, Jak," Malek told him, "and I'll let you try riding a skyboard when we get back."

"Oh? Those are even neater than magical backpacks."

Rivlen blinked.

"Indeed they are." Malek waved for Jadora to follow him to the railing.

He grabbed two of the skyboards leaning there, dropping one down where it magically hovered a couple of inches off the deck, then tucking the other under his arm. They had to ride on the same one?

Jadora stared bleakly at Malek, wanting to object, but she had no magic with which to command the other one. Still, she was reluctant to touch him, nor did she want to end up with her arms wrapped around him because she was afraid she would fall off.

Malek stepped on and offered her his hand. Politely. Such a gentleman. At least he wore a backpack similar to hers. If she had to grab him, they wouldn't end up pressed together with her chest smashed against his back.

She accepted his hand, found it calloused from sword prac-tice, and stepped on behind him. He released her, and the skyboard promptly rose, tilting slightly. Her gut lurched, and she grabbed his shoulders. They were rock solid and made reassuring handholds, but this experience made her tense. The last time she'd been on one of these skyboards, Darv had been alive, riding up at her side to the *Star Flyer*. Where he'd eventually met his death.

"You won't fall," he promised her as the skyboard sped over the railing and back the way they'd come, with hoots, chirps, and croaks floating up from the trees.

Realizing she had a tight grip on his shoulders, Jadora forced her hands to loosen. She'd ridden one of these before without grabbing anyone.

The memory made her frown. "When you kidnapped us the first time, and some of these disks carried us up to your ship, there wasn't a mage on mine with me."

"One of the mage crew controlled it. As I will control this one —" Malek held out the second skyboard he carried under his arm, "—if we find your friend and can bring her back."

Jadora grimaced, thinking that she could have been riding *beside* Malek instead of gripping him for support.

"I wouldn't have minded having one of my own." A part of her wondered if Malek had *wanted* her to share his. And grab his shoulders and notice the rock-like firmness of his muscles through his clothes?

No, she was being silly. He might be her enemy, but as she'd noted numerous times, he wasn't Tonovan. If he longed for female companionship, he could surely have his pick among his people.

Malek looked back but didn't comment on female availability. "It is possible there are many druids down there and that they will consider me an enemy. If we're attacked, it will be easier if I only have to control one board."

"I understand." She almost snorted, realizing he'd been thinking about something far more important than having a woman grab his shoulders.

Feeling foolish, she didn't speak again during the flight.

Clouds drifted in front of the moon as they sailed past two more ships—also Uthari's, she assumed, though she couldn't tell what color their hulls were in the dark—and dipped into a gap in the canopy. They descended, leaves and branches brushing at their clothing. One caught her braid, causing a hard tug that made her gasp softly. A second later, Malek raised a barrier around them. No more branches disturbed them for the rest of the descent.

Since Jadora couldn't sense the magic of druid monuments, she was surprised when they came down only a couple of feet away from giant slabs tilted together in the same manner as the ones in Port Toh-drom. The disk settled on a circle of smooth pebbles surrounding the monument.

After stepping off, Malek conjured a glowing yellow sphere that pushed back the darkness of the jungle and revealed benches that one might expect in a city park. There was plenty of light by which to read the runes, and she wondered if she would find another map with a ring on it.

"Here." Malek handed her the languages book. "Please keep it dry."

The air had grown heavy and smelled of rain.

"I'll do my best," she said.

"I'm going to look around again, but I'll stay nearby in case anything threatens you."

"Such as if a druid jumps out and tries to kidnap me for presuming to touch his stones?"

"Precisely."

"Thank you."

Leaving the light to hover behind her shoulder, he inclined his head and walked toward the trees—the dense undergrowth started up just beyond the circle of stones. Jadora wondered if he truly needed to investigate anything, or if he sensed her uneasiness around him and wanted to give her space. Maybe he was being circumspect and considerate.

She would feel like a heel if she was reading him incorrectly, if Tonovan had lied to her and Malek hadn't done anything wrong. At least not any wronger than being loyal to a man she considered an enemy.

"Malek?" she asked.

He paused at the edge of the light. "Yes?"

"What did you mean back in the cabin? About sleeping with your weapons having something to do with the dreams?"

He hesitated. "My blades are made from lesser dragon steel."

She considered what she knew about the metal. Little other than it had great value, couldn't be melted by normal means, and had magical properties. Seeing them glow would have told her that even if she knew nothing else.

"They have some attributes that can be useful," Malek added. "They've given me flashes of insight before when danger has been imminent, and sometimes, when I want to know something, I'll receive dreams with clues."

"Such as wanting to know which way your escaped prisoners fled?"

"Yes."

"So you weren't intentionally reaching out to me and trying to interrogate me?"

"No. As I said, I wouldn't have guessed you could receive the same dreams that I was having. As far as I know, *you* have not been sleeping with a lesser-dragon-steel blade under your pillow."

"Just vials."

"Naturally," he said, turning again to leave.

"Malek?" She bit her lip, her feelings a confusing tangle. She almost asked him about Loran, almost shared Tonovan's words— his accusation—but she was terrified that it might have been the truth. And what would she do if it had been?

"Yes?"

"Thank you for the backpack and the change of clothes." It wasn't what she wanted to say, but it was what she could get out.

"You are welcome, Professor." This time, he bowed before turning away and disappearing into the trees.

A raindrop plopped onto Jadora's cheek. Afraid they didn't have much time, she opened the book and looked for helpful runes on the monument.

16

Tezi dreamed of falling through trees over and over, branches clawing at her from all sides and smashing her body as she struck them. Pain pummeled her, and regrets flashed through her mind, alternating with the grim certainty that it would all be over soon. But she kept falling, past more and more branches. Were these trees five thousand feet tall? This didn't make sense. She—

Tezi gasped, waking with a confused lurch, her mind scrabbling to figure out where she was and why she wasn't dead. Neither was she among the trees nor on the ground under them. And her body... She expected tremendous agony, and twinges of pain did plague her when she turned her head and tried to look around, but it wasn't as intense as she'd expected. Not as bad as it had been in the dream.

Or *had* that been a dream?

A soft green glow emanated from all around her, and the scent of damp earth filled her nostrils. Her vision was slow to focus, and the memory of stabbing a dagger into Tonovan's eye came to mind, making her shiver. She didn't regret doing it, but she'd added yet another mage enemy to the list she'd never wanted to have. Eventually, one would catch her and kill her. She was amazed it hadn't already happened.

Unless she was in the underworld already, waiting for the slavemasters' approach and to be chained for eternal toil. She had a hard time believing she'd worked hard enough and long enough in life for Thanok to grant her blessed rest in his paradise.

Still, the mattress she lay on was oddly soft for Hell. She patted a blanket underneath her. It was sleek and gray like rabbit fur.

The roots dangling from the ceiling, their gnarled and wispy strands brightened by the green glow, also didn't seem like something from Hell, not as *The Teachings* described it. There were bookcases against the dirt walls, the frames made from the same gnarled wood as the roots. Or maybe the roots themselves had been shaped to create them. As Tezi studied them, she decided that was the case.

"Hm," a woman's voice came from the side, from dark shadows that shrouded the speaker. "Hmmm."

The voice sounded curious, not mean or oppressive.

"Hello?" Tezi asked uncertainly. "Did you help me? Did you find me after I hit the ground? Or..."

Her memory was fuzzy. As she'd been falling, she'd cracked her head more than once. Even though her body ached, she didn't feel like every bone was broken, as it surely would have been if she had ever hit the ground. Could this person have used magic to keep her from landing?

Magic must have been used to coerce those roots to form a bookcase, and that green glow emanated from the walls themselves, not a lamp, so Tezi assumed that her rescuer—or captor?—was a mage.

Or a druid? Wasn't that what the magic users who lived in Zewnath were called?

A woman of perhaps fifty stepped out of the shadows, her gray and green hair—was that dye or its natural color?—bound in an elaborate coif with a few slender braids hanging past her shoulders. Her bronze cheeks were painted, or maybe those were tattoos, with two identical trees, and something akin to vines snaked down the sides of her face, meeting under her jaw. Despite the strange look, she wasn't unattractive or unappealing. There was something warm and maternal about her.

A pang of longing went through Tezi. It had been so long since someone had been warm and maternal with her, and until that moment, she hadn't realized how much she missed it. Even the mercenaries who talked to her, and had been growing willing to accept her, tended toward gruffness. Captain Ferroki had been the most welcoming, and she was the least gruff, but she definitely wasn't maternal.

A lump formed in Tezi's throat, and she blinked, attempting to keep tears from forming in her eyes. After the day she'd had, she didn't think most people would judge her for tears, but she didn't know this woman. She didn't want to cry in front of a stranger.

The woman spoke something in a lilting language that Tezi had never heard before, then held up a wooden bowl. Steam wafted from it, carrying the scent of a meaty stew.

Tezi sat up, though not without wincing. A stab of pain came from her leg, making her doubt she would be able to walk any time soon.

Not that she had anywhere to walk *to*. Tonovan's people had taken her weapons and her money. If she had to walk out of the jungle to get back to civilization, she wouldn't have the least idea which way to go. Even if she did, she doubted she could survive the trek.

The woman reached the bed—she was regarding Tezi almost as warily as Tezi was regarding her—and held out the bowl. She pointed to Tezi's leg, the one that hurt, then made a lifting gesture.

Another rabbit-skin blanket covered Tezi's lower half. Tezi

reached for it to obey the command but paused, realizing she was as naked now as she had been when she'd leaped off the mage-ship. Her clothes were back with the idiot guards who'd stripped her for their master.

She growled and thrust the memories of their hands pawing over her out of her mind. She'd stabbed her primary tormentor and escaped. That was enough. Sadly, she doubted the general was dead, but at least she'd hurt him.

The woman made the lifting motion again. Since she'd already seen Tezi naked, it hardly mattered if she revealed herself. She probably wanted to check Tezi's wounds. The pain in her leg *promised* that she had one there.

Tezi lifted the blanket and gawked, not because there was a wound but because a large green pad lay atop it, pulsing softly. Now that she looked at it, she could feel it on her leg. It reminded her of a pliable, squishy version of the cactus pads from the southern deserts, though it thankfully lacked thorns. Was it *alive*?

The woman nodded and peeled back the edge of the pad to examine a deep gash in Tezi's thigh. It wasn't bleeding, nor did it appear as recent as Tezi would have expected. The sides of the gash were knitting together, the skin around the wound pink. The woman—a healer?—lay the pad back down, and it returned to its soft pulsing. A tingle emanated from it.

"That's a little creepy," Tezi whispered.

Given that the woman smiled and nodded, she probably didn't understand. She pointed to Tezi's bare shoulder, where another smaller green pad was attached.

Tezi gawked, examining herself thoroughly for the first time, and spotted three more of them on her arm, her hip, and the top of her foot. Further, a warm tingle pulsed into her scalp. She reached up and touched a squishy pad attached to the side of her head. How could it do that through her hair? Maybe she didn't want to know.

The woman checked two more of them, nodded to herself, then pointed to a mug of tea on a stone table next to the mattress. She rested the soup there, a ladle sticking out of it, and gestured for Tezi to eat.

Tezi felt self-conscious, especially when her caretaker sat cross-legged on a rug woven from dried plant leaves and gazed intently at her, but she didn't want to appear unappreciative.

"Thank you." She smiled, took the bowl, and tried awkwardly to sip from the large ladle. The shoulder with the green pad on it twinged, and she shifted her grip so she could use the spoon with her other hand. "Are we in an underground... hideout?"

The question prompted the woman to launch into a long explanation, complete with expansive gestures that could have meant they were deep within a subterranean refuge or that the roof might cave in at any moment and they should pray to the tree gods for a reprieve from certain death.

"I'll assume underground hideout." Tezi smiled again and took another sip.

Strange astringent herbs flavored cubes of meat she couldn't identify and chunks of root vegetables she was no more familiar with. The stew tasted like something chosen more for its medicinal qualities than to win culinary competitions, but she made herself chew heartily and keep smiling.

A zidarr raped you? The woman spoke into her mind, the words startlingly understandable even though they weren't in a familiar language. *Their kind are vile.*

Tezi dropped the ladle and fumbled the bowl, almost spilling the stew. The woman leaned forward to help, holding Tezi's hands and cupping them supportively around the bowl.

I do not know your language, but this way, we can speak. The woman touched her temple.

Tezi tried thinking her words, though she didn't know if that would be enough. *He was one of Uthari's generals, not a zidarr, but essentially. He didn't complete the act, but it was... unpleasant.* An understatement. Tezi shrugged, not wanting to go into detail or discuss it at all. *I stabbed him in the eye.*

"Dryka!" the woman exclaimed, eyes gleaming.

Did that mean *yes?*

The woman went back to mental speech. *My name is Gelira of the Earth People. We drove their kind from our land long ago. The mages that serve the self-proclaimed kings are strong in the ways of the Arts, but we are crafty in ways they are not. Also, this land is inhospitable to those who are unfamiliar with it. It took some time, but we convinced them this place was not for them. Now, they rarely come. That so many of them are here and that they brought the harbinger of evil is extremely bad. There have been portents, but... perhaps we did not heed them sufficiently.*

Portents? About... that artifact?

Was that what the woman—Gelira—meant by *harbinger of evil?*

Yes. Gelira nodded. *My people must debate what is to be done. It seems they wish to erect the portal again. We cannot allow that to come to pass. Finish your stew. You must heal more before you rise and walk about. I will find you clothing.*

Thank you. Tezi wanted to ask more questions—what would Jak and his mother think if they learned these people believed that portal was evil?—but Gelira stood, pressed her hands together in front of her, and dipped her forehead to touch her fingers. That must have been a farewell, for she disappeared into the shadows again.

Exhaustion tethered Tezi to the bed as surely as chains would have. She managed to finish the stew before slumping down again, the healing pads continuing to tingle against her skin. Perhaps the next time she woke, they would have finished their work, and she would be strong enough to go... where?

She didn't know. To warn Jak and Jadora? The rest of the mercenaries?

She had no idea if any of them were within a hundred miles, nor did she know if Gelira would let her go. For now, all she could do was hope she didn't dream again.

Rain pattered on the deck, struck the top of Jak's hat, and ran in rivulets off the brim in the back.

Though he was exhausted, he remained at the railing long after his mother disappeared into the night with Malek. The idea of going to sleep while they flew into possible danger did not appeal to him. He also wondered if Tezi was truly alive out there, or if they would find her body on the ground somewhere near the monument.

Since he barely knew her, he didn't know if the thought should distress him as much as it did. He admitted he would be less distressed if one of the other mercenaries was missing and had been in Tonovan's clutches. He liked to think he would still care, but he didn't want to *date* any of the others.

Gradually, Jak grew aware of crew members standing behind him and watching him. They weren't *right* behind him, and nobody was pointing a weapon at his back, but when he glanced over his shoulder, he found five flinty-faced men regarding him with a mixture of suspicion and disapproval. An older sergeant with his meaty arms folded over his chest wore an expression of open hostility.

"I knew I should have gone back to my cabin," Jak muttered.

He was somewhat reassured that the artifact lay on the deck behind the men, but he would have preferred it if he'd been standing next to it with his hand on it. Since Captain Rivlen had berated him for sending telepathic messages to it—and apparently letting everyone on the ship know he was doing so—he hadn't attempted to communicate with it again. But if these people forced him to his knees and started telling him how superior mages were, he would plead with it to help him.

A screech came from the air somewhere ahead of the ship. A *loud* screech.

Jak risked glancing away from the men to check the clouds ahead. Whatever was up there, it was too dark to see.

The sergeant lowered his arms and strode closer.

Jak looked toward the closed hatchway of the navigation cabin. The last time he'd seen Rivlen, she'd gone in there. She ought to be close enough to hear if he bellowed in pain.

But would she care? Or would she pretend she *hadn't* heard him? Malek had asked her to protect Jak, and she'd agreed, but what if she'd been lying? The mages knew how to hide their thoughts, so they couldn't read each *other's* minds.

"Hello," Jak said as cheerfully as he could manage and tipped his hat to the approaching sergeant. "It's a miserable night for stargazing or being outside at all, isn't it?"

"We have to defend the ship." The sergeant stopped in front of Jak. "From *all* threats."

"That's noble. And likely what you're paid for. Maybe if you do a good job, you'll get a medal. I know *I'd* be grateful. I'd draw a portrait of you." Or a caricature. The man had a big forehead that would lend itself wonderfully to such an undertaking.

"You're one of the threats."

"Me?" Jak blinked and touched his chest. "I'm a simple student swept up on an adventure against my wishes. Technically, I was kidnapped, if you want the precise terminology."

"Jinark was on deck by the artifact earlier. He said he *heard* you trying to convince that thing to attack us." The sergeant touched his temple to make the type of *hearing* clear.

So, more than Rivlen had heard Jak's flailing telepathic

attempts. "No, that's not true. I didn't know you at all until you came up just now to glare at me by way of introduction. How are you? I'm Jak. What's your name?"

"You made that *thing* kill people in the battle at King Uthari's castle."

"I asked it to save my life. Your king was hurling lightning bolts at my—" Jak stopped himself from saying friends, since that would only remind them that they'd been on opposite sides, "—at a lot of people and killing *them*. He intended to take me out next."

"A shame it would have been if he'd succeeded, *student*." The sergeant curled a lip. "Why the captain thinks you can be of any use is beyond me. She's new. She'll learn better."

"Maybe you can teach her. I bet she's eager to learn."

"I'd rather teach you."

That was the only warning Jak got before a surge of power rushed toward him. There wasn't time to ask the portal for help. He could only throw up his arms and will it not to strike him.

It jammed him back against the railing but not as hard as he expected. He didn't go flying over it—or break through it—as he sensed his attacker wished.

"Sergeant Dokk," came Rivlen's stern voice from the hatchway to navigation. "Stand down. That's our prisoner, a prisoner we need to keep alive to help with the mission."

"He's a dumb kid, Captain." The sergeant faced her. "He said so himself. He doesn't know anything."

"Ah." Jak lifted a finger. "I didn't say I didn't know *anything*. Just that I'm a student and unlikely to be a threat in any way to you." He thought about also pointing out that he was a guest, not a prisoner, but he didn't know if any of them truly believed that, despite Malek's diplomatic description.

Rivlen squinted at him but only briefly before focusing on the sergeant again. "He is under Lord Malek's protection, and when he isn't here, under *my* protection. I ordered that nobody bother him or his mother, and since you have rainwater in your ears, I'll order it again. Return to your duties and leave him be." Her gaze swept over all five men. "*All* of you."

"Yes, ma'am." Most of the men slunk away.

But Sergeant Dokk remained, his arms over his chest again, and a sullen expression on his face. "You're not Captain Korthan. You're barely older than a kid yourself. I don't think you've got the wisdom for this position, and I'll bet twenty oronis that you slept with someone to get this promotion."

Rivlen strode out of the hatchway, the rain beating on the deck all around her, and faced the man. "I'm not the whore your mother is, Sergeant. I did not *sleep* my way into this position. I did, as second-in-command of the *Night Falcon,* assist my captain in defeating twenty-three enemy ships during my tenure aboard."

"Assist him by holding his prick? We heard from Tonovan that he's screwed you. He said you're not a bad lay despite being clenched up like a mother hen guarding its roost. You've probably slept with *all* of your superior officers, sucking their cocks until they promoted you. Who's next? Malek?"

"*Lord* Malek isn't in the military and isn't in my chain of command." Rivlen didn't so much as flick a finger, but a massive wave of power slammed into the sergeant.

It buzzed Jak's senses, blasting past him like a hurricane gale. Even though he wasn't the target, he stumbled back, ramming into the railing again.

The sergeant flew more than twenty feet and crashed into the ladder leading to the deck of the aftercastle. Boards snapped, and the man's bones might have too.

He roared and stumbled away, barely keeping his footing. "You bitch!"

The wave of power he hurled back wasn't as strong as Rivlen's had been. As Jak gripped the railing, afraid he would be killed simply because he was standing nearby for this, a part of his mind noted that it was interesting that he'd developed the ability to rate magical power, like a seismologist measuring earthquake magnitude.

The sergeant's attack didn't so much as pull a strand of hair out of Rivlen's tight bun. A strong defensive barrier encapsulated her. She managed to launch a counterattack without dropping it, not a wave of energy this time but some insidious mental attack. It felt like a whisper to Jak's senses, but the sergeant clutched both sides of his head and dropped to his knees.

Rivlen strode toward him, her face cold and devoid of emotion. She let him writhe on the deck for several long moments, his gasps and cries of pain competing with whatever creature in the distance kept screeching. Before releasing him, she looked toward the far side of the deck, where several crewmen, including those she'd ordered back to their duties, were watching from behind cover.

Jak expected her to yell at them to get back to work, but she didn't. Maybe she wanted them to witness this so they would think twice about challenging her themselves.

When she finally released the sergeant, he flopped down on the deck, groaning weakly. Jak had little doubt that she could have killed him, and even though he knew nothing about her, he highly doubted she had slept her way into command of a ship. His brain hurt at the idea of her snuggling up to Tonovan.

"Get off your ass and back to your duty, Dokk," Rivlen growled, prodding him in the side with her boot. "If I hear you spreading rumors about me again, I'll kill you. And if you pester the prisoner again, I'll also kill you."

The sergeant slowly rolled to his hands and knees, blood dripping from his nose and landing in a puddle on the deck. Jak stared. He hadn't realized those mental attacks could do real damage. The sergeant stood and stumbled through a hatchway, glowering back over his shoulder at her, and Rivlen squinted at him.

Though Jak was no mind reader, he suspected she was wondering if she'd made a mistake in letting him walk away. It was probably bad form to murder one's crew members, but Jak wouldn't put it past the wizard rulers to have that listed as an allowable punishment in their military.

After the sergeant disappeared, Rivlen strode toward Jak. She still looked pissed, her face frostier than a glacier, and if he'd had anywhere to scurry off to, he would have.

"Thank you for the assistance, Captain." Jak made himself smile and tried to appear grateful—and he *was* grateful, if a little concerned for his life at the moment. "Might I take this moment to acknowledge that you're a fearsome mage, formidable officer, and clearly the rightful commander of this ship?"

Rivlen halted two feet from him, staring straight into his eyes, bringing thoughts of glaciers to mind again. He made himself meet her gaze and didn't try to hide that he was puzzled that she was directing her anger at him. *He* hadn't done anything. He'd been standing here, minding his own business.

"Impressive that you can suck up that thoroughly without making any slurping noises," she finally said.

"I've been refining my skills since I started traveling with mages. Not all of them appreciate my wit. It's flummoxing."

"You defended yourself against him. If the fact that you have power was a rumor before, they'll know the truth now."

"Defended?" Jak touched his chest.

He'd just been standing there. She was the one who'd knocked the sergeant across the ship.

"You used magic to defend yourself when he launched an attack at you. He won't have missed it. The whole damn crew is going to want to know why a wild one is being allowed to wander around the ship—or live at all."

"If that's true, it was reflexive, and only because I didn't want to end up draped over one of those trees down there like a holiday garland." Jak pointed toward the canopy below.

"Next time, if there's trouble, tell me. I *know* you have no trouble with telepathy."

"Just pinpointing delivery, apparently."

"You shout louder than the howler monkeys down there. How do you even have so much magical potential? Your mother doesn't have any. Who in the cosmos was your father?"

"An archaeologist possibly murdered by the man who just went off into the jungle with her." Jak didn't want to believe that was true, not anymore, but he had to admit it was a possibility.

Rivlen didn't scoff and say that Malek wouldn't do that, as Jak thought she might.

"Because he was a wild one and a threat?" she asked, as if that was a perfectly reasonable explanation for it.

"He wasn't either of those things, just someone who didn't want to give his research to bullies trying to steal it from him."

"Lord Malek is not a *bully*."

"Right. Zidarr are known to be the protectors of the little people, not assassins who do their masters' bidding." Jak stopped himself from saying more. He didn't truly believe that. Well, he might believe it about all other zidarr, but he didn't believe it about Malek.

"He's protecting *you*. You should be groveling at his feet. I, and every other mage on this ship, would have killed you by now if not for his order that you're to be kept alive."

"Your bluntness is as refreshing as the rain plastering that flattering bun to your head." He realized he'd gone from sucking up to throwing insults and clamped his mouth shut.

Just because Malek had asked her to protect him didn't mean she couldn't torture him a little. After all, she was having a rough night. Mages probably thought that inflicting torture and torment was a way to blow off steam and relax.

Rivlen squinted at him. Hopefully, she wasn't reading his mind and debating the merits of the idea.

He eyed the artifact, wishing it had knocked that sergeant on his ass for presuming to attack Jak. It pulsed with a blue glow, as it had many of the previous times he'd communicated with it.

Rivlen spun toward it, her hand dropping to her sword.

"Don't attack it," Jak warned, remembering the drakur on the beach that the artifact had slain. They'd presumed to poke it with spears. The artifact might take even more offense at having a mage with a sword whacking at it.

"I hadn't planned to." Rivlen gave him a scathing look.

"My apologies. I thought that you caressing the hilt of your sword might indicate an impending attack."

"You talk too much."

"It's because I'm a student. At the university, we're rewarded for thoroughly articulating our points."

"I should have let Lord Malek take you," she growled and stalked toward the artifact.

It was still pulsing blue, not a regular rhythmic pulsing, but a random and intermittent one. Jak longed to reach out to it and ask if it wanted something, but with the surly Rivlen so close, he dared not.

But the artifact reached out to *him*. The familiar vision of the pool popped into his mind along with the sensation of a question.

You want to know if we're going there? Jak did his best to focus his thoughts toward the portal, hoping Rivlen wouldn't hear them. *We are. I think we're about seven hundred miles away now.*

It was a guess based more on how fast he believed the mageships traveled than any familiarity with the landscape or terrain features. Between the rain and dark, he couldn't have identified any terrain even if he *had* been familiar with it.

Contentment came along with the vision, the waterfall tumbling into the serene pool in his mind, the portal set up beside it, its center a dark energy field filled with stars. The field rippled, and a dragon flew out, the iridescent one he'd seen in the visions before. It flew about over the water, dove down into it, and swam underneath so that the power of the waterfall tickled its scales. Then it sprang out, flapping its wings to dry itself, and settled on a boulder to gaze back at the portal.

Jak hadn't seen this exact version of the vision before, and he held his breath, waiting to see if the artifact relayed something new. He was aware of Rivlen watching him from the other side of it.

In his vision, another dragon flew out, this one with mottled brown and gray scales. It was larger than the first and lacked its vibrancy. The dragon on the boulder screeched and sprang into the air, flying up toward the treetops surrounding the pool. The new dragon roared and flew after it, snapping at its tail. The first dragon tried to escape but wasn't fast enough. As they disappeared over the trees, they were both snapping their jaws at each other, twisting and writhing in the air as they fought like cats.

Trepidation emanated from the portal in the vision. A moment later, the mottled dragon flew back into view, bloody but victorious. It roared before flying off to the north, in the direction Jak now knew was Port Toh-drom and other human civilizations along the coast.

Reminded that it had been thousands of years since the portal had been set up, Jak couldn't assume the port city had been there, but people had been around. People who remembered something bad about the portal, something that terrified their descendants even to this day. Had the mottled dragon attacked their ancestors?

The vision faded, and the portal lost its glow.

Are you warning me about something? Jak asked it.

Though it didn't pulse again, the portal conveyed agreement.

That pissed-off mottled dragons might be waiting to come through you if we set you up again?

Instead of giving a firm sense of agreement again, the artifact flashed a vision into his mind of the dark jungle, the jungle they were flying over.

What's down there? Jak asked. *More artifacts? Like the druid monuments?*

The vision faded, replaced by a notion of uncertainty. It was warning him of something but didn't know what? He hoped there weren't angry dragons waiting down there to attack them.

Rivlen walked toward Jak again, though she kept a wary eye on the artifact.

He grimaced and braced himself, certain she would harangue him again for using telepathy with it.

"Why does it communicate with you?" Rivlen eyed him suspiciously but also curiously. She wasn't radiating as much hostility as she had been a few minutes earlier.

Maybe she'd gotten over being irritated by the sergeant's disrespect. Jak couldn't blame her for that. He highly doubted the male commanders were accused of sleeping their way into promotions or had to put up with stupid comments about not being fit for their duties.

"Rarely," she said, startling him. "I'm surprised you're capable of acknowledging that."

"Because I'm male?"

"And a student with no familiarity with the military or our culture."

"I'm perceptive. Just ask my mother. She says it's a boon and a blessing."

"I'll bet. I will admit that if you're younger than average for your rank, you tend to get crap no matter what your sex. People are envious of those who achieve things they didn't at that age and likely never will. It comes out as suspicion and resentment."

"Easier to be resentful of others than acknowledge our own failures and limitations, right?"

She gave him another squint, this one more assessing than suspicious. He didn't know if he'd said the right thing or if she would accuse him of sucking up again.

"How old are you?" he asked.

"Twenty-five."

"What's the average age that someone gets command of a mageship?"

"Forty-one." She lifted her chin, pride gleaming in her eyes.

"Congratulations. Your record must be exemplary."

He meant it and was trying to make a peace offering, but as soon as the words came out, Jak was *positive* she would accuse him of sucking up. Maybe he should head her off by making slurping noises.

She snorted softly. Reading his thoughts?

"Thanks." It came out gruffly, like she wasn't good at acknowledging compliments. Maybe she didn't get them that often, though that didn't seem likely. Her superiors—those who'd promoted her—had to acknowledge that she was good. "How old are you?"

"Eighteen. But I'll be nineteen in three days. For my birthday, I'm hoping someone will teach me how to use these magical powers I supposedly have. But since Malek says that's forbidden, I'm also open to cake."

"*Lord* Malek," Rivlen corrected.

He doubted he was getting magic lessons *or* cake.

"Why does the portal speak with you?" she repeated. "Instead of me? Or Lord Malek? We are powerful and have training and would be more appropriate allies for it, more able to *help* it, if that's what it wishes. I'll admit it's strange to speak that way about a big lump of metal."

"You may have answered your own question."

"What? I'm not thinking respectful enough thoughts toward it?"

"Maybe it's like mages and gets uptight when people aren't appropriately reverent with it."

She glared at him again. Just when they'd almost been interacting as humans.

"Since it's talking to me instead of you, let me pass along a warning." Jak wiped water out of his eyes; the rain was picking up. "There may be something down in the jungle along our route. Something dangerous."

"That's vague."

"From what I've gathered, vagueness is the norm when communicating with ancient artifacts."

Rivlen gazed thoughtfully at the portal, then toward their route ahead. "I'll do some searching. You go to your cabin. It's dangerous for you to be alone out here."

"So I've gathered."

She headed for the navigation cabin, though she gave him a long thoughtful look over her shoulder before stepping inside. He didn't know how to interpret it, but he jogged belowdecks, not wanting to encounter that sergeant or any other surly crew members tonight. He hoped his mother and Malek returned soon.

17

AFTER CHECKING AGAIN FOR THE MERCENARY GIRL, MALEK crouched on a boulder with his back to a stout tree and settled in to watch the area. He wasn't far from the druid monument or Jadora, who was alternately perusing Uthari's book and running her fingers over the stones while muttering to herself, and he could see decently into the surrounding foliage. The denseness of the jungle growth limited visibility, but between his normal human senses and his magic, he was aware of the animals nearby. If any druids came along, he would also be aware of them.

Of course, if they lived nearby, they might already know he was here. That could be problematic.

Malek hadn't battled druids often in his travels, but he knew of them, and he was certain they knew of him. At the least, they were familiar with the zidarr and could recognize them by their auras. The history between the druids and the kingdoms was one of strife and occasionally war. He doubted their kind had forgotten.

"Huh," Jadora murmured.

Thinking she might have discovered a doorway, Malek focused on her.

Falling rain ran in rivulets from broad leaves and spattered onto the pebbles around the monument. But Jadora didn't seem bothered by it, or even aware of it, other than to lean the book between two of the stone slabs to protect it from moisture. She wasn't looking at it now but at a vine that ran around the ground near one of the benches. She stepped over to it, plucked a long orange flower bud from between a patch of leaves, and started to put it in her pocket. Then she seemed to remember the backpack. She slung it off and tucked the bud into one of the outside pouches.

Malek watched in bemusement as his archaeologist was distracted from her task by the urge to collect a sample. It was a silly thing, but it pleased him that she was using the backpack he'd altered. He wished he'd had some fresh vials to put in it for her, but he'd been limited by what was in the ship's stores. Altering fabric was within his realm of abilities, but making scientific equipment was not. He'd once known a tinkerer who could take a handful of sand and turn it into a glass tea mug. At the time, he'd thought it a trick with little use.

Jadora glanced around, shook her head, and returned to the monument, scrutinizing the runes under the light he'd conjured. She didn't seem to realize Malek was nearby, and that made him feel like a silent stalker, but he was hesitant to call attention to himself. She was more relaxed without him looming next to her.

He regretted that, though he understood the reason. She hadn't been masking her thoughts earlier when she'd been wondering if Malek had been the one to kill her husband. *Tonovan* had put that idea in her head, and it angered Malek, but he'd said nothing. As when he'd first reported that incident to Uthari five years earlier, it would have been Tonovan's word against Malek's, and as he had back then, Tonovan had spoken first, claiming *Malek* had killed the archaeologist, not him.

Malek clenched his jaw at the memory of Uthari's disappointment and of being punished. All Uthari had wanted was the man's journal and information, not his life. Had he been permitted to live, they might have found this artifact years ago.

The rain picked up, a rivulet splashing the back of Malek's neck and running under the collar of his shirt.

He rose, intending to let Jadora know he was keeping an eye on things, and perhaps take cover from the rain under the great slabs of stone, but a rattling of foliage in the other direction drew his attention.

A huge black panther rushed toward them—toward Jadora.

Malek sprang from his boulder, drawing his sword and main-gauche as he landed in its path. The panther hadn't known he was there, but it reacted instantly, changing targets.

It roared and lunged at him with a great clawed paw. The animals on this continent were larger and more formidable than their northern cousins, but Malek matched its speed and didn't give ground. He swept his sword up to deflect the attack and sliced through the deadly paw.

The panther's roar turned to a screech of pain. It jumped at him, fangs snapping toward his throat.

With a surge of power, Malek knocked it back into the jungle. The panther landed on its feet in the undergrowth. He waited to see if it would come at him again—might this be some guardian controlled by the druids?—but it hissed at him and slunk back into the jungle. Perhaps it was a mere predator disappointed that it hadn't found easy prey. He did not sense any magic about it.

"Thank you," Jadora said when he turned to check on her.

Malek started to nod, then remembered her preference for social niceties. "You are welcome."

After cleaning his sword, he sheathed his weapons and joined her by the light.

The rain splashed down on their heads, making him wish he'd brought a hat. He hadn't thought they would be out here for long, but perhaps he should have known an ancient druid monument with hundreds of runes wouldn't be easy to decipher. He tried not to think about the *Star Flyer* sailing farther and farther away and what a long walk they would have to catch up with it, if it flew out of range of the skyboards.

The idea of not being present to complete the mission rankled, but Malek kept himself from querying Jadora about her progress. She'd only gaped into the jungle in the direction the panther had come from for a moment before recovering from her surprise and returning to studying the monument.

"Is there anything I can assist you with?" Malek asked.

"Keeping panthers from eating me is valuable assistance."

"I am capable of doing more than one thing at once."

"Clearly zidarr are talented."

He sensed it was sarcastic but said, "Yes," anyway. It was true.

She gave him an odd look—or a look to suggest *he* was odd?—then waved for him to follow her around to the face of another slab. "I haven't come across anything about a secret entrance or a druid sanctuary yet, but I want you to see this."

Though disappointed, he followed her. "Do you think there *is* a druid sanctuary?"

"There might be. It would explain how Tezi disappeared. They're known to build warrens of underground tunnels that outsiders can't find. From what I've read, they even grow special magical crystals that help them with their architectural projects, everything from burrowing their tunnels in the earth to moving massive stones through the jungle."

"Such architecture would be magical, and I would sense it."

"They're good at hiding," she said.

Malek started to protest the idea that a druid, or mage of any kind, could hide an entire sanctuary from him, but he kept from voicing what would be a statement born of arrogance. Besides, hadn't he been camouflaging the *Star Flyer* earlier? Perhaps the druids could do something similar and more permanent.

"Here's what I want to show you." Jadora pointed at a carving above her head on one of the slabs. "This map. It's similar to the one in Port Toh-drom except for one thing."

Malek studied another version of the map he'd already seen in Jak's mind. She pointed to the ring hundreds of miles inland from the Forked Sea, the spot the *Star Flyer* was heading to. On this map, someone had crossed out the ring.

"Was that done later or at the time of carving?" he asked.

"Later, I believe."

"Like ancient graffiti?"

"Something like that, but it was probably official. From what I've read, the druid monuments have some protective magic about them. I wouldn't recommend taking a chisel to one."

"They do have magical signatures," Malek agreed, though he doubted lightning bolts or anything truly deadly shot out of them if chisels were applied. That ancient portal was the only relic he'd encountered with the power to do that, and it was made from dragon steel. These were just rocks.

"I've encountered a number of warnings of danger now," Jadora admitted. "From everyone from Port Toh-drom's citizens to these monuments to visions from the portal itself."

"Warnings?"

"That returning the portal to that pool and activating it again may be... a bad idea."

While he was mulling the statement, and debating if he wanted to ask for clarification, what had been a hard rain turned into a downpour. It slammed down onto the stones, pelted the tops of their heads, and sounded like drumbeats as it hit the broad leaves around them.

"It should be dry under the stones." Jadora pointed, then

dropped to hands and knees to squeeze into the pyramid the four slabs formed.

For a moment, Malek's mage lamp shone above her, highlighting her back end, her damp clothing clinging to her. Malek averted his gaze while she crawled under the monument, wondering why he'd even noticed that. He wasn't oblivious to women and the fact that they had appealing parts, but he knew better than to be distracted on a mission.

"Do you wish me to join you or wait out here?" The idea of getting out of the rain appealed, but if she didn't want to squat in such close quarters with him, he would endure it.

"If you don't want to face druids in soggy underwear, you should join me."

"I am capable of battling in extreme situations, but I would prefer to stay dry." Malek sent his magical light under the stones first, in case there were runes she could study while they stayed out of the rain, then dropped to all fours and crawled in behind her. He trusted he was agile enough to spring out again in time if another threat approached.

"Does soggy underwear constitute an extreme situation?"

"I've endured worse." There wasn't much room under the stones, and they had to sit shoulder to shoulder, but at least it was dry. "But even mighty warriors find chafing arduous."

"I guess zidarr are human after all."

Malek almost said that the stories about zidarr being something other than human were overblown, but he wasn't certain that was true. He'd been born as human as the next person, but a lot of the training involved strange magic and ancient rites that even he didn't fully understand. During those early years, Uthari had called to half-forgotten gods and channeled power from artifacts as old as that portal, pouring alien energy into him, giving him stamina and strength beyond anything he'd known before, and resilience and regenerative abilities that few mages or even wizards possessed. Was Malek still human? He didn't know.

When he didn't respond, Jadora drew the book into her lap and studied the translations.

Aware of the *Star Flyer* sailing farther away with every passing minute, Malek stretched out with his senses, this time focusing on the ground and the possibility of an underground compound. They didn't have time to leisurely study the runes or wait for the rain to pass.

But with his mind so open, he couldn't help but sense Jadora's thoughts, especially when they crouched so close. They kept straying from translating the runes to wondering if he'd been the one to kill her husband. He'd almost responded to that on the ship, but just because she hated Tonovan didn't mean she didn't believe his lies. And if Malek protested, would that make her more suspicious of him?

The trouble was that he had been at Sprungtown University that night; he'd been searching for that journal when Tonovan killed Loran Freedar. Had Malek been paying more attention to that interrogation, he could have stopped Tonovan.

Further, he had assassinated people before, at Uthari's command, so it wasn't as if he could tell Jadora that he wouldn't do such a thing. He hadn't killed academics—only legitimate enemies who'd plotted against Uthari or his kingdom—but would she care about the distinction?

Rain hammered on the stones and spattered the pebbles and benches, offering no answers.

Malek sighed and pushed a hand through his damp hair. Jadora lurched away, startled by the movement, and clunked her head on the stone, the book dropping from her fingers.

He caught it and lifted a hand, feeling he should apologize for scaring her, though he knew she'd only reacted so strongly because she was wary of him. She kept debating about whether to ask him for the truth but was afraid of the answer she might get.

Sometimes, the ability to read minds wasn't that much of a boon.

"Sorry," she mumbled, taking the book back from him and scooting farther away, so they wouldn't be so close.

People feared the zidarr and had been avoiding Malek his whole life, so it shouldn't have bothered him. But it did. And the thought that he would have to take the blame for that night *again* frustrated him.

"I didn't do it," Malek said quietly, unable to stay silent while she wrestled with her fears and doubts about him.

Jadora looked at him, her eyebrows drawing together, and he didn't know if she'd heard him over the rain.

"Tonovan lied to you," he said more firmly. "He's the one who killed your husband. I'm sure it's of no comfort to you, but Uthari only wanted the journal. That is what he sent us to get that night. He was angry to learn that Loran Freedar had been killed."

She searched his eyes, his face. Looking for the truth?

As he'd feared, she had no reason to believe him over Tonovan. They were loyal to the same king. Maybe to her, their differences were insignificant.

He did have the sense that she wanted to believe him and was inclined to disbelieve Tonovan.

"Uthari was in fact so angry that he punished the person he believed responsible. To avoid that fate, Tonovan blamed me."

"Why didn't you tell Uthari what really happened?"

Malek gazed out at the rain, memories of that night coming to mind. "It would have been my word against his, and I felt I'd failed in not finding the journal, that perhaps I deserved punishment. I also thought that if I told the truth, and Uthari didn't believe me, it would cause him to doubt me again in the future, to think me prone to evasion and dishonesty. Better to take the punishment than be accused of lying or making excuses." He looked at her, meeting her gaze lest he appear dishonest now. "I thought I'd do the same thing with you for the same reason, but... I don't want you to fear me. Or hate me, at least not for that. I know your opinions on mages and zidarr."

"Yes." Jadora looked down at the open pages of the book, though he sensed she wasn't reading. "It is because of that, of what you are and who you're loyal to, that I doubted you."

"I know."

"If you were just a colleague at the university, I wouldn't have believed the accusations, especially not from someone like him. And I didn't, not fully. I just..." She was still gazing down at the book, but a memory formed in her mind. A *fake* memory. The one Tonovan had given her.

Malek clenched his jaw, barely resisting the urge to use his power to push that falsehood out of her mind. But she was considering it. Though it distressed her, she made herself contemplate the memory and look for inconsistencies, signs that it truly was a lie. She focused on Malek's face, on the sneer and naked rage on it before he swept his sword across to behead her husband.

He shook his head, knowing he wouldn't have looked like that, even if he had been responsible. And she seemed to realize that too. Next, she thought of real memories of him, of what he'd looked like when he'd battled Stone Heart and Night Wrath. His face had been a calm mask, never giving away pain, fear, or doubt to his enemies—as he'd long ago been taught.

She didn't know about his training, but she knew she'd never seen him sneer at anyone, even in the heat of battle. That seemed to be what made the difference, what truly made her believe that he was telling the truth and that Tonovan had lied to her, conjuring up some over-the-top Malek-villain.

"I'm sorry." Jadora looked at him with relief softening her eyes. "I wasn't sure. I doubted."

"I understand." Encouraged by her apology, Malek smiled. He didn't want her to feel bad for having those doubts and sought a way to change the subject or lighten her mood. "I'm honored you can envision me as a colleague at the university. My education lacked... breadth."

"You would have excelled in any field you chose to study."

The straightforward way she said it made it sound like an irrefutable fact. Coming from an academic—coming from *her*—it touched him.

Uthari would laugh at him if he admitted it, but Malek found her a little intimidating because of her knowledge, her advanced degrees, and all the respected papers she'd published during her career. He knew he wasn't an idiot, but his zidarr training had focused on magic and combat, with only an hour or two each day spent with tutors educating him on the kingdoms, history, economics, and various subjects that were useful to Uthari for Malek to know. He'd read over the years and filled in the gaps— and he'd read a *lot* about archeology once Uthari instructed him to —but it wasn't the same as having a deep foundation in a subject.

Reluctant to admit any of that, he casually said, "I'll refrain from demonstrating my mathematics skills in your presence to ensure you keep that opinion of me."

"If that's a lack that makes your life feel incomplete, we can go over combinatorics and differential equations later."

"Would it be odd if I found that offer intriguing?"

"You'd be my first student who did."

"So, I'm special."

"Yes, but you know that already." Jadora smiled, and he was pleased his attempt to lighten her mood had worked.

"Yes."

"Thank you," she said quietly, lifting a hand toward him.

If he hadn't been aware of her thoughts, he wouldn't have known what she wanted—or was offering—but he sensed that she regretted not wanting to touch him earlier on the skyboard and thought a hug might be an appropriate way to apologize and make amends for that.

Malek wasn't sure he should allow that, especially since he'd caught himself noticing her physical attributes earlier, but he also didn't want to reject her offer. And he appreciated that she was willing to accept his words as the truth and believe Tonovan was the liar.

He leaned forward and let her wrap her arms around him and rest her face on his shoulder. Not sure if he should reciprocate or even quite how, he patted her on the back with one hand. Hugging wasn't anything he had much experience with, and since she'd flinched away from him a few moments earlier, she might not want a full embrace.

She held him longer than he expected, thinking about how she wished he *were* simply a colleague and not zidarr, not Uthari's man. Malek didn't let himself dwell on anything like that. He was what he was.

He grew aware of the curves of her body pressed against him, the brush of her fingers at the back of his neck, and he sighed and looked upward with the stupid, if belated, realization that he was attracted to his prisoner. His guest. Whatever she was. The woman Uthari wanted him to protect and had ordered him to *win the trust of.*

An elegant rune high up on the inside of one of the slabs caught his eye. Almost thankful for the distraction, he scrutinized it. Unlike everything on the outside of the monument, this wasn't carved; it had been painted on the stone far more recently.

"Jadora," he said, shifting out of her grip, "can you translate that?"

She released him and sat back, giving him a rueful look, but only for a moment before following his gaze. "I think I've seen that one." She flipped through the book. "Door."

"It means door?"

"Yes."

"Door to an underground druid sanctuary right under our feet?" Malek stood up, straightening as much as possible with the slabs slanting inward above him. He rested a hand on the symbol, wondering if he could push it or activate it with magic.

"The definition here doesn't mention all that, but it's possible." Jadora put the book in her pack and pushed away some of the smooth pebbles under them. "There's another slab under here."

When Malek rested his hand against the symbol, it pulsed twice with green light before returning to simple paint. He watched the ground, expecting a door to open, but nothing happened.

"I may have rung the door chime," he said.

"Meaning we have to wait for them to let us in?" Jadora had pushed aside more rocks. The slab was a square set in the earth. It did look like a trapdoor.

"Possibly." Malek squatted, running his hands along the edges of the stone square.

"Wait. If you force your way in, they may not like you."

"They may *attack* me whether I force my way in or not."

"Comforting. If Tezi's down there, I hope she won't get caught in the middle of a fight. I also hope *I* won't get caught in the middle."

"I will protect you."

"And Tezi?"

"If we find her."

"Maybe I should go first. Or alone. The last time I was in Zewnath, I learned enough of the druid language to speak with the ones who live near the coast, so I may be able to communicate with these druids. Also, they shouldn't have a reason to have a grudge against me."

Apparently, she knew about the bad blood between mages and druids. How not? She was a well-read academic.

"Even if that is true," Malek said, "I cannot let you risk yourself while I cower behind you."

"Pride?"

"I've promised to protect you. I can't do that from behind your skirts."

"I'm wearing trousers."

"I noticed. It's an expression."

"You noticed?" Her eyebrows rose.

He tried to decide if he'd said something inappropriate. An unintentional innuendo? He didn't think so, but he wasn't well-schooled in such things.

She smiled slightly. Maybe it was all right, even if he had blundered.

A faint clunk emanated from the slab underneath them.

Malek drew his main-gauche—there wasn't room for the sword—and shifted his crouch, expecting the slab to grind to the side and reveal an earthen passage. But nothing happened.

"I will jump down if it opens," he said softly.

"You can jump down after me, after I've blurted overtures of friendship and showed them how innocuous I am."

Malek frowned at her.

"Also, if you're coming in after me, can you make yourself less... zidarry?"

"No."

"I can see you're going to be a difficult student."

"Special," he reiterated.

"*Very.*"

The stone trapdoor shivered under them.

"Move." Malek pulled her off to the side inasmuch as he could in the confined space.

They ended up mashed against a stone slab as the trapdoor

dropped open and revealed a secret passage. He tightened his grip on Jadora to keep her from falling into what turned out to be a pitch-dark vertical shaft in the ground. There wasn't a ladder or anything to allow one to climb down without a rope or magic.

"I'll go first." He shifted so he could jump down.

"No." She stopped him with a hand to his chest. "We discussed this. They'll be less likely to harm me."

"Less likely doesn't mean they *won't*. I'm sure intruders from foreign lands aren't welcome to pull their door chime, and I must protect you."

"Maybe I can protect *you* here."

"I doubt throwing small explosives at them will do that."

She scowled at him, and he regretted the sarcastic comment.

"Just use your magic to lower me down," she said. "Please."

He sighed and levitated her into the air, slowly, not wanting to alarm her. Surprisingly, no fear flashed in her eyes as he shifted her over the dark shaft. She gazed back at him with trust. Maybe not trust about everything but trust that he wouldn't drop her. He appreciated that and lowered her carefully.

Before, he hadn't detected any magic underneath the ground, but with the thick trapdoor open, some of what was down there escaped, like a scent wafting from a distant kitchen. There was magic down there, and even as he lowered her, he sensed people approaching the bottom of the shaft, people capable of using magic.

Druids. Three? Four? More?

As Jadora neared the bottom, Malek dropped into the hole himself. He breezed past, careful not to bump her, and landed in a crouch with both weapons in his hands.

The blades flared to life, their white glow shedding enough light to illuminate his surroundings. He was in an earthen chamber, roots draping the walls like curtains, and he was confronting not four druids but *eight* of them. Six women and two men, all with faces tattooed with tree and plant symbology, all with hair dyed at least partially green, and several with staffs and other weapons that radiated magic, as the druids themselves radiated magic.

They'd arranged themselves around the chamber, around the shaft hole in the ceiling, in such a way that he couldn't stand without at least two of them at his back. He'd landed with his magical barrier around himself, and he double-checked it now, though against so many magic-users, even he would struggle to maintain it.

As Jadora landed beside him and within his barrier, he eyed the faces of the druids. They guarded their thoughts, as any trained mage would, but he had no trouble determining that they knew what he was—and they wanted to kill him.

Jak was trying to sleep in his cabin when something shook the *Star Flyer*. Right away, he sensed magic crackling somewhere outside. He checked to make sure the mages' defensive barrier was up around the ship. If it was, nothing should have been able to hit them.

He did sense it, but it fluctuated, waning several times before solidifying again. Another magical attack streaked out of the darkness, green light flashing outside of his porthole, and struck the barrier. This time, it held firm, but the amount of power made his mind itch.

This had to mean more of Zaruk's ships, or perhaps ships sent by other kings, had caught up to the *Star Flyer*. He frowned at the thought of Captain Rivlen and the crew defending against multiple vessels without Malek aboard to help. Even though she'd proven herself powerful, and the crew hadn't been defeated yet, he doubted they could win against superior numbers. Who could?

And what if Tonovan and Yidar were pissed after losing their prisoner and blamed the *Star Flyer*? What if they didn't help, as their king had ordered?

Another blast struck the barrier, and it flickered again. Jak imagined the mage crew on the deck, straining to keep it up. Another powerful zidarr must have arrived.

As Jak patted his way to the porthole, the chair locked to the desk so it wouldn't fly out and hit him, more green light flashed outside. Strangely, it didn't seem to come from behind them, as he would expect if other ships had caught up, but from the jungle below.

He pressed his nose to the glass, struggling to see through rivulets of rain on it. What looked like a green fireball streaked out of the trees toward the bottom of the hull. It disappeared from view a second before it splashed against the barrier. He sensed that barrier drop, and dread came over him. These attacks weren't from other mages in ships; they had to be from the enemy the portal had warned him about.

With the barrier down, the mages on deck fired back. Blasts of energy, balls of fire, and bolts of lightning streaked down into the jungle. Some struck trees and blew them into flaming pieces. Others found routes through the branches to the ground below. Jak had no idea if they hit their targets down there. He couldn't see through the canopy, though he did sense someone magical down there now. *Many* someones.

Druids?

Three green balls of energy streaked toward the *Star Flyer* at once. The defenders raised the barrier before any of them hit, but it fell again as the second one struck. The third made it through and slammed into the hull so hard that the ship jerked like a leaf in a tornado. The deck rose up, throwing Jak across the cabin. He tried to will his magic to protect him, the way he'd partially protected himself from that angry sergeant, but he struck the wall hard enough to rattle his teeth. He barely kept from cracking his head against it.

Shouts came from above decks, and a magical alarm buzzed at his senses.

Though he didn't know what he could do, Jak ran into the corridor and through the hold, barely navigating the wobbling stairs without falling. He thrust open the hatch and burst onto the deck.

Rain drenched him immediately. Captain Rivlen was on deck, her uniform sodden, her bun hanging bedraggled at the back of her neck. But her arms were raised, and she radiated power as she funneled her magic into the barrier, reestablishing it with the help of crewmen near the railings.

"Faster," she yelled into the open navigation hatch. "Get us out of here, Lieutenant Harven!"

"I'm trying, ma'am," came the return yell from inside. "But something—"

The deck jolted again as green light flashed, illuminating the sheets of rain pouring down. The ship jerked to a halt, hanging in midair. Even though the barrier remained intact, thick green glowing tendrils grew up from the jungle below and wrapped around it on four sides, holding the *Star Flyer* in place.

Rivlen's face contorted with bewilderment. Whatever this was, she didn't seem to have experience with it.

With the tendrils preventing them from escaping, more green balls of energy sailed upward from the trees.

"I'll manipulate the size and shape of the barrier," Rivlen yelled to her crewmen. "Try to cut through those tendrils when they loosen."

Jak ran toward the artifact where it lay dark and dormant on the deck. Maybe he could convince it to help.

Lightning flashed—natural lightning—and Rivlen saw him.

"Get back in your cabin," she yelled at him.

"I can help!" He hoped.

Rivlen opened her mouth, as if to reiterate the order, or maybe tell him he was an idiot, but then the energy balls struck their barrier. She bared her teeth and threw back her head, her entire body rigid as she concentrated.

For a moment, she stopped throwing her power into the barrier. It sagged inward, and the other mages struggled to keep it in place so the tendrils didn't squash the ship, like some hapless dinghy in a kraken's grasp. Rivlen focused her power on those tendrils. One exploded in a shower of green blobs of light that splatted against the barrier. She snarled and looked at another tendril. It also exploded. Soon after, the last two blew up, and she shouted again for the helmsman to get them out of there.

Though impressed, Jak doubted they were safe yet. He scrambled over the side of the portal and crouched down in the center, pressing his hand against the wet dragon steel.

Will you help us? We're trying to get you to your home pool, but some unknown enemy is attacking us. They want to stop us. As he spoke, the artifact shuddered, as if some invisible being were grabbing it and trying to lift it.

Jak jumped back, afraid he'd made a mistake by jumping into the middle of it. He willed it to settle back down on the deck. Whoever this enemy was, they weren't taking the artifact from him, damn it.

To his surprise, it worked. The artifact flattened to the deck again and grew still. Rivlen squinted over at him, but then someone yelled a question, and she went back to funneling her power into reinforcing the barrier.

Their attackers in the jungle weren't done yet. In addition to spitting more green balls of energy at them, two new tendrils grew up from the treetops, reaching for them like hungry snakes.

The artifact pulsed blue once, and the sensation that it understood the problem came to Jak. And also that it was... conflicted. About *what*?

With his hand flattened to its side, he stared incredulously at it. About the need to defend itself from enemies?

As the battle continued all around, rain pounding the deck and lightning flashing in the sky, the artifact showed him the mottled dragon again. It also showed him something it hadn't before, what had happened to the playful dragon that had come out first. Its carcass hung mangled in the trees, the eyes open but all life gone from them.

"Uh," Jak said.

He didn't know what else to say. Was the artifact having second thoughts about wanting to go home and be activated again?

Another jolt wrenched the deck, and it tilted sideways. The artifact slid toward a railing. Jak yelped and flung himself atop it so he wouldn't be squished.

Rivlen shouted more orders, but the portal shared another vision, and Jak missed the words. Again, it showed him the pool with dragons—the friendly dragons—frolicking in the air and in the water. One basked on a huge rocky area like a lizard, or maybe like a cat, with its tail flapping contentedly as sun beamed down on its side. Intense longing came to Jak from the portal. It *wanted* to go home and be active once more, to have a purpose again, to see those who had made it. But fear and uncertainty mingled with those desires.

There were bad dragons and good dragons? Jak asked it. *And you're not sure which will come through if we set you up?*

It pulsed an affirmative.

He wiped rainwater out of his eyes, not sure what the solution was. Could they set it up, knowing that dangerous beings might come into their world? But he couldn't imagine *not* setting it up, not after all their work, not after his father had died for this.

Besides, whoever was down in the jungle was trying to kill

them. Maybe it was to keep them from setting up the portal, or maybe it was because they wanted it for themselves. Either way, he and the *Star Flyer* were in trouble.

We need your help, Jak told the portal as the tendrils reestablished themselves, despite Rivlen and the mages doing their best to battle them. *Help us stop these enemies from destroying us and taking you. Please. And then we'll go set you up, and we'll see what happens, all right? If bad dragons come through, we'll close you down again, but maybe the ones you like are waiting to return to this world.*

He *hoped* that was the case.

A sense of agreement came from the portal. It nudged him mentally, showing him an image of himself crouching safe in the center.

Trusting it, Jak rolled into the middle and squatted low. The deck was level again, so the portal had stopped sliding around.

Lightning streaked from four points in the artifact, the mouths of the four entwined dragons that made up its frame. He hadn't noticed that before. The branches of lightning arced over both sides of the ship, blasting through the barrier the mages had been making.

A cry of distress came from Rivlen, and a nearby mage pitched to the deck, grabbing his head. Jak worried he'd unintentionally hurt the people defending the ship, but the lightning had to escape so that it could streak down into the jungle. It bypassed the trees, barely stirring a leaf as it found a route to the ground.

From his crouch in the middle of the portal, Jak couldn't see any of that with his eyes, but he sensed it. Maybe the portal was even sharing some of it with him.

Two branches of lightning slammed into a stone monument similar to the one in Port Toh-drom. An uneasy feeling came over Jak along with the certainty that they were indeed battling druids. Another branch of lightning arced through the trees at a trio of men and women who'd been standing with their legs apart, their arms wide, and their heads back as they directed attacks toward the *Star Flyer*. The lightning from the portal slammed into a defensive barrier that surrounded them, knocking it down, then blasting them.

Don't kill them! Jak thought. *Please!*

He knew nothing about the druids, but he was terrified they believed they were doing the right thing, that they, like the citizens of Toh-drom, thought the artifact was a portent of evil. And if killer dragons had once come through it, maybe it was.

The tendrils gripping the *Star Flyer* disappeared, and the attacks from below halted. As more bolts of lightning streaked out of the portal and down to the jungle floor, two of the druids rose and ran for a square hole in the ground. A tunnel entrance? The lightning struck others, putting a halt to any more attacks.

On the ship, Rivlen and the other mages took advantage, sending down attacks of their own.

"They're distracted," Rivlen yelled into navigation. "Get us out of here."

"Same course, Captain?"

"Yes. Don't you dare stray from it!"

"Yes, ma'am!"

Below, more druids fled from the attacks. They disappeared into holes in the ground. Stone slabs slid over them, leaving no enemies remaining on the jungle floor. The monument had been destroyed, the great stones charred and knocked on their sides. Two had cracked and split. They would never stand again.

Jak closed his eyes and leaned his forehead against the portal, knowing he was responsible for that. The druids had been attacking them, and he'd had no choice, but he couldn't help but feel like a marauding plunderer for destroying ancient monuments. What would his mother say?

His mother whom he'd last seen going to *find* druids. Maybe friends of the very ones he'd helped attack. What if they found out, and what if they took their anger out on her?

"I think you can come out now," came Rivlen's voice from above.

She was peering over the side of the portal at him. Her bun had fallen, and damp hair plastered the sides of her face, framing cheeks red from exertion. The urge to draw her came over him, maybe not as she was now, but as she'd been as she hurled her power around, and he stored the memory away for later.

"It's cozy here," Jak said. "More comfortable than my cabin."

"Your knee is in a puddle."

"*All* of me is in a puddle."

"Yes." She extended her hand.

It took Jak a second to realize she wanted to help him up. He hadn't been hit and hadn't been the one doing all the work, so he didn't need assistance, but he didn't want to reject her offer. He appreciated that she was making it and reached up to clasp her hand.

She pulled him up, and they walked together to the hatch. Maybe she intended to escort him back to his cabin and lock him inside. Possibly after giving him a lecture for leaving it.

"Thank you for your assistance," was what she said, stopping at the hatchway.

"Oh," he blurted, startled. "You're welcome."

"We don't have baking facilities, and I'm an inept cook."

"Er, what?"

"You requested cake for your birthday. I don't think I can get that for you. Is there something else you'd like?"

"Can you talk Lord Malek into making me a magical backpack?"

"I think you're closer to him than I am." Her lips pressed together. Was she annoyed by that?

Jak doubted it was true, but he didn't argue. "Can you reach out to him now to see if he and my mother are all right? Those were druids attacking us."

"I know."

"And they went to see druids. They don't have an ancient artifact to protect them. I'm worried."

"Lord Malek can defeat a druid."

"What if there are a *lot* of druids?" Jak didn't point out that he hadn't seen that many down there and that they'd managed to give the *Star Flyer* a great deal of trouble. "This is their home turf."

"I'll attempt to reach out to him." Rivlen's gaze shifted past his shoulder, her eyes going out of focus.

Jak could have tried to speak telepathically to Malek on his own, but since everyone kept telling him not to use his magic and rub his existence in people's faces, he was hesitant.

"I can't reach him," she admitted. "I'll try again later."

"Thank you." Jak headed back to his cabin, worried about what that inability to make contact might mean.

Despite the possible ramifications, when he was alone again, he tried to reach out telepathically to Malek. Maybe he truly did know Malek better than Rivlen, and he would have an easier time finding him.

Lord Malek? he called mentally, imagining his face, as he'd done the last time he'd tried this. *Are you out there? Are you and my mother all right?*

If Malek could hear him, he didn't answer.

Jak sat on the edge of his bunk with his head in his hands, worried about his mother, and worried this whole quest would turn out to be a huge mistake.

18

THE MUGGY NIGHT AIR RUFFLED COLONEL SORATH'S SHIRT AS HE stood in the forecastle of the *Skimmer*, the smallest and fastest—and least damaged—of the mageships Zaruk had sent. His idea to send Night Wrath and his engineer brother ahead to sabotage Uthari's ships wasn't going to plan. Oh, they'd agreed to do it, but they'd demanded Sorath, Ferroki, and all of Thorn Company join them in case the saboteurs were caught and needed to be rescued.

"At least the company is all back together." Ferroki stood next to him, fighting off yawns as the night deepened. "Almost all," she added so quietly that he barely caught it.

"I'm sorry about Tezi," Sorath said.

"Thank you. It's not your fault. I shouldn't have sent her away. I thought I was protecting her."

"You would have been if I hadn't dragged her after Jak and Jadora for a last mission." Sorath should have gone after them alone. "It wasn't right to want to use her as bait because she's pretty."

"It was more because the boy has a crush on her, wasn't it?"

"Yes, because she's pretty."

"I didn't know you'd noticed."

"I'm male. I noticed." Sorath eyed her, waiting for the inevitable comment about him being old enough to be Tezi's father—and then some.

"Should I then feel honored," was what Ferroki said, smiling faintly, "that you also notice older and slightly less vivacious mercenaries?"

"Men aren't particularly singular with their notice, but if you're honored by the admiration of an old, scarred commander dead-set on annoying mages and getting himself killed... then *I'm* honored." His brow creased. Had that made sense? Strange how a lifetime wasn't enough to master flirting.

Not that he was doing that. They'd already agreed that they needed to keep their relationship on a professional level. Though if he somehow succeeded in getting her rookie back for her, and she was moved to kiss him, he wouldn't push her away. Maybe if this sabotage went well, they would have a chance to get Tezi.

Lieutenant Sasko strode out of a hatch, spotted them, and climbed up to the forecastle. "I need to hide behind someone large and imposing." She eyed Sorath, then glanced back toward the hatch she'd exited, and placed herself beside him where she wouldn't be visible to someone peeking out.

"I hope that doesn't mean the engineer we're relying on is harassing you." Ferroki frowned.

Sorath blinked. "Is that likely?"

"He's *experimenting* on me," Sasko said.

Sorath's confusion turned to a scowl. He didn't know what that meant, but it sounded like the kind of thing that mages who thought themselves superior to everyone did to lowly mercenaries. "Is he hurting you?"

"No, he's *hiding* from me."

"I..." Sorath looked at Ferroki. "Are you confused?"

"Yes. Explain, Sasko."

"I'd just snuggled down in my blanket to try to get some sleep on this, the *third* ship we've had to board since this all started, when Vinjo ambled up and asked for a favor. I told him to beat it, that I wasn't having sex with him, but he said he needed my help for this mission. I would have told him to stuff it, but his damn zidarr brother was with him and twitched a finger to rip my blanket out of my hands. I followed Vinjo down to engineering where he's been working on refining some doodads for his sabotage. He has a whole workshop full of crap down there. He made me hold tools for him while he blathered and described his magitational imploding engine assaulter. I think that was the name. Who knows? He kept me there holding things while he blabbed for over an *hour*."

Sasko paused for a dramatic eye roll toward the stars.

"I'm still confused," Sorath told Ferroki.

"I believe the problem is more that our engineer-saboteur is enamored with Sasko than hurting her," Ferroki said. "Apparently, she roused his interest by fantasizing about shoving pencils in Captain Myroth's nose. He liked that."

Sorath rubbed his face, wanting to shoo her away so he could get back to mulling over a way to retrieve Tezi.

"After he finished his assaulter, and I asked if I could go back to sleep, he said he needed to test something on me. He activated his... clandestineness creeper—I think that's it—and disappeared. Sort of. I could see his shadow moving around when he was close to me. He's going to use it to infiltrate Uthari's ships, he said, but he needs to see how well it works. I told him I needed some sleep in case I end up in a *battle* against Uthari's ships. He proceeded to follow me back up to our sleeping area, running ahead and to the side and asking how far away I could see him."

"How did you escape?" Ferroki looked toward the still-closed hatch.

"I told him to hide somewhere on the ship, and I would get

some people to help look for him, so he could test how well it works."

"Which you're doing now."

"While hiding behind the colonel, yes. Sooner or later, he's going to figure out that I'm not looking for him." Sasko peeked toward the hatch. It opened, seemingly of its own accord. She swore softly and positioned herself again so Sorath would hide her. "He figured it out."

Sorath, who'd originally been impatient with this story-telling session, looked toward the hatch. He'd dealt with mages and knew some of them could hide themselves through manipulating illusions—the *Star Flyer* had seemed to do that when it attacked Zaruk's ship in Toh-drom. But a tool that one could flick off and on to hide oneself sounded promising. He wondered if a terrene human could use it.

"Why didn't you ask if *you* could test it?" Ferroki asked. "You might have slept for hours before he found you."

"I didn't think of that. Where were you with your sage advice an hour ago, Captain?"

A throat cleared on the ladder leading up to the forecastle. Sorath turned in time to see a mage in a rumpled, grease-stained blue uniform appear, first as little more than a shadow and then solidifying as he joined them. He clicked a button on a gray box, held it up, and smiled. He peered around Sorath to wave at Sasko.

"Hello, again, Lieutenant Sasko. I trust from the fact that you didn't find me that my clandestineness creeper is as effective as I hoped it would be. Though I did notice you didn't put as much effort into the search as I'd hoped."

"Didn't I tell you I was going to get friends to help with the search?" Sasko straightened and gave up on hiding behind Sorath. "Unfortunately, the captain and colonel weren't that interested in partaking in the late-*late*-night adventure with me."

"No? Neither was my brother." Vinjo's shoulders slumped.

"You'd think he would want to know how well my tools work when he's supposed to partake in this mission with me."

"The magic tarp things you sold us work," Ferroki said. "Perhaps your brother has faith that whatever you invent will be effective."

"Oh, he has no faith in me or my tools at all. I'm not zidarr, you see. Or particularly good at any kind of weapons play. Or athletic endeavors at all. I also get nervous in battles." He shrugged. "Also, they're portable thaumaturge-defier bulwarks, Captain."

"Perhaps you should write that on the side," Ferroki said, "so those of us with simple minds can remember it."

"A good idea. My work *should* be remembered. It's fabulous, after all. Are you sure you don't want to see more of my inventions, Lieutenant Sasko? I didn't get a chance to show you the de-magicifier."

"Yes, you did. It's a black lump."

"With intricate insides and a carefully and complexly woven web of magic around it. It can nullify an engine or other crucial piece of equipment on a mageship. I thought about using it instead of engaging in wanton destruction, but my brother pointed out that all Uthari's engineer would have to do is spot it and remove it."

"Tragic," Sasko said.

"I'll take it along in case I see a use for it. You never know. Lieutenant Sasko, I have numerous other inventions if you'd like to see them. Perhaps, as a woman, you'd be more interested in the auto-hopping ceiling, wall, and machine scrubber."

"As a woman, I would not."

"It's self-frothing."

Sasko eyed the railing, as if she was thinking of jumping over it.

"You can show me your inventions," Sorath said, pegging the

mage as unappreciated and craving recognition. That creeper device was effective. Maybe the rest of his inventions would be too.

"Oh? Lieutenant Sasko said you weren't interested in late-night adventures in engineering."

"The lieutenant is mistaken," Sorath said. "I'm interested. Give me a tour, will you?"

Vinjo's face brightened as if a sun were beaming on it. "*Certainly*, Colonel. As a military man, you'll absolutely appreciate the applications. I'm positive."

"I have no doubt." Sorath let the mage lead him down the steps toward the hatch.

"Your friend may have a new person to ply his affections on," he heard Ferroki say to Sasko.

"May Thanok bless him," Sasko said.

"Vinjo or Sorath?"

"Sorath. He'll need it."

Jadora lifted her hands slowly, having no trouble reading the faces of the eight druids surrounding her and Malek with their weapons readied. Green hair, clothing woven from grasses, and tattoos of flowers and trees on their exposed skin made them seem alien, but she could still gauge their feelings. All eight of them ignored her in favor of focusing on Malek as fear and loathing emanated from them. The six women, in particular, looked like they wanted to eviscerate him.

What if they could? These druids might all be magic users, as dangerous as mages from the sky cities, and together, they might be more powerful than even a zidarr.

Malek hadn't yet moved. He crouched in a ready stance, his sword and main-gauche in hand, the weapons glowing white and illuminating the otherwise dark chamber, and he'd positioned himself so close to Jadora they were almost touching.

She found his presence comforting, as well as his recent reminder that he'd sworn to protect her, and was glad she hadn't succeeded in talking him into letting her come in alone. She briefly wondered what it would be like to have someone like him want to protect her, not out of loyalty to his master who'd requested it, but because he cared whether she lived or died.

Thoughts for another time. She had to stop what the tension in the chamber promised could turn into a battle at any second.

"Greetings," Jadora said in the language she'd learned at the temple near Port Toh-drom, hoping these inland druids spoke the same dialect as the coastal druids. She focused on one of the older women, though she had no idea who in the group was the leader. They all carried weapons, and all appeared equally dangerous. "My name is Professor Jadora Freedar, an archaeologist. This is—" for a second, she thought of introducing Malek as her bodyguard, but magic users could recognize other magic users, and they had to know he was zidarr, or at least a powerful mage, "—Lord Malek. We're sorry to intrude on your home, but we're looking for a friend. She fell from one of the mageships, and she must have been badly injured. We're hoping you've seen her."

The woman she'd been addressing hadn't reacted initially to her words—hadn't taken her tense gaze from Malek—but she glanced at one of the other women. It didn't seem like a bewildered I-have-no-idea-what-this-foreigner-is-saying glance.

"Professor Freedar?" the woman asked, pronouncing her name carefully, as if the syllables were unfamiliar, but it also seemed that she recognized it.

That was surprising, since it had been so many years since Jadora had visited the continent, and she didn't know any of these druids from the temple. Nor did these seem like people who would receive regular news updates from the cities and be aware of the goings on across the world. Maybe making that assumption, simply because they lived in a remote location, was a mistake. They could have the same types of long-range communications devices as the mages.

"I know it's presumptuous for us to show up in your home and ask for favors," Jadora said. "Perhaps you would accept a gift of greeting from me?"

She didn't know if Malek understood any of the language, but he could probably guess what she was talking about from her thoughts. Either way, he glanced at her. A puzzled glance?

"It's a custom among their people," she whispered to him in Dhoran.

"What are you going to give them?" he whispered back.

"I have numerous valuable herbs, though I've lost all the ones I had along from other continents. They might have appreciated those more."

The druids also whispered to each other but not in the language Jadora knew. Uh oh. That meant they *did* speak a different dialect.

Jadora listened intently, suspecting the two tongues had to be related. Or might their dialect be more closely related to the ancient language in Uthari's book, the one used not only on the druid monuments but also on the portal?

"I am Gelira of the Earth People," the woman Jadora had been addressing said, this time in the coastal druid tongue. "Step away from your captor, and show us what you offer."

"He is not my captor," Jadora said reflexively, though she almost snorted at herself.

Wasn't he? The lesser of two evils, as Jak had said. If not for Malek and Tonovan, she and Jak would have succeeded in getting the artifact back to the university, where terrene humans could have studied it in peace.

Except she would be delusional if she believed that was what would have happened. Even if Uthari had never sent his people and had no interest in the portal himself, one of the other wizard kings would have come, and Jadora would now be someone else's prisoner.

"He is zidarr," Gelira said, as if that *must* mean he was her captor.

"Yes, but we're working together right now."

"Because he is your captor." Gelira spoke the words gently, sympathetically.

"Let me show you what I can offer as a gift." Jadora slowly reached for her backpack to remove it, though she hadn't yet decided what she had that the druids might appreciate.

Gelira lifted her hand. "You must step out of his barrier to give it to us." She smiled, then spoke directly into Jadora's mind. *We will talk more once you are away from him and not afraid to speak openly.*

"Uhm." Jadora looked at Malek.

Still in his fighting crouch with his blades raised, he wasn't moving a muscle. He and one of the male druids were staring at each other.

Abruptly, the male looked at his comrades and spoke rapidly in a complaining tone as he pointed accusingly at Malek.

"Are you insulting him?" Jadora whispered to Malek.

Maybe it *wouldn't* be a bad idea for her to try to speak privately with Gelira. The druids shouldn't have any reason to want to kidnap her or treat her badly. She knew all about plants and the earth and how things grew, and that was a large part of their culture, so maybe she could establish a rapport with them.

"I do not know his language," Malek said, "but I am letting him glimpse my thoughts."

"Are *they* insulting?"

"I'm letting him know that I'm well trained and powerful and would slay many of his druids before they succeeded in taking me down."

"So, insulting *and* arrogant."

"One cannot show weakness in front of enemies."

"Pomposity is better."

"I would glare at you, but I'm busy staring defiantly at him."

"Yes, I see that. It's very male."

"That comment ensures I will glare at you later. Pompously and defiantly."

"I look forward to it."

"Please." Gelira waved for Jadora to come stand by her side. "Step out of his barrier."

Jadora hesitated. Even though she didn't *think* the druids had a reason to harm her, they were strangers, and she couldn't know that for certain. Why was Gelira so insistent that she step away from Malek?

"Do you know where Tezi is?" Jadora asked. "She's who I came for."

Yes. She is here and healing. But I will not let her go with another one of them. The other one tried to rape her. Gelira joined the male in glaring hatred at Malek. *His ally.*

Malek doesn't like Tonovan, Jadora replied, though she couldn't deny the ally part. Did she even want to? *He came with me only because I asked him. Also, he helped Tezi get away from Tonovan.*

She freed herself, stabbed him in the eye, and sprang to what she thought would be her death. All to escape that monster. If she is your friend, you will step away from him and let us deal with him.

"Deal with?" she asked aloud.

Malek glanced at her.

Gelira frowned.

I can hear your thoughts, Malek told Jadora. *Hers are too pinpoint and precise for me to intercept, but I get the gist. I will not let them take you away from my protection. I do not trust that they will not harm you. Why do they know your name? They do not wish the artifact to be activated, and I believe they know that you are the one who unburied it.*

Jadora started to object that the druids could know that, but couldn't they? And the citizens in Port Toh-drom had all been afraid of the artifact, so it made sense that the druids on this continent might feel the same way.

What do you suggest? Jadora asked him, aware that Gelira would read her thoughts as easily as Malek did. Could she make use of that? Pretend she *didn't* realize that Gelira would overhear and dole out some ruse?

Tell them to take you to the girl, that I will accompany you to protect you, and that I will not harm any of them as long as they don't harm us. Assure them I am *capable of harming them if they try anything.*

So, I should respond with arrogance?

As I've demonstrated.

Jadora snorted. He had.

Offer to give them fancier herbs than you'd intended, Malek suggested. *Maybe that would work.*

I doubt it. They think you're a rapist, like Tonovan.

Malek's nostrils flared with indignation.

They don't realize that you've fallen in love with me, no longer obey your king, and would behead Tonovan yourself if you had the opportunity. Jadora smiled at him and scooted closer while hoping he could keep from giving her an incredulous look.

She turned toward him—his face was an impressive mask— and slid her arm around his back while patting him on the chest with her other hand. His thin damp shirt made it easy to feel the hard outline of his chest. He wasn't as tense as she'd expected, but she still felt like she was risking her life by presuming to touch a dangerous predator. Right now, he was nothing like the gentle reserved man she'd hugged up above.

The male druid made a disgusted noise and complained more to Gelira and the others.

"As long as your people don't attack us, he won't attack you or do anything to harm your people," Jadora told Gelira, who was squinting at them. "He's here to protect me and help me get Tezi back. That's all."

Jadora did her best to keep her thoughts blank, except what she was thinking to Malek, intending the druids to overhear.

"Back to where?" Gelira asked. "His ship, no?"

"*Our* ship. We're on an archaeological mission together."

"To return the portal to life."

"Yes. So we can find dragons to help humans free themselves from the yoke of their oppressive wizard overlords." Normally she wouldn't have spoken about that to magic users, but the druids had plenty of reason to hate the wizard kings themselves, so...

"A quest which Zidarr Malek, faithful servant of King Uthari for more than thirty years, is cheerfully joining you on." Who would have thought someone with green hair and tree tattoos on her cheeks could convey sarcasm so well?

And those words proved they knew exactly who he was.

"He no longer works for Uthari," Jadora said. "Love moves men to great lengths."

Malek was like a statue, no longer glancing at her or sharing his thoughts with her, and she worried she'd pushed him too far, that he was now as likely to explode in anger at her as to spring at the druids.

"The zidarr are incapable of love," Gelira said.

"Not so. He's a considerate man and a passionate and thorough lover." There. That was the furthest she would try to take this. If they weren't buying it, there was no point in carrying on.

She had no telepathic way to warn Malek without being over-heard, so she only patted his back with the hand under his jacket, hoping she could convey that she was done. If this didn't work, he might have to fight.

Malek finally stirred, slowly sheathing his main-gauche, though he kept his sword out. He angled his body toward Jadora, his chest against her shoulder, and wrapped his free arm around her, his hand resting on her other shoulder. Now, his eyes were locked on Gelira, as if he'd decided she was the leader, more worth focusing on than the male.

"I am not here to threaten you," he stated, perhaps sharing the thoughts as well in a way that she would understand. "Only to protect Jadora as she retrieves the friend of her son."

"Because you are her lover," Gelira stated flatly.

Malek nodded, though what he said was, "I am sworn to protect her."

His unwillingness to lie made Jadora regret opting for a ruse that required it. But he lifted the hand on her shoulder to gently stroke the side of her neck, and a little shiver went through her. Dear Shylezar. This was the worst time to realize that she might be attracted to him. At least it was less horrifying now that she knew he hadn't been the one to kill Loran, and all the small considerate things he'd done for her hadn't been out of guilt, but just because.

It crossed her mind that kissing him might help make Gelira believe this, but she quashed the thought. She didn't think this ruse was working, nor did she want to kiss Malek. At least... not in front of an audience.

Warmth flushed her cheeks as she couldn't make her mind retract that amendment. And Malek glanced at her. Damn it, had he heard her thinking that?

A young voice called from the single tunnel that led out of the chamber, the name *Gelira* the only thing Jadora could understand. Whatever the news was, the druids' faces turned grim as they glanced back and forth at each other.

Gelira sighed and told Jadora, "If he leaves his weapons here in this antechamber, he may enter our abode at your side. We will not touch them." Her gaze shifted to Malek. "And we will guard him and watch his every move. In our sanctuary, we have children and those who are not as practiced at defense. To bring in a tiger is... unwise."

Malek must have understood, for he lifted his chin, the same indignation flaring in his eyes as when she'd accused him of being a rapist.

"I will *not* leave my weapons behind," he said, his voice resonating with power, "but you have my word as zidarr that I will not attack anyone unless your people attack *us* first."

He spoke in Dhoran, but his thoughts must have conveyed the message sufficiently to them. They glanced at each other, communicating in their own language.

Jadora expected a lot of head shakes and for them to end up at an impasse, but after the quick exchange, Gelira nodded. Maybe that sense of power that had accompanied Malek's words had been a magical coercion. She'd forgotten he could do that and wouldn't have guessed it would work on others with power.

"Very well, zidarr," Gelira said. "We accept your oath."

She did not, Jadora noticed, promise that *they* wouldn't attack *him*.

"Follow me." Gelira headed for the corridor that the younger person had called from. "If Tezi wishes to go with you, she may. I am skeptical that she will wish that." She looked back, not at Jadora but at Malek. "Your *ally* is the one who drove her to jump to what she believed was her death."

Jadora missed a step. It hadn't occurred to her that Tezi might not come with them—with *her*. They weren't close, but they had worked together in the escape from Uthari's castle, and they'd traveled together to Zewnath. Granted, they hadn't spoken much, and since then, Jadora and Jak had chosen to join Malek. Maybe Tezi wouldn't want anything to do with her. Gelira was correct that

Tezi wouldn't want anything to do with Malek. Her company referred to his ship as the *Murder Flyer*, not the *Star Flyer*.

As they left the dark entrance, entering a maze of underground tunnels lit with a green glow that emanated from the earthen walls, Jadora considered what she would say to Tezi to convince her to leave. If she was safe here, did they *need* her to leave? The whole point of sending Malek to rescue her had been to get her away from Tonovan. They'd only come here to make sure she wasn't lying near death and in need of help. If she wished to stay, she could, though Jadora couldn't help but assume she would want to be reunited with her company.

But could Jadora offer her that? As long as she was with Malek, if she encountered Thorn Company again, they would consider her an enemy.

Not only Gelira but the entire group of eight druids accompanied them into their warren. Most trailed behind, none doing anything to impede them, but they gripped their weapons tightly, and tension radiated from them.

Was the presence of one lone zidarr enough to disturb them so greatly? In their own home? She had a feeling they could, with their combined might, defend themselves against Malek, but maybe something else was agitating them. Since she'd introduced herself by name, the druids had spent as much time eyeing her as Malek. Maybe he was right that her quest to uncover the portal and put it to use did not sit well with them.

Jadora grew uneasy as they traveled deeper into the maze, aware that they were moving farther and farther from the only entrance she knew about. Already, they'd taken numerous turns at intersections, and the green-glowing, root-draped walls all looked the same. They'd gone through two passages she wouldn't have even noticed if she'd been alone, for roots had grown down over the entrances like curtains, and they kept descending deeper underground. She hoped they weren't walking into a trap.

"Gelira?" Jadora asked. "Or do you have a title I should use?"

"Gelira is fine," she said without looking back.

"I truly did wish to give you a gift. It's my understanding that it's part of your culture."

Gelira paused to scrutinize her. Jadora sensed that she didn't *want* a gift or anything from them. But if it was a part of their tradition...

"It is." Gelira considered her a little longer—searching for duplicity?

No, but Jadora did hope the druids would be less likely to zap her with their magic if she observed proper protocols.

"Is it related to archaeology?" Gelira asked.

"No." Jadora couldn't imagine what archaeological gift she would give a druid. A print of a hieroglyph from a famous henge? "My first passion, and my first career, is herbalism." She didn't know the word for chemistry in the coastal language and wasn't sure druids studied it regardless, so she didn't mention it.

"Oh?" Gelira looked at her backpack. "Follow."

Jadora and Malek were *already* following her, but she didn't point that out.

Gelira took a turn at the next intersection, waving for the druid pack to wait, and stepped through a root-draped doorway wider than most they'd passed. A large chamber glowed green, like everything else, but also pink, purple, and orange, the colors of crystals growing out of beds of a sticky gray-blue substrate. If that was like compost, it was nothing Jadora was familiar with, and she was sure magic was involved.

With a start, she realized these had to be the crystals she'd told Malek about, tools the druids made to help move great rocks and excavate tunnels. She tried to blank her mind of thoughts about them, other than to acknowledge that if the druids *did* try to trap them down here, one of those could be helpful.

"This is where we store our herbs and alchemical ingredients."

Gelira pointed to levels and levels of shelves set into the earthen walls, each filled with jars, crocks, and bags. "Were you here under different circumstances, it would have been interesting to discuss the sciences with you."

Jadora agreed and smiled around wistfully. Hundreds of distinct smells permeated the air, everything from yumquar to flantar lichen to dried peppers, along with many more scents that she couldn't identify. She could have spent weeks in here, exploring all the substances, but they had a more pressing mission, and Gelira turned expectantly, waiting for her gift.

As Jadora slung her backpack off, she casually looked toward the crystals, trying to dredge information on colors from her mind, but she couldn't remember any of the books that had mentioned them talking about the specifics.

They use pink and orange in battle, Malek thought into her mind.

Jadora almost asked for details, but Gelira was watching them and would hear her thoughts. It already concerned her that Malek had sensed her thinking about the crystals.

"Please enjoy these yartof roots and some zemorian tea from the coast," Jadora said, filling her mind only with thoughts of her gift and an apology that she didn't have something more exotic to offer. Beyond that, she wished she weren't making gifts of items she'd taken without paying for in the apothecary shop, but she was a woman without means these days.

"Ah, I do appreciate zemorian tea," Gelira said. "We can't grow it inland. It's too rainy."

As Gelira bowed and accepted the gift, Jadora eyed the purple crystals. If the other colors were used in battles, might those be used for building their compounds? If she could snap one off, dare she do it?

"This place is amazing. I thank you for accepting us into your world." Jadora leaned against a counter near the crystals, keeping her thoughts blank as Gelira turned her back to put away the yartof roots. As she reached for a high shelf, Jadora snapped two purple crystals off at the base, wincing at the noise.

Gelira heard it and started to turn back, but Malek stepped forward. She focused on him, jumping back.

"Do you need help?" He pointed to the high shelf.

"No." Gelira grabbed a stool from a corner so she could reach the spot herself.

When Malek looked at Jadora, she nodded at him, glad for the help. His face was hard to read. No, she decided. It was just hard. Probably more because of her display at the entrance and less because she was trying to find items to help them if they needed to escape. She shouldn't have resorted to subterfuge that could impinge upon his honor or his sense of honesty. His *zidarr*ness.

"I wish we had time to discuss plants," Jadora said as Gelira finished with the stool and turned back to them. "I'm sure your people have a tremendous amount of knowledge, and I know so little of Zewnath's species."

"Another time, perhaps." Gelira's politeness sounded forced.

She gestured for them to return to the tunnel they'd been walking in before. The other druids resumed trekking behind them. Jadora hoped none of them sensed the magical crystals in her pocket. The magic from Malek's weapons might drown out anything lesser nearby. She hoped.

The tunnel they were traveling ended at a cluster of rooms. Gelira parted a curtain of roots, the green glow of a small chamber visible beyond a short hall, and held up a finger.

"I will ask if she wishes to see you. She was gravely injured." Gelira eyed Malek. "She should not be stressed."

He said nothing. This time, his eyes didn't flash with indignation at the implication that he was stressful. Maybe he agreed with that assessment.

That earned Jadora a sidelong look, suggesting he was monitoring her thoughts. The rest of the druids had stopped farther back in the tunnel and were murmuring amongst themselves, as agitated as they'd been since Malek and Jadora's arrival. Gelira disappeared behind the curtain.

Jadora didn't know if it was safe to talk, but with the other druids arguing, nobody seemed to be paying attention to them at the moment. She decided to risk speaking, because Malek's face was as tight and flinty as that of the druids, and she worried she'd offended him. It would be nice to have him looking less fierce and unapproachable when they went in to see Tezi.

"I apologize for my ruse back there," she whispered. "It was probably pointless as far as swaying them, and I'm sure that's not a rumor that you'd want to get out."

Another sidelong look. She couldn't read it at all. He wasn't livid, but he could be masking anger. He was so loyal to his king that any insinuation to the contrary might have infuriated him. Just because he'd been willing to play along didn't mean he'd approved. She'd backed him into that.

He finally said, "When one is imprisoned, it is one's duty to scheme ways to escape."

She nodded, relieved. The words weren't oozing approval, but he understood what she'd been trying to do.

"I like it better when you throw vials of acid at your captors," he added a little glumly.

"Sorry."

He'd probably been affronted and horrified by her fondling his chest.

"That part was all right." He smiled so quickly that she might have imagined it.

Before she could come up with a response, Gelira pushed the roots aside and pointed at Jadora. "She will see you."

Jadora hadn't heard a conversation, but she supposed it would have been telepathic. Tezi didn't likely know any of the languages of the continent.

"She has no interest in seeing *you*." Gelira shifted her pointing finger to Malek.

"As the professor's protector, I will go where she goes," Malek said, that commanding power in his voice again.

Gelira squinted at him. "I am not sense-dead. I know you're attempting to manipulate me."

"As you attempted to manipulate me when you told me to leave my weapons behind," Malek said.

"Unfortunate that it didn't work. You are as powerful as the rumors say." It sounded far more like a statement of disgust than a compliment.

Malek inclined his head once, not taking his eyes from her.

Jadora eased past Gelira, leaving the standoff for them to figure out.

"Gelira?" one of the druids called, then rattled off several sentences in their language.

Gelira sighed, looking at the room and at Jadora and Malek, as if she feared leaving her charge alone with Malek for even a moment, but the other druids moved closer, so she didn't have to go far.

Jadora wouldn't have minded leaving Malek outside with them, so she could talk to Tezi alone, but he stuck with her, his sword still out. He was always alert and wary, but he was hypervigilant down here, and she feared he knew for certain that this was a trap, with an attack imminent.

Tezi sat on a mattress in a sleeveless smock made from woven grass, similar to what the druids wore, and a fur blanket pulled over her lap. Her blue eyes widened when Jadora walked in, then bulged as Malek trailed her. She shrank back against the wall beside the mattress, though she caught herself and straightened, turning her fear into a defiant glower.

"Hello, Tezi. We came to check on you. We were hoping to rescue you from Yidar and Tonovan, but it looks like you did that yourself." Jadora smiled at her, though she also glanced curiously at Malek. He hadn't made any claim of assisting her, but Jadora couldn't help but doubt that Tezi could have gotten away without help. She well knew how difficult it was to wiggle free from the powerful grasps of mages.

But if Malek had helped, he didn't mention it. He merely alternated watching them and watching the tunnel. It was the only exit to the room, and he'd placed himself between it and Jadora.

"Yes, ma'am. I did." Tezi lifted her chin, though a quaver in her voice suggested the ordeal had been traumatic.

"That's good. I'm relieved you didn't need our help and also that the druids found you and helped you." Jadora nodded toward a healing patch on Tezi's arm, familiar with the mixture of magic and myorka pad that was well-known throughout Zewnath. She wished she could get a few to take with her. In her experience, they dried out and the magic faded over time, but that took several weeks, and even after that, they had some efficacy.

"Gelira saved my life," Tezi said.

"I'm glad. Jak was worried." Jadora thought about putting in a good word for her son and saying that he was the one who'd talked Malek into helping, but she'd never gotten the sense that Tezi reciprocated Jak's feelings and didn't want to make her uncomfortable.

"Is he—are you... back with Thorn Company?"

"No." Jadora stifled a wince as she considered how to explain who they *were* staying with. "We ended up on the *Star Flyer*. Colonel Sorath is alive, by the way. I think he might have gone back to your unit. He was injured—it looked like Yidar dropped a stable on him—but I bandaged his wounds, and he should be fine with some rest."

If any of them ever got some rest. The mere thought of sleep made her yawn noisily.

"He dropped the stable on *both* of us, ma'am," Tezi said. "I'm glad he made it out. I wondered."

"You can call me Jadora. And thank you for helping us in that tower. Without you and Sorath throwing those explosives, we never would have slipped away from Yidar. It's not easy to escape a zidarr."

"I know that well." Tezi eyed Malek.

"You seem to be doing fine, but we can take you with us if you want. We're quite a ways from civilization, and I'm not sure if the druids are willing to take you back to Port Toh-drom or another town. I don't know how long it would take, but maybe we can get you back to your unit." Jadora looked at Malek, realizing she should have asked him earlier if that would be a possibility. She didn't even know how Thorn Company had fared in the battle when Malek and the *Star Flyer* had slipped in to get the portal.

Malek's brows rose. "The unit of the mercenaries who've been attacking us?"

"Yes," Jadora said. "I believe Zaruk and his allies hired them and that they're just doing a job. Presumably, they don't have any ill will toward you. Not any more than they have toward all mages in general."

His eyebrows hadn't descended. Maybe that hadn't been the most tactful way to put it.

"Do you have room on the *Star Flyer* for another guest?" Jadora asked.

He must have intended to offer that. Otherwise, why would he have agreed to come to get Tezi?

"She can stay in our cabin," Jadora added.

Tezi's nose scrunched up in a dubious expression as she listened. "Guest or prisoner?" she mumbled.

"You wouldn't be kept in a cell," Jadora told her firmly. "And since Malek is an honorable man who doesn't hold ill will even toward enemies, I'm sure he would let you off in a city his ship was flying over, if not go out of his way to reunite you with your company."

She realized that had come across as manipulative and felt guilty about it. Worse, Malek would see through it. Comments about math weaknesses aside, he was a smart man.

And yes, he was giving her that sidelong look again.

"We can let her off *after* we complete the mission," he said, ignoring the part about her company.

Surprisingly, Tezi's face had shifted from skepticism to grief at the mention of her unit. She swallowed visibly and struggled to mask her features.

Had they been destroyed? Had Tonovan gloated about it to her?

"I can't go back to them," Tezi whispered, looking toward the wall so they couldn't see her eyes.

"Most of your Thorn Company should have survived the battle," Malek said. "Some of Zaruk's ships have crashed, but we did not utterly destroy them and their crews. There were many left alive when we flew away."

"That's not the reason. I just... I don't have anywhere..." Tezi glanced at him, then clammed up.

"Do you want to come with us?" Jadora asked. "With *me*?"

Tezi glanced at Malek again, then shook her head.

Jadora could tell Tezi was trying to hold herself together, that she didn't want to appear weak in front of Malek, and thought she might explain herself further if he weren't there.

"We don't have a lot of time," Malek said quietly. "For more reasons than the range of the skyboards."

Jadora didn't know what he referred to but trusted it was true. In general, a lack of patience didn't seem to be one of his flaws.

"Will you step outside for a moment?" Jadora asked. "Let me talk to her alone and make sure she's all right?"

Malek hesitated, probably not wanting her out of his sight, but he nodded and walked out. The murmurs of the druids in the tunnel fell silent. Maybe they would all glare at each other for another ten minutes.

Jadora stepped closer to Tezi and waved to the end of the mattress. "May I join you?"

Tezi shrugged, reminding Jadora of the teenage girl she probably still was rather than a hardened mercenary. Or even a rookie mercenary, as the women in her unit referred to her.

"If you don't want to come along, I won't try to talk you into it. In truth, we're headed into more danger." Jadora thought of the map on the monument with the portal symbol crossed out. "But I want to make sure you're truly all right before we go, and that you want to be left here. Jak *will* question me when we come back without you."

Tezi glanced at her, moisture filming her eyes, though she'd managed to keep tears from falling thus far. "I appreciate you coming, ma'am, and that you—you and Jak—care, but I'm not looking for... Jak is nice, but..." She groped in the air with her hand.

"Yes, I understand. I've tried to convey that to him." Jadora had been doing that even *before* Tezi had been captured by Tonovan, and she worried that even more calamities had befallen her since then. "But as his mother, I try not to quash his hopes and dreams. He's a good kid though. I'm biased, but I believe if you tell him you're not interested, he'll stop asking you to have drinks with him. Where he thinks you would even *have drinks* in the middle of all this, I don't know. It's not as if there's a pub on the *Star Flyer*."

"Are you... sure you want to take me there?"

"Not really, but it's the only option I can offer right now." Jadora lowered her voice to a whisper. "I do believe that if Lord Malek says he'll drop you off, he will. I won't deny that he works for someone I consider an enemy and a tyrant who doesn't care about anyone without magical power, but within that framework,

Malek seems... he *is* honest and honorable. He won't drag you back and enslave you when he gave his word otherwise."

"Aren't you his prisoner, ma'am?"

The mercenaries must have inculcated that *ma'am* into her.

"Jak and I currently have guest status on his ship. A cabin instead of a cell. We realized we didn't have many options, since so many people were hunting us, and we agreed that we would work with him, to a certain point, if he protected us."

"Some of the people hunting you were *his* people."

"I know. It's complicated." Jadora shrugged.

"I don't know what I should do. I can't go back to Thorn Company. They..." Tezi scrubbed her face with her hands, using the movement to hide brushing away tears. She looked at the wall again. "I've lost..."

Jadora couldn't imagine what could have happened since she'd been with Sorath that morning. Or was that yesterday, by now? It was still dark out, but dawn might be approaching again.

"You can tell me if you want." Jadora used her best supportive voice, the one usually reserved for comforting Jak when he'd been bullied at school and needed hugs and someone to rail to about the cruelties of the world. That hadn't happened since his father died, and he'd convinced himself he always had to be a man, but she remembered the gist. "I'm not going to judge you or tell anyone."

Tezi looked at her, the tears dribbling down her cheeks now, and seemed to be wrestling with indecision.

"I am a mother, you know." Jadora smiled encouragingly, offering an arm for a hug if she needed it.

"Oh, Professor." Like a dam bursting, Tezi collapsed against her, burying her face against her shoulder.

Though a little surprised she'd accepted the offer, Jadora wrapped her arms around Tezi and patted her on the back.

"An awful zidarr—Night Wrath is his name—came down and

read my mind and saw that I've—" Tezi's voice hiccupped, "—I've killed mages. *Bad* mages. One of them killed my mother and father and raped me. He was drunk and fell asleep on top of me, and I drove a dagger into his back. He woke up and almost killed me, but he fell out of bed, and I finished him off. And then Thorn Company took me in when I didn't have anyone, and they started training me, but there was a hotel with idiot teenage boy mages raping women inside, and Sorath shot some of them, and so did the captain and I. Stone Heart saw the truth in our minds, and then this Night Wrath did, and maybe Yidar too. So many of them know now, there's nowhere for me to go where they won't find me. The captain gave me some money and told me to leave the company and hide from them, but then Yidar caught me, and they took my money, and the general mauled me while his asshole men watched and enjoyed it. I got one of their knives, and then something hit the ship, and it was my chance. I stabbed him in the eye and jumped over the railing. I thought I'd fall to my death and that it would end all of my problems, but then the druids saved me, and..." Tezi took in a deep gasping breath, a shudder going through her whole body. "What do I do *now*? They'll *all* be hunting me. As soon as Malek sees what I've done, he'll kill me himself. He *has* to. They have laws about it. All I've ever done is defend myself and other people, but we're not even supposed to do that. We're supposed to *let* them screw us and kidnap us and kill our families, and—"

The words stopped then, as she broke into sobs. Jadora kept hugging her and stroked her hair, even though she was horrified. This was far, far different from comforting a boy who'd been picked on in school, and she hadn't the faintest idea how to help Tezi with this.

Jadora didn't *think* Malek would kill Tezi for defending herself. He hadn't killed Jak when he'd realized he had power, and Malek had *just* said it was the duty of prisoners to try to escape. But even if Malek was reasonable about it, did it truly matter? He was only one zidarr, and Tezi was right that the rest of them would be less understanding.

For killing mages—and taking the eye of one of their high-ranking officers—they would join forces to hunt her down. And if they went back to the *Star Flyer*, wouldn't Tonovan eventually find out she was there? He would be livid. And Jadora couldn't think of anyone worse for Tezi to have on her trail than that awful general.

"It sounds like we need to find another world for you to live on," she murmured, still stroking Tezi's hair.

She said it without thought, a figure of speech, but she paused. Wasn't that... about to become a possibility?

19

It was still dark when Jak woke to a knock on his door.

Hoping Malek and his mother had returned, he lunged to his feet, not bothering to put on his shirt or boots. As he opened it, he realized he didn't sense Malek's notable aura and that his mother would have come in without knocking.

Surprisingly, Captain Rivlen stood there, the light that came from the walls in the corridor softened for night. They almost managed to soften her cool and distant expression of military professionalism, but not quite. She was still in her uniform, and her bun was back up in its tight knot.

"Have you heard from Malek?" Jak rubbed grit out of his eyes. He didn't know how long he had slept but probably only a couple of hours. The thumps, clanks, and bangs that had been going on before as crewmen worked to repair the *Star Flyer* had stopped.

"*Lord* Malek."

Ugh. He lowered his hand. "Is it necessary to be pedantic in the middle of the night?"

"The word you're looking for is *respectful*," Rivlen said, "and that's always necessary, especially for precocious boys with a penchant for getting themselves in trouble."

"I'm not a boy." Jak scowled at her.

She eyed his bare chest, and he blushed. It wasn't a *boyish* chest—back at home, he exercised and played sports and trained so he could go along on Mother's digs—but it was possibly not sprouting as much manly hair as the chest of a twenty-five-year-old might. Or someone like Malek.

Fortunately, she didn't insult it, merely lifting her gaze—her dismissive gaze?—back to his eyes. "Yes, yes, the birthday is coming up. I remember."

"Is there something I can do for you?"

"I'd hoped Lord Malek might have sent a message to you, but from your opening question, I will assume not." Rivlen hesitated. "I still can't reach him, and after that attack, I'm concerned."

"Because if the druids could give this ship and its full complement of mages trouble, they might be able to give him trouble?"

Another hesitation. Earlier she'd said Malek could handle them, but maybe she'd had time to rethink that. "Yes."

She looked tired, and he doubted she'd slept since the attack—or at all. The last time he'd seen her, she'd been grabbing tools to oversee, or personally assist with, the repairs.

"The typical reasons I wouldn't be able to reach him telepathically, given that we shouldn't be that far apart yet, are that he's dead or unconscious. But I wondered if he might be inside a compound that's been magically insulated against mental intrusions."

"Kind of like if dark-eye fabric were wrapped around it?" Jak resisted the urge to touch the pocket that held the key to the portal. He could feel its outline against his thigh.

"Yes. Crafters can weave similar insulating magic into walls. I'm *hoping* that's what we're dealing with, that he's inside a druid sanctuary. But I'm concerned because it's been a while since we were in contact. He should have been able to get the mercenary girl by now." Her lip curled as she said mercenary girl, as if Tezi wasn't worth this effort.

"Maybe the druids didn't want to give *Tezi* up. She has a name. It's *respectful* to use it."

"She's a terrene human."

"We still deserve respect." Granted, he was more affronted on Tezi's behalf than on his own. He didn't care if Rivlen called him *the boy* or *dumb idiot*, at least not enough to get huffy.

She snorted. "You're not one of them, you know."

"Of course I am." Jak realized that wasn't quite true anymore, but he still *identified* with them, and he didn't want anything to do with the uptight, supercilious, tyrannous mage world.

"Dear Shylezar, you even *think* in vocabulary words."

"If you stay out of my mind, you won't need to carry around a dictionary." Jak glowered at her, resenting that he couldn't have peace and privacy even in his own head.

"Why don't you learn how to keep me out, so you don't need to complain about it?"

"Nobody will *teach* me. You'd all rather kill me."

"That's true, but Lord Malek implied he might give you to King Uthari. If the king has any interest in you, he might instruct you."

"That doesn't seem that likely."

"Please. Once he figures out your potential, he'll be eager to turn you into a loyal minion."

That was more horrifying than the thought of mages hunting him down to kill.

"Don't be so melodramatic." Rivlen squinted at him. "Why don't you see if you can reach out to Lord Malek? Assume he's inside a protected sanctuary and that you have to burrow through it to reach him."

"If you can't do that, I'm sure I can't."

"Probably not, but try." Power laced her words, and he had the urge to obey her as eagerly and quickly as possible, perhaps while falling to his knees and gazing adoringly up at her.

He blinked and shoved aside the thought—the compulsion—and glared at her.

She smiled faintly. "A terrene human would have done it without realizing he was being manipulated."

Jak opened his mouth to reply, but one of the young crew women walked past, saluting Rivlen and glancing at Jak. She paused and gave Jak a longer look—actually, she looked at his chest—then smirked at the captain and nodded with approval.

Warmth flushed Jak's cheeks. Maybe his chest was vaguely appealing even if it wasn't covered in manly hair.

Rivlen rolled her eyes, apparently not sharing the opinion. "Try to reach out to him. We're almost out of the range of the skyboards he took. You showed you have potential, and that artifact isn't obeying your orders because you're a sense-dumb shrub. See if you can do it."

"All right." Jak *did* want to know what was happening to Malek and if Mother was all right. He went to his bunk and sat on the edge so he could concentrate more easily.

Rivlen followed him in, raising the lights with a thought, and sat across from him on Mother's bunk. She watched him intently, as if she truly believed he might be able to do something she couldn't. Since he'd seen her utterly destroy another mageship, he highly doubted that, but he rested his palms on his knees and closed his eyes to try.

Malek? Long seconds passed. He formed Malek's face in his mind and tried again.

Nothing.

He thought of the area they'd been flying over when Tezi fell, of the druid monument Malek had described. He imagined it in his mind and a sanctuary hidden in the trees beside it, or maybe an underground sanctuary beneath the monument? Again, he pictured Malek, standing with his mother inside such a sanctuary, and he willed Malek to hear him calling his name.

Since nobody had taught him to channel his power or even how telepathy truly worked, he couldn't do anything except focus hard and think about projecting his thoughts across the distance between them.

Malek?

Busy, came a terse, tense reply.

It was so distant that Jak barely heard it, but he believed it *was* Malek.

Sorry. I just want to know if you and Mother are safe. Your ship was attacked by druids, very powerful druids. Jak attempted to send a memory of the tendrils and the green energy balls, along with the portal attacking back. *The captain is worried because she hasn't been able to reach you for a while.*

Is the ship safe?

For now, but she says we're almost out of range of your skyboards.

I know. Malek didn't say that he was on his way back. What if he was fighting, and he couldn't leave? He was being more terse than usual. A battle would explain it.

Do you want us to come back and help you? Jak offered, though Rivlen hadn't implied that was a possibility.

No. Zaruk's people are coming. Get the portal set up before you're embroiled in another battle. I must concentrate on the druids I'm dealing with. Your mother is fine. As is the girl. Tezi.

Thank you. Jak couldn't keep from sending his relief along with the words.

You're doing well with your telepathy.

Thank you, Jak repeated, ridiculously pleased by the praise.

Malek had *noticed* he was doing something hard. An intense longing filled him to have a teacher, not King Uthari, who cheerfully employed General Tonovan because it was useful to have an unbalanced bastard working for him. He wanted *Malek* to teach him. Damn it.

"That's forbidden," Rivlen said when Jak opened his eyes, apparently still surfing around in his mind.

"Yeah, that's what he said. Zidarr can't have apprentices. But if that's true, who teaches young zidarr?"

"There aren't many who are chosen for that path." Bitterness darkened her eyes as she added, "Almost *no* women. They learn combat from the best weapons masters in the world, and they're taught magic by the kings and queens themselves, the most powerful wizards in the world. It's a tremendous honor to be chosen, but they only take the very best, those with the most potential." The bitterness laced her words as well.

"You applied?" he guessed.

"Yes. I wasn't good enough."

"That's hard to believe."

Rivlen snorted and squinted at him, as if suspicious he was making a joke.

"I've met Yidar. How did *he* get in? I could see Stone Heart—he was formidable—but Yidar?" Jak curled his lip. Maybe he shouldn't have mocked the man to her face—she was on the same side as Uthari's zidarr, after all, so she would probably bark at him for not being respectful.

"You can have great magical potential and the speed and agility of a natural weapons master and still be an idiot," Rivlen said.

"I guess." Jak waved at his head. "Did you get the gist, or do you need me to sum it up?"

"I got it. I'm relieved that he's alive and hope he can get out in time to reach us. If he'd asked for help, I would have gladly turned the ship around." All the bitterness had faded from her tone, and Rivlen gazed wistfully toward the porthole. "He'd be too proud to ask for help even if he needed it. All zidarr are like that.

And they always put the mission above their own personal safety."

There was something else in her tone now, but Jak wasn't sure what. Reverence? *Longing*?

Did she have *feelings* for Malek? That went beyond the respect of two colleagues working together?

"No," Rivlen snapped and stood up. "I do not. And I don't see how someone who can cut through a protected sanctuary with his telepathic power can't keep a wall around his own thoughts. Do you *want* me to hear you?"

"No, of course not." Jak didn't bother to hide his frustration or his annoyance with her condescension. "I don't want that, and I don't want pompous jerk mages to be able to force me to my knees and strut around lecturing me on how superior they are."

He hadn't meant to include her in that group, but she gave him a disgusted look and stalked toward the door.

"I'm sorry," he blurted. "I don't think you're like that. You or Mal—*Lord* Malek. It's just that so many are." He thought of his first meeting with Tonovan, of how he'd forced the entire archaeology team to its knees and blown up the mercenaries' boat with a flick of his fingers.

Rivlen had reached the door, her hand on the knob, but she paused and looked back. Her expression was more contemplative than sympathetic, and he wondered if he should have kept his mouth shut. Maybe she was now having fantasies of forcing him to his knees.

"No." She walked toward him. "Stand up."

Jak did so, and they were face to face only a couple of feet apart.

"Put your hand up." She raised hers, palm toward him.

He tensed, half-expecting to have to defend himself against a slap, and lifted a fist. She gripped it and rolled her eyes again— funny how much younger she appeared when she did that, not like the fearsomely professional military leader but more like one of his peers at the university.

"I'm going to use my magic to try to force you to your knees," she said, "but you push back. For me, that's green."

Jak blinked. "Pardon?"

"The color green is what I imagine when I'm defending myself against an attack or making a barrier. It's a lighter green when I'm making a barrier, almost translucent, the way I want the barrier to be."

Green? Was she messing with him?

"It's not the same for everyone. You'll have to figure out your own colors, if colors even work for you. Everyone in my family thinks about different colors—for me, it's orange for heat attacks, yellow for lightning, blue for manipulating the wind or throwing pure energy, and black for mental attacks. Purple for making things, though I'm horrible at anything craft-related. I can't even thread a needle without stabbing myself."

For some reason, that thought delighted him. The mighty Captain Rivlen sewing a blankie. Maybe some lacy women's undergarments.

"Hilarious," she said. "Now shut off your thoughts and concentrate. If you get this quickly, we can work on walling off your mind. That falls under defenses so is a variation of green for me. But like I said, not everyone accesses their power by thinking about colors. Some people hear songs in their heads for the different things they want to do. Others speak words in their minds, verbal commands basically. I once met a poet who recites rhymes, which sounds tediously slow if you're under attack, but it's whatever works for you. You can usually do some things by willing them to happen, but the mental aids increase your power and reliability. They give you a way to focus when you're in a stressful situation. Ready?"

Jak had been digesting her words and accepting that she was

telling the truth, and he nodded, letting himself believe that she truly meant to teach him. Eagerness and gratitude rose inside of him.

"I'm ready," he said.

Rivlen started slowly, creating pressure all around him and above him, pushing him toward the deck. At first, he tightened his body and locked his knees, but that wouldn't do anything. He already knew that physical power wasn't enough.

He imagined green in the air all around him, a forest of trees—no, the entire *jungle*—barricading him from her power.

"It doesn't have to be that dramatic," she said dryly.

Was she sure? Because the pressure didn't lessen.

He turned the trees into green curtains and willed them to wrap around his body and protect him. Nothing happened. He imagined a bucket of green paint dumping on her head. The pressure remained steady. Frustrated, and feeling silly, he tried other colors. Yellow, blue, brown, pink polka dots...

The pressure only grew, pushing at his shoulders so hard that his legs threatened to give out. He would not only end up on his knees but perhaps with his face smashed against the deck right next to her feet.

Maybe colors didn't work for him. What else had she mentioned? Poems? Songs?

He couldn't think of any lyrics or rhymes that might help with his problem. Cartography was what he knew, not poetry. What he needed were *mountains* to protect him. Big, jagged mountains artfully depicted on a map, drawn by a sure hand. Maybe a ring of mountains all around him would do the trick. Oh, like the Impact Mountains around the Chezhuzan Crater in Northern Agorval. Perfect. He envisioned himself in the ancient crater, protected on all sides by the impervious peaks.

The pressure lessened slightly. Because he was being

successful or because she thought he was struggling and was easing up on him?

He frowned and imagined the mountains growing higher all around him, extending outward toward her and pushing her away from him.

Rivlen took a step back.

"Did I do that?" he blurted. "Did it *work*?"

She scowled, squeezed his hand, and dropped crushing pressure on him as she stepped back in.

Jak gasped, his mountains shattering into a pile of pebbles as his knees clunked to the deck.

"Lesson Number One," she said. "Keep your concentration."

"Right." He hid a grimace, not wanting her to see that he'd hit hard enough to hurt. That had been his own fault, and he appreciated the lesson. "That must be why the mercenaries carry around explosives to throw at you people."

"At *us*," she said, her eyes boring into his.

He swallowed. She was determined to make him believe he wasn't a normal human anymore.

"If you want King Uthari to accept you—for *all* mages to accept you and stop trying to kill you when they see you—you'll have to identify as one of us."

Jak would never do that, but he did his best to keep the defiant thought out of his mind, saying only, "Right," again. He wanted so badly to learn, and if she was willing to teach him, even if it was only this one time, he didn't want to blow it.

Expecting her to release him so they could restart, he tried to push himself to his feet, but the pressure remained, keeping him on his knees in front of her. The recalcitrant thought surfaced that maybe she *liked* that.

No, he'd already decided she wasn't like that. This was part of his lesson.

"You want to get up?" Rivlen asked. "Use your power to force the pressure away."

He brought back the mountains, the jagged peaks rising in a circle around him, stretching toward the sky, high enough to protect him from even overhead attacks. The pressure lessened, and he made them higher and larger. She pushed harder. He imagined nothing but mountains, stretching away from him for miles and miles, not letting any mages close enough to attack.

Gritting his teeth, he focused as hard as he had when he reached out to Malek, making them precise and perfect in his mind, each snow-capped peak chiseled from stone and layered in ice. Gradually, the pressure lessened. A groan escaped his lips at the effort this took, but he didn't care. He was doing this.

Once the pressure disappeared entirely, Jak climbed to his feet, again facing Rivlen from a level position. Actually, he was a couple of inches taller than she, something he could barely tell because he saw mountains instead of her face. He had to mentally command them to grow transparent so he could see her through them.

The pressure didn't come back. Jak smiled fiercely, pleased that he'd done it. He didn't think she'd *let* him up. No, he'd succeeded in pushing back and rising on his own.

Maybe it was silly, but pride swelled inside of him. Then he realized he was panting, as if he'd run a race, and a bead of sweat ran down his chest. He'd probably looked like an idiot grunting and straining from his knees. His sense of pride dwindled, though it didn't disappear altogether, and he tried to keep the mountains around his body to protect himself. Maybe they could even protect his thoughts from mind reading. But it would be difficult carrying such large imagery with him all the time when he was around mages. Maybe something smaller would do. Like a jaunty bandana with mountains on the fabric. He could envision himself wearing it under his hat. Stylish. The kind of thing women liked. Maybe even older women.

Jak raised his eyebrows, aware that Rivlen hadn't stepped back and was still gripping his hand. They still stood face to face, him with his bare chest heaving as she contemplated him.

Maybe she was impressed that he'd fought her off during his first lesson. Maybe she was even... *attracted* to him.

Not that *she* was panting or sweating, alas. She'd doubtless applied only the amount of pressure that she thought a neophyte could wade through.

Rivlen smirked, released his hand, and swatted him on the chest. "Not bad, kid."

Kid? He stifled a groan. She definitely wasn't attracted to him. What had he been thinking?

Besides, wasn't it *Tezi* he wanted to invite for a drink? Not some flinty mage who thought terrene humans were a lesser species and agreed that Malek should hand Jak over to Uthari for *training*. What kind of soul-selling would *that* involve? He barely kept from shuddering as he imagined being turned into someone like Malek who was sent out to hunt down and kill people who got in the way of his king.

"Thanks." Jak eased back a step from her and stuck his hands in his pockets.

"You're hiding your thoughts better now."

"Oh, good. I put on a bandana."

"What?" She glanced at his head.

It was devoid of hats, bandanas, and anything but sleep-tousled hair.

"Green didn't work, so I put mountains on it."

"Ah." She didn't say anything to suggest that was weird. "Good. Do you want to do it again? It takes a lot of practice."

He was tired, and a little wary now of how stupid he'd ended up looking in front of her, but he nodded anyway. He couldn't pass up a chance to learn this stuff.

"Wait." He lifted a hand. "Will you get in trouble for this? You and Malek—Lord Malek both said it was forbidden to teach me, to teach a wild one."

"What I said was that it's forbidden for a *zidarr* to teach anyone, but if King Uthari knows about you, it's likely he'll take you in, and you won't have the status of wild one for long. They must have some use planned for you."

Jak made sure the mental bandana was snug around his head as he thought about how repellent the idea was of being of *use* to Uthari and how he had no intention of becoming his minion.

"And as an officer in the military, it's my job to train the up-and-coming officers," Rivlen said, not commenting on his defiance —was it possible she couldn't read his mind now? "Maybe you'll end up serving in Uthari's army one day."

No way. He made himself say, "Huh. Well, thanks. This is better than cake."

He thought she wouldn't remember the reference, but she said, "Better than a magical backpack?"

"That would be amazing too." Jak lifted his hand in case she wanted to grip it again—maybe contact made the magic flow more easily. "But if I ever end up face to face with Tonovan again, I'd *really* like to be able to protect my mother from him. And myself, but especially her."

She gripped his hand but didn't respond right away. Maybe he shouldn't have mentioned wanting to fight Tonovan, since they served the same king. Hell, he was her superior officer. She might feel it her duty to report all of this to him. At least he hadn't blath-ered about *killing* Tonovan, though if the man ever leered at his mother again, Jak would be tempted to try, especially if he learned enough and gained the power to do it.

But it was delusional to think he ever would have *that* much power. Just because Rivlen thought he had some strong potential didn't mean he could beat all of Uthari's best mages.

"Maybe someday," Rivlen said quietly, her eyes intense and her hand tightening around his, "if I train you and if we end up facing him, you can stand with me, and we can defeat him together."

Thus far, he'd never sensed the thoughts or feelings of other mages, but something flashed into his mind, Tonovan pinning a younger and inexperienced Lieutenant Rivlen against a wall, tearing her uniform open, and instructing her how she could best *serve* him.

A wave of such loathing rolled over Jak that he almost dropped to his knees, not because of magic this time, but because the emotion was so intense. He locked them as the image disappeared, and Rivlen's face smoothed—for a moment, that loathing had been twisting her usually attractive features. But she had control of her face again, only the burning intensity in her eyes remaining as she imagined defeating Tonovan.

"That seems fair," Jak whispered, not wanting to bring up the rest—her thoughts. He suspected she hadn't meant to share them. But if they had been true, he had another reason to hate that man.

"Good. Sometimes superior officers disappear, and officers below them are promoted. There are a lot of people who are tired of that man running the fleet." Rivlen smiled fiercely, ambition replacing the loathing in her eyes.

Jak realized he shouldn't have let his emotions—*her* emotions —make him agree too hastily to things. Maybe he should have asked Malek about all this.

Rivlen opened her mouth but stopped before saying more. Her gaze drifted to the side as she concentrated on something.

A message? Was Malek reaching out to her?

She released him and stepped back. "My lieutenant has informed me that King Uthari has contacted the ship via the dome-jir and wants to speak to me."

A lurch of fear went through Jak. Could Uthari somehow know from halfway across the world that Rivlen was teaching him? Despite what she'd said, Jak questioned if it was allowed. Maybe Uthari would punish her for presuming to show Jak—a wild one—something about magic. Or maybe he would punish her for plotting against General Tonovan. Because that was what she was doing, wasn't it? Thinking of training Jak to assist her in confronting him. Or in... assassinating him?

Dear Shylezar, he hoped he hadn't agreed to that.

"I must go to the dome-jir so I can receive his orders." Did she look a little nervous, or was that his imagination? If she did, she quashed the emotion quickly, then bowed formally to him, the expressionless soldier mien returning, and headed for the door. Before walking out, she paused. "Practice with your mountains. I'll come teach you more when there's time. And you'll remember our deal."

There was something triumphant and even possessive as she looked over her shoulder, meeting his eyes.

"I will," he whispered, holding her gaze.

Jak wouldn't forget. He was terrified that he'd made a huge mistake, but he was also certain he would do it again. He detested Tonovan, and he wanted so badly to know how to use his power, to defend himself and his mother.

Sasko dozed for a while with the rest of Thorn Company—they'd been given a section of the *Skimmer*'s deck—until voices woke her. Lieutenant Vinjo was standing at the railing with Night Wrath, Sorath, and the captain of the ship, Night Wrath and Vinjo with skyboards tucked under their arms and packs on their backs. In addition, Night Wrath carried his weapons. Vinjo wore a tool belt and gripped that invisibility box he'd been showing off earlier. The clandestineness creeper. If the man ever sold his gizmos, he would have to hire someone else to come up with names.

"You should go see your new admirer off, LT," Tinder said.

She and Dr. Fret were at work nearby, Tinder making new grenades, and Fret with spools of suture, healing tinctures, and rolls of bandages that she was adding to her medical kit. They must have found time for a supply run in Port Toh-drom.

"If one of you two learned to cook," Sasko said, "you could provide everything the company needs."

"I can cook," Tinder said.

"Charring meat over a campfire doesn't count as cooking."

"Why not? It's efficient and doesn't dirty pans. And I'm serious." Tinder pointed at the group of mages. "If you kiss him and give him a reason to come back, maybe he'll try harder to not be discovered, captured, and tortured for information that includes the location of our ship."

"I'm not kissing him. Besides, he's making puppy eyes at Sorath now."

"Maybe we could get Colonel Sorath to kiss him," Fret said. "He seems lonely."

"A kooky mage inventor isn't going to solve that problem for him."

Probably. Vinjo was smiling expansively as he demonstrated something—an explosion, if his whole body bouncing and arm movements properly conveyed the notion—to Sorath.

Night Wrath rolled his eyes and muttered darkly to the captain.

Sorath nodded, patted Vinjo on the shoulder, and pointed off to the south. Vinjo nodded vigorously, then pulled something out of his pocket and handed it to Sorath. A gift? Another odd invention?

"Too bad," Tinder said. "If he liked you because you fantasized about shoving pencils up a mage's nose, he ought to *love* Sorath. I'm positive his fantasies involve larger and pointier objects."

"Given how much he loathes most of the mages," Fret said, "he has a curious knack for befriending the atypical ones."

Sasko started to correct that to *kooky*, but she remembered that helmsman from the *Dauntless*—Nobber—who'd also been eager to obey Sorath over his captain. He hadn't been kooky as much as young and impressionable. That he'd been willing to crash his ship—or *pretend* to crash his ship—for Sorath had been remarkable.

"I don't know if they're atypical as much as low in the pecking order." Tinder paused in trimming a fuse so she could flap her arm like a chicken wing. "They probably like a big dominant male showing interest in their ideas."

"Sorath isn't that dominant." That was a word Sasko tended to attach to *overbearing* and *arrogant*. "I've actually been surprised he's reasonable and hasn't tried to take command of the company from Ferroki."

"He's big, scarred, and has lots of muscles. Close enough."

"That might be the secret," Fret said.

"To what?" Tinder asked.

Fret gazed speculatively at the men, probably thinking about something more profound than scars and muscles. She read a lot when she wasn't doctoring and tended to get philosophical.

"I'm afraid to say." Fret peered around the deck of the ship. "There might be a mage around reading minds."

"Nobody bothers reading the minds of doctors," Sasko said. "They're never thinking inimical thoughts."

"I'm thinking them now. Well, less inimical—at least from my point of view—and more..." Fret glanced around again before whispering, "incendiary."

"I knew it started with an i."

"Maybe revolutionary is the right word. Or even seditious."

Tinder eyed her with concern. "You're right. You should keep those thoughts to yourself, especially with them close." She nodded toward Night Wrath and the ship's captain.

"They're busy planning mayhem," Sasko said, though if Fret was plotting against mages, she shouldn't encourage it.

"It just occurred to me," Fret said quietly, "that there have to be more mages who are low in the pecking order than high, and if someone with a knack for befriending them could unite them..."

"Against their superiors?" Sasko asked.

"Remember what Jak and Jadora talked about? The reason they dug up that portal in the first place?"

"No," Tinder said firmly.

"You don't? They want to find allies to get rid of the tyrannical governments run by wizards and create equality and opportunity for—"

Tinder clamped a hand across Fret's mouth.

Fret raised her eyebrows.

"I don't remember," Tinder said firmly, glancing at Night Wrath. "And neither do you."

"Ah," Fret said when Tinder released her. "I remember now. I mean I *don't* remember."

Sasko lifted her eyes toward the stars. None of the mages had looked over, so they wouldn't likely get in trouble, but Tinder was right. It was too dangerous to think about such things on a ship full of mind readers.

Fortunately, Sorath was gesticulating with his voice raised, and the mages at the railing were focused on him. He was asking to go along.

"I can only keep two of us clandestine." Vinjo waved one of his gizmos.

"You've got no magic," Night Wrath told Sorath. "You would be a liability."

"This was *my* idea," Sorath said.

"Yes, and I'm so thankful that you volunteered me for it," Night Wrath said.

"I'm willing to go along with you in case there's a fight."

Night Wrath squinted at him. Scouring his thoughts?

"Not to watch our backs, I see, but because you want to rescue that *girl*. That girl who's killed mages." Night Wrath snarled. "If she's Tonovan's prisoner, she's getting what she deserves."

"Nobody deserves that."

"She deserves it and *worse*." Night Wrath put up a hand, using magic to push Sorath back from him before Sorath could throw a punch.

Vinjo stood to the side, not interfering but looking back and forth between them with concern.

"You're not coming, *Colonel*." Night Wrath gave the rank in a mocking tone.

Sasko wished Sorath had succeeded in punching him.

Night Wrath pushed him farther back, then waved for Vinjo to step up to the railing with him. They exchanged a few parting words with the captain, while Sorath glared daggers at Night Wrath's shoulder blades, then readied their skyboards. Night Wrath looked irritated but determined. Meanwhile, Vinjo had gone from grinning to peering into the dark jungle with a daunted expression on his face. Or was that a terrified expression?

Maybe he *did* need a kiss to give him a reason to come back. Or impart bravery, if lips could accomplish such feats.

Perhaps thinking something similar, Sorath stepped around Night Wrath to clap Vinjo on the back. "You'll do fine, Lieutenant. Just remember to hide behind your brother if you get in trouble."

"That never worked with our parents," Vinjo said, "but I'll try."

They sprang onto their skyboards, Night Wrath like the natural athlete he was, and Vinjo with a wobble that caused a pencil to fall from behind his ear, bounce off the railing, and disappear into the jungle below. He recovered, and they zipped away into the darkness, flying ahead of the ship.

"I have concerns about that mission succeeding," Tinder said.

"That's why we're up in the middle of the night readying grenades and medical supplies," Fret said.

The ship's captain headed to the navigation cabin, and Sorath came over to join Thorn Company.

He pointed at the grenades. "Make some extras of those. I think we'll need them."

"Because the sabotage mission will fail, and those two will blab and lead our enemies back to us?" Sasko asked.

"Because whether it succeeds or fails, Uthari's people are going to be furious with us, and we're now the closest ship to his." Sorath squinted toward navigation. "I'm going to suggest to the helmsman that we fly off to the west, so we're not in a direct line between the *Star Flyer* and Port Toh-drom. That might make it harder for them to find us if they retrace the route."

"Good idea," Sasko said.

An even better idea would be for them to leave the continent altogether, but she doubted anyone would go along with that.

20

MALEK STOOD IN FRONT OF THE ROOT CURTAIN TO TEZI'S ROOM, aware of the girl crying as she talked to Jadora, but his focus was on the druids conferring scant feet away. They protected their thoughts well, and he couldn't understand their words if they didn't share them telepathically with him, but their body language told him much. They were plotting against him and had been since he'd dropped down into their sanctuary. Only their fear of losing some of their people had kept them from attacking him.

He was also positive they wanted Jadora dead—or at least incapacitated—so she couldn't help Malek get the portal operational. They feared what would happen when it was—as did everyone on this continent. He'd sensed it from the natives during the brief time he'd been in Port Toh-drom, though they hadn't been able to articulate anything beyond big-round-artifact-bad. The druids, he was certain, knew more, but unless they let him glimpse their thoughts or told him...

Gelira held up a hand, nodded to the group, and turned to face Malek.

He hadn't sheathed his sword since he'd entered their sanctuary—their underground *fortress*—where the walls were rein-forced by strong magic to withstand attacks and also to keep anyone from sensing they were down here. He'd been surprised earlier when Jak had managed to get a message through to him. The boy had impressive potential, and Malek truly hoped Uthari took him in to train.

"Zidarr Malek," Gelira said, then switched to telepathy, sharing images as well as words, so he could more easily get the gist of what she meant. As it often did, the magic of his sword supplied flashes of insight that helped. *Are you in command of the ship flying inland with the ancient dragon gate?*

The ship that allies of yours attacked and tried to strike down? Malek asked to let her know he was aware of what had happened.

Thanks to Jak sharing his thoughts, Malek had seen enough of the attack to confirm that it had been druid magic. Her people had declared themselves enemies with that act, and from what Malek had seen in Jak's memories, they might have destroyed the *Star Flyer* if not for the assistance from the artifact. Later, Malek would thank Jak for that help. He would try to think of a favor he could grant that wouldn't put him at cross-purposes with Uthari and his wishes. He'd already walked a fine line by arranging interference to Tonovan's ship, interference that had let Tezi take his eye. Malek planned to confess that to Uthari and fully expected to be punished for it, but he couldn't regret it.

The ship that is flying without permission into our territory and carrying a deadly artifact that my ancestors long ago worked very hard to get rid of and bury where it wouldn't be found again, Gelira said. *Imagine our horror to sense it arriving on our shores once again.*

How is it deadly?

Because of what can come through it when it is seated in place and able to be activated from the other world.

Worlds, Malek almost corrected, but she might not know that. He wouldn't dismiss what she had to say though. Her ancestors had always been here on this continent, and it was the ancient druidic tongue that was one of the thirty-two languages engraved on the inside of the portal.

Explain, he said.

Tell your captain to divert and bring the gate here, so that we can properly bury it again, this time where nobody will ever find it.

You'll definitely *have to explain if you want me to do that.* Malek didn't point out that he wouldn't do that under any circumstances. Uthari wanted it activated, at least long enough for someone to retrieve plenty of the plant he sought, and it was Malek's duty to make that happen.

Gelira tilted her head. *If I explain sufficiently, would you consider it?*

He didn't want to lie, so he avoided answering the question directly. *You must convince me that it is dangerous even to a zidarr and a ship full of mages. I have a hard time believing anything but dragons themselves could be a threat to us or to your kind.* He waved at the druids to acknowledge that they were well-trained and powerful, more so than he'd expected.

There are many *dangerous creatures in the other world, including the dragons. Not all of them are the benevolent rulers that were the basis for one of your people's religions. They may have been like that in the beginning, but things changed after a time. Cruel dragons came through and preyed on us and on other dragons. There was a great war between them. We took advantage of their distraction to pull down the gate and take it halfway across the world. Only because it has been buried all this time has our world been safe from the deadly predators who once traveled through the portal to dine on human flesh.*

Grisly, Malek said, *but what evidence can you give me? Ancient stories aren't reliable resources. I'm sure Professor Freedar would agree.*

Gelira pursed her lips as she scowled through the curtain past Malek. For a second, emotion escaped the defenses wrapped around her mind, and he sensed her frustration and anger at Jadora for having unearthed the artifact.

Malek growled and stepped forward, his grip tight on his sword.

Gelira blinked and stepped back, raising a hand as if to create defensive magic. Several of her people pointed their weapons at Malek.

He and Gelira froze, neither attacking, but both tense. Reminding himself that he couldn't win against so many, and that he needed to return to the ship and complete Uthari's mission, Malek forced himself to step back.

Puzzlement creased Gelira's brow as she asked, *Are you truly her lover? I'd assumed that was a ploy, but...*

The memory of Jadora stroking his chest came to mind, but Malek pushed it away. That ruse had not pleased him, and when Jadora had said he'd sworn his loyalty to her instead of Uthari, it had taken all of his control not to spring away, lest someone believe it true. The thought that she could come up with such a scenario, even as part of a ploy, disturbed him, and he hoped he hadn't done anything to put that idea into her mind.

I am loyal to my king, he replied.

That's not what I asked.

It is all that is important. Do you have evidence of this past in which people were preyed upon, or do you not?

Thankfully, Gelira dropped the uncomfortable line of inquiry about Jadora. *If I show you something that proves it is the truth, will you put an end to your mission?* She tilted her head again—she looked like she was regarding some odd growth found in the back of a laboratory cabinet when she did that. *For a long time, our kind and your kind have been enemies, but I believe that in this matter, you will agree it would be wise if we were in alignment and acted together.*

Perhaps you should have had this conversation with me before *attacking my ship.* Malek suspected they were only having it now because their attack had failed and they weren't sure they could take him down without great losses.

Yes, she surprised him by agreeing. *You are correct.*

She waved to the male druid Malek had been trading glares with earlier and said something aloud. He trotted back up the tunnel and disappeared.

We have an old text. You would need to translate it to read its contents, but it was scribed two centuries ago by one of my kind who gathered information from all the ancient monuments and cave paintings in this land. He gathered together the stories from those who were eyewitnesses to the events of that time.

Malek debated if a book of old stories copied from cave paintings counted as evidence. Fortunately, he had an archaeologist along to consult.

"Jadora," he called through the curtain. "They have an old book they're going to show us. I'd like your opinion on it, such as if you've heard of the author—the scribe who gathered the ancient stories in it—and if it is a reliable resource."

She pushed aside the roots and joined him.

"She said it would need to be translated," Malek added, "but I'd appreciate your first impressions."

"I understand."

Malek lowered his voice. "I'd also like to know if it's legitimately two centuries old or if they're cobbling together something right now to fool us. Would you be able to tell the age of a book by examining it? Or if someone used magic to make it *look* old?" He sensed the male druid returning.

"I'd like to think so," she said dryly.

The male druid bowed to Gelira and handed her a leather-bound tome with yellowed pages. It appeared as old as they'd promised, but Malek knew what could be done with magic.

Gelira took the tome, brought it to them, and offered it to Jadora with a smile. *We would like this returned to us one day, but you may take it long enough to examine it thoroughly and translate the stories within.*

Remembering the burst of anger Gelira had let slip out about Jadora, Malek eased closer to her, his sword between the two of them. His blade gave him another flash of insight, awareness that Gelira was feigning friendliness and still resented Jadora's role in unearthing the portal.

Jadora must have noticed his movement, for she glanced at him, but she said nothing, only accepting the book. She carefully opened it, the binding crackling with age, and studied the opening page.

I have heard of the scribe, she thought for Malek's sake. *The druids don't have archaeologists, in the sense that we use the term, but he was known to gather ancient languages and stories to make records of everything for posterity.*

Will you be able to translate it using Uthari's book?

That is not a complete lexicon, but I believe I can get the gist by translating the known words. Jadora ran her finger down the runes on the first page. *I recognize some of these from the work I started on the monument.*

Malek nodded. A large rune at the top in the spot where a chapter number or short story title might have been in a modern book looked familiar to him, though he didn't remember from where. Likely the monument.

I assume it will take time? he asked.

Jadora carefully turned the brittle pages. It was a thick tome. *A few weeks, I would guess. Perhaps I could translate the first section in the next day or two.*

"We will study this with an open mind," Malek told Gelira.

Good. But it will take time for you to translate. If you will allow it, I will show you the story that the first section of the tome shares.

Malek hesitated, not trusting that she would give them the truth.

But Jadora responded with a "Yes, please" and a firm nod. Her eyes radiated curiosity.

Gelira dropped her chin to her chest while the other druids waited behind her. Instead of sharing only words with them, she shared imagery, a story that played out in Malek's and Jadora's minds.

He expected it to feature the portal resting beside the familiar pool deep in the forest, but Gelira showed them a village by a stream, the jungle cleared away from wooden huts, gardens, and pens of chickens and other small livestock. The villagers were out tending the land and the animals, wearing simple clothing similar to what the druids today favored, long tunics of coarsely spun fabric or woven grass. Sun beamed down upon them, and they appeared happy until a long and sinuous creature flew over the trees and into view of the inhabitants.

It wasn't a dragon but a giant worm with wings. It dove over the trees and down toward the villagers, its body as wide as some of the huts and easily a hundred feet in length. The wings were huge and diaphanous, strangely graceful on the body of what was essentially a fat giant worm.

Malek raised skeptical eyebrows and looked at Jadora. He had never heard of such a creature.

Her eyes were closed, and she appeared engrossed in the vision, so he couldn't get her opinion.

Gelira continued to share the story. No sound came with the images, but the villagers appeared to scream. They ran for the cover of their huts, but the worm swooped down. It spat streams of green ichor from its mouth, each wad enough to knock a person down when it struck. More than that. It knocked the villagers down and pinned them to the ground under the sticky stuff. The worm rapid-fired the ichor, taking down dozens of people within a minute.

A group of druids strode out of the trees, coming to the

defense of the villagers. They launched magical attacks at the worm, crude early versions of the tendrils and green balls of energy that their descendants had used on the *Star Flyer*. But the worm was impervious to the attacks and spat ichor at them with pinpoint accuracy. It ate through the barriers they attempted to raise. The druids fell to the ichor and were as trapped as everyone else. A few villagers made it into huts, but the worm flew over the structures and used its flexible back end like a whip to smash them to the ground.

Malek eyed Gelira and the druids, continuing to be skeptical of all of this. The faces of the men and women behind Gelira were grave, and they glanced uneasily at each other, as if they not only believed this had truly happened but feared it would happen again.

After the winged worm pinned down all of the villagers, like a spider trapping prey in its web, it landed among them. It flattened its wings against its body and undulated through the destruction. It opened a huge round mouth full of fangs and ate its prisoners alive.

The image faded, and Gelira sighed, opening her eyes. *That book is the only resource we have that collects the stories of the past in one place, but they are also on our monuments and on the walls of caves all throughout this land. They were written in the ancient language, but there are those among us today who can still read the words. We know what our monuments say, what happened in the past.*

"Thoughts?" Malek asked Jadora.

"There were carvings of deadly creatures on the monument in Port Toh-drom. Without your king's book, I could not translate the stories around them, but some of them were familiar to me because they are in druidic mythology. That giant flying worm is mentioned. There are a lot of large predatory creatures in their ancient tales, and there are even stories they tell their children about not wandering into the jungle lest the sky lizards eat them. Some believe those refer to dragons."

Gelira nodded at her.

Malek was still skeptical, but if Jadora wasn't scoffing, he would try to keep an open mind.

"However," Jadora continued, "there's nothing in the fossil record that suggests anything like that giant worm ever existed. We *do* have evidence of dragons, so we know they were here, but not the other creatures described in their mythology. Most of the truly large creatures we've found fossils of came out of the oceans and ate nothing more than fish."

That is because they came here only to hunt, Gelira told them. *They did not die here. Once they feasted on our helpless ancestors, they returned to their world.*

"There's a *keyhole* on the portal," Malek said. "And a corresponding key. Isn't it required to open a passageway between worlds?"

"We believe so," Jadora said.

Gelira spread her arms. Malek couldn't tell if it was because she didn't know the answer to his question or she wasn't aware of the keyhole.

"It's possible the dragons added it later," Jadora said. "Perhaps to try to keep such creatures from using the portals. Also, if few of the worms died on Torvil, that would explain their lack of bones in the fossil record. Only a very small percentage of all the animals that existed long ago died in such a way that their remains were preserved. We've found very few dragon skeletons, only two fully intact."

If you set up the dragon gate, Gelira continued, *it is possible these creatures will once again come to prey on humans. Maybe this time, they won't limit themselves to our continent. Had my ancestors not acted quickly enough, the flying predators might have gone all over the world, and they might have stayed instead of returning to their home.*

What if they had devoured all humans and our species had gone extinct? She pointed at Jadora. *Do your scientific records not agree that the population of Zewnath is relatively low compared to the other fertile continents in the world? What they do not likely say is that it's because we lost so many people ten thousand years ago and that it's taken a long time for our populations to grow again.*

"That is true," Jadora told Malek. "Numerous scientists have noted that Zewnath seemed to have an extinction-level event around that time. There is a hypothesis that an asteroid struck, altering the climate of the landmass for a time, because many of the larger species had a significant population decline."

It was not only humans that they hunted, Gelira said.

"Let us go, and I will discuss this with King Uthari." Malek would report it to him, especially if Jadora translated the tome and found the story had been accurately shared, but he doubted it would change Uthari's mind about anything. If there were large predatory creatures in other worlds that they would have to worry about, Malek believed he could handle them. And if a key was now required to use the portal, such creatures shouldn't be able to come back to Torvil.

If we let you go, you will return to your ship and take her to help you activate the artifact. I sense that you do not believe us. Gelira frowned at Malek, then pointed at Jadora. *Though I believe maybe she does.*

Jadora opened her mouth but closed it again.

Do you want to discuss this in private? Malek asked her silently.

Is there privacy to be had here?

If you wish to rejoin your comrade, we will remain out here and give you privacy. Gelira nodded toward Tezi's room.

Her face remained bland, and there was nothing blatantly suspicious about the words or her movement, but she was plotting something. Malek was certain of it.

If Jadora hadn't walked back into the room, Malek might have challenged Gelira, but they'd already been posturing at each other, and all it had done was waste time. He needed to grab Tezi, if she was coming, and get them out of there.

Tezi was standing when Malek returned to the room, evidence of her tears staining her face, but she lifted her chin with determination. As much determination as one could have while standing barefoot in a druid smock with her hair in tangled knots.

"You're coming?" he asked.

"To another world, yes." A smile ghosted across her face.

"You'll have to explain that to me later," Malek told Jadora.

Uncertainty troubled her eyes, and Jadora only nodded. Had Gelira's shared vision truly put doubts in her mind?

"We should talk about it later," Jadora whispered, "but for now, we'd better—"

Magic pulsed in the tunnel, and Malek whirled toward it, but nobody walked in. It soon faded, and at first, he couldn't tell what had happened. But then he saw it.

"They altered the roots." He strode toward the curtain in the tunnel, but the roots had grown thick and emanated magic. A *lot* of magic.

He tried to push them aside, but they'd grown so thick that there were no gaps between them. What had been a curtain was now a door. No, a *wall*.

"So we can't get out?" Jadora asked.

Malek lifted his sword. There wasn't enough room for a good swing, but the blade had enough magic of its own that he believed it would cut through. He hesitated. Afterward, he would have to face the druids, and he sensed the whole group waiting in the tunnel to see what he would do. Though Malek couldn't see them, he was certain they were crouched to attack.

Gelira had left. To speak with the druids who had attacked his ship? Or with others elsewhere in the jungle? Perhaps near the spot the *Star Flyer* was taking the portal?

Malek imagined another group of druids leaping out and attacking while Rivlen and the crew were setting it up. They might target Jak if it was apparent he had the knowledge to activate it. That thought made Malek grimace. He'd offered to protect Jak as much as Jadora. Jak had been the one to surrender—to make a deal with Malek.

"I think I can break out," he said, backing into the chamber, "but they're out there expecting it. A lot of them. I would guess they only have orders to keep us here, but I *know* they wouldn't hesitate to kill me."

"I gave her tea." Jadora sounded affronted, as if the gift should have eliminated any hard feelings about raising up an artifact these people were apparently sworn to keep from being activated.

"And stole some of her crystals. Any chance those are the ones that dig holes?" Malek's gaze drifted upward. He didn't know how far underground they were now, or how much the magic that protected the sanctuary would fight the magic of the crystals, but the druids might not anticipate them making a back door and leaving that way.

"We can find out." Jadora removed the two glowing purple crystals that she'd snapped off like asparagus stalks and handed them to Malek. "I believe they take magic to activate."

"It's not anything I'm familiar with, but let me try." Depending on how deep they were, Malek might be able to blast a way out on his own, but the addition of the protective druid magic in the walls and ceiling of the sanctuary added complexity. His method would also drop any dirt he moved down on top of them if he didn't blow it upward with enough force.

With that thought in mind, he opted for the back wall instead of the ceiling, taking one of the crystals and jamming it into the dirt between roots. Most mage tools weren't that difficult to use, so he started simple, willing it to carve a tunnel starting at that point.

To his surprise, a hole appeared right away. Little dirt tumbled back into the room. It was as if it compacted or melted together, leaving the walls smooth.

Tezi's eyes grew round as she watched. Jadora, who'd known what the crystals could do, only nodded.

The magical tool advanced through the dirt of its own accord, as if it were a drill bit, but the hole it created was much wider than the crystal itself. Much, *much* wider. It was identical to the tunnels they'd traveled through to get back here.

Realizing it was boring happily along horizontally, Malek willed the crystal to tilt upward. It obeyed, disappearing from view.

"What happens if it tries to come up under a tree?" Jadora whispered.

"You're the one who stole it," Malek said.

"Yes, but you're zidarr. You're supposed to know everything about magic."

"Not druid magic. I—" Malek sensed the druids approaching the entrance to the room. The root wall was still in place, but he had a feeling they'd figured out what was going on. "Go." He pointed for Jadora to lead Tezi out through the new tunnel. "I'll catch up."

A thump, followed by a ripping sound came from the root wall. Jadora and Tezi hurried out the back without questioning him.

Malek held his sword at the ready as he faced the roots. He would buy them time to reach the surface, then find a way to follow. Without him, they wouldn't be able to ride the skyboards back to safety, so he had to survive.

Captain Rivlen smoothed her uniform and her face as she sat in front of the dome-jir in a tiny cabin near hers that was reserved for its use. King Uthari had never asked to speak personally to her before, always dealing with her superiors when she'd served under others, but now that she was the captain of one of his mage-ships, she had to expect such attention. Especially when Malek wasn't here.

After she rested her hand on the crystal communication node to acknowledge that she was ready to talk, long seconds passed with the air above it remaining empty.

Nerves tangled in her gut since she'd just been doing something questionable. As she'd told Jak, there was nothing wrong with her teaching her young officers magic and practicing skills with them, but he wasn't a part of her crew. He wasn't even a mage citizen. The fact that he had potential to become powerful didn't change that. If anything, it might make others question her choice, believing she wanted to do... exactly what she'd envisioned doing. Training him and using him as a secret weapon to help her defeat Tonovan.

She hadn't intended to do any of that when she'd gone to his cabin. All she'd wanted was what she'd asked, to know if he could contact Malek.

Normally, she wouldn't have asked a prisoner—or even a guest —for assistance, but she'd seen glimpses of his power, his potential. She'd also felt more kindly inclined toward him since he ran up on deck to convince the artifact to launch counterattacks at the druids. Even though she'd heard it could do that, she wouldn't have known how to make it do so. She could sense its magic but not how to manipulate it.

The air above the dome-jir wavered, and Uthari's face appeared.

"King Uthari." Rivlen saluted and made sure her thoughts were locked behind a barrier, even though he shouldn't be able to read her through a communications node. "Captain Rivlen reporting."

"Good evening, Captain," Uthari said calmly. "I had hoped to speak with Malek, but I understand from your officer that he left the ship?"

"Yes, to retrieve a prisoner."

"One of the archaeologists?"

Belatedly, it occurred to Rivlen that Malek must not have reported his self-appointed rescue mission to Uthari, and he might not appreciate it if she blabbed the details. Even though she doubted a loyal zidarr kept many secrets from his king, she didn't want to risk irking Malek.

Malek was... someone whose trust she wanted to have. To *deserve*.

"Captain?" Uthari prompted.

She'd already said too much. If she withheld information, that would make Uthari suspicious.

"I don't know the girl's name," Rivlen said, as if that had been what she'd been debating. "It is a young mercenary that the archaeologists asked him to retrieve."

"She has some... archaeological value?"

"I don't think so, Your Majesty. I haven't been told everything."

"Interestingly, General Tonovan recently reported to me about how he *lost* a prisoner, also not one of archaeological value."

"That is interesting, Your Majesty." Rivlen struggled to keep her face neutral. How had she ended up being the one answering questions about this? "Perhaps Lord Malek can fill you in on what happened."

Uthari's lips thinned. "I am unable to reach him telepathically."

Rivlen almost pointed out that few people could reach anyone from across the world, but Uthari probably *was* one of those people. "I believe he's in a druid sanctuary."

Uthari's gray eyebrows flew up. "Why?"

"The prisoner ended up there. It is a long story, Your Majesty, and I haven't been given all the details." Rivlen changed the subject, hoping Uthari would allow himself to be diverted. "I do not know if Lord Malek has told you yet, but we retrieved the artifact and are on our way to what we believe is the place it must be set up to operate. Jak provided a map."

"Jak?"

"The archaeologist boy." When had she started thinking of him by name?

"I know who he is. I didn't realize you were that close." Uthari's tone was dry, but there seemed to be a warning in there too.

"He assisted us with a battle earlier tonight. Druids in the jungle attacked the ship, and he convinced the artifact to shoot lightning at them."

"The druids are objecting to your presence? That's not without precedent, but it is unexpected."

"It certainly was." Rivlen had expected attacks from the mage-ships following them, not from the dark jungle underneath them.

"You will continue on the course that *Jak* has given you."

"Yes, Your Majesty." Rivlen wiped her damp palms on her trousers, certain she'd handled this conversation badly.

"And you will explain everything you know about this prisoner and why Malek is retrieving her at the behest of *his* prisoners."

Damn, he hadn't been diverted after all.

"Yes, Your Majesty."

Rivlen took a deep breath and started telling the truth insofar as she knew it, beginning with the fact that Malek considered the archaeologists guests and not prisoners. Even though she wanted to protect him from Uthari's wrath, if he was doing something that would irk the king, she wasn't willing to risk her own career by lying to their monarch, not even for him.

21

ON HANDS AND KNEES, JADORA LED TEZI UP THE SLOPING TUNNEL, the sides strangely warm and slick, freshly carved by the purple crystal. They glowed a faint green, as the ones in the sanctuary did.

The earth shuddered, and one of the druids yelled. Jadora couldn't tell if they were in the room or still behind the wall of roots they'd made. Nor could she tell if Malek was battling the druids. She didn't hear the clangs of a sword fight, but casting magic wasn't noisy.

Jadora hoped he could escape, and not just because she and Tezi couldn't power the skyboards and leave the area without him.

She crept upward as fast as the purple crystal parted the earth ahead of them. Unfortunately, though its magical tunnel-cleaning progress was inexorable, it was not rapid.

"How much farther to the surface, ma'am?" Tezi whispered from behind her.

"I don't know."

As they crept after it, the crystal started pulsing with purple light.

"What does that mean?" Tezi asked.

"I don't know that either."

"Where'd you get it?"

"A crystal planter in the druid's storage room."

"You stole it?"

The ground trembled, and dirt dropped on their backs. Jadora gulped and tried not to imagine the entire tunnel collapsing.

"Is this the time for judgment?" She clawed dirt out of her hair as they waited for the crystal to burrow farther.

"Sorry, but I wondered if they're angry and they want to kill us because they found out."

"If they want to kill us, I promise that's not the reason." Jadora felt a faint draft of warmer, more humid air. She squinted, searching for light up ahead, but it was probably still dark out. She couldn't yet hear any jungle sounds.

"That's less reassuring than you might think, ma'am."

"The crystals were growing, so it's less that I stole something they'll miss and more like snipping a cultivar from a desirable plant." Admittedly, that was something Jadora wouldn't do in her normal life without asking for permission. She missed being an upstanding citizen.

More shouts wafted up from behind them, but Jadora couldn't decipher any of them other than reading the frustration in the voices. They all belonged to the druids. Whatever Malek was doing, he wasn't yelling about it.

A great wrenching of the earth came, knocking Jadora into a newly formed wall. A wave of dusty air whooshed up from behind them. Someone coughed—Malek?—but it was muted.

Jadora feared the tunnel behind them, or the room they'd left him in, had caved in. Worse, the crystal stopped making progress.

Another draft of muggy jungle air wafted in, making her certain they were close. She prodded the crystal, but the purple glow disappeared, leaving them in the dark.

"Uh," Tezi said.

"Hold on. I have a second one." Jadora pulled it out of her pocket, the crystal still glowing a cheerful purple, and thrust the pointed tip into the ground next to the dead one.

When nothing happened, she tried pushing it and twisting it, hoping vainly that she could replicate whatever Malek had done to get it started. It didn't move.

Jadora wiped sweat and dirt off her face. "I think we dig now. At least we have light."

Wishing she had some of her archaeology tools with her, Jadora removed the crystals to claw at the damp dirt with nothing but her fingers. As Tezi squirmed up beside her to help, the earth shook again. A thunderous snap sounded behind them, followed by the muted roar of more dirt falling. Were they burying Malek alive?

"They really want him," Tezi whispered.

"I think what they want is for *us* not to get back to his ship and get the portal set up." Jadora scowled as she tore at dirt and small rocks with nothing but her fingernails.

A heavy piece tumbled from above and thudded down on her calf. If she and Tezi didn't want to be buried alive, they needed to get out of here soon.

Another chunk fell, striking the back of her head. Jadora remembered the explosives she'd made back on the ship. They were in her backpack, and she'd designed them to work similarly to Sorath's pop-bangs—to detonate on impact. She envisioned herself blowing up because a rock landed on one.

Swearing, she tore off the pack and put it under her body to protect it as she dug. She was tempted to pull out one of the explosives to clear the way more quickly, but that might collapse the tunnel. If she was wrong and they weren't close to the surface, the weight could crush them to death.

"Uhm, ma'am?" Tezi patted something in their way. "There's a big rock. We may have to divert our route."

She was right. The rock—no, the *boulder*—was huge and completely blocked the way they'd been digging. Maybe it was the reason the crystal had burned out.

"I guess we try explosives, after all." Jadora pulled two of them out of her pack.

They didn't have a large amount of black powder in them, so she didn't know if they would be sufficient for the task. She'd designed them to distract mages from hurling magic at her, not excavate tunnels.

"Sergeant Tinder would approve," Tezi said.

"Is she the one who makes grenades while your doctor knits?"

"Yes."

"It's important to have hobbies." Jadora carefully nestled her explosives into a gap next to the boulder. "Back up."

Tezi did so but glanced warily behind them. The shouts had all stopped. Jadora didn't know if that was because so much dirt had fallen behind them that it muted the noise, or if the druids had succeeded in burying Malek and didn't have anything to yell and curse about anymore.

A thud came from somewhere above them. Jadora swore again. If the druids had figured out what she and Tezi were doing, they might have gone outside to wait for them to come up.

She grabbed a couple of rocks and shifted awkwardly in the tunnel to make room to throw. "Be ready."

Tezi turned her back and covered her head. Though Jadora wished she had a detonator and a long fuse, she didn't. With no other options, she threw a rock.

It clanged off the boulder, missing her explosives by a foot. She threw a second rock and missed again. Maybe she should have tried throwing the explosives at the boulder. It was a much larger target.

"Here, ma'am." Tezi held out her hand. "I was learning to be a marksman. Markswoman."

Jadora gave her the last rock. Tezi threw it like a sports champion, and it slammed into one of the explosives, causing both of them to blow.

They spun away and protected their heads as rock and dirt pelted them in their backs. Then the ceiling tumbled down all around them, wet earth slapping against their clothes.

Afraid they would be buried, it took Jadora a moment to realize the moisture proved they were close to the surface, the rain-soaked surface. Along with dirt, bits of leaf matter and vines spattered onto the back of her neck. Rainwater dribbled down after them. They'd made it.

"Up," she whispered, grabbing her backpack and jumping to catch the crumbling lip of the hole they'd created.

But as she and Tezi scrambled out, Jadora spotted a pair of bare legs and sandals standing on solid ground nearby. A grim-faced male druid pointed a staff at them, as if it were a magelock rifle capable of firing blasts of energy. Maybe it was.

Jadora looked in the other direction and spotted another druid. She slumped. This had all been for nothing.

Then rocks and dirt erupted ten feet behind her like a geyser. The druids spun toward the disturbance, pointing their weapons at it. Before they could shoot, invisible waves of power struck them, hurling them backward. Somehow, the power missed Jadora and Tezi.

Malek, covered in dirt and pieces of roots, sprang out of the hole he'd made. He spotted them, lifted his hand in another direction—Jadora could make out the stone monument in the distance—and the two skyboards sailed toward him.

"Get on," he barked, directing one straight to Jadora and Tezi.

As they scrambled aboard it, the two druids recovered and

pointed their staffs at them. Jadora almost sprang off to take cover behind a tree.

"I'll protect you." Malek formed a barrier between Jadora and Tezi and the druids, and the green energy balls that shot from their staffs were deflected. "Stay on."

The skyboard was already moving, and they had little choice. With no way to control it themselves, Jadora and Tezi could only clutch each other and squat low for balance.

Malek jumped onto the other skyboard and sped over to join them. The druids split up and fired from either side, trying to find a gap in his barrier, but he spread it to cover all three of them.

The skyboards rose into the air and darted away, swerving between tree trunks. Even though Malek's barrier protected them, Jadora couldn't keep from ducking every time it looked like a branch would hit them. His magic broke the branches away, tearing a hole for them to escape through.

Green balls of energy chased them toward the canopy, lighting up the night sky as they struck Malek's barrier. Under the dirt, his face was tense with concentration. Jadora remembered him saying it took extra effort for him to steer someone else's skyboard, and he had to keep his barrier up at the same time. Those blasts hitting it couldn't be insubstantial, not if druids with similar weapons had almost taken down the *Star Flyer* earlier.

"You're doing well," Jadora called softly to him, not sure if he would appreciate encouragement or if it would distract him. She waved and added, "Thank you."

He glanced over, nodded once, and returned his focus to the route ahead.

As they breached the canopy and flew up over the treetops, angry shouts came from below. More druids had rushed out of their sanctuary, but they were too late to make a difference.

"Don't set up that portal, archaeologist," came a call in a

language Jadora could understand. "You'll bring death and destruction to the entire world!"

"Translate the book!" another voice added. Gelira.

"I will," Jadora said, though she didn't know if it would make a difference.

She looked at Malek, his face tense with concentration, and wondered if he and Uthari would stop this mission under any circumstances. She had little doubt that Uthari would sacrifice a great many people to get the plant he wanted and who knew what else.

And Malek? As much as she wished otherwise, she believed he would stay loyal to his king and do whatever Uthari asked.

The blue-uniformed helmsman, whom Sorath had dubbed Lieutenant Chow, because he was eating something every time Sorath walked into navigation, had his feet propped up on the wheel and was reading a book as the *Skimmer* waited for Night Wrath and Lieutenant Vinjo to return.

It was Sorath's third time checking in, hoping for an update. The sabotage mission had been his idea, so if it went horribly wrong, he would be held responsible. Normally, responsibility didn't bother him, but he would regret voicing his idea if Thorn Company ended up captured by Malek. Further, now that he had quasi befriended Vinjo, he would also regret sending the kid to his death. His inventions had been creative and surprisingly useful, at least as far as Sorath, a non-mage, could tell. He was surprised Vinjo's colleagues didn't respect him more.

Chow grabbed his fourth or fifth frosted cookie from a plate. Surprisingly, the six-and-a-half-foot tall dessert-devourer was rail thin. Maybe he had worms.

"Any word from Night Wrath yet?" Sorath glanced at the

dome-jir embedded in a panel near the wheel, though he suspected Night Wrath would communicate with the ship's captain telepathically.

"Not since the last time you asked."

Sorath paced. It had been more than an hour since Night Wrath and Vinjo left, and he didn't think Uthari's ships were that far ahead.

The helmsman kept looking up from his book to glower back at him, and Sorath was about to leave when the communications device lit up. A hooded face formed in the air above the crystal dome.

The helmsman put his feet down. "Lord Night Wrath?"

"Yes, who is this? The captain is either sleeping or ignoring my attempt to communicate with him."

"He's sleeping, my lord. This is Lieutenant Chakower, the helmsman."

Sorath thought Chow was a better name, but he didn't say so.

"Tell him we've succeeded in planting one of my brother's explosives on the engine of the rearmost of Uthari's ships. The *Dread Arrow.*"

"Yes, my lord."

"Something has Uthari's people discombobulated. They were focused on the jungle instead of paying attention to us sneaking in from the side. We were happy to take advantage. My brother came up with a system to delay the detonation, so we may be able to plant another of his devices before they're discovered. We're angling for the *Star Flyer* right now, and not only is the crew busy repairing damage, but I don't sense Malek aboard. This mission could go better than we expected."

Sorath gripped a ceiling beam, relieved, though he wondered who had damaged the *Star Flyer*. None of Zaruk's other ships were close enough. Sorath also wondered where Malek was. What if

Uthari's zidarr was flying around on a skyboard of his own and sabotaging *Zaruk's* ships?

"I'll report in when we're done," Night Wrath finished, his face fading.

"Yes, my lord."

Sorath thought about banging on the captain's hatch and passing along the news, but there wasn't much for any of them to do until Night Wrath and Vinjo completed the mission. Once the explosives detonated and, hopefully, forced the ships to land, Zaruk's fleet could swoop in and take advantage.

A servant in a blue dress and carrying a tray knocked on the open hatch before entering.

"About time," Chow growled, waving her in. "A helmsman can't navigate all night on cookies alone."

The woman walked in, her glazed eyes vacant. A silver slave-band encircled her head, contrasting with the lank black hair that hung to her shoulders. She glanced at Sorath as she hurried to the helmsman's side with the food.

Chow reached over and squeezed her ass, letting his hand linger. She froze, fear twisting her face, until her headband flashed faintly, inserting who knew what thoughts into her mind. She relaxed an iota, though Chow's fondling didn't stop, and placed dried meat and fruit on the helmsman's plate.

Sorath strode forward, intending to disentangle her from the helmsman's grip.

"You didn't bring a clean plate? Are you kidding?" Chow released her and flicked a finger. She reeled backward, shoulder ramming the wall, and almost spilled the tray's contents. "Nobody wants cookie crumbs stuck to their jerky."

Sorath caught her before she tripped over her feet and went down. She bobbed her head, muttered, "Thank you," and promised to return with another plate.

Sorath clenched his jaw and fantasized about shooting Chow in the back of the head.

"You're welcome to try, Colonel," Chow said without looking back, "but I've had my defenses up since you walked in. As if I'd trust some rabid mage-hating merc at my naked back."

"I'd shoot you in the head, not the back." Or maybe he would break the man's neck. Too bad he'd used all of his pop-bangs. Sorath wondered if Tinder could make something similar. Grenades were serviceable but large and didn't detonate upon impact.

Chow turned, apparently not approving of this line of thought. "Amazing that a grown man doesn't know his place around mages."

"Amazing that your captain doesn't berate you for the food stains all over your uniform."

Scowling, Chow glanced down. Sorath could have lunged across the cabin and snapped his neck in that moment of distraction, but that would only get him killed—and Thorn Company punished. Besides, the *Skimmer* needed Chow to pilot it. Sorath longed for Nobber from the *Dauntless*. Or any of the handful of mages he encountered now and then who weren't snotty bastards.

Chow had started to brush the crumbs off his uniform, but he must have read Sorath's thoughts, for he jerked his head back up. "I should punish you for your fantasies." His lips curved into a smile. "The captain wouldn't mind. Neither would Night Wrath. Cocky terrene humans who don't know their place *should* be punished."

"Or we could act like mature adults and focus on our mission." Sorath doubted that would happen and rested his hand on the hilt of his dagger.

"No. I think you should get on your knees and beg for my mercy." Chow clenched a fist, applying pressure on Sorath from above.

Which likely meant he wasn't defending himself. Sorath didn't fight the pressure—he knew from experience how futile that was —but threw his dagger as he dropped.

Chow squawked and flung himself out of his chair. The dagger lodged in the wooden wheel, as Sorath had intended, and it startled the helmsman, making his magic falter. Sorath lunged across the cabin, wrapped a hand around Chow's neck, and hefted him to his feet by the grip.

"I'll kill you," Chow wheezed, though he couldn't concentrate with Sorath's fingers squeezing.

"Why do I suspect your captain wouldn't miss you?"

Let go! Chow roared into his mind, no longer able to get the air to gasp the words out loud.

As much as Sorath wanted to kill him, he didn't. He didn't know if there was another helmsman, nor did he believe he could get away with killing one of the crew without ramifications for Thorn Company. He pulled his dagger out of the wheel and used it to shave a few chin hairs off the kid. Or maybe those were crumbs.

"I'm going to let you live, but if you decide to *punish* me again, we'll have another discussion. One where my dagger doesn't intentionally miss its target. Do you—" The running lights of a ship outside caught Sorath's eye.

They had deliberately flown west, out of the path of Uthari's vessels. No other mageships should have been out here.

Chow shoved at Sorath's chest, attempting to knock him back. He tried to do it with physical force instead of magic. Sorath didn't budge. He did release the kid, shoving him aside and pointing out the front window.

Though he glowered and wheezed for air, Chow looked. And turned his glower on the running lights. There were *many* sets of them out there.

"Is there any chance those are more of Zaruk's ships? That

caught up to us from the beach?" Sorath didn't know why he asked the question. There were too many sets of lights for that. It looked like an entire fleet out there. Out there and coming this way.

"No." Chow forgot his notions of punishing Sorath and planted both hands on the control panel, squinting as he used his senses to probe the ships. He swore and knocked his plate of food away. "Those are Uthari's people."

"The *Star Flyer, Dread Arrow,* and *King's Courage*?" Sorath couldn't imagine why they would have deviated from their course. Also, unless Malek was casting illusions to make his fleet seem larger than it was, there were more than three ships out there.

"No." Chow grabbed the wheel and spun them away from the oncoming ships. "Go wake up the captain. And get your mercenaries ready for a battle."

Against that many ships? This wouldn't be a battle but a massacre.

"Can you outrun them?" Sorath asked, remembering that this ship had been chosen for this mission because of its speed.

As Sorath headed for the hatchway, something like a giant invisible hand grabbed the *Skimmer* out of the air with a jolt that sent the helmsman to the floor again. Sorath caught himself on the ceiling beam but barely managed to keep his feet as the deck tilted wildly.

"No," Chow said. "We're screwed."

22

DAWN WAS CREEPING OVER THE JUNGLE AS THE BLACK-HULLED *Star Flyer* came into view. For the last ten minutes, the skyboard that Tezi rode with Jadora had been shuddering, a tiny glowing circle on the surface pulsing yellow. Tezi had little experience with the magical devices but was certain it was letting them know it was at the end of its range. Even so, she didn't know whether to be relieved or not by the ominous black ship flying over the trees.

Jadora believed they would be safe on Malek's ship, and before everything had gone crazy back in the druid sanctuary, she'd mentioned the possibility of Tezi going through the portal to leave Torvil—and the zidarr who wanted her dead—behind.

Tezi didn't know if she could imagine that, especially if there weren't any other humans in the world of the dragons, but the idea of spending a year off on an adventure was a little intriguing. If she could survive. And if she could one day return, ideally after Night Wrath, and every mage who knew her secrets, had forgotten about her.

Jadora twitched and jerked her head up, as if she'd fallen

asleep. If she could do that while standing, that was impressive, though the ride had been smooth since they escaped the druids.

The silent Malek rode right beside them, controlling both of the skyboards. Whenever Tezi glanced over at him, his face was cool and impassive, his eyes alert as he scanned the jungle canopy. The times their eyes had met, there hadn't been any warmth there, and she kept worrying that she'd made the wrong decision. Malek had helped them escape, but until he and Jadora had shown up, Tezi hadn't *needed* to escape.

Had she asked to stay with the druids, *they* might have hidden her for a year, long enough for Night Wrath to forget about her. Of course, they might have killed her themselves when they learned of her past. They were magic users themselves after all.

On the ship's deck, red-uniformed mages watched them come in for a landing. The skyboards shuddered again and gave out as they flew over the railing. Tezi hurried to jump to the deck and offered Jadora a steadying hand.

"We made it." Jadora smiled and patted her on the shoulder.

Tezi felt sheepish and uncomfortable after breaking down and crying in front of her, but she doubted Jadora would tell anyone. As a mother, she was probably sympathetic, and Tezi believed she would keep confidences.

She hoped she didn't end up on the opposing side from Jadora again, but as several armed mages walked up to them, Tezi worried that was about to happen. Was she truly to be treated well until such time as she wanted to get off the ship? Or would she end up in another cell? *She* wasn't a valuable archaeologist who had secret knowledge of how to work the portal, the portal now resting on the deck of this ship.

"Lord Malek." A female officer stopped in front of them and saluted him as a young crewman came forward and took the skyboards for recharging. She looked briefly and dismissively at Tezi. "King Uthari contacted me while you were unavailable. He had... questions about the fact that you were after a prisoner and that General Tonovan had lost a prisoner at the same time."

"I see," Malek said.

At this news, Jadora bit her lip and watched Malek, but he didn't look at her.

Back in the druid sanctuary, they had almost seemed close, like partners, but now he was distant and aloof, making Tezi wonder if she'd imagined that. It was hard to imagine a zidarr chumming around with a terrene human. Or anyone.

"I will contact him immediately." Malek stepped toward a hatchway, but the officer stopped him.

"Sir? Is the new girl a prisoner?" She cast another dismissive glance at Tezi. "Or a guest?"

Malek only considered Tezi briefly—not dismissively but not with much interest either—before looking at Jadora. She arched her eyebrows but didn't say anything.

"A guest," Malek said, his voice loud enough to be heard by all the nearby crewmen. "Under my protection."

"Does she get her own cabin? Or...?"

Or a cell?

"Have her stay with the professor and her son for now." Malek nodded curtly and strode for the hatchway.

Jadora watched him go, her face hard to read, then nodded to Tezi.

"This way." Jadora led Tezi toward a different hatchway, knowing where to go without an escort, but two more crewmen hurried to walk in front of and behind them. Two *armed* crewmen.

Tezi wondered if there was much difference between being a prisoner to a zidarr and a guest to one. At least Malek hadn't looked her up and down like someone planning a sexual conquest. One of the crewmen eyed her curiously, though that might have been because she was barefoot and in a sleeveless smock possibly woven from flower stems.

When she followed Jadora into a cabin, a familiar voice blurted, "Mother!"

Jak sprang from his bunk and hugged her while Tezi hung back.

Maybe she should have asked for her own cabin—or cell. As well-intentioned as Jak seemed, Tezi didn't know if she could deal with any more interest from men this week. Or this year. She was dirty and grimy after digging her way out of the druid compound, but she felt even dirtier from being manhandled by Tonovan. She longed to scrub herself with soap and wondered if the mageships had anything as luxurious as bathtubs. She would have settled for being dropped off by a jungle pond.

"Rookie Tezi," Jak said after releasing his mother and spotting her. He took a step toward her, as if he might give her a hug too, but maybe he read her face accurately, for he stopped short and gave her a vigorous wave and head bob. "I'm so glad they found you. Was it in time? To get away from Tonovan? Before he— you know." He glanced at his mother, who had a finger to her lips. "Oh, never mind." Bleakness swam in his eyes, but he covered it up with a forced smile. "Here, you can have my bunk. You must be tired."

"I know I am." Jadora lay down on her bunk, slinging off a backpack, but not bothering to take her boots off. She rested her head on the backpack as if it were a pillow and closed her eyes. "And haunted and afraid for the future."

"Uh," Jak said. "Are you going to tell me about your trip?"

"Later." Jadora draped her arm over her eyes. Outside, the sun was coming up, brightening the cabin. "I have some translating to do, but I need to rest first."

"Do you want to hear about our battle? And how the artifact and I helped drive away druids? And how Captain Rivlen was appreciative and came and showed me how to use some of my magic?"

Jadora lowered her arm and frowned over at him. "I *didn't*, but now I'm worried that I'd better hear this story."

"Your magic?" Tezi whispered.

"Uh, yeah." Jak shrugged at her and sat in the cabin's only chair. "It seems like I have some. I didn't know until recently."

"The story, Jak. Share it, please." Jadora watched him intently. "Especially the part where Captain Rivlen, who's been looking down her nose at us since we came aboard, is teaching you magic. Is that *permitted*?"

Tezi sank down on the free bunk, made uneasy by Jak's revelation, even though she didn't know him well. He was friendly and earnest and seemed like a decent person. If he developed the powers of mages, would he change? Would he turn into one of *them*?

She wished she were back with Thorn Company.

"She didn't say it *wasn't* permitted," Jak said, "and I figured I should learn from anyone who's willing to teach me. I want to be able to protect you, Mother. And Tezi too. And myself. Anyone who needs it. I'm tired of them pushing us around."

"I understand," Jadora said, "but why would she help you?"

"Because I'm charming and delightful and great company?"

"I hope you don't truly believe that."

"As my mother, you're supposed to bolster my delusions, not quash them."

"You *are* charming and great company, but she didn't strike me as someone who would appreciate it."

"She's... all right, once you talk an ancient artifact into saving her ship, but I admit, I think she wants to use me."

"*Use* you?" Jadora asked. "In a way similar to how King Uthari and Malek want to use us?"

"Probably, but not related to the artifact, as far as I can tell. More some revenge plot and personal ambitions."

Jadora's jaw dropped. "Jak... That's not anything good for you to be involved in."

"None of this is anything good for us to be involved in." Jak waved to encompass the ship. "But if I can learn something useful, I *have* to do it."

Jadora gazed at him with a conflicted expression but didn't argue further.

"I trust you'll do the right thing," she said quietly, then draped her arm back over her eyes.

"I will," Jak said, though doubt lurked in his own eyes.

It was the first time Tezi had seen more than affable friendliness on his face, and she wasn't sure she liked the glimpse of more troubled emotions—or the thought that he had the power to become a mage.

Jak took a blanket off the bunk and waved for Tezi to have the rest. "You're probably exhausted. You should sleep too. I got a few hours last night, so I'm fine."

Despite the words, he spread the blanket on the deck. If he'd been in a battle the night before, he probably hadn't gotten much rest either. Tezi felt guilty that he would sleep on the deck while she had a bunk, but she was too exhausted after the night's events to reject the offer. Even though she'd slept for a few hours in the druid sanctuary, her body had been busy healing, and she didn't feel refreshed.

"Do you know how much farther it is to... this place we're going?" Tezi asked Jak quietly, suspecting Jadora was already sleeping.

"Hard to say, since I don't know how far we've gone. It was about nine hundred miles from the coast, and the mageships travel quickly, so we should get there today. If I put it in the right spot on the map." Jak frowned. "I had to estimate based on a carving in a thousands-of-years-old stone monument."

Tezi might have asked him for more details, but someone knocked.

"It's Malek," Jak whispered. He glanced at his mother—she

hadn't stirred—and called a little louder, "Come in."

Tezi sat up and eyed the door warily. If Jak truly sensed magic, he would know if a zidarr was standing out there, but she was surprised Malek would come to see them himself. She would have expected, if they were lucky, some lowly soldier to be tasked with bringing them food and water.

But when the door opened, Malek was indeed the one standing there. He'd shaven, combed the dirt out of his hair, and changed clothes, from dirty forgettable brown and tans to clean forgettable brown and tans. He held folded towels, with a bar of lye soap on the top, and a couple of clean uniforms—for them?— stacked underneath.

"There's a washroom three hatches down that you can use." He delivered the towels and clothes to the desk. "Nobody will bother you." He glanced at Tezi and Jak, then let his gaze linger longer on Jadora, who hadn't stirred.

"I'll let her know when she wakes up," Jak offered.

"She's using her backpack as a pillow," Malek observed.

The statement puzzled Tezi. Why would he care?

"That means she likes it," Jak said. "Clearly, it's a superior gift."

"Hm," Malek said.

"Is using it for a pillow not permissible?"

"I don't know. Is she keeping her explosives in there?"

"Yeah, but I don't think they can go off if you drool on them."

"Dampening them with saliva could render them less effective," Malek said, the strange conversation bewildering Tezi.

"I'll let her know," Jak said.

Jadora lowered her arm and looked blearily at them. She must have truly been sleeping because she seemed confused by their presence.

"Malek is worried that you're drooling on your explosives," Jak said.

Jadora touched her mouth.

"She *wasn't* drooling," Tezi whispered, surprised Malek hadn't corrected Jak for not saying *lord* in front of his name. "She's only been asleep for five minutes. There hasn't been time."

"I came to see if you need anything." Malek waved at the towels, then looked at Tezi. "Do you require medical attention?"

"No." She wouldn't have said yes even if her leg had been falling off. What if *he* was what passed for a healer on this ship? The idea of a zidarr putting a hand on her, even for healing, made her shiver. "Thank you."

He glanced at the side of her neck. "I see."

Tezi touched her neck, finding one of the druid patches still there. That gash and numerous other wounds did still ache, and maybe he could tell, but he didn't push the issue.

"Is everything all right?" Jadora asked. "With you and your contact with... King Uthari?"

"He wasn't pleased by my diversion." Malek didn't look again at Tezi, but there was no question as to what he meant. "Even if Tonovan hasn't figured out that I've got his prisoner and had a hand in her escaping, I'm positive Uthari has."

Wait, *Malek* had a hand in her escaping? How so?

Tezi frowned, but neither of them looked at her.

"Will he punish you?" Jadora whispered.

"It doesn't matter."

"That's a yes, isn't it? It *does* matter." Her weary eyes grew stricken as she watched his face. "I asked you to do this."

"*We* asked you," Jak said, though they weren't looking at him either.

They barely seemed aware that he and Tezi were in the cabin.

"And now it is done, and we will continue on." Malek nodded gravely to Jadora. "Rest. When we arrive, we will need you to help set up the portal. And if you can translate some of that druid text, I would be interested to read what it says. I informed King Uthari that there are possible dangers."

"Let me guess. He still wants you to erect it."

Malek held Jadora's gaze. "And visit the dragon home world, yes."

"For his plant."

"For his plant. If there are dangers, he's confident I can deal with them." Malek smiled faintly, a surprisingly human gesture for a zidarr, then bowed and left.

"What did he mean he had a *hand* in me escaping?" Maybe it wasn't the most important thing to ask, but Tezi couldn't help herself.

Jadora rubbed her face. "He didn't explain it, but I assumed that if you got away, it was because Tonovan was distracted by more than his penis. I've met him. He's... powerful."

Tezi stared at the deck. "The ship hit something. A tree, I think. A bunch of them. I already had the knife, so I was ready to stab Tonovan, but yes, he and the guards were distracted."

At the time, it hadn't occurred to her to wonder *why* the ship hit the trees. Had Malek been responsible? She didn't want to think she owed anything to him. She also felt a little cheated of her victory, however modest a victory it had been.

"You *stabbed* him?" Jak beamed a smile at her. "Tonovan? That's wonderful. Malek didn't give us any details. Just said that he was flying in and missed seeing you go over the side." He shuddered. "I can't believe you jumped. Or did you fall? When the ship hit the trees?"

"I jumped," Tezi said tersely, not wanting to think about it. "Once I stabbed him, I knew I'd be dead if they caught me. And I didn't want to be a prisoner any longer." She swallowed, her eyes losing focus. She both wished she were alone and didn't want to be alone. A paradox. Was that the right word? Sergeant Words would know. Bleakness filled Tezi. She hadn't realized she would miss the mercenaries so much.

"That's understandable," Jadora said quietly.

"But *horrible*." Indeed, Jak did look horrified, like he feared she would jump off the *Star Flyer* the first chance she got. "Don't give up, Tezi. There's always hope."

Was there? Tezi looked to Jadora and thought of what she'd hinted at, another world where one could disappear.

"Let her rest, Jak," Jadora said softly.

"It's fine." Now that she had the option, Tezi would rather wash herself than rest. She took a towel and the soap bar and peeked into the corridor before stepping out, expecting a guard. Or worse, for Malek to be standing out there, but the corridor was empty. She glanced back, gave Jak a wave, since he still looked worried, and went to bathe.

No, she decided as she scrubbed herself in blessed privacy. Not worried. He'd looked innocent, like he still believed the world wasn't irrevocably broken and that there was a way to fix it, and he wanted her to believe that too. But this last year had left her with little but pessimism, and she couldn't. All she could hold on to was this new hope that there might be another place, somewhere to escape.

The ship shuddered so hard that Jak would have fallen out of his bunk if he hadn't been sleeping on the deck. Something *did* fall out, thumping down next to him. At first, he thought it was his mother, but it was one of her books. She'd been sitting up in bed translating something.

"What's going on?" Tezi whispered.

As Jak sat up and tried to sense who or what was attacking the *Star Flyer,* someone burst into their cabin. The deck tilted wildly, and the hatch slammed all the way against the wall.

Jak jumped to his feet, facing Rivlen and two of her crewmen as they stared in at him—at all three of them—with suspicion on their faces.

"They're all here," Rivlen called back. "Keep searching!"

"It could have been one of them," one of the crewmen said. "They could have done it, run back in here, and be feigning sleep."

"Someone would have seen that, and—"

"It wasn't them," came Malek's voice from the corridor. "It was one of Zaruk's people who sneaked on while I was gone."

Rivlen swore and slammed the hatch back shut. The ship lurched again.

Jak rubbed his head in confusion. After two nights of barely sleeping, he had been dozing, so he had no idea what time it was or how far the ship had traveled.

"Is it... not an attack?" Tezi asked.

Mother leaned over and picked up her book, appearing no more enlightened than the rest of them.

"It sounded like sabotage," Jak said.

Now that he'd been awake for more than ten seconds, he didn't sense anyone attacking the ship with magic, nor was the air outside buzzing with the kind of power it would have if crewmen had erected a barrier.

A thump rocked the deck, followed by a terrible scraping sound.

"We're hitting the trees," he said.

"We're going to crash?" Tezi asked.

More thumps and scrapes sounded, as if giant branches were trying to tear the *Star Flyer* out of the sky.

"That may already be happening." Jak put a hand on the hatch, tempted to go out and offer to help, but what could he, or even the artifact, do if this was mechanical sabotage? Lightning bolts wouldn't fix that.

"Stay here," Mother said. "They already suspect us. If you wander around out there, that could make it worse."

Remembering Rivlen checking on them, Jak realized she was right. That stung, given that he'd helped out the night before, but maybe they thought Tezi had done something. As far as Malek's crew knew, she was one of the mercenaries working for the other side.

Still, Jak couldn't keep from saying, "I wasn't going to wander. I was going to purposely stride about, looking for a way to help."

"Well, don't. We don't know anything about mage technology."

The ship struck something else, the deck jolting sideways.

"I know it's bad when you run into trees," Jak said.

Outside their porthole, the sky had disappeared, replaced by leaves and vine-draped tree branches. A snake on a trunk reared back, flicking a forked tongue at them as they flew past.

A crunching noise emanated from below, followed by wood snapping. The ship tilted so wildly that Mother tumbled out of her bunk, almost landing on Jak.

"The deck is safer," he said, gripping her shoulders to keep her down with him. "There's nowhere to fall."

Tezi remained in her bunk, flattened to it and gripping the edges.

More branches streaked past the porthole until the ship slammed into something underneath them. The impact sent Jak and his mother flying a foot into the air before thumping back down on the deck.

"I take it back." Jak rubbed his backside.

The deck wobbled, then rocked.

"We landed in water," Mother said. "Were there any significant lakes or rivers along our route?"

The map on the druid monument hadn't included many bodies of water, but Jak mentally reviewed other maps of the continent he'd seen and guessed how far they'd flown while he slept.

"This might be the Neenak River. If so, it's a big one."

"Hopefully, without any waterfalls in its path."

"Uhm." There *were* waterfalls, but Jak didn't mention it, since he wasn't sure where they'd landed or even if they were in that river. They might have come down in a lake. "Hopefully not."

Other than the faint rocking of the ship in the water, it had steadied. Fewer shouts came from outside, and Jak longed to go see what was happening, but his mother's warning kept him in the cabin. He did get up and peer out the porthole.

A monkey in a tree at the edge of the water hung by one arm as it gaped at them.

"I guess we're not a common sight," Jak muttered. The ship was moving, and the monkey and its tree were soon out of sight. "I think we are in a river." He pressed his nose to the glass, trying to see down to the water. "At least it seems to be slow moving."

Mother picked up her book again and settled back on her bunk, rearranging papers and another book that hadn't fallen off. Judging by the pages of translations she'd done, she hadn't slept that much during the day.

"Did you trade something to the druids for fresh reading material?" Jak didn't recognize the new book, but it looked older than the three of them combined. "The classic druid murder mystery?"

"They lent it to me. They think the stories recorded in it will make me change my mind about the wisdom of setting up the portal. Though... it's more Malek's and Uthari's minds that need changing." Mother flipped a yellowed page. "And if they wanted that done quickly, they should have given me a book that wasn't written in an ancient language that I need to painstakingly translate word by word."

"The druids don't want us to activate the portal?" Jak asked. "Is that why some of their people attacked the ship last night?"

"It's possible."

"I wonder if they were responsible for this." Tezi waved to indicate the ship bobbing in a river instead of flying through the sky.

Mother shrugged without taking her gaze from the books. "So far, everyone we've met who lives on this continent is certain that portal is a horrible portent of evil, if not itself a delivery mechanism for evil."

"Evil? That's vague." Then Jak remembered the most recent vision he'd received, of the mottled dragon having slain the frolicking dragon. Though Mother was busy, he detailed it for her, pacing while he spoke.

"I've been getting visions of unpleasant occurrences from it from the beginning," she said.

"I've also gotten nice visions of dragons having fun and playing in the water," Jak said, "but when the portal shared the last one, it seemed concerned that killer dragons could be a possibility. I told it we would take it to its home, activate it, and investigate. If we find something bad in one of these other worlds, then we can take the key out and close it down."

"The druids are concerned about something from another world coming *here* if the portal is open again."

"Wouldn't the key have to be in it for that? We could remove it when we weren't using it."

"I don't know." Mother wrote a couple more words on her page of translations. "Maybe a key is only required to leave through the portal, not return through one."

Malek knocked on the hatch. Jak sprang for it, eager for information.

The hatch opened, and Malek looked past him. Checking to make sure nobody was skulking about?

"Captain Rivlen already did that," Jak said, stung that Malek might not trust him.

"I was making sure nobody's here threatening you." Malek's gaze lingered on Mother, who'd only glanced up for a moment before returning to the translating. "Such as the saboteur."

"Oh." Jak remembered the zidarr who'd come after them back

in Uthari's courtyard, wanting to deny Uthari of his helpful archaeologists. "Thanks."

Malek nodded and started to withdraw.

"Wait." Jak lifted his hand. "What happened? Can I help?"

"Someone sabotaged the perpetual engine. It powers the vessel and keeps it aloft."

"Can it be fixed out here?" Jak envisioned the crew having to go to a repair shop back in a sky city to order new parts.

"Yes, but it'll take time. Likely enough time that Zaruk's mageships that we crashed back at the coast will finish repairs and catch up with us. And they could have reinforcements by now."

"Did you catch the saboteur?"

Malek's face darkened. "No. I'm waiting for a more thorough report, but it looks like someone sneaked aboard while I was gone and placed an explosive with a delayed detonation meant to deliver a crippling blow to the engine after he or she got away. Whoever made it must be a talented engineer."

"Does that mean it was one of Zaruk's people? And not a druid? Mother said the druids don't want us to set up the portal."

"I know they don't." Malek glanced at her again.

"Do you know why?"

"Only the story they told." Malek stepped back into the corridor. "I must help with the repairs. Stay in your cabin. Though we haven't found anyone, it *is* possible someone is hiding out and waiting to take advantage of our distraction."

"Can I come with you and help?"

"With the engine? I doubt the artifact can assist with that."

"I know, but I meant me." Jak touched his chest. "I'm learning how to use my magic, you know. Captain Rivlen taught me a little."

His face grew masked. "Did she?"

Even though Malek's tone was neutral, Jak wished he hadn't blurted that out. Rivlen had been vague about whether she was permitted to teach him. What if Malek reported her to someone?

"Just a little," Jak said. "After I helped—or convinced the artifact to help—with the druid attack."

A long moment passed as Malek considered him. Jak fought the urge to squirm, hoping he wouldn't get Rivlen in trouble. And hoping *he* wouldn't get in trouble.

Remembering the trick with the mental bandana, he wrapped it around his mind to protect his thoughts. Though as soon as he did it, he wondered if he should. Malek had given them the monk book and suggested he and Mother learn to guard their thoughts, but would Malek be suspicious of Jak if he could no longer see into his mind?

"Come then," Malek finally said. "We'll see if you can lend your power to the engineer fixing the engine. He'll do the crafting, but he can use my power—*our* power—to aid him and work more quickly. Jadora, yell if anyone bothers you."

Mother waved a hand in acknowledgment, then penned another line on her paper.

As Malek led the way toward the big hold with the engine and all those glowing tendrils, Jak bounced after him. He couldn't hide his excitement, his eagerness to learn more. Maybe this would be a way to study someone good at crafting. Then he could learn how to make things. Like his *own* backpack of extra holding. Or a pen that never ran out of ink. He'd seen one of those for sale in the university bookstore once, but it had been too expensive for a student to buy.

"I see you want to use your power for great things," Malek said over his shoulder.

"Pens *are* great." And oops, Jak had forgotten about his bandana and trying to block his thoughts.

"You'll get better at it. In time, protecting your thoughts

becomes second nature and something you don't have to think about. I did have trouble reading you back there."

"Oh, good. For how long?"

"Ten or fifteen seconds," Malek said dryly.

"I'll work on that." Jak wondered a bit at Rivlen's suggestion that he might be truly powerful one day.

"Good."

Two mages in coveralls instead of uniforms knelt next to the magical sphere embedded in the bottom of the hull, the sphere that had been glowing every previous time Jak had passed through the hold. It wasn't glowing now.

Captain Rivlen paced nearby, answering questions from crewmen who ran in and out of the area. Others worked on the tendrils stretching from the sphere—the engine—to different parts of the ship. They had also stopped glowing, and the crewmen painted a grayish-green goo on charred spots.

As Jak followed Malek around to the back side of the engine, a fissure came into view, the surface to either side blackened. There were also scorch marks on the hull and the deck around it.

"My lord?" One of the engineer mages in coveralls frowned at Jak. "What's your prisoner doing here?"

"My *guest* offered to help."

"We don't know if he... if one of them... was responsible for this." The engineer glanced toward Rivlen.

She was squinting thoughtfully at Jak. He again fought the urge to squirm as he wished he hadn't said anything to Malek about her lesson. Jak didn't want to keep secrets from Malek, but he also didn't want to get Rivlen in trouble.

"The archaeologists want to see the portal erected as eagerly as King Uthari. They weren't responsible. Trust that I could figure it out if they were." Malek's voice was cool.

The engineer lowered his gaze and shrank inward. "Yes, my lord. My apologies. But the mercenary girl..."

"Was sleeping in her bunk," Rivlen said. "I checked."

"Yes, ma'am."

"I suggest you focus on repairing the engine and leave finding the saboteurs to me."

"Yes, ma'am."

Someone else ran up to give Rivlen a report, and Malek pointed to the platform the sphere was mounted into.

"We'll sit there," he told Jak and stopped where he could see the engine and the engineers.

He sank to his knees, his hands on his thighs, and closed his eyes. Jak sat beside him in the same pose, emulating him.

Watch the engineers and try to sense what they're doing, Malek spoke into his mind. *Once you're ready, we're going to feed a steady stream of our own power into them so they can make their repairs more quickly.*

I understand, Jak replied.

Don't feed yours in too fast, or they'll struggle to make use of it. Also, it's not good to drain yourself to the extent that you grow exhausted. You don't want to be defenseless if someone attacks or to underperform if you're needed in battle.

Jak nodded. With his eyes closed and his mind open, he already sensed the engineers using their magic. One was doing something like weaving, using strands of different types of power to repair the surface of the sphere. The other was pouring his own energy into the core, causing something similar to a chemical reaction inside.

Jak paid attention to them for several moments, wondering if he could learn simply by watching and sensing how to do what they were doing. Then he noticed a tendril of power flowing from Malek and splitting into two, half going into each engineer. They gasped audibly as the power infused them, as if it felt good— maybe it did—and seemed to bask in and enjoy it for a moment before leaning back into their work.

Don't try to do a split at first, Malek said. *Just feed yours into the mage pouring energy into the core.*

All right. Jak almost asked what color this was for him, but Rivlen had said different people used different aids, and the terrain features on maps had worked much better for him than colors. He debated what feature might work for this. A valley or a canyon? With the spring melt rushing through it toward the distant sea?

He envisioned a canyon and his power like water flowing through the channel. To his surprise, he could feel a tangible trickle of *something* leaving his body. His magic? His power? He'd never sensed anything like it and was amazed as it rushed through the narrow passage he'd formed in his mind, waves and currents carrying fallen logs and other debris out of the mountains he envisioned.

The engineer gasped, but more in pain than pleasure, and Jak shrank back, the imagery shattering in his mind.

Malek gripped Jak's arm. *Easy, remember? You can also hurt people if you feed power too quickly.*

Sorry, that was dumb. I got excited. Realizing that might sound bad, Jak hurried to add, *At being able to do it and feel myself doing it. Not at hurting people.*

Save the hurting for your enemies. With allies, you want them to want to work with you again.

I get it.

"That kid has power," someone muttered.

"Yes," Rivlen said.

Her voice was as calm and professional as usual, so Jak was sure it was only in his mind that she was thinking about one day using him to help her with Tonovan. But when he opened his eyes and looked at her, he found her looking back, watching him with an intensity that was a little scary.

He licked his lips and closed his eyes again, trying not to think about her. He wanted to do this right, so Malek would find him useful and teach him more.

Wait, *was* this teaching? Malek had said it was forbidden for him to teach Jak.

He thought about asking, but Malek was focused on funneling his power into the engineers. *Afterward*, Jak would ask.

In his mind, he replaced the steep-walled canyon with a valley, the sides gently sloped. He imagined water flowing into it, a deep but slow-moving river, and he sent it toward the engineer waiting at the end of the valley. A more contented sound came from the man this time, and Jak could sense him adding the flow of power to his own, altering it into something different, something that could rebuild the engine.

Minutes passed, and Jak realized this wasn't as easy as he'd imagined. The concentration required to maintain the image and the power flowing out of him drained him, and it was almost as if this were a physical workout.

A bead of sweat traced the side of his face. He wasn't panting, the way he had been when pushing hard to drive back Rivlen, but he worried that he was feeding too much power, too much of his energy. If this took hours, and he was supposed to maintain the same steady flow the whole time, he would black out in a useless heap beside Malek.

You're doing well, Malek told him, reading his thoughts.

Jak couldn't concentrate on keeping those to himself while he was doing something else. Not yet. Maybe someday...

Thanks.

Rest if you need to.

Jak sensed Malek's power still flowing into the men, a perfectly steady stream that split in two—that couldn't be easy to do—while Jak's own seemed to wax and wane. He struggled to even out the flow of his river through the valley, smoothing the walls, and keeping the surface placid. Without fluctuation. Despite Malek's praise, he wondered if he was truly being helpful. Or was Malek humoring him?

Extra power always helps, Malek told him. *Don't belittle yourself. You're learning.*

And... are you teaching me? The word *forbidden* popped into Jak's mind again. Malek's own word.

No.

Are you sure?

Malek sighed and rested a hand on Jak's shoulder. *No.*

What if I meet King Uthari again? And he asks? Should I lie to him? I don't want you to get in trouble.

You will meet him again, but don't lie. Just don't develop some notion of wanting to challenge him or any of the other kings. He should allow this if you're willing to serve him in the end.

Panic welled in Jak, and he struggled to keep his river flowing. He didn't *want* to serve Uthari. Or any of those kings and their vile governments that oppressed the rest of humanity. He wanted to learn to use his power to *help* people. People who needed help, not megalomaniacal jackasses in castles.

Jak halted the thoughts, afraid he was too late, that Malek had caught everything and would send him away. He genuinely wanted to help with repairing the ship, and if *Malek* had asked him to serve him, that might not have been so repulsive. Though he knew he shouldn't want that either. Malek was Uthari's man, and serving him would mean serving Uthari, but Jak didn't believe that Malek would make him do anything awful. Like making enemies disappear in the dead of night. Or hurting people who had no means of defending themselves, those who needed protectors, not bullies.

I'm sorry, he thought, aware of Malek's silence. He was surprised the hand on his shoulder hadn't turned into a vise at these defiant thoughts. *I'm not unappreciative. I just... I'm not one of you.*

I was the same when I was younger, Malek surprised him by saying. *I came from your world, from the streets of Amuri in Zar. King Werok ruled then, the father of King Zaruk. Werok's people spotted me when I was twelve and tried to have me killed. They hunted me for almost a year. I fled across the Forked Sea to Uth, but I had a lot of power and had learned enough to be dangerous—noticeably dangerous. Some of Uthari's people learned of me, hunted me down, and dragged me before him. I believed he would kill me and told him to screw himself, among other things. I'd lost my mother the year before and was very angry at the world and at the mages. I'd taken her to a mage healer who could have cured her, one of Werok's selected minions, but we didn't have any money, so he wouldn't treat her. She died later that week. So you see, I also had a reason to hate mages.*

You were thirteen? Is that too old for training? Jak was amazed by the story. He had assumed Malek had been born in one of the sky cities to powerful and wealthy mage parents.

Technically, yes, but Uthari saw my potential and offered to make me a zidarr if I passed the training. I was shocked and told him I would only use my power to kill mages, because I hated them all. He said I had to serve him, and that he would never let me kill the mages under his protection, but he also said he would allow me to kill King Werok if I successfully finished my training. Only then would I be strong enough to slay him. I said yes immediately. I didn't know zidarr training was ten years long.

What happened? Did you wait ten years and still want to kill him? Jak knew that Zaruk had ruled more than twenty years, since his father's death, but he wasn't familiar enough with recent history in that part of the world to know if it had been an assassination.

True to his word, it was the first assignment Uthari gave me. He had reason to hate Werok himself, but he would have sent me even if he hadn't. It had been... the price for my loyalty, and I have served him faithfully ever since.

Jak couldn't think of a price for which he would sell *his* loyalty.

The idea of being a mindless minion serving a king without question turned his stomach. Oh, he didn't truly believe Malek was mindless—if anything, he was dangerous because he *wasn't*—but...

Perhaps if you loyally serve Uthari, he'll work on your behalf to make a deal with the dragons, so you can ride one. Malek's tone was light—surprisingly, he didn't seem angered by any of Jak's thoughts.

That would be fun, but I would like to think I could charm a dragon myself.

You think highly of your charisma.

I do. Uthari would have to swear to protect my mother for me to even consider working for him. As soon as the words came out, Jak wanted to retract them. He hadn't meant to promise that he would swear his undying loyalty to Uthari for the rest of his life. And he would much prefer to figure out a way on his own to keep his mother safe.

We all have our price, was all Malek said.

When did you stop hating mages?

As I grew older, I became less angry. These days, someone has to go out of their way to make an enemy of me.

Tonovan's sneering face popped into Jak's mind. He hated the man for what he'd done to Tezi and Rivlen and for what he'd hinted he would do to Mother if he got the chance.

He killed your father, Malek said so softly into his mind that Jak thought he'd imagined it.

He went rigid, all thoughts of his river and helping the engineer dashed from his mind by this cold splash of water. Hot fury replaced the cold shock.

Before, he'd wondered if Malek had done it, but now that he knew Malek, he had no problem believing that Tonovan had been responsible. Jak had already hated Tonovan, but now... now he thought he could kill him. His father wouldn't have wanted him to kill or take revenge on anyone, but Jak shook as he thought of how much Tonovan had wrenched from him and his mother. He *deserved* to die.

He told your mother that I did it, Malek added. *Just as he told Uthari the same five years ago. Uthari had only wanted the information in your father's journal, not for your father to be killed. Tonovan knew Uthari would be angry at his loss, so he blamed me. I did not correct him back then, since Tonovan was a colleague I had to work with, and I did not know if Uthari would believe me after Tonovan had already told him otherwise. But he recently told your mother the same lie. I do not wish her to believe I was responsible.*

Because she matters to you? Jak didn't know why he asked that. It wasn't like he wanted Malek and his mother to fall in love or something silly, but he longed to know that Malek cared about them. That all this wasn't just because Uthari had ordered him to keep them alive.

She matters, Malek said, then squeezed Jak's shoulder and let it go. *So do you.*

Malek was still funneling his power to the engineers, so Jak tried to do the same, but his mind was whirling. What would he do if Uthari offered to train him and promised that he could one day kill Tonovan? Would that be worth it?

Jak opened his eyes, trying to reset his focus so he could go back to being useful to the engineers. He noticed Rivlen was still there, but she wasn't watching him anymore. She was focused on Malek now, her gaze full of appreciation—or was that *attraction?*—as he sat like a statue, that outflow of power steady and reliable and, now that Jak could sense such things, impressive. Already the engine was far less damaged, that fissure only a crack and the sphere glowing once again.

Rivlen touched her chest as she watched Malek. Yes, definitely attraction.

It was a far different look from the one she'd given Jak. He almost snorted at his memory of them standing face to face in his cabin and his brief thought that she might be interested in him. It had been a silly thought. Rivlen might want to use him, but it had nothing to do with sex.

Jak closed his eyes and tried to get back to helping. In the back of his mind, a faint detached and rational part of him wondered if Malek had told him all that to manipulate him. Maybe all Malek wanted was to use him too. To make him want to agree to serve Uthari.

That Malek would wish that seemed so obvious, but if it was true... it would sting Jak a lot more than anything Rivlen could do. But he shouldn't assume anything. Wasn't it also possible that Malek cared? That he was doing this not because of some nefarious desire to give his king another useful tool but because he didn't want all the mages in the world hunting Jak down for being a rogue? That he wanted Jak to live?

An alarm gong sounded, and Malek sprang to his feet. Rivlen sprinted for one of the stairways leading above decks.

"Stay here," Malek told Jak.

"What is it? An attack? Druids?"

"Zaruk's fleet. They'll be within attack range soon. Tonovan's ship is coming to help, but our other ship was also damaged by a saboteur. We need to get the engine back online, so we can get back in the sky." Malek pointed at the engineers. "Keep helping, Jak, and I'll make you a backpack."

Malek's slight smile before he charged up the stairs after Rivlen was friendly—even *fatherly*—and it filled Jak with longing, longing for the relationship they were developing to be real, not some awful manipulation for King Uthari's sake.

23

LIEUTENANT SASKO KNELT BY THE RAILING, HER RIFLE POINTING AT one of the eight ships surrounding the *Skimmer*, the rest of Thorn Company lined up to either side of her. Sorath and Ferroki stood behind them, listening to the ship's captain rant in a panicked tone. Their mageship had been immobile in the air for the last twenty minutes as the fleet of black-hulled vessels flew in to surround them. As many blue-uniformed mages as mercenaries were lined up to face the threat, but the enemy had far, far more resources.

"What can we do?" the ship's captain demanded, turning pleading eyes toward Sorath.

"Surrender," he said. "And hope they accept it and don't kill us all."

"That's not acceptable!"

"Then by all means. Toss some fireballs at them."

Red-uniformed mage soldiers gazed indifferently at them from the decks of all eight ships. There were two more craft flying farther back, one more of a large yacht than a military vessel, though numerous weapons bristled from its sides.

"That's got to be half of Uthari's fleet," the captain said, a whiny note to his voice. "Wasn't he worried about defending his city from further attacks? Who commits so many forces to chasing some big metal ring around the world?"

For once, Sasko couldn't blame a mage for whining. She feared Thorn Company might not get out of this. Uthari's people had a lot of reasons to be mad at them and mad at anyone associated with Zaruk and his alliance.

She wondered where Vinjo was. If Uthari's people boarded the ship, his *clandestineness creeper* could have come in handy.

Vinjo and Night Wrath were probably out over the jungle somewhere on their skyboards, maybe witnessing this from afar and wondering what they were supposed to do now. Maybe they'd already been captured and were being tortured for information. They might be the reason Uthari's fleet had found the *Skimmer*.

If so, Sasko hoped they'd tortured the zidarr and not Vinjo. He was too goofy to deserve that fate. And... affable. For a mage.

Belatedly, Sasko wished she had said something to him before he left. She wouldn't have *kissed* him, but she could have wished him luck.

A strange pressure built in her ears. At first, she thought she was the only one who felt it, but Tinder, Words, Basher, and several others juggled their firearms so they could use both hands to cover their ears.

Wood snapped somewhere underneath them. One of the trees in the jungle below? Something in the framework of the ship?

More snaps followed, and the pressure built.

"They're squeezing my ship to pieces," the captain yelled. "Mages, defend!"

"We're *trying*, sir!"

A board in the deck snapped under Sasko's knees. More boards followed. A wrenching noise came from somewhere below, and the glowing sphere that was the ship's engine levitated out through a hole in the hull, the broken power tendrils that provided magic for the entire ship dangling from it.

The ramifications didn't sink in fully for Sasko until gravity caught up with the *Skimmer*. They plunged downward toward the treetops, never even getting a chance to fight against their attackers.

The *Skimmer* smashed into the densely packed trees, hurling Sasko and the rest of Thorn Company into the air. The ship caught in the branches but tilted sideways, and mercenaries and mages slid across the deck in a jumble as more thunderous snaps filled the air.

Sasko flailed for something to grab on to, afraid they would pitch over the side of the ship and plummet all the way to the jungle floor hundreds of feet below. Ferroki struck the railing and crashed through. She disappeared over the side.

"Ferroki!" Sorath cried, tumbling right behind her.

Horror and terror filled Sasko at the certainty that she would be dead within seconds. Somehow, she caught the railing and it didn't break, but her feet dropped over the edge, and she dangled from the wrecked ship. The ship's captain tumbled past her, bumping her and almost knocking her free. He tried to grab the railing but missed it and reached for her instead. Sasko twisted to avoid being pulled down with him. The bastard could probably levitate. *She* couldn't.

Or so she thought. Scant seconds later, invisible power wrapped around her and pushed her upward from below. Sasko tried to keep her grip on the railing, not wanting to be pulled upward any more than she wanted to drop below, but the magic was too powerful.

Screams sounded below as people crashed through the trees— or hit the ground. Not everybody was being grabbed by Uthari's mages.

Nearby, Tinder swore and called out for Fret.

"It's lifting me too," Fret yelled back from several feet away.

"I almost dropped my grenades!"

"We may need those."

"May? We *always* need grenades."

Sasko caught sight of them as the magic levitated them away from the wreck and above the trees. The whole company was getting this treatment. There were Sorath and Ferroki, thank Shylezar.

Sasko's first thought was that the entire crew was being saved —or at least captured for some nefarious purpose—but then she realized that only brown uniforms were visible. Thorn Company. Thorn Company and Sorath.

Uthari's people had let the mages fall.

Sasko didn't know why they wanted Thorn Company, nor did she know if this was a better fate than death.

While the engineers finished repairs, Malek joined Captain Rivlen in the forecastle with several other mages who would help them defend the *Star Flyer*. The engineers had made great progress below, and in another fifteen minutes, the ship should be ready to take to the sky again, but he sensed enemies flying toward them quickly.

He also sensed Tonovan's *King's Courage* heading this way, but would it once again fight and help them? Or would Tonovan stand back and get his revenge as the *Star Flyer* was annihilated by superior forces?

Malek had to hope that Tonovan's loyalty to Uthari and the mission would keep him working with him, at least for now. But even if Tonovan charged in, they were outnumbered. Malek sensed six enemy mageships and realized it had been a mistake not to obliterate all of them back at the coast. Because Uthari hadn't commanded him to be ruthless with their competitors, Malek hadn't ordered their ships utterly destroyed and the crews killed. Malek might regret that.

"The kid's got potential, doesn't he, my lord?" Rivlen gave him a sidelong look, though she stood with her hands clasped behind her back, waiting for their enemies to come within range.

"Yes." Malek returned the sidelong look. "I understand you were teaching him last night."

Rivlen froze, her eyes those of a rabbit stumbling onto a leopard in the briar patch.

Malek hadn't meant to accuse her of anything, especially since *he'd* just been showing Jak how to share his power with others, but her reaction made him wonder about her motivations. The way Jak had reported the lesson had suggested Rivlen might have been thanking him for helping defend the ship, but maybe it was something else. Did she think she could use Jak somehow? Malek hadn't missed that she was ambitious. He didn't mind that, if it made her a good officer, and so far, he had no qualms about her work.

"He helped us in the druid fight," Rivlen said. "I'm ashamed to admit it, but we might not have gotten out of that mess without the artifact shooting lightning at our attackers. As far as I know, he's the only one who can convince it to do that."

"I haven't tried, so I don't know how difficult it is, but yes." Malek would call Jak up to communicate with the portal again if they ended up in trouble. For now, he was still helping in engineering. It shouldn't take much longer for the crewmen to get the engine working again.

"I decided to show him something as a *thank-you*." Rivlen shrugged, and he sensed it was a partial truth. "He wants to be able to defend himself when mages try to force him to his knees. Apparently, terrene humans don't like that."

"Shocking."

"He picked it up very quickly and even pushed me back at one point."

"Are you hoping he'll apply to join the military, so he can serve under you, and you can legitimately teach him?"

"That would be acceptable, but I assumed that you and King Uthari have some use for him."

The first blue-hulled ship came into view over the river. Malek sensed the others closing in as well, though the trees still hid them. The fleet was splitting apart, intending to surround the *Star Flyer.*

"I do not know what Uthari will wish for him," Malek said, "but I did suggest Jak could be useful in some capacity. A young cartographer might not be a natural fit for the military. Especially if he doesn't like being on his knees."

"Not *all* officers force their troops to their knees, my lord. Occasional lessons must be taught, but competence, respect, and professional courtesy are all I require. Besides, he didn't assume I'd slept my way into my position. I appreciate that."

"I doubt many who've seen you in battle assume that."

"Then you would be surprised."

"I didn't assume that." Malek sensed the *King's Courage* and Tonovan flying behind Zaruk's formation.

"And I appreciate that too, my lord." Rivlen snapped a salute. "It will be an honor to go into battle with you."

That struck him as the kind of thing someone who didn't believe they would win would say. He intended to make sure they won.

You appear to have a problem, Malek, Tonovan drawled into his mind. *How does it feel to have your mighty* Star Flyer *reduced to a dinghy bobbing about in the water?*

We're repairing our problem. Are you going to assist us or watch while our enemies take the artifact?

They're demanding our surrender and promising to blast us out of the sky if we fire upon them. We let them pass without comment. I was waiting for you to let me know if you have something sneaky planned.

You don't think engaging them in open battle will be sufficient?

Two against six is poor odds, especially when your ship is kissing the fishes.

We'll get it in the air, Malek said. *Where's the* Dread Arrow?

Also repairing damage. They won't arrive in time for the battle.

I see. Are you and the Courage *with me?*

I hope the enemy obliterates you and plasters pieces of your body all over the trees in the jungle, but of course I'm with you for the battle. I know what Uthari wants, and it's in both of our interests to see that he gets it.

Yes.

A surprisingly large horde of people yelled and waved rifles, swords, and shields from the deck of the visible ship. Had Night Wrath hired a lot more mercenaries? Maybe they'd brought down some of the companies that had assisted them with the siege on Utharika.

No, none of those people wore uniforms. They looked more like roamers. Ah, they *were* roamers. Malek snorted. Night Wrath was so desperate that he'd hired pirates?

And what had happened to the Thorn Company mercenaries? Malek was pleased not to have to face soldiers following Colonel Sorath's orders but couldn't help but wonder what else the man might be up to. Could Sorath have been behind the sabotage? A mage had planted the magical explosive, Malek had no doubt, but the idea reeked of the mercenary colonel.

Malek made a note to check on Tezi, to make sure she didn't receive orders from her commander or anyone else on Zaruk's ships, someone who might try to get her to do something from within. He doubted they knew she was there, but it was possible.

When the sabotage of the engine had first been discovered, Rivlen and several crew members had assumed Tezi had done it and wanted to wring her neck. Even after Malek had pointed out that a mage would have been required to activate the device that had delivered the damage, the crew had been suspicious until they'd confirmed Tezi never left her cabin.

They're about to open fire, Tonovan said.

As are we. I'll keep you apprised of our planned sneakiness.

I so look forward to it.

"Tonovan is with us," Malek said. "Open fire."

Rivlen gave the order, and Malek lifted his hands, summoning his power in the hope that they could deal a few devastating blows before all of their enemies positioned themselves with their defenses up. He hadn't traveled all the way down here to fail at his mission.

In her cabin, Jadora sat at the desk with books spread before her and did her best to ignore the alarm gong and the shouts echoing down from above decks. She also ignored the sway of the ship as it rocked in the river, though the latter threatened to give her motion sickness. Seagoing voyages didn't usually bother her unless a storm came or she was trying to read and write, as she was now. The druidic symbols moved on the page, right along with the rocking deck, making her miss the smoothness of being in the air.

Tezi paced between the bunks, looking strange in the red uniform Malek had brought for her. Jadora wore one herself while she waited for her clothes to dry, and she half-wondered if they could wander above decks without anyone noticing they weren't part of the crew.

But if a battle was about to break out, she didn't want to be in the middle of it. It worried her that *Jak* had gone off to do who knew what with Malek. She doubted Malek would be able to keep an eye on him while a battle raged all around, though he'd kept her and Tezi from falling off their skyboard as they'd fled the druids, so maybe he could.

Outside, a flock of large birds sprang out of the tree in front of the porthole, taking flight with alarmed squawks. A moment later, a faint shudder reverberated through the *Star Flyer*. It seemed to come more from the water than the air, but light flashed, so she suspected that some of Zaruk's mageships had caught up with them and started attacking. Their magic might be bouncing off a barrier and hitting the surface of the water, making waves.

"I almost wish they would give me a weapon so I could help," Tezi said as she paced, "but I might be fighting my own people if I did that."

"Possibly so." Jadora flipped a few pages, looking for the translation for an unfamiliar rune. "Unless they never got paid and refused to continue fighting."

"I suppose I shouldn't hope for that, since Thorn Company needed the money, but it would be distressing to have survived almost falling to my death only to be killed by my own people."

Almost *jumping* to her death, Jadora thought but did not say. Whichever verb was more correct, Tonovan and Yidar were to blame, not Tezi.

Jadora flipped to the next page, enthralled and horrified by the story unfolding as she translated. It was the first of many in the book and matched what Gelira had shown them, except it was a much more detailed version that listed the names of the people who'd died to the worm, and also listed the physical damage done to the village—one of several that had been destroyed.

She wouldn't have time to translate the rest of the tales before they reached the pool, but if she could get through the first one and share it with Malek, maybe it would be enough to change his mind. To change *Uthari's* mind.

Assuming she wanted to do that. Did she? The thought of throwing away the last five years and Loran's life's work depressed her vastly, but she could already tell this story—this historical accounting, if the druids could be believed—would confirm that setting up the portal would be dangerous. The idea of not seeing it placed and activated was distressing, but unleashing a malevolent dragon or some other creature on the world would be far worse.

Maybe Jak was right, and the key-keyhole system would keep that from happening, but if a key was firmly in place on the portal in the world that the creatures came from... it wouldn't matter if the portal here on Torvil had one or not. She kept hoping to see the keys explained in the druid book, but so far, they hadn't been mentioned.

Jadora checked to see how many pages she had left in the first story and groaned. "This is going to take several more hours."

Lightning flashed outside again, and the *Star Flyer* trembled.

"We might not have them, ma'am, if the ship is destroyed."

"I'll trust Malek and Captain Rivlen can keep that from happening."

Tezi sat on the bunk and looked at her. "Before I left, the zidarr Night Wrath said Zaruk's allies had several more ships on the way. With this delay, they might have had time to catch up. I'm sure that was the point of the sabotage."

Jadora had little doubt. She wished she could say Malek could still drive them off, but even he couldn't beat so many when he was that outnumbered. Yidar and Tonovan were supposed to be around to help him, but maybe they would accidentally fail to show up. If Tonovan knew that Malek had been responsible for Tezi stabbing him and getting away...

She translated another paragraph and grimaced at a gory description. Maybe it wouldn't be the worst thing if the artifact and the key—and her and Jak's knowledge—were separated again. But that wasn't what would happen. If Zaruk's army defeated the *Star Flyer*, their mages would sweep in and get everything, her and Jak included. They would find themselves prisoners once again.

The hatch opened, and an older crewman shoved Jak inside. "Stay in your cabin for the fight."

"You're welcome," Jak called after him.

"Yeah, yeah, thanks for the juice, kid." The hatch slammed shut.

"They're an ungrateful people," Jak said.

Jadora gave him a quick look over to make sure he hadn't been injured, then returned to her work. She had a niggling feeling that finishing translating at least the first story was important. Maybe it was possible that Malek and Uthari would see reason if she presented them with irrefutable evidence about the dangers that had once come through the portal.

Not that the druids' tome was irrefutable, as they would likely point out.

"Who was that?" Tezi asked.

"One of the engineers." Jak sounded a little smug as he added, "I helped him."

"How?"

"Sort of the magical equivalent of holding his tools. Malek helped a lot more, I'll admit. I kept getting distracted. Uhm, Mother?"

His tone had taken on an odd note, and she looked up at him.

"Did Malek tell you..." Jak glanced at Tezi, as if he wished they had privacy, but there was nowhere to ask her to go. He came and sat on the bunk, his knees clunking the edge of the desk. He lowered his voice to a whisper to ask, "Did Malek tell you Tonovan killed Father?"

"When I was dwelling on the question so thoroughly that it had to be battering him in his mind-reading head, yes. It had been prominent in my thoughts since Tonovan told me that *Malek* had done it." Jadora shrugged, indicating they couldn't know the truth, but she was far more inclined to believe Malek. If it turned out he'd lied about that, she would be devastated. They were both supposed to be her enemies, so it shouldn't matter... but it would.

"Tonovan telling you that makes me *positive* Malek didn't do it," Jak said.

"You don't think he would lie to you?" The ship rocked violently in the water, making Jadora wonder if their enemies were targeting the river specifically now and trying to capsize them. Would a magical barrier protect against that?

"Not about that. I do think maybe... he told me on purpose."

Jadora frowned, not positive what he meant, and hunted for the translation for the next rune. She wanted to listen and be there for Jak, especially since the concerned furrow to his brow suggested he was trying to work something out, but she *had* to finish this.

"I think maybe he was intentionally manipulating me," Jak admitted. "He wants me to want to serve Uthari."

Jadora didn't know how Tonovan having murdered Loran could result in that, but she paused to focus fully on him. "I trust you don't want to do that."

"Of course not. I want to help people. *Real* people, not mages."

"They're real people too, but I accept there's a big distinction."

"I wonder if I could learn from them, even as they think they're turning me into some loyal minion, and then one day use my power to help overthrow them."

Tezi had sat at the far end of the bunk, giving them their privacy, but it was impossible for her not to hear, and she glanced at Jak.

Jadora would prefer it if Jak didn't want anything to do with his power at all, but his eyes burned with a desire to learn how to use it. She couldn't blame him for wanting to protect himself, but this seemed like a dangerous road to walk.

"You had better keep that thought to yourself. Actually, you better keep it out of your head altogether." She touched his temple.

"I know, but Rivlen showed me how to keep them from reading my mind. I need to practice a lot more, since it's hard to do while you're doing anything else, but eventually, I'll be able to think freely without anybody knowing what's in my mind."

"Well, I haven't mastered *The Mind Way* yet, so don't tell me anything you don't want them to know."

"Oh, good point."

"And be careful. You don't want to, in feigning to be one of them, start sympathizing with them and truly end up on their side."

Jak shook his head, though he paused after a moment. "I won't, but that is what happened to Malek, at least if he was telling me the truth."

Her pen paused. "He wasn't always one of them? He told you his background?"

He'd never told *Jadora* his background. Not that she'd asked. If she had, maybe he would have. Though *she* wasn't some potential future mage that he was cultivating and trying to win to Uthari's side.

"Yeah." Jak dropped his whisper even further. "He was one of us. A wild one, like me. Mages were *hunting* him and trying to kill him until Uthari took him in and offered to train him as a zidarr so he could take revenge on the man who killed his mother. Or the king whose doctor refused to treat her." He shrugged.

"The story sounds complicated."

"It is a little, but the point is, he's deep down one of us. Or he started out that way. Maybe that's why he's not a huge jerk now like the rest of them."

"Maybe," Jadora said neutrally, not pointing out that if Malek was taking Jak under his wing and telling him secrets as a way to manipulate him, he might qualify as a *huge jerk*.

Jak looked toward the ceiling, his eyes growing unfocused. She'd caught that vacant-eyed expression on him more frequently lately and had come to recognize it as his trying-to-sense-magical-things look.

She'd much preferred the days when he didn't *have* a look like that. His eagerness to learn from these people scared her. Even though she didn't believe he would ever turn on her, she worried that this was a path that would change him irrevocably, and not for the better.

But what could she do? Now that they were surrounded by mages and being attacked at every turn, it would be foolish for Jak *not* to learn everything he could. She had to support him, not judge him, not push him away. The last thing she wanted was to risk losing him.

With emotion welling in her throat, she wrapped her arms around him.

"Mother?" Jak patted her back, though he seemed confused by the hug.

"I guess you can't read minds yet," she murmured.

"No, I don't know what terrain feature that is."

"I'll pretend I know what that means."

"I'll explain later. I need to go. We're surrounded by a *lot* of enemies, and they're demanding the *Star Flyer* surrender. Captain Rivlen wants me to come up and convince the portal to attack them. The engine is repaired, but we can't go anywhere unless we have the room to take off." Jak squeezed her, then released her and strode for the hatch.

"Be careful," she called after him.

"I will."

As soon as he was gone, Jadora wiped her eyes. She wouldn't let the tears fall, not with Tezi in the cabin.

"I wish I could help, ma'am," Tezi said softly.

"I wish we didn't *need* help."

"Maybe I can get one of Malek's people to give me a weapon, so I can protect you. You did offer to take me to another world. That would be the least I could do."

Jadora smiled at her, trying to make it sincere, but the idea of one mercenary stemming the tide of mages who wanted to use or kill her and Jak and get the artifact wasn't heartening.

"I know I'm young and don't look as tough as Sergeant Tinder or the captain, but I'm a good shot. If I could get them to give me a magelock, I could be useful, maybe keep mages from kidnapping you."

Something she would only be willing to do until her own people showed up with those mages. Maybe she hadn't considered that yet.

"Do you think Malek would? Or is he..." Tezi trailed off and clasped her hands in her lap.

"Lying to us?" Or manipulating them, anyway. Jadora didn't think Malek was a liar, but she could never forget that his loyalty was to Uthari, not to her and Jak.

"I wasn't sure if you believed the story Jak shared. Malek's story."

"It's probably true." Jadora remembered Malek appearing disgruntled when she'd once voiced—no *thought*—that he was the pampered son of wealthy mages who'd dropped him off for zidarr training in his youth. "His reasons for sharing it are what should be questioned. Still, if anyone here *would* be willing to give you a weapon, he would be the one."

More alarm gongs reverberated through the walls.

"This may not be the time to ask him." Jadora sighed. "In case we get out of this, I'd better finish this translation."

"What's the book telling you?"

"That setting up the portal may be a very bad idea."

24

Though Rivlen had requested he come up on deck to help, Jak crept out warily, afraid someone would yell at him. Or—a fireball slammed into the ship's barrier directly over his head, and his heart tried to leap out of his chest—afraid an enemy would pick him off.

Four ships were visible in the sky above, three blue and one black, and he sensed three other ships over the trees lining the river. Those were all Zaruk's forces.

Malek and Rivlen stood in the forecastle, casting magical attacks at the enemy craft. Several ships showed signs of damage, and the *Star Flyer's* defenses were firmly in place, but Zaruk's people kept targeting the water around them. Waves formed and crashed into the barrier, bobbing the *Star Flyer* about like a soap bubble. At one point, they were thrown against the shore, only their barrier keeping them from wrecking on the trees. Instead, they bounced off, the deck wobbling precariously.

Abruptly, the *Star Flyer* lifted into the air, and Jak clenched a triumphant fist. When the engineer had sent him away, it had been because the man was almost done and hadn't needed more power, so Jak had expected this.

As the ship rose, continuing to fire at its enemies, Jak ran across the deck to the artifact. Unfortunately, as the *Star Flyer* climbed above the trees, the view confirmed that there were six ships to Uthari's two.

Jak prayed to Shylezar that the portal would deign to help them again. The last time, it had been uncertain about its desire to return to its home for activation. He had no idea if it was capable of mulling its fate and impact on humanity, the way a person might, but it could be.

As he vaulted over the side and into the center, a ship barreled down on them, as if it meant to ram them. Hordes of wild-eyed warriors roared and waved their weapons from the deck. Roamers.

He trusted they wouldn't get through... unless the barrier went down. As long as Malek was up there in the forecastle, it shouldn't.

Jak rested his hand on the cool dragon steel of the portal. *Hello, my friend. We're almost to your home, but we're in trouble again.*

Artillery weapons boomed, and the shouts of the roamers grew louder. Maybe he should go straight to urging the artifact to attack, but it wasn't a firearm. He couldn't simply pull the trigger. It was always a negotiation.

The artifact didn't respond with a blue pulse or any kind of acknowledgment. That concerned Jak, since it usually let him know in some way that it was aware of him.

Given all the enemies around, maybe the lack of pulsing blue magic was a boon. The *Star Flyer*'s crew would have to lower their barrier, at least above the artifact, for it to strike at the other ships. Sooner or later, their enemies would realize the artifact was a weapon and that they should attack en masse and focus on destroying it—or the person using it.

Not that he wanted to give them ideas. Jak glanced up at the ships looming over them in the sky and spotted a *lot* of people peering down at him.

Even though he doubted they could read his mind from that far away, Jak wrapped his mental bandana around his head to keep them from prying.

Are you ready? We'll lower the defenses so it can attack. Malek's face was tense as he looked down at Jak from the forecastle—the faces of *all* of the mages defending the ship were tense.

Jak knew he couldn't delay. *Yes.*

As the barrier protecting the ship partially dropped, Jak closed his eyes, focused on the portal, and willed it to once again send out its powerful lightning bolts to attack those who wanted to capture it—and kill him.

Thus far, the portal had been amenable to keeping Jak alive, something he appreciated deeply, but he still didn't get a response from it. It was as if the artifact had fallen asleep. Or—his gut twisted—been *damaged*.

But it still radiated its usual powerful aura. And as he'd jogged up, Jak hadn't seen anything amiss about the portal, nor had there been holes or char marks on the deck nearby to suggest it had been targeted. Even if it had been, wasn't it supposed to be nearly indestructible? Mother had said no smith on Torvil could melt dragon steel. Even the lesser dragon steel, such as Malek's weapons were made from, was too impervious to be melted down by mere flame. It required the great magic of a dragon to shape.

"Portal," Jak whispered, his shoulder blades itching with awareness of the gaping hole in the ship's defenses above him. "Wake up. We need your help. Badly."

Again, he envisioned it coming to life, sending lightning bolts up to attack the ships firing magic at the *Star Flyer*.

In the past, the portal had sometimes refused to obey orders to attack, and had shared its reluctance, but this wasn't like that. It wasn't responding at all.

Had someone somehow turned the sentient entity within it *off?* Was that possible?

He and his mother had crawled all over the portal when they'd taken measurements and done the rubbings. If there was anything like a toggle or a switch, they would have seen it.

Jak's eyes flew open. Could the same engineer who'd damaged the engine have figured out how to sabotage the *artifact?*

A fireball slammed into the deck a few feet from it, blasting through to the hold below as scorching heat roasted the air. With his heart hammering against his rib cage, Jak ducked low, hoping that being in the center of the portal would protect him.

But one of the enemy ships was visible directly above him. Shouts of triumph came from its deck where mages were lined up along the railing, mages who were now targeting him.

Jak? Malek asked.

The artifact isn't responding! Jak plastered himself against the inside of the portal as more attacks plummeted down, fireballs and lightning strikes hammering it and the deck around it. *I think it might have been sabotaged somehow.*

Can you fix it? Malek's voice sounded calm in Jak's mind. That calm might have been reassuring, but then he added, *Even with Tonovan's help, we can't survive against so many without it.*

I'll try! Jak patted around the inside of the portal, looking for a device or anything out of place.

Return fire streaked upward from the forecastle as the *Star Flyer's* mages fought back. One of Malek's powerful attacks slammed into the chest of a man who had been targeting Jak. It blasted the mage across the deck of his ship and off the other side. He plummeted down, features and clothes charred black, and wasn't moving by the time he hit the water.

But more mages stepped up to take his place. Fireballs roared back and forth, the crews of both ships opting for offense instead of defense.

Malek's eyes blazed as he tried to single-handedly take out every member of the enemy crew. He might have done it, but another ship floated closer to help, the ship with the horde of roamers aboard.

Jak shook his head, not finding anything on the inside of the portal. He would have to check the top and the outside. The idea of being in the open and so vulnerable made him cringe, but it had to be done.

As he vaulted over the artifact, trying to stay low and use it for cover as much as possible, the ship with the roamers drew close enough for its warriors to throw ropes over the sides and slide down to the *Star Flyer*. Malek and Rivlen and others blasted many of the men before they reached the deck, but Zaruk's fleet had picked up a *lot* of those warriors. Through sheer numbers, some made it down, drawing weapons and roaring as they charged the crew.

All trained mages, the *Star Flyer's* crew raised barriers to protect themselves, but that meant they couldn't launch attacks of their own. That emboldened the mages on the ships above, and more attacks rained down on the deck—and on Jak.

A fireball streaked toward him, and he scrambled around the portal, trying to get away, but two roamers fought a crewman right in his path. A barrier appeared around him, protecting him as the flames would have enveloped him. Malek.

Jak gulped. Malek glanced at him as he sprang down from the forecastle, his weapons in hand. Somehow, he attacked with his blades, targeted other enemies with magic, and protected Jak all at once.

Certain that couldn't last, that even Malek would be overwhelmed, Jak ran around the portal as quickly as he could. He patted all over the surface, searching by hand in case there was something his eyes couldn't detect.

With the chaos all around, smoke now hazing the air and

flames crackling all along the nearby railing, Jak almost missed a bump on the side of one of the four entwined dragons of the framework. It blended in so perfectly with the blue-black of the dragon steel that he'd missed it. Even looking right at the four-inch-long oval bump, he could barely detect it. But it wasn't made from dragon steel, and he knew it wasn't part of the artifact.

With no idea what it was, he tried to pry it off, hoping that would fix the problem. Maybe it was designed to disrupt magic or interrupt telepathic communication. With his hand right on it, Jak could sense that the device was magic, but since the artifact itself radiated so much power, it had been easy to miss.

He tugged at it with his fingers, nails barely able to dig into the slight seam. It was affixed as surely as if his mother had glued it with that super-powered concoction of hers. Why didn't he have a dagger, damn it? He jammed his hands into his pockets, looking for a tool he could use, but he'd put them all into the new backpack. The backpack he'd left back in the cabin.

He almost called to Malek for help, but so many people were attacking Malek, both from the deck of the *Star Flyer* and from the ships above, that Jak dared not distract him. The barrier that had protected Jak earlier disappeared as Malek was forced to focus on his enemies.

Jak had to do this himself. He gripped the smooth oval and willed it to release, trying to use his magic, since his fingernails weren't enough. But it wouldn't budge. He needed a mental aid for his magic. Like the mountains.

He formed a map of the continent in his mind and groped for what terrain feature might help him pry something free. An earthquake was what he needed, great tectonic plates shifting along a fault line, driving the ground apart. He imagined that happening, the portal as one plate and the foreign device as another.

It started to give, but a group of roamers landed not five feet away from Jak. Their bearded faces were tattooed, their eyes wild with battle lust, and they charged for him with huge axes and spears raised. Malek was behind them but too busy to help.

Jak swore, knowing he had to get out of the way, but he had to get the damn device off. With a last desperate burst of power, he envisioned the tectonic plates shifting hard. The device came free in his hand. He threw it at the men, hitting a spear-wielder in the chest, but it didn't deter him in the least.

Jak sprang up and backward, trying to throw himself inside the portal where its mass would help protect him. But the warrior was faster than he and leaped after him.

As Jak came down on his back in the center, pressing a hand to the side, the man landed on the portal above him. Jak willed the artifact to come to life and help him, to hurl its magic at their foes, and he sensed it stirring, waking from its sleep. But it was too slow.

The roamer slammed the spear downward. Jak rolled, trying to evade the strike, but the point slammed into his abdomen, scraping against his hip bone. He couldn't keep from shrieking as agony tore through him.

An instant later, a fireball engulfed the roamer, knocking him out of sight as flames incinerated half of the spear shaft. The heat scorched Jak's face, but it wasn't heat that made him pant with pain. The spear had gone all the way through, pinning him to the deck. Only through sheer will did he keep one hand on the portal, pleading with it to fight, to protect him and the *Star Flyer*.

Thankfully, lightning bolts sprang from its sides, zagging upward and striking two of the attacking mageships.

"Get the barrier up!" someone yelled. Rivlen.

"No," Malek yelled back. "It's attacking now."

"Shit!"

That was an understatement.

Gritting his teeth, Jak panted, the deck hard against his back, the remains of the spear keeping him pinned in place. More pain than he'd ever experienced lanced through his body. But he kept his hand planted, in case the artifact required that. He even tried to feed some of his power into it, the way he had for the engineer, but the agony made it too hard to concentrate on magic, on anything.

Knock them out of the air, he begged the artifact as sword clashes rang out all around him. The roamers were still on the deck fighting. They either hadn't noticed the lightning and that the tides might be turning, or they didn't care. They just wanted to kill mages. *All of them. Please.*

More lightning sprang away, targeting ships farther away, hitting them with enough power to tear through the barriers protecting them.

A roaring warrior sprang onto the portal and pointed his axe at Jak. Oh, Shylezar. Not again.

The man lifted the axe with both hands, like a logger about to cleave a stump in half. Or cleave Jak's head from his body.

Then someone came out of nowhere, landing inside the portal with him, one boot to either side of Jak's chest. A blade glowing a brilliant white swept upward, catching the axe with a thunderous clang. The bigger weapon seemed like it should cut the slender blade in half, but Malek's lesser dragon steel broke the axe. And then drove into the roamer's belly.

As the man bellowed in pain, Malek spun and jumped, rising high enough to kick his foe in the crotch. The roamer flew backward and out of sight. Malek landed in precisely the same position, not so much as brushing Jak.

With the spear lodged in his gut, Jak couldn't manage to appreciate much, but he was glad not to be stepped on as Malek defeated more enemies, if not with his blades then with his magic. He hurled attacks at anyone who tried to get close to the artifact and Jak.

Blackness threatened Jak's vision, and he closed his eyes, focusing on keeping his connection with the portal. If he lost contact, it might stop helping, and the *Star Flyer* might yet be overwhelmed.

Aware of the lightning bolts streaking out and slamming into enemy ships, he tried to concentrate on that. Anything to keep from noticing the pain and from wondering if he would die before this battle ended and someone could help him.

The din of shouts and swords clashing lessened. Because the fight was ending? Or because he was passing out?

It grew silent, save for the sound of Rivlen barking orders. Jak tried to open his eyes, but all he could see was blurry brown. Malek.

A hand rested on his chest. *I need to pull out the spear, Jak,* Malek spoke into his mind.

Ship... safe?

For now, yes. You were a tremendous help. This will hurt.

It would hurt *more* than it already did? Jak groaned. *That's a crappy... reward.*

I know.

The hand patted him, then intense pain flooded him as the spear was pulled out. It was too much, and he lost consciousness.

Lieutenant Vinjo sat cross-legged on his skyboard, hovering in the treetops hundreds of feet above the ground, hidden by leaves as he glumly watched a fleet of black-hulled ships floating in the air where the *Skimmer* had once been. Now, only smoke wafted up from the jungle below, a few fires burning in the treetops. Vinjo could still sense magic from the crashed ship, and he could also sense the auras of mages, so at least *some* people had survived, but he doubted many had.

Vinjo and his brother had returned from their sabotage mission too late to help, arriving just as their battered ship plummeted out of the sky. They'd been lucky to avoid notice themselves —at least for now.

His brother stood on his skyboard, also staying hidden in the foliage, but he was close enough for Vinjo to see him clenching and unclenching his fist, his jaw locked as he glared at the fleet.

"Don't do anything," Vinjo whispered. "There are too many of them. Even for you, Veejar."

"I'm not an idiot. And don't call me that."

Vinjo rolled his eyes and didn't point out that his brother had been named Veejar at birth, that *Night Wrath* was a stupid appellation, and that not *all* zidarr felt compelled to change their names. Pointing out that Malek hadn't would only irritate his brother further, and he wasn't above lashing out at Vinjo. Something Vinjo knew well.

He shook his head, distressed at this turn of events. They'd worked well together—surprisingly so—and successfully planted devices to not only sabotage two of Uthari's ships but to nullify the dragon-steel portal, at least until one of their people noticed Vinjo's concealed magical power disrupter and removed it. Thanks to a recent battle with druids, the ships had been distracted, and it had been easier than they'd expected for Vinjo and his brother to sneak aboard.

Little had they known that another entire enemy *fleet* had arrived on the continent. How had they found the *Skimmer*? Vinjo didn't know.

"It was the mercenaries," Veejar snarled, as if reading Vinjo's thoughts.

Vinjo didn't think he'd had his mental barriers down, but maybe his brother had been able to read them anyway. Zidarr training had changed him a great deal, giving him powers Vinjo could only guess at. Their parents were proud—at least Father was. Vinjo was fairly certain that her first son scared Mother now.

"Uthari's people wouldn't have spared them otherwise." Veejar thrust a hand toward the ships and scowled at Vinjo. "You saw that, right? Those people Uthari's mages were plucking up as the mageship crashed were those damn Thorn Company mercenaries." His eyes flared with fury. "*Sorath*. I bet he was the one who made the deal, sold us out to Uthari. What payment do you think they offered him?"

Vinjo shook his head, not wanting to believe the mercenary colonel would have betrayed them. He'd shown genuine interest in Vinjo's inventions. Something his own people hardly ever did.

Terrene humans knew how to value magical tools—and those who invented them. Some of them anyway. The Thorn Company captain had quickly seen the value of his portable thaumaturge-defier bulwarks and had paid him fairly for them. Lieutenant Sasko... possibly didn't see their worth yet. Or *his* worth.

Maybe he'd come on too strong with her. He'd been so amused and delighted to realize she was fantasizing about shoving pencils up Captain Myroth's nose at the same time *he* was fantasizing about something similar that he'd immediately been smitten. Most terrene humans tried to tamp down such irreverent thoughts, especially with a zidarr in the room, but she'd been so *brazen*.

"What in all the lava pools in Hell are you thinking about?" his brother snapped. "It's not that mercenary woman again, is it? Wipe that stupid expression off your face. They *betrayed* us."

"Sorry." Vinjo admitted this was not the appropriate time to contemplate such things, but he did take a moment to hope Lieutenant Sasko and the others would not be tortured by Uthari's troops. *He* did not believe they'd voluntarily betrayed the ship, which meant they were now Uthari's prisoners, not his allies. And prisoners tended to be tortured and interrogated. "Should we check the wreck and see if we can help anyone? I think there are survivors."

"We can't until—" Veejar peered toward the fleet again.

Uthari's ships were on the move, leaving the smoke and heading south, deeper into the continent. None of their crewmen seemed to have noticed the two brothers skulking in the branches and watching from afar.

Why would they? They had obliterated the *Skimmer*. They should have no reason to believe opposition lurked anywhere nearby.

"Follow me." Veejar led the way toward the jungle floor, dodging branches and vines and avoiding clearings, so nobody flying past above would spot them.

Vinjo was careful not to draw upon his power for anything and hoped no alert mages on the enemy ships would sense the magic of the skyboards.

But now that it was moving, Uthari's fleet departed quickly, heading to whatever its next destination was.

The smell of smoke guided Vinjo and his brother toward the wreck. Even though Vinjo expected it to be bad, he winced at the carnage spread across the jungle floor. The ship had been torn to pieces by the attack and the subsequent fall. Burning pieces were caught in the tree branches, and dead servants and a few mages littered the ground. They'd struck down too hard to be saved.

Numerous mage crewmen had survived, and Vinjo recognized the captain and the tall surly helmsman poking about the wreckage, pulling comrades out from under debris. Those with healing powers were figuring out who were most wounded and tending those mages first.

Even without looking at what remained of the engine and the magical components that had powered the *Skimmer*, Vinjo knew they would not be able to repair the craft and fly out of there. If they couldn't find an ally ship in the area to pick them up, one that had avoided being obliterated by Uthari's fleet, they could be stuck in the jungle indefinitely.

"We'll find someone," his brother said, eyeing the carnage with disgust. "We'll find someone, we'll get a ride, and we'll catch up with Uthari's fleet. And *you*—" he pinned Vinjo with his gaze, "—will craft more magical devices capable of sabotaging their ships. *Permanently.* This will not go unpunished." He flung his arm out toward the bodies and the burning pieces of wreckage. "And I will personally kill those treacherous mercenaries, starting with Colonel Sorath."

Vinjo watched bleakly as his brother flew down to report to the captain. His brother the zidarr. His brother who'd become someone Vinjo dared not defy.

Jadora had finished translating the first story and was pulling out the explosives in her backpack when all fell quiet outside. A minute earlier, she'd heard a cry of pure unadulterated pain that she feared belonged to Jak. Tezi stood by the desk, her gaze locked on the porthole as she tried to see the sky above and what was happening.

Jadora didn't *care* what was happening. She had to get to her son.

With two of her explosives in hand, she slung the backpack over her shoulder and charged for the hatch. What she could do in a huge battle, she didn't know, but if Jak had been hurt, she would fight her way to him to help.

As she reached for the hatch, it opened. Jadora halted short of crashing into it.

A crewman stepped into the cabin to hold open the hatch so Malek could walk in carrying Jak. The side of Jak's shirt above his waistband was dark with blood, and a hole had been torn in the material—a hole torn in *him*.

"Jak!" Jadora scooted back to give them room to come in, though her instinct was to leap in and gather her son in her own arms. He was too big for that, but as Malek laid Jak on her bunk, she slung off the backpack, already digging for bandages.

"Rivlen is mopping up. I'll heal him." Malek knelt on the deck beside the bunk and pushed Jak's shirt up, revealing a massive puncture wound. Whatever had done it had gone straight through him.

"Let me clean the wound first," she whispered, hands shaking as she pulled out a bottle of antiseptic and a clean cloth.

Jadora didn't know how much Malek could do with his magical healing, but she hoped it was a lot. A gut wound like that could be fatal when treated only with normal medicine. Her hands steadied as she gently swabbed it clean, though she felt like she was still shaking inside.

"It looks like a sword went straight through him," Tezi whispered, staying back to give them room.

"A spear," Malek said, letting Jadora clean it, then resting his hand on the wound. "We have many injured. The saboteur attached a device to the portal, so Jak couldn't call upon its power until he found it. We didn't know."

Malek closed his eyes. Though it didn't appear he was doing anything, Jadora trusted he was drawing upon his magic. She kept from asking or doing anything that would disturb him, only kneeling beside him so she could stroke Jak's head. His face was clammy and cool, his body in shock from the wound.

"We're flying again," Tezi said quietly, looking out the porthole. As the ship turned, altering what she could see, she sucked in a breath. "There are three wrecked mageships in the water down there. All Zaruk's. Blue hulls. Charred." After a pause, she added, "I hope Captain Ferroki and Thorn Company weren't on them."

Jadora understood why she was concerned, but she couldn't muster the words to answer. Once she knew Jak would be all right, she could think about other things, but not now.

"Help us," he mumbled, shifting and squirming on the blanket. "Help the ship."

"Jak, the battle is over." Jadora glanced at Malek for verification.

The noise and strikes to the *Star Flyer* had faded, so she *hoped* it was over, but it was possible enemy ships behind them were giving chase. Malek's eyes were still closed, his chin to his chest, and he didn't respond.

"You'll be fine, Jak," she whispered, in case the words penetrated his subconscious. If she made light of his injury, maybe he would believe it wasn't that bad and be reassured. "Though I understand you used your body to block a spear. As your mother, I can't recommend such activities to you. They're bad for your longevity."

I apologize for not being able to protect him, Malek spoke into her mind, though he hadn't moved his hand from Jak's injury or lifted his head. *We were overwhelmed, and nobody realized the artifact had also been sabotaged and that it would take him time to figure out how to fix it.*

Jadora knew she should tell him it was all right, that it hadn't been his fault, but her emotions wrestled with her rational mind. It was all she could do not to blurt out that this had only happened because of King Uthari and his quest. Even though she knew that wasn't entirely true, that she and Jak would have ended up in trouble, one way or another, as soon as she carved the artifact from the lava rock that had buried it, it was hard not to blame Malek. To blame *all* of the mages.

Tears leaked from her eyes as she struggled to get control of her feelings. She couldn't know what had happened up there, but Jak was probably only alive because of Malek.

"Will he be all right?" she finally asked, pleased that the words came out calmly and without accusation, though maybe it didn't matter. Malek had surely read her mind as it spun with anger and reproach.

Yes. Whatever he'd read from her, he didn't comment on it.

"Thank you."

Tezi glanced over, making Jadora aware that she was responding aloud to his telepathic communications.

Instead of questioning anything, Tezi said, "I'm going to see if they'll let me up on deck to look around. And if I can find out..."

"I did not see Colonel Sorath or any of your mercenaries in the battle," Malek said. "If Sorath had been there, he would have been among those shooting at me. I would, however, not be surprised if the sabotage was his idea."

He kept focusing on healing Jak and didn't turn his head to glare icily at Tezi, though the words seemed like they should come with some rancor. Maybe he was too focused on what he was doing to summon rancor.

"Oh." Tezi bit her lip and looked at Jadora.

Jadora managed a smile for her, hoping Tezi didn't regret coming with them. At least she was alive. All three of them were alive. For now.

"I'll go check anyway." Tezi headed for the hatch, as much to give them privacy as to look for evidence of Thorn Company, Jadora thought. They'd likely already sailed too far away from that river for her to see back to the wreckage.

Malek didn't forbid her to leave. Jadora hadn't thought she *wanted* privacy, but with Tezi gone, she felt less need to put up a brave front. She slumped and caught herself shifting closer to Malek, wanting... something. To not be alone in worrying about her son. Support.

Malek wasn't the right person to want that from, but she leaned her forehead against his shoulder anyway. Her earlier anger and accusations seeped out of her, replaced by gratitude and relief that he was there to help. If he said Jak would be all right, he should be correct. Who better than he to know his healing abilities? And she didn't have a reason to doubt his honesty, to think he would lie about this.

Besides, Jak's cheeks seemed a little pinker. He'd stopped squirming, and his breathing was even.

She blinked back tears of relief, though she doubted Malek would judge her for them. She hoped he didn't mind her leaning on him for support. In a minute, she would get up and leave him to finish without distractions.

Again, Malek didn't comment on her thoughts, but he shifted his free arm to wrap around her back.

Thank you, she thought, not sure this time if the words were for Jak or herself. *Later, I need to show you something.*

You've translated the book?

The first story in it. The whole book will take some time. She was bemused that he thought she might have translated all three hundred pages of an ancient foreign text in less than a day.

Until tomorrow?

Longer than that.

Tomorrow night?

She swatted him in the chest.

The memory of lovingly stroking his chest for the sake of the druids came to mind, but she didn't consider that now. There was nobody to fool this time, and he wouldn't appreciate such famil-iarity. Besides, nothing had changed between them. She was simply glad he was helping her son.

After a while, she extricated herself from his supportive hug, rose to her feet, and sat at the desk. When a soft knock came at the hatch, Malek didn't stir, so she answered it.

Captain Rivlen stood in the corridor, her uniform dark with dried blood, her temple split with a gash that she hadn't stopped to tend. She had the harried mien of someone doing a dozen things at once and only frowned briefly at Jadora before looking past her to Malek.

"He's busy healing my son." Jadora hoped she wouldn't drag Malek away.

Rivlen watched for a moment, perhaps considering doing exactly that, but she finally nodded curtly. "When he's done, tell him that King Uthari's *captain* sent a message and wants to talk to him."

Jadora didn't understand the emphasis on the word, but she had no trouble perceiving that a message from the king, or his captain, was important. "I will."

Without a *thank-you*, or even another nod, Rivlen closed the hatch again. By now, Jadora was used to a lack of social niceties from the mages, but the reminder that Rivlen was cold and aloof only made her more concerned that she'd taught Jak some magic. Jadora couldn't imagine why she would unless it benefited her somehow.

She returned to her chair and thought about starting to translate the next story, but she struggled to focus, instead glancing frequently at Jak. She could work on the book later. Assuming there was a later. If the *Star Flyer* was back on course, it might arrive at the waterfall pool this very day.

With a faint sigh that exuded weariness, Malek lowered his hand and leaned back from Jak. He'd been on his knees on the hard deck for a long time, and Jadora rose to offer him a hand up if he needed it. *She* would have needed it after sitting in that awkward a position for so long, especially after running around and battling people, but Malek rose easily enough, and when he turned toward her, she was facing him self-consciously, her hand still outstretched.

He gazed down at the hand, and she lowered it. "I thought you might have stiffened up. Do you want a painkiller or anything?" She didn't see any obvious injuries on him, but it was hard to believe he hadn't been knocked around during the battle.

Hell, *she'd* been knocked around, if only from the jostling of the ship, and her hip ached from when she'd been pitched out of her bunk earlier.

"What do you have?" he asked, surprising her by not dismissing the offer.

She rattled off a few of the painkillers and anti-inflammatory medicines she'd taken from the apothecary shop. Maybe he had heard of tiger wort for he agreed to that.

"Captain Rivlen came by," she said as she pulled out the herb and measured a dose. Back home, she could more easily make capsules for powders, but all she'd found in the apothecary shop was some of the berry-flavored paste she occasionally used to hide the taste of bitter medicines.

"I heard."

"You probably need to go speak with your king's captain immediately, but I did want to show you this first." Jadora handed him the tacky ball of paste with the bitter herb inside, then lifted the sheets of her translations. "Or sum it up for you if you don't have time to read it. It's similar to the tale the druids showed us but more detailed and talks of other villages that were destroyed by the giant flying worm. The agoratha, as the druids call it. Maybe you should tell your king about it, in case... it changes his mind."

Malek held up the ball of paste, a bemused crinkled to his brow. "Did you put the medicine in candy for me?"

"It's not exactly *candy*, but it'll hide the taste, yes."

"You didn't think a mighty zidarr could swallow a bitter medicine without complaining?"

"Jak can't."

"His mightiness is only nascent."

"I doubt any power he develops will improve his ability to take medicine without scrunching up his face like a mewling baby." Jadora looked fondly at her son, hoping he would wake soon, whether it involved mewling or not.

His shirt was still rucked up—she would need to wash it for him to remove the blood—so she could see that the wound was noticeably better. Not gone, but the puncture had been sealed, and the skin puckered around it looked like what she would expect weeks into the healing process instead of the same day.

"Go ahead and summarize it." Malek put the paste in his mouth and swallowed it, apparently trusting that she hadn't opted for poison instead of medicine. "King Uthari and his *captain* will expect me to contact them without delay."

"I understand."

He opened his mouth, perhaps to say that she didn't truly— she had no idea why they'd both emphasized this captain—but he closed it again and gazed out the porthole as she shared key lines from the translation. He didn't charge off the second she put the papers down.

"I will tell him," Malek said. "But I don't think it will change much, especially now."

"Now?"

Malek shook his head bleakly, lifted a hand in parting, and left.

"Why do I have a feeling that more bad things are going to happen?" Jadora sighed.

"Mother?" Jak asked weakly, his eyes open, his fingers probing his wound. He shifted onto one side and patted at the matching spot on his back. The wound there wasn't as large, but it was impossible to miss. Fortunately, it was also healing.

How long had he been awake? Long enough to hear the story?

"Hello, Jak." Jadora sank down on the side of the bed and patted his chest. "I'm glad you're awake." She was glad he was *alive*.

"Me too. Did Malek heal me?"

"You're sure I didn't do it?"

"Uh, not unless I've been out a *lot* longer than I thought." He rolled onto his back again, tugged his shirt down, then scratched his wound through the material with a grimace. "Your methods are lovely but a little slower acting."

"They're *normal* acting. And yes, he brought you down and healed you."

"He saved my life." Jak rubbed his face.

Jadora almost pointed out that Jak's life had only been in danger because Malek and Rivlen had called him up to the main deck in the first place, but if they hadn't, and if the artifact hadn't helped, they might all be dead now. And in truth, she was grateful to Malek, even if she continued to be frustrated that Jak kept being put in danger over and over.

"More than once up there." Jak plucked at the dried blood on his shirt. "Things went unexpectedly."

"If you can take that off without too much pain, I'll wash it for you."

"You're volunteering to do my laundry? I must have come close to dying."

"I do your laundry more often than you do. That is not unusual."

He peeled out of the shirt, only wincing a little at his twinges. "It's unusual for you to do it without reminding me that I'm a grown man now and should be able to do my own chores."

"That's because that's true." She found his backpack and pulled out the spare clothing Malek had provided, grimacing because it was another one of their military uniforms, but it was better than wandering around naked.

"Do you really think we should stop the quest?" Jak waved at the papers. He must have heard most of her summary. "All our work? *Father's* work?"

"I would be curious for the rest of my life if we didn't try to activate the portal," she admitted, "but I'm now scared of what will happen if we do it without studying it a lot more first. If the druids weren't able to stop the creatures that came out of it, except by pulling down the portal and moving it, isn't it hubris to believe we can?"

"Malek is more powerful than a druid," Jak said with hero worship in his eyes.

Every time Jak saw him fight—or fought with him—he seemed to be more under Malek's spell. What would happen when the day came that King Uthari, with the faithful Malek at his side, asked Jak to swear his allegiance and join them?

"I doubt there are many *people* who can challenge him one on one, but those creatures sound like they were far more powerful and deadly than human beings. If a village of druids couldn't defeat one, that doesn't bode well." Jadora glanced at the pages. "We already know dragons were more powerful than humans, so we might as well assume that other beings were too. We know so little about the dragon home world. It's possible they weren't the apex predators where they came from."

"I hadn't considered that."

"What if dragons came here to get away from predators who hunted them?"

"That's a bleak thought." Jak sat up and faced her. "Remember what I said about the last vision the portal gave me? About there being evil dragons that killed the fun, frolicking ones? We wouldn't want the evil dragons to visit Torvil."

"I agree. We should avoid activating the portal," Jadora said. "At least for now. Maybe if we had a year or two here on Zewnath and could do more research—talk to more druids and translate the rest of their ancient texts and monuments—we could more wisely approach activating the portal."

"That's probably smart. And probably something Uthari will say no to."

Jadora gazed out the porthole, at the clouds passing by above as they soared inexorably toward their destination. "That's what I'm afraid of."

25

MALEK TOOK THE SHIP'S DOME-JIR TO HIS CABIN SO HE COULD contact King Uthari—or Captain Reynok of Uthari's personal yacht—in person. He could reach out telepathically to Uthari, but Uthari also could have reached out telepathically to Malek, and he hadn't. The choice to have Reynok contact the *Star Flyer* instead seemed like it was meant to send a message.

The obvious message was that Uthari was letting Malek know that he was aboard his yacht and on his way to Zewnath in person, perhaps to make sure matters were handled to his satisfaction. But was there also an implication that Malek, whom Uthari had previously trusted to oversee this mission for him, was not performing sufficiently? Perhaps it even conveyed a loss of trust. Because of Malek's choice to go against Tonovan to take his prisoner? Malek hadn't thought Uthari would care about that, but he also had consciously made the choice not to ask permission or share what he was doing ahead of time.

Malek made a disgusted noise and set a hand on the dome-jir to activate it. Worrying and trying to guess at hints wasn't worthy of a zidarr. He would bluntly ask Uthari how he felt, and if he thought Malek had made a mistake, what he needed to do to rectify it.

When the orange crystal lit up, Captain Reynok's face formed in the air above it. With neatly combed, short gray hair and a trimmed beard, Reynok always appeared the epitome of professionalism. Over the years, the captain had refused several promotions that could have led to him commanding the entire fleet, instead continuing to serve Uthari aboard his personal craft.

"Lord Malek." Reynok nodded politely.

"Captain Reynok. I apologize for the delay. We recently engaged in battle, and there were injured to tend."

"Yes, there are a great many enemy ships on this continent." This continent. Meaning Uthari's *Serene Waters* had already arrived in Zewnath? "We've encountered a few of them ourselves. This permitted us to acquire a few potentially valuable prisoners."

"Oh?"

"I believe you had a run-in with Colonel Sorath recently."

"I encountered him. He was injured and didn't trouble me."

"Interesting that you didn't kill him," Reynok said. "He certainly wishes to kill *you*. And he's informed me that he would happily wring my neck and the king's as well. Such a surly man."

"He blames us for the loss of his company." Malek searched for a respectful way to ask to speak with Uthari. Reynok was giving him useful information, but Sorath wasn't Malek's priority.

"So I understand," Reynok said. "I told him we'd intended to kill *him* with that ruse, and were indifferent to his unit, but that did not change his feelings toward us."

"Odd. Where are you, Captain Reynok? Port Toh-drom?" That was the last place Malek had seen Sorath.

"We are on the way to meet you and assist you with the placement of the portal. King Uthari decided to see to that himself, that it was too important to leave to chance." One of Reynok's gray eyebrows arched, as if he were conveying that *Malek* represented chance.

If Uthari believed that, Malek would have preferred he convey it to him personally instead of complaining to Reynok, though the two of them had worked together even longer than Malek and Uthari, so perhaps Reynok was an understandable confidant. Still, it concerned Malek that he'd made a choice that had led Uthari to believe *him* someone he needed to discuss with a confidant.

"I believe I have the situation in hand," Malek said, "but I welcome his presence of course."

Was that true? Malek hadn't intended to lie, but as he thought of Jadora's warning—and the warning of the druids—he wondered if it would be safe down here for the king.

Against most foes, Uthari had more than the necessary power to take care of himself, but even he hadn't been strong enough to defend against the might of the dragon portal. And if some malevolent dragon—or giant flying worm—came through, it might be strong enough to threaten Uthari. What would happen to Utharika and the Kingdom of Uth if the king fell down here? He didn't have a son, and whatever was in his will regarding heirs was a secret to Malek, maybe a secret to everyone. If Uthari planned to find immortality through that plant, he might not have even named an heir. The kingdom would be open to whatever opportunistic ruler swept in with the power to claim it. Malek's lip curled as he imagined Yidar trying to step in and obtain the realm he craved.

"I will tell him that you are prepared to speak with him now," Reynok said.

"I am always prepared."

"You were unavailable earlier when he tried."

"For a short time, I was inside a druid sanctuary with walls that could muffle magical messages." Malek was still surprised Jak had been able to get through when others who'd tried to contact him had failed.

"Retrieving Tonovan's prisoner?" Reynok's eyebrow arched again.

That story had gotten around.

"Yes, and acquiring a druid tome with information on the portal." Admittedly, it hadn't been Malek's intent to get that, but since he had, Uthari might be less inclined to believe that side trip had been frivolous. "Professor Freedar is translating it now. I believe His Majesty should be warned of the contents."

"He will contact you soon." Reynok ended the communication, and the glow of the crystal faded.

Malek stepped over to the meditation area in the corner of his cabin, acknowledging weariness as he removed his weapons belt and sank to his knees. After using his power for the engine repairs, the battle, and healing Jak, he needed to replenish his reserves. If Uthari did not contact him promptly, he would use this time to rest.

Before setting the weapons aside, he held his sword by the hilt, wondering if it would give him any insight into his conversation with Reynok.

An image flashed into his mind, not of the captain but of the past. Uthari stood in his suite back in Utharika, gazing out the window and gripping his chin as he considered the conversation he and Malek had shared about bringing Jak into his service. Uthari was developing a burgeoning belief that Malek was growing close to Jadora and Jak, and that he might, because he cared for them, do something that went against Uthari's wishes, such as setting them free in the dragon home world instead of keeping them captive until Jadora found the Jitaruvak and turned it into a drug he could use.

The image faded, and Malek set his sword down. He usually trusted the dreams and visions the lesser-dragon-steel blade shared, but he wasn't sure how much it could truly know. Could it have read Uthari's mind from across the world? Malek was skeptical about that. It was possible, maybe *probable*, that these were Malek's own concerns manifesting rather than a display of something that had truly happened.

Good afternoon, Malek, Uthari spoke into his mind. The telepathic words resonated strongly, proof that Uthari wasn't far away. *You are available to speak now?*

I am, Your Majesty.

I have come to assist you in this final and most important step.

Very good.

Do not mistake me. I believe you are capable of doing it yourself. I have learned that you were the one to reacquire the artifact, as well as our archaeologists and their key. It seems young Jak was indeed willing to turn himself over to you.

I offered him protection, as we discussed.

And he believed you would give it. As you said, it was easier to gain his trust than that of his mother.

Yes.

Though it sounds like she may trust you now too. Uthari smiled into his mind.

Malek considered whether that was a sincere smile or one that hinted of suspicion. What had Uthari heard and from whom?

He thought of Jadora's ruse with the druids, but it was hard to imagine that Gelira or any of them would have shared details of their encounter with Uthari. They should distrust and dislike him as much as they distrusted and disliked Malek. He couldn't imagine that Uthari had a *spy* among the druids. Before this, he'd had no reason to cultivate an interest in or contacts on this continent—as far as Malek knew.

I do not believe she trusts me fully, Malek said carefully, *but I think she believes I will protect her for as long as it serves you. She knows my loyalty is to you and that if you one day order me to act against her, I will.*

That is not what she told the druids.

Malek rocked back on his knees. Uthari *did* have a spy. Or one of the druids—that male, perhaps—had seen the opportunity to get Malek in trouble and had taken it, perhaps out of a desire for revenge. Malek *had* damaged their compound.

She sought to manipulate them with a ruse, Malek said, not letting himself pause too long before replying, lest it be suspicious. *I know she doesn't believe that, and I highly doubt the druids were fooled, but you have seen her with her acids and various concoctions that she makes. She does not lie down and accept her fate lightly.*

You admire that in her.

Malek sighed, knowing he dared not be anything other than honest with Uthari. *Yes.*

Do you have feelings for her?

Romantic feelings? No. Malek remembered feeling attraction to Jadora as they worked in the rain—and as she'd stepped close and touched his chest. *I don't know,* he amended.

He almost said yes, but acknowledging a sexual attraction wasn't the same as having romantic feelings for a person. He'd had sex many times in his life without forming an attachment. The knowledge that zidarr were not allowed to marry or have romantic entanglements had always been sufficient reason not to allow himself that. Whenever he'd caught himself favoring a partner, he'd walked away from the woman and took any urges to the training-room floor. It was the way of the zidarr, and it suited him. He'd never regretted his choice. Or at least only rarely and briefly. Insignificantly.

Uthari chuckled into his mind. *I wouldn't have guessed it possible for you to develop an interest in a woman.*

Malek resisted the urge to respond defensively or say anything. He could not tell Uthari's mood. Despite the chuckle, suspicion was more logical. Even if Uthari was amused momentarily, suspicion might underlie it.

If I don't know *means yes, and you simply don't grasp that yet, then I have myself to blame,* Uthari continued. *I did encourage you to get close to her, so she would trust you.*

Malek also resisted the urge to blurt an emphatic, *Yes!*

Whatever I feel, it will not interfere with my duties, Your Majesty, he said instead.

Good.

Malek wished Uthari had said he believed him rather than simply *good.* The fact that he'd heard about the incident with the druids made Malek uneasy. Even if Jadora had been attempting a ruse, and nothing more, he shouldn't have allowed those words to fall on others' ears without denying them. He might believe it was the duty of prisoners to do what they had to do to escape, but there was a line that should be drawn. One couldn't give up one's honor and dignity in exchange for freedom. That was too high a price.

I do trust you and have great faith in your abilities, Uthari continued, *but it is possible I made a mistake in wanting Professor Freedar to trust you. If she believes you an ally, to the extent that she dares such a ruse as she did with the druids, perhaps she will not believe there could be ramifications for... poor performance.*

Poor performance? I do not believe she is capable of that.

Poor obedience then. A failure to carry out my wishes fully.

To obtain the plant? I do not think she objects to that.

To obtain it and synthesize it into a compound that I can make available to the world. For a price.

Malek didn't think Uthari had mentioned a *price* before, but it didn't surprise him. All of the kings sought to gain riches and resources to increase the reach of their kingdoms and grant privilege to those who lived within their realms.

I would, of course, invite her to take her own compound, should she be willing to stay in Utharika and work for us. As I would gift you with it and any whose extended lives could benefit the world. Our *world. I would, however, not be willing to let her take it and grant it to the millions of milling terrene humans who seek to overthrow us. I should not, for example, wish Colonel Sorath to live a longer life. I believe he shall live a very short life.*

Yes, Your Majesty. Malek knew that when Uthari rambled, he didn't necessarily want input, simply to muse. Malek was happy to let Uthari do it; it was better than Uthari voicing suspicions about him.

Because of my stipulations, it is possible Professor Freedar will be unwilling to work wholeheartedly on my behalf, even though she may wish to please you.

I do not think that is a desire for her. Malek might have her trust, but he had a hard time imagining Jadora wishing to *please* any man.

If not, then I have made a wise choice. When I decided to fly down and oversee this mission myself, I picked up some insurance along the way. In truth, I thought I might need bait, to lure her to us if you hadn't succeeded in finding her. After all, the most efficient way to hunt is to lure your prey to you. But now, I believe it is only insurance that I need, to make sure she works to accomplish my desires.

Malek frowned, remembering the colleague Jadora had lost. Tonovan had also wanted him brought along for *insurance*. Admittedly, Malek had agreed with the reasoning then, and he'd been the one to choose the professor, but that had been before he knew Jadora. Now... he had no wish to see someone else Jadora cared about used to enforce compliance, so he hoped that was not what Uthari meant.

We already have her son, Malek said.

True, but as you have pointed out, and as even Captain Rivlen has admitted, the boy Jak could be useful to us. It would be a shame to kill him to force compliance.

So you found someone else that could work in that capacity?

I did. When we meet, you'll bring Professor Freedar to my ship, so she can see for herself who we have and what is at stake, should she fail to return to our world with the Jitaruvak.

Malek closed his eyes. He did *not* want to do that, but he made himself say, *Yes, Your Majesty.*

The crew of the *Star Flyer* was so busy with repairs that nobody noticed Tezi as she came above decks to check on the damage—and to see if any blue-hulled or green-hulled vessels that might contain Thorn Company soldiers were visible on the horizon.

But when she reached the railing, only one other mageship was in view. A black-hulled ally of the *Star Flyer*. She couldn't tell if it belonged to Tonovan or Yidar but hoped that Tonovan's ship had crashed during the battle, with the general drowning in the river.

That river had disappeared from view, replaced by a never-ending canopy of green to the north, west, and east. The greenery continued to the south, but it ran up into mountains with black cliffs and stony peaks breaking up the foliage. With rounded instead of jagged outlines, and no snow blanketing the tops, these mountains were much different from the peaks in the northlands where Tezi had grown up.

Tiny black clouds hovered in a cluster partway up one of the mountains. Or were those birds? Tezi squinted, trying to identify them, but they weren't close enough yet.

It wasn't important. What she wanted was to find Malek and

ask him for a weapon. She'd offered to help protect Jadora and Jak, and she intended to do that.

Captain Rivlen walked onto the deck, spotted Tezi, and threw an alarmed glance toward the other black mageship. Only then did Tezi realize it had navigated closer and was flying alongside the *Star Flyer*. As with this ship, most of its crew was busy with repairs, but a familiar officer in a fur-lined cloak stood at the railing, his arms crossed over his chest as he glared at Tezi.

Tonovan.

The surprise on his face—he must have just noticed her—shifted to fury. He wore an eyepatch over his left eye, the one she'd stabbed. Had he lost his eyeball? She'd assumed that with their magic, someone would have been able to repair it.

If he hadn't been glowering at her, she might have felt pleased to have delivered a lasting blow, but she realized she'd made a grave mistake in allowing him to see her.

Idiot, she told herself, scooting away from the railing and out of his line of sight, though it was too late. Would he attack her? Would he attack *Malek* for his part in retrieving her?

Rivlen gripped Tezi's arm and led her toward the navigation cabin. "As much as I'd normally approve of an escaped prisoner *taunting* Tonovan with her existence, now isn't the best time."

Rivlen sent a long look back over her shoulder.

Tonovan was glaring at her—at both of them.

How interesting that your ship located my missing prisoner, he spoke into Tezi's mind—or maybe into both of their minds? That message seemed to be for Rivlen.

If she answered, she directed the words solely to Tonovan.

Did you play a hand in her escape, Captain? he continued. *Our ship inexplicably ran into trees, which gave her the opportunity to stab me with a knife. An attack from an ambitious mage officer who's forgotten the honor of serving her superior and covets his position is irritating but somewhat understandable.* His tone was cold but not full of loathing with the message for Rivlen, but when he shifted to speaking of Tezi, pure rage accompanied his words. *An attack from a worthless soldier who doesn't acknowledge us as the gods that we are to their kind... that presumptuousness must be punished. With great pain and finally death.*

They were only a few steps from the navigation cabin when a crushing power wrapped around Tezi from all sides and slammed down on her from above. She was forced not only to her knees, but to her stomach, her face grinding into the wood deck. What felt like icy metal claws wrapped around her neck, cutting off her air as pain raced down her spine.

You dumb bitch, Tonovan snarled into Tezi's mind. *How stupid do you have to be to stab me and then show your face to me a day later? You've killed others of my kind. How is it that you've lived this long? If Rivlen helped you, it was to spite me, not because she cares about you. And after this mission is over, I'll punish her for her presumptuousness as well. As I have before. Women must know their place, even mage women.*

Rivlen gasped and dropped to her knees beside Tezi. Would he kill her too? Rivlen hadn't *done* anything.

Hands planted on the deck, Tezi tried to push herself up, but she was once again helpless before that man.

Rivlen's gasp turned into a snarl, and she managed to rise back to her feet. She must have cast some counterattack, for the pressure and pain enveloping Tezi waned.

Wishing she had a weapon, Tezi pushed up to her hands and knees. Maybe she could get Malek to help?

I know you think you're my equal, Rivlen, Tonovan growled into their minds, *but you're as young and immature as that mercenary.*

"I'm not the one who took your prisoner from you, you ass." Rivlen's face contorted with concentration and effort as she threw her hands out, her fingers splayed.

Whatever attack she launched, it distracted Tonovan enough

that the rest of the pressure holding Tezi disappeared. Tezi lurched upright and pushed open the hatch to navigation. A helmsman standing at the wheel stared past her toward where Rivlen staggered back even as she kept her arms up. Her braid of hair lifted and wrapped around her neck, as if it were a python that Tonovan would coax into strangling her. Rivlen snarled, and it went limp.

"Where's Malek?" Tezi demanded of the helmsman.

"*Lord* Malek," the man snapped, though he was riveted by the battle and didn't look at her. "I think he still has the dome-jir and is communicating with someone."

"*Where?*"

"His cabin. Are you supposed to report to him?"

"*Yes.*"

The helmsman scowled at her but pointed downward, flashing an image of the hopefully correct corridor and hatch into her mind. Tezi ran out again, intending to race belowdecks, but a blast of power targeting Rivlen clipped her and smashed her against a wall. She rolled away as Rivlen roared and threw a counterattack at Tonovan.

As soon as she escaped the influence of their magic, Tezi hurried belowdecks. She would have thought them both idiots for fighting each other when they had so many other enemies down here, but she was the reason for the battle, so she couldn't. Besides, a wild part of her hoped Rivlen would somehow win and get rid of the general.

Unfortunately, it hadn't looked like she was winning.

Tezi sprinted down the steps through the cavernous hold, ignoring a crewman who yelled at her, telling him only that she was supposed to get Malek. That was as good as a passcode, for nobody questioned it.

She found his hatch and banged on it. Malek stepped out,

buckling his weapons belt on, and only glanced at her face for a second before charging back the way she had come.

"Mind reading makes it easy to deliver messages," Tezi muttered and ran after him.

Maybe she should have gone to hide in the cabin with Jak and Jadora, but the battle above decks had started because of her. It would be cowardly to hide while Rivlen was hurt on her behalf.

Malek ran faster than she and reached the deck first. Only seconds passed before Tezi caught up, but it was enough time for the battle to end. Maybe it had ended before Malek arrived, but she doubted it.

Rivlen slumped against the wall of the navigation cabin with Malek at her side, a hand on her shoulder as he glared across at Tonovan. The general stood at his railing, knuckles white as he gripped it hard. His glare for Malek was full of ice instead of the white-hot fury he'd shown to Rivlen, but it was equally hostile.

Whatever conversation they were having, Tezi didn't hear it this time.

Rivlen looked over at her, blood dripping from one nostril. She'd recovered enough to mask her features, and Tezi didn't know if she was furious with her for allowing herself to be seen or thankful that she'd gotten Malek. Probably the former. The uptight captain didn't seem like someone who *thanked* people often.

Tonovan spun away from the railing, his cloak flapping around his ankles. Tezi wished it would tangle around his legs and trip him, but she wasn't that lucky. Tonovan stalked through a hatchway and disappeared. Unfortunately, his ship continued to sail along beside the *Star Flyer*.

Rivlen slumped forward and gripped her knees, like a runner who'd finished a long race. She wiped her nose with the back of her hand, eyed the blood, and snorted with disgust.

"I guess you were right, my lord," she said without looking up at Malek. "I'm not ready to duel him."

He released her shoulder and clasped his hands behind his back. "You will be more powerful than he by the time you're his age. If you live that long."

"Are you calling me reckless? You who leaped into a druid's den last night?"

"Ambitious, perhaps, but not reckless. Though I have not known you long, I believe you are cunning and calculating."

"I'll take that as a compliment then."

More softly, Malek said, "I appreciate you protecting their friend."

They turned together to look at Tezi. Their friend? Jak and Jadora's? She supposed that was better than being called *the girl* or *the prisoner*.

"I'm sorry I let him see me," Tezi said. "I didn't realize his ship was flying right beside this one."

"Go back to your cabin, and don't let him see you again." Rivlen pointed downward.

Tezi stepped toward the hatch but paused, remembering what she'd wanted to ask. "Will you lend me a weapon, Lord Malek? They took my magelock."

"A *weapon*?" Rivlen's eyebrows flew up, the reaction assuring that she considered Tezi a prisoner even if Malek hadn't called Tezi that.

"Such a weapon would not allow you to defeat General Tonovan," Malek said calmly, not showing any surprise that she'd made the request.

"I didn't think it would, but I promised Jadora that I would help protect them."

"That is not necessary." Malek lifted his chin. "*I* am protecting them."

"Aren't you busy sometimes?" Tezi looked toward Rivlen to

point out that he apparently hadn't been aware of that battle. "I'm not working for Thorn Company anymore, so I'm free."

Very free, she thought bleakly.

"Are you *sure* you're not?" Rivlen grumbled, squinting at her.

"Yes." Tezi kept her focus on Malek, judging him far more reasonable—and more likely to agree to something that might help Jak and Jadora. "When you're not around, I can be there to help. I'm young, but I'm a good shot."

"Your aim with a dagger is accurate." Malek smiled slightly.

It wasn't a facial gesture Tezi would have guessed a zidarr capable of, and she didn't know how to respond other than to stare at him.

"Anyone's aim is accurate from that close a range." Rivlen eyed her dismissively.

"Not necessarily. Not against a wizard." Malek looked at Rivlen and a spot on her uniform jacket where blood had dripped from her nose. "Tend to your wounds and uniform, Captain. We'll meet Uthari soon, and we should look our best."

"Yes, my lord. Thank you for your assistance." Rivlen's bow was formal but grudging, and Tezi guessed she longed for the day when she didn't *need* assistance with anything or anyone.

"I will get you a rifle," Malek told Tezi.

"Thank you, my lord. Uhm, you said we'll meet King Uthari soon? I didn't think any of the kings left their castles. I thought they just sent their troops." As she finished the words, Tezi remembered the mercenary-hiring event in Zarlesh and how some of Zaruk's allies, maybe even Queen Vorsha and King Dy, had been in the tower there, watching over things. That meant they left their castles sometimes, but that had only been to travel to another king's city, not to some wild land with mageship battles taking place in the skies over it.

"That is typically the case, but this mission is important to King Uthari." Malek glanced toward the mountains.

Since last Tezi had looked, the *Star Flyer* had sailed closer. What she'd earlier thought were strange dark clouds or birds were large enough to see in more detail. Her stomach sank. They were ships. At least a dozen. And they all had black hulls.

Uthari had brought a huge portion of his fleet, far more ships than Zaruk and his allies had sent. And Zaruk's alliance had even fewer now after so many had been destroyed back at the river.

If Thorn Company was still out there and still committed to fighting for Zaruk... they were on a suicide mission.

26

ON THE DECK OF A SLEEK BLACK YACHT THAT DIDN'T MATCH THE military warships of the rest of Uthari's fleet, Sorath sat back to back with Ferroki, waiting to see why he and Thorn Company had been plucked free of the *Skimmer*.

From what he'd seen, its captain and the rest of the crew had been left to die in the jungle—those who'd used their magic to manage to avoid instant death from the fall. Sorath had no idea what Lieutenant Vinjo and Night Wrath would think when they found the wrecked ship, and he was doing his best not to dwell on them. Mage guards monitored their group, which included every soldier from Thorn Company, and were no doubt browsing the thoughts of their prisoners.

Ferroki had been surprised but relieved that everyone except the already-missing Tezi had ended up on the yacht with them. Sorath sat scanning their surroundings, more worried than relieved. He and Thorn Company had helped Zaruk's alliance steal the artifact from these people. It was possible that Uthari's mages had plucked them all up simply so they could torture them and give them a particularly excruciating death.

Hours had passed since they'd been brought aboard the yacht. Since then, it had rained on them twice, they'd received no food or water, and they'd been forbidden from going anywhere except to a nearby latrine with fancy marble floors and sinks and washouts made from hammered copper. Two female servants in the men's side waited with pitchers to wash their butts after they used the head. Sorath hadn't asked if the women's latrine featured the male equivalent. Maybe women were trusted to be able to wash their *own* backsides.

"This has to be King Uthari's yacht," Ferroki said, resuming a debate they'd been having off and on for the last hour.

"I don't doubt that." Sorath shifted, his pistol clunking on the deck. Surprisingly, their captors hadn't disarmed them. "I'm just skeptical that *he's* here. It's not like he has a bunch of heirs—or even one—he can leave behind to rule over his city while he takes a jaunt to the Southern Hemisphere."

"He has trusted people who watch over his city while he's gone. I've been to Utharika before. And this portal is clearly important to him. He risked starting a war over it."

A mosquito whined in Sorath's ear before biting him on the neck. He smacked it with his hand. The air had grown extra muggy with the rain, leaving them all sweating, and the mosquitoes were feasting on the mercenary company. He hadn't noticed any of the blank-faced guards having trouble. Maybe mage blood didn't taste good to insects.

"If he *is* here," Sorath said, "why would he want us? Torture? Revenge? He was among those who arranged for the destruction of my company, so I don't know how much more revenge he can take on me."

That wasn't true. Sorath could imagine Uthari putting a knife to Ferroki's throat to manipulate him. Or Tezi's. Or any of the mercenaries. It hadn't been that long since he joined up with Thorn Company, but he'd started thinking of them as colleagues and himself as being a part of a unit again. Maybe that had been a mistake. He was too reckless these days, too unafraid of consequences. Consequences that could end up hurting them.

"If he is here," Ferroki said, "and he speaks with us, I'm going to ask him for Tezi back. I wish I could offer him something in trade."

"Maybe you can. He must want us for some reason."

"Intelligence? We don't know much. No more than the mages his people left in the jungle to be eaten by panthers."

"Maybe he wants to hire Thorn Company," Sorath said.

Ferroki snorted. "Because we're such elite soldiers? He's clearly in need of us, since he's only got ten ships and two zidarr down here with him."

"We must have some value to him."

"Even if he did want to hire us, we signed on with Captain Myroth."

"We don't know if he's still alive," Sorath said.

"Night Wrath should be."

"We don't know if he's alive either. He and Vinjo may both have been captured. And Night Wrath isn't the one who had you sign the contract, is he?"

"No, it was the captain. I believe he was also writing up something for the roamers before we left."

Sorath had been relieved to leave them behind, people who looked like him but whose language and culture he knew little of, only what he remembered his mother sharing when he'd been young. He'd feared someone would try to stick him in command of them.

Two uniformed men walked out of fancy gilded double doors and to the group of mercenaries. "Colonel Sorath and Captain Ferroki. The king will see you now."

"It *is* King Uthari," Ferroki said. "Huh."

"I'd say I'm delighted, but I'm not." Sorath pushed himself to his feet.

"Don't tell him that."

"He'll know. All they have to do is look at my grumpy face, and they always know."

The double doors led into a wide wood-paneled corridor. After swatting a couple more mosquitos off the back of his neck, Sorath was relieved to step inside, even if it meant meeting with Uthari.

The air was noticeably cooler in the corridor, scented faintly by a citrus cleaning solution, and free of insects. An ornate carpet runner ran over a polished wood floor toward another set of double doors at the end, where a female servant held a tray of glasses of water with ice cubes and lemon slices floating inside.

The crewmen led Sorath and Ferroki through the doors to a foyer with upholstered furniture and walls of bookcases. Sorath hoped nobody asked him to sit, because he would leave a sweaty butt print on the floral chairs.

"Who are you?" Ferroki asked a bespectacled man sitting quietly in the corner. It wasn't King Uthari. The man was in his sixties or seventies, with tousled white hair and a matching beard, and he clutched a worn copy of Thanok's *The Teachings* to his chest as he eyed them warily.

"A priest." The man's gaze lingered on their weapons, as if Sorath and Ferroki were the dangerous ones here.

"Any chance the king is dying, and you're here to pray for his soul before he passes?" Sorath asked.

"I have been praying for his soul, but if his death is imminent, I'm not aware of it." The priest smiled sadly. "He is not repentant for his sins."

"Because I do not sin," a male voice said from an office to one side.

King Uthari walked out, a pale lean man with a sharp face and sharper blue eyes. He was rumored to have lived for centuries but looked no older than the priest, perhaps younger, with only the bald pate and wispy white tufts of hair over his ears lending him an elderly mien. If not for the power radiating from him and the icy eyes, he might have passed as someone's grandfather.

Uthari looked them over, then waved for Sorath and Ferroki to follow him into the office and gestured toward a desk with two chairs in front of it. The guards stayed in the foyer, but the servant followed them in and set three glasses of iced water on the desk before bowing to Uthari and walking out.

"Your Majesty." Ferroki saluted him, the appropriate greeting for a soldier in uniform addressing a king, though she also bowed deeply.

Sorath crossed his arms over his chest and glowered, unable to summon an *appropriate greeting* for one of the rulers who'd conspired to take out his unit. If Sorath had believed he could wring his neck before Uthari could kill him, he would have tried, but this wasn't a dumb young mage with cookie crumbs on his shirt. He would be able to defend himself and wouldn't be easily distracted.

"That's correct, Colonel. Do sit." Uthari waved to the chairs and sat opposite them.

The seats were of wood, so butt stains were unlikely, but Sorath stood behind the proffered chair instead. Ferroki, more diplomatic, as always, perched on the edge of hers.

"A week ago, I was extremely perturbed with you," Uthari said, "and would have killed you with gleeful satisfaction if I'd had the opportunity."

"You're the one who stole the artifact from Zaruk's land," Sorath said. "You can't blame me for being available for hire and capable of stealing it back."

"Zaruk is an idiot who didn't know it was there for ten thousand years. Even if it were not originally from Zewnath—" Uthari waved out a wide window, the canopy of greenery stretching up the slopes of nearby mountains, "—and even if he had a legitimate claim to it, he would not deserve it. He is a brute, not a scholar, and should not be the owner of a dragon-steel pencil, much less a powerful dragon-steel artifact that could change the course of history."

"A debate for you political types. I'm just a soldier. What do you want with me? With *us*?" Sorath glanced at Ferroki, though, so far, Uthari had focused on him.

"I have reacquired the portal, as well as the archaeologists with the key and intimate knowledge of it."

"No wonder you broke out the fancy drinks."

"I now know where the portal must be placed to be of use to us," Uthari said, "and we'll arrive there soon."

"It looks like you've got everything you could ever want."

"I don't appreciate your belligerent tone or lack of respect, Colonel," Uthari said.

"Darn."

"You should know from our past encounters that it is more preferable to work with me than against me."

"*Past encounters*? Are you referring to when your zidarr helped wipe out my entire company?"

Ferroki reached back to grip Sorath's arm in warning. "We've signed a contract with Captain Myroth on King Zaruk's behalf, Your Majesty. Even if, given our current predicament, it would be wiser for us to work with you, we are unable to break our contract."

"Myroth is dead," Uthari said matter-of-factly. "When we flew over the coast, Zaruk's ships that were finishing up repairs there challenged us before they knew how superior our numbers were. We destroyed them and left them wrecked on the beach."

Sorath gritted his teeth, hoping Queen Vorsha's *Dauntless* hadn't also been wrecked. He had few friends back on that ship, but he'd liked the mage helmsman who'd worked with him during the invasion.

"Zaruk's remaining ships here in Zewnath are few," Uthari said. "It would be imprudent of you to throw away the lives of your people by attempting to reunite with the handful of his officers who no doubt care nothing about Thorn Company."

"As I'm sure *you* care," Sorath said.

"I do not," Uthari said, "but Captain Ferroki leads a disciplined and well-trained unit. I believe it would be useful for us to have extra troops, and I find that option superior to rounding up unpredictable riffraff pirates to toss at my enemies."

Sorath had a feeling Uthari's people had already encountered the ships with the roamers on them and defeated them. He sighed, trusting that meant the sabotage had not worked.

"Oh, it worked," Uthari said. "It was inconvenient. Was it your idea?"

"What makes you think that?"

"I know Night Wrath, as I know most of the zidarr. They are full of pride and rarely think of employing guerrilla tactics." Uthari's gaze shifted to Ferroki, as if he were digging in her mind to see if it might have been *her* idea.

"I thought of it, yes," Sorath said, not because he wanted credit but because he didn't want her to be blamed.

"You are known for creative solutions in battle."

"So known for it that mage monarchs want me dead."

"Earning a reputation for defeating the troops of such monarchs can lead to one being targeted."

"No kidding."

"Have a drink, Colonel." Uthari waved to the untouched water. "Perhaps a refreshing beverage will cool your temper so you can think more rationally."

"Your Majesty." Ferroki took one of the glasses. "What is it that you want from us? With your clearly superior forces, there's nobody here to oppose you for the artifact."

"Not *yet*, but my spies have informed me that other rulers have sent fleets. Some ships have already reached Zewnath and have likely learned of our destination. Just as I have spies, so do they—in a fleet this size, there are always a few." Uthari's lips twisted with displeasure. "Further, the powerful signature of the artifact makes it difficult to hide. And I cannot take it back to Utharika, not if I want to use it. I judge that it may take several tries and some weeks to find what I seek." Uthari sipped from his glass. "I need to retain control of it for *at least* that time, though I hope not to lose control of it at all. It may take a clever soldier familiar with guerrilla tactics to advise my officers on how to achieve that."

Sorath was stunned that Uthari thought highly enough of him to want his advice—and daunted that he seemed to genuinely believe they could hold off fleets of mageships sent by other rulers. How was Sorath supposed to tell ships full of mages what to do? They would never listen to him.

"If your ideas are good, I will ensure they do," Uthari said. "And I am prepared to pay you for your time, of course."

"You tried to kill me last year."

"No, I helped finance efforts to have you killed. You were dangerous then, as I'm sure you're dangerous now. But if you work for me instead of against me, I am willing to let you live."

"How generous." Sorath glared at him.

Ferroki slid a warning look over her shoulder and squeezed his arm. She hadn't let go of it.

Sorath understood that she wanted to keep him from mouthing off and getting himself killed, but this was ludicrous. They couldn't trust this man.

"What do you want Thorn Company to do?" Ferroki asked with impressive calm.

Maybe because Uthari had never helped finance efforts to kill *her* people.

"Obey the colonel's orders and keep him from doing something foolish, like exploding at a king who, should Sorath attack, would be forced to act in self-defense and kill him." Uthari raised his eyebrows toward her. "You have a calming influence on him."

Ferroki's mouth twisted. "Yes, I've spent thirty years building a company so that my main duty can be calming a man."

"You are a mercenary, Captain. Surely, you must be accustomed to taking whatever work pays the bills, and I will also remunerate you for your time. I'm certain we can find plenty of enemies for you to shoot when you're not busy calming your colonel."

"I'll expect double pay for this onerous duty."

"Really, Ferroki." Sorath withdrew his arm from her grip.

"I'd ask for triple pay if I were you," Uthari told her. "I understand he's already been fantasizing about ripping the balls off some of my men."

"The one who told us to shut up when we asked for somewhere to sit out of the rain," Sorath said. "I also willed exotic jungle insects to lay eggs under his skin and itchy, pus-filled rashes to break out all over his body."

"Triple pay," Ferroki agreed, looking back at Uthari.

He smiled slightly. "I will have my secretary draw up a contract. I will also reunite you with your missing soldier."

Ferroki raised her eyebrows.

"The blonde girl. Zidarr Malek retrieved her from General Tonovan and Zidarr Yidar through a rather roundabout way. She's offered to help guard my archaeologists."

"Is she all right?" Ferroki asked softly.

"Better than Tonovan's eye," Uthari said.

Sorath didn't know what that meant, but the connotations concerned him.

"Now that we're agreed about your new duties," Uthari said,

"you may return to your unit. We'll find somewhere *covered* to house you."

"Yes, Your Majesty." Ferroki stood, bowed politely, and headed for the door.

"Sorath," Uthari said, his voice cool, "someone will be by to question you later."

"Question me?"

Why did that sound like a polite way to say *torture and interrogate* him?

"About the saboteurs and the devices they used. I trust you know more than you'll willingly tell me."

Sorath held back a grimace. He would cheerfully blame it all on Night Wrath, but if Lieutenant Vinjo had escaped, he didn't want to see the kid tortured or killed.

"As I thought," Uthari said softly. "We'll speak later."

Sorath bared his teeth at the king before walking out. He hated working for mages.

Jak absently rubbed the scar on his abdomen, glad it ached only a little, though he was so engrossed by the view out the porthole that he might not have noticed even true pain. After Malek's healing, he'd slept for hours, and during that time, they'd arrived at their destination.

The *Star Flyer* hung low over the treetops, and he could make out a deep pool below, the rush of a waterfall flowing into it audible through the glass. The lush undergrowth and flat rocks around the pool were the same as in his dream—his vision—though there were no dragons sunning themselves on the rocks or frolicking in the water. Nor were any animals or birds howling or squawking or chirping from the trees. They'd probably been stunned to silence by the arrival of the newcomers.

So *many* newcomers.

When the *Star Flyer* had glided along the foothills of the mountains and drawn into this spot, a dozen other mageships had already been waiting. Maybe Jak should have been relieved, since they were all Uthari's, meaning there wouldn't be another big battle, but Tezi had said the king himself was here. Jak worried about what that might mean, about why he would have come.

Was it possible that Uthari had lost faith in his people—in *Malek*—and come to oversee this himself? Jak didn't know what Malek could have done wrong besides helping Tezi, but if that was the reason for all this, it would be Jak's fault.

At least Malek didn't seem to be irritated with them. Earlier, he'd shown up with Tezi, having given her a magelock rifle. At her request, apparently. He'd also said he was glad Jak was on his feet and asked if he needed anything. All he'd offered Mother was a sad smile that Jak hadn't been able to interpret.

He hoped Malek wouldn't treat them differently around Uthari. Even if he was the king's loyal servant, Jak preferred to think of Malek as his own man. There was something wrong with someone with that much strength and power being subservient to someone else. Though Jak had no idea what Malek would work for if he was motivated only by his own goals and desires. He didn't seem to crave much.

Jak knew it was pointless to wish Malek would want to work with him and Mother, toward the same goals they had. Or that they'd once had. He worried the trip to the druids—and the things in that book—had changed her perspective about the portal.

Mother came to stand at his side to gaze out the porthole, but she rested her hand on the notes from the tome she was continuing to translate. She hadn't mentioned anything about the second story she was working on, but her face was glum and defeated, so Jak feared it was as grisly as the first.

To one side of the porthole, something large and metallic descended into view, the edge just visible. Jak jumped.

It took him a second to recognize the familiar blue-black framework of the portal. The crew was lowering it down to the side of the pool.

"I thought they might wait until morning," Mother mumbled.

Outside, the sun was setting, the pool in deep shade cast by the surrounding trees.

"So you would have more time to translate?" Jak asked.

"And to dread the uncertainty of this path."

"It's a shame they're taking that away from you." He smiled.

She didn't.

"They're probably worried about other fleets showing up and taking the portal from them again."

"I have no doubt." She looked down at the open pages of the druid book.

"Just because bad things happened ten thousand years ago," Jak said, "doesn't mean they will again now if we activate the portal. If you think about it, it's pretty unlikely that they will. Look at how much has changed here on Torvil in that time. Humans didn't have cities or large civilizations of any significance back then. It's possible that the evil flying worms have gone extinct."

"The agoratha. It's also possible dragons have gone extinct."

"I'm trying to cheer you up, and you're trying to depress me, Mother. This isn't right."

She smiled sadly and wrapped an arm around his shoulders. "I know. You're right. I'll try to think positively about this. A lot *has* changed. After all this time, we don't even know if we'll be able to activate the portal."

"There you go trying to depress me again. After all we've worked toward, we *want* this to work. And we want a delightful world full of helpful dragons to be waiting for us. Including at least one dragon that adores me and wants to let me ride him."

"I see your supposedly growing maturity hasn't stolen all of your childhood fantasies."

"Of course not. And don't pretend you don't *also* want to ride a dragon."

"You never saw me acting out that fantasy by cavorting around the kitchen on a broomstick."

"That's because you usually wear dresses at home. Broomstick-dragon-riding doesn't work in a dress."

Someone knocked at the hatch before Mother could retort.

"It's Malek," Jak said.

She lowered her arm and turned to face the hatch. Tezi, who'd been cleaning her new rifle, hopped off the bunk to do the same.

"King Uthari's yacht is adjacent to our ship," Malek said when he opened the hatch, only glancing at Jak and Tezi before holding Mother's gaze. "He's instructed me to bring you to meet with him."

"Just her?" Jak stepped in front of Mother.

"Yes."

"Will Tonovan be there?" Jak demanded, glancing at Tezi, who grimaced at the name.

"I don't know," Malek said.

"I want to come."

"Captain Rivlen is coming to get you," Malek told him, "and take you down to the pool where you'll instruct the crew on how and where to set up the portal."

"Mother needs to come down for that too. Or it can wait until we *both* meet with your king." Jak wasn't that worried about Uthari harassing Mother, since he seemed too old to have Tonovan's disgusting sexual urges, but he could threaten her in other ways. Jak wanted to make sure that didn't happen. What he could do against Uthari, he didn't know, but he *had* to be there if Mother needed him.

"I will protect her from any physical threat," Malek said. "You have my word."

Rivlen showed up in the corridor behind him, glancing curiously—or with concern?—at the back of his head. Maybe zidarr weren't supposed to make promises to lowly prisoners.

"Go with the captain, Jak," Malek said. It was a gentle order, but it was an order nonetheless.

Jak looked to Mother, still hesitant to leave her to walk alone among the enemy.

"I'll be all right." She patted him on the shoulder and picked up the books and her sheets of translations to take along. "I appreciate your concern, but if one of us isn't down there to help the crew, they may erect the portal upside down."

"I'd think even idiots could guess that the words go right-side up."

"The words are in Ancient Zeruvian," Mother said. "I doubt many of the crew read it and know which side is up."

"True."

"Go see if you can activate it and find a dragon to ride." She smiled at him, though they both knew it was forced.

Jak watched glumly as she walked out with Malek. Even though he believed Malek would protect her from threats—was it strange that he'd specified *physical* threats?—he had a bad feeling in the pit of his stomach. Everything from Uthari's presence down here to his desire to see Mother alone concerned him.

"Come on, kid." Rivlen waved for him to grab his backpack and follow her. She was armed with a sword, pistol, and backpack of her own. Maybe she thought this would take all night. Or all week.

"Jak, please. I explained my upcoming birthday and the manliness it would convey upon me."

"Developing your power is more likely to convey that."

"I hadn't realized powerful mages were considered manly. In Sprungtown, that word is reserved for large men with muscles and chest hair."

"That's because your people are barbaric. Mages are attracted to the mind and one's ability to manipulate power."

"Next summer at the lake, I'll take my hat off instead of my shirt and see if I can win female attention with my mind." Jak paused in the hatchway.

Tezi stood behind him, rifle in hand, as if she intended to follow. He wouldn't mind the company—especially since she was less likely to insult him than Rivlen—and having someone friendly watching his back while he worked, but he didn't know if she would be allowed to come.

She met his eyes, her chin set with determination, and he decided not to ask. If she acted like she belonged, maybe Rivlen would agree and bring her down.

Jak smiled and tilted his head for her to follow.

She's not planning to have sex with you, Rivlen spoke into his mind as they climbed the stairs toward the deck.

Jak lamented that there were no rails, because he almost pitched over the side.

Unless you force the matter, Rivlen added, *but you don't seem like the type for that.*

I'm not. And I'd prefer to keep both of my eyes.

Wise. Especially since Lord Malek armed her again. She's like those small dogs that you could break in half with two hands but that delude themselves into believing their bite will slay you.

Jak scowled, not liking her talking about Tezi in such a manner, essentially behind her back. *You'd be furious if Tonovan said that about you. Why say such things about someone else?*

Because she's beneath you.

That's not true, and why would it matter to you anyway?

Rivlen didn't answer immediately, instead pushing open the hatch and walking out onto the deck. The *Star Flyer* had descended over the pool, so that they were below the canopy, and the deck lay in shadows. The waterfall roared, the ship close enough that Jak could feel its spray on his cheeks.

I am instructing you in how to be a mage, Rivlen finally said as they headed for the railing, *am I not?*

In how to use my power. Jak didn't say, *Not how to be one of you,* though he was tempted. Even if she was condescending, he would prefer to learn more from her and wouldn't go out of his way to irritate her. *And we've only had one lesson.*

At the railing, she faced him and smiled while ignoring Tezi. *There will be more. Don't forget that you've agreed to help me with my problem.* She glanced toward another ship—*Tonovan's* ship— though it was higher than the *Star Flyer*, and its crew wasn't visible from their vantage point.

Jak didn't think that was *exactly* what he had agreed to, and he doubted he could learn enough soon enough to be much help in a battle against Tonovan, but he would stand with her against the man if he got the chance. Whether it was good for his health or not.

Good.

He realized he hadn't been protecting his thoughts and sighed. Why was that so hard to remember to do around these people? He resolved to work on that and on everything else he'd been learning.

Good, she repeated, smiling and patting his cheek.

It was far more condescending than caring, and he glared and snapped the power of his mountains around himself like a cloak, wanting to push her back, to at least show enough capability that she wouldn't treat him like a child.

She jerked her hand back as if stunned. Or hurt?

He hadn't meant to do that and almost dropped the defensive cloak he'd created, but she seemed more surprised than hurt. She even smiled again, more appreciative than condescending this time, and inclined her head toward him.

Tezi, who'd stopped beside them, her rifle in hand, looked back and forth between them. "Everything all right?"

"Yes." Rivlen twitched her fingers, and Jak and Tezi rose into the air and levitated over the railing. "We'll join the others below."

Which color is levitating people for you? Jak asked.

Sky blue. Rivlen reached for a rope someone had tied to the railing, as if she meant to descend by hand. Could a mage levitate others but not oneself? *Did green work for you? For defense?*

Mountains, actually.

Mountains?

The colors didn't work for me, so I tried terrain features on maps. There aren't usually clouds on maps, but I wonder if that would work for me for levitation. Jak peered toward the pool below, worried that Rivlen would drop them in the water, but a breeze nudged them toward the rocky ledge where the artifact lay and a half dozen mages were arguing about where to put it and how to tilt it upright.

Try it on me. Rivlen had grabbed the rope, but she paused astraddle the railing and gazed down at him. *Levitation is a more advanced technique, but you have more aptitude than most.*

She said it matter-of-factly, not as if she meant to give a compliment, and she kept scrutinizing him thoughtfully. He was her puzzling pupil.

Jak and Tezi landed on the rocky shelf, the mages by the portal ignoring them.

If I screw it up, will I drop you? If he was going to mess up, there were far more people Jak would rather drop than Rivlen.

I'm so honored. Try it, and keep me over the water, so I'll land in it if you drop me.

Jak was surprised Rivlen would let him practice on her. More than that, she was *urging* him to. Maybe she thought he could learn to be a threat—or a suitable distraction—to Tonovan sooner than he did and wanted to teach him as quickly as possible.

I'll try. Jak took a deep breath, focused on her, and imagined clouds forming under her body to lift her into the air. Nothing happened.

"Is she coming?" Unaware of their telepathic exchange and his efforts, Tezi peered up at Rivlen.

"As soon as I can figure out how to levitate her down."

"What?"

Jak shook his head, trying again. The mental clouds evaporated in his thoughts. Rivlen frowned, and he worried she would lose patience. That didn't seem fair, since she'd said levitation was advanced. After her words about him having aptitude, he wanted to show her that she was right. He *did* have aptitude, and he was worth teaching.

But the clouds did nothing. Maybe his brain knew they weren't true cartographic features and refused to accept them for this practice. It didn't seem like it should matter—after all, she thought in terms of *green* and *sky blue*—but another idea came to him. He shifted from envisioning clouds to thinking of a geyser erupting, a stream of hot water and hot air bursting up under Rivlen.

She rose into the air rapidly, flying up thirty feet before Jak swore and adjusted his mental geyser, willing its force to lessen and to arc outward, so she wouldn't come down in the pool.

"Are you doing that?" Tezi gaped as Rivlen descended toward them.

Jak, struggling to keep gravity from taking over and crashing her down like a meteor, didn't answer. Instead, he imagined the geyser stream shifting so that it was still under her, slowly losing steam as it finished erupting, dropping her down gently beside them.

Rivlen smiled as she landed, a more authentic smile than the others she'd given him. "For a moment, I thought I would end up catapulted over the trees and all the way back to the coast."

"Sorry," Jak said sheepishly.

"Don't be. It was well done. You'll learn to regulate your power as you practice more. We all have to learn such methods and figure out what works best for us. I am wondering, however, what odd quirk you added that heated up my ass." She arched her brows and rubbed her butt.

Embarrassment scorched his cheeks. He hadn't expected *that*.

"Sorry," he muttered again. "The clouds didn't work, so I used a geyser."

She laughed shortly. "That'll do it."

"I hope it didn't, uhm..." He glanced at her backside, relieved the seat of her trousers didn't appear scorched or wet. "Burn."

"It wasn't *that* hot. It felt kind of good." She wriggled her eyebrows at him. "I'll know who to call when we get back to the north and winter comes."

With that, Rivlen walked away and started barking orders to her men and demanding an update.

"She really is teaching you how to use magic?" Tezi asked, watching him warily. Like he was some strange alien creature that had crawled out of the pool.

No, even worse. Like he was one of *them*.

Jak hoped Tezi wouldn't start thinking of him as an enemy, as someone like Tonovan. That notion horrified him.

"A little bit, yes. I recently learned I have some aptitude for it." Jak shrugged, trying to convey that it wasn't a big deal. And it wasn't, right? It wasn't as if he had changed or *would* change. "I'm still the same person. Academic, goofy, incapable of making my own lunch or cleaning my room. Just ask my mother."

His mother, who was currently meeting with—or being interrogated by?—King Uthari. The thought reminded Jak that he had more to worry about than how people were perceiving him today.

"I believe you," Tezi said. "I just... It's weird that she's teaching you. She doesn't seem like someone who would care."

"About me? No, I'm sure she doesn't."

"Then why would she help you possibly become a threat to them?"

"I think they want—*she* wants—to use me. I can't say I love that idea, but if it means I can learn how to better take care of myself and those I care about, you can understand that, right?" He waved to the rifle she'd somehow finagled from Malek.

"I can, but that could be..." Tezi's mouth dropped open, and she lowered her voice to a whisper. "I bet I know why she's helping you."

"Why?" Jak asked, though he already knew.

"Tonovan saw me on the deck earlier and thought Captain Rivlen had helped rescue me. He attacked her and was winning in their battle until I ran and got Malek for help. I could see it in her eyes that she detests Tonovan."

Jak nodded. "Yes."

"You already knew?"

"I didn't know about the attack—that's unfortunate that Tonovan saw you and knows you're alive, but since we all ended up here together, it was inevitable." Jak warily eyed the general's ship, wondering if Tonovan was roaming about while Malek and Uthari were meeting with Mother. Hopefully, he had little interest in coming down and seeing the portal set up. "But yes, Rivlen admitted she doesn't like him."

"She hates him with the intense heat of a gout of dragon fire, and if you're not careful, you'll get caught in the middle." Tezi rested a hand on his arm. "I don't know these people well, and I don't want to, but I'm positive she would sacrifice you to get what she wants."

Jak had told himself not to flirt with Tezi anymore, not after all she'd been through, but he couldn't control the little zing that went through him at her touch. Even though he should have drawn his arm back and nodded polite but distant agreement, he instead held precisely still in case she wanted to touch anything else.

"I don't think you're wrong," he said. "I'll keep your warning in mind."

"Good. Also consider avoiding her like you would a snake spitting venom."

"Over here, Jak," Rivlen called coolly, eyeing Tezi's hand on his arm from where she'd stopped in front of the artifact. She pointed to the ground at her side, a hunter calling over a hound.

Tezi dropped her arm.

Though a recalcitrant part of Jak wanted to disobey, he'd been waiting too long to see if they could get the portal working, and he didn't want to delay. Besides, as Tezi had pointed out, it would be wise to walk lightly around Rivlen.

27

JADORA SHOULDN'T HAVE TAKEN COMFORT FROM HAVING MALEK walk at her side, not when he was taking her to see his master, but in a short time, he'd come to feel like the protector he kept saying he was. How many times now had he saved their lives? Though she kept warning herself not to trust him, not to forget who and what he was, having him at her side reassured her.

As they traveled through the elegant yacht, they passed servants in magebands and red-uniformed crewmen at posts along the way, but no escort showed up to lead them to Uthari's suite. As had been the case back in the castle, Malek was trusted to find his own way, and nobody questioned his passing.

Malek stopped before double doors at the end of a wide corridor and gazed at her, his expression glum. The unease she'd felt since they came aboard blossomed into fear. Whatever lay inside, she wouldn't like it. But he'd promised to protect her from threats, so it couldn't be that bad, could it?

Except that he'd said he would protect her from *physical* threats. Why had he felt the need to specify that?

"I did not know about this," Malek said softly, tilting his head toward the doors, then switching to telepathy for the rest. *I did not know King Uthari was coming or that he would bring someone. I regret that I may not have served him thoroughly enough and adequately enough. This may have caused him to develop some doubt about me, and that prompted him to take this action.*

What action? Jadora thought of Darv. Dear Shylezar, would this be something similar? Something *worse*?

Malek started to respond, but the doors opened first. He touched the small of Jadora's back, then led the way inside. Trusting her to follow.

She did. Where else on this ship would she go to escape this fate?

They entered a foyer with doors open to the sides and in the back. Uthari sat at a desk in an office to the left, calmly penning something in a ledger. The room was lined on all sides by shelves full of books, with a few pieces of art here and there. Not the erotic or gladiatorial art that Tonovan had favored but a mixture of diagrams of plants and inventions, blueprints of architecturally interesting buildings, and maps from around the world. It was the kind of office she'd seen often among her colleagues at the university. She herself had once had such a space full of books and diagrams of plants.

"Jadora?" came a whisper from a plush armchair in the corner of the foyer.

Her jaw dropped. She'd missed seeing him at first—hadn't *expected* to see him, not here.

It had been two years since that last awkward holiday gathering where they'd fought, yet another heated argument over the teachings of science and the teachings of Thanok and all the ways they clashed. It had been the kind of argument that her mother had always mediated, stepping between them to act as peacekeeper, until she'd passed away. After that, the visits had been too strained, too uncomfortable to endure.

Jadora stared bleakly at him, his *Teachings* in his lap, looking little different from the last time they'd spoken—fought. His white hair was a little thinner, his face a little leaner, with more wrinkles at the corners of his eyes, the creases of his forehead deeper.

"Father," she whispered, spreading her hand toward him in futile distress.

Even though he didn't appear to have been abused, the awareness that he could be at any time sprang to her mind. He didn't know anything about archaeology, and frequently told her how deplorable it was to seek evidence that anyone but the god Thanok had created man or manipulated human beings in any way. The only reason Uthari would have plucked him up from his church was to use him as a handle on her. To ensure her compliance.

"Why?" she whispered, turning to face Uthari again. "You already had *us*."

"At the time I picked him up," Uthari said, "we did not."

"But now you do. We turned ourselves over to you. To *him*." Jadora thrust her arm toward Malek, who stood silently to her side, his hands clasped behind his back. "Jak told him we'd get the portal working, if at all possible, and find the Jitaruvak. That's everything you asked for. You *win*. You didn't have to *kidnap* anyone else."

Father watched her with fear in his eyes. Fear for her or for himself? Or both? Even though there weren't any shackle scars on his wrists or outward signs that he'd been tortured, she doubted he'd sat in that chair and been waited on by servants for the entire flight down.

"He had a cabin and was not abused," Uthari said dryly, picking right up on their habit of reading her thoughts. "I even offered him reading material." He gestured toward the expansive shelves. "Should he grow weary of that one simple book."

Father gripped his *Teachings* to his chest, as if it were a shield, and muttered, "In the reckoning, he who has worked long and hard will be welcomed into the final serene rest."

"You will go through the portal, Professor, with Malek, Jak, and a mercenary escort, including the woman you two insisted was worth more than my general's eye." Uthari gazed at Malek for the first time.

"If he'd keep his penis in his pants, women wouldn't try to kill him," Jadora snapped. "Don't you *dare* blame us for helping someone get away from that monster."

She shouldn't have yelled at Uthari, but she couldn't bring herself to grovel at his feet. If he lashed out at her, so be it.

No sooner had the defiant thought occurred than she realized he would lash out at her *father*, not her. She closed her eyes, trying to quiet her frustration. When she opened them again, she found Uthari smiling.

"I do appreciate a fast learner. Really, Professor. There's no need for all this drama. As I said before, if you help me in this endeavor, I'll reward you. If you don't wish to live and work in my city, I'll return you to yours. Once we have the plant and you've synthesized a drug and shown my people how to reproduce it, I require nothing more from you. Although..." He tilted his head, glancing at Malek before looking back to her. "It would behoove you to allow your son to learn from us. Perhaps even from *me*—" Uthari rested a hand on his chest, "—should he prove as promising as some have suggested."

Father's brow furrowed in confusion.

"That would be far better for him than to be labeled as a wild one and hunted by those sworn to protect our people from such threats." Uthari's look toward Malek was longer this time, far more significant.

The idea of Malek hunting down Jak like an elk in the forest horrified her. It would be worse than some stranger doing it. Jak *liked* Malek. He might not admit it, but he did. And so did she, damn it.

Tears threatened to film her eyes, but she blinked and didn't let them fully form.

It didn't matter. Not when Uthari could read her every thought.

He smiled again. "It would be far better for the boy to join us. Better for him, and better for you. And as his mother, you would be welcomed into our world."

Sure, she would. The all-mage academics at the universities in his sky city would welcome her with open arms.

"Jak?" Father whispered, a puzzled tilt to his head. "A wild one? He is not—our family is not..."

Jadora almost said she would explain later, but all she had was a hypothesis regarding Jak's talents, not one she wanted to think about with mind readers around.

"I trust we understand each other when it comes to your father," Uthari said. "If you go through the portal to the dragon home world, find it a wondrous place and decide not to return with my plant, then I will send your father to meet the god he so devoutly worships."

Father's face grew pale, but he didn't beg Jadora to do as Uthari said so his life would be spared. Hopefully, he knew he didn't need to, but even if he doubted her, he would have been too proud to ask for her help, even in this.

"I had no such plans," Jadora said.

"Yet you promised your young mercenary that *she* could stay in the other world and avoid the wrath of those who would avenge themselves upon her."

"I did. I didn't think you were waiting for *her* to bring you back a plant."

Uthari snorted. "It is true that the world won't miss her. I will also allow her to live if you do your part."

Magnanimous.

"But should you need sacrifices to deter any hungry predators you meet along the way—" Uthari slanted another look at Malek, who must have shared the druids' story with him, "—they will do. The only mercenary I care about keeping alive will be staying with me to help defend the fleet."

Who was that? Sorath? Jadora had no idea how many Thorn Company soldiers were left alive, but if he was among the living, she was glad.

She took a deep breath. "May I have a minute to speak with my father before leaving? I assume you want us to go as soon as we can activate the portal."

"You assume correctly. I've brought suitable backup with me, but the whole world now knows of this portal and wants to claim it for themselves." Uthari rose from his chair. "But I will be generous and give you *two* minutes to speak with your father." He walked past her toward the door. "Come, Malek. We will allow them privacy."

Jadora highly doubted Uthari wouldn't use his telepathy to spy on their conversation, but she wanted to make sure her father was as well as possible and to apologize to him for inadvertently causing this.

Malek trailed obediently after Uthari without looking back. Even though she shouldn't have expected anything else, that stung. She didn't know what she wanted from him—even a long look at her might get him in trouble—but an acknowledgment of some kind would have been nice.

The doors thumped shut. Afraid that the two minutes would be literal, Jadora rushed forward. She would have clasped her father's hands, but he still gripped his *Teachings*.

"I'm so sorry, Father." Jadora peered into his eyes, looking for evidence that he'd been wounded—traumatized. "I don't know how they even knew we lived in the same city. I didn't say anything about..."

She trailed off, remembering she *had* mentioned her father. Only once and only to Malek. Had *he* suggested this to Uthari? Maybe not now, but earlier on? Before they'd become... whatever they'd become. Maybe nothing. She had no idea. It was hard to believe the hug he'd given her when Jak had been wounded had meant nothing.

"We live less than ten miles apart, my girl. I'm sure they thought to look up your relatives." Father lowered his arms enough to hug her, though he didn't relinquish the book. The corner clunked her in the spine. A metaphor for their relationship.

She shook her head and hugged him fiercely. "Don't worry. I'll do what they ask. He'll have no reason to hurt you."

"I must admit I haven't followed your recent... diversion, and I don't even know what exactly they want, but I do hope that's the case. It was troubling enough watching them torture the mercenary."

Her first thought was that he meant Tezi, but when would Father have met her?

"Mercenary?"

"The colonel. They plucked his company off their ship during a battle, and they questioned him thoroughly. Correction: Uthari questioned him thoroughly while one of his officers tortured him. I am not certain what they learned, since even with the awful torture, he said nothing out loud, but I believe they successfully got what they wanted from his thoughts. Afterward, they set us upon this course to what is apparently a desirable destination." Father looked toward a porthole, the waterfall visible outside, and appeared flummoxed.

"That must be why Thorn Company wasn't at our last battle. They were busy with Uthari's fleet. They—"

The doors opened again. Their two minutes were up.

Malek walked in, no doubt sent by Uthari. In the brief time he'd been gone, he had acquired a large backpack and a blanket roll, as if he were about to leave on a dig in the wild. Uthari must have believed it would be a simple matter to get the portal working and that they could leave right away.

"It's time to go," Malek told Jadora.

"It's getting dark." She gripped her father's arms, wishing she could stay longer. She hadn't had a chance to ask him how he was doing or what his life had been like these last two years. Granted, that last was her fault. As he'd pointed out, they lived in the same city. Their separation might have kept them from arguing, but she could have been stronger, could have made more effort to spend time with him, no matter how uncomfortable it was.

"Whether it's dark here will have no effect on whether it's light or dark at our destination," Malek said.

"Yes, but it'll make it hard to see the runes on the portal."

"I will provide light." Malek extended his hand toward the exit.

"Such a gentleman." Jadora couldn't keep the sarcasm out of her voice.

"When you go into darkness," her father said, quoting his beloved book, "you must carry a light with you."

"Or a mage, apparently." She sighed and hugged him again.

He surprised her by holding the hug longer and whispering in her ear. "I don't understand this fully, but they're vile, my girl. Don't let them use me against you, or against the world, if that is what they plan."

The tears she'd fought down earlier returned, and her throat tightened, stealing her words. She could only hug him harder, then turn away and walk out, her face to the floor so neither of them would see the haunted terror in her eyes.

As crewmen gathered packs of supplies for Jadora, Jak, and the mercenaries who would go along, Malek waited on deck and tried to focus on the mission, not the haunted look in Jadora's eyes as she gazed down at her son and the team attempting to activate the portal. He wanted to apologize to her on Uthari's behalf for kidnapping her father, but she wouldn't appreciate any such gesture from him, not when he worked side by side with Uthari. And he couldn't disparage Uthari to her. A loyal zidarr did not speak poorly of his king.

"Malek." Uthari walked up to him carrying three skyboards, pausing only to eye Sorath, Ferroki, and the rest of their mercenaries.

Malek questioned his choice to capture them and get them involved, but he accepted that Uthari might have some grander plan and know more than he.

"Having transportation on your journey may be helpful." Uthari handed him the skyboards. "Unlike a mageship, these will fit through the portal with you."

"A good idea, Your Majesty."

After glancing at the listening mercenaries, Uthari switched to telepathy. *Assuming our archaeologists can open the portal, you will head this expedition.*

Malek nodded. He'd assumed that.

I'm not going to send any other mages with you, Uthari added.

Why not? If we face something with the magic of a dragon, we may need more firepower than I can provide.

You will find a way to handle even a great enemy such as that. I am certain. Uthari gripped his shoulder and nodded, sharing his sense of confidence in Malek's abilities with him.

Malek appreciated that, but it seemed unwise to take so few allies with power. He'd envisioned leading at least twenty strong mages through the portal with him.

Since Yidar betrayed me, Uthari explained, *I am hesitant to trust anyone I haven't known and worked with for a very long time, especially since you now believe the portal goes to more places than our world and the dragon world. If you end up finding a treasure trove of powerful magical artifacts or meeting dragons who'd be willing to ally with humans, I don't want to risk anyone stabbing you in the back, taking the key and prizes for himself, and disappearing to another world, never to return to Torvil.*

I think it is unlikely that we'll find any great prizes, Your Majesty. On this first mission, we'll be lucky to find anything at all. We don't even know which world holds the dragons.

Actually, we might. Uthari held up a finger and drew something out from under his tunic, an oval-shaped disk made from blue-black steel. From *dragon steel.* The artifact, whatever it was, oozed only faint magic, but something was engraved on the front. *Show this to our archaeologists once you're down there.*

Yes, Your Majesty.

I have faith in you, Malek. If there are great treasures, I would prefer to have them—if only to keep rulers of competing kingdoms from getting them and using them against us—but you know what I truly want. Bring back the plant.

And you will free Jadora's father without harming him?

Uthari's eyes narrowed slightly. Perhaps Malek shouldn't have brought that up, but he wasn't pleased that Uthari had not trusted him to take care of everything and had felt the need to take matters into his own hands.

As long as she cooperates, I will not harm her or any of her family. I see that she has come to mean something to you, Malek.

Yes, he admitted. There was little point in denying it.

I trust you have not violated the Zidarr Code and do not intend to.

I have not and will not. As always, my loyalty is to you. Malek doubted he needed to make gestures, but he dropped to one knee and bowed his head.

I believe you, my son. Uthari rested a hand on his shoulder. *You have been my greatest student, and it has been an honor to teach you.*

Thank you.

Now, get my plant. We have a legacy to bequeath to this world.

We? You're sharing your legacy with me?

Of course. I know you do not seek glory, but all the world will know of Malek's contribution and what your loyalty has meant to me. Uthari squeezed his shoulder, sending a comforting wave of magic through him, as he'd once done when Malek had been a boy, haunted by the loss of his mother.

He no longer needed such comforting, but he still liked to be appreciated. Who didn't?

When Uthari stepped back, Malek rose, catching Jadora watching him, though she turned back to the railing as soon as their eyes met.

Succeed, Uthari added softly, *and I'll ensure her contribution is remembered as well. And that she and her son receive the Jitaruvak. Whether they love us or not, I will reward them for their assistance.*

That is good, Your Majesty.

28

JAK PROPPED HIS FISTS ON HIS HIPS AND WATCHED AS FOUR MAGES used their power to move the portal around, per his instructions, while also applying enough magical force to keep it upright. They had figured out which way was up without his help, but they didn't know where it was supposed to go, so they were letting him guide them. Though, judging by their exasperated glares after twenty minutes of moving it around with nothing happening, they were losing their patience. Rivlen stood off to the side, squinting at Jak.

No, he wasn't making them move a twenty-foot portal around because it was funny, though it *was* amusing. He was trying to put it in the precise place where it had been in his vision. The trouble was that the trees and foliage were all different after so much time —he didn't think the same *species* were even growing here now as had thrived thousands of years ago. It was amazing the waterfall and pool looked so similar. He'd studied enough geology in his cartography courses to know that rivers dried up and changed course over the millennia.

"Isn't it supposed to be able to stand up by itself?" one of the mages asked.

"I think it will if we get it in the right spot." Jak didn't know if that was true. He *did* know there weren't any switches or anything to press or turn, unless one counted putting the key in the keyhole. He thought that was only required for travel, not to place and activate it. But maybe he was wrong? He touched his pocket.

"Shouldn't you be reading a *book* to figure this out?" the mage asked. "Not standing there like my mother advising on the furniture arrangement in the parlor?"

"*My* mother took the book that might offer advice on this." Jak held up a hand and approached the portal. "Let me talk to it and see if it will tell me where it wants to be."

"Yeah, talk to the big stone ring, kid. That'll work well."

"It's a *dragon-steel* ring."

"Imagine my embarrassment."

Jak thought about asking Rivlen if her loyal troops were supposed to be this lippy, but she was scrutinizing him with narrowed eyes. He had a feeling she would prefer it if they got this done sooner rather than later. Jak hadn't had many interactions with Uthari and didn't know how patient he was with his troops in general, but since Rivlen was newly appointed to her position, she might worry about looking good for her king.

Less looking *good than* being *good,* she spoke into his mind. *Do you have a clue what you're doing?*

Not when it comes to consistently keeping mages out of my thoughts, no.

Clearly.

As the other mages kept the portal upright, the bottom hovering a few inches above the undergrowth, Jak pressed his hand to it. *Do we have the right place, portal friend?*

It pulsed blue, the glow noticeable in the fading daylight, and emanated a feeling of pleased contentment.

The mages skittered back, and the portal wobbled, threatening to fall.

"Don't let go," Jak barked, even as he tried to think of what cartographical feature might let him levitate the portal himself. Not another geyser. He didn't want to give it a warm backside.

The mages firmed up their grips, so he didn't have to figure it out. Later, he could try. For now...

Do we have to do anything to make it so you can stand upright on your own?

A thoughtful pause followed, as if the artifact were dredging the information from its ancient memory. Then it made a noise in Jak's mind, something between the screech of a crow and the siren of the flatlands bellbird. Even though it was mental, it made Jak wince.

Did you mean to do that?

The portal made the noise in his mind again, then pulsed.

I guess so. Is that... what dragons sound like?

Another pulse.

Is that a word in their language? The command to activate you?

A pulse.

"What's he doing to it, ma'am?" one of the mages whispered to Rivlen.

"Getting it excited with his sensuous touch," she replied.

"Huh."

Jak would have jerked his hand away, but it made communicating with the portal easier. *One more time, please. I'm going to have a hard time emulating that.* Not to mention that it would be embarrassing and get him teased by these people. *Does it have to be aloud?*

The artifact issued another cheerful blue pulse.

I'm not sure I believe you, but here goes...

Jak opened his mouth and did his best to emulate the squawk. That startled the mages almost as much as the first pulse had, and the artifact wobbled again before they caught it. Maybe he should have warned them.

"What are you doing?" Rivlen asked.

"What it tells me to do."

"What if it tells you to jump on one leg while picking your nose?"

"I don't know. What would you do if Tonovan asked you that?"

"Probably make a noise similar to yours."

Nothing had changed with the portal.

Did I not get it right? Jak asked.

The portal made the noise in his mind again, this time with more emphasis. Jak didn't know if he could get his human vocal chords to issue the right sound. The alarming idea that they wouldn't be able to activate it without a dragon here to squawk came to him. What then? Maybe he should try inserting the key and hope for the best.

Jak pulled it from his pocket and unwrapped it, but the portal conveyed to him that the key wouldn't work until it was activated, then made the noise in his mind again.

All right, all right. Jak opened his mouth and imitated the cry once more.

He tried five different variations and was about to give up— one of the mages had covered his ears—when the portal glowed blue. Not a pulse this time but a steady glow.

It shifted under his hand, a wave of power emanating from it, and Jak scurried back, almost tripping over a bush.

The portal lowered to the ground as the mages glanced uncertainly at each other, then magically pushed dirt aside to form a ditch several inches deep. Strands of power that Jak could sense unfurled from its sides and attached to the ground, drilling in deep to create anchors. The portal pulsed once more, then fell dark again, but now it stood upright of its own accord.

The mages lifted their hands and backed away. "We're not holding it anymore."

"I see that," Rivlen said.

The portal continued to emanate more power than it had before, creating a soft hum that competed with the crickets and other insects buzzing around the pool.

"I believe we've effectively activated it. Now it should be available for anyone with a key to use." Jak lifted his medallion and slid it into the matching hole on the surface.

A *thunk-clunk* sounded, though the portal didn't pulse or otherwise show a sign of further readiness. Jak made sure he could remove the medallion again. He could. He placed it back in, eliciting the same noise.

He let his hand linger and silently asked, *What's next? How do we travel to another world?*

This time, when the portal pulsed, it highlighted the thirty-two sets of star symbols—constellations—on its inside surface. It highlighted *all* of them.

Does that mean I have to pick one? What do I do? Press the constellation to activate it? Jak tried the one closest to him, resting his hand on it. When nothing happened, he tried pushing. Again, nothing.

"Hm."

It was getting darker, and someone sent a few spheres of light into the air around the portal. That made it easier to see the symbols, but he already knew them by heart after spending so much time studying the rubbings. *Seeing* them wasn't the problem.

"Maybe we have to wait until our own constellation is visible in the sky," his mother's voice came from the trees.

Jak spun, relieved to spot her. Malek walked at her side, three skyboards tucked under his arm. They both wore backpacks, and Malek carried another, presumably for Jak.

He wanted to ask if Mother was all right and what Uthari

had done to her, but the mages that all turned to look at her made him save the questions. Also, Mother and Malek hadn't come down alone. A few armed men walked into the light with them. No, armed *women*. Three of the Thorn Company mercenaries trailed them, two also wearing packs and carrying an extra.

"Captain Ferroki," Tezi blurted. She'd been sitting cross-legged with her rifle in her lap, watching Jak work, but she jumped to her feet. "And Dr. Fret and Sergeant Tinder. I didn't think I would see you again."

She jogged over, as if to hug them, but paused, uncertainty stealing the delight from her voice. What, she didn't think they wanted her back? Jak hoped that wasn't true.

"We've been tracking you, Rookie." Sergeant Tinder stepped forward and thumped Tezi on the shoulder hard enough that she staggered to the side.

"Really?" Tezi asked.

"No." Ferroki gave her a more sedate pat.

Only the petite Dr. Fret delivered what Jak would count as a real hug.

"We were captured," Ferroki said, pointing up at one of the dark ships looming overhead. Uthari's yacht. "King Uthari is sending along a couple of our people to help the exploration team." Ferroki shifted her pointing finger to Mother and Malek and Jak. "Specifically, Dr. Fret and Sergeant Tinder. And you, Tezi."

"But..." Tezi's face scrunched up. "We were—you *are*—working for a different king."

"Is that right?" Sergeant Tinder asked. "You know, I think she's right. I *knew* something was off."

"Captain Myroth, who gave us our contract, is dead," Ferroki said. "Uthari is giving us the choice to help him or, if we insist on remaining his enemy, be killed."

"Magnanimous of him." Tezi glanced at Malek, as if she'd expected more from him—or his leader.

Or maybe that was how *Jak* felt.

"I don't understand," Jak said, walking over. "Why would Uthari send mercenaries along? You don't have any expertise that would help, do you?"

Colonel Sorath had known quite a lot about archaeology, or at least finding ancient relics, but none of the others had mentioned such interests, not in Jak's hearing.

They exchanged long looks with each other.

"Ostensibly, my people are being sent along as combat forces to help in case you end up in a fight." Ferroki pressed her lips together. "He may have said they could be used as sacrifices if you need to throw someone into a predator's mouth as you run away, but I trust you wouldn't do that to other people. I think Uthari also wants some of us tied up on your mission as a way to ensure Sorath's cooperation. He was also captured." Ferroki pointed up at the yacht again.

"His cooperation with what?" Jak asked.

"King Uthari acknowledges that Sorath is a renowned tactician," Malek said, "and may be of some use if enemy forces come upon the fleet while we're in the middle of our mission."

Malek looked toward the portal, hopefully not thinking badly of Jak for not yet having figured out how to open up a passageway to another world. He ought to at least be able to detect that it was emanating more magic now.

"Never mind that *King Uthari* was one of the people who conspired to get Sorath's unit killed last year," Sergeant Tinder whispered to Jak. It was a loud whisper that everyone heard, even with the waterfall roaring in the background.

Malek gazed coolly at her.

Jak rubbed his face. Was this truly the team that would go with him and Mother? Wait, maybe that wasn't a bad thing. If the mercenaries weren't loyal to the mission, Malek would be the only one along who truly was. Jak wrapped his mental bandana around his mind before considering that further—and whether it would be possible for their group to somehow overpower him and get away.

But get away to what end? If they wanted to come home, they still had to come back *here*.

If they wanted to come home. If Jak couldn't return to his old life, did he care about that? Mother had already promised Tezi another world to hide in. Maybe the mercenaries wanted the same thing, and that was why they'd allowed themselves to be coerced down this path.

"Mother?" Jak lifted a finger. "You mentioned the stars. Can I have a word with you?"

He walked to the rocky ledge beside the pool, hoping neither Malek, Rivlen, nor any of the mages followed them to eavesdrop. Of course, they could spy on Mother's thoughts whether they were close or not. Jak would start out talking about the portal and then, only if the mages appeared distracted, bring up his other thought.

"I wondered," Mother said, "if we might have to wait until that constellation is visible in the night sky in order for the portal to work."

"If that were the case, it wouldn't work on cloudy nights."

"It might have to be there, not necessarily be visible to our eyes. The portal doesn't have eyes. But there might be something with the alignment of the stars being required for it to operate."

"That's an interesting thought."

Though Malek hadn't followed them to the pool, Jak could see him out of the corner of his eye. He was watching them.

"Uthari has your grandfather," Mother said. "My father."

Jak rocked back. "What? Back in his castle?"

"Here."

"*Why?*" Jak hadn't seen Grandfather in two years, not since he and Mother had argued vehemently over religion and how she wasn't a heathen for not believing in his faith. The thought of him being here—and in danger because of them—distressed him greatly. Jak didn't follow Grandfather's faith either, but he didn't see why that meant they couldn't still have holiday dinners together. Grandfather had always praised his maps and given him candy when he'd gotten good marks in school.

"To ensure our cooperation."

"There's a lot of that going around."

"I noticed," Mother said tightly. "Uthari wants the Jitaruvak and will threaten whomever he wishes to ensure he gets it."

Jak thought of the apparatus in Uthari's suite back in the castle. Mother had said the mixture of magic and drugs pumped into his system was keeping him alive longer than normal but that it wouldn't work forever. And if he ever missed his doses...

"Any chance he didn't bring his contraption along and, if we take a long time, he'll die?" Jak whispered.

He didn't have to look at Malek to be certain his eyes were boring into them. No doubt he was eavesdropping.

"I would guess he has it along." Mother looked at the portal, the symbols on the inside still glowing a soft blue. "It's beautiful, but I can't help but think that because it's now set up, other... creatures could come through."

"I doubt predators have been lurking near portals on their own world for ten thousand years waiting for ours to come back to life so they can pounce on us."

Mother considered that for a moment, then nodded. "Yes. You're right. We may be able to accomplish Uthari's mission without ever seeing another living being, at least one that wants to threaten us."

"And if we do, we'll push Malek into its path as we dive back through the portal to come home." A home where Uthari and his mageships would be waiting. Maybe Jak shouldn't hope for that particular vision to play out.

He glanced toward Malek again, intending to give an apologetic wave—he didn't truly wish to sacrifice Malek, not when there were so many other mages he would like to see eaten—but he wasn't watching them anymore. He'd walked to the portal and was studying it.

"Let's figure out if we can open a pathway to another world first," Mother said. "It's all moot if we can't do that."

Jak nodded and followed her over to the portal.

"I already tried touching and pushing the symbols," he said.

"With your hand or your mind?" Malek asked.

"My mind doesn't know how to push buttons yet."

"No? You removed the saboteur's device on the portal."

"By imagining a cataclysmic earthquake on the map of my mind. I would hope something less dramatic would suffice for button pushing."

Malek gazed at him.

"That's weird, isn't it?" Jak guessed. "Using map-related mental imagery for manipulating magic."

"I've not heard of anyone using such mental aids before."

"Thus weird."

"Atypical."

"I didn't know zidarr were diplomatic," Jak said. "Or are you only refraining from insulting me because my mother's next to me?"

"She's not." Malek looked not at the spot where Mother had been standing but where she was now, kneeling in the undergrowth beside the portal, pulling out roots and plucking leaves from some of the plants that had been upturned when the artifact settled itself into the ground. "I doubt she even heard us."

Malek didn't smile, but there was a fondness in his voice as he watched Mother clean off her samples and open a pouch in her backpack. He mentally nudged one of the illumination spheres over to provide more light for her.

Jak felt more exasperated than fond. "*Mother*. We're focusing on the portal and how to use it right now."

Mother murmured thoughtfully in what was either a foreign language or the plant taxonomy.

Malek's gaze shifted upward, toward the darkening sky. "You believe we need the Dragon's Tail constellation to be visible for the portal to work?"

Mother had suggested that. Jak didn't know if a portal that only worked a few hours a night made sense, but he shrugged.

"It's possible," Jak said. "Why don't you try pushing a symbol with your mind? Maybe that's all it takes. Though that would imply that only those with magic would be able to use the portals."

"Perhaps that is the case. The dragons may not have wanted lesser beings to travel to their world."

"*Lesser beings,*" Jak said, still including himself in the category of terrene humans who had no magic, "like the giant man-eating flying worm in the druid story? I still don't get how some dumb animal could have come through if a key was required."

"We don't know that it was dumb," Mother said, joining them again. "The dragons clearly weren't."

"Whether it was intelligent or not, the worm's ability to so easily defeat the druids in that village might suggest it had magic," Malek said. "Perhaps with sufficient magic, one can activate the portal without a key."

"Or as we discussed before—" Mother nodded to Jak, "—a key only has to be inserted in the departure portal, not the arrival one. There could be one permanently installed on some of the other worlds."

"We will learn more with exploration." Malek pointed to the symbols. "King Uthari gave me an artifact that may indicate which one we should visit first, but what do you two think? Based on your research, is there one constellation more likely to lead us to the dragon home world than to a place of danger?"

"Not that one." Mother knelt back from her sample-taking and pointed at one of the constellations on the portal. No, she was pointing to the language symbol adjacent to it, a rune with three squiggly lines.

"Why not that one?" Jak asked.

"It was at the top of the first story I translated in the druid tome." Mother tugged out the book and brought it over to Jak and Malek. She opened it to the first page and pointed at a header symbol that Jak had assumed was the title for the story.

He rocked back, glancing from the page to the symbol she'd pointed at on the portal. They were identical.

"Nor this one, I should think." Mother flipped to the next chapter or section of the book, tapped another symbol on top, and pointed to a matching one on the portal. "I've only translated a few lines of this story, but it starts out with, *Death came like a swarm of wasps.*"

"Remarkable." Malek took the book from her and flipped through it, pausing on the pages that included the larger header symbols and glancing up to locate the corresponding ones on the portal. "Are all thirty-two in here?"

"No. Nineteen." Mother pointed toward the back of the book. "Actually, twenty, but there are blank pages under the twentieth, like whoever was recording what happened was halted before he or she could finish."

"Because something even more awful killed him?" Jak asked.

"There's no way to know but probably not. At least not from creatures coming through the portal. This book and the scribe who wrote it lived only a couple of centuries ago."

"*Only*," Jak said, though he understood what she meant. The portal had been buried far longer than that.

"If the scribe was copying from ancient druid monuments, perhaps this story was never told," Mother said. "Or maybe the monument was damaged, so the carvings weren't legible."

Malek flipped through the book more slowly, pausing to study each header symbol. He stopped in the middle, touching a symbol that started a long entry—that particular story took up a third of the book.

"It might be a good idea to let me finish translating the text before picking a destination and taking a journey," Mother suggested.

"How long do you think that would take?" Malek asked reasonably, as if he were considering it even though his team was picked and packed and ready to go.

"The first entry was short and took me last night and today." Mother shrugged. "Maybe two weeks to do the whole book."

Malek handed it back to her and gazed up at Uthari's ship. Contacting the king?

A long minute passed before Malek shook his head. "The king says many more enemies are on the way, and that even with this fleet, we may not be able to keep control over the portal."

Jak imagined the fight for this portal starting the great world war between kings—between all mages—that some people believed could cause them to kill each other and leave Torvil ungoverned, ushering in an era where terrene humans could finally rule themselves.

"More likely, after a prolonged squabble, they'll come up with a treaty and share it." Malek eyed him. "But many people could be killed first, mages *and* terrene humans."

Mother winced, glancing toward the yacht. Thinking of her father?

Jak sighed. They had to help Uthari find his plant. After that, maybe they could figure out something better, something that would help their people.

"We can't pick at random," Jak said, though the idea of exploring—and *mapping!*—thirty-one new worlds delighted him. If there hadn't been anything else to worry about, and if they'd been down here on an expedition with years to study, he would have loved to be a part of that.

"No." Malek shrugged off his pack. "Uthari wants us to find the dragon home world, and the source of his Jitaruvak, on the first try. Then, even if we're not able to retain power over the portal indefinitely, he will have acquired what he wants most."

Malek drew a flat blue-black disk out of his pack, an engraving of a dragon on the top. If it hadn't been made from the same lesser dragon steel as the portal, Jak would have guessed it the lid to a bowl or something equally mundane.

Malek pointed at a symbol on the portal that looked more like two crescent moons facing each other than part of a written language, then tapped something on the disk. A matching symbol was nestled in the curve of the dragon's tail.

"This is the world he thinks we should try first," Malek said. "He told me he found this more than a century ago and has had it as artwork on the wall in his lavatory. It wasn't until last week, when I was showing him the rubbings from the portal, that he realized it might be related to our quest."

"King Uthari keeps priceless dragon-steel artifacts in the lavatory?" Mother asked.

"He said it was too small to serve as decor for his office," Malek said.

Mother rolled her eyes.

"This is great," Jak breathed, tracing his finger along the dragon. "It might mean that it's the symbol to the dragon home world."

"That's what we're hoping."

"That's the symbol for the longest entry in the book," Mother said.

"I should have had you translate that one first." Malek shook his head. "I didn't realize that symbols from the portal were in there."

Jak gazed at the twin crescent moons on the portal and the matching constellation next to it, twelve dots that reminded him of a hunter drawing a bow. Excitement welled up in him as he realized they might truly know how to reach the dragon home world.

"Press it, Malek," he breathed.

"*Lord* Malek," came a correction from behind them. Captain Rivlen had come over and was listening.

"Press it, Lord Malek," Jak said, too intrigued by the possibilities ahead of him to care about pompous corrections.

"I already tried," Malek admitted, returning the disk to his pack. "Maybe you should try, since you're the portal's favorite person."

"I think it's just that I'm the only one who talks to it."

"I've tried to communicate with it," Malek said.

"Oh?"

"It ignored me."

"Oh," Jak repeated, surprised. It hadn't occurred to him that the artifact might have chosen him, like a diplomatic envoy or some such. Maybe it was only because he'd been the first one to try to communicate with it. "Or maybe it's just that the person who inserted the key has to push the button."

"That could be," Malek said. "Try gently nudging it. No cataclysmic events necessary."

"What do you use as a mental aid for telekinesis?" Jak asked him.

Malek opened his mouth, then closed it again and glanced at Rivlen. Would answering the question be too close to the teaching he was forbidden from doing?

Malek nodded sadly.

"It's the color yellow for me," Rivlen offered.

Jak formed a map of Torvil in his mind and envisioned the winds that had long ago helped shape the mountains and mold dunes in the desert. Wind wasn't a terrain feature, but it affected terrain features. Maybe he could use it to push things around.

He imagined channeling a gust through a tunnel to push against something at the other end. The crescent-moon symbol.

The portal pulsed blue, as it had done many times, then did something it had *never* done, at least not in their presence. The blackness of space filled the center, then stars formed in it and spun about, swirling streaks of white.

Tremendous power flared around the center of the portal, buzzing in Jak's mind like mosquitoes. They all stepped back, watching warily, not certain what to expect. It felt like the portal was building to something greater, like a volcanic eruption. But after a flare of power that made Jak's entire body buzz and his skin itch, the power faded, and the swirling in the center stilled. What remained was a starry sky with the hunter constellation in the center of the portal.

"It worked!" Jak blurted and hugged his mother.

She hugged him back, though her face was more troubled than elated.

Jak was too excited to decipher her feelings. He released her and hugged Malek, momentarily forgetting propriety and that he was technically an enemy. It was Malek who'd brought the disk with the dragon on it after all.

The gesture seemed to startle Malek, but he recovered and patted Jak on the back. Jak released Malek and spun toward the next closest person. Rivlen.

She held up a hand. "We're not that close."

"Are you sure?" He grinned. "I've warmed your butt."

Malek arched his eyebrows.

It had been a joke, but Rivlen looked horrified as she rushed to tell Malek, "I was teaching him to levitate people. Me."

"That required butt warming?" Malek asked mildly.

"The way he does it." Rivlen rubbed her face, hiding red cheeks.

Jak hadn't meant to embarrass her and blurted, "Sorry," before turning back to the portal. "We should go through. I don't know how long it will stay open."

He might have stepped through right then, but Mother stopped him.

"Hold on. Let's make sure we've figured out how to get back. Loran always assumed there would be a corresponding portal on the dragon home world, so I've—"

"If there are thirty-two worlds, there have to be portals on *all* of them," Jak said.

"There had to have once been portals. What if they don't all exist anymore?" Mother pointed at the artifact. "*Ours* was buried for thousands of years. Presumably, nobody could travel here during that time. That has to be why the druids did it, to keep travelers from coming. What happens if the world we're trying to visit has had something similar happen? We might never reach the other side. We could die."

"Send someone expendable through." Rivlen looked at Tezi and the other mercenaries.

They scowled at her and fingered their weapons. Though they'd stayed back with the mages, they had been watching and listening to what was going on.

"Tezi isn't expendable," Jak snapped. "None of them are." He resisted the urge to say Uthari was and that he could, if he wanted to find his plant so badly, go through himself.

Malek lifted a hand. "It would have to be a mage, someone who could activate the portal on the other side, so he could return."

"Assuming there's a key on the other side," Mother said. "Or are we supposed to take ours with us for travel? And use it again when we want to return?"

"Good question. Let's see if taking it out causes the passageway to close." Jak approached and touched the key, but he mentally spoke to the portal before removing it. *Do I leave this or take it?*

For the first time, the portal showed Jak a vision of himself. In it, Jak removed the key, returned it to the band on his hat, and strode through the center, leaping into the constellation and disappearing. The vision didn't show what would happen when he reached the other side—did the artifact even know?—but it showed one of the iridescent dragons frolicking in a lavender-blue sky. It looked at Jak, soared down to him, and landed. Jak patted the dragon on the side, then climbed onto its back, and they flew off together to see this new world from above. The Jak in the vision pulled out map-making materials and started drawing.

Someone poked Jak in the shoulder. Mother.

The vision faded. "Well, it sure knows how to entice me."

"Did it give you a warning?" Mother asked.

"No." Jak removed the key and tucked it into its spot on his hat. "I think it's all right."

Mother lifted her brows.

"I think... It didn't tell me, but I'm guessing we wouldn't have been able to form a connection to another world if the portal on the other end didn't exist and wasn't set up to receive visitors. None of those creatures or dragons or anything else have been able to come *here* since the druids took down the portal, right?"

"As far as we know," Mother said.

A sensation came over Jak, a certainty that they had a limited amount of time to use the portal now that he'd taken out the key.

"It's time to go, for whoever is going on this first trip." Jak licked his lips, nervous but bolstered by the vision into believing this wouldn't be certain death. "If you don't want to risk the entire group... I can go alone. I know how to push the button now to come back. It should just be a matter of inserting the key on the other portal and pressing the Dragon's Tail constellation."

Mother shook her head. "You're not going alone." She lifted the druid book. "The danger out there could be immense. Something might attack you as soon as you arrive. If anyone were to go alone, it should be Malek. *He* can take care of himself."

"Thank you for letting me know how inept you believe me to be," Jak said.

"You don't even have a weapon."

"Yes, he does." Malek stepped forward and gave Jak and Mother charged pistols. "We're going together. With our fighters." He pointed to the mercenaries.

"Oh, good," Sergeant Tinder said. "I was afraid he'd forget us, and we'd be forced to lounge by this tropical pool and eat bananas from that tree over there."

"Those are plantains," Mother said, "and they're not ripe."

"You're ruining my fantasies, Professor."

"Come," Malek ordered the group, a hint of magic adding compulsion to the words. Maybe he also sensed that they had limited time to step through.

Malek, Jak, Mother, Sergeant Tinder, Dr. Fret, and Tezi lined up in front of the portal. Nobody compelled Jak, magically or otherwise, but he sprang through first. For the last five years, he'd been waiting for this. It was time to see what was on the other side.

29

Yidar stood in the forecastle of the *King's Courage* as it floated over the waterfall tumbling into the pool next to the portal. He watched as the starry field in the middle faded, returning to empty air. Malek, the two archaeologists, and three mercenaries—including the girl Yidar had captured back in Port Toh-drom—had disappeared through it.

He supposed he shouldn't hope that they failed utterly or died instantly and never returned, but it was hard not to feel bitter. *He'd* wanted to capture the portal and travel through it, to find dragon allies in this other world that supposedly existed. Dragon allies and who knew what resources and riches could be out there. He could put such things to good use.

Uthari did not need any more resources. Yidar did. If he was to carve out his own kingdom and become a ruler in his own right, subservient to no one, he needed more than his magic. As he'd learned with his failed attempt to get the best of Uthari, his magic was not as sufficient as he'd believed. Unfortunately.

He wouldn't challenge Uthari again. For whatever reason, his old mentor had allowed him to live, even humoring him with the suggestion that he might not object to Yidar creating a kingdom of his own. But Uthari had made it clear he expected Yidar to continue on as his faithful zidarr for now.

And since Yidar hadn't been the one to recover the artifact, the key, or the archaeologists, he suspected Uthari believed him a failure. Once again, *Malek* had shown up and acquired everything.

Yidar curled his lip, again hoping some horrible fate befell Malek wherever he arrived.

Hope, however, wasn't a plan. If Yidar wanted a kingdom, he had to come up with a plan. And that plan had to include acquiring allies and resources of his own.

He'd watched carefully as the boy had placed that key and activated the portal. It was unlikely that Yidar could wrest the key from him when they returned, not with Malek at his side and Uthari's yacht floating nearby. But was that the only key in the world?

If this portal had once been used by many for travel, that was hard to believe. Perhaps there were other keys out there, and perhaps Yidar could acquire one. If he did, he could lead his *own* teams through the portal. With Uthari monitoring so closely, Yidar might have to sneak out in the middle of the night, but once he was in another world, he doubted Uthari would follow and risk losing control of his kingdom here. It was already surprising that he'd flown so far from home.

"But where do I find another key?" he murmured.

When Malek had been trying to locate the first one, he'd contacted the artifact-hunters guild. Perhaps Yidar could send them a message and offer a reward, but if those people knew of multiple keys, wouldn't they have already contacted Malek and Uthari? As far as Yidar knew, nothing had come from Malek's attempt to hire them.

Yidar gazed out at the jungle canopy and the mountains, wilderness extending in all directions as far as the eye could see.

From what he'd gathered, the portal operated in this location, and this was where it had been set up thousands of years earlier. As strange as it seemed, wild and uncivilized Zewnath had been the hub of travel from this world to the dragon world.

"If other keys exist, they are probably *here*," he mused.

The druids might be the ones to ask, but the druids had made it clear they opposed Uthari and his desire to activate the portal.

"But they should have no qualms with *me*." Other than defending his ship when they'd attacked, he'd had no interactions with the druids, and they shouldn't have any reason to hate him personally. Oh, they might dislike him because they believed him one of Uthari's loyal servants, but perhaps he could show them that he was his own man and that he might even have things to offer them.

He wasn't sure yet what those things might be, as he wouldn't dare act against Uthari when he was so close, but what if Yidar could serve as an informant to the druids? If they had an extra key, would they trade it for information about Uthari and what Malek found in the other world?

Playing the role of spy would be dangerous, however, and Yidar found himself reluctant to reach out and volunteer himself for such a position. For now, he would be patient and watch and wait to see if an opportunity presented itself.

If the druids wanted the portal brought down, they might soon appear in the area. Perhaps they would even reach out to Yidar. Especially if he could find a way to let them know he would be *amenable* to them reaching out.

Yidar, King Uthari spoke into his mind.

A wave of panic washed over Yidar as he glanced toward the king's yacht. He'd been guarding his thoughts, as he always did. Uthari couldn't have sensed them. It was impossible.

Yes, Your Majesty? Yidar made himself reply calmly.

Report to the Serene Waters *for a meeting.*

Yes, Your Majesty.

Yidar blew out a slow breath and headed to his cabin to grab his skyboard, so he could fly over. It was probably only a coincidence that Uthari had contacted him at that moment, but he resolved to keep his thoughts of druids and spying out of his mind. At least for tonight.

With luck, the coming days would bring the opportunities he craved. He would not be a slave to Uthari forever. He swore it.

Stars streaked past as they soared weightlessly through a magical passageway, dreams and awareness mingling in a disorienting jumble.

The return to reality came with blinding light and harsh frigid wind that battered at Malek's cheeks. He landed with a jarring thud that almost pitched him to the ground. It was as if he'd fallen twenty feet without knowing where the bottom was or being able to prepare himself. Beside him, Jak, Jadora, and the mercenaries tumbled to the frozen earth, some rolling several feet before stopping.

Malek drew his weapons and peered around, squinting as his eyes adjusted to bright sunlight. He used his magical senses as much as his vision to assess the area around them and search for threats.

Wind moaned across a frozen white tundra, and a bright but cold sun gleamed in the lavender-blue sky. A few hazy clouds wafted past high above, the same types of white clouds as back on Torvil.

There wasn't any sign of vegetation, not a single tree or shrub, and the disappointed certainty that Uthari's plant wouldn't be found here came over Malek. It was possible the Jitaruvak grew on this world, but it might be thousands of miles away in a different climate zone. The three skyboards he'd brought couldn't travel that far, and Malek had no way to recharge them here. Without a mageship, a journey of thousands of miles would be arduous and time-consuming. If such was required, they wouldn't be able to return until long after Uthari's enemies reached the fleet.

"The portal neglected to mention it was *winter* when it showed me that vision." Jak pushed himself to his feet and stuck his hands under his armpits as he looked around. "*Very* winter."

"There are gloves, wool hats, and extra clothes in the packs my people gave you," Malek said. "We anticipated this possibility."

"There's no portal," Jadora said. "Did you anticipate *that* possibility?"

She'd risen to her knees to look all about, including behind Malek.

She was right. Ahead of them, the tundra stretched, flat and white and devoid of life. Behind them, a cliff of pure ice rose up hundreds of feet. Not a cliff, Malek realized. The edge of a glacier. Beyond it, there might be mountains, but he couldn't see them from the foot of the glacier.

"That can't be right," Jak whispered. "It *has* to be here."

"Did the portal tell you that?" Jadora asked.

"Not exactly, but it couldn't have worked without another portal to connect to."

"That was our hypothesis, not a proven fact," she said gently.

Jak winced, and Malek sensed his distress, his fear that he'd led them here, and they would all be trapped and die.

Malek would have gone through regardless, since Uthari had commanded it, so he did not blame Jak. This was disturbing, however, since if they couldn't get back, Malek wouldn't be able to complete his mission.

"We only have food and water for three days," Dr. Fret said, helping Tezi, who'd taken a harder fall as they landed, to her feet. "This is not good."

"I don't think *water* is going to be the problem." Sergeant Tinder thumped her boot down on the icy tundra, then eyed the pure ice of the glacier. "Though melting it might be a challenge. I don't see anything around here to burn."

Malek removed his pack to dig out his spyglass while debating the best course of action. He could start a fire with magic, so that wasn't a problem, and they could survive weeks without food if need be, but it might get a lot colder here at night. Whatever the temperature was now, with the sun blazing in the sky, it was well below freezing. He'd packed jackets, tents, and blankets, but if it dropped much colder than this after dark, even magic might not be enough to insulate them.

Perhaps unwisely, Malek had assumed that wherever the portals were placed, the climate would be hospitable for life. Human life, he'd believed, but in hindsight, it only would have needed to be sufficient for dragons. They might be much hardier than humans.

"This has become a survival mission," Malek said. "We'll have to find or build a shelter and make sure we can last the night. Then we can figure out what to do next."

The mercenaries spread out to look around. Thus far, they didn't appear alarmed, but he didn't think they'd yet realized what the lack of a portal on this world meant. Jak and Jadora understood. They kept exchanging concerned glances, and that feeling of regret from Jak increased.

Jadora walked to the glacier and tapped her finger to it before sticking her hands in her pockets. Since the glacier appeared to stretch for miles—if not dozens of miles—Malek saw little point in searching in that direction. It was possible there might be a cave or crevice that they could hunker in that would protect them from the elements, so he would keep it in mind for that, but he hoped to find evidence of something more promising, something that would allow him to fulfill the mission, make Uthari happy, and ensure Jadora's father wouldn't be in danger.

Using the spyglass, he scanned the horizon in the opposite direction, slowly searching from one end of the tundra to the other. Malek wanted to believe Uthari wouldn't do anything to Jadora's father other than keeping him there as an incentive to motivate her, but he also hadn't expected there to be a need to kill her university colleague. And there *hadn't* been, but Tonovan had acted of his own accord on that. And it was possible Uthari would let Tonovan act of his own accord again, which Tonovan might do simply to spite Malek.

It was unfortunate that Tonovan had seen Tezi, prompting that spat before they'd arrived. When Malek had stepped in to help Rivlen, it had infuriated Tonovan. Again.

On the horizon, a lone rocky butte covered in snow made him pause and refocus the spyglass. Halfway up the butte on the side closest to them, a cliff held a cluster of symmetrical white bumps. Domes?

Malek boosted the spyglass to maximum magnification and used his magic to amplify it further. Yes, they *were* domes, all resting atop the cliff, and all attached to each other. Man-made domes? Or *something*-made domes. Perhaps dragons had built them.

It was hard to gauge their size from this distance—more than ten miles, he guessed. The way they were clustered together reminded him of a castle or fortress or some other compound. Most of the domes were opaque, the same snowy white as the rest of the tundra, but a couple were almost translucent, like frosty windows. Or like... greenhouses?

For a moment, he envisioned Uthari's plant cheerfully growing in the protected domes, but he snorted at himself. It was unlikely that the very thing he'd come for would be so handily placed near their arrival spot.

Or was it? If the legends were correct, the dragons had valued the plant; they'd brought it to Torvil and had given it to their human allies—or perhaps human *servants*—to extend their lives. What if the dragons grew it right there so it would be conveniently close to the portal in case they needed to take some through to their servants on other worlds?

"What portal?" he mumbled.

Though maybe it was located there too? Could the dragons have created some way to divert travelers so they wouldn't pop up in their fortress?

"Jadora," Malek called, keeping his tone even, though he was excited at the possibilities. Until they explored the compound, there was no point in getting anyone's hopes up.

She lingered at the glacier for a moment, her now gloved hand on the ice as she considered it curiously, then walked away and joined him. She was also thinking about the portal and where it might be, but as she approached him, wariness and concern for her father returned to the forefront of her mind. She wasn't thinking about Tonovan, but she worried about what Uthari was doing to her father while she was gone, and what he might do if they failed to return.

Malek held out the spyglass to her, wishing she wouldn't associate him with all that, but he was Uthari's man, so what else could he expect?

"Look in that direction." Without the spyglass, it took him a moment to find the butte and point it out. To his bare eyes, the domes weren't visible. "It looks like a fortress, and I'd like your opinion on whether it's possible for the portal to be located there and for the occupants to have set something up to divert new arrivals outside of their compound."

He also wondered if she would think those translucent domes looked like greenhouses, but he didn't want to bias her and would wait to hear her thoughts.

Hope stirred within Jadora at this first hint of civilization, and that heartened him, making him glad he'd been able to show it to her. An icy wind blew through, and she shivered. Malek resisted the urge to wrap an arm around her, judging that she wouldn't appreciate that familiarity, but he tried to subtly use his magic to warm her clothing. If the compound proved to be something they could access, they could spend the night there. Assuming its owners didn't object.

They were too far away from it for him to sense magical beings. Once they got closer, he would be able to tell if anything like a dragon was home. If dragons were half as powerful as the legends said, he ought to be able to sense their auras from miles away.

"Those look like greenhouses," Jadora mused.

"I had that thought too."

"And what are those platforms in the butte above the compound? Landing pads?"

Beyond the domes, Malek hadn't thought much about the butte, but he had seen the platforms, and now that she mentioned it, he could imagine an avian creature using them to alight on.

"We can take the skyboards over to check it out," he said.

"Check what out?" Jak joined them.

Jadora passed the spyglass to him.

"*Yes!*" he exclaimed as soon as he spotted it, then danced and bounced around while pumping his arms. "I *knew* there had to be something epic here."

"Domes are epic?" Jadora smiled at him.

"Those domes look epic."

"Do they also look like a warm spot to spend the night?" Dr. Fret, her arms under her armpits, was jumping in place in lieu of exploring.

"Maybe. Can we get there on the skyboards? Can I fly one?" Jak grinned at Malek.

"You can try," Malek said. "Providing whoever rides with you is willing to put up with the learning curve. I can also control three myself if nothing untoward happens that requires my concentration."

Such as if they were attacked by giant, magic-slinging predators. Malek wished Uthari had agreed to wait for Jadora to translate the rest of that book before sending them. Leaving the world without as much knowledge as they could possibly gain seemed unwise.

"Mother won't mind," Jak said.

"I planned to take her with me." Malek tossed the three skyboards to the ground, willing them to hover a couple of inches above while waiting for riders. "And that your favorite mercenary would go with you." He glanced at Tezi who was exploring around the area with Tinder.

"Oh, that's all right. If Mother doesn't mind." Jak thought of his grandfather as he looked from her to Malek. When Jak concentrated on it, he could hide his thoughts, but he hadn't learned to subconsciously do it all the time yet, so Malek usually still got the gist of what he was thinking. And he thought Jadora was irked with Malek.

He sighed, knowing there was truth to that. Jadora wasn't irked as much as disappointed. That saddened him more.

"It's fine," Jadora said.

"Mercenaries." Malek pointed to the other two skyboards as he stepped on one.

"We have names," Tinder muttered.

Malek wished Uthari had given him mages instead of mercenaries. In lieu of that, he would have preferred to be here with only Jak and Jadora.

Fret elbowed Tinder. "You're supposed to say, 'We have names, *my lord.*' Don't piss him off. He probably has orders to use us as shields or trade us to the dragons as slaves."

"Any dragon that wants to enslave me will get a grenade up the butt," Tinder said.

"Do dragons *have* butts?"

The mercenaries looked at Jadora, as if she were the expert on such matters.

"As far as the fossil record suggests," Jadora said, "despite being scaled like lizards, dragons are anatomically similar to birds. Their bones are lightweight and pneumatized, and we believe they were warm-blooded."

"Did that answer my question?" Fret whispered to Tinder as they stepped onto the same skyboard, gripping each other for support as it wobbled slightly.

"If birds have butts, yes," Tinder said.

"They have cloacas," Mother said.

Malek waved for her to join him as Jak and Tezi took the other skyboard.

"I don't know what that is," Tinder said.

"Something you might find it difficult to insert a grenade into," Fret said.

Malek shook his head. Not only had Uthari saddled him with mercenaries, but he'd given him a failed troupe of entertainers.

Jak scrutinized his skyboard, concentration furrowing his brow. Later, Malek would give him lessons, but it might be better to simply get to their destination as quickly as possible now.

"Follow," he said, nudging his skyboard into the lead and willing the others after him.

He navigated carefully, not wanting Jadora to feel compelled to grab on to him for stability. She gripped his shoulders without comment, but he sensed that her willingness to be close to him had changed since Uthari's arrival. Maybe he should have taken one of the mercenaries and let her go with Jak, so she wouldn't be uncomfortable.

I regret that your father was brought into this, he told her as they skimmed across the tundra.

You mean you regret that Uthari chose to kidnap my father? I note that your sentence arrangement attempted to eliminate blame.

Yes. I'm hoping that compound does indeed contain a greenhouse, that the Jitaruvak is grown there, and that we'll be able to get a sample.

What makes you think they're growing it there?

Malek shared his earlier thoughts.

We haven't seen any sign that there are dragons here yet, she pointed out. *I haven't even seen a bird.*

"Something lives out there," Tezi said, as if she were privy to their conversation. But she wasn't looking at them, instead pointing to a dark frost-covered mound off to the side. A pile of animal scat.

"Did that come out of a cloaca?" Tinder asked.

"I thought you didn't know what that was," Fret said.

"I read between the lines."

Malek kept them flying toward the butte and the domes, but he did take note of the animal scat. Whatever had made it had been large, and though not that recent, it was evidence that something lived out here on the tundra.

They were halfway to the fortress when Malek started sensing magic from it. He couldn't detect living beings, but the structure itself exuded power. That gave him hope that perhaps dragons had indeed constructed it.

"Is that a city?" Tezi looked toward Jadora. "Do humans live here?"

"I don't know," Jadora said. "If any humans from Torvil ever traveled to the other worlds and stayed there, nobody wrote it down—or carved it in stone—anywhere that archaeologists have found."

"I don't think humans made that place," Jak said, his eyes locked on the fortress.

By now, he likely also sensed the magic emanating from it. As they drew closer, Malek could tell that it was alien magic, not similar in feel to anything he'd experienced before, and he agreed it was unlikely humans had constructed the place.

"Are you keeping me warm?" Jadora asked quietly.

Malek glanced back. He'd been trying to do it without her noticing, but she was an observant woman, as evinced by her growing specimen collection, full of presumably medicinal or otherwise valuable plants spotted in the jungle.

"Yes," he said.

"Are you keeping the others warm?"

"No." He wasn't as moved to help them. He could have, but he was focusing on flying three skyboards and paying attention to their surroundings. "They're not standing next to me."

"So, this is overflow heat from you warming yourself?"

He used his magic to warm himself, so he could answer honestly, though he felt compelled to vagueness. "Something like that."

"Ah."

A distant screech floated across the tundra. Malek scanned the sky in that direction but didn't see anything. He withdrew his spyglass again, but if something was flying out there, it was too small to find. At least for now.

"Who wanted to see birds?" Jak asked.

"Just evidence of life," Jadora said.

"The screech and the poo suggest it's here."

"Comforting."

As they neared the fortress, Malek realized the butte and plateau that the domes perched upon had also been made by magic. The rocky butte rose a couple hundred feet from the surrounding tundra, with the plateau chiseled into one side about halfway up. The vertical cliff below it lacked a staircase or ladder or anything that would have made climbing up easy, and Jadora's suggestion that the creators were creatures of flight seemed plausible.

Their skyboard took them over a bone lying on the ground, what looked like a human femur snapped in half. Maybe he was mistaken, and it had belonged to some other animal of similar size to a person. But they passed others as they drew closer to the butte, and they all looked like human bones.

"Er." Jak was looking at them too.

Most were broken, snapped by powerful teeth, and had been chewed on, though they didn't appear that old. They weren't yellowed from exposure, nor had they been buried by snow. The lack of nearby footprints was surprising. Malek would have expected scavengers, but maybe whatever had chewed on the bones had come from the sky.

Where had the *humans* come from was a question that popped into his mind.

Were there other explorers out here who'd been using the portals all the time the one on Torvil had been buried? Or did humans live on this world? Maybe the dragons who'd visited Torvil long ago had taken humans back with them to serve them or for some other purpose.

Malek had expected to encounter other creatures, dragons perhaps, and whatever animals lived on their world, but it hadn't occurred to him that humans might live here. Or *had* lived here.

"Maybe visiting this place wasn't such a good idea," Dr. Fret said.

"How many people have *died* here?" Tinder pointed at a skull, a few shreds of muscle and tufts of hair attached to the top. "And how recently?"

"Recently," Jadora said grimly, eyeing not the bones but the domes above them. She pointed upward at something flapping in the breeze. A rope anchored to a metal eyelet embedded near the top of the cliff. "It looks like whoever's fortress this is, they don't like visitors."

"I don't sense anyone alive up there," Malek said.

"Then maybe the *fortress* doesn't like visitors."

"That is possible." He lowered the skyboards to the ground and considered the domes and the butte looming above them.

If dragons lived up there, they might not like being disturbed. Maybe these humans, wherever they had come from, were scavengers and the inhabitants had protested their intrusion. Admittedly, Malek was here to get a plant, a specific plant cultivated by dragons, so that might make *him* a scavenger too.

Malek had few options but to investigate the compound, since this was why Uthari had sent him, but he didn't want to endanger Jadora or Jak. And if some automatic defense system lashed out at him, he might lose his concentration and control of the other skyboards. It would be better if he left the rest of the group down here while he explored alone. Unfortunately, he couldn't guarantee that they would be safe here, or that if something happened, he could get back to them in time.

It irritated him that Uthari hadn't let him bring other mages along out of some fear of someone betraying him. Maybe it was understandable that he'd worry more about that after Yidar's betrayal, but Malek couldn't help but feel Uthari had endangered this mission by not giving him a full team of capable people. Instead, he had these fighters, fighters who would be useless against magical creatures.

"I'll go up to investigate." Malek nodded for Jadora and the others to step off their skyboards. "If something attacks me, I might not be able to defend you adequately or keep the skyboards in the air."

"I'm fine with staying here," Tinder said.

"I'm not sure I am." Fret eyed a nearby rib cage, several bones shattered from the broken sternum, as if a giant had stepped on the person's chest.

"This shouldn't take long." Malek looked at Jadora. "If I need a clever archaeologist to help me figure out a way in, I'll come back."

"I'm offended that he looked at you instead of me when he said that," Jak whispered to her.

Jadora didn't smile. She probably had more of an idea about the threats here than any of them.

"What happens if whatever attacked them attacks us?" Tezi pointed her rifle at one of the skulls.

"Attack back," Malek said. "More effectively than they did."

None of them were heartened by that advice. Again, Malek wished for a mage ally, someone who could put up a barrier to protect their group. It might not be effective against something as powerful as a dragon, but it would be better than huddling there helplessly, waiting to be picked off by aerial predators swooping down.

He did have Jak, but did Jak know how to make a barrier? Malek couldn't imagine that Rivlen had found time to engage him in many lessons yet.

"You're looking at me." Jak touched his chest. "Am I the one who's supposed to attack back effectively?" He drew the pistol and eyed it skeptically.

"Has Rivlen taught you to make a barrier?"

"No. Just to push back when someone is trying to force me to my knees, and earlier tonight, she was showing me how to levitate her."

"Jak's a *mage*?" Fret whispered to Tinder.

Tinder shrugged back.

Tezi didn't look surprised. Maybe she'd been privy to the levitation lesson. Jadora only looked grim. All along, Malek had sensed that she didn't want her son to have power, to potentially turn into a mage—into one of the *enemy*, as she thought of them.

That saddened Malek, and he wished he could convince her that she need not think of all mages that way. Most simply lived out their lives in the sky cities without bothering her people. But these past weeks hadn't given her any reason to believe that, and since she associated Malek with Uthari and considered *him* an enemy... he couldn't do anything to alleviate her fears.

"You'll have to learn," Malek told Jak.

When they returned to Torvil, Malek might be punished for teaching someone magic, but since Uthari had given him no mages, maybe he would understand. There wasn't much choice. Someone had to be able to defend Jadora when Malek wasn't right beside her.

"Oh?" Jak looked curiously at him. Raptly. "Are you going to show me?"

"I will show you how to defend yourself and those around you with a protective barrier. As you've seen, it works against magical and physical attacks, so long as those attacking are not more powerful than you. A barrier is a reflection of your innate power and ability to concentrate, as well as magical stamina, which is something you will develop over time."

"Yes. I'm ready." Not only did Jak not try to hide his thoughts, but a burst of hope and gratitude filled him.

The intensity of the emotion surprised Malek. It was understandable that Jak was eager to learn to master his abilities, but this seemed like more than that. Relief? Because he worried Rivlen only wanted to instruct him to use him as a pawn? Yes. Jak longed for a teacher who didn't want to use him and who was someone he respected.

That made Malek feel bleak, since his motivation wasn't any purer than Rivlen's. He could only justify doing this because he believed Jak would be willing to work for Uthari in the end.

"We'll take the shortcut." Malek wiggled his fingers for Jak to step closer. "It's usually better for people to muddle through and figure it out on their own, but I need you to learn this right away. We'll link minds and do it together."

Jak didn't hesitate to come stand beside him. His trust and lack of questions was surprising but convenient. They didn't have a lot of time for him to figure this out.

Jadora watched with far more wariness, alternating between eyeing Malek suspiciously and Jak with open concern. Malek tried not to think about how she might have trusted him more before Uthari had shown up with her father.

The mercenaries stood farther back, huddling together as a frigid wind swept across the tundra, and they regarded Malek with more fear than suspicion, as if they thought he would turn Jak into a monster. Malek doubted that was possible, even if he wished it. Jak didn't have the heart of a killer.

"What's a mind link?" Jak asked.

"This." Malek rested his hand on the back of Jak's head. "The first time, watch me make a barrier. You'll be able to sense what I'm doing. Then we'll do a few together. Then you'll do it on your own."

"All right."

A screech came from the sky, identical to the one they'd heard earlier but much closer this time. A huge furry brown creature flew into view. It had the leathery wings and face of a bat but was the size of a horse.

It spotted them and flapped its wings faster, flying toward them. The creature wasn't magical, or Malek would have sensed it earlier, but he had no doubt it was a threat.

The mercenaries raised their weapons.

"Hold." Malek gestured for them to come closer. "This will make the practice more realistic. I'll protect the group with a barrier, just as we do for the mageships in battle."

"I haven't seen the mageships battle a giant killer bat yet,"

Tinder grumbled, though Malek had added a note of compulsion to his words, so the three mercenaries hurried over.

"If our barrier fails, you can shoot it," Malek said.

"Terribly magnanimous of you."

Had Uthari been there, or someone who cared more than he did, Malek would have demanded they add *my lord* when they spoke to him. But the lack didn't bother him, and Jadora would roll her eyes if he was a stickler about that. Besides, for her sake, he would rather not teach *Jak* to develop the arrogance that was as prevalent as eating and breathing among the mage community.

"I'm raising it," Malek said quietly, cuing Jak to pay attention.

As he formed a barrier around the group, Malek did it more slowly than he usually would, gathering the magic and weaving it together in his mind. Jak watched with an eager intentness that any teacher would love from a student. He wanted to learn, to master it more quickly than most, and he wanted Malek to think well of him. Malek recognized the feeling, because he'd been the same way as a boy when he'd been learning from Uthari.

After being raised without a father and fending for himself on the streets after his mother died, he'd wanted the one person who'd been willing to be a mentor to believe in him, to think he was worth the effort and that it wasn't time wasted. It was strange all these years later to be on the other end of that, to have a boy who'd also lost his father long for someone to fill that emptiness in his life. Jak was older than Malek had been when he'd started learning, more a man than a boy, but maybe it didn't matter. Human beings of all ages could have gaps in their lives and long to have them filled.

The mercenaries dropped to one knee, their rifles aimed at the winged creature descending toward them, beady black eyes hungry, fangs ready to tear them into shreds. But they'd worked for mages before, and they understood that a barrier protected them—and that they couldn't fire through it.

Aware of Jak studying it and learning from his technique, Malek made it stronger than usual. Even those who couldn't sense magic would likely know it was there.

The creature didn't, or if it did, it didn't care. It extended its talons as it neared them, but it struck the barrier and bounced off. It screeched and flew back in a frustrated rage, its wings battering the barrier, its fangs gnashing at it, though from its point of view, it must have been like beating a rock.

When it drew back, flying upward to angle down from another direction and try again, Malek dropped his barrier. He wanted to make several so Jak could watch, so he knocked the creature away with a blast of power. It flew tail over snout, wings flapping wildly as it righted itself.

Help me this time, he told Jak.

I'm not sure what to use, but I'll try. You seemed to weave it together.

Yes. My mother was a seamstress, and I helped her when I was a boy. She sewed, knitted, spun, just about anything related to making garments that you can imagine. Malek had been teased by others in the zidarr training for using craft imagery to make his magic, so he'd stopped admitting it to people long ago, letting those who wondered believe he used colors, as was so common, but he thought Jak might appreciate knowing, since he also had a unique way of looking at the world.

Oh! Jak radiated pleasure at what he also perceived as a commonality. *I'm going to try envisioning us in a cave, a deep metamorphic rock cave without any exits. Oh, even better: a diamond cave. Nothing will break through that.*

Good. It's coming back. Do it now.

Again, Malek weaved the barrier slowly so Jak had time to work with him. He nodded as he sensed Jak layering a barrier on top of his. Again using his weaving imagery, Malek demonstrated how to meld their efforts together to make them stronger than two separate barriers would have been.

This is how mages do it when they're defending a ship, he explained calmly as the bat-creature reached them and flailed at the barrier again. *Even if individual mages use different imagery to form their magic, they can still work seamlessly together.*

The mercenaries kept their rifles pointed at the creature, tense and afraid the barrier would fail. No, not against a creature that didn't have magic of its own. For even a new mage without much power, keeping a mundane predator at bay wasn't that hard, assuming one didn't have to do it indefinitely. Stamina was required for a prolonged attack.

Of the four of them, only Jadora didn't seem worried about the creature gnashing at the barrier above them with its fangs. Her gaze stayed on Jak and Malek, her worry for her son.

I won't lead him astray or harm him, he told her silently as Jak remained focused on maintaining their barrier. *You can trust me in this.*

Only in this? She raised her eyebrows.

In many things.

Except those that go against your king's wishes.

Yes. You know I have sworn to obey his orders.

You'll pardon me for not being pleased that you're trying to turn Jak into his faithful follower too.

Malek knew what she meant—and wasn't that exactly what he was doing?—but he felt the need to justify his choice. *I want him to learn this so he can protect you in this place.*

I believe you, but the consequences, whether intended or not, will be profound. If anything, Jadora's face grew more concerned as she watched Jak concentrating.

Consequences? Do you believe he will turn on you because he embraces his power? Nothing like that need happen. He is grounded and has a sympathetic heart.

He looks at you the way he used to look at Lor— at his father. She didn't say more, but Malek sensed the rest and understood. She feared Jak would end up working for Uthari, not because he wanted to but because Malek asked it, and Jak wanted Malek to like him. Like a father would like a son.

Malek didn't know how to respond to the accusation—*was* it an accusation?—since he'd long felt like that toward Uthari, who'd taken him in and trained him. It was natural to develop feelings of loyalty for a mentor.

We don't have to be enemies, Jadora, he said.

As long as you work for someone who thinks nothing of kidnapping people and blackmailing them into working for him... we do. Jadora thought of Darv, of Tonovan hurling him against a wall and breaking his neck, and she looked away, bringing her fist to her mouth and closing her eyes.

Malek didn't know how to address that, to assuage her concerns—maybe he couldn't—so he focused on the training. *See if you can make it by yourself, Jak.*

Malek knocked the creature away again, dropped his barrier, and drew his sword. Whether Jak succeeded or failed, Malek would kill the pernicious predator so it wouldn't threaten the group while he was gone.

Jak bit his lip and replicated his barrier. He got it up quickly, channeling power into it so it was as rock-solid as Malek's had been. He truly did have a lot of potential. Not for the first time, Malek wondered how that was possible since Jadora didn't have any power, and she'd claimed Jak's father hadn't either.

"I did it," Jak blurted as the creature struck the barrier, scratching uselessly at it with talons before screeching and landing a few feet away.

It hissed, a startlingly loud noise that assaulted their eardrums, and Jak stumbled back, clasping his hands to his ears. His concentration faltered, and the barrier dropped.

The creature screeched and sprang for him. Jak swore and tried to raise the barrier again, but like many new—and even experienced—mages, fear blasted into him and made concentration difficult.

Malek reacted more quickly than the mercenaries, springing with his sword raised and keeping the creature from reaching Jak. His blade glowed white, eager for battle even on this foreign world, and as the furred foe snapped at him, Malek swept his sword at it. With its magic enhancing his strength, he easily slashed through its snout. The creature clawed reflexively at him, even as its hot blood gushed onto the frozen snow, but Malek slashed again, cutting off its short taloned arms. Finally, he drove his blade into its chest.

The creature pitched sideways, spilling more blood onto the snow. When he was sure it was dead, Malek cleaned his blade and turned back to the group. He was in time to see reverence in Jak's eyes, and in that moment, he understood Jadora's concern more clearly. She had to worry that nothing good would come from her son idolizing a zidarr, at least nothing good from her perspective.

Malek wondered if it was awful that, since he'd never had a son, he didn't mind Jak's appreciation. It was too bad he couldn't legitimately teach him, not beyond this one day, this rare circumstance.

"Sorry," Jak said, sheepishness and shame replacing his reverence as the moment passed and he realized his failure. "I wasn't expecting that horrible noise. But that's no excuse. I should have been concentrating harder. I shouldn't have let anything surprise me."

"You won't be taken off guard again." Malek sheathed his sword and stepped onto his skyboard. "I'll be back as soon as possible. Stay together. If something happens to me, Jak will help you find the portal and a way home."

Jak lifted his brows, but he didn't object. He accepted the

responsibility and stepped close to his mother, as if to say he would do whatever it took to make sure she stayed safe.

"Well, that's reassuring," Tinder muttered, rolling her eyes.

"One day, perhaps it will be," Malek said, pinning the three mercenaries with his gaze, but only for a moment. He rose into the air and headed up toward the compound.

30

After Malek and the others stepped through the portal, and its starry center disappeared and the magic returned to its usual soft hum, Captain Rivlen returned to the *Star Flyer*. Assuming King Uthari would want the valuable artifact guarded, she left several crew members down below with orders to alert her if anything happened.

Full darkness had fallen, and she looked forward to a meal in her cabin, but she'd no sooner sat down than a telepathic summons came.

Join us on the Serene Waters, *Captain Rivlen,* Uthari spoke into her mind.

Yes, Your Majesty, she answered promptly, though nerves twisted in her stomach.

Other than for her promotion, during which Uthari had stood at the back of the formation, Rivlen had never interacted with him in person before. Unless one counted her uneasy communication with him via the dome-jir. She worried he'd detected her half-truths, her attempt to protect Malek, and intended to punish her for them.

Even though Uthari had signed the orders that promoted her to captain of the *Star Flyer*, and he presumably believed her a capable commander, she worried she might not be living up to his expectations. She longed for recognition and the promise of future promotions, not punishment, and hoped that any failing she'd demonstrated could be corrected.

After alerting her second-in-command that he was in charge of the ship, she flew to the *Serene Waters* on a skyboard, grimacing before she landed. General Tonovan was already there, as was Lord Yidar. He'd never offended her in the past, but the fact that he now stood shoulder to shoulder with Tonovan, as if they were good buddies, made her wary of him. She wished *she* had someone to stand at her side.

Almost laughably, Jak's face flashed into her mind, but he would need a lot more training before he could serve sufficiently as an ally. She had no idea if he would even return from the mission to the other world. If he did, King Uthari might take him away to train himself. The lessons Rivlen had given Jak might have been a waste of her time, though they hadn't taken long, and she hadn't minded them. She'd felt she owed him after the battle with the druids. And then he'd been injured helping them a second time. He deserved a few rewards.

Besides, it pleased her that he'd genuinely believed that the crewman who'd questioned her competence, who'd believed she must have slept her way into her promotion, had been an idiot. *Jak* hadn't had trouble believing her capable of her job. Even if he was a naive kid, she appreciated that.

Colonel Sorath and the female mercenary captain also stood on deck, shoulder to shoulder themselves as they faced Tonovan and Yidar. As Rivlen landed, the yacht's commander, Captain Reynok, also joined the group. Two captains from the other mage-ships arrived, and Rivlen realized this was a meeting, not necessarily a punishment Uthari had called her over to deliver. Maybe he wasn't irritated with her at all.

Rivlen stood as far from Tonovan as she could while remaining in the area, but that didn't keep him from glaring and speaking telepathically to her.

Do you actually care about that mercenary girl, he asked, *or did you only protect her to irk me?*

I do enjoy irking you, Rivlen said, meeting his eyes—his *eye*—though she should have been more circumspect. When he'd attacked her, he'd been even stronger than she remembered. Years had passed since he'd forced her to have sex with him, since she'd been a weak young lieutenant who'd had little choice. She'd thought she'd grown so much in power that she would be close to a match for him by now, that all it would take was someone distracting him for her to get the upper hand.

But her memory couldn't be trusted. It embarrassed her that he'd driven her to her knees and that only Malek's timely arrival had kept him from truly hurting her. She should have thanked the mercenary girl for running off to get Malek, but she'd been too chagrined by her failure.

It's dangerous for young captains to irk generals. Tonovan probed her defenses with a mental dagger.

Had she not been prepared for an attack and raised protection around her mind quickly enough, that would have hurt with the power of a *real* dagger.

Especially when Malek is no longer babysitting you, he added.

Rivlen gritted her teeth, tempted to attack him back, but she sensed that he was goading her into doing exactly that. Maybe he wanted to embarrass her in front of their colleagues and even those powerless mercenaries. Though their telepathic conversation was private, everyone was looking back and forth between Rivlen and Tonovan. Even the terrene humans sensed the tension between them.

We have a mission to complete, Rivlen told him. *Why don't you grow up before someone stronger than you stabs out your other eye?*

Stronger than I? Who would that be? Only Uthari and Malek equal my power, and they know my value.

They more than *equal your power, you pompous prick.*

Malek and I have never dueled. Someday, we will, and perhaps my power will prove greater than his.

You could have dueled him today if you wished. You fled to your cabin with your tail between your legs.

Rivlen sensed anger rising within Tonovan, bubbling closer to the surface. She needed to swallow her pride and shut up. Even better, she should suck up to appease him, but it was so hard when she loathed him so very much.

I should duel him while you wait nearby to pounce and take advantage while we grapple? Tonovan asked. *I'm no fool. Unlike you, I know not to tempt fate, or enemies who could crush me with a thought.* He sent a mental dagger at her mind again, stabbing at her defenses with the power of a steam hammer.

Even though she was protecting herself, the power was too much to deal with, and she grunted in pain, unwillingly stepping back and bumping into someone. Surprisingly, the attack vanished. Her relief was short-lived, for now she could sense that Uthari was behind her and had witnessed her weakness. The torch of shame seared her cheeks.

"Captain Rivlen." Uthari rested a hand on her back, sending a surprising wave of healing magic through her. It faded quickly, but she felt better than she had before Tonovan's attack, invigorated, as if she could go into battle with any foe now. "Thank you for coming. Join us."

Everyone in the group greeted him politely, bowing their heads with murmurs of *Your Majesty.* Only Colonel Sorath glared darkly at him with no respect in his eyes. Surprisingly, Uthari only smiled at the mercenary's defiance.

"As you know," Uthari addressed them, radiating power and calm, "several rulers have sent fleets to Zewnath. Until a few moments ago, they were milling around over the jungle, having little idea where the artifact was located. But when it activated... I trust you all felt that tremendous burst of power."

Everyone except for the mercenaries nodded.

"The fleets close enough for me to sense are beelining in this direction." Uthari extended his hand toward the portal, still standing erect below without anyone propping it up. The waterfall roared as it poured into the nearby pool, but the power of nature was nothing compared to the power of its magic. "I expect the first of them will arrive before dawn."

"We could face one fleet, Your Majesty," Captain Reynok said, "but even if you lure this supposedly brilliant military mind—" he gave Sorath a scathing look, "—into helping us come up with a clever ploy, I don't see how we can defeat as many ships as you believe are coming."

"I have an idea," Uthari said, "and Captain Rivlen is going to escort me down to the artifact to investigate the possibility."

Rivlen arched her brows, surprised to be singled out, but she quickly said, "Of course, Your Majesty."

Tonovan squinted at them but didn't object, at least not out loud.

"Yidar will also join us," Uthari said.

"Yes, Your Majesty."

Rivlen hadn't spoken often with Yidar and didn't know what to think of him. He was fit and radiated the tremendous power of a zidarr, as Malek did, but the similarities ended there. There was a sullen set to his jaw that reminded her of a recalcitrant teenager.

They walked to the railing, and Uthari sprang atop it, as if he were twenty instead of eighty—or, if the myths were to be believed, *two hundred* and eighty. He jumped down, drawing wind underneath him to slow his descent, and landed lightly near the waterfall.

Yidar jumped after him, not slowing his descent at all, but showing off his physicality and zidarr indestructibility by landing in a deep crouch. Rivlen could have emulated Uthari's trick but had her skyboard with her, so used it to soar down.

Uthari waited in front of the artifact with the crewmen Rivlen had left to guard it. They were down on one knee, bowing their heads toward him. Ignoring them, Uthari prowled around the portal.

Maybe he meant to establish a link to it, the way Jak had, so he could draw upon its power to attack their enemies. Rivlen nodded to herself, thinking it was a good idea. If they were claiming it and didn't want others to take it, why not channel its powers? Maybe it could do much more than Jak had figured out. A wizard as ancient and powerful as Uthari ought to be able to draw out all of its hidden magic.

"What kingdom do you envision yourself ruling, Yidar?" Uthari asked, though his gaze remained toward the artifact.

Rivlen arched her eyebrows. Zidarr were supposed to loyally serve their kings, not claim their own lands.

Yidar stirred, not appearing surprised by the question. The remains of a mage mark that someone had given him brushed against Rivlen's senses and unsettled her. It was strange to see a trusted zidarr with such a mark, and she wondered what he'd done.

"I thought to carve out my own, Your Majesty," Yidar said carefully.

"There are few unclaimed lands left in the world and none of value. Zewnath is the largest, but the druids would object to a foreign ruler. If your ambitions drive you to claim a kingdom, you'd be best served taking over an existing one."

"That would be a daunting task, unless I could convince this artifact to help me find allies to stand with me." Yidar also prowled around it, regarding it curiously.

"The artifact *is* an ally. It was for the boy, and it could be for us." Uthari looked at Rivlen for the first time since coming down. "I saw Jak call upon it in my courtyard and use it against me, but it was difficult for me to discern how he summoned its power. At first, I was too busy attacking our enemies to more than glance at him, and then when I realized what he was doing, he convinced the portal to attack *me* before I could kill him."

Jak had tried to kill Uthari? Rivlen hadn't realized that. Teaching Jak might have been a mistake, especially if Uthari was irked and thinking of killing him. Of course, Uthari might have admired the kid's audacity and be more interested in taking him in.

"He called forth lightning from it twice while he was aboard *Star Flyer*," Rivlen said. "Both times, he made sure his hand was on it. I sensed him rouse its power, but I don't know what mental command he used. As with you, Your Majesty, I was busy fighting and unable to watch him closely."

"Unfortunate. I wonder if Malek has figured out how to call upon the portal's powers." Uthari stepped close and dared put his hand on it for the first time. "It hums with the power of dragon steel. It's magnificent." He slid an appreciative hand along its surface.

Yidar stepped up on the other side of the portal, glancing dismissively at Rivlen and placing his hand on it. His eyes said that he was thinking that he might beat his king to figuring out the puzzle and make the tool his.

Rivlen gripped her chin and stayed back, suspecting Uthari would be the one to master it, if anyone could.

"Jak had a key that he put in that indention over there," she said after a moment when nothing seemed to happen. If either of them had roused its magic, she couldn't sense it. There was no change in the artifact itself. "He took it with him when they left. Maybe it has to be near the artifact to call forth its power."

"That's a possibility," Uthari murmured, his chin to his chest, his eyes closed. "But I do not believe he had the key when he called upon its magic in my courtyard."

"Weren't the mercenaries nearby with it?"

"They were."

"It does not respond to me in any way." Yidar sounded frustrated. He lifted a boot, as if he might kick the portal.

"Do not," Uthari said. "It defends itself from those who threaten it. It can do that whether the key is nearby or not."

Yidar grunted and lowered his leg.

"Come here, Captain Rivlen," Uthari said. "I want you to show me what you remember of the two battles, of how Jak touched and accessed the portal."

Though nervous at the request—Uthari was asking her to lower her mental defenses so he could read her memories like the pages of a book—he was her king, and Rivlen dared not disobey. She joined him in the shadow of the portal, though she didn't touch it herself.

As she stood next to Uthari, she was aware of his tangible aura, his magic not diminished in the least by his age. He radiated the same power as a zidarr, maybe even more, as if he were a wine that had only grown more potent with time.

She let out a slow breath and made herself peel back the mental barriers she habitually kept wrapped around her mind.

I appreciate your willingness to open your mind, Uthari spoke quietly into her thoughts. *If we are not able to master this artifact and use it the way Jak did, we will have a difficult time keeping the others from taking it.*

I understand. Rivlen did her best to think of the battles, though she'd only glanced at Jak. She'd been too busy defending the ship.

During the first battle, when the lightning had shot out, annihilating those grasping vines, she'd been as startled as the druids. She'd gaped at Jak as he knelt in the center of the portal, his hand on it, whispering who knew what to it. Whatever his link was to it, she'd been so thankful that she'd wanted to give him a gift.

You taught him our ways, Uthari thought.

The words weren't accusing, and he didn't lash out at her after saying them, but a shiver went through her. She hadn't meant to show him *that*.

Just a couple of lessons, Your Majesty. I thought... Well, based on something he said, I thought you and Malek knew about Jak's potential, and that you'd decided to find a use for him instead of killing him as a wild one.

That is so. I do not care that you gave him a lesson.

A breath she hadn't realized she'd been holding trickled out of her. *I am relieved, Your Majesty. I seek only to serve you to my utmost, to one day take the place as the leader of your military forces.*

It was a bold thing to admit, especially when General Tonovan was not that old. He might serve another twenty years if he were not killed, but she was positive some enemy's blade would find his chest before then, if not hers.

I see that. Uthari chuckled into her mind. *It will keep him on his toes.*

No king or queen currently living has a female military leader. It would be without precedent. Assuming you would not forbid it?

Certainly not. He or she who is best qualified for the job must be chosen, though I hope you'll be pleased at your current rank for some time. As a newly appointed captain, there is much to learn.

Yes, Your Majesty. I understand.

Uthari ran his hand along the frame of the portal. *It does not respond to me. I am not able to cause it to pulse blue or draw upon its power in any way.* He regarded her curiously. *What do you think it sees in Jak, besides that he has potential and that my loyal mages would rather cultivate his power than kill him?*

Rivlen hesitated. The question seemed like a trap, and she couldn't tell if Uthari truly wanted Jak or resented his people's interest in him.

Maybe it's simply bonded with him because he was the first to touch it and attempt to communicate with it? Is that true? He and his mother found it, did they not?

They did, but Malek and Tonovan arrived shortly after.

No artifact would want to bond with Tonovan, she said before she could catch herself.

No? What about with Malek? He has a less offensive personality.

Indeed. Rivlen thought of the times she'd seen Malek fight. Though they were serving together on the same ship for the first time, she'd seen him in battle more than once before, seen his power, his skill with the blades, how appealing he was when training on the deck with his shirt off...

Uthari's white eyebrows rose.

Rivlen had her mental protections back in place and was *positive* she hadn't shared fantasies of shirtless Malek with him, but something about the amusement in his eyes suggested he'd gotten the gist anyway.

Since he is zidarr, he is unlikely to return your interest.

I... had not realized zidarr have to be celibate. She couldn't believe she'd said that to her king or brought up this topic at all.

They do not, but they may not marry or allow themselves to develop strong feelings for a sexual partner. Their first loyalty is to their king. His eyes narrowed slightly.

Rivlen, worried Uthari would think she wanted to align with Malek to oust him from power, hurried to explain. *I've no fantasies about marrying anyone. I just thought he might be... stimulating.*

Uthari laughed. *And here I thought my Malek too aloof to stimulate a female.*

He is a competent warrior, Your Majesty. Rivlen was too embarrassed to go into more detail and prayed that Uthari and Tonovan weren't drinking buddies and that this wouldn't get back to the general. The last thing she needed was for Tonovan to have another handle on her.

Fortunately, Uthari returned to his assessment of the artifact. *I did not see the answer in your memories. We have a few hours to figure this out, Rivlen. No more.*

Do you truly believe we'll be in trouble if we can't?

It depends on how quickly Malek returns with Jak. As much as I hate to depend on an unproven boy, so far, he's the only one this artifact is speaking with—and defending.

You'll have to turn him into a loyal subject then.

Malek is working on that. Impressionable young men also find him stimulating.

Are you teasing me, Your Majesty?

Not with malice. Uthari smiled gently at her, seeming more like a grandfather than a ruler over all and one known to punish those who crossed him, and patted her on the shoulder.

Nearby, Yidar watched and glared at her.

Tezi shivered and jumped up and down in her jacket, wishing she had one of the fur-lined parkas she'd worn during the winters in her northern homeland. Funny how quickly her body had forgotten the cold. Though she'd once been acclimated to it, now she shivered.

This wasn't what she'd envisioned when Jadora had spoken of a world where she might hide until the angry mages of Torvil forgot about her.

"Come sit between us, Rookie." Dr. Fret crouched with her back to the cliff, staying out of the wind as much as possible. Tinder huddled beside her, but Fret patted the ground between them. "Sergeant Tinder has so much muscle that she makes a wonderful barrier against the wind."

"That's my ass that's blocking the wind," Tinder said.

"A muscular ass." Fret winked at her.

Their cheeks were pink with windburn, and frost crusted their eyelashes, but they managed to share flirtatious smiles. A couple of weeks ago, Tezi had rolled her eyes at such open displays of affection, but now she found it comforting.

"I don't think you're supposed to call me rookie anymore," she said, "since the captain... asked me to leave. I'm not a part of the company."

"You're a part of this mission that we've been forced on," Tinder said. "That's good enough. Besides, if all the mages kill each other while we're gone, there'll be nobody left who wants you dead."

"We shouldn't hope for that, right?" Tezi asked wistfully.

"Not while Malek is around, but the rest of the time, sure."

Tezi accepted their offer and squeezed in between them. "I don't think he would punish us for fantasizing about the death of his people."

"You don't? Why not?"

"He seems less... *less* than the others." Tezi shrugged.

"According to his reputation, he's more... *more* than the others," Tinder said.

"I think his reputation has mostly been established by people he defeated in battle."

"Those people are dead."

"Then the people around the people he defeated in battle."

"That could be accurate." Tinder raised her voice. "Professor, if you get cold, you can come squat with us too."

Jadora had to be as affected by the temperature as the rest of them, but she paced about in the open, alternately looking up at the compound, in the direction Malek had disappeared, and back toward the vast glacier they'd left.

Even from ten miles away, or however far they'd traveled on the skyboards, the shelf of white-blue ice was an impressive landmark. Impressive but desolate. If there was anything atop it, Tezi couldn't see it, and she couldn't imagine what kept drawing Jadora's gaze. Hopefully, she hadn't seen more huge bat-creatures.

Jak was prowling around the remains of the dead bat, practicing, or so he'd said, his barriers on it. The stiffening carcass didn't look like something worth protecting, but maybe it helped to have a target.

Jadora waved an acknowledgment, but she didn't join them, instead turning her focus toward the sky. It was getting dark, and the stars would be out soon. Tezi hoped the night sky would be normal, not tinged with lavender. Thanks to that strange coloring, the sunlight and everything about this place was surreal.

"After I got away from my captors," Tezi said, "the professor suggested I might be able to hide out on one of the worlds the portal can take people, but I didn't envision anything like this. A single person couldn't survive here. I'm not even sure a group could."

"I hope it doesn't get vastly colder at night," Fret said, "or even Tinder's muscular ass won't be enough to keep us warm."

"One of the worlds?" Tinder asked. "I thought the portal was supposed to go to the dragon home world, and that's it."

"She implied there are lots of destinations."

"If they're all like this, maybe you want to rethink your plans."

"You do know," Fret said, "that Captain Ferroki only asked you to leave to protect you, right? Not because she doesn't want you in the company."

"I gathered that. And I appreciate it." Tezi didn't admit that she'd lost the money Ferroki had given her and that she would be in a tough situation if they went back and she had to fend for herself.

"How many zidarr or mages know about your past?" Fret asked. "The mage you helped kill at that hotel and whatever happened before?"

"Stone Heart did."

"He's dead."

"Night Wrath does."

"I'm not sure if he's dead," Fret said, "but he's on what is currently the losing side."

"And Uthari's General Tonovan knows I stabbed him in the eye, so he'll kill me the first chance he gets."

"He's the problematic one then."

"They're *all* problematic," Tinder said.

"Yes, but if we could get away from those two," Fret said, "or if they were killed in battle, and if we could keep Tezi away from more mind-reading mages in the future... maybe she wouldn't have to leave the company."

Malek probably knew Tezi's secrets by now too. She shook her head bleakly, unable to imagine a future where all of the mages and zidarr who were threats to her were dead.

A screech came from somewhere above the butte and the fortress.

"That sounds like another of those creatures." Tinder rose, pushing her hands out of her sleeves so she could grab her rifle. "We may have to fight this time."

"Get together." Jak waved to his mother and ran toward Tezi and the others. "All in one place so I can make a barrier around us."

"What are the odds that he learned how to do that from Malek rubbing the back of his head?" Tinder muttered.

"I don't think there was rubbing," Tezi said, "just teaching."

"To me, it looked like rubbing and the oozing of mageness onto him. He'll probably demand we start calling him *lord* soon."

Jak and Jadora joined them in the shadow of the cliff, and Tezi didn't respond. A part of her wondered if Tinder was right. Oh, she doubted Jak would change in one day, but over time?

The idea of someone she'd considered normal—or at least a terrene human like her—turning into one of them made her uncomfortable, but it wasn't as if she knew Jak well and would feel betrayed by him changing. His *mother* might.

"Keep your backs to the cliff," Jak said.

"Are you sure?" Tinder asked. "I thought we should run around and flail our arms to draw its attention."

"I'm going to try to make a barrier around us all. It might be easier if one side is already protected." Jak gazed upward, as if expecting something to fly into view any second.

"He's not responding to my sarcasm," Tinder said. "That means he's not a real mage. A real mage would be forcing me to my knees now."

"Then maybe we don't have to call him *my lord* yet," Fret said.

Jadora frowned at them, and Tezi elbowed Fret and Tinder to knock it off. Even if they were stuck on this mission against their wishes, they should try to work together and be civil. Jak and Jadora were *also* here against their wishes.

Another giant bat creature flew into view.

Tinder lifted her rifle to aim at it.

"Wait." Jak lifted a hand. "I think I've got a barrier up. Don't shoot."

"You *think*?" Tinder asked. "When will we find out? Half a second before it swoops in and eats us?"

"Probably more like a quarter of a second. A creature plummeting at more than the speed of gravity would be fast." Jak's brow furrowed, and he looked at his mother. "Is that right? Are birds faster than gravity, or do they match it when they dive?"

"Depending on air resistance, terminal velocity is a little over a hundred miles an hour. I don't know about these creatures, but back home, daragoth falcons are believed to dive at well over two hundred miles an hour."

"My quarter second estimate would be high then."

"Yes. But to accurately calculate the time, we would need to know the gravity on this world. It feels similar to Torvil—almost surprisingly so—but I doubt it's precisely the same."

A second creature came after the first.

"Am I or am I *not* shooting at those?" Tinder demanded.

Tezi also rose, her weapon ready. If Jak and his mother were talking about science, it didn't seem like he could be concentrating on magic.

But he said, "No," and kept his hand up.

The big, winged creatures circled the area over the group, flying so close to the cliff that their wingtips knocked ice free. The pieces crumbled toward the tops of their heads. Tezi lifted an arm to protect herself, but they landed on an invisible shelf ten feet above them. An invisible *barrier*.

"Hah," Jak said.

His barrier was tested further when one of the creatures dove toward them, talons outstretched and fangs on display.

Tinder cursed, her rifle pointed at it even though she didn't fire. Tezi did the same. Even Jadora shifted uneasily at this test of her son's power. Fret clutched her medical kit close and crouched low.

The creature struck the barrier and bounced off, leaving pieces of brown fur floating in the air. The second one hit right behind it, striking at such an angle that it rolled away on the ground.

It recovered, springing to its feet, and screeched at them. The other one managed to stay in the air, but it hissed like an angry cat as it flew back and forth in front of the cliff, glaring at them.

High above, a dark shadow flew into view, and Tezi groaned,

thinking a third creature had arrived. But it was Malek on the skyboard, looking down upon them. Checking on them?

Jak looked up and waved. Malek's return gesture, his palm toward Jak, wasn't a wave, but it seemed to be an acknowledgment that Jak had handled the situation.

The creature in the air spotted Malek and flew upward at him. Tezi thought he might also form a barrier to thwart his avian attacker, but Malek drew his sword and main-gauche and crouched in a fighting position.

The giant bat flew up above him before banking and diving toward him. His skyboard darted sideways, evading outstretched talons, and Malek swept both blades out, striking fast enough to catch the creature as it flew past at two hundred miles an hour, or whatever Jadora had said.

Malek lopped off one of its wings and took a chunk out of its backside. With only one wing, it couldn't fly, and it plummeted down, hitting the ground so hard Tezi felt a tremor under her feet. It groaned and rose up, flapping its remaining wing uselessly, and hissed up at Malek.

Instead of following it down to finish it off with a blade, he created a fireball. As the orange blaze streaked toward it, the creature tried to hop out of the way, but it wasn't fast enough. The fireball engulfed it. One final dying squawk sounded before death cut it off.

What speed, Tezi wondered, did fireballs fly at?

"Oh, sure," Tinder said, "he can throw fireballs around to roast bat birds, but we're stuck freezing."

"Do you *want* him to roast you?" Fret asked.

"No, but a nice campfire placed five feet away wouldn't be unappreciated."

"Maybe you can huddle up to the burning corpse."

The remaining creature flew a few dozen yards away before landing again. It peered over at the group and up at Malek.

Malek either didn't deem it a threat or thought Jak could handle it, for he lifted a hand toward him again, then sailed out of view on his skyboard.

"You still got the barrier up, kid?" Tinder asked.

"Yes."

The other creature was doing the equivalent of preening itself and didn't look like much of a danger, but maybe that was a ruse.

"Good," Tinder said. "Keep it up."

"I will." Jak's chin had a determined set.

Jadora patted him on the back. "You're doing well."

"Thank you."

Her gaze lifted to the sky again. It had grown noticeably darker in the last few minutes.

"The stars are coming out," Jadora murmured.

"Is that significant?" Tezi asked.

"Beyond the fact that we're more likely to freeze now?" Tinder muttered.

"Perhaps," Jadora said softly, her gaze locked to them.

31

SORATH LEANED AGAINST THE RAILING OF THE *SERENE WATERS*, dully watching Uthari and Rivlen at the portal. As night deepened, he fought the urge to yawn. Given that Uthari thought Sorath was valuable and could be useful, he could have provided a cabin and a hot meal.

Captain Ferroki joined him at the railing.

"I'm sorry you're caught up in this," Sorath said, "and that your people are... who knows where."

Not dead, he hoped. Or irrevocably stuck on another world.

"It's not your fault," Ferroki said.

"Are you sure? Sending saboteurs was my clever plan that got us all stuck on the ship that Uthari's fleet swooped down on and annihilated."

Something that Uthari, thanks to Sorath's earlier torture session, now knew all about. Uthari had also plucked the location of this pool out of his mind, making Sorath regret that he'd visited the druid monument in Port Toh-drom to find that map. Who knew what else the powerful wizard had gotten?

"I've heard that the ship with the roamers was also defeated,"

Ferroki said. "We might have already died if we'd been with them."

"There's no way to win here, is there?"

"Is a master tactician supposed to say things like that?"

"One bitter and beaten down by the world is, sure. Also, most wars presume that you want the side you're fighting for to win. I'm hoping these power-hungry megalomaniacs all kill each other off."

"I'd be more inclined to hope for that if we weren't on one of their ships." Ferroki sighed and rested her forearms on the railing, hands clasped. "I was thinking about walking away back in Tohdrom. Accepting that we wouldn't be paid and trying to extricate the company while it was still possible."

"Why didn't you?"

"They swooped us up to another ship—literally. They brought us in to sign another contract and paid us for the last. I also had the sense they wouldn't let us go, even if I said no."

"Who wants to fly into a war without cannon fodder?" Sorath peered toward the north, in the direction that enemy ships would likely come from. So far, no lights were visible over the canopy of green, but Uthari had promised that a fleet was coming, and he would know. Sorath wondered what had happened to Night Wrath and Lieutenant Vinjo.

"Uh oh," Ferroki murmured, her gaze downward.

Sorath turned back to the portal, expecting Uthari had figured out how to get it to spit lightning bolts.

It *was* doing something, but lightning wasn't involved. The frame of the portal glowed blue, and judging by the reactions of Uthari, Rivlen, and the nearby mages, they hadn't been the ones to cause it. They all scurried backward while sharing uneasy glances with each other.

What could make someone as powerful as Uthari uneasy?

Blackness formed in the center of the portal with stars swirling all around, the same as it had when Jak activated it.

"Is our team coming back already?" Sorath wondered. "If so, that didn't take long."

"What else could it be?" Ferroki didn't sound as concerned.

Because she didn't yet realize all the ramifications.

"It could be someone—or something—from another world coming to visit us," Sorath said.

"How would they have known that after thousands of years our portal is once again available for use?"

"I don't know, but I'm not a mage or, despite years of battling against it, an expert in magic. I wouldn't be surprised if there's some way to communicate with the portal and get news from it. It must be linked with all the other portals in some way, right?"

Ferroki shook her head. "I know nothing about these artifacts."

Sorath rested his hand on his black-powder pistol, watching and waiting. He wasn't the only one.

But before anything appeared, a shout came from the crewman standing watch in the forecastle. "Enemies sighted!"

He pointed not toward the pool and the portal but back in the direction of the coast. Several ships had come into view, their running lights visible on the dark horizon.

"Uthari better get back up here," Ferroki said, "unless he's succeeded in figuring out how to use the portal as a weapon."

"I don't know whether to hope for that or not." Sorath eyed all the sets of lights. "That's a lot of mageships."

People swore, not only on their deck but on the decks of the nearby vessels in Uthari's fleet.

"Look out!" someone down by the pool yelled.

Down below, the stars had solidified in the center of the portal, a different constellation hanging there than had before. Something huge, long, and winged flowed out of the center.

It wasn't a dragon. It looked like a giant snake—no, more like a giant earthworm with a great round maw full of pointy teeth. Its single set of wings shouldn't have been able to keep that long body in the air, but it didn't slither out of the portal. It *flew* out.

At first, it stayed low, undulating a few feet above the ground, its creased body glistening with slime or mucous. All of the people left down there were mages, and all save one got defensive barriers up, but one man gaped at the thing approaching him, too shocked to defend himself. The worm, more than ten feet high and wide and perhaps a hundred feet long, was like nothing Sorath had ever seen.

As he raised his pistol, certain this creature was dangerous, the mage in its path sprang to the side, trying to dodge. The worm swung its maw toward him and caught him in midair. Dozens of pointy teeth bit into him, clamping down before drawing him deeper into its body, chomping vigorously as the man screamed.

Sorath and Ferroki opened fire together, his black-powder pistol cracking and her magelock rifle buzzing. Bullets and charges slammed into the creature.

At the same time, Uthari and the other mages below hurled lightning and fireballs at their alien foe. The attacks all landed— or seemed to—but the great worm absorbed them as if they were nothing.

It continued forward without pause, the last twenty feet of its body acting like a tail, lashing from side to side. Several of the mages ducked to avoid it. One braced himself, a defensive barrier raised, but when the tail struck the barrier, it knocked it and the mage across the clearing. His defenses dropped as he crashed into a tree.

Captain Rivlen stepped up beside Uthari and blasted the creature with a wave of flames. The huge worm screeched, but it was hard to tell if that represented pain or was a battle cry. Could it even *feel* pain?

Sorath pounded several more bullets into its flanks, but it was like hurling pebbles into a snowbank. They disappeared without doing noticeable damage.

"This isn't going to work." He holstered his weapon. "We're going to have to find a lot more firepower to throw at it."

Lightning crackled from Uthari's fingers, striking the huge worm. A few tiny blisters appeared in its slimy skin, but it wasn't perturbed. It swung its huge body back toward the portal, toward Uthari and Rivlen.

"Protect the king!" one of his bodyguards yelled.

Up on a nearby mageship, General Tonovan and the zidarr Yidar appeared, and each cast lightning attacks similar to Uthari's. They struck the great worm, but again, it didn't slow it. With speed surprising for its bulk, it undulated toward Uthari.

Sorath couldn't help but think that some of their problems would be solved if it caught and ate the king. But Rivlen and Uthari combined forces, raising an invisible wall between their people and their great enemy. Unlike with the other mage, the worm couldn't knock them and their barrier aside. It crashed into the invisible wall.

That didn't deter it for long. The worm turned again, flapped wings that shouldn't have been large enough to carry it aloft, and rose into the air. It flew straight for the *Serene Waters*, and Sorath swore.

"I'm lamenting that we never got to share a kiss, Captain Ferroki," he said, scanning the ship's deck, seeking inspiration.

"Why?" She smiled at him, though it was fleeting. "Do giant worms make you randy?"

"Not that I know of, but impending death has a tendency to fill me with regrets."

"Ah. I know the feeling."

"All mages combine to create barriers," the ship's captain yelled.

Ferroki stopped firing and lowered her rifle. There was no point.

"Did Tinder leave any of her grenades behind?" Sorath asked.

"Yes, but—" A magical blast struck the ship's barrier, and Ferroki broke off.

It hadn't come from the worm, which hadn't reached them yet, but from the jungle behind the yacht. The enemy ships had closed to firing distance, but they weren't shooting the alien creature. No, they were taking advantage of the distraction and firing on Uthari's fleet.

"—I don't think it's going to matter," Ferroki said grimly.

Sorath swore.

After Malek was certain that Jak could protect Jadora and the others from the local wildlife, he committed fully to exploring the compound, at least from the outside. The powerful magic emanating from the structure made him hesitant to force his way in before making a thorough assessment.

So far, he'd found one breach in the interlocking domes, a huge hole with jagged sides that wasn't part of the original design. It looked like a meteor had crashed through.

Surprisingly, there weren't any doors or entrances other than that. At least not *visible* doors. He probed the walls, searching for variations in the magic that would have suggested hidden entrances. He also tried to detect what was inside the compound, but most of the walls were as opaque to his senses as they were to his eyes.

Earlier, he'd been certain there was no life inside, because he couldn't sense any magical beings, but now, he was less certain. The magically and materially dense dome walls might be keeping him from detecting life.

Still riding his skyboard, Malek flew closer to one of the two domes with nearly transparent walls. They were the ones he'd seen from afar, greenery visible inside, plant life growing up high enough that he'd been able to see it from the ground. Frost on the domes obscured the foliage, but he had an impression of everything from trees to raised garden beds sprouting vining plants, some with great leaves. It was impossible to tell if any of the species were familiar, but an image of Uthari's Jitaruvak came to mind. Jadora would know more, but from what Uthari had said, it was fern-like with fronds for leaves.

Malek floated closer to one of the walls until he hovered within a foot of it. Rather than flying in through the hole on the other side of the compound, he was tempted to cut into one of these domes. The structure had already been damaged once and not been repaired, so maybe nobody was left to care about it.

That didn't mean it was empty. Something had been killing the humans who'd visited it. Some bird or animal using the compound as a den? Maybe a whole flock of those bat creatures lived inside. One or two weren't a match for him, and he suspected the mercenaries' magelocks would have injured them if he hadn't been there, but he could imagine a group of explorers being overwhelmed by ten or twenty.

Malek drew his sword. If he cut in here, the creatures might not notice his presence.

But tremendous magical energy emanated from the walls, making his senses buzz. It was nothing like the magical structures in Utharika or other mage-made cities. Instead, it reminded him of the magic of the portal, especially when it had activated, its aura growing tremendously strong.

He sucked in a breath as the ramifications of that struck him. This compound might also have been made by dragons.

If so, was it thousands of years old, like the portal, or had it been constructed more recently? He almost flew down to get

Jadora and ask her opinion as an archaeologist, but the magic radiating from the structure felt dangerous to him, as if it might lash out at any second. To be safe, he was keeping his defensive barrier up as he explored, but he would have to lower it to cut into one of the domes.

As he shifted his grip on his sword, prepared to slice into the wall, one of its premonitions flashed in his mind. It showed power striking him so hard that he flew off his skyboard, was knocked unconscious, and plummeted to his death.

Malek lowered his blade. The insights he received from his weapons didn't always tell the future; they were more warnings. But sometimes, they predicted it accurately, especially if he wasn't wise enough to heed them.

"The hole it is," he murmured and willed his skyboard to take him around the compound. It was likely he would need to explore it thoroughly anyway. If the portal was inside, it was probably in a protected room.

A gust of wind tugged at his jacket and chilled his face. The temperature had dropped even further since the sun set, so he resolved to hurry. He could keep himself warm with magic, as long as he stayed awake, but the others couldn't. And even he couldn't stay awake forever.

As he navigated around the compound, he glanced below, making sure the others were still all right, and spotted them huddled together for warmth. All except Jadora, who was eyeing the darkening night sky.

On the way out here, she'd glanced back toward the glacier often, as if some idea were niggling at her mind. As soon as he finished here, he would ask her if any new ideas had come to her.

When he reached the hole, he couldn't make out much through it. There was no moon in the sky, only stars coming out, and they did little to brighten the interior of the compound. He conjured an illumination globe and sent it inside ahead of him.

It shone over debris on a stone floor, rubble from the broken wall and more bones strewn among it. *Human* bones.

If there were hungry carnivores living inside, it was strange that they would only target humans. It was even stranger that so many people would come here. Where were they coming from? Did they live on this frigid world? Or, like his group, had they arrived through the portal from elsewhere?

Maybe they'd arrived and been *trapped* here. When they'd eventually died, the creatures might have brought them here to eat.

But he remembered the rope anchored on the wall for climbing. At least one group of humans had come intentionally. Drawn to this place the same as they'd all been? By the promise of the greenhouses?

A purple beam burst out of an inside wall and struck his globe of light. The two magics collided, and his lost, discomfort pinging in his mind from the backlash of energy as his globe disappeared.

His sword had been right about the danger, but Malek doubted entering here would be any safer than cutting a hole in the wall.

He sent another globe of light inside, willing it to zip deeper into the dome in the hope of seeing more before the defensive magic destroyed it.

This time, it made it farther and illuminated a back wall and a huge rounded doorway that led into the next dome. That doorway was large enough for a dragon to fly through if it tucked its wings.

Another beam blasted out and destroyed his globe. Before the light disappeared, it illuminated stone objects in the second dome, what might have been large chests and other storage units, as well as the side of a huge blue-black ring. It looked exactly like the portal on Torvil.

"This is the spot," he murmured. "No choice but to go in."

They would need to use that portal in order to leave. Malek

drew his sword again, hoping he could destroy the compound's defenses before they destroyed him.

The great bat creature that had attacked them earlier was now feasting on the carcass of the one Malek had roasted with a fireball. Jadora tried to ignore the tearing noises as it ripped off flesh to eat. Instead, she stomped around with her arms inside her buttoned-up jacket, her gloved hands under her armpits as she waited for the constellation she hoped to see appear in the sky. A couple of stars that *might* be a part of it were visible, but it still wasn't fully dark. Though, with a lavender glow on one of the horizons, she worried the stars might not ever be as visible as they were back home.

Jak came over and touched her shoulder. "You sure you don't want to huddle together with the rest of us?" He waved toward the cliff where the mercenaries crouched with their backs to the rock. "I'm trying to figure out fireballs."

"Maybe try to figure out sparks first."

"I suppose. There's nothing to burn to keep a fire going even if I *do* create flames, but it's a way to pass the time." Jak peered up at the plateau, the tops of a couple of the domes visible. "Do you think he found a way inside? It's been a while."

"He hasn't given me an update. *You* could ask him."

"I thought about it, but I don't want to pester him. I want him to think I'm polite and delightful and not an annoying student. Someone he wants to continue to teach, even if it's forbidden."

"You are delightful," Jadora said without commenting on the rest.

"No thoughts on whether or not I'm annoying?"

"You don't annoy *me*, but I'm not a powerful zidarr. I couldn't even tell that you'd created that barrier until the ice fell on us. Or *didn't* fall on us."

"I've been thinking about that. Do you still think I developed this ability to use magic because of this?" Jak removed his hat and fingered the medallion. "Because I had it so close to my head for so many years?"

"Unless you've learned something different, it's the best hypothesis I've got."

"And you don't think my abilities will go away, even if I stop wearing it, right?"

Jadora shook her head. "*If* close proximity to dragon steel is what was responsible for humans developing magic all those years ago, then it not only doesn't require continued contact with dragon steel, but whatever changes it makes to your blood will be passed along to your children."

"Then what if you wear it for a while? If not the hat, you could keep the medallion in your pocket."

"You want me to be able to make barriers too?"

"Well, it's a handy skill, but I was thinking more that it would be a good idea for you to have some magic so you could learn to keep mages from reading your thoughts."

"Have *you* been able to do that?"

"Sort of. When I'm thinking about it, but I'm sure you'd be better at it. You can concentrate for long periods of time without being distracted. I can't even finish one map without starting to fantasize about my *next* project."

"Yes, speaking of maps—" Jadora pointed toward the sky, noticing that more stars had come out.

"Wait." Jak waved his hat. "Don't change the subject yet. I mean it. Do you want to hold the key?"

"Didn't you say it took a couple of years before you started noticing anything different?"

"Yes."

"And it was only when we were captured by the mages that you realized you could do more than sense whether tools were magical? That was five *years* after you started wearing the hat."

"I might have been able to do things earlier if I'd known. Why not wear the hat and start soaking up its magic now? Even if it does take a while—hopefully not years—to develop power of note, it might not take that long to be able to do something easy, like blocking your mind off from them."

Jadora considered the offer. He had a good point.

"Malek might find it suspicious if I suddenly start wearing your hat," she said. "If our hypothesis proves to be true, we... probably don't want their kind knowing about it. It would be more advantageous if terrene humans were the ones to figure it out, found some dragon-steel artifacts to snuggle with, and eventually developed powers to rival the mages. Though I'm not sure we should wish for that either. Our people might simply become more like them."

Jak removed the medallion from the hat's headband and pressed it into her hand. "He won't think anything odd about you holding the key. We're a team. Just don't think about other stuff that we don't want them to know."

She snorted softly. "You know how much luck we've had with *that*."

She did, however, accept the medallion and button it into one of her pockets. Even if she had no desire to hurl fireballs, she admitted that being able to protect her thoughts *would* be helpful. Especially since she'd had so little time to practice the methods hinted at in *The Mind Way*.

"Thank you," she said.

"You're welcome. Now, come huddle with us?" He pointed toward the group.

Jadora checked the stars again and held up her hand. "There it is. In the sky in that direction." She almost said south, but with no familiarity with this world, she doubted she could assume the sun set in the west and rose in the east.

"Hm?"

She pointed toward the constellation, trusting he would recognize it. From their position, it was just visible—the butte blocked a chunk of the night sky. From the glacier where they'd come out of the portal—or been spit out by the portal—the constellation would have been directly in front of them.

"Ah, I see it," Jak said. "The constellation for this world. I've been thinking of it as a hunter with a bow."

"It's prominently visible from where we popped into this world," she said. "In almost exactly the same position as the Dragon's Tail constellation is in our sky. I don't think that's a coincidence. The Dragon's Tail is almost exactly over the southern pole, and it's used for navigation for those in the Southern Hemisphere, much as the Goat's Horn is used in the north."

"Yes." Jak knew those things, but he didn't sound like he'd caught what she was getting at yet.

Maybe her guess didn't mean anything, but the fact that the constellation on the portal had appeared exactly where she'd thought it would suggested she was on to something. "I bet this hunter constellation is also south. And if I'm right, the portal isn't up there." She pointed to the compound. "But back where we arrived. Maybe buried in that glacier."

"How could we have come out of it if it's embedded in ice? Wouldn't something like that render it unusable? Like our portal being buried under lava?"

Yes, she'd been mulling that over since they arrived. "I'm not sure, but maybe it was an instance of *close enough*. If the portal is right at the edge of that glacier, maybe its magic was able to overcome the ice and spit us out at the closest safe spot."

She expected Jak to keep arguing about how unlikely that was —it did seem a lot to ascribe such abilities to a lump of metal, but one of those lumps of metal had been giving them both visions for weeks.

He eyed the compound, the domes shadowed by the top of the butte rising above them. The elevated terrain would hide the constellation from anyone or anything inside the domes. Next, he looked toward the glacier and finally turned toward the southern sky.

"I see what you're saying. We believe that how the portals work is through more than magic, right? That the magic has to be interwoven with science. They can only operate in a spot where the constellations they're linked to are visible in the night sky, and the stars over the poles on Torvil are the only ones that don't move much with the time of day and the seasons. That's why the Dragon's Tail works as an anchor point."

Jadora nodded. "That's what I believe. Which means that if we get the opportunity to travel to other worlds through the portals, we'll always be able to find our way, because we'll always know the chosen constellation doesn't move in the night sky. That is, if we can dig out the portal here so we can get home again. Of course, we wouldn't necessarily *have* to go home. We could go from world to world, now that we know how to activate the portal. Assuming you can figure out how to use your magic to push the buttons."

"I *can*. I was the one to do it back on Torvil. My nascent abilities are vast and deep and blossoming into greatness."

"I would ask if Malek told you that, but I'm positive he would never say something so goofy."

"No, he's not as poetical as I am. *Mother*." Jak grinned and gripped her arm. "If I know which way is south, I can start *mapping* this place. Oh, and I can map the night sky too. This is brilliant." He peered up at the stars as if he were scorching them into his memory until he had an opportunity to draw them. Maybe he was.

"That could be a constellation over the north pole, and we could be in this world's Northern Hemisphere."

"True, but it's unlikely we're going to walk all the way into another hemisphere from here. It doesn't matter if I'm technically drawing the map upside down if it's designed for future explorers stepping out of the portal. Did you know putting north at the top of a map is a relatively recent historical convention anyway? What went at the top used to be decided by cultural preferences or what the cartographer wanted to emphasize. All I really need is a reference point that doesn't move." Jak waved at the constellation. "That's *perfect*."

"This does lead me to another question. If the portal is back there—" Jadora pointed toward the glacier, "—what's up there?"

"Didn't you and Malek see a greenhouse?"

"Something that might have been one, yes. There were two translucent domes with greenery visible inside."

"I didn't see them, but I trust they were there if you two did."

Jadora frowned, surprised her observant son had missed that. "What did *you* see?"

Something else more intriguing must have distracted him.

"All the domes I noticed were opaque, so not much. I did have the thought that the view from up there would be amazing, and that if I went up there, I would be able to see all of the terrain features for miles and might be able to start a map. For a moment, I thought I even saw a viewing platform up on that peak and envisioned a telescope waiting up there, but that would be farfetched. Besides, my vision isn't that good."

"I didn't see anything like that." An inkling of suspicion burrowed a small, worried hole in her gut. "Maybe we should ask the mercenaries what they saw."

Jak's brows rose. "You think the compound is somehow capable of showing us all different things? If so, to what end?"

Jadora gazed at one of the human skulls dotting the ground. "A trap?"

"If so, Malek is walking into it."

32

LIEUTENANT SASKO REPORTED TO FERROKI AND SORATH, BRINGING them the bag of grenades they'd requested. Tinder had taken some along with her for her adventure, but she'd left plenty aboard Uthari's yacht for the rest of them.

Most of Thorn Company crowded behind Sasko, afraid but standing their ground and waiting for orders. Sasko was afraid too. The huge flying worm was attacking Uthari's fleet from one side while enemy ships closed from the rear, launching cannonballs and fireballs to weaken the barriers the mages were struggling to keep up. The worm struck so hard, using a mixture of magic and the sheer bulk of its body, that it delivered greater damage than most mage attacks.

The worm had broken through one ship's barriers already, snatching up two of its crew members and devouring them whole. Sasko had expected King Uthari's lightning bolts to fry the creature—he'd annihilated entire enemy ships when Thorn Company had been invading his city. But the worm barely reacted to direct hits.

Nor had she seen anything else do much damage. The last

she'd heard, the mages were cycling through different attacks, trying wind, pressure, frost, and everything else in their repertoire. The worm, a magical being itself, was nearly impervious to it all.

Sasko couldn't imagine grenades accomplishing what magic couldn't.

"Ideas?" Sorath asked them over the din of battle.

"You're asking for them?" Sasko asked. "I was hoping you had some. My idea is to flee. Flee now and flee fast and hope we're faster than some of the other ships fleeing."

"I already told Captain Reynok to maneuver around and try to get the worm attacking their enemies," Sorath said. "I doubt it can tell us apart or cares which ship it attacks. But he says he can't draw back as long as Uthari is on the ground below."

"Is there some way we can lure the worm away from this area and toward them?" Ferroki pointed at the oncoming ships. "I don't know that they deserve this fate any more than we do, but..."

"They're firing at us when we're dealing with a horrible monster from another world," Sorath said. "They deserve whatever we can cast onto them."

"We need a lure." Ferroki raised her voice to be heard over mages shouting for help reinforcing the barrier. "What does the worm like?"

It had been striking one of Uthari's ships on the other side of the pond, but it flew back toward them, its slimy body gleaming orange as mages on the ground launched fireballs at it. Though a few char marks and blisters dulled its glistening flesh in spots, the creature seemed to absorb the magic and didn't notice the wounds. It undulated toward the yacht at top speed, as if it meant to ram them.

It shrieked, its round fang-filled maw opening. Sasko crouched to spring away if it made it through the yacht's defenses.

"It's projecting magic at us when it screams," a mage yelled. "It's going to tear through our barrier."

"Reinforce, reinforce!"

"Blast it!"

"Look out, Yarvort!" someone cried to a mage near the railing.

The worm lunged for the mage, the pink insides of its gullet visible as it opened wide, preparing to swallow him. He jumped over the railing to avoid that fate. The worm's teeth gnashed down, but it missed him. It reared up, issuing something between a hiss and a screech.

It didn't have eyes, but somehow, it saw the mercenaries and angled toward them.

Sorath grabbed two grenades.

"Fire into its big ugly yap!" he yelled to everyone who stood their ground and didn't scatter.

Ferroki remained at his side, shooting into the maw as Sorath hurled a grenade toward it.

Sasko grabbed two from the bag, almost fumbling them as the huge worm flew closer. It reached them as Sorath's grenade sailed into its mouth and blew.

Sasko's hope that the creature would explode didn't come true, but it did jerk and screech, hurt by the grenade. Gray smoke wafted out between its teeth. But the blow didn't keep it from lunging for the group.

Sorath and Ferroki dove to the side, barely avoiding the worm as it flew past, its massive bulk smashing the ship's railing and breaking boards on the deck. The grenade exploding inside its gullet had discombobulated it—it was the first thing that had. Before it could recover and snap at anyone on deck, the nearby mages unleashed their magic at it. Waves of raw energy and fireballs slammed into its side.

Afraid the attacks would strike her, Sasko scurried out of the way of its thrashing body. Its wings almost slammed down on a mage as the worm tried to lift off the ship and into the air. Sasko hurled her grenade. It struck the undulating body and exploded, but the outside was so impervious to everything that it didn't do any damage. Only the gullet had proven vaguely vulnerable, but as the worm flew past, its mouth was no longer a target.

A hapless servant was running alongside the far railing, carrying ammunition for the ship's big guns. He saw the worm but too late.

Sasko, Sorath, and several others opened fire on it, trying to keep it from snapping down on the servant. Once again, their bullets and charges failed to hurt it.

The servant leaped away, but the worm darted after him with far more speed than something so large should have had. It caught the man by the head and chomped down.

Sorath roared and ran up to its mouth, slamming his pickaxe into its fangs as he tried to yank the servant free. The worm wouldn't relinquish its prize, and bone crunched audibly along with the man's dying screams. Snarling, Sorath released him and pulled out another grenade. He used his pick to pry open the worm's mouth enough to throw the grenade down its gullet.

Abruptly, the worm rolled sideways. It knocked Sorath to the deck with its bulk, and if he hadn't been fast enough, it would have crushed him. Sorath somersaulted out of the way. He came up with his pistol in hand as the grenade blew within the worm's gullet.

Again, it reared up and screeched with pain. Instead of wheeling to attack him, it flapped its wings and flew up toward the night sky, leaving the remains of the servant's body on the deck.

Sasko holstered her pistol long enough to rub a shaky hand over her face. It had taken—or *eaten*—the man's head, leaving only the bloody stump of his neck and body behind.

Though possibly hurt and still screeching, the worm didn't go far. It banked and turned to come around to attack the yacht again.

"Get that barrier up, now!" Captain Reynok yelled.

"What it *likes*," Sorath said, answering Ferroki's earlier question as he looked grimly at the dead servant, "is to eat *us*."

He ran to the bag to grab more grenades.

"Sounds like another good reason to flee." This was not what Sasko had signed on for. How had Thorn Company ended up in this mess? That creature made the giant sand lizards in the desert back home seem like helpful little garden critters.

"I guess we know what would make a useful lure," Ferroki said, as grim as Sorath.

Sorath nodded. "Exactly right. We need to find someone delicious to hurl over at the other ships and see if it'll follow."

"*Someone*?" Ferroki asked. "We can't use human beings as bait."

"You mercenaries, get your asses to work and *do* something," an angry mage called.

"Are you sure?" Sasko asked. "Because that idiot just volunteered."

"I wish," Sorath muttered. "Let's try to use the corpse. Let the poor man's sacrifice mean something."

"Do you think the worm will be drawn by... not-live prey?" Ferroki asked.

"There's one way to find out."

Orange light flared as fireballs struck the yacht's barrier, attacks from the other fleet. The enemy ships, no doubt seeing their problem, hadn't drawn closer, but they were well within firing range.

"We'll get the mages to levitate it over there," Sorath said.

"I'll do it," came a voice from behind them. Captain Reynok stood close enough to hear their conversation. "You mercenaries better hope *live* bait isn't needed."

Judging by the rage on Sorath's face and the way he clenched that grenade in his fist, he was thinking of turning the captain into their live bait, but several other mages gathered around him as Reynok levitated the headless corpse into the air. They watched

Sorath warily as the group collectively opened a gap in the barrier so the body could float through. Reynok whisked it toward the enemy ships.

"Make sure the worm sees it." Sorath pointed to where it was attacking another of Uthari's ships, having been drawn by a barrier falling.

"Right, of course." Reynok's brow creased as he manipulated the corpse closer to the worm, bashing it against its side to draw its attention.

Sorath audibly ground his teeth. Sasko's gut twisted at the disrespect, but maybe the man's life could save others. Could save *theirs*.

"It's turning to look at it," someone yelled with excitement. "Hurry, Captain. Don't let it capture it until it's lying on top of the barrier of an enemy ship."

"I'm not stupid. I know what to do. You focus on keeping *our* barrier up."

"Yes, sir."

"If we do this right," Reynok muttered, "we won't need to feed it mercenaries."

Sasko joined Sorath in teeth grinding.

"We have more servants," one of the mages offered, nodding to Sorath, as if to say he appreciated the mercenaries.

But not, apparently, the ship's servants. Sasko shook her head. Working for these people was like turning one's bare back to the whips of the slavemasters in Hell. She deeply regretted advising Ferroki to stick with them until they got paid. No amount of money was worth this.

At least the worm chased the bait, wings flapping and its huge body undulating as it flew above the treetops toward the enemy fleet. The mages on the ship Reynok was targeting were too distracted by the creature's approach to notice the relatively small body. They lowered their barrier to fire at the worm, and Reynok dropped the corpse onto their deck before cursing and bending over to grab his knees. Apparently, levitating something that far away was a workout.

Fireballs lit up the night as the enemy ship targeted the worm. When they tried to raise their barrier, it tore through it with its magic. The worm soared down, crashing through their railing and snapping at their people.

"We've got a reprieve but only for a moment. They're not going to have any more luck killing it than we've had." Reynok straightened and looked at Sorath and Ferroki. "Figure something else out, mercenary geniuses."

Judging by the tenseness of Sorath's fingers around the grenade, he wanted to see if shoving it down a mage's gullet worked as well as down a worm's.

"Teamwork," Ferroki said.

"What?" Reynok asked.

"We've wounded it, but this looks like it'll be a battle of attrition," she said. "Perhaps you should speak to your king and the enemy commanders and put aside the issue of the portal for now. We all need to work together to defeat this creature."

"The king isn't going to like that plan."

"Are you sure?" Ferroki asked. "He's been shooting lightning at it and watching it do little. Maybe he'll be wise and agree."

Reynok spat on the deck and stalked away.

"We may have to pitch that idea to Uthari directly," Ferroki told Sorath. "Unless you have something better in mind."

"I don't. I'll see if I can get his attention." Sorath gazed back at the other vessels—the entire enemy fleet was firing at the worm now. It kept flying, moving from ship to ship, trying to find undefended humans to snatch up and eat.

"Don't forget to mention that our people aren't available for sacrifices," Sasko said.

"Maybe I'll suggest that his captain looks plump and delicious." Sorath strode off to find Uthari.

Malek left his skyboard outside the dome and stood on the narrow ledge between it and the edge of the cliff. He would need all of his focus for defending himself inside.

Once he'd poured all of his power into his defensive barrier, he jumped through the jagged hole, landing in a crouch with his weapons in hand. His heel came down on a bone that hadn't been visible from outside. It discombobulated him, but he recovered immediately. A good thing, because not one but *three* purple beams lanced toward him. They struck his barrier and were deflected, but their tremendous power made him glad he'd put far more energy than usual into this effort. They would drain him quickly if he didn't stop them.

The beams came out of square black devices mounted high on the dome walls. He couldn't throw fireballs while he had his barrier up, so he directed a telekinetic attack at one, trying to crush it with an invisible fist.

He'd used such a method to shatter boulders and break steel before, but the magical device resisted him. He willed even more power into the attack, as much as he dared without weakening his barrier too much. Finally, the device imploded with a soft *crunch*, and one beam disappeared.

Gritting his teeth and focusing like he hadn't had to since he'd been a boy in training, Malek attacked a second device. It crunched to pieces, the beam going out. By the time he destroyed the last one, sweat pricked at his armpits, never mind that the temperature inside wasn't any less frigid than outside.

The last beam went out, leaving him in darkness. He took a moment to reinforce his barrier, then conjured another light, sending it ahead again and hoping it would trigger any additional traps further along his path.

There was little in the first dome that he hadn't already seen. Rubble, dust, and scattered human bones, long femurs and tibias snapped by strong teeth. Shards of what had once been skulls. A broken pelvis bone with frozen gristle stuck to it.

He didn't see any animal scat. Maybe, unlike bats on Torvil, the creatures were smart enough to leave their den for that.

As Malek proceeded to the second dome, directing his light ahead, two more beams lanced out from the sides and destroyed it. He stopped in the doorway, a doorway that rose more than thirty feet above his head. There was no doubt that this place had been built for something or someone much larger than humans.

Destroying the second set of beams wasn't any easier than the first, but at least he knew what he was dealing with now. He broke the devices and started to advance, but the ceiling drew his eye. Unlike the simple dome in the last chamber, this one showed the stars, as if it were translucent. Since he'd seen it from outside, he knew it wasn't.

The stars slowly drifted across the ceiling as if he were seeing the movement of an entire night in a couple of minutes. Interesting, but that wasn't what he'd come for. The greenhouse domes were ahead and to his right.

He started forward, but he halted with the realization that the portal he'd seen from the entrance wasn't here. It *had* been here. Unless it had been an illusion?

He squinted at a long dust-free rectangle on the ground. It was as if something—the portal?—had rested there on a pedestal for a time and recently been moved.

But seconds ago? And if so, by what? Not those bat creatures.

Something else was in here with him.

Malek advanced slowly, stretching out with his senses. Though the magic of the place still made it difficult to discern if anything lived inside, he thought he sensed... something. A presence. Something watching him.

If not for believing the portal was in here and that the plant Uthari needed might be in the greenhouse, Malek would have turned around and left. He was used to being one of the most powerful people on Torvil, capable of handling almost any single foe, but this place, and whatever lurked deep inside, unsettled him deeply. He was barely handling the security devices; what would he do if he came face to face with the being who'd created them?

A familiar energy pinged at his senses, magic identical to what he'd felt when the portal activated back on Torvil. Strange.

He crept to the next dome, again conjuring his light to draw the attack. It came without fail. Three beams again.

After dealing with them, he paused in the doorway and wiped sweat from his brow. Uthari should have sent every zidarr and mage in his forces to infiltrate this place.

The third dome had writing all over the walls, runes that glowed a soft blue. He didn't recognize the language but thought it matched one of the symbols on the portal. In fact, it looked similar in style to the symbol Malek had pressed to bring them to this world, the one next to a dragon on Uthari's ancient decorative disk.

This place *had* been made by the dragons. Malek was more certain of it than ever. And he knew Jadora would be delighted to see this chamber... *if* she wouldn't be in danger.

As Malek conjured another light, the scent of fresh plants and something flowering drifted to him. He was nearing the greenhouses, or where they had appeared to be from the outside.

At the next dome, he sent his light ahead of him, expecting the beams, but nothing happened. From the doorway, he looked for the familiar black devices on the dome walls, but this chamber didn't have any. He directed his sphere to float all around, hoping to trigger any other traps that might lurk, but nothing happened to it.

He shook his head slowly, not trusting that he'd reached a safe room. Nothing about this place seemed safe.

Before he could take a step inside, his sword flashed another premonition into his mind. This time, he saw himself stepping onto a particular portion of the stone floor identical to the rest, and a hidden explosive blowing him all the way to the ceiling.

Wonderful.

Malek let the light extinguish and summoned his power to apply pressure to the floor. It was a vast dome, and he might only need to do it along the path he would take, but it was easier to apply blanket pressure.

Three explosions erupted at the same time, one right along the route he would have walked to get to the next doorway. They were magical instead of mundane, so neither smoke nor the acrid odor of spent powder filled the air. Instead, the sweet scent of flowering plants and lush foliage wafted to him from a dome to the side.

It wasn't anything Malek was familiar with, but he suspected it was the scent of Uthari's plant.

And that made him suspicious.

All along, he'd been lured to this place by the promise of what he wanted to find. The portal and the plant. And he kept being teased, led deeper into the compound. Far enough that he wouldn't be able to escape when whatever had set this trap sprang out at him?

He didn't know how some alien entity could have read his mind when he habitually kept his mental defenses up, but perhaps what was effective against mages—against other human beings—was not effective against this foe.

With his weapons in hand, he crept toward the side doorway. The greenhouse chamber should have been in that direction, but he'd begun to doubt he would ever find that plant or the portal. His instincts promised something far more dangerous.

What had Uthari said about hunting? That the most efficient way was to lure the target to oneself...

When Malek stepped into the doorway and could fully see into the next chamber, he wasn't surprised at what awaited. Not plants and not the portal. A pair of slitted reptilian eyes stared at him from above the scaled snout of a dragon.

"We have to go help him." Jak stretched imploring fingers toward his mother, though they were with the mercenaries now, and he was addressing the whole group. "You said it's a trap, and I think you're right."

"How could *we* help?" Tinder waved at the cliff towering above them. "We can't get up there."

Mother looked toward the frozen rope hanging from its anchor. Dr. Fret also looked but shook her head in horror.

"That doesn't even go all the way to the top," Tinder said.

Jak pointed, not at the rope, but at the two skyboards Malek had left leaning against the cliff. "I can fly those."

"Did Malek instruct you?" Mother asked. "Were you navigating yours across the tundra before?"

"No, I was trying to figure it out, but he took control, and we flew off before I had time. He said he'd show me later, but I was paying attention to what he did, and I'm sure I can do it now without lessons. I'll just imagine... the surf. Waves crashing to the shore, carrying logs atop them and to a beach."

"Did you say *crashing*?" Tinder asked. "Because that's not something I want to happen while I'm on one of those."

"I can do it." Jak rushed and grabbed the two skyboards.

When Malek had lowered them, they'd floated right away.

Though Jak could sense the magic of the devices, they clattered down when he dropped them, not looking like they were going anywhere.

He willed them to float, as if they were in the water. Thinking his coastal-wave imagery was too rough, he envisioned them on a placid pool, bobbing gently. They wobbled, but neither rose.

"Just try one," Mother suggested.

"We can't all go up on one. Malek navigated all three."

"You're not Malek, and I don't think they want to go up anyway." Mother waved at the mercenaries.

"To help Malek?" Tinder shook her head. "No."

"I'll go if you can take me with you," Tezi said.

Tinder elbowed her. "What are you *doing*?"

"If Malek dies, none of us are getting out of here," Tezi said.

Jak wanted to say that wasn't true, but she might be right. Even though he had the key and could operate the portal without Malek, they didn't know where the portal on this world *was*. If it truly was buried in the glacier, he had no idea how he would get it out without Malek's help.

"He's not going to die," Tinder said. "He's a *zidarr*."

A roar wafted down from the compound above. Even muted by distance and the walls of the domes, its tremendous power made Jak's knees shake. It reverberated with magic, deadly magic.

"Whatever that was," Tezi said, "I think it's more powerful than a zidarr."

"Another reason not to go up there." Tinder looked at Fret. "Right?"

Fret nodded and held up her medical kit. "I will be here with my sutures, should you be injured in your endeavor."

Jak swallowed. If whatever had made that roar injured them, they would need a lot more than sutures.

Though daunted, Jak focused on the skyboards again. He

willed them to float, not on the hard tundra but on the surface of a placid bay, moved only by the gentle movement of waves.

The skyboards lifted into the air.

"Got it." Jak clenched his fist and stepped on. The skyboard bobbed but kept floating in the air. He pointed for Tezi and anyone else who would come to get on the second one. "Mother?"

She hesitated but only for a second before stepping on behind him. The skyboard sank down, bumping the ground, but it lifted up again.

"Wait," Tinder blurted. "You can't take your *mother* up there. There's something huge and horrible and probably with a lot of teeth *roaring*. She doesn't even have a weapon."

Jak started to point out that she would be safer with him than down here—that they all would—since only he could make a defensive barrier, but that might not be enough to protect them. Tinder was right. Whatever had made that noise sounded terrifying.

"I have small explosives and vials of acid," Mother said.

Tinder rolled her eyes, then pulled out a spare pistol and gave it to her. "Don't get yourself killed."

"Maybe we should all go." Fret glanced at the half-eaten carcass nearby. The still-living creature had disappeared at some point, but it couldn't be that far away.

"Will we all fit?" Tezi stepped gingerly onto the other skyboard. It sank to the ground.

Jak growled with concentration and willed it back into the air. It lifted three inches off the ground.

Tezi's face twisted with skepticism, but she didn't step back off. Jak only had to get them to the top of the cliff. He could do this.

Tinder waved for Fret to step on behind Tezi. "She doesn't weigh that much. I bet three could go on one if they're light."

The skyboard sank again as all three mercenaries stood on it, but Jak willed it up and envisioned a strong wave coming to sweep all of them toward the top of the cliff.

It took three tries. With the first one, Mother grunted and stumbled into him, as if a wave had struck her in the back.

Jak winced. This was harder than he'd expected. He wished he'd tried this back on the ship or somewhere it didn't matter.

Malek? he called up. *Are you all right? Do you need help? And if you do, do you have any advice on flying the skyboards?*

Do not come up here. Malek flashed an image into Jak's mind: a dragon.

And not one of the fun, frolicking dragons from his visions. It looked like the mottled brown and gray dragon that had *killed* the frolicking dragons.

Jak swore.

Take the skyboards and get back to the glacier. Malek shared the image of a river carrying the oval disks downstream. It seemed far better than the tidal waves Jak had been using. *Find a cave, somewhere to hide. I'll try not to let it know you exist.*

Thanks. Do you need help? I can—

No. Get out of here.

Jak worried the terse replies meant Malek *did* need help. How was a human, even a zidarr, supposed to defeat a *dragon*?

Using the river imagery, Jak willed the skyboards to rise up. It was harder to get the second one into the air, either because of the extra weight or because it wasn't the one he had direct contact with, but with more focus, he coerced both to float side by side.

He lifted them five feet and looked toward the glacier and toward the compound. The desire to make sure his mother and the others were safe wrestled with his desire to make sure Malek didn't die.

"Jak?" Mother gripped his shoulder.

"It's a dragon. Malek said so. One of the bad dragons."

Tinder groaned.

"He wants us to flee back to the glacier and find a hiding spot," Jak continued, "but I think he's in trouble."

"We could try to find the portal," Mother said, her voice uncertain, like she also hated the idea of leaving Malek. "We could dig it out and get it ready for him, in case he has to flee."

"That could take *days*. I don't know if he has *minutes*. And I'm afraid he doesn't think he'll make it, that he's willing to sacrifice himself to buy time for us to escape." Scarcely aware of the decision, Jak found himself guiding the skyboards higher, not toward the distant glacier but toward the domes above.

"Uh," Tinder said.

Jak expected Mother to object, to implore him to choose the more practical option, finding the portal and getting out of here, but maybe she knew as well as Jak that they would never escape a dragon hunting them. Or maybe she refused to leave Malek behind.

She squeezed his shoulder and said, "We'll find a way to help."

"Dragons can't like acid."

"Nobody does."

As Jak flew them upward, the skyboards wobbling with every gust of wind, he tried not to think about how little he knew about magic and how useless he would be in a fight with a dragon.

33

THE DRAGON'S ROAR FADED, ITS POWER LEAVING MALEK SHAKEN, though he kept his weapons up and didn't let his fear show. He was facing a great predator, steel muscles visible under the sheen of its mottled brown and gray scales. It parted its jaws to show fangs like spears, each tooth capable of puncturing a man clean through. Even a man wearing a full suit of armor, such as the set rusting over by the wall. The warrior who'd worn it had died long ago, perhaps one of few to make it this far into the lair. For all the good it had done him.

The magical power that radiated from the dragon daunted Malek even more than its physical attributes. He had never faced something with such a tremendous aura.

More sophisticated prey than usual has wandered into my lair. The dragon wasn't speaking in Dhoran, but as with the druids, Malek understood it through the telepathic link. *I will enjoy defeating and slaying you more than the others.*

Malek lifted his chin and stared defiantly back at the dragon, though now that he was in the chamber with it, he had no doubt that he was outmatched. For the first time in a long time, he wished Tonovan were at his side, or Yidar or Gorsith or *all* of them.

Why do you hunt humans? Malek asked. *Once, on my world, humans and dragons were allies.*

Those were different dragons from another time. They are gone, and my kind rule the realms. The dragon rose to all fours, its powerful muscles rippling under its sleek scales. The chamber was large enough for it to spread its wings, perhaps even to fly. *You are from the first human world, yes? The one that is populated by* many *of your kind.*

Malek knew without a doubt that this was an enemy, an intelligent enemy, so he dared not give it information. The last thing he wanted was to be the catalyst for an invasion of his world.

Our kind have long memories, it added, *and we remember that the hunting is* very *good there.*

Where I came from doesn't matter. That I am powerful enough to defend myself against you does. Malek doubted that was true, but he kept his mental barrier wrapped tightly around his mind so the dragon could not read his thoughts. While he spoke, he did his best to exude power, in the hope that it would let him walk out of here without a fight. *Tell us how to leave this place, and I will destroy no more of your insignificant security baubles.*

You will not leave this place. Why do you think I have created illusions to bring your kind here?

They were more than illusions. They were somehow *smart* illusions that had read Malek's mind and shown him exactly what he wanted to see. He'd even *smelled* what he wanted to smell.

Because you are bored here and have nothing better to do than play games?

Because we enjoy the taste of your flesh above all others. The dragon's eyes glinted with ravenous hunger.

Malek crouched, sensing the impending attack. There was no point in running. A dragon could fly faster than he could run, even in here. The doorways had been designed to accommodate its kind.

We? Malek asked, trying to get a last snippet of information. If there was more than one dragon here, he truly was in trouble. Great trouble.

We are here. The dragon crouched, prepared to spring. *And we are hungry.*

Malek put all of his power into his barrier, but he didn't trust it would be enough. He leaped aside as the dragon lunged and snapped its great maw at him.

Despite dodging, those fangs grazed his barrier. Grazed it and blasted it out of existence. Like a bubble popping.

Malek was so startled that he barely remembered to swing his sword. Thankfully, he did, because the snout darted sideways after him. Jaws clacked together like a bear trap.

Sword met fangs in a jarring clash that sent Malek flying backward. If not for the blade, he would have lost his arm.

He rolled backward and leaped to his feet only to find the dragon lunging after him, jaws snapping again. Steamy breath washed over him, like a blast furnace in contrast with the frigid air.

This time, Malek held his ground. As the snout darted in, he jumped into the air, throwing his magic into his muscles to gain greater elevation.

The dragon didn't expect it. Malek came down on its snout, scales slick under his feet, and drove his blade downward.

His sword glowed fiercely as it sank in, but it only pierced a few inches before the dragon reacted. It whipped its head on its long neck, and a surge of raw power slammed into Malek like a battering ram.

Barely retaining his grip on his sword, he flew all the way across the chamber. He would have struck the wall with bone-shattering force, but he twisted in the air like a cat. He hit it feet first, using his magic to soften the landing, as he did when he jumped from great heights. Gravity caught up, dropping him ten feet to the ground, but he got his feet under him again and came down in a crouch.

Instead of charging after him, the dragon cast another magical attack. Malek saw it coming in time to raise his barrier. It railed at him like a hurricane wind, but he managed to keep his defenses up. For now.

Those cold reptilian eyes didn't appear perturbed at all by his ability thus far to avoid death. No, the dragon seemed to be playing with him—and enjoying itself.

It launched another attack. Having to put so much energy into his defenses was draining Malek. This was nothing like a battle with a human opponent. The dragon would wear him down long before he could wear it down.

Well, he wouldn't let that happen. He would go out fighting as fiercely as he could for as long as he could.

Growling, he raised his weapons and charged the dragon.

With a pouch of grenades slung over his shoulder, Sorath picked his way through charred foliage, around fires burning in the undergrowth, and over uprooted trees as he maneuvered toward the clearing and the portal. Captain Reynok hadn't been willing to fly him closer. Sorath spotted King Uthari up ahead, numerous uniformed mages around him, protecting him while he hurled a variety of attacks at the worm.

After their bait delivery, the worm had harassed the other fleet for several minutes, but the newcomers had flown closer to the pool and Uthari's ships, risking being fired upon in the hope that the worm would return to attacking them. It had. It was flying back and forth while the fools on the mageships continued to fire at each other as often as at the worm.

Why they couldn't figure out that they needed to work together, Sorath couldn't guess. As Ferroki had stated, it was their only chance to defeat it. The mages couldn't focus on the worm while they were busy fending off attacks from each other.

A part of him wondered why he was risking himself to reach Uthari. The worm attacked the people down here twice as often as on the better-protected ships, and he had no way to defend himself from it at all. It might swoop down and eat him before he delivered his message.

Even as Sorath had the thought, a shadow fell over him. The worm.

It was a hundred feet above, but it had spotted him maneuvering through the brush by himself. It banked and flew downward, wings flapping as the round mouth opened wide, blood dripping from its fangs.

Sorath gripped one of his grenades. "I'm right here, you ugly bastard!"

He doubted it had ears any more than it had eyes, but he didn't care. As he hefted the grenade to throw, he crouched to spring behind an uprooted tree. Whether he would be able to move fast enough to avoid being eaten, he didn't know. But he'd been prepared for his death for the last year, maybe for his entire life, and he wasn't afraid now. He only hoped he could destroy the thing.

When the maw was less than twenty feet away, its pink insides slick, with slime dripping to the ground all around Sorath, he threw the grenade. As soon as it left his fingers, he dove over the fallen tree.

The grenade sailed into his target, but that didn't slow the worm. The mouth darted for him as he ducked down behind the log. The grenade blew, slime and ichor and who knew what flying everywhere and spattering Sorath's face, but it didn't stop the worm. Like lightning, it snapped for his head.

Sorath ducked and scrambled under the log, trying to buy time to pull out another grenade. The worm grabbed the fallen tree as if it were a toothpick and hurled it away, its remaining roots tearing from the ground and littering dirt everywhere.

Swearing, Sorath rolled to the side and jumped up. Without any cover, he was an easy target.

The worm lunged after him and might have caught him, might have snapped its fangs down on his head, but a barrier formed in the air above him. The worm butted against it and screeched.

Sorath leaped over a body, ran around a boulder, and spotted Uthari and a female captain near the portal. As the captain kept the barrier up behind Sorath, Uthari blasted a wave of power over it, striking the worm. The magic hit it hard enough that its body thumped to the ground, knocking down more trees.

Sorath made it to them, running behind the portal for cover.

Uthari switched to lightning as the worm recovered, trying to angle it down the vulnerable gullet. Several of its fangs had been blown away by Sorath's grenade, and black ichor oozed from wounds to that pink interior flesh. But it snapped its maw shut, denying the lightning entrance. With a few fast wingbeats, the worm surged toward them.

"Barrier up!" Uthari lowered his arms and stopped attacking, adding his power to that of the captain's and several mages around them.

The worm struck the invisible wall again, battering it a few times, then flew back up toward the ships to find another target.

"You have a message, Colonel?" Uthari asked blandly, though sweat dampened his wispy white hair, and he and his mages looked as frazzled as Sorath.

"Yeah, you people need to work together."

"We *are* working together." Uthari gestured to Rivlen and the red-uniformed mages.

"*All* of you. Your ships and the ships from the other fleets."

"We have been debating that," Uthari said. "Getting everyone to agree has been difficult. They all believe that they can lurk in the background while the worm destroys *my* fleet and then take the artifact."

What a bunch of idiots.

"Tell them the worm can't be destroyed," Sorath said, "and that the only way to get rid of it is to work together to drive it back through the portal to its world."

"Interesting," Uthari said, as if he were discussing literature with his book club instead of standing in the middle of a battle-field with carnage all around them. "Do you believe that's true?"

"How would I know?" Sorath doubted they could activate the portal without the key, but all he cared about was getting these people to work together. "Tell them anyway."

Even as Uthari considered it, a man on a nearby ship screamed and leaped over the railing to avoid the worm. He tried to slow himself with magic to keep from falling to his death but that only gave the creature, with its insatiable appetite, time to catch him and devour him.

"Captain Rivlen," Uthari said. "We don't know which world it came from, do we?"

"No, Your Majesty."

"Earlier, our team pressed one of the symbols to activate the portal, but we would not wish to send this problem through to them." Uthari raised his voice to address his mages. "Did anyone see one of the symbols light up before the worm came through? We could perhaps force it back to its own world."

"Just send it *anywhere*," Sorath snapped in exasperation as the creature tore into the hull of another ship.

"You are not properly respectful to your superiors, Colonel."

Sorath wanted to tell Uthari to shove his respect up his ass on a pointy stick, but Uthari and Rivlen *had* saved him from being eaten. He managed to keep his retort to, "I know. It's a problem. I'm working on it."

"Good. Self-improvement is something to strive for." Uthari turned his back on Sorath, lifting his arms to renew his attack on the worm and—Sorath hoped—tell all of his allies and enemies the update to the plan.

Jak flew the skyboards up to the top of the plateau and stopped in front of a massive hole in one of the domes. Worried he couldn't navigate both boards through it without crashing one, he let them drop to the ground.

Another powerful roar echoed from within. It was laden with magic that made every hair on his neck stand up.

Malek? Jak struggled to sense him—or the dragon—through all the magic emanating from the compound itself, but he'd communicated with Malek from below and expected to get an answer now. *How can we help you?*

Mother slung her backpack off and pulled out her vials of acid and the modest explosives.

"Will you give me a couple?" Jak whispered, though he couldn't imagine them bothering a dragon in the least. He also doubted the magelock pistol that Malek had given him would help.

Too bad the portal wasn't inside the compound, as they'd once thought, because he might have drawn upon its power to fight the dragon, but he feared his mother was right and that it was buried back in the glacier.

"Here." She pressed two of her homemade pop-bangs into his hand before climbing through the entrance hole.

Startled that she would lead the way, Jak hurried to follow. The mercenaries had grenades and their magelock weapons out as they climbed in after him, but he doubted any of them had enough firepower to be useful. Would even Malek be strong enough to fight a dragon? Would human weapons—even blades made from lesser dragon steel—pierce its magical scales? He highly doubted his mother's acids would.

Jak caught up to her in the second dome. She glanced around, her eyes wide as she took in the stars on the ceiling and the writing on the walls visible through the doorway to the next dome. But they couldn't stop to sightsee. Determination and the sounds of battle kept them pressing forward.

The gnawed human bones on the ground unnerved Jak, but he owed Malek his life several times now. Even if he was their kidnapper, he was also... Jak didn't know what. A friend? A mentor? Would Malek admit to being either? Even if he didn't, Jak felt that way about him. He couldn't help it.

A thud and a grunt of pain—a *human* grunt of pain—came from ahead and to the right. The roar of the dragon drowned it out, thunderous—almost eardrum-splitting—as it echoed from the walls of the compound. Steel clashed against tooth more than once, the only proof that Malek was still fighting.

When the group passed through another dome and the battle came into view, Malek had maneuvered onto the dragon's back. He crouched astride it as if it were a giant horse. As Jak had feared, it was one of the mottled dragons, maybe the very one the portal had shown him—warned him about.

The dragon tried to buck Malek off, but he drove his longsword down into his back. The tip of the blade sank in, but not as far as it should have given the power behind Malek's blow.

For the first time, the dragon screeched in pain instead of roaring in triumph, and Jak thought they might have arrived to see the killing blow. But with a thrust of magical power that Jak felt from a hundred feet away, the dragon blasted Malek from his back. He flew upward like a bullet and slammed into the high ceiling with an ominous thud before tumbling downward.

Though pain stamped his face, and he appeared stunned from the blow, Malek managed to twist in the air, softening his landing as he came down on his feet. But he'd lost his sword. It was still embedded in the dragon's back, far out of reach as the creature spun toward him, its great fanged maw opening.

All Malek had left was his main-gauche. How could such a small weapon bother a dragon?

"Fire," Jak urged the mercenaries, as he waved his mother forward, pointing her toward one side of the wide doorway leading into the chamber as he ran to the other side.

The mercenaries exchanged we're-in-huge-trouble glances, but they did raise their weapons. As the dragon charged Malek, they opened fire, the blue charges of their magelocks buzzing away. They whizzed past Jak and Jadora and struck the side of the dragon. Their aim was true, but the blasts bounced off the dragon's scales, as surely as if a magical barrier wrapped around it.

Even worse, the dragon didn't seem to notice them at all. Without hesitating, it sprang at Malek.

He dodged, slashing with his main-gauche as he evaded snapping jaws. His blade cut into the scaled snout, doing more damage than the rifles, but it was one of several slashes he'd landed, and it fazed the dragon no more than the firearms.

It whipped its head sideways, trying to bite him in half. He ducked and jumped away, but a magical blow landed, hurling him all the way to the wall.

Malek whirled before he struck it, raising his arms to throw an attack of his own. Instead of throwing a broad wave of energy, he angled a pinpoint burst at one of the dragon's eyes.

Jak sensed the power and knew it would have been strong enough to knock over a building. The dragon reared back, squinting its yellow reptilian eye shut and roaring, but it sounded more angered than truly pained. Still, it gave Malek time to recover and charge in, springing more than twenty feet in the air, his magic boosting him far more than muscles ever could. Once again, he landed on the dragon's back. He yanked out his sword an instant before another blow knocked him off the other side.

As his scaled foe whirled to stomp after him, Mother threw her first explosive.

Incoming! Jak telepathically warned Malek.

It blew up under the dragon's belly. Maybe explosives were unfamiliar, for the boom startled the dragon more than the mage-lock charges had. It leaped into the air.

Encouraged, Jak threw one of his own explosives, trying to strike it in the head.

Malek hurled his main-gauche like a throwing knife, aiming again for the dragon's eye. With telekinetic power, the dragon knocked the weapon from its trajectory, not as distracted as they'd hoped.

Jak's explosive struck the side of its neck and blew, smoke and the acrid scent of black powder filling the air. For a moment, he lost track of the dragon in the hazy cloud, so he was startled when it charged out of the smoke toward them.

"Look out!" Jak cried, scrambling back from the doorway.

On the other side, his mother did the same, though she readied one of her vials to throw, no doubt hoping that it would somehow eat through those diamond-hard scales.

The mercenaries backed away, firing as they tried to outrun the oncoming dragon. Again, their weapons did nothing, not even when Tezi hit it right in the eye.

Jak threw his other explosive at its side, only hoping to distract it. Unlike Malek, the mercenaries couldn't survive being hurled at walls and ceilings.

A clink sounded as Mother's vial of acid struck its opposite side. The dragon roared and flung power at the mercenaries. Tinder and Fret flew backward, somersaulting all the way into the next chamber. The blow flattened Tezi completely, and the dragon sprang, lifting its talons to smash her—or pierce her.

"No!" Jak cried, out of explosives.

Malek leaped through the doorway, landing on the dragon's tail. He drove his sword into its scales, piercing muscle and bone.

The dragon screeched in pain, halting before pinning Tezi, and she rolled away. The tail jerked off the ground with Malek still crouching on it, twisting his sword as he forced it deeper. The dragon didn't fling Malek across the chamber, as Jak would have expected, but whipped its tail right toward its open jaws. Malek yanked his sword out and tried to spring free, but the dragon moved as fast as a viper, catching him in the air. Fangs drove through his torso, puncturing flesh and organs.

This time Mother cried, "No!" as Malek yelled in pain.

Somehow, though pierced by those awful fangs, Malek twisted and stabbed his sword upward before the jaws could snap together fully. The point drove into the top of the dragon's mouth, tilting back toward its brain. The creature's jaws flew wide as it whipped its head about, trying to get rid of the pain.

Malek, sword still in hand, slid off the fangs and thudded to the ground. He wasn't able to land on his feet, not this time.

One of Mother's explosives struck the creature's side, but its greatest distress came from within its mouth. It kept whipping its head about, tongue darting around its fangs as it tried to soothe its pain.

Malek rose to his knees, the garish wounds in his side and stomach horrifying—and likely deadly. He clasped one hand to them, trying to staunch the flow of blood as he kept his sword up with his other. He pointed it at the dragon, but he couldn't rise to his feet, couldn't attack again, not physically. Jak sensed him pouring all of his power into a magical attack.

The memory of the engineers in the *Star Flyer* came to mind, of how Jak had helped one of them. Maybe he could do the same now to give Malek more power for his attack.

As the mercenaries fired uselessly at the dragon, and Mother threw the last of her vials, Jak envisioned his power flowing into Malek. First the wide, calm river that he'd given the engineer and then, realizing Malek needed more and all at once, he funneled all of his energy into him, a torrent that he prayed Malek could use.

Though blood flowed from his wounds, and the intense pain should have distracted him too much to do anything, Malek kept his blade pointed at the dragon, attacking again with a pinpoint spear-strike of power. Jak sensed his own power flowing into him, Malek knowing how to accept it and mingle it with his.

The strike hit as his sword had, piercing into the roof of the dragon's mouth. Their combined magic was stronger and more effective than the blade, and it drove deeper, crunching through bone and into the vulnerable brain inside its skull.

Another screech ripped from the dragon's throat, battering Jak's eardrums and almost making him falter. But he funneled power into Malek until he had nothing left to give.

With a final blast, Malek punched his magical attack through the dragon's brain and out its skull on the back side. Its head whipped backward so hard that its neck snapped. The great beast tottered and pitched to the ground, dead.

Jak's legs gave way, every ounce of power sapped from him, and he pitched down where he was, though he managed to catch himself on his hands and knees. He was exhausted but not injured. Malek was the one to collapse next to the dragon, blood pooling under him.

Jak was too weak to run over and check on him and terrified of what he would find if he did, terrified that Malek had used his last breath to kill the dragon.

34

AFTER MAKING SURE JAK WAS ALL RIGHT, JADORA RAN AROUND THE great scaled body and dropped to her knees beside Malek, afraid he was as dead as the dragon.

He lay flat on his back, his arms out, his sword still in hand, but his fingers limp. An alarming amount of blood pooled on the ground underneath him. The dragon's fangs had punctured his abdomen in several places, leaving his jacket and shirt shredded and his side a macerated piece of meat. Even though she'd tended numerous wounds in her life, the sight turned her stomach, and it was with shaking fingers that she reached for his throat to check his pulse.

Dr. Fret knelt beside her, her medical kit already open. She pulled out bandages and bottles of antiseptic and water.

A pulse beat under Jadora's fingers. Thank Shylezar.

"He's alive," she said.

"It takes a lot to kill a zidarr," Fret said.

Jadora shook her head. "Without his magic, he's just a man."

"I'm not sure that's true, but I will admit this is beyond me. I can bandage him and try to slow the bleeding—those punctures may need to be cauterized—but I think he'll need magical healing from someone experienced and powerful if he's going to survive."

"I have yebthar powder. It helps stop bleeding." Jadora dug into her own pack.

"Uhm," Tinder said from behind them. "Are we sure we *want* him to survive?"

Jadora glared back at her but didn't deign to respond, only opening the jar of yebthar powder.

"Yes." Jak had summoned the energy to rise and also stood behind them, his fist to his mouth.

Only Tezi was elsewhere, eyeing the dragon and looking around the inside of the compound.

"Be careful," Jak told her. "The walls of this place emanate powerful magic, and I saw some broken devices back in the other chambers. I think they may have been booby traps that Malek destroyed. There could be more."

"I understand," Tezi said.

"I only ask," Tinder said as Fret cleaned the puncture wounds —the horrible bites had gone all the way through Malek—and Jadora spread the powder over them, "because he's our captor and the only person between us and escape."

"Escape where?" Fret asked. "We have to go back to the company."

"The company is in Uthari's clutches. Do we really want to go back to that? And even if we do, do we want to take *him*? This is our chance to deprive Uthari of one of his zidarr. We originally signed on to fight *against* Uthari, and Zaruk's people paid us for our first mission. We were supposed to—"

"We're not letting Malek die," Jadora snapped.

She was thankful that Fret kept working, even as Tinder argued why they shouldn't. *Jadora* wasn't working for Zaruk. She didn't need to deprive Uthari of anything.

Even if she wished Malek didn't loyally serve Uthari, she

wouldn't let him die because of it. She owed him her life numerous times now, and he was… not expendable.

"Get the skyboards in here, Jak," Jadora said. "We're going to fly him to the glacier, find the portal, and take him back to his people before he can die on us."

"Yes, Mother." He jogged back to where they'd left them.

Tinder paced, muttering who knew what while Jadora and Fret worked. Metal scraped as Tezi poked at a dusty suit of armor by a wall.

By the time Jak returned, Jadora and Fret had Malek bandaged. It took three of them to maneuver him onto one of the skyboards, and his legs hung off the end. He didn't open his eyes or so much as groan through any of this. The amount of blood he left behind on the ground was as disturbing as the puncture wounds.

"I'd better fly on this one so I can control it better and keep him from falling off." Jak perched on it with Malek, gingerly straddling him so they wouldn't fall off.

Jadora hurried to clean Malek's sword and main-gauche and carefully sheathed them for him, so he would have them when he woke up. Which would be soon, she hoped. Even if everything Tinder had said was right, Jadora couldn't imagine wishing for anything other than his health.

Fret and Jadora got on another skyboard. Tinder and Tezi jogged over, Tezi carrying a battle-axe made from blue-black metal. Dragon steel.

"Where did you find that?" Fret asked.

Another time, Jadora would have been curious, but all she wanted was to get Malek out of here and to someone who could heal him.

"By the charred armor and the remains of the dead man inside it. Someone who challenged the dragon and didn't make it, I'm guessing."

"That was almost Malek." Tinder looked like she would say more, such as that it still *could be* Malek if they left him here, but Jadora and Fret glared at her. "Fine." She threw up her arms. "Are you going to be able to fly all these skyboards, kid? I can't help but notice they're flat on the ground."

"Yes." It took Jak a couple of minutes and a lot of forehead crinkling as his face twisted with concentration, but all three boards rose into the air.

The group flew slowly toward the exit, and Jadora held her breath as they sailed outside and over the edge of the cliff. Wind buffeted them, but Jak had a better command of the skyboards the second time, and they only wobbled slightly.

A squawk came from below, and Jadora feared they would have to somehow fight off another bat creature while they flew across the tundra, but it had returned to the corpse of the other one to eat. Busy with its feast, it didn't give chase.

When Jadora looked back at the compound, it was less interesting than before, less lustrous. No, it was more than that. The two domes that had been nearly translucent with greenery visible inside were now the same dull white as the others.

"Did you ever see greenhouses, Jak?" she asked before remembering that she shouldn't distract him.

He glanced back. "No. Only that platform with what I thought might be a telescope, but all I see now is the natural top of the butte."

"It was an illusion all along then, tailored to each of us, to draw us into the trap." For her and Malek, it had been the greenhouse, the promise of the Jitaruvak. For Jak, a place from which to draw maps. Later, she might ask what the mercenaries had seen, but for now, all she wanted was to get out of there.

They wouldn't be welcomed home with open arms, not when they'd failed to find anything of value, but they could worry about that when they were safely back. Hopefully, Uthari would realize the probability of them finding anything valuable on their first trip had been low all along, and he wouldn't punish them.

"Do we... fly along the glacier and look for fissures?" Jak asked as they drew nearer to the vast wall of blue-white ice. "Or do we go back to the spot where we appeared and try to drill into the ice behind it? With... something."

With the tools they didn't have? Maybe if Tezi hacked at the ice with that battle-axe, the dragon steel would have the power to chip into the glacier faster than typical.

"Start there," Jadora said, watching Malek's face.

If he woke up and had any power left, he might be able to magically melt a hole in the ice faster than anything they could do, but he hadn't stirred. He barely seemed to be breathing. Jadora worried that if they didn't find that portal and get him back to his people soon, it would be too late.

"This is where we arrived." Jak pointed to their footprints in the snow, then peered at the wall of ice and shook his head. "I don't sense anything back there, and Malek must not have either. If it were anywhere near the surface, we should have felt it."

Jadora pointed for him to start searching. It *had* to be here somewhere. She refused to contemplate that they'd been wrong about how the portals worked and that there wasn't one on this world.

Jak steered the three skyboards in one direction along the glacier, and the group scanned it for holes or fissures, anything that might lead back into the ice. The darkness of night made it hard to see what might have been gaps, and Jadora worried they would fly past an opening without seeing it, but she dared not suggest they wait until morning.

"Sorry, I can't manipulate these things to split up so we could look in different directions," Jak said.

They could have searched on foot, but he was zipping them along quickly, and they covered a lot of ground.

"It's a solid wall of ice all along here," Tinder said. "We're not going to find a cave or anything useful in that."

"How far should we go?" Jak asked, ignoring her.

"Take us back to where we arrived," Jadora said after a mile.

Maybe she was acting based on an incorrect assumption, but she had to believe they had emerged near the portal on this world.

Jak continued two miles in the other direction before turning them back toward their arrival spot.

A three-quarter lavender moon appeared in the sky, creeping over the top of the glacier. Jadora looked up at it, as if it might hold answers. Aside from the color, it was as cratered as their own moon, the shape almost comforting in its familiarity. Though there was nothing familiar about the lavender sheen it cast on the ice.

"Oh," Jadora blurted and pointed upward. "Try taking us *up*."

They'd been flying along at ground level.

"I think I see something." Jak pointed to a spot thirty feet up.

The skyboards rose toward a split in the ice, the fissure Jadora had hoped for. They flew into it, a narrow but tall gap in the ice.

It wasn't open all the way to the surface but instead formed a tunnel of sharp angles and protrusions. It was a tight fit, and the skyboards scraped against the sides as Jak struggled to navigate all three at once. In several spots, they had to duck to avoid cracking their heads.

A clunk sounded, Tezi's new axe striking the ice. She grunted, almost falling off her skyboard.

"We need some light," Tinder said.

"I don't know how to do that yet," Jak admitted.

The skyboard that Jadora shared with Fret scraped against something and tilted, pitching sideways. They fell off, and it stuck in the side of a snowy mound.

"I need a break," Jak admitted with a groan. He stepped off his skyboard, careful not to bump Malek, and slumped against a mound of ice.

Bluish light brightened the area, and Jadora spun toward Malek, thinking he'd woken up and provided it. But he was still unconscious. The glow came from Tezi's axe.

"Uh." She held it at arm's length. "I was thinking that some light would be nice."

"Tell it a steak dinner would also be nice," Tinder grumbled.

"Or the portal," Jak said.

"Up," Malek rasped.

Startled, Jak sprang away from him. Jadora rushed to his side as Malek tried to sit up, his face contorted with pain.

"What are you doing?" She tried to press him back down to the skyboard.

"It's above us."

"That's not what I asked. You need to rest. Your *intestines* could fall out."

"I trust you and the doctor bandaged them sufficiently," he said, his voice still raspy and etched with pain.

Malek resisted her efforts to keep him down—to keep him resting and *healing*—and rolled to his hands and knees. He squinted over at Tezi's new axe, the weapon awkwardly large in her hands, but he didn't say anything about it, instead gritting his teeth and using the ice mound to claw himself to his feet.

"Follow me." He stumbled with his first step.

Jadora cursed at him, decided there was no way he would lie back down, and grabbed his arm to drape over her shoulders. She put her own arm around his waist, careful not to touch the bandaged area. If he stubbornly refused to ride the skyboard, she would help him.

Maybe it was for the best. Jak's face was pale from the effort of learning and using all this new magic, and he sighed with relief as the mercenaries picked up the skyboards to carry them.

With Malek leading, they wound their way deeper into the fissure. It led only a little farther back before turning, running parallel to the cliff and rising in elevation. The narrow passage branched in several spots, but Malek picked their route with certainty. In some spots, they had to climb, and once, they encountered a slick slope downward, and they all slipped and grunted over the challenging terrain.

Malek's face contorted with pain, and more than once, he left blood on the ice. That made Jadora grimace. Either he had wounds that they hadn't found and treated, or he was bleeding through the bandages.

At least, thanks to Tezi's find, they could see where they were going, the blue light reflecting off the ice. Until their fissure dead-ended. Jadora stared at it, defeat making her shoulders slump.

Unfazed, Malek lifted a hand and blasted away huge chunks of ice, sending shards flying. Jadora and the others covered their faces as he drilled out a cave in the glacier. His face was a rictus of concentration and pain, and soon he was panting.

"You need to rest," Jadora said, worried he might yet kill himself for their sake. "Please, Malek."

He pushed on, deepening the cave, even as sweat beaded on his forehead and dripped down his face.

"Can I help?" Jak asked, though he didn't sound like he had any energy left either. "Wait, I can sense it!"

Malek lowered his hand, bent over, and gripped his knees. He was panting, as if he'd sprinted miles.

At the back of the newly formed cave, the ice was darker. Tezi squeezed past Malek and lifted her axe, the light glinting off the walls. The ice in the back was darker because something blue-black was encased behind it.

"The portal," Jadora breathed, such relief filling her that she almost sank to her knees.

Malek *did* drop to his knees, slumping against the side of the cave, his face as pale as the ice. He closed his eyes, as if to say they could handle the rest. And they would.

"Our turn." Jadora pointed the mercenaries toward the ice and started to pull off her backpack but remembered that she'd used all of her explosives. "Malek, would you be offended if I asked to borrow one of your blades to chip ice?"

"*They* would be offended." His chin remained drooped to his chest, but he drew his main-gauche and gave it to her.

Fret and Tinder clambered to the back of the cave and started chipping ice with daggers. Tezi used her new weapon. Even though she had the skinniest arms of any of them, the dragon steel hewed great chunks out of the ice.

"Be careful not to hit the portal," Jadora said as she joined them, awed that its magic had managed to spit them out through pure ice. After winding around within the glacier, it was hard to tell how deep they were now, but she guessed the portal wasn't far from where they had arrived. "If it's like the other one and thinks you're trying to damage it... Uh, we've seen it kill drakur and people."

Tezi had been hefting the axe for another swing but hesitated.

"Clear as much as you can without risking striking it," Jadora advised her. "Once we get close, we may have to switch to less deadly tools. Since it's made from the same material, that axe might actually have the power to damage it. I don't know."

"I'll be *very* careful." And she was. After the warning, Tezi swung the axe gingerly, but it was still more effective than the smaller blades.

At least the mundane blades. Malek's main-gauche chipped large pieces away, as if she were carving from a block of butter instead of ice. It didn't glow white the way it did when he held it, and she wondered if it *was* offended to be used for such a task, or if he'd been joking. Not that he was in a position to joke.

The group was so intent on the project, their heavy breaths

clouding the air with frost, that several minutes passed before Jadora noticed Jak wasn't helping them.

Her first thought was that using the magic to fly the skyboards had been so draining that he needed to rest, but he'd wandered into a three-foot-wide crack to one side of the cave. Jadora didn't know if Malek had made it, or if the fissure had been inside the glacier before.

"Jak?"

He didn't answer. Thinking of the time the other portal had compelled him into danger, Jadora rushed to check on him. Maybe this portal was also communicating with—*compelling* —him.

"Jak?" She pulled away from the light as she patted her way down the jagged fissure. "Are you... you?"

"I'm here." His voice had an odd note to it. "I had this feeling, like I needed to check down here."

"You sensed something magical?"

"Maybe. Or maybe the portal told me. I'm not sure. It *is* active under the ice."

Jadora rounded a sharp bend, and a faint blue glow came from up ahead. Another dragon-steel artifact? Or weapon?

Jak came into view, his back to her as he gazed at a dead-end in front of him, the end of the fissure.

The clinks and grunts from the women hacking at the ice drifted to them, making Jadora feel guilty for leaving. She walked up and put her hand on Jak's shoulder, intending to guide him back so they could help, but the source of the glow came into view. As with the portal, something was embedded in the ice. A *lot* of somethings. Dozens and dozens of oval-shaped objects, each glowing pale blue.

"Those look like eggs," she said.

Very large eggs. She'd seen ostrich eggs, and these were much larger. The ice had cracked and shifted in front of the spot where

Jak stood, and one of the eggs was partially free of its frozen sheath.

"They *are* eggs," he said. "And I need to get that one out of there."

"Uh, I think they're fine where they are."

"It's not fully encased in the ice anymore. When spring comes, it'll thaw and hatch, and with nobody here to take care of it, the hatchling will die."

"If they're frozen, they're long dead already. Things that freeze don't come back to life." Even as she said the words, Jadora doubted herself. These eggs were glowing with magical power. Since they weren't artifacts or tools made by mages, didn't that imply they had to be... alive?

Jadora rubbed her face, her nose numb. Her whole body was numb. She wanted to get out of here and rest. And to make sure Malek was taken care of and that *he* could rest.

Jak shook off her grip and stepped forward, trying to dig away the ice with his fingers. Though she feared she would regret it, she handed him the main-gauche.

"Thanks." He chipped at the ice before realizing what he had. "You took Malek's dagger?"

"He gave it to me."

Jak went back to chipping, but in a quiet voice, he asked, "Is he going to be all right?"

"If the portal works and we get him back to his people." In time, she added to herself but didn't say aloud.

"I don't want him to die."

"I don't either."

"Shit." Jak spun back toward the tunnel. "We left him alone with them. They want to kill him."

"The doctor won't allow that," Jadora said, but he'd roused the fear in her as well. "I'll check on him. Get the egg."

He hesitated, then went back to hacking at the ice, his hands moving twice as fast as before.

Even though Jadora didn't want to think Tezi, Tinder, and the kindly Dr. Fret would spring at Malek with daggers as soon as she was out of the area, she couldn't keep from running back to the chamber. Her feet slipped on the slick ground, and she smacked her hip on a protruding chunk of ice. She almost tumbled back into the cave, looking left and right.

The women were still cutting the ice away from the portal, though Tinder was glaring over her shoulder at Malek. It was a sullen glare. He remained slumped against the ice wall, but his eyes were partially open, and he watched them intently. Warily.

Jadora swallowed, something telling her there had been an exchange. An unfriendly exchange?

She made her way to his side and sank down, resting a hand on his shoulder. "Are you all right?"

Tinder turned her back on them and chipped at the ice. They'd half-revealed the portal. At least something was going right.

"I am unable to meditate and rejuvenate my body when there are enemies nearby," he said, his voice still raspy with pain.

She thought he would continue, explain that Tinder had threatened him, but if she had, he said nothing of it.

"I'm sorry. We're trying to get you back to your people. I assume—I *hope*—one of them is as good at healing as you are." Jadora thought of Jak's wound that Malek had so effectively repaired.

He turned his head to regard her, his eyes still half open. She hoped he wasn't wondering if he needed to worry about *her* as an enemy. She didn't know what he was to her exactly, and she worried she might one day regret that she hadn't listened to Tinder and left him behind, but she couldn't imagine doing that.

"You should have," Malek whispered and touched her cheek.

"Left you behind?" She assumed he was reading her thoughts, but his words didn't make sense. Maybe he'd lost so much blood that he was delusional.

"Yes. If you wanted to escape."

"And go where?"

"Thirty other options." He looked toward the portal.

"Because option thirty-one here is so delightful. Clearly, the others would also be paradise."

"What if this had been a paradise?" He lowered his hand and closed his eyes, leaning his head against the ice.

Could she have lived out her life on another world? And left him to die? No.

"Some prices are too high to pay for one's freedom," she murmured, not sure he was still awake. Still conscious.

A long moment passed, and she was about to leave him, certain he wouldn't rouse again until a healer worked on him, but he touched the sheath where his main-gauche usually hung.

"You lost my dagger?"

"No," she said. "Jak needed it for something... important."

"I got it," Jak's voice came out of the fissure ahead of him. He staggered into view carrying a two-foot-long egg, his grinning face barely visible above it.

Malek opened his eyes and stared at him for a long moment, but all he said was, "Huh."

The mercenaries, sweating from their exertion, didn't react much more strongly. Everyone was too numb to ask what Jak was clutching.

"I'd better help." Jadora stood up to take a turn at the ice.

"Wait." Malek lifted his hand. "Stand back."

She did, then realized the order might be for all of them and waved the mercenaries away from the half-revealed portal.

Malek took a deep breath and glared at it—or maybe concentrated on it. The ice that was still affixed to the portal and the piles of shards they'd chipped away melted. At first, it was gradual, but heat radiated throughout the area, and a pond of water formed.

As soon as the center of the portal was clear, Malek said, "Key."

He glanced at Jak, frowned, then looked at Jadora.

She took it out of her pocket, hoping he wouldn't wonder why she had it again, and placed it in a hole identical to the one on the portal on Torvil. Without comment, Malek activated the symbol with their familiar Dragon's Tail constellation. She waited for the stars to form in the center, then removed the key and started back, intending to help Malek.

But he held up a hand, used the wall for support, and stood on his own. His jaw was clenched with determination as he walked toward the portal by himself, pausing only to take his main-gauche back from Jak and sheath it.

Jadora hadn't minded helping him, but she wasn't surprised he wanted to return without showing a need for support. Uthari and Tonovan and who knew who else would be there waiting. He wouldn't want to appear weak.

Malek led the way through, followed by Tezi, Fret, and Tinder.

Jadora joined Jak on the threshold. "Are you sure you want to take what I assume is a dragon egg back?"

"I have to. I got a vision from the portal implying... I'm not sure exactly what. A mixture of hope and a promise of answers."

"If there's one thing I know about children, it's that they come with a lot more questions than answers."

Jak shrugged and shook his head.

If the egg hadn't been glowing, Jadora would have assumed that the embryo inside was long dead, but her main thought was that it might hatch and they would end up with another monster like the one they'd battled. Or that *Uthari* would end up with a monster.

"They might confiscate it," she said.

Why had she said *might*? She couldn't imagine a scenario in which Uthari or one of the other powerful wizards wouldn't take it.

"I'll have to figure out a way to keep that from happening."

Before she could ask how, Jak strode through the portal.

An ear-splitting screech met Tezi as she stepped out of the portal behind Malek, the humid jungle air wrapping around her.

The massive thick tail of something swept past not ten feet in front of them, smacked into a tree, and tore it from its roots. It wasn't the only tree down. Smashed bushes, uprooted trees, wrecked mageships, and bodies littered the area around the pool, and puddles of blood darkened the flat rocks around the waterfall.

Her instincts told her to hide—to *flee*—as she gaped up at more than a dozen mageships circling the area, the crews throwing magic and firing cannons at a great winged worm that somehow remained aloft, biting through their barriers and into the hulls of their vessels. Some were Uthari's black mageships, but others had arrived as well, several blue, one green, three yellow, and a number of brown and red. They might have come to fight each other, but they were stuck joining forces to battle this... *creature.*

Even larger than the dragon they'd fought, the worm flew about, biting and smashing and launching magical attacks that threw even the powerful mages to the decks. It bled from dozens of wounds in its slimy wrinkled flesh, dark ichor oozing out of them and dropping to the ground, where it burned the foliage and caused smoke.

The worm screeched again, and one ship flew backward without being touched, at least not by anything physical.

A white-haired mage on the ground, with uniformed guards all around him, lifted his hands and fired red lightning from his fingertips. It wrapped around the worm, then branched and snaked into its gullet. That angered the beast, making it screech again, but Tezi couldn't tell if the attack was hurting it.

With a start, she realized that was Uthari. If one of the most powerful wizards in the world couldn't kill this creature, who could?

"It's wounded," Malek said as Tinder and Fret appeared behind them. "They've driven it back here. They're trying to force it to leave, but they didn't have a key for the portal, so they couldn't open it."

"I think they just want to *kill* it," Tezi said, though he'd probably read people's minds and knew more than she.

Jak swore when he and his mother popped out of the portal, Jak still carrying that egg. He stumbled to the side, flattened his palm against the dragon-steel framework, and closed his eyes.

As it had several times before, blue lightning streaked out of the portal. It slammed into the worm, and its body went rigid in the air. Its wings ceased flapping. The worm should have plummeted to the ground, but it hung above them, defying gravity.

It screeched again, and another ship flew backward, slamming into the treetops. The worm couldn't move, and might have been dying, but how much more damage could it do before it was destroyed?

The battle-axe Tezi had found glowed blue again, imparting eagerness and a desire to join the fight. She shook her head, rooting her feet to the ground. Even with a magical weapon, she was certain that running up to hack at the worm's tail would get her killed. Besides, it hung in the air high enough that she couldn't have reached it.

Malek looked over, his eyes locking on to the battle-axe. He startled her by snatching it from her grip.

Holding the long haft in one hand, even as he gripped his

bandaged side with the other, he leaned back and hurled it like a throwing axe instead of the massive weapon it was.

The big double-headed blade glowed brighter as it spun toward the worm. It thunked into the creature right in the center, lodging so deep that one of the heads disappeared. That didn't keep the weapon from flashing blue again, the magic of the axe mingling with the lightning from the portal.

Finally, the creature toppled to the ground, the earth reverberating under Tezi's feet. The axe wriggled free. Malek's doing? Or its own magic? It flew back to him, landing in his grip.

Tezi stared at him, glumness replacing fear as she realized she wouldn't likely get it back. She'd been delighted to find a prize in that fortress, a magical weapon that might make her a more effective warrior against mages, but it was too great a prize, even more powerful than the lesser-dragon-steel weapons Malek carried. Of course a zidarr would claim it for himself.

Malek let out a deep pained sigh, looked at her for a long moment, then handed her the weapon. The ichor from the worm dripped off the blade to sizzle between their feet.

Tezi gawked as she accepted it, shocked he would give it back.

"Others will try to take it from you," Malek said. "Learn how to use it, and sleep with it under your pillow."

"Under my... pillow?" The haft was more than four feet long, each of the double blades larger than her head.

"A *big* pillow."

"Mercenaries don't get big pillows, my lord."

"Might consider a career change."

She didn't know if that was a joke or not. Did zidarr *joke*?

Jadora came up to Malek's side. "You're bleeding through your bandages. We need to get you—"

"We'll take care of it," Uthari said as he approached, his voice ringing with power.

He strode up with his soldiers trailing him and regarded Jak, who'd lowered his hand and stepped away from the portal, with exasperation. He gave Jadora an assessing squint and ignored Tezi, Tinder, and Fret altogether, though he did glance at the battle-axe.

His gaze settled on Malek, and he looked him up and down. "What did *you* battle that wounded you so?"

"A dragon. I don't recommend it."

"I will make the same recommendation about giant winged worms."

"Wise."

"As all rulers should be."

Uthari wrapped an arm around Malek's back, and perhaps some healing magic flowed from his fingers, for Malek's face grew less tense. He leaned against the king and let his chin droop to his chest.

"Come." Uthari led him to a skyboard that one of his men tossed out to float above the ground. "We'll get you healed. And you can give me a thorough report. I'm positive that an *egg* is not what I requested you get."

Jadora watched as Uthari took Malek up to his yacht, her expression somewhere between relief and disappointment. Malek looked back at her, holding her gaze for a long moment, before he disappeared over the railing.

Tezi hoped a telepathic message accompanied it, something along the lines of *Thanks for not leaving me there,* and *I'll make sure my people don't treat you like dung.*

Maybe that was a vain hope, for Uthari's remaining soldiers approached Jak and Jadora with weapons drawn and wariness in their eyes.

"Come with us," they said.

Jak looked at the portal, as if he didn't want to leave it. Since he could command it to lash out at even the most powerful enemies, why would he?

Jadora gazed wistfully toward the jungle, as if she wanted to disappear into the wilds instead of putting herself back in the mages' custody. Tezi understood the feeling perfectly well.

But the mages surrounded Jak and Jadora, forced them onto skyboards, and they were taken up to the same ship as Malek.

"He'll watch out for them," Tezi told herself.

"Who?" Dr. Fret asked. "Malek?"

"Yes." Tezi didn't know *why* Malek was less of a bastard than the other ones, but she was glad he was and that he seemed to like Jak and Jadora.

"For the next few weeks, he'll be struggling to survive those wounds and heal," Fret said.

"Their magic is powerful. I'm sure they'll be able to heal him sooner than that."

"I still think we should have left him there," Tinder grumbled. "He's Uthari's man, and we're all fools if we let ourselves forget that."

A couple of ropes were tossed over the side of the yacht, the tops tied to the railings. Captain Ferroki stepped into view, waved down at them, and slid down one of the ropes. Colonel Sorath, his clothing torn and slimed with worm goo, limped out of the trees to meet her.

"I'm glad they're alive." Tezi's shoulders slumped with relief. Given the number of bodies around the clearing, she wouldn't have been surprised to hear the entire company had been killed.

"As am I." Fret fidgeted with the hem of her shirt. "I was positive they wouldn't make it. I was positive *we* wouldn't make it."

"Such a worrier," Tinder said.

"It's my job."

Sorath and Ferroki walked past the carnage to greet them, Sorath thumping them on the shoulders and Ferroki giving hugs. She didn't usually do that, so it was a testament to how much she'd worried about them—and likely about the entire company.

"Glad to see you're still alive, Tezi," Sorath said, "and that you came back with something powerful enough to lop a wizard's head off. There are rumors about you and General Tonovan's eye."

Tezi tried to smile, but her main thought was that she might be in more trouble than when she'd left. If that world hadn't been a frozen wasteland full of things that wanted to eat humans, she might have stayed.

"I don't suppose Tonovan and Night Wrath died in the fight?" Tinder asked, maybe thinking the same thing.

"We don't know where Night Wrath is," Ferroki said. "He and the engineering lieutenant never showed up here. As for Tonovan, the last I saw, he and Yidar were integral in wounding that creature and keeping it from destroying Uthari's ships. Some of the other mageships weren't so well defended." Ferroki looked toward wrecks that hung in the treetops or burned on the ground. There were likely more farther back in the trees that Tezi couldn't see. "Though Malek will be remembered for landing the killing blow."

"And that'll irk them." Sorath sounded smug.

"I'm sure more than a few will have noticed that the portal's lightning was also more effective than that of Uthari or any of the mages." Ferroki glanced at it. "Uthari is also going to be irked."

Sorath nodded.

"Why?" Tezi asked.

"While you were gone, he and Captain Rivlen spent hours trying to figure out how to summon the portal's magic. Uthari wanted to use it to defeat the other mageships that were approaching, but he never got it to do anything."

The portal had fallen dark, the starry center gone, the symbols no longer glowing. It remained upright though, standing of its own accord, and Tezi feared another giant killer creature could come through at any time. The warnings from the druids had been correct.

"Let's hope all of these mages are smart enough to realize they need to keep working together for a while," Sorath said, perhaps thinking along the same lines as Tezi, for he was also eyeing the portal. "As long as that's still standing, more enemies could show up. It only took a matter of *hours* for something to realize the route to our world was open again."

"Is there any chance our grand rulers will realize how stupid it is to leave the portal active?" Tinder asked. "And drag it off and bury it again?"

Sorath shook his head. "I don't know what Uthari is looking for, but he's definitely driven by the desire to find *something* out there. Even if he weren't, you came back with what I'm assuming is a dragon egg and an incredibly powerful weapon." He pointed at the battle-axe. "Weapons made from lesser dragon steel are rarer than shooting stars, at least here in our world. I'm not sure there are *any* made from full dragon steel. I can count on my fingers and toes the dragon-steel artifacts that exist in museums and private collections around the world. There might be a few more squir-reled away that nobody knows about, but they're rare."

Ferroki frowned at Tezi and the weapon, concern in her eyes. "What did Malek say when he gave it back to you? I admit I'm surprised he did. And... I'm not sure that was a favor."

She looked toward one of the black-hulled ships, and Tezi spotted General Tonovan glaring down at them. Her gut twisted as she wondered how she could avoid him. They were in the middle of the jungle, a thousand miles from anywhere, so it wasn't as if she could run away.

"He said people would want it," Tezi said, "and to sleep with it under my pillow."

"You have a pillow, killer?" Sorath asked. "I haven't seen a pillow in weeks. I'm envious."

"I can't rejoin the company, can I?" Tezi met Ferroki's gaze, trying not to let on how much she missed them and wanted to come back, wanted to have people around that she trusted.

Ferroki hesitated, and before she spoke, Tezi knew the answer.

"You're going to be more of a target than ever if you keep that axe," Tinder said. "Maybe you should give it to Malek."

Tezi looked up at Tonovan again. He'd shifted his glower to someone else on one of the other ships, but maybe he sensed her looking at him, for he glanced back down. He sniffed dismissively and walked away.

"I think my only chance at staying alive may be to keep it." Tezi didn't know if it could defend her from magical attacks, but she dearly hoped so.

"I would love to have you back in the company someday," Ferroki said, "but between having that weapon and having Tonovan's wrath, you're going to be a target, and the people standing next to targets tend to get hit a lot."

"I know, ma'am. I understand."

"I also don't want to leave you to fend for yourself." Ferroki looked at Sorath, as if he might have an answer.

"I would volunteer to stick with you," Sorath told Tezi, "but I'm not sure Uthari is going to let me go. I can't tell you how delighted I am to be forced to work for one of the men who banded together to destroy my company."

"Maybe I should give you the axe," Tezi told him.

His nostrils flared, and his dark eyes gleamed as he envisioned that—or perhaps envisioned driving it into Uthari's chest. Tezi doubted it would be that easy, but maybe Sorath, with his background in artifact hunting, knew more about the weapon and its potential than she did.

But he shook his head, letting the vision go. "You found it. It's yours. Just promise me you won't let one of those zidarr or some other mage that already has far more power than he needs take it." He glanced to where Tonovan had been, though he'd disappeared from view.

"I don't know if I can make that promise." Tezi wished she could, but Malek had snatched the weapon out of her grip before she'd realized what was happening. If he could catch her off guard, another could as well. "Unless I can talk Malek into hiring me to keep an eye out for Jak and Jadora. He sort of agreed that I could do that before, even when I didn't have any real way to protect them."

"Do you want your destiny tied to theirs?" Tinder asked skeptically.

"I... don't know if I have a choice."

EPILOGUE

MALEK WOKE TO SUNLIGHT STREAMING THROUGH A PORTHOLE, THE pain in his side much less than the last time he'd been conscious. Before he opened his eyes, he sensed Uthari sitting at the desk and that they were in his cabin on the *Star Flyer*. That was a relief.

He'd needed healing before when he'd been on a mission with Uthari. The last time, he'd woken up in a giant plush bed, with servants shaving his face and sponging off his chest. Since he'd never cared to be touched by strangers, and he disliked comforts that threatened to take away his edge, it had been almost as disturbing as receiving the wound in the first place.

A chuckle from the desk prompted him to open his eyes, and Malek realized he hadn't been guarding his thoughts. It was often difficult to do in that groggy state between dreams and wakefulness.

"Do not worry, my friend." Uthari grunted and shifted on the chair. "I know your preferences and have acceded to them this time, at great expense to my backside. You're not as young as you once were. You might want to consider a cushion for your desk chair."

"My butt likes firmness."

"Everything in this cabin is firm, including your mattress. I dropped a pen on it earlier, and it bounced all the way to the ceiling."

"You're in an interesting humor today, Your Majesty." Malek squinted at the porthole, wondering how many hours, or perhaps days, he'd been out. For part of the time, he'd consciously meditated to help heal his wounds, but eventually he'd dozed off.

"We've placed and activated the portal. That's a promising development. I'm without my plant, but I didn't truly expect that would be easy to find. I am pleased that in the scant time you were in another world, your party found a dragon-steel weapon and what might be a dragon egg. That's quite intriguing and suggestive that there might be great treasures out there to be discovered, beyond what I originally sought."

"We also found a dragon that lured me into its trap and almost killed me." Maybe he shouldn't have admitted to being tricked by the dragon, but Malek didn't want to downplay how dangerous the creatures were. What if there had been more than one? His whole party would have been devoured, no amount of zidarr power sufficient to stop it. He doubted he would have been able to defeat even this one if Jak hadn't been there to help in the end.

"Yes, I noticed the large fang wounds in your abdomen when I healed them," Uthari said. "I will confess that I was relieved when you arrived with a weapon capable of finally destroying that giant worm. I dare say that thing was even more powerful than a dragon, and it may be a mere teaser of what's out there—and what else might come through the portal."

"Will you take it back to Utharika so that more creatures can't come out of it?"

"We can't explore the other worlds ourselves if we do that."

"Perhaps it would make sense to wait on that for a time, until we've learned more about the threats out there and how to defeat them."

"I don't see how we could do that without using the portal and exploring more. While you've been resting, we've been making preparations, should more creatures come through. As soon as you're ready, you will start leading teams through. You may have to take mages and zidarr from other kingdoms. I'll be meeting with other rulers later today to hash out an agreement. As much as I'd like to keep the portal for myself, this has shown me that it would be tremendously difficult to do that when it must be kept here, and we may also need powerful allies from other kingdoms to battle whatever else comes. But they'll need us too. As much as it pains us all to work together, that may be necessary for the near future. I will, of course, keep planning ways to come out on top."

"Of course," Malek murmured.

"How did you survive the dragon? Judging by those wounds, it had you in its jaws."

"I managed to get my sword into the roof of its mouth." Malek hesitated before confessing to the rest, but he wouldn't be surprised if Uthari already knew. He might have questioned Jak or his mother—or the mercenaries who'd been there as witnesses. Though Malek doubted they quite knew what had happened in the end. "Then Jak assisted me by lending me some of his power, enough to finish it off."

"I see. And how did he learn to do that? Rivlen?"

Malek hadn't realized Uthari knew Rivlen had taught Jak a few things, but it didn't surprise him. Maybe he could have implied Rivlen had taught Jak this too, but no. He'd known when he opted to show Jak how to use his magic that it was forbidden, and he'd chosen to do it anyway.

"I showed him how to do it to help the engineers repair the engine after the sabotage. And then, when I was sent through the portal without any other mages—" as Malek spoke, he was careful not to imply he blamed Uthari for that, even if it had been Uthari's choice, "—I showed him how to make a barrier in case he needed to protect the others while I was busy."

"I see," Uthari repeated, shifting again on the hard seat. "You know it was not *I* who wrote the Zidarr Code or the rules, but as was agreed upon by the original wizard rulers long ago, I promised to enforce them."

"I understand, and I am prepared to accept punishment for my choice."

"A choice that may have ultimately saved your life."

"I will not pretend it was through great foresight and anticipation of that need that I taught him. I simply... like him."

"He must be less irreverent with you than he is with me," Uthari said.

"Sometimes. Sometimes not. He has potential, though, and is worth cultivating for your service, as we discussed."

"You're lucky I don't believe you want an apprentice for yourself, to train up to assist you in bids for greater power."

"No." Malek considered the other person who'd taught Jak. "It might behoove us to keep an eye on Rivlen though."

"You think she could be a threat to my rule one day?"

"Perhaps not, but she longs for revenge on Tonovan."

Uthari snorted. "I'll be utterly shocked if one of the women he's raped doesn't come back to kill him one day. She has the potential to become powerful enough to do so. Though I admit..." Uthari's eyes gleamed with rare open humor. "It amused me *tremendously* when the girl who took his eye walked out of the portal with that battle-axe. A *dragon-steel* battle-axe. Dear wizard ancestors, I had no idea such a thing existed anywhere in the world. The *worlds*. I hope Tonovan wet himself when he saw that."

"I doubt he acknowledges it as a threat in her hands."

"I was bemused that you gave it back to her."

"She's the one who found it. I was too busy bleeding half to death on the floor of the dragon's fortress to notice it."

"So, you don't think I should take it for my personal collection?" Uthari asked. "I admit that even with all I've accumulated in my life, I'll be fantasizing over that axe like a lusty teenager drooling over a busty barmaid." Uthari stroked his chin. "If I don't take it, someone else will. It's wasted in the hands of a human who can't even sense the power of what she has."

"If you take it, she won't be able to lop Tonovan's head off with it."

"He's your ally. You're not supposed to long for such things. And besides, it's his penis she would lop off. If he's not careful, that girl will dismantle him one body part at a time. Perhaps losing something else to her would finally teach him a lesson, that it's better to entice people with rewards than cow them with cruelty."

"Perhaps," Malek murmured, though he doubted it.

He sat up with a twinge from his side and swung his legs over the side of the bunk, wondering if he could return to some light exercise. If Uthari meant to send him through the portal on further missions, he would need to resume his training with even greater tenacity than ever. Fortunately, that appealed to him. Losing oneself in exercise and blade work was simple, pleasing, and it kept him from worrying about other things.

"Will you set Professor Freedar's father free?" That was one thing Malek wanted resolved so Jadora wouldn't have to worry about it.

"I've let her see him again, but no, not until she finds the Jitaruvak and synthesizes it for me. I do not trust her to do my bidding, though it would be ludicrous of her to work against me."

"It may take a long time to find that specific plant."

"And you do not approve of me holding a bargaining chip in reserve?"

"It is not necessary. She will help me."

"Oh?" Uthari arched his brows. "Have you succeeded in winning her trust? Or, as the druids suggested, in *wooing* her?"

Though Uthari teased him, Malek did not take his questions lightly. It disturbed him that the details of Jadora's ruse had made it back to him, a ruse that had implied not only wooing but insurgence.

"There's been no wooing, but..." Malek met Uthari's eyes with honesty and earnestness, wanting him to see that he wasn't joking or being evasive, "she didn't leave me."

"What do you mean?"

"You saw my wounds." Malek gestured toward his bare abdomen, though bandages still covered it. "They could have left me—one of the mercenaries argued for it—but they wouldn't. Neither Jak nor Jadora." They'd thought him unconscious when they'd been arguing about that, but he'd been meditating, doing his best to self-heal. In such a state, he was too focused on helping his body regenerate to speak or communicate, but he'd heard them. "They carried me back to the portal."

"If they'd left you for dead and returned without you, I would have seen the truth in their minds and punished them for their betrayal."

"They are prisoners. They've sworn no oaths to you or me. It wouldn't have been a betrayal but exactly what I would have done if I'd been forced into another's service. Logically, they should have left me to die. And they could have gone to another world instead of returning here to face your wrath. I'm sure not all are as frozen and inhospitable as that one." He *wasn't* sure of that, but with thirty-two worlds total, it seemed likely.

"That is good then," Uthari said lightly, though it was after a long contemplative moment. "Perhaps you've succeeded in winning their trust."

"Perhaps."

"I am not going back to Utharika until I'm sure the situation is stable down here, ideally when I have the plant in hand, so the professor's father will stay with me as my guest. I am pleased that she trusts you, but I will not relinquish an advantage."

"I understand," Malek said, though he didn't truly. He didn't believe it was necessary to hold the man. But until some of the ships were heading back up north, there was no way for him to be returned to his life in Sprungtown regardless. So be it. With luck, he wouldn't be endangered by creatures that came through the portal, and Malek would find the Jitaruvak soon.

"You would truly object if I took the axe?" Uthari asked, still dwelling on the weapon. Maybe he *had* been fantasizing about the thing while in bed with his hand around his prick. Given his age, such vigor was impressive.

"It is not my place to object to your choices, Your Majesty. You are my king, and I trust you to do what you believe is right." Malek looked toward the Zidarr Code, the only framed decoration on the wall. Integrity, duty, courage, austerity, and honor.

Uthari followed his gaze and snorted. "Yes, yes, integrity. You won't object but make me feel guilty by gazing avidly at your Code."

"As you trained me to do."

"As I recall, I only insisted that you memorize it, not that you hang it above your bed." Uthari rose, rubbed his butt, and gave the hard wooden chair a scathing look. "Rest up, Malek. I'll need you again soon, perhaps more than ever."

"I'll be ready. Thank you for healing me, Your Majesty." Malek knew Uthari had done it personally and that there were few people he would do that for.

"You deserve it, Malek. And I always will." Uthari bowed to him, as if they were equals rather than master and zidarr, before walking out.

~

Jak sat cross-legged on the bed in one of the rooms he and his mother had been given and considered the glowing pale-blue egg taking up the bottom third. A full day and night had passed since they'd been brought aboard Uthari's ship, and nobody higher ranking than servants had been by to check on them. Terrene-human servants with silver slavebands or copper magebands encircling their heads.

They'd brought food and drink several times, and that morning, four of them had carried in giant pitchers of hot water, struggling under the loads, to fill the tub in the small bathing room. Mother had tried to assure them their efforts weren't necessary, not because she hadn't wanted a bath, Jak was sure, but because she hated the idea of anyone laboring on their behalf.

Jak didn't like it either, the glazed expressions on the faces of the servants troubling him. They changed only slightly, not when someone spoke to them but when the magical headbands gave them a zing of pleasure. Before he'd grown so aware of magic, he hadn't been able to sense when that was happening, but now he could see how the ubiquitous tools worked, how they delivered pleasure whenever the slaves started to feel disgruntled.

On the *Star Flyer*, a fully military ship, there had been few servants, the lower-ranking crew members being responsible for most of the labor required to keep the vessel running. Despite copious amounts of weaponry, Uthari's *Serene Waters* was his personal yacht, designed to pamper him and whatever allies he wanted to entertain. Servants abounded. Even this guest suite was a reminder of the posh mage lifestyle with soft mattresses and luxurious blankets, chilled air wafting from a vent and making the rooms much cooler than the humid sun-bathed air outside.

Thunks sounded beyond the porthole. A handful of burly servants in headbands were using machetes to hack large, green-hulled fruits out of trees, sweat drenching their faces and bare chests. Jak would have been shocked if the mages couldn't twitch their fingers and acquire the fruits themselves, no sweat required.

Mother knocked on his door, and Jak waved her to the desk and chair. She had an identical bedroom on the other side of a nicely furnished sitting room and the washroom.

Most of the damage that Uthari's yacht had taken during the battle was above decks. Jak had been surprised to learn it had been at the forefront of the battle, with most of Thorn Company aboard, helping the mages to fight the worm. Nobody would accuse Uthari of cowardice, especially when he'd been down by the portal for the whole encounter and had fought as hard as anyone.

Jak wished Uthari *were* a coward. Maybe it would have been easier to talk Malek into leaving the king then, but when Jak thought of the way they'd walked away from the portal together, Uthari offering his support and Malek accepting it, he feared such a fantasy could never come to fruition.

The fact that Uthari ruled a gilded city built on the backs of terrene-human laborers didn't bother Malek, or at least not enough to walk away from being a loyal zidarr. It seemed strange, given the story he'd shared of how he had come from an impoverished terrene mother himself, but maybe too many years had passed, and he'd forgotten what it was like to be someone like that. Someone helpless in the face of the manipulation and power of the mages. Maybe Malek was just glad he'd escaped that fate.

Jak shook his head, hoping *he* never became like that. The thought that he might change now that he was learning magic worried him, and he knew it worried his mother too.

She sat, watching him as much as she watched the egg, though when she spoke, it was to ask about it. "Do you think there's a living dragon embryo in there?"

"I do."

"I don't know how it could have survived being frozen, for however long it was in that glacier, and now thawed."

"Magic," was the only explanation Jak could offer.

He remembered the sense of recognition he'd received from the new portal when they'd approached it. Even though it had been ensconced in ice, it had been as aware of its surroundings as the one here on Torvil. And it had directed him hopefully down the passage with the eggs in it. He wasn't sure how many had been frozen in the ice, but he'd gotten the sensation that the portal wanted them all freed.

One egg had been all Jak could carry and all he dared take. After the battle in the fortress, he worried what would happen if he let even one dragon loose in their world.

"I'm surprised he hasn't been by to take it yet," Mother said.

There was no doubt that *he* was Uthari.

"Maybe he's been busy healing Malek," Jak said.

"You think he would do that personally? I'm sure he has mages who are trained as healers."

"Malek healed *me* personally."

"Yes, but he's..." Mother extended a hand, as if the answer might alight on her palm.

Different. Jak understood. "I know, but I think their ability to heal is to some extent a reflection of their power, and those two are among the most powerful here. Malek has admitted there are things he isn't good at—crafting—but healing is probably something all zidarr, and mages and wizards who go into battle often, practice."

"I suppose. I'm afraid of them taking that egg and raising whatever hatches from it to serve them." Mother lowered her voice. "Maybe they'll put a slaveband on it to ensure it's a loyal minion for Uthari."

"I doubt that would work on a dragon." Jak was also worried about the possibility of Uthari claiming it for himself. Supposedly, all he wanted was that plant, but that might only be because he hadn't known *dragon eggs* were a possibility. "Maybe I should have left it where it was, especially since nobody but me knew they were there, but I got the impression this one would eventually die because it wasn't fully ensconced anymore. The portal wanted them *all* freed."

"*All?*"

"Yes. I should try to communicate with our portal here to see if it knows anything about the eggs and what it thinks. If they let me go back down there." Jak waved toward the porthole. Through it, they could see the top of the waterfall, and his senses told him that the portal was still active. He'd half expected Uthari to order it buried, though he didn't think that would work—not after they had come through the one in the ice—not unless it was also moved far from the Dragon's Tail constellation.

"It sounds like you're having more detailed conversations with it than I envisioned."

"Probably not. I ask it a lot of questions and it pulses at me. You have to be able to read between the lines. Or the pulses."

"I wonder why only you seem to be able to."

Jak didn't know. It had surprised him to learn that Uthari had tried and hadn't been successful. Though it sounded like Uthari had tried to force the portal straight into being a weapon instead of communicating with it first. As Jak well knew, the portal didn't like to attack unless it was defending itself or defending him. Presumably, he wasn't *that* special, and there were others it would defend, but he didn't know how it determined who qualified.

"I'm a lovely human being," he said, "and I drew a portrait of it the other day."

"That must be it. It's vain and enjoys knowing it features in artwork."

"Let's hope Uthari isn't a gifted artist and can only draw stick figures." As soon as the words came out, Jak realized he sensed a powerful presence in the corridor outside their rooms. Not Malek but Uthari.

The door of the suite opened, no warning knock first, and Jak wiped away what were probably considered blasphemous thoughts as he affixed his mental bandana around his mind.

Earlier, a couple of guards had brought Grandfather by, letting him stay for an hour, though they had remained in the room and watched, as if he were some heinous criminal or they'd feared the three of them would plot anarchy. After Mother and Grandfather had hugged, they'd sat awkwardly facing each other.

Jak had stepped up to fill the time with an accounting of their adventure. He'd enjoyed sharing the tale of how they'd barely survived, though he'd left out the parts about him learning magic, having a feeling Grandfather might have lectures about the sinful nature of being able to do with his mind what good hard-working men did with their hands. He'd wished Mother would have said something more to Grandfather than apologizing for him being brought here and asking after his welfare, but maybe she'd felt inhibited by the guards' presence. Or just by Grandfather himself. With all that was going on in their lives now, Jak wished they could make amends and get along better. But the guards had taken Grandfather away before that could happen.

Two servants preceded Uthari into the suite and set a tray of drinks and cookies on a low table between the chairs in the sitting room. Ice clinked in the pale-orange liquid in the glasses, condensation beading on the outside.

"Come out, my guests," Uthari said, his voice ringing with power.

Though reluctant to leave the egg—Jak had made a nest around it with blankets so it wouldn't fall—he stepped into the sitting room with his mother. The servants departed, but two bodyguards remained, uniformed men glowering from either side of the door.

Jak looked around with his eyes and his senses, hoping he would detect Malek coming to join them, both because he would be more comfortable with him here for this meeting and because he wanted to know that Malek was all right. It was encouraging that he'd gotten to his feet and thrown that axe, but he was the kind of person who would die fighting or sacrifice himself for others. He wouldn't have been injured so badly if he hadn't been trying to keep the dragon from killing Tezi.

"He is recovering from his injuries." Uthari picked up one of the three glasses, but before he sat, he walked over to Mother and held out his hand. "You'll forgive me if I get business out of the way before we discuss more mundane matters."

At first, Jak thought he wanted the egg, and Mother also appeared confused.

"The medallion," Uthari said.

She sank back, leaning against the wall for support.

Jak, realizing his mental bandana with mountains on it wasn't enough to hide his thoughts from Uthari, kept his mind empty and didn't allow himself to feel disappointment. He'd hoped that Mother would be able to keep it for long enough to develop some powers. It also would have proven if their hypothesis was correct, if dragon steel could, over time, permanently alter humans close to it. The idea of Uthari sleeping with the thing under his pillow and possibly gaining even more power was depressing. Jak hoped there was some sort of a cap and that something else besides time of exposure played into the amount of power one developed.

"I understand that you resent me for taking that which your late husband labored to find," Uthari said, "but as long as you have it, *I* do not control the portal, which is unappealing to me. Further, it would be a reason for others to target you in an attempt to acquire it. They will find it far more difficult to steal it from me."

Mother probably wasn't swayed by his words, but she had no choice. She drew the medallion from her pocket and placed it in his palm. Jak could only watch glumly, wishing he'd kept it in his hat, though that wouldn't have changed anything.

"Excellent." Uthari walked to a chair, his ice cubes clinking in his glass. "Now, join me for a discussion."

Jak and Mother faced him from a sofa where they sat on the edge. Neither of them could relax in the presence of this man.

"You should also be less of a target now that we've succeeded in opening the portal and know how to visit other worlds." Uthari sipped from his glass and gestured to the tray. "Please, enjoy the snacks and drink. It's a juice made from a local fruit. Quite refreshing."

The fruit the servants were out there cutting down, no doubt.

"You should relish this brief quiet time," Uthari continued, "because as my advisors and the various fleet commanders here have pointed out, it's highly possible something else dangerous will come through the portal, and we'll have another battle on our hands."

"Your Majesty," Mother said, "why keep the portal here and active when we now know for certain that there's a threat? Even with all of these forces down here, it looked like you—like everyone—struggled to defeat one creature. What if two had come through together? Or more?"

Uthari's eyes narrowed, as if she shouldn't *dare* accuse him of not being able to handle the situation.

"That would have been even more of a challenge," was all he said. "But we learned from our first battle and know now what works."

"A zidarr with a dragon-steel axe," Jak mumbled before he could think better of it.

The last he'd seen, Tezi had that weapon, and he didn't want to prompt these people to think of it and take it from her, but maybe that was inevitable. Uthari might already have it in his cabin, leaning against the wall.

"The worm was in its death throes when you returned," Uthari said calmly, "but I do acknowledge that Malek played a role in defeating it. As did you." He smiled and looked frankly at Jak.

"As did the *portal*." Jak tried not to squirm under that gaze.

"The portal that thus far only you have been able to convince to attack enemies."

"I'm sure someone else can figure it out, Your Majesty."

"We'll figure it out together. You'll show me how you communicate with it, just as Malek showed you how to share your power with him."

Panic flared in Jak's chest. Had Malek admitted that to Uthari? Or had Malek hoped Uthari wouldn't find out? And if he had, *how* had he? Malek's words about it being forbidden for a zidarr to train someone and how it would result in punishment sprang to mind. Dear Shylezar, what if he'd been punished instead of healed? Or healed and then punished such that he needed to be healed again?

"Relax, boy." Uthari sipped from his drink. "Don't hyperventilate in front of your mother."

Judging by Mother's pale face, this conversation concerned her as much as it did Jak. His mouth was dry, and he wanted to sip from one of those drinks, but he didn't want to sit here in this magically cooled room, enjoying something at the expense of those who labored outside in the heat.

"Malek is fine. And he told me what he taught you and why. It *is* forbidden, for the very reason that I'm watching play out in front of me like one of Egarath the Eternal's dramas. You've developed feelings for him, and he you." Uthari's gaze shifted to Mother. "Both of you. Were he another of my zidarr or one of my officers, I would put an end to this, but I trust him. Through him, you will serve me."

Jak wanted to shake his head defiantly, but he didn't move a muscle. It would be better if Uthari believed that. As long as

Uthari thought Jak and Mother would willingly work for him, he shouldn't hurt them.

Mother was also careful not to show sign of defiance. She gazed at the drink, and Jak imagined her carefully trying to keep her mind free of thoughts.

"As I pointed out before, there are far more reasons for you to serve me than to work against me. I would like you to translate the rest of that druid text, and I still want the Jitaruvak. As soon as Malek has recovered, I intend to send you out to the other worlds until you find it. Now that I know the portal can go many places, I insist that we explore thoroughly before dismantling it again. There may be many things out there that can serve mankind and better our lives in addition to granting immortality. This opportunity and the legacy we could bequeath our people is tremendous. And I'm giving you the opportunity to be a part of it."

Jak nodded, intending to play along.

"Just to be clear," Mother said, "when you say mankind and people, do you mean all human beings or those with power?"

"I am not opposed to the lives of terrene humans being improved, though I can't imagine most of them need *immortality*. They barely do anything useful with the time they have. They are not like our kind, with the power to change the world and shape the future of humanity." Uthari smiled at Jak, including him with that *our*. "Oh, I'll admit there are a few special souls with the passion, intelligence, and work ethic to make a contribution. That is why, Professor Freedar, that from the beginning, I offered you a place in Utharika. That offer remains. You may work for me and enjoy my hospitality while I train your son. I cannot allow you to work for my enemies, nor to work against our kind out of some idealistic notion that terrene human beings en masse can contribute in a meaningful way and are worth coddling. They work in their farms and factories, doing what they are capable of, and providing for others who can contribute more. That is the way it has been since our kind evolved and came to power, and it is the way it will always be."

"I see," Mother said, her face a mask, but Jak had no doubt she wanted to throttle Uthari.

He hoped she was keeping that thought out of her mind.

"As your reward for agreeing to work for me and going out with exploratory parties until the Jitaruvak is found, I will allow your son to have a hand in raising anything that hatches from that egg. I know you are concerned that I will train it to become some monster in my service." Uthari smiled blandly at her.

She hadn't managed to keep *that* thought out of her mind. Jak wondered if, once he grew better at protecting his own thoughts, he could learn to protect hers as well.

"And as I said, I will allow your son to train with Malek." Uthari watched Jak as he took another sip.

Jak didn't want to be elated, and certainly not *appreciative* to Uthari, but he couldn't keep from grinning with wild hope. He would much rather learn from Malek than Rivlen, trusting that Malek wouldn't simply be using him to further his own ambitions. As far as Jak could tell, Malek already *had* everything he wanted. If he ever decided he wanted Tonovan dead, he would handle it himself, not train a boy to throw in the general's path.

"I see you approve." Uthari chuckled at him, then looked at Mother again. "And what say you, Professor? This is a great honor and opportunity for your son. Such training is not permitted by the Zidarr Code, but should anyone else hear of it and object, Malek and your son will be under *my* protection. Perhaps I will even teach Jak a little myself, to further legitimize the endeavor."

"I will never step in the way of my son's education," Mother said.

Jak didn't know how to interpret that, but he hoped Uthari didn't either.

"Good. I must meet with the other rulers now and fashion an

agreement over how to deal with the promises and threats of our newly revived portal. I shall bid you good evening." Uthari set down his glass and rose but held up a finger to Mother before heading to the door. "There's one more thing. Malek already knows this, and I suspect he knows better than to attempt to stretch this rule, but I will not be as lax on this point. I *forbid* the two of you from having any sort of physical romantic relationship." His eyes narrowed at the stricken expression that flashed across Mother's face before she masked it again. Stricken because she couldn't believe he'd suggested such a thing? Or... because he was taking away something she wanted? "As I said, at this juncture, I would trust Malek with my life and my kingdom, but women always tend to complicate matters of loyalty between men." For the first time, his tone took on an icy chill. "If I deem it necessary, I will remove the complication. Don't assume your value to me is infinite."

Mother said nothing, offering neither defiance nor acceptance. Uthari watched her for several long seconds before walking out, his guards trailing behind him.

Only when the door closed did she sink back into the sofa, a hand to her eyes.

"You didn't want to, right?" Jak asked, though he wasn't certain. He'd never seen his mother flirt with anyone except his father, and he didn't think he'd seen anything that could be construed as that between her and Malek. She hadn't even wanted to surrender to him. That had all been Jak's idea. "Be like that with him—a zidarr? Not like with Father."

"That wouldn't be wise, no," she said without removing her hand from her eyes. "Even if Uthari hadn't just threatened to kill me."

Jak frowned, well aware that she hadn't answered his question, not fully. But he didn't ask it again.

"I need to rest." Mother returned to her room, closing the door behind her.

For a long moment, Jak wrestled between being excited about training with Malek and worrying about what would ultimately happen to him and his mother. Eventually, he returned to his room, intending to draw a map of what he remembered of the area around the portal in the other world.

But a slight snap distracted him from that task. A faint pale-blue pulse came from the bed, drawing his eye to the egg. His breath caught as he stared at it. A hairline crack had appeared in the surface.

The egg was hatching.

THE END

Made in United States
North Haven, CT
26 January 2022

15272328R00400